The EMBROIDERED BOOK

KATE HEARTFIELD is a *Sunday Times* bestselling author and a former journalist. Her debut novel won Canada's Aurora Award, and her novellas, stories, and games have been short-listed for the Nebula, Locus, Crawford, Sunburst, and Aurora awards. Kate lives near Ottawa, Canada.

Also by Kate Heartfield

The Chatelaine
The Valkyrie

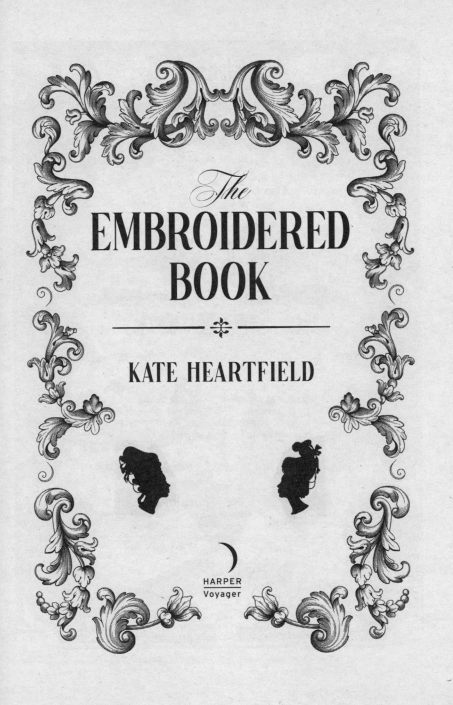

The EMBROIDERED BOOK

❖

KATE HEARTFIELD

HARPER
Voyager

Harper*Voyager*
An imprint of
HarperCollins*Publishers* Ltd
1 London Bridge Street
London SE1 9GF

www.harpercollins.co.uk

HarperCollins*Publishers*
Macken House
39/40 Mayor Street Upper
Dublin 1
D01 C9W8
Ireland

First published by HarperCollins*Publishers* 2022

This paperback edition 2023
2

A catalogue record for this book is available from the British Library

ISBN: 978-0-00-838063-2

Printed and bound in the UK using 100% renewable electricity
at CPI Group (UK) Ltd

This book is produced from independently certified FSC™ paper
to ensure responsible forest management.

For more information visit: www.harpercollins.co.uk/green

For my sister

DRAMATIS PERSONAE

— ❖ —

THE HOUSE OF
HABSBURG-LORRAINE

MARIA THERESA ...... *sovereign of Austria, Hungary, and Bohemia, and, by marriage, Holy Roman Empress. Widow, statesman, fanatic, matriarch.*

JOSEPH ...... *eldest son of Maria Theresa. Holy Roman Emperor and co-regent of the Habsburg domains. Thwarted philosopher.*

MIMI ...... *formally Maria Christina, favourite daughter of Maria Theresa.*

LIESL ...... *formally Maria Elisabeth, most beautiful daughter of Maria Theresa.*

AMALIA ...... *most terrifying daughter of Maria Theresa.*

JOSEPHA ...... *most terrified daughter of Maria Theresa.*

LEOPOLD ...... *son of Maria Theresa. Grand Duke of Tuscany.*

FRANCIS ...... *son of Leopold.*

CHARLOTTE ...... *formally Maria Carolina. Said to be the daughter of Maria Theresa most like her mother.*

ANTOINE ...... *formally Maria Antonia. Known for her sweet nature and charm.*

MAX ...... *Maria Theresa's youngest child, more than a little spoiled.*

AUSTRIA

ANGELO SOLIMAN ...... *soldier and scholar. Friend of the Emperor Joseph.*

PRINCE LOUIS DE ROHAN ...... *nobleman with titles in France and the Holy Roman Empire.*

COUNTESS LERCHENFELD ...... *governess: first to Charlotte and Antoine, then to Charlotte alone.*

COUNTESS BRANDEIS ...... *governess to Antoine.*

GENEVIÈVE ...... *a mysterious visitor to the Austrian court.*

NAPLES

FERDINAND ...... *young ruler of Naples and Sicily, third son of King Carlos of Spain, terrible reputation.*

FILIPPO ...... *Ferdinand's older brother, ineligible for the throne because of a lifelong medical condition.*

BERNARDO TANUCCI ...... *corrupt lawyer, Ferdinand's chief adviser and former regent.*

CATERINA DE' MEDICI, MARCHESA OF SAN MARCO ...... *lady-in-waiting who knows everything that happens in Naples.*

FRANCESCO D'AQUINO, PRINCE OF CARAMANICO ...... *Neapolitan noble who refuses to appear at court.*

VINCENZO LUNARDI ...... *secretary to the Prince of Caramanico, inventor.*

ALESSANDRO CAGLIOSTRO ...... *magician and 'count' from Sicily.*

ISAAC LARS SILFVERSPARRE ...... *Swedish nobleman and violinist.*

WILLIAM HAMILTON ...... *British ambassador, lover of antiquities and volcanoes, owner of a monkey.*

EMMA HART ...... *Hamilton's mistress, famous for her performance art.*

JOHN ACTON ...... *expatriate Englishman, naval commander.*

ANGELICA KAUFFMAN ...... *successful Swiss painter.*

HORATIO NELSON ...... *captain in the British navy.*

FRANCE

LOUIS-AUGUSTE, DAUPHIN OF FRANCE ...... *orphaned heir to the throne.*

LOUIS XV ...... *King of France, the Dauphin's grandfather.*

JEANNE BÉCU, COMTESSE DU BARRY ...... *mistress to King Louis XV.*

LOUIS-STANISLAS, COMTE DE PROVENCE ...... *the Dauphin's arrogant brother.*

CHARLES, COMTE D'ARTOIS ...... *the Dauphin's charming brother.*

ÉLISABETH ...... *the Dauphin's devoted sister.*

PHILIPPE D'ORLÉANS ...... *royal cousin and prince of the blood.*

'MESDAMES' ADÉLAÏDE, VICTOIRE AND SOPHIE ...... *eccentric unmarried daughters of Louis XV, the Dauphin's aunts.*

ANNE D'ARPAJON, COMTESSE DE NOAILLES ...... *'Madame Etiquette',* dame d'honneur, *principal lady-in-waiting at Versailles.*

HENRIETTE CAMPAN ...... *lady-in-waiting at Versailles.*

MARIE-THÉRÈSE LOUISE DE SAVOIE ...... PRINCESSE DE LAMBALLE, *beautiful widowed French noble.*

YOLANDE GABRIELLE DE POLASTRON, COMTESSE DE POLIGNAC ...... *equally beautiful married French noble.*

JOSEPH BOLOGNE, CHEVALIER DE SAINT-GEORGES ...... *brilliant composer, violinist and fencer.*

GILBERT DU MOTIER, MARQUIS DE LAFAYETTE ...... *young French noble bent on revenge for his father's death at the hands of the English.*

LÉONARD AUTIÉ AND JEAN-FRANÇOIS AUTIÉ ...... *collectively 'MONSIEUR LÉONARD', hairdressers at Versailles.*

AXEL VON FERSEN ...... *Swedish count.*

THE CHEVALIER D'ÉON ...... *French spy living in exile after a falling-out with Louis XV.*

ÉLISABETH LOUISE VIGÉE LE BRUN ...... *successful French painter.*

LOUISE-ÉLISABETH DE CROŸ ...... THE MARQUISE DE TOURZEL, *French noble.*

PAULINE ...... *daughter of the Marquise de Tourzel.*

CHARLOTTE'S CHILDREN

TERESA ...... *born June* 1772

LUISA ...... *born July* 1773

CARLO ...... *born January* 1775

MARIANNA ...... *born November* 1775

FRANCESCO ...... *born August* 1777

MARIA CRISTINA (LITTLE MIMI) ...... *born January* 1779

GENNARO ...... *born April* 1780

GIUSEPPE ...... *born June* 1781

MARIA AMALIA ...... *born April* 1782

MARIA ANTONIA ...... *born December* 1784

CLOTHILDE ...... *born February* 1786

ENRICHIETTA ...... *born July* 1787

CARLO ...... *born August* 1788

LEOPOLD ...... *born July* 1790

ALBERTO ...... *born May* 1792

ISABELLA ...... *born December* 1793

ANTOINETTE'S CHILDREN

MARIE-THÉRÈSE ...... *affectionately 'Mousseline', born December* 1778

LOUIS-JOSEPH ...... *born October* 1781

LOUIS-CHARLES ...... *born March* 1785

SOPHIE ...... *born July* 1786

PART ONE

1767 TO 1768

CHAPTER ONE

The Empress Is Unmoved — You, Lucky Habsburg,
Marry — Charlotte Voices an Opinion — Death and
Decay — The Embroidered Book — Sacrifices

━━━━━━━ ✞ ━━━━━━━

If only Antoine could find a love spell. A potion, a ribbon, a ring. With the right magic, she'd open Mama's heart, and save her sister from marrying the beast of Naples.

It's not as if the Empress Maria Theresa, sovereign of half of Europe, is incapable of love. She loved Papa so fiercely that she tallied every minute she spent with him in her diary. And after Papa's death, the year before last, Mama loved her daughter Mimi enough to let her marry the man of her choice.

Charlotte says that Mama was just relieved that Mimi did fall in love with a man, since her only romance before that had been with her sister-in-law. But Charlotte is uncharitable.

It is undeniable that Mama shows no signs of bending when it comes to Josepha. Josepha must go to Naples. It has been decreed.

Bella gerant alii, tu felix Austria nube. The family motto. *Let others wage war; you, lucky Habsburg, marry.*

Even Antoine, who has not studied much Latin, knows *nube* is in the imperative case.

At her sigh, Mama looks up sharply.

3

Mama has brought Antoine and her sisters to do their needlework in the Porcelain Room today. All the unmarried archduchesses, except for pretty Liesl, who is away visiting cousins. The remaining girls work furiously, silently, like mice trapped inside a teacup. Shadow-coloured plaster vines climb creamy walls on indigo trellises, between masses of gold-framed drawings.

Josepha is sixteen, which is very grown up, but she looks terrified. Her eyes go wide at Antoine's sigh, but she doesn't lift her head. She pokes her needle into the cloth in her lap.

Charlotte is slightly less grown-up at fifteen, but she looks angry. Dear Charlotte. She's the only one who's a match for Mama, and she thinks Mama hates her for it. But hasn't Mama said she plans to send Charlotte to marry the heir to the French throne? The most important of all the alliances? Only Charlotte could manage that, because she is just like Mama, though Antoine would never tell her that for fear of the look Charlotte would give her.

Antoine, at eleven, is still young enough to sigh and get away with it. She should be more prudent, though. Everything depends on Mama's love.

'Are you worried about your performance tomorrow?' Mama asks Antoine.

'No, Mama,' she says with her best smile. 'I've practised and practised. I just hope the ambassador likes it.'

The Neapolitan ambassador. The man who wants Josepha to marry his horrible king.

'Don't frown, Josepha,' murmurs Mama. 'Your forehead.'

Josepha smooths her expression, but her eyes go feral, like the cats the groom chased away from the stable last year. She stares at the cloth, unable to see where the threads went awry.

'You've pulled a thread clear through, Josepha,' Mama says.

'Ah. Thank you, Mama. I don't know how I didn't notice that.'

'Distraction is not a luxury we can afford,' says Mama. She sips her coffee, out of a cup the same colours as the walls.

Mama, as a young woman, drank coffee in secret, defying her father's ban on the drink during the wars with Turkey. Now Mama drinks coffee openly, because she is the Empress and can do what she likes. Only she will decide what can and cannot be done within the walls of Schönbrunn Palace in the year 1767.

Including everything her unmarried daughters do and think.

'Josepha,' Mama says, 'I suspect you're still nervous about your upcoming marriage. You should accept God's will. Pray for the strength to do so.'

'Yes, Mama,' says Josepha. Her face goes white.

Charlotte coughs.

'You have an opinion, Charlotte?' Mama looks at her. 'Say it plainly, if you do. I will have no coughers and tutters among my children.'

Charlotte looks at the white gloves in her lap, at the tiny knots of white silk thread in the monograms. 'I have heard nothing good of King Ferdinand of Naples. People say he is a monster.'

'He is a sixteen-year-old bachelor king,' says Mama. 'Of course he is a monster. His whole life he has been surrounded by flatterers and, and . . . Italians. He needs a good Christian wife to keep him away from the brothels and turn his mind towards his responsibilities, that's all. And we need Naples on our side.'

'Why me and not Amalia?' Josepha whispers, her face red. 'She is stronger than I am, and older. She is downright terrifying.'

'Ferdinand refused her,' Mama retorts. 'He doesn't want a wife five years older than he is. Not even Liesl, despite her beauty. Which is all to the good, as your brother and I have several possibilities in mind for Liesl. Anyway, Amalia will do for Parma. We must all do our duty, Josepha.' She pauses, and raises one formidable finger. 'The current Empress of Russia began life as the shabby daughter of a shabby soldier in a shabby town. But her mother made her a good marriage. And now Catherine rules an empire!'

'Catherine rules because she had her husband killed and seized his throne for herself,' Charlotte says with a little smile.

'Well,' her mother replies with a wave of her hand, 'Russians.' For Mama, it sufficed to say 'Italians' or 'Russians' to explain events in other lands. 'And she would not have had a throne to seize, had she married some local count's son who called her pretty.'

'Mimi married the man she loves,' says Charlotte, quieter, and without the smile.

Why test Mama? She'll only anger her. Antoine holds her breath.

Nobody speaks for a moment; the only sound is thread moving roughly through muslin. Nobody disputes, least of all Mama, that Mimi has always been Mama's favourite.

'The circumstances were different,' Mama mutters, her voice sinking so low that Antoine stops pulling her thread, to hear. 'We need Naples, and Naples has a king of marrying age. Josepha will be queen of the lower half of the Italian peninsula, and Sicily besides. It is not such a terrible fate.'

Charlotte lifts the white glove she's been embroidering, and looks at Antoine pointedly. Charlotte has been insisting on trying an enchantment to change Mama's mind. Trying to direct Mama's thoughts seems awfully dangerous, and Antoine has been arguing against it. But what choice do they have?

If only Antoine could find a love spell.

She starts to sigh again, and realizes halfway through, and tries to stop it, but it turns into a cough.

'Goodness,' Mama says, dropping her embroidery into her lap and raising both hands to God. 'All my daughters are coughing today. I'll have the cooks prepare my thyme tea for all three of you tonight. We can't afford any more illness in this family.'

The first death Charlotte remembers was her brother Charles. Smallpox. He was the same age Charlotte is now; he made desperate, horrible jokes right to the end, and she wishes that wasn't how she remembers him.

Not long after that, their governess, Countess Ertag, was murdered.

The next death was her sister Johanna. Johanna and Josepha were a pair, just as Charlotte and Antoine are. There are so many siblings in the family that their ages stretch over two decades, with ten-year-old Max at the bottom. And there are some gaps, from deaths. So the children tend to be closest to one or two of their siblings who are nearest to them in age. Johanna and Josepha did everything together and were always merry.

Johanna didn't even seem to mind being betrothed to Ferdinand of Naples; but then, she was young, and Ferdinand hadn't yet made his reputation as a beast. The year after Charles died, smallpox took Johanna, two days before Christmas. Josepha took it hardest; since that time she's never looked anything but afraid. And now she's heading off to Naples in her sister's place, if Mama gets her way.

The next death was their father's. Two years ago, a messenger came to say Papa had died – suddenly, of a stroke – far from home.

Their brother Joseph lost both his wives to smallpox: the first, he passionately loved (while she passionately loved Mimi). The second wife, poor woman, he did not love at all; and now she lies in the family crypt too.

The girls are powerless over death.

But Mama was not. When Joseph's second wife fell ill, so did Mama, but Mama got better. Let Antoine believe it was the ribbon enchanted 'for mending' they put under Mama's pillow; Charlotte knows it was sheer stubbornness. And when the Empress heard that her daughters had been crawling under hedges in the garden (they were looking for dropped coins, for sacrifices), she declared that Charlotte was an unfortunate influence on her younger sister. From then on, they were to see each other only at dinners or with other family present. Different governesses from then on, and different tutoring sessions, and rooms at opposite ends of the children's wing.

They found ways of coping, of meeting in secret at night to talk about magic.

But they still have no spell that will save a life.

Charlotte opens Antoine's door, softly and soundlessly, and steps in.

Antoine is standing at her dressing table, with a pewter powder box in her hand. 'There you are,' she says brightly. 'Did you bring it?'

Charlotte nods, and pulls the book with the embroidered cover from the false pocket sewn inside her nightgown, the pocket that can hold a vast quantity of things (so long as each is, itself, a pocket-sized thing) and still seem empty from the outside.

Antoine kneels and sprinkles ash from the powder box.

'I'm glad you have ash,' says Charlotte, pulling the items for the sacrifice out of her pocket. 'It's been so hot lately that there's nothing in the fireplaces and the kitchens are always crowded.'

'Herr Bauer gave me some.'

'Who?'

'The gardener. He puts ash into the soil around the roses. He is very clever and shows me all the new roses he invents.'

'People don't invent roses,' Charlotte says, before realizing she knows nothing about it; perhaps they do.

She opens the embroidered book. On the thirtieth page, there is the spell she needs, in her long-dead governess's patient and frilly handwriting:

For an item of clothing, reproducible and inexhaustible, to confer on the wearer persuasion of a listener's mind beyond the natural, these proofs have been found: convaincre ⟳→ convaincre ⟳→ ccovaicore ⟳→ cccaaicore ⟳→ cccaaiccue. For the prime magister, these were the sacrifices corresponding to the letters of power, in sequence dextral: ccc, for the love, an affection, written; aa, for the body, clippings of all fingernails; i, for the hope, a passing fancy or appetite, written; cc, for the second love, a fondness, written; u, for the memory, one jape or trifle, written; and at the last, e, for the treasure, a clipped groat.

'It's mostly writing this time,' Charlotte murmurs. 'You have pen and paper? I brought the other things.'

The other things are a velvet coin-purse filled with her own fingernail clippings and a small copper coin, with the shield of Austria on one side and '1 HELLER 1765' on the other. She doesn't have a clipped groat, and she hopes this will do.

She goes now to Antoine's dressing table, where her sister has laid a few scraps of paper, an inkwell, and a quill. Charlotte has already decided on the hope: for chocolate cake tomorrow. A passing fancy or appetite. The memory, small as it is, is harder than she thought it would be: the people who used to tell jokes were Papa and Charles, and they are both dead, and she doesn't want to sacrifice her memories of them. Finally, she remembers the way her little brother Max dramatically lifted his coat-tails to sit down at dinner the other day, in imitation of a certain cousin. She smiles and writes that down.

The loves are difficult. For the fondness, she writes the name of Mops, Antoine's little pug. It's hard to imagine not being fond of Mops, with his perpetually confused face and delightful little ears. The affection is a little trickier, but ultimately she settles on Lerchenfeld, her new governess. She's been a good governess, even something like a friend.

Charlotte folds the papers, so that Antoine won't see what she's written. They do this to spare each other.

Into each point of the star, she puts her sacrifices, walking around twice clockwise so she can place them in order as they are in the spell.

Then Charlotte pulls the final item out of her pocket: the long white gloves with her monogram on them. Mama says it is a waste for the unmarried archduchesses to monogram anything; soon they will have new initials, once they're married. But Charlotte likes to mark the things that are hers.

She steps gingerly over the ash lines of the star, places the gloves in the middle, and steps back.

'I give these things,' she pronounces.

She takes a deep breath, pulls out a handkerchief and puts it to her nose. She can hear Antoine doing the same. But she smells nothing, sees nothing.

Perhaps the sacrifices aren't worth enough. The coin is wrong, or the memory too trifling. Or they misunderstood the spell altogether. They've never tried this one before.

Then, small but real movement: the little pile of fingernail and toenail clippings darkens and shifts. The coin rusts and wears, going green and then bright orange and then brown. The bits of paper become ragged and thin and, as with every spell, there is a horrible moment when the words come off the paper, in a stream of ink that rises into the air as if someone were tugging on them. Little currents of dark ink in the air, dissipating, gone. The paper itself is a pile of brown threads, and the pile of nail trimmings is now a kind of sludge. Everything goes brown, eventually. The coin, the paper, the nails.

It's working.

Charlotte watches it all with her usual fascination. It distracts from the fact that she is losing things, including some she will not remember. No matter how small, these losses are deaths, unnaturally hastened. They have given death more than its due. But now she is fifteen, and she has need of important magic.

There it is at last: the smell of decay and death. They hold their handkerchiefs tightly to their faces, but the smell fills Charlotte's nostrils anyway.

The coin lasts the longest. For several minutes, the pile of brown dust remains, smaller and smaller, until a breath of unseen wind takes it. The items in the points of the star are gone, as if they never were. She doesn't care what they eat for dessert tomorrow, and Lerchenfeld is just an old sycophant in a bonnet. She glances at the pink-lined basket where Mops is snoring gently, disgustingly.

As for the memory, it was there – a moment ago – but it is gone. She can see her hand setting down the words, but her mind's eye can't make sense of what she wrote. Her breath catches – it always comes with a lurch, this loss of memory – but she is fairly sure that it was nothing of any importance, this time.

The embroidered book is still lying open on the floor. Charlotte closes it gently, gratefully. The stitches of the book's cover are familiar to her fingertips: the hard knots at the centres of the forget-me-nots, the feathered chain stitch of the vine at the edge. She can even feel the slight change in the length of the stitches where her own work begins.

Countess Ertag was governess to both Charlotte and Antoine when they were young. She had been working on the embroidery for a book cover for months. A week before she died, she stitched the worked canvas onto the binding, and sat staring at it, resting her hand on it, as though it were the portrait of one dead.

'It isn't finished,' Charlotte said; she was then nine years old. 'Look, the bottom right corner is empty.'

'I left that to finish later. See how I've left it open here, just a little flap? I'm going to put a poppy there, the same design as the petticoat I made for you last year.'

A week later, a servant found Ertag with her throat cut in her bed.

The children were not supposed to know, but Charlotte and Antoine overheard. They listened at keyholes. All of Ertag's possessions were found strewn about her room: her petticoats and prayer books and letters. Everything stained with blood. Her window, a palace window, wide open to the cold air.

Nobody talks about this now; Mama must have covered it all up.

The embroidered book was still in the needlework basket, which was in the nursery, so nobody noticed it. One day, Charlotte took it out, and flipped through the blank pages. Then she closed it and laid her palm on the cover and sat with it, just as her governess had done.

'Why don't you finish it?' Antoine suggested. Charlotte can still see Antoine as she was then, at six years old: her taffeta skirt spread around her on the nursery floor, her golden ringlets tumbling. Antoine has a way of making herself into a picture, of sticking in the memory that way.

And she has a way of being wise about things. Charlotte did finish the embroidery, in memory of her governess. She filled in the poppy, just as it was on her petticoat. She stitched the corner of the embroidered canvas to the binding. What would she do with those blank pages? What had Ertag intended to do? She'd opened the book again, idly, and then dropped it.

It had filled, somehow, with Ertag's handwriting.

Spell after spell, written in a style that was nothing like the way Ertag spoke.

And on the first page, a five-pointed star drawn in golden ink, with the word 'cindres' written across the bottom, and in each point of the star, a word: 'l'amour', 'le corps', 'l'espoir', 'la mémoire', 'le trésor'.

This was a book Ertag kept secret, and Ertag was killed, her possessions examined. Charlotte and Antoine have never told anyone about the book, and never will. They don't even need to discuss it. They simply know.

The spells are written confusingly. There are dozens of them – it's hard to say how many, as some have variations, and it's difficult to say where one leaves off and another begins. Some spells stretch on for pages of notes and commentary, even bizarre drawings. Only thirteen of the spells make the slightest sense; with the rest, Charlotte and Antoine aren't sure what item one is meant to enchant or how. The sisters haven't even tried all thirteen that do make sense – there is one for a shroud to remember the dead, which Antoine finds frightening even to read. And some of the ones they've tried, they can't make work.

Still, they've enchanted dolls and ribbons and silk fans. They can remember a pretty speech without memorizing it, cause a twinge in each other's hands, and cool a hot ballroom, a very little bit, on a summer night.

Now they can add one more spell to their list of successes: the spell for an item of clothing that makes the wearer persuasive to listeners.

'It worked!' Antoine stands up and claps her hands. The smell of rot lingers, but they know it will be gone in minutes.

'It worked,' Charlotte agrees, plucking the gloves off the floor.

'Are you sure this is a good idea?' Antoine asks, flopping onto the bed. 'Remember what happened when you enchanted Wolfgang Mozart's shoe.'

One of the first spells Charlotte ever managed. 'I do remember. He tripped, which was just what I intended. So the spell worked perfectly. And the little beast got plenty of attention, not to mention mollycoddling from you, so it did him no harm.'

'He could have tripped in front of a carriage, or off a cliff. You promised me then—'

'Believe me, Antoine, I won't do any harm to anyone. I'm

trying to prevent harm, remember? Do you really want Josepha to go off to marry that horrible boy?'

Antoine bites her lip. 'Just be careful.'

'I will be. And anyway, unlike Mozart's shoe, I'll be the one wearing these. I'll be the one in control.'

Charlotte pulls the gloves onto her arms, one after the other. They look just the same as they did, but now they are enchanted. Now they have power.

'Tomorrow,' Charlotte vows, 'we'll make Mama see reason at last.'

CHAPTER TWO

A Conversation with the Emperor —
Unbreakable Ciphers — Charlotte Tests her Gloves —
Consequences — Pandora Dolls

———————— ✤ ————————

Charlotte has never seen her brother Joseph looking more content than he is behind his desk, writing. The oldest son of Maria Theresa, Holy Roman Emperor since Father died.

Joseph has been a grown-up for nearly as long as Charlotte can remember. She learned how to navigate the court and manage her mother from the older siblings closer to her in age: Amalia, for example, is the one who told her and Johanna what to expect from their monthly courses, which all the girls in the family call 'the General', for mysterious reasons. Before he left for Tuscany, Leopold advised her to think of her eventual marriage to the Dauphin as freedom, a chance to make a life of her own. Joseph has never given her any advice.

But she needs to understand politics, and she can't think of anyone else who can explain it to her.

The glove spell promised *persuasion of a listener's mind beyond the natural*. But it can't tell Charlotte what, exactly, she should *say* to Mama. Persuasion is not command, and she wants to give the magic the best possible chance of working. Mama doesn't seem to care about Ferdinand's terrible reputation, or Josepha's ill-suited character. She only cares about alliances and pacts. So it is time Charlotte learned to speak that language.

Her governess frowns when she asks for philosophy books, saying Charlotte wouldn't understand them anyway. But she does understand. Her chess teacher, Joseph's friend Angelo Soliman, gave her a copy of Montesquieu's book *The Spirit of the Laws* and she understood it perfectly. Besides, she has eyes and ears and a brain. She understands that if there's land to be worked and people to work it, nobody should be hungry. She understands that the alliances Mama wants so badly are no protection against war; all the alliances in Europe have changed in the course of her lifetime and she's only fifteen years old. She understands more than any of them think – or she could, if they would only tell her more about what's really happening.

'What is it, Charlotte?' Joseph asks. He looks tired, irritated.

She steps into the big, red-walled room, her hands behind her back. 'I have some questions, about the Empire. Shall I come back at another time?'

'Some questions about the Empire.' He looks at her as though she's just said something ridiculous, holding his pen just off the paper. 'Don't you have tutors? A governess?'

'Yes, but they won't tell me any of the things I really want to know.'

'And what is it you really want to know?'

She swallows. 'Why must we marry Bourbons?'

At that, Joseph actually smiles, and lays down his pen. 'We don't always marry Bourbons. My second wife was not a Bourbon.'

'But so many of us are promised to members of that house.'

'Yes, because Mama wishes it, and I leave that business to her.'

'But why does Mama wish it? She says we need the alliance, and I understand that much, but why is that one alliance so important that we must repeat it over and over again?'

'Well, if you ask me, it isn't,' Joseph says abruptly. 'But with Britain and Prussia plotting against us, the House of Bourbon seems a natural friend. So Mama looks south and west, to France, Spain, Italy.'

'But you disagree, Joseph,' she encourages him.

'I don't disagree, exactly, but I think we should look eastward, too, to Russia and even the Turks. And, most importantly, we must strengthen our own dominions. We can't rely too much on any of them.'

Charlotte considers this. There's an argument, then: we can't rely too much on the House of Bourbon. She can make that argument, and Mama will listen, because Charlotte will be wearing enchanted gloves. But she needs to know more.

'And how do we make ourselves stronger?'

He looks at her for a moment, as if considering his words. How he must see her as a child still. 'We've brought in some new laws in Hungary, which might make things better.'

'Laws to free the serfs?' Charlotte has heard that this is something Joseph wants.

'Not yet.' The smile he had when she asked her first question has faded with every answer, and it is entirely gone now. 'One day, soon, I hope. I'm trying to convince Mama.'

Charlotte purses her mouth. She knows what that's like. 'I think that if the serfs were free, they would make their own food. Montesquieu says—'

'Montesquieu! I didn't know you were reading him. Do you know Hume?'

Charlotte shakes her head. 'Montesquieu is the only philosopher I've read.' She feels embarrassed, and then angry at being embarrassed. Is it her fault her governess doesn't teach her any of the things she'll need to know?

Joseph seems to read some of this on her face. 'Well, borrow my copy of Hume, then. You can't go out into the world having read only one book, for God's sake. Worse than reading none at all. Borrow all of my books, any time you like, and maybe you'll make better use of them than I can.

There's so little I can do – in my current situation. But at least I can get out, travel, see how things are. I'd advise you to do the same, Charlotte. When you go to France, when you're queen there one day, you must be sure to get out and see how the common people are living, so you'll know what is really happening. Don't trust anything but your own eyes. And don't trust anyone, either.' His face relaxes a little, and he holds up the piece of paper. 'That's why you must cipher everything. Even the silliest letter, about Christmas presents or what-have-you. Because if you only cipher the dangerous letters, spies will know immediately which letters, and which relationships, are dangerous. You do know how to cipher, don't you?'

'I know the kind where one letter substitutes for another,' she says uncertainly.

'Yes, but that one's easy to crack. That one's for children. Mother hasn't had you taught to do it properly? Of course she hasn't. Charlotte, listen to me. You mustn't wait for Mama to allow you to do anything. You wait and wait and then one day you realize that there could have been a time when you might have—'

Joseph runs his hands over his close-cropped head – she likes seeing him without his wig. He's only twenty-six years old, but he talks like a bitter old man. She would like to tease him about it, if she knew him better.

He is rummaging in his desk. At last he finds a steel ruler, with which he marks a blank paper along both the top edge and the left side; then he uses the ruler to make a grid. He writes the letters of the alphabet along the top, and then down the left side, in neat rows.

'Here,' he says, holding the paper out to her. 'You do the rest. For each row, write the alphabet in order, but start with a different letter each time. So, the first row starts with A, then the next row starts with B, then C, and so on.'

Joseph sits and opens a book while she works at his desk. Her letters are uncannily like his, she notices. How strange, that simply being brother and sister would give them the same handwriting.

When she has finished writing the table of letters, she hands him the paper.

'This is the *tabula recta*,' he says. 'That just means a lined tablet.'

That Charlotte knew, although she doesn't say so. She's gone many times to the Latin grammars and dictionaries in the children's library. She went looking for *magister* and found 'a teacher or leader, a master, as of the arts, an authority, or an owner or keeper; rarely, an instigator or author' and, further down the page, '*magistra*: a female teacher'. A governess might be called *magistra*, then, but though the book was Countess Ertag's, the word in it is always *magister*.

'This cipher is unbreakable, but a little tricky to learn,' Joseph says. 'Say, for example, you wanted to write the word Charlotte – that's the message you want to send. First you write the letters of a keyword over top – let's make the keyword, oh, *mot clef*. See, write *mot clef* over Charlotte, at the bottom of the page, and see what you get. Just start again at *mot* when you run out.'

She does so.

'See? In the place of C-H-A-R-L-O-T-T-E, you get M-O-T-C-L-E-F-M-O.'

'But the L is still L.'

'That doesn't matter. Now match each letter in "Charlotte" to the letter of the keyword you have written underneath it, and you'll get the coded letter. See, find "C" on the left-hand side of the table, and "M" at the top, follow your finger along . . . *voilà*. The first letter of the enciphered text is now "O". Do you see?'

She stares at the letters. It reminds her of the letter substitution in the embroidered book, of how a word in French becomes something that looks like nonsense, but is really magic. Where did they come from, these 'proofs' that turn words into spells? Surely Countess Ertag didn't think of them all herself.

'Charlotte?' Joseph prods. 'Do you understand?'

She frowns. She doesn't understand – not enough. Still not enough. 'But if everyone knows what the *tabula recta* is, can't anyone decode it?'

He shakes his head. 'Everything depends on the keyword. You see, nobody would really use *mot clef*. They might use anything. The last letter I had from Leopold used *cheval*. If you don't know the word, you can't break the code.'

She nods. 'I'll practise. And I'll teach Antoine. Shall I?'

'Good girl,' Joseph says, and folds the paper into a paper dart, and sends it flying. It hits an ugly landscape painting, and his eyes go wide in mock horror.

The private theatre at Schönbrunn rises to a gilt-framed painting of the heavens. Charlotte always feels a little vertigo here, though the imperial box is not so terribly high. Everything seems poised on an edge, from the strains of violins tuning in front of the stage, to the rustle of conversation. It's warm. From her seat, Charlotte can see through to the backstage, where Antoine and little Max stand, fidgeting. They're dressed in Turkish style, bright as parrots with beads and feathers, and Antoine in an orange turban.

Charlotte feels as though she's in costume herself. Ordinarily, the archduchesses would not wear full court dress to an evening of family entertainment, but Mama insisted tonight, because the Neapolitan ambassador is here. So Charlotte stands stiffly in a rustling skirt that juts out a full foot on either side. Her hair has been teased and tugged so tightly that even her eyebrows are reluctant to move.

She doesn't actually mind it, this costume that flattens her, forces her to be the image of Her Imperial Highness the Archduchess, rather than a mere living girl.

But the panniers and powder can be annoying. And here,

in this golden room, she feels restless. The theatre always feels as if it is opening onto the world, somehow; perhaps it's the blue sky and clouds of the fresco on the ceiling, although the palace is full of such scenes. Perhaps it's the backdrop on stage, the landscape reaching into some imaginary distance.

Mama is dressed in her perpetual black; she will never stop mourning Papa. She looks angry.

'He's late,' she murmurs. 'I don't like this ambassador. He knows I can't afford to be anything but kind to him. They've been more than patient with us, God knows. After dear Johanna died, Ferdinand could have chosen a new bride then, and he didn't. So, now the Empress waits for the ambassador, and will not frown when he arrives. Put your gloves on, Charlotte. Are those the ones you've been embroidering? They're not suitable with that dress.'

Charlotte looks down at the long white gloves in her hand. She thinks they're very suitable. She thinks they're fit for a queen.

She draws them on, pushing each finger right to the end, holding them out like a conjurer. 'Mama, I think we can afford not to send anyone at all to marry Ferdinand of Naples.'

Josepha's mouth gapes.

Mama's mouth twists upward and, for a heartbeat, Charlotte believes she's succeeded. But the smile is not agreement.

'Is that so, Charlotte? You think we can afford that, do you? That we can afford to lose the support of half of Italy and also of the entire Bourbon family? To make an enemy of the King of Spain?' Mama closes her eyes, a sure sign she's losing what passes, with her, for patience. 'Good God, I really am alone.'

Charlotte lifts her chin and carries on with what she rehearsed. 'I think we ought to look to the east, and to our own dominions, to make sure that our own people are well fed, well trained and able to fight for us. We cannot rely too much on a single ally, which the House of Bourbon really is. We should draw our strength from many sources.'

Mama stares at her, astonished. Charlotte has never seen her mother speechless before. Is this the effect of the gloves?

It doesn't last long.

'Charlotte, you are speaking about things you don't understand. I am ashamed. Ashamed and disappointed. What has possessed you?'

Joseph walks into the imperial box at just that moment, and tightens his mouth, nodding briefly to his mother before squeezing past the wide skirts.

'He's here, Mama,' Josepha whispers, and indeed, there is the Neapolitan ambassador. Grinning as he comes into the imperial box behind Joseph. Showing no shame at all for being late, he kisses Mama's hand, and greets the archduchesses.

Behind the ambassador stands a young man, richly dressed. When he bows, a crucifix swings from his neck. As he stands up, he looks fixedly at Charlotte. He has a very smug expression on his face, accentuated by the peaches-and-cream of his make-up and the pale curls of his wig.

'Your Imperial Majesty, Your Imperial Highnesses,' says the ambassador, 'may I present Prince Louis de Rohan, Bishop of Canopus and Co-adjutor of Strasbourg.'

Mama holds out her hand for Rohan to kiss. Charlotte tries not to scowl and then gives up, deciding she doesn't care enough to make the effort. Was there something more she needed to do to make the gloves work? Some magic word or gesture?

'I have heard so much of the talents of the archdukes and archduchesses of Austria,' says this Rohan, still looking at Charlotte.

She looks pointedly at the back of Mama's head, but Mama is focused on the ambassador, and impervious to pointed stares, as to everything else. What went wrong? The gloves should have had some effect!

Charlotte has memorized the titles of every courtier who might greet her at a ball, especially the ones who have something to do with France, where she'll be sent in a year or two. She knows well enough who Rohan is. He's usually in Paris, but he comes to Vienna from time to time. 'Prince' means very little in his case; the Rohan family is a branch of a branch of a family that might once have been kings in Brittany. But he's in line to become Bishop of Strasbourg, and that city is an ecclesiastical principality within the Empire, so then he'll have something to rule. Charlotte can't imagine a worse way to run things, for either the Church or the state. At the moment, Rohan has nothing but his name, and whatever scraps the Church gives him to make it look as though he has some use in the world.

He's smiling at Charlotte now, altogether too benignly. She decides she dislikes him.

'The dance is about to begin,' says Mama, clapping her hands, and they take their seats.

Charlotte sits to the left of Mama, and glances with a little envy over at the right-hand side of the imperial box, where Joseph sits with a few people he's invited: the young composer Antonio Salieri, who looks nervous; the scholar Angelo Soliman, in a golden turban and long silver coat; and the comfortable, pink-and-white face of Christoph Gluck, Antoine's music teacher. Joseph glances at her, and gives her a conspiratorial, apologetic smile, as if to recognize that she's stuck at Mama's end of the box.

Charlotte feels as though everything happening in the theatre is on the outside of a glass box that surrounds her. She is a person of no consequence and her actions have no effect. How could the gloves not have worked? Perhaps the effects are subtle. Perhaps Mama is simply too stubborn to be convinced, even by magic. Or perhaps magic doesn't work on Mama at all. But how? Why? Mama is no magister – of that, Charlotte is sure. Maria Theresa would consider it unnatural and un-Christian, no doubt, but it's not only that. If the

Empress knew about magic, she would do whatever it took to make sure her daughters never used it.

So what, then, is the solution to the riddle? The spell didn't work, but the gloves are enchanted. The sacrifices vanished, and every time the sacrifices have vanished before, the object in the centre of the star has been enchanted.

Charlotte breathes heavily, which the stomacher of her gown does not allow, so she breathes noisily. Mama flicks her gaze her way, just once, as the lights dim and the music skirls.

The concertmaster walks in and takes his position before the little orchestra, bows to the Empress, and the violins begin.

Max and Antoine enter the stage from opposite sides, Max mincing out like a miniature potentate. Over their heads, the red stage curtains hang heavily, their golden fringes seeming to mimic the loops of ribbon on Antoine's sleeves. Charlotte nearly forgets about the gloves, about everything, watching her sister dance as though nothing in the world weighs anything at all. How does Antoine make the angles of her elbows match so perfectly, through every change of her arms?

Charlotte clasps her gloved fingers together in amazement. Her little sister has grown up lately. She moves with such precision. She never falters, never forgets. Is it tiresome to be so perfect all the time? To have to be so perfect? What would it be like if Antoine were to . . . Charlotte unclasps her fingers, and lifts one index finger, and half imagines before she can form the words—

Antoine stops her pirouette abruptly, and stands as lumpen and perplexed as a milkmaid transported to the opera house from some alpine pasture.

The family stays perfectly quiet and composed, as if they are under a spell too. For this is a spell; no doubt about it. This is not Antoine. The gloves work, damn them. Damn them! Max frowns at Antoine, and the moment stretches on. The ambassador coughs, not precisely politely. Charlotte tears the gloves off, finger by finger, getting them stuck.

The French Prince de Rohan is staring at her. Let him stare.

Then too late, too late, she realizes what to do, and she shoves the gloves back onto her hands. What must she do to make them work? She didn't do anything before, only let a stray thought enter her mind. *Come on, Antoine! Move!*

At last, Antoine glides into a chassé. She performs every move perfectly, but her mortification is like a roar in the ears. The dance continues, and everyone pretends not to take any notice. But Mama is frowning, and Antoine's cheeks are scarlet.

Charlotte is already out of bed when she feels the sudden twinge in her hand that means Antoine has stuck a pin into the Pandora doll. Not the first time she's regretted giving that doll to her sister!

They began life not as toys, but as miniature models that dressmakers brought to court as samples, to show the Austrian ladies what the ladies of Paris were wearing, and to offer the same fashions for sale. Somehow, these two prim-faced dolls had gone unclaimed at some point, and ended up in the nursery.

Charlotte enchanted one to represent herself, and the other Antoine. A pin in the hand of the doll means pain to the hand of the girl. So they always know when one of them needs the other. It's a panicky, unmoored ache that causes her to clutch her elbow as though her whole arm is rebellious, but when she forces herself to identify the pain, calmly, to locate it, it's bearable.

Perhaps not the best mode of communication between sisters. Especially not when one of those sisters doesn't take the pin out right away.

Charlotte grits her teeth and slips through doorways in silent shoes that won't wake her governess, past ushers and guards trained to mind their own business.

She opens the door, and Antoine's face is hard, all bunched

up like a batch of bad knitting. But the moment her eyes meet Charlotte's, her expression softens and she pulls the pin out. The pain softens too.

Charlotte comes to the bed, sits next to her. 'You didn't have to use the doll. I was already on my way to apologize.'

'No need,' says Antoine. 'I'm sure you had a reason for testing the gloves that way. Rather than in private, I mean.'

'I didn't. That's the thing. It was an accident.'

Antoine's brows bunch together. 'You were wearing the gloves and you—'

'Had a thought. Half a thought, really. The gloves work. They work much better than I realized. I never would have done that to you on purpose, Antoine. Please believe me.'

Antoine purses her lips. 'I believe you. You didn't intend – I did tell you, you know—'

'I know.' Charlotte puts her arm around her sister and pulls Antoine's head onto her shoulder. They sit for a moment, the doll on Antoine's lap that looks a little like Charlotte did a few years ago, dressed in the fashions of 1764.

The fashions of Paris, where one day, Charlotte will live, as dauphine, as queen. As a sovereign, she won't be able to travel much – there are dangers on the road, and worse dangers in leaving one's country unattended – but if Antoine marries one of the French princes, she will have many opportunities to come to see Charlotte. All will be well.

But, in the meantime, they must save poor Josepha from having to go to Naples, beyond the Alps, to marry a king who already has a worse reputation at sixteen than most men manage by sixty.

And somehow they have to do it without the gloves, for it seems they won't work on Mama. Charlotte tells Antoine about her efforts to affect Mama's behaviour.

'There's no changing her mind, not even through magic,' Antoine says sadly. 'Why do you think she's so cruel to Josepha?'

'I don't think she intends to be cruel. She's just so used to being afraid.'

'Afraid!'

'Papa was Holy Roman Emperor. And now Joseph. But Mama is the one who rules, even so! It's quite the trick she's managed, especially when you consider that all the powers of Europe tried to stop her, when she first took the throne. I think she always keeps herself ready in case someone comes along and says, Now wait a moment, Frau Habsburg, things don't seem to be in order here. We're not just her children. We're her weapons. But we have weapons of our own, don't we, sister? And nobody expects us to have any, that's the thing.' Charlotte pulls the embroidered book out of her secret pocket. 'Nobody looks in the needlework basket.'

Antoine takes the book from her and smiles. 'All right. I'll try to think of my needle as a weapon. It might make my embroidery go better.'

'Your embroidery is perfect, like everything you do.'

Antoine casts her gaze down, disbelieving.

'Everything is perfect when your meddling sister doesn't ruin it. Am I absolved, Antoine?' Charlotte asks, putting her hand on Antoine's shoulder. 'May I go? Or will you summon me back with the pin?'

'I didn't summon you here to absolve you, Charlotte. I wanted to see the book, in fact.'

'The book?' Charlotte frowns. She only brought it because she always carries the book with her when she leaves her bedroom at night, for safekeeping. 'What spell do you want? It's late, Antoine.'

'I don't want to do a spell tonight. I just want to see something.' She flips through the pages. 'Ah, here it is. I thought I remembered—'

Charlotte reads the page upside down: 'For an anointment to confer resistance, a simple spell, to be performed only on a clean vial containing no matter saving the liquor found in the inner coffin of a human inhumation . . .'

'Clever girl,' Charlotte says. 'That must be it!'

'It?'

'The reason the gloves didn't work on Mama. Isn't that why you thought of it?'

'Yes, that's it, of course. Horrible, isn't it? The liquor – what is that, exactly, Charlotte?'

'The liquid remains of a rotting corpse, I suppose. I can't imagine Mama willingly anointing herself with such a thing. Perhaps someone did it without her knowing?'

'Or perhaps there's a similar spell that's less gruesome. I don't think Countess Ertag knew every spell in the world. There must be other magisters, with other spellbooks, and perhaps one of them sent Mama a present. Perfume, or something.'

'That must be it. Oh, Antoine, I feel so much better. Knowing, I mean. Why the gloves didn't work.'

'They didn't work on her. They worked on me. Because I'm not resistant.'

Charlotte nods, slowly, and puts her hands over Antoine's to close the book. 'We'll find out. Somehow, we'll find out what made Mama resistant, and we'll get some for ourselves. But first, we have to find a way to change her mind. Josepha is set to leave in less than a month.'

Antoine nods. 'But if magic won't work on Mama, what can we do, Charlotte?'

What indeed? 'Let me worry about that. Am I absolved, then?'

Antoine's face falls into a mockery of a jowly old priest as she says, dramatically, '*Ego te absolvo.*'

Charlotte kisses her quickly on the cheek and slides the book back into her apron pocket.

CHAPTER THREE

*The Empress Lectures — The Court Moves — Noises in
the Crypt — Magic Lantern Demonstration — A Tilt
in the Axis of the World*

———————— ❖ ————————

The next morning, Antoine waits, straight-backed on the newly upholstered settee in Mama's anteroom, until Josepha comes out of Mama's study. Josepha's face is pale except for two irregular patches of red on her cheeks, like rouge applied by a monkey.

'How is she?' Antoine asks, stepping close to Josepha so she can speak without the door usher or Mama's secretary overhearing. But Josepha just widens her eyes, breathes deeply, and shakes her head. She pulls a copy of *Don Quixote* out of her apron pocket and opens it in front of her to read while she walks out of the room and into the corridor.

Mama is still recovering from the smallpox she had in the spring; she still begins work early in the morning, but she does it from her bed, with heavy curtains drawn and standing orders that she is not to be disturbed until after Mass. But she summoned Antoine and Josepha first thing, today.

Antoine steels herself and goes in.

The golden room is as dark and sour as a dough-cupboard. Mama is sitting up, but even so it is strange to see her in bed. Mama, who always said no one needs more than six hours' sleep a night.

'Antoine,' Mama says.

'It was an error, Mama. I am mortified.'

'No doubt. Antoine, you are nearly twelve years old. You do not dance to please yourself, or even to please me. Soon enough, ambassadors will be sending reports back to their princes of your suitability.'

'Yes, Mama.'

'I can't think what came over you. I've been negligent, I see. I've left you too much in the hands of governesses and cousins, and they all fawn over you. Of course they do. You're a beautiful child, and you're sweet-hearted and good by nature. Everyone loves you, as well they should. But you also need proper instruction and sternness of character, and there, I've failed you.'

'Oh, Mama—'

'Don't contradict me, Antoine. I have. You were always your father's favourite, so I've tried to keep you little, for his sake. My last sight of him was when you ran after him as he left, and he came down off his horse to embrace you. So for him – I thought I'd have time to – but you're growing up so quickly. You must make yourself beyond reproach in everything. Good heavens, girl, don't look so stricken. Manage yourself.'

He came down off his horse. Down off his horse? Antoine has no memory of her father saying goodbye to her. The family's last sight of him was of an embrace with Antoine, and she has forgotten it.

She has sacrificed it, surely. Her father's final touch, a moment of desperate affection for her alone. And she can't even remember what she bought with that sacrifice.

'Mama, I am so, so sorry.'

'You've said so. Don't repeat yourself and never make yourself craven with apologies. What you must do is be more attentive in your lessons, and remember that in everything you do, you affect the reputation of this family.'

Antoine bows her head. This is the moment for the request that she rehearsed. She knows she looks sorrowful and remorseful, and she has good reason for that, better than Mama knows. And she knows, guiltily, that her real pain will serve her purposes well now, and she wishes that she could for one moment separate the Antoine who *is* from the Antoine who performs, but what would happen if she did?

'Mama,' she whispers, her head still bowed, 'I shall ask God to help me be a more attentive student.'

'Good,' says Mama, leaning back, satisfied. 'Tomorrow you will attend Mass twice.'

Antoine nods solemnly. 'Perhaps I should pray in the crypt, as you do?'

There's a silence, for two beats of Antoine's sparrow heart. The imperial family crypt is in the heart of Vienna, near the Hofburg palace, where the family spends its winters. It's nearly October, and the servants are already packing for the move. One of the first things Mama does, every autumn, is visit the dead.

'I don't think that's necessary,' Mama says uncertainly.

'When Papa said goodbye to me,' Antoine says, hating herself with every word, 'I wonder if he knew . . . what was to come. I would like to ask for his help. I need his help to be a better daughter.'

It's a perfect performance, and it's entirely genuine. How can both be true? She looks up and sees Mama's face. It looks different, suddenly. The lined face of an old woman, though she's only fifty. Without rouge, in her black sleeping bonnet in the dim room, the Empress looks as pale and worn as a market woman. And she looks tired in her eyes, too: tired and sad.

'Very well,' Mama says at last. 'We're scheduled to move to the Hofburg next week. After we're settled there, we'll go to the crypt together to pray for the late Emperor's soul, and that of dear Joseph's lately departed wife, and the others we have lost in these last terrible years. Josepha will come with us.'

Antoine holds her face steady and thinks as quickly as she can. Poor Josepha. The last thing Antoine wants is to put her through anything more!

'Josepha?' she asks. 'Couldn't it be just the two of us, Mama?'

Mama is resistant to more than magic. She shakes her head, so that her bonnet ribbons flap. 'Josepha has great need of courage and faith. She needs, as you need, to be reminded of her duty to her father and to the Empire. Dear heavens, what – Come forward, Antoine. Come, come, so I can see you.'

Antoine does a subtle *pas de bourrée en avant*. She reaches the foot of her mother's bed.

'That hairline,' Mama says. 'Has it always been so crooked? We'll have to find another way of dressing it in the front, hide it somehow.'

Try as she might to avoid it, Antoine always adds to Mama's burdens. She puts her hand to her hairline.

'Don't touch your face, dear,' the Empress commands. 'You're nearly of the age for pimples.'

There are only five miles between Schönbrunn and the Hofburg palace, but to Antoine the annual move from summer residence to winter always feels like a tilt in the axis of the world. Antoine prefers Schönbrunn, surrounded by nothing but gardens, open and bright. The Hofburg is in the heart of Vienna, all shadows and whispers.

She does like the plain, cheerful Capuchin church just outside the palace, but the crypt beneath the church is neither plain nor cheerful.

On the morning after the move, Antoine, Mama, Josepha and a half-dozen servants with lamps file through the quiet nave and down the stone steps, and enter the vault where the dead lie. Antoine's grandfather's sarcophagus looms great and terrible in dark metal, with death's heads on each corner bearing the imperial crown. They walk past, and the newer vault opens before them, its ceiling soaring high overhead.

Antoine tastes marble and metal. There is the tomb of her brother Charles. She tries not to think of him lying there, of his heart in a silver urn in another church, where the Habsburg hearts are kept. What will happen to the hearts on the last day? She would like to ask someone, but Charlotte will think it's a silly question, and anyone else will scold her for asking it.

At the sight of her sister-in-law's sarcophagus, with a portrait of Maria worked in a bronze disc at its head, Antoine stops short. What a terrible notion this is! Surely she can't open a tomb. It's unthinkable. The price is too high. She can live without the corpse liquor, without the spell. Can't she?

Without it, a magister could work a spell on her at any time. She knows now what that feels like, to be powerless. It felt like losing herself entirely.

She closes her eyes, and shudders. No. She must be strong. She must do this, for Mama and for Austria, if not herself. Antoine is not like Charlotte or Mama. Not clever like them. She has no weapons other than her smile and her dancing and her wit. If someone can take those away, she has nothing, and she will let everyone down.

She opens the vial of enchanted oil in her pocket and shakes one drop on a marble finial near the entrance to the current vault as they walk past. No one sees. She knows the oil works to make metal and stone pliable; she and Charlotte made it early in their experiments with the spell-book, but have found few good uses for it, and after they mangled a gargoyle in the courtyard outside the Hofburg chapel last winter, they haven't used it since. A single drop is enough.

Mama kneels by the tomb where Papa lies, where Mama will one day lie too. Josepha and Antoine kneel behind her. Antoine waits, trying to pray for strength.

A grinding sound, unlike anything from this world, comes from behind them, from the entrance. Antoine's oil at work.

'What in God's name?' Maria Theresa rises and follows the servants to the source of it, bustling back the way they came. Antoine takes her chance. This must be Maria's tomb; Joseph's second wife was put to rest within a few hours of her death, with no embalming, because no one wanted to handle her smallpox-riddled body. Antoine shakes one drop of her oil onto a lion's face sculpted on the side of the sarcophagus.

The lion yawns.

Out of the lion's mouth trickles a dark umber liquor, into the bottle that Antoine tucks back into her pocket as the servants and courtiers return.

Maria Theresa is annoyed. 'Come, Antoine. It's nothing.'

'Rats,' whispers Josepha, wide-eyed.

As they kneel again to make their devotions, Mama cries out, and points at Maria's sarcophagus. The lion's face is motionless now, but its mouth remains slack, and something drips from it.

'It isn't sealed properly,' Maria Theresa says, and stands, covering her mouth with her handkerchief. 'Come, girls, quickly. Good God.'

Charlotte can think better at the Hofburg. At Schönbrunn, everything is built to Mama's specifications. But there is no single mind behind the cluster of old buildings at the heart of Vienna, the dark rooms and connecting courtyards, busy with soldiers and horses.

The servants' passageways behind the rooms also make it easier to sneak to Antoine's chambers. All day, it's been clear that something new is bothering Antoine. She sat listless at dinner, and she and Josepha both looked stone-faced as they sat embroidering with Mama. At last, Charlotte has a chance to ask her, sitting in her room by the light of a few candles.

She can hardly believe the answer.

'You opened a coffin? Antoine, what were you thinking?'

Antoine's mouth is set. 'We had to get it from somewhere.'

Charlotte sits next to her on the narrow bed, stares at the tiny vial in Antoine's shaking hand, and wrinkles her nose. 'I know you're angry with me over the dance—'

'It's not only that.' Antoine's cheeks are flushed. 'Charlotte, Ertag was killed because she knew about magic. Don't you think? Why else would anyone kill a governess? And whoever killed her got past the palace guards and through her window on the second floor. Someone out there knows about magic, and probably knows how to do magic. What if they find out we have the book?'

Charlotte looks away. These are thoughts she's had before, but she never spoke about her fears with Antoine. Her sister was too young, before, to understand the danger. No longer.

The sky outside the window is soft indigo, and outside it, only a few guards and walls between them and Vienna. The palace can't protect them; Ertag's death is proof of that. A few weeks until Josepha is set to leave for Naples, if Charlotte fails. Mama has been playing three different suitors off each other for the beautiful Liesl but that will have to end soon, as Liesl is getting old at twenty-four. And in a year or two, Charlotte will leave too, off to marry the Dauphin of France, leaving Antoine here alone. Antoine and Max, the two youngest children, are the only ones whose marriages haven't yet been arranged.

Antoine's blue silk dressing screen casts one corner of the room in shadow, and the candlelight catches on the silver basin on her washstand. They're sitting on the little bed in the middle of the room, and knowing that there are guards at the doors, that their governesses are not far, doesn't bring much comfort. They were sleeping near Ertag when she died.

Charlotte looks back at her sister's earnest face. Antoine is so clever, though she never realizes it. She's the very best girl in the world, and Charlotte loves her. She'll do anything to protect her. Charlotte looks again at the vial of unspeakable liquid in Antoine's hand, and shudders.

'All right,' Charlotte says, opening the book. '"For an anointment to confer resistance . . ."'

The spell is simple enough, and the sacrifices decay. Then it's a matter of determining what the embroidered book means by 'anointing', whether a dab on the forehead would be enough. They decide to start with that, and then they will test the gloves on each other.

It doesn't feel like protection when they dip their fingers in and touch a drop to each other's brow. It feels like penitence, and Charlotte is oddly grateful to share in it. The girls both shudder, and Charlotte has to block out all thoughts about what they've just touched, or she'll retch. It's lucky there's such a tiny quantity, barely enough to wet two fingertips.

They try the gloves, eventually dissolving into nervous giggles as they try to make each other walk like chickens or speak poetry. Nothing happens. They are immune.

Charlotte feels strangely powerful. She can't change her mother's heart, but she can find a way to stop Josepha's marriage. She has almost a month. There's still time.

The move to the Hofburg always exhausts Mama, who has to oversee every reinstallation of wood panelling, every arrangement of paintings. So when the bustle of the first few days has quieted, Mama goes to her private rooms, and there is a day or two of peace. She has a tiny chapel built onto her bedroom here, so even morning Mass at the Hofburg chapel is a quieter affair, without the presence of the Empress.

Joseph pulls Charlotte aside as they're leaving the chapel.

At that moment, he doesn't look like a twice-widowed emperor. He looks like her oldest brother, those familiar watery blue eyes smiling down at her.

'Will you bring Antoine and Max to my study after breakfast? I've sent word to your governesses. Angelo Soliman is coming by to show me a new kind of magic lantern – it has a stronger lamp inside, and projects clearer images on the wall. He suggested the youngest members of the family might like to see it. You can ask Josepha too if you like, but she's in bed with a headache, last I heard.'

Charlotte nods. 'Antoine loves magic lanterns. She'll be pleased.'

Joseph steps in closer, quieter. 'And will you make sure to tell Max to behave himself? I'm trying to convince Soliman that royal children aren't so bad.'

Charlotte suppresses a grin as they walk past the font, the crush of people ahead slowing them down. Angelo Soliman has been a friend of Joseph's for years; he organized everything for Joseph's first wedding, seven years ago. He heads the household of the Prince of Liechtenstein, whose palace is a short walk from the Hofburg, so Soliman has been a fixture in the children's lives. Charlotte likes to play chess with him and Antoine loves it when he takes her to see the warhorses.

'Has Dr Soliman developed some new fear of us?' she asks, joking.

'Keep this to yourself, but Soliman's leaving Prince Wenzel's household soon. He's getting married and he'll need some new employment. I've been trying to convince him to tutor Max.'

Charlotte duly gathers her two younger siblings and they traipse through the middle of several vast rooms and into Joseph's study. It's a square room, with the Emperor's desk in one corner, and one of the Hofburg's ornate white stoves in another. Smaller and duller than his study at Schönbrunn, but this one seems to suit Joseph better. The stoves are fed from the passageways behind the walls, so servants seldom come into the rooms at the Hofburg, unless they're called.

Joseph closes the doors as Angelo Soliman, standing in the middle of the room, bows to the children. Antoine gives her pretty curtsey, and Max a military bow. Soliman catches Charlotte's eye, with an expression of camaraderie.

Charlotte likes Soliman. He doesn't frown when Charlotte talks, or warn her against being prideful, or tell her there are only certain things she needs to know. In that, he is unlike all her teachers and her governesses, and certainly unlike her mother.

And today, he's brought his sabre, which pleases Max mightily. Max pulls it out of the scabbard and brandishes it, baring his teeth. Joseph has to put out an arm to protect his prize astronomical clock from the sabre's dull edge.

'Did you take this from a Turk, Dr Soliman?' Max asks, breathless.

Soliman smiles. 'No, Your Highness. I bought it so that I'd look dazzling at your brother's wedding. The war with Turkey was before my time. I fought against the Spanish, the Neapolitans, and the French, in the war over your mother's succession.'

There's an odd smell in the room: familiar but misplaced. A smell like wet leaves or old coins. Something musty – perhaps it's the magic lantern on the cart in the corner, although it looks quite new, all painted in red and yellow. It's a smell like – like the one that comes when sacrifices decay, Charlotte realizes. The smell of magic.

She glares at Antoine, looks her up and down, but doesn't see any enchanted items on her that she knows about. Antoine looks back at her, a little grumpy at being glared at. She looks nervous, though, too. Surely if she were up to something magical, she would have told Charlotte? Or is this something furtive like the business in the crypt all over again?

Charlotte takes a breath, and decides that she's imagined the smell. She, Antoine and Max take the chairs Soliman indicates, all in a row.

Joseph leans back, his elbow on the back of the unoccupied, upholstered yellow chair next to his, his fingers playing at his mouth. 'Max, Dr Soliman fought at the Battle of Piacenza, our great victory over the Bourbon forces.'

Max's eyes go wide.

'That was twenty years ago, when I was a young man,' Soliman says in his slightly accented German. 'But that was where I met His Highness Prince Josef Wenzel, and I have been in his service ever since.'

'But why are you in Vienna?' Max asks, his sabreless hands now at his hips. 'Why don't you go home?'

Soliman frowns slightly. 'Oh, I see. It's confusing, I know – my master is Prince of Liechtenstein, but he doesn't actually live in Liechtenstein. I don't believe he's even been there. He's always lived here in Vienna, and since I am head of his household—'

'No, I mean . . .' Max pauses. '. . . you come from Africa, don't you?'

'Ah,' Soliman says, and looks at Joseph, who makes a half-apologetic gesture. 'I was born in the Bornu Empire, but I was taken from there when I was a little younger than you are now. Do you know where the Bornu Empire is, Your Highness?'

Max does not.

'I've told you, the palace tutors are abysmal,' Joseph says. 'And geography's not even their worst subject.'

Soliman turns to Antoine and Charlotte, his expression quizzical.

Antoine says, 'I'm afraid Countess Brandeis doesn't emphasize such things in the education of girls.'

'What do governesses teach, I wonder?' Soliman asks Antoine, looking at her quite seriously.

It's an innocent question, but it makes Charlotte nervous all the same. Antoine glances at Charlotte, but she doesn't look nervous – she's only looking to her for commiseration. Charlotte had Brandeis for a governess until recently too.

'Oh, all sorts of rules.'

'Rules, Your Highness?'

'How one ought to greet a count, or how to signal that an audience is at an end, or what sort of rewards to give for service. That sort of thing.'

Charlotte has been trained in these things too, though at least she knows to what end. She has heard that Versailles has even more rules than Schönbrunn.

'Ah,' Soliman says, the shoulders inside his golden jacket relaxing slightly. 'Well, Your Highness, that does sound tedious, but necessary training for imperial children.'

'I don't see why,' Max says, still petulant.

'Because', Charlotte says, 'rules help everyone understand what to expect. Without rules, everything happens according to the monarch's whim, and that's despotism.'

Soliman turns to her. 'I see you've been reading your Montesquieu, Your Highness.'

She nods, partly in thanks for his gift of the book. She wants to say more about it – to discuss the definition of 'civic virtue', which she never feels she has quite understood – but she has learned not to show off. Soliman, at least, isn't looking at her as though her intelligence is a problem to be managed. She doesn't know quite how he's looking at her. There's satisfaction, but also . . . what? Not quite sadness. Reluctance. Perhaps there's something else he wants to say, too.

Or perhaps she said something wrong, and he doesn't want to embarrass her.

Soliman pulls the cart with the magic lantern into the middle of the room. He picks up a bundle of wooden slides, each of them with painted glass set into it. In his other hand, he holds a bit of chalk. 'You must each mark your slide, according to which one you think will be the most spectacular, and then we'll see who chose best.'

Antoine takes the chalk first, and looks through carefully, finally marking a pretty 'A' on a long slide that contains four pictures of animals. Max marks an 'M' on a slide with a stick protruding out of it. Charlotte chooses one with a windmill and a round pulley. She can smell magic again; she's sure of it.

Soliman takes a spill out of the vase, lights it in the fire and touches it to the small lamp inside the magic lantern. Joseph closes the window shutter and they are in darkness, save a circle of blurry light on the far wall, one of the few plain walls in the palace.

'We begin with His Highness's tightrope walker,' says Soliman with a grandiloquent manner. As he moves the stick, the figure walks across the rope, and Max claps his hands.

'This one', Soliman says, 'has an oddity to it. You do see that bird, above the tightrope-walker's head, all of you?'

'Of course,' says Max, pointing.

There is no bird on the image. The sky over the tightrope-walker's head is plain blue paint, not a spot on it.

Antoine opens her mouth, but Charlotte nudges her ankle under their chairs. She can smell magic, and she can sense a little too much interest in the set of Soliman's shoulders as he waits for their answers. Better to say the same as Max.

'You mean that little one, there,' she says. 'Oh yes, I think I see it. You see it, Antoine?'

'Of course,' Antoine says tightly.

Soliman's shoulders relax. 'Sometimes people can't see it from certain angles. The way the light bounces off the paint just there, a small chip in the glass, I suspect. Well, shall we move on to these handsome bears and leopards?'

There's a bang of a servant's rod outside the door, and it swings open, and the image of the tightrope-walker fades in sudden light from the next room. At the door stands Countess Brandeis. For a moment Charlotte thinks: We summoned her by gossiping about her; but then she sees the expression on Brandeis's face.

'Your Imperial Majesty, Your Highnesses,' Brandeis says. 'The Empress would like to see you immediately.'

Joseph rises. 'What's the matter?'

He goes to the door of the study, speaks quietly to the countess, then turns back, his fingers to his temple and his eyes downcast. 'It's Josepha. Her headache – it's smallpox.'

CHAPTER FOUR

*Red Curtains — Notes from a Harpsichord — The Empress
Changes Her Plans — Recriminations —
A Conversation Overheard*

———————— �֍ ————————

The court adopts its familiar smallpox practices for the second time that year. Performances and balls are cancelled, not only at court but throughout the city, because, in Vienna, when there's an outbreak in one there's an outbreak in the other. Everyone eats alone in their rooms, and when they pass in the halls, they keep their distance.

The doctor is old fashioned. Every time Charlotte passes Josepha's room, she sees covered porcelain pans being removed. Blood. She can't see her sister in the dim room; all she sees, in those brief moments when the door opens, is red. Red blankets, red curtains. Why the colour red ought to have any effect on smallpox, she can't say, but the doctor always does it. Ties bits of cloth around people's arms and necks.

A week passes like this, and Charlotte speaks very little to anyone. Antoine stays away from her, even at night. Maids dress her quickly, from behind, and leave again. She spends a lot of time looking out of the window and reading: sometimes the embroidered book, sometimes Montesquieu, sometimes Hume, thanks to Joseph. She thinks about the smell of magic and Dr Soliman's questions, and the more she thinks about it, the more she convinces herself it was all her imagination. But sometimes she lets herself wonder if perhaps he is a magister after all, if her decision to lie to him may have been a mistake. Perhaps he wants to teach them! But then again, perhaps he would tell Joseph or, worse, Mama, and they would take the embroidered book away.

She does not see Josepha ever again. Josepha dies on 15 October, the very day she was meant to leave Vienna for her new home in Naples.

Mama calls her children into her study at the Hofburg the day before the funeral, to say a prayer in private together. It's a warm room full of gilt and wood, and the air is stuffy. Everyone is in black. Even now, they stand some distance apart, like guards arrayed in the courtyard.

Charlotte has a tune in her head, a set of five notes, rising, falling. Harpsichord notes – it's a piece Josepha used to play. The notes light, melodic, almost frivolous. The harpsichords are silent – no one would dare play while the court is in mourning – but the notes press into her mind all the same, dampening everything else. Mama's red eyes, red knuckles on the edge of her desk. Josepha always held her hands so prettily at the harpsichord, her left little finger crooked; Charlotte can see it.

Not all the children are here. Liesl is unwell and still in bed; she has caught smallpox too but is expected to recover. The doctors say that Liesl will be horribly scarred, though. Pretty Liesl.

Joseph loved Josepha so; she was his favourite. He holds his own little daughter close to him, the only two people in the room who aren't standing apart.

Charlotte. Antoine.

Max, whose ten-year-old face is red and puffy.

Amalia, who, as an unmarried and unscarred Habsburg of

twenty-one, is on borrowed time, stands like a soldier near the door, as though she expects an ambush.

But the first shot is directed at Joseph.

'I'm told there's a delegation of Protestants come to meet with you,' Maria Theresa says, levelling her gaze at the Holy Roman Emperor.

'They will wait until after the funeral, of course.'

'They will wait longer than that.'

'They wish to discuss the restrictions on their own worship, Mother. Restrictions that are in dire need of reform.'

'Joseph, you think everything is in dire need of reform.'

He says nothing, which says a great deal. His little daughter stands upright, looking at his face, while he looks at the Empress.

'If we were not Catholic monarchs of a Catholic nation, what would we be?' Maria Theresa says, spreading her delicate hands wide. 'Despots. There would be no higher law, no restraint, and men could do as they liked. We must be humble before God, in this sacred hour. We must take refuge in Him, and put our Empire fully in His hands.'

Joseph raises his chin. 'Then I'll tell the Protestants to go away, and perhaps while I'm at it, we can expel the Jews from Prague again.'

Charlotte freezes, and everyone in the room freezes too. Mama's deportation of the Jews happened before Charlotte was born, and she knows little about it, or how it ended.

'I have agreed that was an error,' Mama says evenly. 'I am fallible. I make mistakes, but I put my faith in God, and I ask him to guide me to do better. What do you use for guidance, Joseph? Faith? I don't think so. No, with you it's all books and bons mots. Wit! All your clever, barbed conversations, but there's no decency in any of it.'

Joseph burns; Charlotte can feel it, and she burns on his behalf. She breathes heavily, wanting to defend him but seeing the pain on her mother's face too. Mama blames herself for Josepha's death. Indeed, the whole court blames Mama. The story of the improperly sealed tomb, leaking unspeakable liquors, has made the rounds. Josepha caught smallpox from her dead sister-in-law, people say, because of the Empress's obstinate piety.

'I will send the Protestants away,' Joseph says, even more quietly than Mama. Their voices always get lowest when they are angriest; it is the Habsburg way.

'Good,' Mama says. 'We have problems enough without going looking for more. I have had letters from all the Bourbons, who send their condolences. We cannot much longer delay the wedding with Naples.'

'But Josepha is dead!' says Max. 'How can she be married?'

'Max, it's time you learned to hold your tongue and think,' snaps Mama. 'I have other daughters, do I not?'

Sixteen years, Josepha lived. Sixteen years, she smiled with her hand over her mouth, and played quietly with Max on the floor with his toy soldiers, and ran through the gardens with her favourite sister, who's now in the crypt with her.

Charlotte remembers, pointlessly, the name of the piece Josepha used to play, the one that is playing now in her head, the notes rising and falling mockingly. The Sarabande from Handel's Suite in D Minor.

In the doorway, Amalia puts her hand to her waist, as if she wears a sword there rather than a pannier.

'Amalia, be at ease. Ferdinand of Naples does not want a bride five years his senior,' snaps Mama. 'Charlotte, it is Naples for you, I'm afraid. Amalia is too old and Antoine is too young.'

Charlotte . . .

The final notes of the Sarabande.

. . . it is . . .

The right hand reaching, the left hand pulling back.

. . . Naples . . .

Josepha's hands poised over the keyboard.

. . . for you.

Charlotte hears the 'No' escape her lips before she thinks the word. In her head there's no more music.

No.

Charlotte was never meant to go to Naples; she has always been promised to the Dauphin of France. She's trained for France! All her planned enchantments, starting with the gloves, are for diplomacy. She's prepared for politics, not whatever the boorish King of Naples might want of her. Decoration? Submission?

'No?' Mama asks in a whisper.

Charlotte breathes, and starts again. 'God has taken away the bride you prepared for the King of Naples, Mama. Perhaps He considers the matter closed.'

'Oh, it's blasphemy now, is it?' Mama says. 'Charlotte, I expect you to do your duty. Naples was ruled by Austrian Habsburgs when I was a child. Now you have a chance to win it back for us: in fact, if not in name. You can do what an army cannot, and all you need do is be pleasant, stand up straight, bear children, whisper wisdom into your husband's ear, and speak prudently on those rare occasions when you must speak in public at all.'

If only there were an odious substance she could paint on her body to protect herself from this. But Mama doesn't need magic to do her harm.

And Charlotte doesn't need magic to survive a wound. She lifts her chin, opens her mouth, and asks, 'When must I go?'

Mama shrugs. 'The King of Naples knows you are bereaved. They won't insist that you come right away. But we can't leave it too long.'

For once, Antoine's face is not a mask. She is stricken. And well she should be. If Charlotte could be angry with her, this might be easier for both of them. Charlotte makes an attempt at petulance, says, 'Send me to Naples, then, and forget me.'

She isn't speaking to Mama but to Antoine.

Mama snorts. 'This is not a pantomime, Charlotte. Spare us your dramatic speeches.'

'We are left with the question of who will marry the Dauphin,' murmurs Joseph.

Mama spreads her black-taffeta arms wide. 'Amalia is for Parma. Liesl, poor dear, will never lose her smallpox scars. She will make an abbess, and pray for all our souls. Antoine is the only one left to me. Antoine will have to do for France.'

'But she is . . .'

'Antoine is eleven. The Dauphin is thirteen. We have a year or two to get Antoine into condition.'

Charlotte can barely look at Antoine, for fear of what she'll see on her face.

Charlotte, it is Naples for you. Antoine will have to do for France. The word of the Empress.

For once, Charlotte is glad that she is separated from Antoine for the hour before dinner, when they each are meant to take their exercise. She tells her governess she's going out to the gardens and while Lerchenfeld is fussing with her cloak, Charlotte runs ahead into the bright cool air.

The Hofburg is just inside the walls of Vienna, an irregular ring of bastions and open slopes that separate the old city from its suburbs. Unlike Schönbrunn with its acres of orangeries and lakes, the green spaces here are mostly tucked inside the palace, in courtyards or squares. The one place to get a good walk is the narrow strip of private garden outside the palace proper, and just inside the fortifications. A central path leads from one section to the next, each laid out with trees, topiary and neat hedge walls.

It's cold today, wonderfully cold, though the grass is still green. The world smells like moss and bark: an October smell. Nobody's here. Charlotte strides towards the little maze at the centre of the garden, pauses for a moment, and then runs into it, her black cloak streaming behind her. She turns down one path and then another. For a moment, at least, she'll be alone.

It's a childish thing to do but Charlotte can't bear anyone looking at her or talking at her now. She's too angry to think straight, and what might happen if, for once, Charlotte did or said something without thinking?

She sags against a statue of Minerva. She's worn out, panting from more than the sharp October air. It takes everything Charlotte has to anticipate the blows before they come, from her mother, from the grinning, looming courtiers, from governesses and teachers. To find ways to fend them off, or cushion them, or heal the wounds they leave. She works all the time; she watches all the time. She doesn't have the energy to do all that and not be angry.

Josepha is dead. Josepha deserved better; she deserved a moment to sit and read a book or play her harpsichord in peace. Charlotte would have gladly taken Josepha's place to save her from going to Naples, but now she is taking her place and it saves no one, helps no one. No one but Mama and her schemes and alliances.

Charlotte puts her hands to her cheeks.

Rage is a relief. Easier than some other possibilities. And here, for a moment, she can be angry in peace, and hurt no one. The hedges are half a foot higher than her head, and thick. A maze is a kind of magic: a way to escape without leaving; a way to hide under the dove-grey sky.

A crunch on the gravel: a footstep. She whirls and sees Antoine, holding her black skirt in both hands and looking nervous. As though she's found a monster in the middle of the labyrinth.

'You'll get a lecture, Antoine, if Mama finds out we've been together. My terrible influence and all that.'

'What more can she do to us?' Antoine asks, her voice a mix of bright and sweet and sad.

'She'd think of something.'

'Charlotte, I'm so—'

Charlotte shakes her head. 'Antoine, leave it.'

'But – but Charlotte, I – How horrible that you—'

Charlotte feels the words surging at her teeth, demanding escape. They fly like knives. 'Stop. Just stop.'

'You'll be a wonderful queen, Charlotte,' Antoine says earnestly. 'You'll be just like Mama. A great ruler.'

Charlotte winces. 'I am *nothing* like her. I'm nothing but one of her spare parts. And you – you're not even that yet. Try to remember it, before—'

'Before I get anyone else killed.'

Charlotte turns to her then, and the anger, damn it, dissipates. Why wouldn't Antoine leave her alone? Antoine is shivering, her arms wrapped around herself.

'I didn't say that,' Charlotte says. 'And you must not think it. Not for a moment. You and I painted that – that horrible – If the infection came from the coffin, you would have taken ill too. Perhaps Josepha was sick before she even went into the crypt, and it has nothing to do with you.'

Antoine looks down the gravel of the path, at a brown leaf caught in an eddy of wind. It flies past her toes and catches on the base of the statue. 'Mama thinks I had a mild case as a baby. Perhaps I'm immune to smallpox. I was a vain little beast, to be so upset by making a mistake in the ballet. And now Josepha is dead and you – I'm so sorry, Charlotte. I can't tell you how sorry I am. I don't have words for it.'

The air has gone out of Charlotte, the anger, the hurt, everything. She feels nothing but grief.

She and Antoine sink to the ground, their skirts on the damp gravel, and hug tightly, black taffeta cold in each other's arms.

They are just putting their hands to the ground to raise themselves up when they both freeze. They hear adult voices, passing by on the path that encircles the maze, and Charlotte puts her hand out to stop Antoine.

'Dr Mesmer and Dr Hell are always going to be at each other's throats.' The voice is familiar, someone speaking Parisian French. Charlotte kneels, cranes her neck and catches a glimpse. Louis de Rohan, the French prince-bishop. Charlotte half forgot he was still in Vienna; she hasn't seen him since the move from Schönbrunn. He says, 'Take my advice, Soliman, and don't let Mesmer spout his reformist ideas. Before you know it, you'll have rogue magisters performing spells in every alley in Vienna.'

Soliman! Charlotte catches a glimpse of a red turban, and then they've walked on, past them.

She crouches back down with Antoine and whispers, 'Come on. I want to hear what they're talking about.'

Antoine's eyes go wide, but Charlotte doesn't stop to argue. She creeps along the hedge, silently cursing the crick in her back. This little maze is nothing like the grand labyrinth at Schönbrunn – if they'd been standing, Rohan and Soliman would have seen them. She creeps to the corner and looks; the men are farther along the path, up on a raised circular court surrounded by a low stone wall. She can see them, their backs to her.

Charlotte gestures to Antoine and they run across an open area to the wall, crouch below it. She doesn't think the men have seen them, but she can hardly hear over her heart.

'I'm sure of it, Brother,' Soliman says, his voice low. 'My chalk left no mark on their hands. It would have, if they had done any magic within the last month. Five years I've watched them, and I've found no evidence. I had a suspicion, yes, after that strange moment during the ballet performance, but now I know it was wrong.'

Antoine grasps her arm, but Charlotte avoids her gaze, her own hand to her mouth.

'Perhaps the girls fooled you somehow,' Rohan says. 'Perhaps they've put a spell on you.'

'They can't put a spell on me, of course.'

'Well, how am I to know what your practices are here?' Rohan retorts. 'You've said yourself it's as much as you can do to keep everyone in line. And whether the governess told the children anything or not, the fact remains she was a rogue magister in the imperial court. You and your Vienna friends must decide whether you are a chapter of the Order of 1326 or just another nest of rogues.'

'I would have handled that whole business with the governess differently,' Soliman retorts. 'But what was done was done, and I have done my best to make sure it left no trace.'

'There's still too much we don't know about that governess, and you've had five years to find out.'

'It seems there isn't much to find out. She was what rogue magisters always are: unlucky enough to find out something they should never have known. I don't think she had many spells. We know she didn't make herself immune.'

'That's true enough,' Rohan says, with an edge to his voice Charlotte dislikes. 'You don't suppose the girls, though—'

'I think it's highly unlikely they could have obtained what they need, even if they knew about it. Anyway, I tested them for that as well; they saw an illusion they would not have, if they were immune.'

'Well, we'll lose our chance to take their memories soon enough, and it'll be death or nothing, if you're wrong. They'll be anointed when they're crowned. One for Naples and one for France, I suspect. Our last chance to make sure of this business without mess.'

Death or nothing. Rohan looks out at the garden, over the girls' heads. They crouch as low as they can.

'If we act,' Soliman says, 'if we intercede to take their memories, that too presents a risk of discovery. I believe that risk is unnecessary and imprudent, given the lack of evidence. They were very young when Countess Ertag died. Even if she did say something to them, it would be no more real to them now than fairy tales. And I don't think she said anything.'

There's silence for a few moments, and Antoine's breathing so loudly. So is Charlotte, for that matter. They should get away, but they don't dare move. She grips Antoine's hand in her own.

'All right,' Rohan says at last. 'An end to it, then, Dr Soliman. You'll be glad to spend your time on more important things, I'm sure. I'll make my report to Paris. And I'll take that illumination spell, too, thank you, although I think something other than shoes . . .'

The two men are walking again, away from the girls, and their voices trail off.

Charlotte and Antoine look at each other with wide eyes, holding each other's arms, their breath fogging together. There are magisters in Vienna, right in the very heart of the imperial court, and they have spells to share and opinions to debate. They knew about Countess Ertag. And they have been watching Charlotte and Antoine, for years, watching for signs that they know something they should not.

CHAPTER FIVE

*Black Silk — The House of Bourbon — Antoine Is
Twelve — Charlotte's Trousseau — Leave-takings*

A few days after Josepha's funeral, Mama calls Charlotte into
her study. One wall is cluttered with the children's landscape
paintings. When Charlotte was small, when Papa was still
alive, all the children used to come in here and chatter away
while Mama signed papers, a smile on her face.

Now, Mama and Charlotte face each other in black silk.
Mama is standing, so Charlotte stands too.

'You must stop,' Mama says, without so much as a greeting.
'Charlotte, from this moment forward, your complaining
stops.'

There's no point in arguing. 'As you say, Mama.'

'You are fifteen and yet you act like a child. The world
does not conform itself to your wishes, and it never will. It
would be best if you resigned yourself to that fact now, before
you do your family and your country damage.'

'I am sorry, Mama.'

Charlotte is only half listening. She is thinking, as she has
been thinking for days, about what spells Angelo Soliman
might have. Would he be able to explain the mysterious
spells in the embroidered book? If not him, well, he and

55

Rohan spoke of other magisters. Of 'rogues'. Perhaps the world is full of people who know about magic.

Mama comes around the edge of the desk, closer. 'Naples is very beautiful.'

'So I have heard, Mama.' Charlotte can't help adding, with a little smile to show she's not entirely serious but also that she is not going to forgive anything, 'The volcano must keep it interesting.'

Mama's mouth shows her disapproval of irony, but she stays in diplomatic mode. 'And not only the city. The whole southern portion of Italy is yours, my dear, and Sicily too.'

'Mine? I don't think the House of Bourbon will see it that way.'

'You always knew you would marry into that family,' Mama says sharply. 'Do not act as though this has surprised you.'

'I believed I would marry the Dauphin, and go to France. You always told me so.'

'Surely one Bourbon is as good as another.'

She's shaken out of thinking about magic, now. Irritated. 'But, Mama, the King of Naples does everything his father tells him to do. Naples is ruled from afar by the King of Spain. In France I could be of some *use*. Some purpose.'

'In France, your purpose would have been to hold the Bourbon alliance and hold the support of France and Spain for Austria and the Empire, against our enemies. England is rising, and Prussia will never be satisfied. Your role in Naples is the same: to cement the compact between the families, and rear children who will ensure the continuation of the Empire.'

'But, Mama, if the King of Spain is the true power in Naples, I'll be powerless.'

Mama turns away, looks down at her desk, at the perpetual stack of papers, the coffee set, the inkwell, the engraved brass globe.

'I know what it's like to have one's childhood expectations

exposed as the fragile things they are. My father spent the last years of his life bartering with every European power, getting promises that they would recognize me as his heir. Oh, the treasures he traded away for those promises! I was twenty-three when he died and, immediately, the vultures descended. This king and that king, all portioning up my lands for themselves, claiming to be horrified at the thought of a woman inheriting. Monsters. Most of Europe was against me. My father had left me a handful of promises but he had not thought to leave me much of an army. Do you know what I did?'

'You went to Hungary.' Charlotte has always liked this story.

Mama grips the side of her desk, as if for support, and indeed she is shaky on her feet these days. 'I went to Hungary. I rode a black horse up to the top of a hill and I brandished my sword and I swore to defend Hungary to my last breath. I gave myself to Hungary in return for an army. And with that army, I won back nearly everything. But do you know what it says on all the official documents, my daughter?'

Charlotte frowns. She doesn't know this part. This is a departure from the usual tale. 'I don't, Mama.'

'It says that I am *King* of Hungary, and Austria, and Bohemia, of all my other lands. I am king. Because one cannot be both a woman and a sovereign at once, you see. And as for emperor, well, I had to ask your dear papa to take that title on for me. Do you know what they shouted in Hungary, when I rode my black horse? "Our lives and blood for King Maria Theresa!"'

Mama is a king. Just as Charlotte is not a magistra but a magister.

Mama steps forward and puts one hand on each of Charlotte's shoulders. 'You will not be powerless in Naples, my dear daughter. Power is not something you are given. Power is something you take. When you are a woman, it is a little more difficult, that's all. You have to give people a way to believe they don't see you taking it. Your power, as a woman, is in submission, as I submitted to Hungary.'

Charlotte bends her head, in acknowledgement, if not submission. 'Mama,' she says, quietly, 'will Antoine be all right?'

'Better than all right. They say the Dauphin is very sweet, by the standards of thirteen-year-old boys.'

'Well, perhaps it is for the best, then,' Charlotte says with a grin. 'I couldn't stand a sweet husband.'

'No, indeed!' Mama lets her hands drop from Charlotte's shoulders. 'All of France will fall in love with Antoine. Our dear little pet. How could they not adore her? Of course, we have a great deal of work to do to make her ready. All her tutors are unsuitable, and I shall have to send to France for others. French history, etiquette, deportment. And then there is the matter of her spelling. I had thought of asking Angelo Soliman to take over her language instruction, because Joseph speaks so highly of him, but he's run off to get married, so I'll have to find someone else.'

Charlotte blinks. 'Run off?'

'Yes, my dear. Joseph tells me she's a Kellerman, so from a good family, and widow of Countess Harrach's secretary – what was his name?'

Charlotte should be relieved; she doesn't need to worry about Soliman discovering them, with him gone from Vienna. Instead she feels strangely desolate.

'I didn't know he was going so soon.'

'Mmm, so soon after your sister's funeral. It would have been better to postpone it.'

Very quietly, Charlotte asks, 'And my wedding? When is that to be?'

'We'll perform it here in April, at the Augustinian church, with one of your brothers standing as proxy for the groom. That gives you a full six months to prepare. Then you'll travel to Naples, and I'm sure they'll want to have another ceremony there after you arrive.'

'And Antoine? How long before she goes to France?'

'I think we can make it two years at least. The Dauphin is young too, and not yet king. There is time for them. Speaking of churches, I have an idea. The Abbé Vermond might be able to help Antoine with her French. I think she'd do very well if she only applied herself.'

'I'm sure you're right, Mama,' Charlotte says, and means it. She kisses her mother on her powdered cheek, and to her surprise, she means that too.

Antoine turns twelve while the court is still in mourning. She feels terribly old, now that her marriage is being arranged.

In February, they ask Joseph about Soliman as casually as they can, and he says Soliman's wedding took place, very quietly with just a few witnesses because the Prince of Liechtenstein did not approve. Soliman has, in fact, left the prince's service at last, and taken his wife travelling. He said something about Trieste.

Mama sends for a new doctor, to inoculate Joseph's daughter and Max against the smallpox; the older children are deemed to have been exposed to it often enough. The inoculation is dangerous: the doctor takes a scraping of a smallpox sore from an infected person and places it inside a cut in the skin of the healthy patient. For several days, the only reports anyone makes about anything are the latest count of pustules, the incidence of fever. But both children recover, and Maria Theresa declares that she will begin a programme of inoculation for anyone who wants the procedure and cannot afford it. Gradually, the balls and concerts resume, as smallpox abates again, for months, years if they're lucky.

While all of this occupies the Empress, Charlotte and Antoine make the most of their time together. In the six months between Josepha's death and Charlotte's proxy wedding, they do as many spells as they can, making Charlotte a kind of magical trousseau, with all the weapons she might require.

She has some things already: a fan that can cool a room, the Pandora doll and, now, her white gloves. She won't be taking her childish old nightgown with her, the one with the enchanted pocket on the inside where she hides the embroidered book. She and Antoine enchant a new pocket for her, a portable one of the kind they wear under their skirts. A pale, rose-coloured pouch of plain linen, with ribbons for tying it around her waist. They also attempt a couple of new enchantments: a thimble that can break something – a thread, a piece of fabric – into even pieces, and a spell to make the contents of a book seem like the contents of another book to anyone but its owner.

They do the enchantment to make a little more of the oil that makes metal and stone pliable, in case it's useful.

There is a spell they've never been able to make work, for crumbs that show a path, and they try it again, with no success. Magic mending is of no use to them at the moment: they have nothing to mend. As for the shoe that rises in the air, which Charlotte once used to play a prank on Mozart, it seems of little use now.

That leaves only two spells that they can make sense of. One is for a drink that confers loyalty, but its sacrifices are unimaginably high. The other is the enchantment for 'a shroud to remember the dead', which is not something Charlotte wants in her trousseau.

The fourteenth spell they puzzled out, for immunity, is something Charlotte only needed once.

They've never found the spell for the embroidery within the book itself. Antoine thinks it's probably there, written so confusingly that she and Charlotte have no idea what it does. There must also be a way to make secret writing appear. What wonders might be in the book, but hidden to them! Perhaps there's even a love spell, somewhere?

Charlotte and Antoine put off the work of deciding how they will continue to share one book between them, with a mountain range in the middle.

So, on their last night together, a spring evening, they sprawl on the floor of Antoine's room, each with a pen and an inkwell and a sheaf of papers, copying out spells: the ones they understand and the ones they don't.

'I wonder where Ertag found these,' Charlotte says. 'The way they're written – she wouldn't have written them that way herself.'

Antoine copies the words that appear in nearly every spell: 'these proofs have been found'. What does it mean? It sounds as though spells are things that magisters can discover, or even invent. She thinks of saying something about it, but remembers Charlotte chiding her, months before: *People don't invent roses.*

Charlotte stops, puts down her pen and sits up, sighing.

'What is it?' Antoine asks. She's still lying on her front, copying out spells.

'All of this,' Charlotte says, gesturing at the piles of paper. 'So much we don't understand. What do we have? Fans and dolls and ribbons.'

'We puzzled out the immunity spell. Maybe we'll puzzle out these others too.'

'Maybe. But this is only one spellbook! We know there are other magisters in the world, and they must have amazing powers. We know they keep magic secret, and they don't seem to want us to know about it. If they were to find out, Antoine, what would they do?'

Antoine thinks of Countess Ertag's bloody bedsheets and shudders. 'They won't find out.'

'We must be very careful, and not ever mention magic to anyone. Antoine, if someone comes to you and says they're a magister, asks what you know, you must not say anything about it. Don't do any new magic that might go wrong in ways you can't predict – yes, I'm thinking of the gloves. If you see Rohan, write to me. When Soliman comes back to Vienna, if he talks to you about anything at all, write to me. Do you promise, Antoine?'

'Of course. We've kept it secret this long.' Antoine looks over the papers filled with strange instructions. *Fans and dolls and ribbons,* Charlotte said. 'But how will we ever learn any new spells if we can't do new magic?'

Charlotte pauses, and gives voice to something she's hardly allowed herself to think about until now. 'Do you remember Rohan saying, "They'll be anointed when they're crowned"? When we're queens, they wouldn't dare act against us. Maybe there's something they've done to Mama and Joseph, but Mama and Joseph didn't understand it, but we will. I'll find out what I can. Perhaps there are books about it in Naples. Once I have a son, I'll be on the Council there, and then I'll be able to order all sorts of scientific enquiries, as queen. Perhaps when you are a queen, you can do the same. But for now, we must be careful. I promise, I won't let anyone find out about you. And whatever you do, keep the book hidden.'

'Aren't you taking the book, Charlotte? I think you should. You're the one travelling.'

'You'll be travelling too, dear, soon enough.'

'But you were the one who finished the embroidery. It's yours. It's always been yours, really. I don't think it would be right if it stayed with me.'

Charlotte leans closer on one elbow and kisses Antoine's cheek. She seems glad; she has always been protective of the book. 'All right. You keep these copies, then, and I'll take the book. But you must be very careful to keep them safe. Put them inside an enchanted pocket and put that under the floorboards. No one must ever see them.'

Antoine nods. 'I don't know what I'll do without you, Charlotte. I can't imagine it.'

'You won't be without me,' Charlotte says, and takes her hand. 'Not ever. Don't forget. If anything ever happens, if you need help, I will help you. Always. Even if you're in the wilds of America.'

'I'm not going to the wilds of America,' says Antoine,

giggling. They used to play at living simple lives in nature, or at exploring strange islands and ruling pirate bands, but she's too grown up for that now. 'I'm going to Paris.'

'All the easier for me to reach you, then. No matter what, I will help you. I promise.'

Antoine purses her lips, and nods. 'I promise too.'

They have always known they would be separated one day. They have known it as they have known that one day they will die. That doesn't make it any easier.

Charlotte stands in the grey morning courtyard, looking at her sister in her blue jacket and dress. Antoine looks older, suddenly. A dauphine in the making.

'I wish I could climb into your pocket,' Antoine whispers, 'and go with you.'

'Climb in,' Charlotte whispers back. 'This is my enchanted one.'

At that, Antoine grins. Then: 'If something happens in Naples,' she says, her smile gone, 'if—'

'Write to me often. Always use the cipher. The one that Joseph taught us. And change the keyword with each letter; do you remember the order?'

'*Amour, corps, espoir, mémoire, trésor,*' Antoine recites.

Charlotte wants to say that everything will be fine, but she can't. It isn't true, and she can't hide it from Antoine. Antoine is, despite her smart little jacket and pile of curls, not a child any more. They're being sent away like packages to the men who've ordered them, and nothing will ever be entirely fine now.

Charlotte holds her sister close, warm in her arms. Then she looks one last time into Antoine's cornflower eyes and wonders which of them will sacrifice this memory. She turns. She walks away.

Countess Lerchenfeld, their old governess, is waiting by the carriage that will deliver Charlotte to Naples. She packs Charlotte in with her attendants and her furs and books. For the next three weeks, this carriage will be Charlotte's world, taking her over the Alps and down into Italy.

'Lerchenfeld, I have one request, for when you return here without me,' Charlotte says. She's seated now, but the carriage door is still open, and Lerchenfeld is holding her gloved hand.

'I will make a good report of you to your mother and brother.'

'You're very kind. But would you also . . . write to me, often, and please be sure in every letter to send word of Antoine. Write the smallest details: what she says, what she does, almost what she thinks. If anything happens, tell me.'

Lerchenfeld looks at her quizzically.

'She will soon be a bride herself,' Charlotte supplies, because Lerchenfeld seems to want an explanation, 'and I wish I could prepare her for the ordeal. She is so young and so soft-hearted. Please – please love her, for my sake.'

Lerchenfeld nods. 'I will be a friend to your sister. And I will write you letters, every week. More.'

Charlotte nods, absently, as Lerchenfeld closes the carriage door. Charlotte puts her hand to the window-glass to cover the small figure of Antoine, her warm-hearted sister nothing but a cold, blue blur.

Then she opens the carriage door and runs out, before they can stop her, before she can stop herself. She gathers Antoine into her arms and they fall into tears, shaking, laughing at each other between their sobs.

PART TWO

1768 TO 1775

CHAPTER SIX

Charlotte Travels to Italy – Conversations with Leopold –
Conversations with Ferdinand – The Wedding –
The White Gloves

———————— ❖ ————————

Maria Theresa, to her credit, is a formidable negotiator of marriage contracts: as soon as Charlotte bears an heir, she will be given a seat on the Council of Naples. The better to do what the Empress expects of her daughter: protect Austria's interests and keep her mother and brother apprised of what the Bourbons are doing. This, along with the rearing of good Catholic children, is what Maria Theresa expects. She has made that clear over the course of the last six months.

Charlotte has quietly used these six months to read all of Joseph's philosophy books and decide what sort of queen she can be and will be, in Naples. It's true that she can't count on her position giving her as much respect or influence as it might have in France. But Charlotte knows she can be more than the protector of Habsburg interests. She can be a great queen, and she intends to be one.

And Joseph, in his conversations with her over the last few months, has given her some practical advice.

'Nobody pretends that the King of Naples is anything but a figurehead, so his advisers report directly to the King of

Spain,' Joseph said after she returned his copy of Hume's *Treatise of Human Nature* and gave him her impressions of it. 'That's a problem, but also an opportunity. Think of the people in Naples who will feel aggrieved and neglected. The writers and artists and philosophers who have no royal patron. The local nobility, who have been told they don't matter. You can be the champion of those people, and they'll love you for it.'

So Charlotte has been preparing, when she wasn't spending time with Antoine, mining Joseph for all the information about wars and diplomacy that she could, or asking the Italians at court about customs and history. Now she has a journey of 873 miles, and she still has work to do. By the time the carriages reach Salzburg, she has a notebook full of comments on the opera, which Neapolitans are said to love, and she has memorized the names of all the King's relatives and advisers.

Salzburg is the border of the Alps, and marks the place where Antoine's future journey will diverge from Charlotte's. Charlotte's carriage turns to the south, towards a horizon that ripples and rises.

At Innsbruck, Charlotte writes to Lerchenfeld and asks for news of Antoine. It's a beautiful city, all cold whites and blues even on the sunniest spring days, surrounded by snow-capped mountains. She prays in the room where her father died, now converted into a chapel by Maria Theresa. She makes a list of expressions she likes in the Neapolitan language. *Ô paese mio*: in my country or in my opinion. *Meglio sulo ca male accumpagnato*: better alone than in bad company.

By the time they reach the Brenner Pass, she is spending more time than she likes staring out of the window, her thoughts wordless, as fanciful as the sinuous clouds and the sparkling veins of quartz in the cliffside. The people watch the imperial carriage train as if it were a stray dog; they wear coloured feathers in their hats.

The convoy stops at an ugly inn, and by morning she has

her paper and pencil in hand again. She makes an inventory of the sacrifices she can make, as the carriage rattles downhill into a land of hillside vineyards. Hopes she would rather bury; affections that hurt.

One day, it's warm enough in the carriage that she wishes she had her enchanted fan, which cools down any room so nicely. But it's wrapped inside a fur deep in one of her trunks, because it cools down everything around it even when she doesn't want it to. She always wears gloves when she uses it, because it's like ice to the touch. Yet another girlish enchantment that is of very little use.

In golden Florence, she meets her brother Leopold and his Bourbon wife, who is a sister of Charlotte's new husband. She hasn't seen Leopold in three years, not since he became the Grand Duke of Tuscany. More importantly, he hasn't seen her in three years, and he treats her almost as if she were a stranger, a visiting ruler who needs to know the lay of the land. She loves him for it.

Even better, Leopold and his wife accompany her south to her new home. She sits in a carriage with her brother as they roll on to Rome.

'Your wife is lovely,' she says. 'Such beautiful blue eyes.'

'Yes, she's very good.'

'Not like her brother then.'

Leopold laughs shortly. 'Ah, no. Not much like her brother. They both have the same long nose, but I must admit it suits Luisa much better.'

'Is he awful?'

He shrugs. 'Your husband? Ferdinand is a nonentity. An irritation. You'll have no difficulty getting around him, so long as you don't have any unrealistic expectations.'

'Love, you mean.'

He looks out of the window, where the trees are bright with green. 'Ha! Yes. Love. But I meant, well, common decency, really. Reason. Respect. He's not . . . sound. Do you know what I mean? He's rotten to the core. But as long as you don't try to lean on him, he can't hurt you too badly. I think.'

'You fill me with hope, Brother.'

He looks back at her, very serious. 'Hope is something we all have to set aside, sooner or later, if we're realists. You'll get on all right, Charlotte. There's a mountain range between us and Mama now. We can make our own lives here. And I won't be far. Don't worry too much about Ferdinand. Give him enough freedom to keep himself occupied and he won't get in your way. The man you really have to watch out for is Bernardo Tanucci.'

'He was the head of the council of regency when Ferdinand was still a minor, yes? The Tuscan lawyer.'

Leopold nods. 'Tanucci is still the real ruler of Naples, though he reports to Ferdinand's father in Spain. Any policy that keeps money flowing into the coffers, and thus Tanucci's purse, is the official policy of Naples. There's no military to speak of, because that would cost money. And anyone who *has* money must give it up or shut up. Taxes upon taxes. The people don't like it, but there's not much they can do about it, and Ferdinand being such a vulgar oaf protects him from criticism – the King is a man of the people, you see. The Church is another matter. Tanucci's practically at war with the Pope – His Holiness had the gall to think himself above him.'

Charlotte's expression says something like: 'Well, well.'

'So the question is', Leopold says, crossing his legs, 'whether you want to be Queen of Naples in reality, or just in name. I recommend the latter course as the easier option. But somehow I doubt that's the path you'll take.'

She smiles. 'If I weren't a queen, what would I be?'

Leopold shrugs and grins. 'Charlotte, I suppose.'

She shakes her head, but she's grinning too. 'I left that waif behind on the road, somewhere north of the Alps.'

They've been told to drive straight through Rome, because of Tanucci's troubles with the Pope, but Charlotte insists they stop long enough to have at least a look at Saint Peter's. They sleep in Marino that night, and she stays up late and writes a letter to Antoine.

Three days, and they reach Terracina, on a warm day. Everything smells like rotting fish. On one side, mountains; on the other, the sea. On a tiny spit of land surrounded by marshes, a pavilion waits, with her husband inside it. No escape.

Ferdinand is not as ugly as his portrait led Charlotte to believe. He looks insouciant, almost dashing, in his bright blue coat, thick with medals and sashes. It brings out his eyes, which are intelligent enough, or perhaps it's only that they are appraising, and confident. He looks her up and down when she enters the pavilion.

She does as she's been taught: she kneels before him. He snorts. What does that mean? What is he snorting about? She's done something wrong, or – no, he's breaking the formality to keep himself comfortable. He takes Charlotte by the hand and lifts her to her feet, and grins at her.

Another eight hours by carriage to the Palace of Caserta, and this time she cannot ride with Leopold. Charlotte and Ferdinand change out of court dress and into travelling clothes; Charlotte wears a dove-grey Brunswick, the jacket flaring nicely out over the slim skirt. No more panniers today, thank God.

They put her into a carriage with the man who is technically already her husband. Charlotte has already married him once, by proxy in Vienna. But they'll have to be married again, tomorrow. That way, both countries get a wedding. She'll have to go through it all twice: the standing, the swearing, the music in the streets, the nauseatingly long party.

The doors close; the carriage rolls.

'Well, Carolina,' he says in Neapolitan. 'How do you think we'll get on?'

'Charlotte,' she says. 'My family calls me Charlotte. We use the French versions of our names. Our father was from Lorraine, you know.'

He cocks his head, as though surprised to hear her speak Neapolitan back. She's been studying.

'But you're in Italy now,' he replies.

'And yet I remain Charlotte.'

'Are you a virgin?' he asks, switching into French.

She nearly chokes. 'What?'

He laughs, and looks out of the window. 'I can see we'll have great conversations.'

She was caught off guard, not embarrassed, but there's no way to tell him that now, and why does she care what he thinks, anyway? The bully. But she should at least try not to make an enemy of him. A nonentity, Leopold called him.

The road skirts the coast, along a dark green promontory named for Circe. She pulls a book out of her velvet travel bag. Thanks to the enchantment she and Antoine did, it looks like a French translation of Smollett's *Travels Through France and Italy*. It is, in fact, Joseph's copy of *Candide*. He can get another, when he finds it missing. Maria Theresa would never approve of her daughter reading Voltaire, least of all this irreverent book.

But Charlotte isn't really reading it at the moment. The carriage turns, and she shifts in the seat, bringing her husband into view.

He drops his tongue out of his mouth, a glazed pink monstrosity, and she drops her book.

He laughs hysterically, bends and picks it up. 'Thank you,' she says, anticipating. But he doesn't straighten. He takes the opportunity to seize the hem of her skirt in both hands and agitate it, flapping and worrying it.

She flinches, pulling her legs as close to the edge of the seat as she can. Ferdinand lets go, with a grin on his face, and leafs through the book, lazily, not taking care with the pages. He reads aloud: '"The old philosopher, whose name was Martin, embarked then with Candide for Bordeaux. They had both seen and suffered a great deal . . ." Looks boring.'

Then he tosses it to her. He leans back.

'You'll have to learn how to have a bit of fun, *Charlotte*.'

She stares at him, stunned. He seems not to have recognized what he was reading, but he was reading it all the same: *Candide*. He should have seen a travel diary. The enchantment on the book had no effect on him.

Charlotte goes cold. Surely Ferdinand cannot be a magister.

'I'm looking forward to meeting some of the natural philosophers in Naples,' she says, in French, casually, as though the book has given her the thought. 'In Vienna, many proofs have been found of fascinating theories, of late.'

She emphasizes *proofs have been found*, in case that is a common formula for magic spells; Ertag would certainly never have come up with such a phrase on her own. But Ferdinand's face just wrinkles into a bemused, mocking expression.

'Great conversations,' he mutters.

No, he cannot be a magister. But, like Mama, he seems to be immune to magic. She remembers Rohan saying, *They'll be anointed when they're crowned.* But Ferdinand seems to know nothing of magic, any more than Mama or Joseph did. If they've been anointed to make them immune, they were unaware. The thought makes her shudder. In any case, if Ferdinand is immune, she won't be able to use her gloves on him, or anything else. She has never felt so powerless, and she has felt powerless all her life.

They ride on in silence for a painful hour, and at some point she realizes that he is, mercifully, asleep.

It's nearly midnight when they arrive at the top of a low hill, with a starless night above a vast façade of pale stone in all the colours of a blushing bride. Caserta Palace. They show her to a room with walls and paintings she does not know, and sheets that do not smell of home. She falls asleep at last, reciting the exports of Naples and Sicily: olive oil, wheat, silk, wool, sulphur, wine.

At the wedding supper, Charlotte sits on a dais beside her husband. She's glad to be out of the stiff armour of cloth of silver she wore for the ceremony, and the heavy purple cloak, lined with ermine. A queen's wedding finery. Now, she's in one of the ninety-nine silk gowns from her trousseau, but it's still a court dress, stiff, with wide panniers. Blood red. She doesn't sit so much as arrange herself, with plumes on her head. And she's not hungry.

It doesn't help that there's no table. Everyone sits against the wall, balancing their plates on their knees.

'Spanish etiquette dictates that no one else may eat at the King's table,' says Leopold, on her other side. 'And they follow Spanish etiquette here. So Ferdinand did away with tables altogether, so he could eat with his friends. You'll get used to it – eating without a table, I mean. And the rest.'

Charlotte's husband, at her side, is not looking at her. He is looking at the men at the further reaches of the room, and laughing with most of the arm of a braised octopus falling out of his mouth. Her husband's face is florid – the wine, perhaps. His nose is not as big as she was led to believe – she had heard that the people call him King Big-Nose – but it will soon be covered in red veins if he keeps carrying on like this.

She doesn't want him to look at her, as a man looks at a horse he bought for too much money.

'I've heard the Jesuits have all left Naples,' says Ferdinand. 'Who will the Pied Piper lure away next? Maybe all the lawyers, eh, Tanucci?'

Bernardo Tanucci, sitting across the room from Charlotte, does not touch his food either. He watches everyone from under his terrifying eyebrows.

'I am afraid I cannot do anything about the lawyers, Your Majesty, because a man cannot act against his own interests,' says Tanucci with an evil little smile. 'But yes, I've rid the city of the Jesuits. They were too powerful.'

'Surely everyone is only just as powerful as I allow them to be.'

Charlotte sips the white Tuscan wine in her glass. It's sweeter than she likes.

Tanucci inclines his head. 'Of course. But these not-so-secret societies think they run Naples, and we must remind them from time to time that they do not. The Freemasons, the Jesuits – they're no better than criminals.'

'I suppose you're right, Tanucci. You know best. Though I do stick my nose in, from time to time, eh?' Ferdinand looks around, basking in the laughter at the joke he has made at his own expense.

Charlotte clears her throat. 'Begging Your Majesty's pardon.'

'My wife speaks!' Ferdinand crows, looking at her. 'The German mouse squeaks!'

Everyone laughs.

Charlotte smooths a rumple in the white glove on her left wrist. Time to see whether the white gloves work on anyone here. There's a lump in her throat. The last time she used the gloves, inadvertently, they needed only a passing thought, and that thought froze Antoine in place for what seemed forever. She must be very precise, and very deliberate.

'I wonder who will run the schools,' she says in her most persuasive tones, 'if the Jesuits are gone. Expensive, aren't they, schools?'

Tanucci, she thinks. *You will agree.*

'Expensive, aren't they,' Tanucci says woodenly. 'Schools.'

His face is impassive as he says it, and afterwards his mouth quirks into a short, nervous chuckle. He's surprised by what he just said.

But everyone else interprets it as mockery, his parroting her own words back to her as though they are ridiculous. They think his little smile at the end was triumph, not nerves or surprise. They laugh, and she fights the urge to pull the damned gloves off her hands.

'You don't have any scars,' says Ferdinand, peering at her.

'I'm sorry, Your Majesty?'

'I mean, I knew the smallpox killed half of Maria Theresa's whelps, so I expected you to be covered in bumps when you arrived. But perhaps that is what those two little lumps are there, under your bodice.'

As the hall fills with laughter again, he reaches across and puts his hand on her breast. She tries to pull away, but the heavy, carved chair doesn't move.

The laughter stops.

'You have no right to pull away from me,' he says, his voice low.

Then he turns and looks around the silent room, and Charlotte thinks for a moment she has misheard the next thing he says, because the blood is beating in her ears.

'I need to take a shit,' Ferdinand groans, his hand on his belly. 'Who's coming to keep me company?'

A half-dozen men rise dutifully from their seats and follow the King down the corridor to his close-stool.

The only magic she has doesn't work against her husband, and it hasn't been much help with Tanucci, either. She sits alone in the room full of discarded plates and glasses, the ushers at the door not meeting her eyes.

The wedding night.

Charlotte sits in bed in her nightgown and thinks as hard as she can. For a few days out of every month, at least, she can send word to Ferdinand that she is unwell. Will he know what she means? God knows what he calls the General. It might not even put him off, but some men don't like blood, her sisters have told her, and he might give her five days' peace out of every month. A week's peace? Can she get away with that?

If only there were some spell to make him believe, falsely,

that he's been in bed with his wife. She can see nothing like that in the embroidered book, though, and she needs to give birth to an heir. When she has a son, she gets a seat on the Council of Naples. And then she can start doing something real with her life.

Three weeks out of every month. That's not so bad. And maybe it won't be every one of those nights. He will have mistresses, no doubt, and so long as they don't try to legitimize their children, Charlotte is happy to let them take some of the burden.

Perhaps, all in all, it will be bearable. She folds her hands in her lap and looks at the courtiers giggling at the doorway, waiting for the King. Courtiers whose names she does not know, giggling about her private life. About what's going to happen, any moment now.

Or, perhaps, giggling because it hasn't happened yet. Where is Ferdinand? Passed out drunk somewhere? God damn him: he seems intent on embarrassing her. If she'll have to get it over with some time, it might as well—

The door opens, and the room is full of people. Liveried people, except for Ferdinand, who swaggers in to general applause.

Charlotte goes over everything her sisters told her in her mind. What to expect. It won't hurt too badly, they said.

She expects Ferdinand to undress, but he just leaps at her, making a show for the audience. They all roar with laughter as his first kiss lands like a blow on her mouth, as he puts his hand on her leg and pushes her onto her back.

'Go on, leave us!' he roars, laughing.

She stares at the interlaced gold crowns that decorate the underside of the top of the bedstead.

Ferdinand attaches himself to Charlotte, every one of his kisses draining her, his arms binding her.

Then he pulls back, and says, 'I haven't forced anyone in my life. If you're unwilling, there are plenty of other fifteen-year-old girls in the palace.'

She hesitates; then she says, 'I am your wife.'

He grins, and for a moment she can understand why he thinks himself handsome. 'You are. Carolina.'

Charlotte tries not to freeze, but can only bring herself to return a fraction of his kisses. She gives him her cheek, her neck. She sings songs in her head.

She cries out once, from the pain. And then Ferdinand leaves, mercifully, and she weeps, alone.

CHAPTER SEVEN

The French Ambassador — Antoine's Shortcomings —
Alliances — A Very Good Likeness — Turpentine
and Blood

The new French ambassador to Vienna, the Marquis de Durfort, has the most amiable expression Antoine has ever seen. It's so beatific, with such rosy cheeks and sparkling eyes, that she feels sure he could send men to their deaths and they'd go happily. She tries to copy it, discreetly, as she sits across from him at dinner, but she's sure she isn't getting it right.

Durfort has made it perfectly clear, without ever saying so, that Antoine is unsatisfactory.

Antoine knows the list of her shortcomings as well as she knows the Ten Commandments.

She speaks French with a German accent, the tutors say – and when she protests that she speaks the same French as her father and has since she was a baby, her tutors say, well, but the late Emperor was from Lorraine! Entirely the wrong vowels. Her written French is even worse.

She is too short, and short-sighted. She gets pimples. Her bosom is too small. One shoulder rides above the other. Her hairline is too high – and if that were not bad enough, she's losing patches of hair along her temples from the wool band that scrapes her curls back under the constructions of her hairstylists.

Most painfully, her teeth are crooked. For three months, a doctor has been adjusting them, pulling on some of the bottom teeth with a set of pliers called a pelican, and wrapping golden wires around the top. Her jaw aches all the time, but the teeth haven't moved.

'After dinner, I will show you my collection of French royal portraits,' says Maria Theresa, her soup spoon quavering. She's been shakier of late, and heavier on her legs. The soup spoon clatters down into the bowl as she raises one finger to make her next point. 'I have every member of the royal family now, and they are all quite recent and done by the very best painters. The King of France has been very good to me. I'd like to reciprocate. We shall have one made of Antoine for him, especially if she is going to marry his grandson. No doubt the young Dauphin wants to have a look at her, too.'

'What a gracious offer, Your Imperial Majesty!' Durfort beams. 'Perhaps next year, when the subject is a little older? There is no rush.'

Did Antoine imagine that before he said *older*, he let his gaze linger over her disappointing lack of bosom? She blushes, which is not the end of the world, even though it is not quite for the reason they'll all assume.

Mama does not smile. Despite what Durfort says, she is indeed in a rush.

Austria and France used to be enemies, before Antoine was born. Then France finally took Austria's side in the most recent war against Prussia and England. France came out of that war poorer and with fewer colonies. Many French people blame Mama and hate Austrians.

But Mama's old enemy, Prussia, has allied with England, and rich England has gained territories in America and Africa.

So Mama must seal the French alliance. Antoine understands this very well. France may be a bankrupt and reluctant friend, but Austria needs all the friends it can get. Besides,

France is ruled by Bourbons, and Mama is joining Habsburgs to Bourbons all over Europe.

But the French King has been non-committal about the plan to marry Antoine to his grandson Louis.

'It takes time to make a good picture,' Mama says.

'Indeed,' says Durfort, tenting his fingers and leaning back to regard Antoine. 'I know of a painter with just the right touch. Joseph Ducreux. Yes, I think it must be Ducreux.'

'He's in Paris?' Mama asks dubiously.

'And very sought after there. But I'm sure he would wrap up his affairs and travel here, for such a commission. It would be a mere matter of months, and in the meantime . . .' He smiles indulgently, and pauses, and says, '. . . the archduchess can only grow more beautiful.'

Mama stares for a long time at the finished portrait of Antoine. She stands, breathing heavily, scowling.

'It's a very good likeness,' Countess Lerchenfeld ventures at last. She's standing on one side of Mama, and Antoine on the other. They're alone in the Mirrors Room, where Mama can get a sense of the portrait from a distance. On an easel, the girl in the painting waits.

'Is it?' Mama asks. 'Hmm. I don't see why the painter couldn't have moved that shoulder down. She looks as though she's cringing. You didn't cringe, did you, Antoine? Your smile is strange.'

She did not cringe, all through the many hours of sitting still. The smile is strange because of the wires, although it is some mercy at least that formal portraits never show the mouth open. Still, Antoine's mouth looks as uncomfortable as it feels.

'It doesn't have . . .' Maria Theresa waves her hand. '. . . her sweetness.'

'Yes, well, she's growing up,' Lerchenfeld says encouragingly. 'She's to be a bride. The King will see how sweet she is, certainly, but he will also see that she's no longer a child.'

'Indeed, indeed. Antoine, Lerchenfeld tells me you've had your monthly courses! Is that so?'

Antoine blushes. 'Yes, Mama. Just yesterday.'

'What is it your sisters call it? The General? Ha. Well, that's good news at last. I'll inform the ambassador. But this painting – no. We can't afford a bad impression. We'll have to have a new one. Or perhaps that French painter can fix it. Have it put in storage, Lerchenfeld, until we can find out what can be done. What a shame.'

Mama will ask the painter to try again. Which means Antoine must sit for more hours. And it won't ever be good enough. Antoine knows as well as anyone that it is impossible to please Mama entirely. No human painter can make this portrait match the image in Mama's mind.

She feels a sudden warmth of feeling for Wolfgang Mozart, who played for her once in this very room, when they were children. Now she is nearly thirteen, and off to be married. And he has written an opera, which was meant to be performed this past spring, but it keeps being postponed. The reasons aren't entirely clear. Some people say it's because it's so very bad – what can one expect from a twelve-year-old boy? Others say the problem is the opposite, that it is so good, it must be a fraud, written by the boy's father, perhaps. Making fools of everyone in Vienna.

Antoine is caught in a similar bind: the painting shows that she is not pretty enough, but if she were to use magic to make the painting show a beautiful woman, nobody would believe it was her.

But perhaps there is a way to make the painting just a *little* different. Antoine imagines asking Mama to take a second look; imagines the Empress cocking her head and saying, 'Perhaps I was unfair. It does catch the eye, doesn't it?'

There is one spell about paintings in the embroidered book, but it's confusing and it says nothing about the desires of the beholder: 'For a painting to preserve the subject as he is, these proofs have been found, with the prime magister's later warning that the body will indeed age, although it may seem otherwise to observers, and thus the reversal spell that follows may be employed . . .'

The subject as he is? That's no help. A painting that showed Antoine as she really is, flaws and all, is the last thing Mama wants. In fact, she wants the opposite.

Antoine bites her lip. Tonight, when she is alone, she'll read the spell again. She can feel an idea forming in her mind, and only needs the courage to put it into action.

The painting spell is a costly one. By the light of one candle, the sacrifices in the star around the painting rot, curl, disintegrate.

Some of these sacrifices are harder than others, but they are all losses.

Antoine's baby teeth yellow and crumble. The embroidered leash for Mops that Charlotte gave her as a farewell gift rots and withers.

A scrap of paper turns to dust and, with it, the memory of a French essay she'd written, covered in a second shade of ink where her tutor has corrected her spelling.

She can't look at the paper that contains her hope of seeing her family again once she leaves for France. Why not? She wants to lose that hope; it will be easier without it. And yet she can't look at that one, or the one containing her affection for her little brother Max.

How can the love in her heart just disappear, as if it never was? Can love be a thing, a substance, independent of its causes? And if so, why can't a spell create it, out of nothing?

She shivers, and then coughs. She'd forgotten about the smell and does not have a kerchief to hand. Never mind. She gets to her feet and walks over the lines of ash to the easel in the centre of the star. The sacrifices disappeared. The painting is enchanted.

It does look more like her, strangely. The shoulder is even higher, and, look, there is a pimple that did not exist when she sat for the painting. Even if it had, the painter would have left it out. This is Antoine as she is, and as she will always remain, if the reversal spell doesn't work the way she hopes it will. What has she done? She shivers again.

And she opens her paintbox.

Like all of Mama's children, Antoine has been taught painting. Her perfectly adequate landscapes grace one wall in the nursery wing still. She is no genius, but she doesn't need to be, for the tiny alterations she has in mind. Nothing that anyone will find impossible. Little changes that an observer, even one as eagle-eyed as Mama, might believe they simply hadn't noticed before.

She mixes a silvery colour, a fat paint with plenty of oil in it, so it will dry properly over the layers below. With the tiniest brush, she fills in her high, uneven hairline, just a little. She feels a sting on her forehead, as though someone had dragged nettles across it.

Antoine rushes to the wall hung with many mirrors and checks. Yes, her hairline does look smoother now. She can change herself!

The next thing is the right shoulder, which is higher than the other. Ducreux chose an angle that would disguise that, but it's still perfectly apparent to anyone who looks closely. Antoine takes up the palette knife and scrapes a tiny line away from the top of her shoulder.

That pain is not stinging, but deep. Her bones shift and shudder. A crack like lightning racks her body. She's on the floor, writhing, and she doesn't even know whether she's cried aloud, or whether it's only in her mind. She's bitten the inside of her lip, the rough patch created by the ends of the wires on her teeth.

If they find her like this, what will they do? She can barely bring herself to care through the red haze of agony.

After a very long while, the ache subsides enough for her to get to her feet. She's still alone. But she can walk; she can stand.

84

There's a pale line above her new shoulder, on the painting. It will always be there as a ghost image, but luckily Ducreux painted a sort of glow around her, fading into the darker background. When Antoine (using her less sore left arm) paints a thin line of darkness onto the canvas, the ghost of her flesh becomes a bit of *sfumato*.

It's a more difficult matter to change the teeth, which weren't showing in the portrait anyway. She settles for trying to shift the jaw a little, to reduce the thrust of her bottom lip. A little dab of white there and a curve of shadow there—

And she's holding her mouth to stop from screaming in pain as blood runs out between her lips. She grabs a rag and holds it, breathing in the smell of turpentine as she collects the blood on her palette. Blood is a useful sacrifice, and it must never go to waste.

The reversal spell is simpler, but feels just as momentous. Antoine almost convinces herself she can feel the change when her link to the painting disintegrates. She stares for a moment at the girl on the canvas, then does a small test. A red dot on one arm of the painted girl; nothing appears on Antoine's own arm. It worked! Exactly as she'd planned. She figured out the spell and made it work, all on her own.

To be certain, she scrapes a dress-pin across the back of one hand, making a red line she can cover with gloves until it heals.

The perfect girl in the painting shows no sign of the scratch. They are no longer linked. Antoine bids her goodbye.

CHAPTER EIGHT

Charlotte's Plans Are Frustrated – A Long Winter –
Letters from Home – A Glass of Nocillo – Allies

———— ✢ ————

Charlotte does not understand her husband. Unlike Joseph, Ferdinand doesn't have to contend with a fractious empire, a patchwork of laws and languages. He is king; he could make his country into a place where doctors can save the lives of children, where great writers and artists work without interference from superstition and cant, where the streets are clean and safe, where laws and treaties create peace where before there was tribalism and violence. She straightens her shoulders and breathes more freely, just thinking of it. If she were king, she would do all those things, and more. She *will* do them. After all, Mama made herself king, despite being a woman. Charlotte can see that future for herself, hiding behind every marble pillar or shadowed doorway in the palace, tempting her to run after it.

Her ladies-in-waiting don't see that future, she's sure. They see a stiff, reserved sixteen-year-old who speaks their language haltingly and doesn't laugh at anyone's jokes. The only one who smiles at her is Caterina of San Marco.

Caterina is twenty-one years old, five years older than Charlotte. She has brown curls, a sharp nose, a slight smile, and heavy-lidded, appraising eyes. A Medici on both sides, she is married to a marquis forty years her senior. Forty years! Charlotte can hardly imagine it. Caterina, it seems, can hardly imagine it either, because she is engaged in a very public and unabashed affair with the dashing Austrian envoy. That connection with Austria is one reason Charlotte asks Caterina to sit with her one rainy afternoon, in her bedchamber. They embroider flowered needlecases and look out of the window at the expanse of grey sky and green slopes, marked with pale pathways. Caserta is vast, bigger even than Schönbrunn. Charlotte feels very far away from everything here.

'When do we move to the Palazzo Reale?' she asks.

Caterina pulls her needle through a piece of silk. 'In October, usually, but it changes every year. Everything is smaller there, and older of course, but I like it better. I like to see Vesuvius when I look out of the window.'

Charlotte laughs, surprised. 'The volcano doesn't make you nervous?'

'No, it's fascinating. But what I like the best is on the other side of the palace: the Phlegraean Fields. The craters there smoke all the time, and I've picked yellow sulphur off the ground, pieces as big as my fist. Do you know about Laura Bassi, the first woman who graduated from the University of Bologna? She explained to me the workings of the acid in the boiling mud pits there. And there's a mountain that's only as old as our great-grandfathers, at least by Mr Hamilton's estimate. But I'm boring you, Your Majesty.'

'Not at all!' Charlotte protests. 'I'm afraid I don't know as much as I'd like about the natural world, but I hope to encourage its study. That's one of the things I would very much like to do, as queen.'

Caterina gives her a look she can't interpret. 'Yes, well, the Phlegraean Fields are best known at court for their wines

– there are vineyards at the mouth of the underworld. Isn't that a beautiful thought? But the wines the palace buys are always terrible. Favour-trading and old contracts, you know. If you'd like the best for your own rooms, Your Majesty, I'm happy to help. I know a supplier of Maraschino from Venice: half the price and twice the quality.'

Charlotte laughs again, out of sheer amazement. The world of Naples is not as constrained as it feels.

She sends out invitations to the half-dozen notables on the top of the list she made so carefully on her journey.

The Neapolitan nobility and the intellectuals: that was Joseph's advice. She already has a list a dozen names long of the people she wants to meet: poets, philosophers, the heads of ancient families. She gives the list to the Superintendent of the Queen's Household, only to be told that all events within the palace must be approved by the Master of the King's Entertainments. The Master of the King's Entertainments informs her that the calendar is, alas, full for the foreseeable future.

So she sends invitations one at a time, starting with Francesco d'Aquino, the Prince of Caramanico, a Freemason with an interest in natural philosophy who stays in his own town and does not come to the palace. That means he is outside of Ferdinand's orbit, and a potential ally.

But she receives only a polite refusal with the vaguest excuse about the needs of his estate.

The problem is that those who avoid Ferdinand's court have no reason to believe his new queen is worth changing that practice. She could try to explain in letters, but that's risky, even with ciphers.

She asks Caterina for an explanation, over coffee in her rooms.

'Your Majesty, court life is not for everyone,' Caterina says, her usually staccato speech uncharacteristically slow and careful. 'The prince does not come to the palace.'

'Because he doesn't like my husband. But I am not my

husband.' She picks up her coffee cup, but her hand is shaking, and she puts it down again. 'I could write him a letter, but would it convince him?'

And, she thinks, *would ciphers be enough to keep it private? I don't know who I can trust, if anyone.*

'Your Majesty, of course I am happy to speak to the prince and anyone else, on your behalf. But . . . may I speak frankly?'

'Always.'

'Those who don't come to the palace survive by staying out of Tanucci's way. If they were to accept the Queen's invitation, after refusing the King's . . . Well, Your Majesty, it would be poking the bear.'

Charlotte grits her teeth. 'Do what you can, please, Caterina,' she says.

She asks for Tanucci to come and see her, but the request is ignored. Finally, she corners him in the King's antechamber one day, as members of the Council stream past: men with stern jowls, watery eyes, and sharp noses, who make the smallest possible courtesies to her as they race away to run her kingdom.

Charlotte stands before Tanucci and demands to know why the Queen may not see people.

'You may invite anyone you like, Your Majesty,' he says smugly. 'Of course, it is not within my power to make them come. You must understand that you are new to this country, and its customs.'

'I would like to get to know it better,' she retorts. 'Soon enough I'll have a seat on the Council. I need to learn all I can.'

He smiles, almost conspiratorially, and lowers his voice as he sneers at the old men now on the far side of the room. 'Your Majesty, the Council's business is not very arduous. I would not worry about it requiring much of you.'

Of course. He's taken power away from the Council, too. The one thing she has been clinging to, naively.

Now he's looking at the papers in his hand, impatiently,

as though he has better things to do than talk to a sixteen-year-old girl. Than talk to the Queen.

'May I at least have a carriage to go calling on people?' She doesn't like the pleading tone to her own voice. She wanted that to sound colder, more confident.

'Whenever the expense of outfitting the proper guard for such an outing can be justified, of course. I don't know how things are done in Vienna, Your Majesty, but here even the royal family must consider the palace budget before acting on their whims.'

She grits her teeth. She might try the gloves on him again, to force him to approve an outing or a salon, but what would stop him from rescinding the approval the moment she was out of the room? Besides, her last attempt to control him didn't work very well.

'It is not a whim to wish to speak to someone other than my ladies-in-waiting,' she protests.

He spreads his arms wide. 'Your Majesty, there are card parties and billiards parties, dances and masquerades, several nights a week here in the palace. Is that not sufficient entertainment for you?'

And all of them filled with Ferdinand's lackeys. She gives Tanucci a brittle smile and leaves him smirking at her.

That night, Charlotte draws the blue and gold silk curtains around her bed, and opens the embroidered book. The rough paper feels so familiar to her fingers. As a child, she had thought all the world's possibilities were open before her. One day she would be a queen, and she was already a magister. But both of those titles are paper crowns.

Her life will be what her mother always planned it to be. It's so simple, so plain before her eyes now. Years upon years of letting Ferdinand into her bed and body, of standing beside him for portraits and ceremonies. Watching the flames of Enlightenment gutter in Naples as anyone with a brain leaves, while those who have no choice but to stay starve in body and mind. Her brother Joseph will have no partner here for his plans. Leopold seems content to merely survive in his own kingdom. And Antoine—

And Antoine is going to Paris, where anything might await her. Where Prince de Rohan is. Charlotte had assured her sister that they would learn more about magic, once they became queens. But here she is, Queen, and she knows nothing and no one.

She flips through page after page of spells that she can't decipher. Reads them over again, reads them aloud, in dry whispers. If she could work even a few more spells in this book, what might she be able to do then?

There must be magisters in Naples. She hears Rohan's voice in her memory: *You and your Vienna friends must decide whether you are a chapter of the Order of 1326 or just another nest of rogues.* If this Order of 1326 is different in every place, who's to say whether the same Order in Naples would be a danger? But who's to say that it wouldn't? And she promised Antoine to keep it secret.

She also promised that when they were queens, they would be safe.

Charlotte's ignorance gnaws at her, but she has no way of finding anything out. Her only accomplice is Caterina, but she can't say anything to Caterina about the Order without breaking her promise, and risking discovery. The marchesa is a pleasant companion – and Charlotte's only friend in Naples – but the moment Charlotte spoke the words, everything could shatter. She could put Caterina in danger. Or, more likely, she could give Caterina the tools to betray her, in a court where she has no influence at all of her own.

She makes claws with her hands in frustration, and hot tears rim her eyes. Roughly, she turns the pages, until her eyes land on a spell that she and Antoine had never quite understood and never dared to try:

For a pearl to be dropped into one-third of one demiard of eau-de-vie then to be quaffed equally by two from a single cup, exhaustible, to confer on the second drinker eternally pain pro tempore on the threshold of betrayal of the first, these proofs have been found.'

She thinks about it for five days. The threshold of betrayal. If Caterina could not betray her, that would be the same as trust, the same as secrecy. Wouldn't it?

The spell requires minor sacrifices when it comes to love, hope, treasure, and memory. The body sacrifice, though, is a more difficult matter.

The embroidered book says that the prime magister sacrificed 'a flaying of the skin'. If it's to be of any size, and it must be, according to the long string of 'a's in the spell formula, then Charlotte would require some explanation. She is willing to fake a carriage accident or something of that kind, but the trouble is that if the initial amount of skin she takes is wrong, or from the wrong part of the body, then it will all be for nothing.

She and Antoine have made other substitutions for the sacrifices the book lists as those of the 'prime magister' for any spell: hair when they ran out of fingernail clippings; two copper coins for a silver one. Once or twice, they simply couldn't get a spell to work no matter what they sacrificed. But in general, they have found, substitutions *can* work. Perhaps the only question is quantity.

So Charlotte starts bleeding.

Mama's doctors used to bleed her when she was ill; she knows how to do it with a razor and a pan. But it will take a few tries, she thinks, to get enough for this spell. She'll have to keep the blood somewhere in the meantime.

There are many drawers that lock in Charlotte's rooms at Caserta: inside her massive jewellery cabinet there are three alone. But she doesn't keep those keys. The only key she has is to a document box of ebony that Joseph gave her, which she keeps on her writing table. It's just big enough inside for a slightly elongated ashen star, and for her enchanted fan, to keep the blood cold.

In the centre of the star, one perfect pearl, for the enchantment. In one point of the star, she keeps the pan of blood, and adds to it day by day, as much blood as she dares. She speaks the words.

But the sacrifices do not decay.

She almost can't remember, now, what it feels like not to be tired, to have headaches. She can't bear noise and has great difficulty bringing herself to eat. When she walks, even a few steps, she gets dizzy and her heart races.

The court moves to the Palazzo Reale, and she insists on carrying her document box on her lap in the carriage. The old palace is a maze and she doesn't know where anything is. She walks through room after room, looking at the people in them as though they were portraits on the walls.

People don't keep their voices low enough when they murmur about how the King will have to take a new wife. Ferdinand, to his credit, looks genuinely concerned, although most of the time he's out hunting and whoring as usual.

Just after Christmas, the doctor offers to bleed Charlotte, and she laughs in a manner that seems strange and desperate even to her own ears. She insists they leave her the blood. And when she takes it, resting after every step, her heart dancing a bourrée, and adds it to her pan, at last the blood dries and rots, and the bits of paper and silver coins decay, and Charlotte has lost a little more hope and memory, and she crawls back to bed with the pearl clutched in one palm.

For months, she rests.

1768 turns to 1769. The winter passes into spring. The court returns to Caserta.

Charlotte remains in her bed, because she lacks the strength to get out of it.

10 June 1769
Antoine to Charlotte

My dear Charlotte,
  My teeth and shoulder are much straighter now and the French ambassador has made the formal offer for my hand at last. Mother is pleased. So am I, of course, if a little terrified. At least I have your good example to show me how to be brave.
  I hope you are feeling less unwell now and I'm so sorry your husband is such a beast. Once you have a child and get onto the Council of Naples, things will change.
  Now that the General has arrived for me, Mother says her youngest girl has grown up and is ready to do her duty. I will do my best to prove her right!
  Please don't sacrifice any memories of me, if you can help it. I'm going to be very lonely in France. Do you think they'll like me?

    Your loving
    Antoine

Charlotte is a little stronger every day. Ferdinand is getting impatient; these are months gone to waste, months when she could be giving him his heir.

By October, she's well enough to sit up most of the day and even take short walks. She asks for Caterina of San Marco to come sit with her and talk, to bring her a bottle of this year's nocillo, so she can see what all the fuss is about. Charlotte is in her bedroom, wearing a white lace dressing gown. She takes the edge of it between her fingers, thinking of the hours of women's work that lace represents, and how quickly it would tear, or take a stain.

Caterina comes in, and tells the guard to wait outside the door. They're alone in a room that has very little of Charlotte in it: her bed, with coverings and curtains she still doesn't quite recognize when she wakes; two upholstered chairs and a walnut table; and two long silk settees in dark blue. Charlotte, for the first time in a long while, is on the settee rather than the bed.

Caterina quickly covers up her expression of concern. She's brought a glass bottle full of dark liquid; she does as she is told. She comes forward, puts the bottle on the little round table at Charlotte's side and kneels, taking Charlotte's cold hands in her own.

'I'm overjoyed to see you looking so well, Your Majesty!'

Caterina is the picture of health, and suddenly Charlotte feels as if their ages have reversed.

'Please, sit, Caterina,' says Charlotte, indicating the place next to her on the settee. They speak French together, which is a relief. 'What are they saying about me? About my illness?'

'The palace has managed to keep the secret rather well, for once. The common people know nothing, although the rumour is that you're with child and ill from that, and the palace does nothing to dispel that idea. As for the courtiers, well . . . Two of them will argue, and the following day they'll have the same argument but will have switched sides, forgetting what they thought the day before. You know how it is, Madame.'

'Well, soon I'll be back at my regular duties and they'll have to find something else to argue about. Is that the nocillo, Caterina?'

'It is, Your Majesty. As you asked. The first of this year's bottling. My mother is a great believer in its medicinal properties. It ought to perk your appetite. Shall I pour it for you?'

'Let me,' Charlotte says, and takes out the stopper. There is already one small crystal glass on the table. Charlotte pours the nocillo in, up to the line she measured.

Caterina explains that the walnuts were green when they went into the spirits, but the resulting concoction is as dark as ink, as viscous as blood. It smells sharp, spicy, like pine trees and cloves. Charlotte surreptitiously drops the enchanted pearl into the glass, and it dissolves, as though it were made of sugar.

She turns to Caterina with her best attempt at a bright smile, and takes a sip. It's smooth, herbal at first, then nutty. Bittersweet.

'Very good,' she says.

She starts to offer Caterina the cup, but then hesitates.

The only power Charlotte has is in magic; that is her only advantage over Tanucci. But she can't find other magisters on her own; she can barely leave the palace. She needs Caterina.

Pain, the spell promised. What sort of pain, and how much? Of course, Caterina will have nothing to fear so long as she is loyal, and is loyalty not something she has already promised, as Charlotte's lady-in-waiting? Still, it seems only fair to give her something like a choice.

'My father', Charlotte says, thinking as she goes, 'came from Lorraine. Sometimes you can hear it in my French, I'd wager. He said they had a tradition there that the second person to drink from a cup would suffer great pain if they ever betrayed the one who drank first.'

'A quaint belief,' says Caterina. 'Then again, people here eat snails to keep their friends loyal, so we all have our stories, don't we?'

'We do. Would you drink from my cup, Caterina, if that were true? If you knew you would suffer if you ever betrayed me?'

In answer, Caterina curls her fingers around Charlotte's, and takes a sip. 'Most willingly,' she says.

It's done, Charlotte thinks, and she puts the nocillo down on the table.

'I do trust you, Caterina,' she says. Her heart hammers. It is so difficult to step over the line and speak of the things she's kept secret forever. Even now, even after the magic is done and Caterina can't turn on her.

But the secret is not only hers; it is hers and Antoine's, and she promised to keep it between them.

'I have a commission for you,' Charlotte says, her voice low. 'Have you ever heard of a society that calls itself the Order of 1326?'

'I have not, Your Majesty. I thought Tanucci had banished all the secret societies. Are they like the Freemasons, or like the Jesuits? Are they in Naples?'

'These are the questions I need answered. Will you go out into the city for me, and find out what you can? And, Caterina, you must not breathe a word to anyone about my interest in this. Gather what information you can, but don't let them realize I've sent you. And if you find them, keep yourself safe. Don't let them think you know anything.'

Caterina smiles. 'But I don't know anything, Your Majesty.'

'It's a strange task, I know. But I will be most grateful.'

Caterina nods. 'If they're in Naples, I'll find them.'

24 January 1770
Joseph to Charlotte

My dear Charlotte,

I believe Antoine told you in her last letter that my daughter, my darling Thérèse, had contracted pleurisy shortly after the new year. Yesterday, she died. She was seven years old and I don't think I will ever be happy again. I was at her side, holding her fevered body in my arms, and praying to God to give me my daughter back. It was only later, when I got to my own room, that the full horror of it struck me, and I think I shall carry that horror with me until I die.

On New Year's Day, she gave us a puppet show all about her grandmother's reign, and now, not a month later, she is gone.

I'll write to Leopold and ask him to come to Vienna for a few weeks. He's the heir now – I won't marry again – and he will need to be ready to rule this empire.

How odd it feels to not be a father any more. So often, these last years, I have felt as though that was all I had, my one joy and comfort.

I am sending you a few of her little writings and drawings, as you always liked to see those. I know your first years in Naples have been difficult ones, and you haven't been able to establish yourself there as you planned. We can't control our fates; we can only keep going as best we can.

Finally, I will give you a report on Antoine because you will chastise me if I don't: she is healthy and well and, by all accounts, studying very hard for her life in France.

With all my devotion,
Joseph

CHAPTER NINE

The Court Grieves — The Court Sees a Marvel —
Concealments — A Gold Watch

The spring of 1770 is a desperate one in the Austrian court.

Antoine could not save Joseph's little daughter, any more than she could save her sister Josepha. What can she do that is of any use to anyone? She can practise matching the correct forms of address to the long lists of names the ambassador has given her. She knows what to say and how to move, and she makes an appearance at masquerades and balls, half of them in her honour. Even Joseph, grim and grieving, does his duty as emperor and hosts a magnificent feast, with supper served in shifts of one hundred courtiers each. There are plates and flags and drawings everywhere in Vienna, praising the nuptials between France and Austria in the most poetic language.

Every day, her mother tells her how vital it is that Antoine impresses the French: she will be the embodiment of Austria and the alliance.

The Marquis de Durfort, the French ambassador, sits with Antoine and Mama one day to report on the vast trousseau being assembled for her in Paris.

'I think you'll find it quite sufficient, Your Imperial

Highness,' he says, smiling as he shows her several Pandora dolls wearing the latest fashions.

'I have a new *robe à l'anglaise* almost exactly like that one already,' Antoine says, pointing to a pink silk confection.

'But of course, the Dauphine owns no such gown,' he says with a twisted smirk.

She lets her confusion show. 'I will be the Dauphine, will I not?'

'And the Dauphine will bring no item with her from Austria. Not so much as a ring or a dressing gown.'

Now it's alarm, not confusion, but she still doesn't try to hide it. 'Mama?'

Mama nods. 'You must remember, Antoine, that an entire generation of French people were brought up to hate Austria.' She spreads her knobby hands, as if to say that it is one more inexplicable French quirk. 'It seems strange to you, I know, as your papa was French. Both countries have always been part of your heritage. But to them, you are an Austrian, and they need to believe you are not a spy. You will have to renounce all claims of inheritance through me, and you will have to bring nothing with you, to show that you are ready to become a French dauphine, entirely.' She pauses. 'I'm afraid even little Mops must stay here with me. Oh, just for a little while. Don't look so stricken. I'm allowed to send you gifts, my dear. After you've been in France for a few months, I'll send Mops to you, and any little items here you particularly want – a prayer book, that sort of thing. But for now you must take nothing. And . . .' Mama pauses, and looks at Durfort.

'And?' Antoine prompts. 'What more is there, Mama?'

'When you enter into French territory, you are not to bring even the clothes on your back. You will undress, in the presence of a few noble ladies of the court, before crossing the border.'

Nothing. Naked. Naked? Antoine shivers, as if she's already stripped. She must think. Her enchanted items may be few but she sacrificed so much to create them! And the spells themselves, which she is working so hard to understand. She keeps them safe with her at all times in her pocket. Travelling without them would be unthinkable.

What can she do? Can she memorize all the book's spells in the few weeks that remain before she must leave? She can't leave them behind. She could destroy them, ask Charlotte to recopy them and send them on to her in France. But what courier could Charlotte trust with such a mission, even if the spells were ciphered? Between Naples and Versailles, there is a great deal of road.

And those weeks on the road, without any magic and without the spells that might give her some small advantage. Heaven knows she has few natural advantages, as Mama and Durfort make plain at every opportunity. Those first months in France, when she cannot put a single foot wrong, lest the whole alliance suffer, and the people of Europe fall back into war and hunger. It's too much to ask of her. It should have been Charlotte; France is too important for Antoine.

'My dear, it's natural to be nervous about it, but the ladies will dress you again quickly,' Mama says kindly.

It's barbaric, Antoine wants to spit, but she holds her tongue, because the French ambassador is present, and Mama wants the French ambassador to tell his king that Mama is sending France an angel.

'I'm only a little surprised,' Antoine says, and puts on her sweetest smile. 'I didn't know.'

Countess Ertag used magic herself to hide her spells, to keep them safe. Surely Antoine should be able to do the same. But if there are spells that could help her in the embroidered book, they're hidden in words and phrases she can't understand. She reads them over and over anyway, looking for some thread she might grasp and begin to unravel.

It's tricky even to know what item a spell is meant to

enchant. There is a spell 'to test gold', but does the gold itself go into the centre of the star, or some instrument? There's a spell 'for a winnowing basket' but with no clue as to what the enchantment might be; perhaps the basket would simply winnow better.

And then there are the sacrifices, some of which are written as references to other things. 'For the love, a sacrifice equal to twice that of the whetstone enchantment', reads a spell for creating an accurate map, but there seems to be no whetstone enchantment in the book. The book reads like a collection of scattered things, found at random, and perhaps that is precisely what it is. Antoine wonders, often, how many of the spells Countess Ertag managed to make work herself, and, always, whether the spell for the embroidery is somewhere among them, in words that disguise its meaning.

Finally, she catches a tiny thread-end of meaning she hadn't noticed before. There's a spell for a 'cap of Hades, to steal shadows' and, in desperation, she asks Joseph for a book on Greek legends. There she finds it, in the Perseus story: a hat that renders its wearer invisible.

The sacrifices, though, are written in equally obscure phrases. Still, Antoine puzzles over them, and makes notes as she tries the spell every night. If she cracks it, that might help her understand the other spells, or show her some way to hide them. The more magic she does, the more she will understand. It's only a matter of hitting on the right sacrifices, and that is only a matter of doing the work. But she is running out of time.

Three weeks before Antoine's proxy wedding, everyone is in the Small Gallery at Schönbrunn, waiting for a spectacle to begin.

It's a bright room, thanks to the gleaming white walls broken only by gilt sconces and large windows that let in the daylight. A painted sky opens above their heads. Courtiers wait on their chairs, an army of dolls in their finery. Antoine is wearing her robin's-egg *robe à la française*, her skirt spilling beyond her chair. Perhaps the reason the French ambassador whispers so loudly to Mama is that it is hard to get close to any woman wearing panniers.

Antoine feels alone, apart, despite the crowd in the room. She's losing everything and everyone, very soon. She would like to be in her room, studying spells, reading them over to try to commit them all to memory even if she can't make them work. But she, like the rest of the court, was commanded to witness a marvel.

A young engineer called Wolfgang Kempelen wants the contract to redesign the water pipes at Schönbrunn. The Empress asked to see some example of his work.

So here is the engineer, looking rather uncomfortable in stiff new jacket and breeches, opening the door from the adjoining Round Chinese Cabinet Room. He bows low to Maria Theresa. The courtiers gasp, not at Kempelen but at a turbaned dummy in an ermine robe sitting inside a cabinet on wheels.

The turban makes her think of Angelo Soliman. He's known for his skill at chess, and ordinarily he would be present at any scientific demonstration. But he often accompanies Joseph on his travels, and her brother the Emperor has been travelling a great deal lately. He's always inspecting provinces or going to diplomatic meetings. Antoine suspects Joseph is unhappy at court, with the reminders of the people he's lost. He and Mama seem to be ever more irritated with each other, and Joseph doesn't get along well with Leopold either.

Since that day in the garden at the Hofburg, Antoine has only seen Soliman once or twice, in crowded rooms, after he returned to Vienna with his wife. It's a relief, of course, because it means he isn't spying on her any more, or so she hopes. But it also makes her feel even more that magic is slipping away from her, that soon it will all be a half-remembered childhood lark. She will be stripped, remade, powerless.

On the surface of the cabinet is a painted chess board.

'Behold, my artificial man!' says Kempelen, his voice breaking. 'Will anyone here challenge the Turk to a game of chess?'

Automata can do marvellous things. A Frenchman named Vaucanson built a metal man who could play the flute thanks to a system of bellows. But to play a game of chess?

Antoine's brother Max stands and bows histrionically to the audience for a laugh. Antoine, irritated, doesn't smile along with everyone else, until it occurs to her with a jolt that she might be smiling if she hadn't sacrificed her love for him. Then she does smile, falsely, though no one is looking at her anyway. Max walks to the open area of the gallery, where the Turk sits. He walks around the Turk, bending down to look below it. Then he moves a pawn.

The Turk moves an opposing pawn.

The audience applauds lightly.

'Well, but it can't really play,' says Max. 'It doesn't understand.'

Max lifts up a knight and moves it diagonally across the board, as if it were a queen or a bishop. An illegal move.

There's a pause, then the Turk slowly shakes its head.

Everyone gasps.

Someone in the crowd says, 'Perhaps there's finally someone in Vienna who can beat Angelo Soliman at chess.'

Someone else shouts, 'There's room for a man in that cabinet. A monkey, at least!'

The engineer bows his head. 'I'd be delighted to show the court the inner workings of my machine.'

He flings open one small door covering about one-third of the cabinet. Wheels and spiked cylinders fill the space. Kempelen throws open a door at the back of the cabinet and waves a candlestick behind it, so they can all see that the space extends to the back.

Max's face is red.

Antoine leans forward in her seat. It must be magic! Surely

there is no other explanation. An enchanted automaton – the thought makes her shiver. Or an enchantment to conceal someone inside? Any spell that hides a thing or a person could be useful to her.

'If Your Highness would like a closer look,' says Kempelen loudly, and sweeps his arm, bowing. He's looking at Antoine.

They are all looking at Antoine.

She must know more. Antoine looks at Mama for permission and Mama sighs. Good enough. Antoine stands and says nothing; she got into the habit of keeping her mouth closed when her teeth were wired.

She approaches the cabinet with a surreptitious sniff, wondering whether she might smell magic the way Charlotte thought she did in Joseph's study, when Soliman showed them the magic lantern. But this room is big and airy, and Antoine smells nothing.

It looks ordinary. There is no magnet she can see, no strings. Kempelen showed them the inside, and there didn't seem to be room for a hidden compartment. If Kempelen is a magister, it would be dangerous to reveal that she knows anything about magic. And she promised Charlotte. But surely it's safer to be sure of who is and who isn't?

She knows so little. But she knows her own skills, at least; they are listed in every diplomatic document between Austria and France.

She can dance, at least when her sister is not putting spells on her. That will not help her here.

She paints competent portraits. More competent than anyone knows. That will not help her here.

She sings and plays both harp and clavier.

She is clever at games of cards.

She can bluff.

Antoine moves a pawn, saying lightly, 'I think you must be a magician, Herr Kempelen.'

The Turk takes the pawn as Antoine glances quickly at Kempelen's face, to see if she can see a secret on it.

What Antoine sees is a momentary glance beyond her, over her shoulder, at the little room off to the side of the Great Gallery. The room where Kempelen made his preparations. The Round Chinese Cabinet Room.

Antoine shrugs prettily and walks through polite laughter back to her seat.

And when the crowd moves to the Grand Gallery for dinner, she manages to slip into the little adjoining room, alone.

The Round Chinese Cabinet Room is empty.

The only furnishings are a few large porcelain vases, and two upholstered chairs. The room is its own adornment, its walls covered in gilt-framed lacquer panels, and its floor a pattern of inlaid exotic woods: black, orange, yellow, every shade of brown. It dazzles the eye, but there can be no doubt: the room is empty.

Antoine turns, about to open the door to exit, when her mind catches up to her eye. An imperfection in the pattern of the variegated wood on the floor. She turns slowly, looking down.

In the centre of the floor is a six-petalled, stylized flower, from which linear patterns stretch to fill the floor. Just to one side of that flower, a crack between a dark strip of wood and a light one is slightly too wide.

Antoine catches her breath, remembering. She and Max used to play here, until Mama caught them. The line must show where the floor used to open up to allow Mama's 'conspiracy table' to rise through. Antoine barely remembers what it used to look like; Mama had this room redecorated when Antoine was a small child, and the table has not been in operation since. This room was for private conversations – very private, with Mama's counsellors, ambassadors, allies. So that they would not be overheard, not even by servants, Mama would have the servants place all the food and dishes and even the candles and flowers onto a table far below, on the ground floor of the palace. Then an apparatus would hoist the table up in the midst of the dinner guests. The name *table de conspiration* survived despite Mama's efforts to have everyone call it the *table d'union* instead.

There must still be a gap, under the floor. The secret to the workings of the Mechanical Turk, perhaps? She is probably wrong, but if she is, there is no one to mock her for it. She can test her theory.

Antoine forces herself to breathe, to think, as she quietly walks through the door. She leaves the room. But she doesn't walk back to the crowd in the Great Gallery. Instead, she grabs her skirts and runs lightly down the small staircase to the floor below.

The chamber underneath the Round Chinese Cabinet Room is much plainer, and dim despite the pale plaster walls. In the centre rises a thick rectangular column of cheap, plain wood. Covering the old workings of the table? One panel is swinging free at one side.

'I know you're there,' Antoine says, though she doesn't.

The panel swings open to reveal a woman holding an open fan before her face: a fan with round glass lenses in each blade, like a peacock's tail.

Antoine reaches into her pocket, searching for something that could protect her, and she pulls out the thimble that breaks small items into pieces. What will she do with that? She knows as she holds it out that it's ridiculous, and puts it back in her pocket as the woman drops her fan, and looks at Antoine.

She's older than Antoine; perhaps about forty, with a strong nose and a sweet, wry little mouth.

'A magister,' the woman says. 'Aren't you? I'm not going to hurt you, child. I do like a surprise.'

Antoine takes refuge in diplomacy. 'I'll keep your secret if you keep mine,' she says.

'We have an agreement,' says the woman, and puts out her hand.

⁂

After she says her prayers, Antoine sneaks back down to the room beneath the Chinese Cabinet Room. She half expects it to be empty. But she is still there: Geneviève. The only name she would give. They didn't get much past introductions before Antoine knew she'd be missed upstairs, and left, swearing to return.

Her other promise, to Charlotte, weighs on her heart. But if this woman wanted to do her harm, she could have done it already. And she already knows, or suspects, something about Antoine, so surely it would be more dangerous to let her get away from the palace without learning something about her?

Geneviève has procured a bottle of red wine and two glasses. Antoine, at fourteen, is allowed to drink wine at meals and balls, but she doesn't much like it. She keeps a little in her glass for toasts and otherwise drinks mineral water. Still, for a clandestine meeting with a magister, she nods in a grown-up fashion and Geneviève pours into both glasses. They sit on the floor, their skirts spreading around them, tucking their feet to one side.

'*Voilà*,' Geneviève says, holding up her glass. 'To my health. I need it more than you do, my dear. Sitting on the floor reminds me of my age.' She speaks French with a Parisian accent; how Antoine wishes she could learn that from her, as well as all the other things she wants to know. She will sound like a foreigner when she goes to Paris, or so the French ambassador says, even though she's been speaking French all her life.

'So you are not here for me?' Antoine asks before she sips. 'Are you not a . . . member of the Order of 1326?'

Geneviève's mouth twists. 'I most certainly am not. I am what the Order calls a "rogue". As you are too, I think? Believe me, my dear, there are worse things women can be called, and I've been called them all.' She takes a sip of the wine, closes her eyes, leans back.

'Then you are hiding from them too,' Antoine says conspiratorially.

That makes Geneviève smile. 'The Brothers are aware of me, but their attempts to deal with me have been, shall we say, more trouble than they were worth. I keep my activities out of public view so as far as those pompous asses are concerned, I don't pose a very great threat. Their biggest fear is that magic will become public knowledge, you see. So if I were to start being open about my abilities, well, then suddenly I would find myself declared insane, or something of that nature. It is a détente.'

Antoine wishes she understood more of this. She frowns. 'And they don't ask you to join them?'

Geneviève snorts, which is all the answer she gives.

'Hmm,' Antoine says. 'I didn't know that one could be a magister and not be in the Order. I mean, I did know, but I thought—'

'You're a magister and not a Brother. You asked if I was one, remember?'

'Yes, but I'm an accident.' She smiles. 'And they don't know about me. I think. And I don't know any other magisters, Brother or otherwise.' Charlotte, of course, but she must keep that secret. A thought occurs to her, about her future, about the journey she is soon to take. 'Are there many rogue magisters in Paris?'

'Paris? Yes, there are rogues in Paris, of course, but how many, I can't say. I haven't been there in some time.'

Geneviève's snort sends the long white lappets of her bonnet flapping. On each one there is a large, furry moth embroidered in many hues of brown and gold. It gives the effect of two moths flying about, as Geneviève is rather animated when she talks.

'I thought – your accent—'

'I am French, yes,' Geneviève says, 'but I live in London now. Where I have very good friends and, yes, some rogues are among them. But everyone's trying to kidnap me in London at the moment. It's very tiresome. So, sometimes I find it pleasant to disappear for a few weeks. Kempelen needed help, and I have always had a gift for machines and devices. He doesn't know I'm actually doing magic. It drives him mad, not knowing how I do it.'

'And how *do* you do it?' Antoine asks, leaning closer and matching Geneviève's wry smile.

In answer, Geneviève pulls her fan lorgnette out of her pocket. 'All the lenses of this fan show me somewhere different, you see. They let me see certain places, even when I am not precisely there. But the trouble with it is that one has to be quite close to the place one wants to see; I can't look through a lens and see Constantinople, for example, though believe me I have tried. This one in the middle lets me see through a similar lens, disguised as a jewel in the Turk's turban. I also have a glove that acts as a kind of possession spell: whatever one glove does, its twin does as well. So I keep a chessboard in front of me, and whatever I do, the Turk does.'

Geneviève gets to her feet, groaning a little and putting a hand on her hip. She swings open the panel on the side of the column in the middle of the room, the one that once held the workings of Mama's table. Inside, Antoine can see the space where Geneviève was concealed. There's a smell of oil and metal. Two great wheels gleam on either side, in the dark. The vestiges of the mechanical table.

'It's not a terribly comfortable spot, but it serves the purpose. I didn't count on a magister snooping. What sort of spell did you use to find me?'

She says it admiringly, and Antoine feels, for the first time, as though magic is something she can be proud of, not just a secret she loves and has to hide away. As though she's done something of merit, although of course she hasn't. She was simply lucky. Still, she would like to do something of merit. She likes the feeling of being admired for something other than her dancing and her posture.

'I didn't do any spell. I just guessed.'

'Guessed! It seems Maria Theresa's youngest daughter is

intelligent as well as beautiful. Oh, yes, I keep up with the great families of Europe. Old habit. And you're off to Paris, if my gossip is up to date? To marry the Dauphin? Well, that's a waste. They won't know what to do with a young woman of intelligence there.'

'Geneviève, how long are you staying in Vienna?'

She makes a non-committal shape with her mouth, shrugs one shoulder. 'Not for long, but I don't have to leave right away. A few days, perhaps. If you will visit me, perhaps I can convince Kempelen to stay a little.'

Antoine nods, eager to please her new acquaintance. A magister! She may be able to teach Antoine how to decipher the rest of the spells in the embroidered book. She may even be able to find a way for Antoine to take the book with her to France. 'Please stay as long as you can. I will bring you anything you need from the kitchens.'

Geneviève lowers her face, raises her eyebrows and looks at her as though she ought to know better. 'My dear, I can get whatever I like.'

For three nights in a row, Antoine meets Geneviève at midnight and talks until close to dawn. Antoine is beyond tired, but she's hungry for more of these conversations, and afraid that Geneviève will vanish as inexplicably as she appeared.

Antoine doesn't ask Geneviève how she gets in and out of the palace for their meetings; she has so many other questions to ask. Tonight, Geneviève has spread a rug on the floor with a candelabrum, a plate of fresh bread and strong cheese, two glasses, and a dark bottle of port. Antoine doesn't ask about them either.

Geneviève looks at every page of Antoine's spells with great interest, and points out a few places where Antoine might try something she hadn't considered. But she says most of the spells are new to her too.

'I don't know anything about this governess of yours.

Which may mean she found out about magic not from another rogue, but in some way she wasn't supposed to. Perhaps she stole spells from one of the Brothers, or happened upon them by accident somewhere. Of course, it's possible she did know other rogues, and I just never heard about it. We don't all know each other. Unlike the Order, we don't work together very well, and it is often safer to work alone. And you have managed to keep these spells secret all these years?'

Geneviève looks at her shrewdly, arching an eyebrow.

Antoine hasn't mentioned the embroidered book, because she can't think of a way to explain why she made the copies and doesn't have the book any more – a way that doesn't point to Charlotte.

'Angelo Soliman and Prince Louis de Rohan were suspicious, but I overheard them say they had found no evidence that my governess had taught me.' She changes the subject, quickly, and asks about the Order.

'The Order of 1326 is a cult of secrecy and snobbery,' Geneviève says bluntly, pouring the port. 'They want to make sure that only the people they approve can do magic. No one else. So the Brothers hunt the rest of us, as if we were animals. They take our memories of magic away, if they can, but that is tricky. Sometimes they find it more useful to undermine a magister's reputation, so everyone believes them to be a fraud, or insane. But if the Brothers truly want to do away with a difficult magister, and if they think it's worth risking the attention that murders tend to draw, they kill them.'

Antoine's eyes go wide.

'I've stood over the coffins of several of my friends,' Geneviève says, pointing her bejewelled finger at Antoine's chest. 'They kill. They hunt us and they will not hesitate to kill us. Who do you think killed your governess? A rogue magister dies in a locked room in a palace, and nobody seems to remember it afterwards or speak of it ever again? I'd say that was the Order's work.'

Antoine can't imagine Angelo Soliman as an assassin. She remembers his voice in the garden: *I would have handled the whole business differently.* It isn't Angelo Soliman she has to fear. It's Rohan, and who knows how many others. These Brothers could be anyone, anywhere. She shivers. She's so sick and tired of being afraid. In France, she must be the perfect dauphine, secure the alliance, and keep herself safe from unseen magisters. It's too much.

'Geneviève, I need to find some way to learn more magic, to help me when I'm in France. At the very least, I need some way to carry my spells with me.'

'What do you mean?' Geneviève asks sharply, a piece of cheese halfway to her mouth. 'Why wouldn't you have your spells?'

'I can't bring anything of my own with me. Not even the clothes I wear. I'll be stripped at the border. So that I'll be entirely reborn as French.'

'Ah,' Geneviève says, and puts down the cheese. 'I'd forgotten how fucking ridiculous they are at Versailles. More rules and rituals than the Order. Poor child. You're going to travel without any of your enchanted items? Without your spells? Good God. I'm not sure anything could induce me to do that, in this dangerous world. You want so desperately to go to France?'

Antoine hasn't ever thought about it in those terms. She must go *somewhere*; unmarriageable archduchesses go to abbeys. It would be lovely, of course, to be closer to her family. The French royal family does not travel much outside the borders of France, and she knows full well she might never see Austria again. But what cold comfort it would be, to be near to everyone, and watch helplessly as the French alliance faltered, as Prussia invaded, as Joseph and Mama were dethroned and the Empire dismantled.

'I want to be *worthy* of France,' she says.

Geneviève snorts and pulls up her Belgian lace engageantes, as if she's about to begin work on something, but instead she just pours another glass of port for each of them.

'France will be lucky to have a magister as its queen.'

'Well,' says Antoine, 'I'm hardly a magister at all.'

Geneviève grins. 'We'll see about that.'

CHAPTER TEN

Farewell to Austria — The Pavilion at the Rhine —
The Invention of Marie Antoinette —
Lorrainers — An Old Enemy

Distant shouts of coachmen. Antoine's gilded carriage rolls to a stop. After two weeks on the road, they have reached the edge of the Habsburg universe: the Rhine.

It's nearly May, but no warmer than when they set out. Her last sight of her mother was a dark blur of widow's clothing through a carriage window fogged with Antoine's own breath, through rebellious tears. She still feels guilty that she wasn't able to manage a smile and a wave for the people who lined the streets to say goodbye to her; it was so kind of them to come out so early on such a cold morning.

Now all her tears are dry and Vienna seems very distant and long ago. She gave away most of her things. Books and embroideries to her siblings. Clothing to the daughters of courtiers. A self-portrait for Mama. Her enchanted items wait in a chest to be mailed to her after her arrival at Versailles: her Pandora doll, her thimble, her book ribbon. The treasures of a girl, worthless to a world that does not know about her sacrifices.

Fifty-six coaches and carriages accompany her, carrying

256 people. None of them will go with her into France.

She kisses the two cousins who have come all this way, playmates from childhood, and they all wipe tears away. She holds her dog Mops to her heart. It hurts to leave him behind, after all. She doesn't love him – she sacrificed that – but she knows she should, and that is nearly the same.

Antoine steps out of her jewel-box carriage of gold and glass. She steps onto the hardened mud and looks at the trees, all slanted rays of bleak sunlight and green shadows, like a wood between worlds.

Three Frenchwomen, pinch-faced, drop to their knees. She raises them up and embraces them, and their faces become even more pinched. They say their names but she immediately forgets them; Geneviève gave her a spell for earrings that will whisper a forgotten name, but Antoine cannot wear those today.

The women lead her into a wooden pavilion. She'll enter from the Holy Roman Empire, and emerge into France.

The thin walls are hung with tapestries in rich colours, showing pale faces staring off at something unseen. The tapestries do nothing to warm the air that whistles through the slatted walls.

A woman wheels over a cart bearing Antoine's new French clothes. The *grand habit*, the court dress, for the handover. She's wearing a beautiful new *robe à la française* already, and it was even made in France, but the ritual is what matters.

The first things they strip from her are the muslin cap on her head and the satin shoes on her feet. One woman unpins her gown, and then her stomacher. Someone, standing behind her, is unlacing her stays. A woman in front of her unties the silk gown petticoat, then the hip roll. Then the modesty petticoat, and she is standing in her chemise, shivering, as a woman kneels before her, unties her garters, rolls down her silk stockings.

'Soon you will meet your husband, Your Royal Highness,' says one of the ladies, trying to distract her from her own nakedness, perhaps. 'How exciting! You will call him Monseigneur le Dauphin and he will call you Madame la Dauphine.'

Durfort has briefed her on French etiquette, and she bristles at the reminder she did not need. But these women are kind. They are trying to help.

'I hope in private he will call me Antoine,' she says with her warmest smile. 'Do you think that would be all right?'

'In France, you will be Marie Antoinette,' says one. 'Much more suitable. Much prettier.'

She hesitates, then nods. Is she not here to be pretty and suitable? What does it matter what her name is?

Poor Joseph's second wife never did make a place for herself, and she was miserable throughout their marriage. Antoine won't make the same mistake. She'll make her husband love her. She'll make everyone love her. Antoine has a perfect hairline now, and straight teeth. Her jaw aches as she smiles.

She glances at the cart to see what they'll dress her in. A chemise. A tightly boned golden bodice with lace trim. Wide panniers. Hooped petticoat. Cloth-of-gold skirt and stomacher covered in gemstones and silk bows. Lace engageantes for her arms, gold-embroidered silk stockings for her legs. Diamond-buckled silk shoes with little heels. A gold brocade train to go over the skirt.

Gold is not the prettiest colour on her, but gold means power. Gold means *we can*. A shining new dress, an enormous dress, conforming to the traditions laid down as gospel by the Sun King.

All of this is magic of a kind.

Pots of powder and rouge, which will at least help hide the effects of her shameful crying.

Outside the pavilion's thin walls, there's distant thunder and the rumble of men's voices.

The tears threaten, the tears she has stifled at such great pain on her journey, in her glass box.

One woman takes her old clothing back out through the German door, to give to the cousins, Antoine's final gifts to them in gratitude for being her last friends on Habsburg soil.

For one last moment Antoine stands as Antoine, naked. But not quite naked. She smiles.

Invisible for the moment, around her neck, hangs the golden device that Geneviève created for her. The one bit of gold that no one can see. Its heavy, cold weight lies just below her collarbone.

They worked together, for three nights. The workings came out of Antoine's big gold watch, which had been a present from her mother. Inside, Geneviève affixed six copper wheels. She has access to all of Kempelen's instruments, and some enchanted ones of her own. With a magic pen, she engraved tiny numbers on one wheel, and wrote letters of sacrifice on five wheels beneath it. Each of the numbers corresponds to one of the spells in Antoine's papers, plus seven that Geneviève has given her.

Antoine wrote a legend on a little scroll in tiny handwriting, to show which number goes with which spell. The scroll fits inside the glass watchcase. Most of them are still mysterious to her, but she notes them down anyway, in the hope of a day when she can use them.

A book, made of gears. Now if Antoine wants to know what sacrifices go with which spell, she need only consult her watch. And, most importantly, Geneviève even enchanted it so that it can become invisible at the touch of a tiny button on the side. Geneviève made her own sacrifices for that; it is the best gift Antoine has ever received.

The night after the watch was finished, Geneviève was nowhere to be found. Kempelen had stopped showing the mechanical Turk to the court, and had moved on to his commission to change the water system. Geneviève left no note, no vestiges of her presence.

Antoine holds back tears, sniffing as quickly and discreetly as she can; she has no handkerchief. She smiles violently and holds up her arms as the new chemise drops over her head, and the world, for one brief moment, goes white.

Strasbourg, just over the border, is the first city to welcome the new Dauphine. They let off fireworks and there is a magnificent ball. It seems strangely sombre, all the same, but perhaps people are more sombre here. Antoinette greets everyone – the local girls and boys in shepherd dress, the officials, the nobility – just as she has been taught. There are mountains of flowers and the whole city is alight.

In the episcopal palace, she comes face to face with Prince Louis de Rohan, and she stops breathing for a moment.

'Your Royal Highness,' he says, bowing low. 'I welcome you to France.'

A hundred people are watching them. She tries not to look like a magister. How does one look like a magister, or not like a magister? She tries not to look wary, but she is.

'The people of this country appreciate the sacrifices you have made,' the prince says lightly. 'We appreciate that you have left your family behind. Although of course you have the examples of your sisters ahead of you.'

She must say something.

'If I am pleasing to the people of France, that is all I desire.'

He smiles, not prettily. 'How could they not be pleased?'

'They don't look pleased,' she says, looking around, and realizing that she's spoken too frankly. Oh well. Frankness can be one of her charms. Let him think she wants to be friends, that she has no reason not to want to be friends. She steps closer to the prince, and says almost conspiratorially, 'Everyone looks a little sour here today.'

'Ah, well, as to that, Your Royal Highness, there is an explanation,' says Rohan. 'His Majesty in his wisdom gave a princess of Lorraine, about your age, the honour of the first dance after the royal family's. This broke with precedence and half the nobility threatened to boycott. They're here but they're still not happy about it.'

'About when a princess dances?'

'About whether it has anything to do with our new dauphine being a daughter of Lorraine on her father's side,' he says. 'And whether her being a daughter of Austria, on her mother's side, will affect the way the King of France does business. Today, it's which princess dances first; tomorrow, it may be which side we take in the next disastrous Habsburg war. The great families of France make it their business to understand the significance of the slightest change to etiquette. Your arrival has set the cat among the pigeons.'

She feels cold. 'I did not know about any of this. The King only meant it as a kindness, I'm sure.'

He shakes his head, smiling. 'Of course. Between you and me, Your Highness, these are pigeons in urgent need of a visit from a cat.'

She smiles back, and the line of people who want to speak to her is moving, pushing the Prince de Rohan away from her. He seems content to be pushed, making his farewell. Perhaps everything will be fine.

The King of France is handsome, Antoinette decides. The ballroom at the Château de Compiègne, the last major stop before Paris, is full of eyes watching her: eyes couched in feathers and powder, lace and rouge. Antoinette dances perfectly in dove-grey silk shoes, pointed in the front with a small but sturdy heel.

There are eight dancers in the contredanse allemande, and the rest of the ballroom observes, with drinks in their hands. A walking gavotte step now; a sprightly rigaudon, and back to the refrain. She feels light in every vein, like going downhill on a sled in the snow.

The King is handsome, yes, but in the way of old men – he must be sixty if he's a day; she should know his exact age: it was in her notes – with a fine nose and dark eyebrows beneath a very plain, powdered coiffure. He has been king since he was a child – France barely remembers any other – and he seems to wear it as if it is a part of him. Every one of his feelings appears on his face; why should he bother to hide them? He is king, and his feelings are everyone's business.

His grandson, Antoinette's husband, doesn't seem to have any feelings at all. The Dauphin greeted her very nicely, and the two of them danced a minuet, before everyone, perfectly. But he has not spoken much to her since. He is dark-haired, big-featured, heavy-set. He watches everything in a stolid way that Antoinette has decided is the sign of great intelligence. He keeps his thoughts to himself; and isn't that wisdom? No one seems to pay him any mind, but he is the future king, and perhaps they are showing deference.

She rotates on the ballroom floor, her arms interlaced, her hands resting lightly in those of Philippe d'Orléans, a man she just met. One of her husband's highest-ranking cousins. The music stops, and they separate.

D'Orléans's face is florid, and he bows stiffly, his expression sour. She wonders what she could have done wrong. She is sure she got all the steps right. As she's puzzling it over, he slips away into the crowd.

Antoinette has a moment to rest, now. She steps out of the way of the dance floor and into a group of women. She smiles at the young Princesse de Lamballe, who was presented to her earlier. Madame Adélaïde, the eldest surviving daughter of the King, says that Antoine danced beautifully. She and the Dauphin's other three aunts at Versailles are unmarried. She's terrifyingly beautiful, with piercing grey eyes and glowing skin. Antoinette feels like a child next to her.

'I'm afraid I have to keep reminding myself to dance the Parisian way, and not the Viennese,' Antoinette says with a friendly smile. 'Some of the steps are a little different. I hope I remembered.'

'You've shown them all how to dance in the Austrian

style, Your Royal Highness,' says Adélaïde. 'Soon they will match their steps to yours, and not the other way around.'

That wasn't what Antoinette intended at all, but she can't think of a way to say so.

'Everyone was quite dazzled,' Madame Adélaïde continues. 'You must not pay the slightest attention to Philippe. He's as bitter as a lemon, and has been from birth. If your husband and his brothers were to die childless, he'd be *it*. He never forgets that. Not for one moment. After all, stranger things have happened, haven't they? My father was fourth in line for the throne one moment, and then smallpox and measles did their work, and there he was, king at five years old.'

'Thank you,' Antoinette says, a little befuddled but genuinely grateful. 'I studied very hard, but I'm afraid I still have so much to learn.'

'Do you? Then you must ask me for help. Come, don't be shy, I like nothing better than gossip. What do you want to know?'

'Well, I did wonder about that very elegant woman with the high voice, there by the King.'

The woman in question, as if she's heard, turns her doe-like gaze and perpetual half-smile in Antoinette's direction.

'And well you might wonder, my dear, well you might. That is Jeanne Bécu. She calls herself the Comtesse du Barry.'

'Calls herself?'

Madame Adélaïde makes a dismissive gesture that might mean anything. 'She's the illegitimate daughter of a seamstress. A shop assistant and errand girl.'

Antoinette frowns, trying to frame her question. 'But why is she here?'

'She's here because she pleases the King.'

Antoinette smiles. 'I should like to please the King too. I suppose I'll be her rival!'

Madame Adélaïde snorts, and covers her face with a bit of lace as she laughs. It's only after the fact that Antoinette realizes, to her great embarrassment, what Madame Adélaïde meant by 'pleases'.

Everyone around them is listening, and people who didn't hear are whispering to their neighbours, asking what the Dauphine said.

The Princesse de Lamballe is not staring or whispering. She is one of the prettiest creatures Antoinette has ever seen, with laughing eyes and a wry little smile under her pointed nose. She's a little older than Antoinette but she's as tiny as a girl in her mauve bodice all covered in shining ribbons. She's so thin that the force of her weight comes as a surprise when it smacks into Antoinette's shoulder as the princess falls to the floor.

'She's fainted!' one of the women says.

'She does that quite a lot,' says Madame Adélaïde wryly.

Louis appears at Antoinette's side and offers Lamballe a hand. 'Are you all right, my dear?'

'I'm quite all right, thank you, Your Royal Highness. It's only a bit warm in here, isn't it? Oh, I'm so sorry, Your Royal Highness!'

This last is addressed to Antoinette, for hitting her on the way down.

'You must think no more of it,' she says to Lamballe, as they both stand and smooth their skirts. She steps forward and embraces her, saying in her ear, 'In fact I think I shall love you forever for rescuing me from my embarrassment.'

'Sometimes we simply need a distraction,' Lamballe whispers back with a faintly Italian accent. She turns to the other women, reassuring them and smiling and taking the offered water.

Louis, overhearing, takes Antoinette's arm lightly, and speaks in her ear. 'Is everything all right?'

How lucky she is, to have such a gallant and perceptive husband!

'I'm afraid I am tired, and danced badly,' she says.

'No,' says Louis very seriously. 'You dance with such grace. I'm quite jealous. Everything you do is perfect.'

CHAPTER ELEVEN

A Man Who Talks in His Sleep — Meetings in the
Palazzo Reale — Promises — Roman Ruins — Risks

———— ⁕ ————

Caterina meets Charlotte in the garden at Portici, on the slopes of Vesuvius, on a spring morning in 1770 when the air is full of moisture and the cries of sea birds. They walk together on an open path lined with orange trees, where they can see others coming.

'It has been slow,' says Caterina. 'I didn't want to be seen to be investigating, so I only dropped the phrase here and there. I let people think I'd encountered it in an old book. But no one ever reacted to it in the slightest. I was starting to despair. And then I had lunch with my cousin.'

Charlotte stops walking and turns to her. 'Your cousin—'

'Knows nothing,' Caterina says, holding up one hand. 'But he has a tendency to fall in love with the beautiful men who come through on the Grand Tour – you know, the foreigners. Diplomats. Artists. He had his heart broken by a German scholar named Johann Winckelmann, who came here to study the ruins at Pompeii a few years ago.'

'He had just come to Vienna when I left,' Charlotte says. 'If I'm thinking of the right man. Isn't he the one who was murdered in Trieste a couple of years ago?'

Caterina nods. 'Not by my cousin, I hasten to add. But this Winckelmann was a man inclined to talk in his sleep or in his drink, my cousin says. He used to mutter about the Order of 1326. My cousin once followed Winckelmann to a Freemasons' lodge, but he said he never came out, and he thought Winckelmann had simply been trying to elude him. I found the lodge; it is still meeting in secret here in Naples.'

'Despite Tanucci?'

'Despite Tanucci. I found a place where I could see the entrance, watch them come and go. And I saw a very peculiar thing. Three of the people who went into the Masons' meeting did not come out again. At least, not by that door, and not at the time when everyone else did.'

'Their names?'

Caterina looks slightly smug. 'One of them is the Prince of Caramanico.'

Charlotte puts her hand on Caterina's. The very man she invited to the palace when she first came to Naples; the one who snubbed her.

'He's the grandmaster of the Masonic lodge, you see,' Caterina says.

'And you are sure it was him? He doesn't come to court, you said.'

'I've met him several times at demonstrations and lectures. I'd know him anywhere; he has a very recognizable profile.' Caterina lifts her face into an impression of a haughty aristocrat. 'It doesn't surprise me that he would be a member of any society that's thumbing its nose at Tanucci.'

Caterina seems to have made some assumptions about the Order, which Charlotte ignores.

'And the other two men?'

'The prince's friend Vincenzo Lunardi, a handsome young clerk – I've seen him at lectures as well. The third man I didn't recognize, but he wore a very distinctive cloak with stars embroidered on it – not the best way to be inconspicuous. I gave his description to a few actresses I know, and they said he's a Sicilian alchemist, recently arrived here with his young wife after they left Rome under some sort of scandal. He calls himself Alessandro Cagliostro, and claims to be a count, but I know all the noble families of Sicily. Whoever he is, he did not begin life as Count Alessandro Cagliostro.'

Charlotte thinks for a moment. The sun is hot on her face, and the air smells clean. 'Well, Caterina, I want you to find out everything you can about these men – their families, their interests, their debts, their desires. You've found the Order of 1326. I have no doubt.'

'And what is this Order, Your Majesty? What do they do?'

Charlotte feels a surprising affection for Caterina in that moment, giddy with the knowledge that she has an ally, that she can discover things about the world beyond Ferdinand's palaces, beyond her mother's reach. Something terrifying is happening beyond those walls, but Charlotte is going to terrify it right back.

So she pulls an enchanted thimble out of her pocket and, with it on her thumb, flicks a silver piastra coin in the air. It falls to the earth in a shower of 120 grana coins; the thimble splits anything into its constituent parts, literally or figuratively, unpredictably and wonderfully. She has not quite found a good use for it yet.

'They do magic,' she says, answering Caterina's question, enjoying the look of astonishment on the marchesa's face. 'Would you like to learn?'

Charlotte sits in the library at the Palazzo Reale and grips the smooth dark wood of the chair's armrest, trying to hold on, to make reality stay in position.

Three stuffed heads – a pine marten, a quail, a badger – look at her, unimpressed. The old library is horrible, but it serves her purpose for today. No fear of Ferdinand or his friends turning up in a library, least of all this one. It's a dingy room with more taxidermy than books, and with little brown landscapes on the walls. It was last decorated in the time of Ferdinand's father, before the old man left Naples to take up the throne of Spain.

More importantly for her purposes, it has three doors: one leading to a stairwell, one leading into the suite of royal antechambers, and one leading out into the galleries and ballroom. She can have her conversation with each of the three men alone, without giving them any time to consult each other in between.

With Caterina's help, she arranged to have the Prince of Caramanico brought in through the gallery door, while Vincenzo Lunardi waited in the immense and richly decorated antechamber. The prince agreed to her proposal, kissed her hand, and left through the door ahead of her, and then Lunardi came in from the door on her left. He, too, was persuaded, and left how he came in.

Now that only leaves the man waiting beyond the door to the right, in a stairwell, but that couldn't be helped, and besides, it is a very grand stairwell, even if it is only a minor one stuck in a corner of the palace. Everything here is grand, and Count Cagliostro can wait very nicely, surrounded by pink and blue marble, gold finials and inoffensive oil landscapes rising far above his head. 'Count' Cagliostro. Caterina says that he makes his living by frightening superstitious old ladies who take one look at his spangled blue robe and heavy amulet and hand over their money.

Today, at least, he has the good sense not to be wearing the robe. He's dressed in sober indigo velvet, with lace at his throat. He's younger than Charlotte expected, stout, with a face that is pleasant enough. He doesn't look as though he is in touch with the dark forces of the universe. Is that good or bad for his business? Caterina ushers him in and waits by the door; they have sent away the footmen so there is only the guard outside the room's main doors.

And then the meeting proceeds as it did with Caramanico and Lunardi.

'Will you take something?'

Caramanico, as expected, requested a glass of his favourite wine, the sweet golden Constantia, imported from Africa at great expense. Lunardi, as expected, enjoyed a sweet white as well, but in his case the Italian Picolit.

It's warm in the room – summer now, as it took some time for Charlotte to make her plans and send her letters. It's a thirsty sort of day for a man who's been kept waiting.

For Cagliostro, it's champagne, in a thin crystal flute. The table is arrayed with silver plates carrying each man's favourite cheese and nuts, and Cagliostro takes a few chestnuts in his beringed fingers.

'I will save Your Majesty from saying it directly,' the count says, once he has swallowed. 'I would be overjoyed to supply an elixir. For fertility, or . . .?'

Charlotte nearly laughs. She's still exuberant from the easy success of the other two interviews. 'I do not want an elixir, Count. I will do you the same courtesy you showed me, and speak directly. I am a magister, and I wish to join the Naples chapter of the Order of 1326.'

Cagliostro almost chokes on a chestnut. 'Your Majesty,' he says, recovering, 'I must confess my ignorance.'

She waves a hand, and turns away from him, and launches into the explanation that worked so well with the other two. She has some spells of her own, but she wishes to learn more. She wishes to work with other magisters for the good of the country and the world.

The prince objected here, helpfully telling Charlotte more about precisely what rules she was breaking. It was forbidden for anyone to use magic who had not first been initiated.

To which Charlotte replied that she had learned magic before she knew of such a rule, and now she wanted only to regularize her position.

More than that, though, the prince explained, there was a rule against monarchs being members of the Order, lest they become too powerful. And besides – here he paused, and she had to prompt him – there had never been a female member of the Order, at least not in living memory.

By the time Cagliostro makes these same objections, Charlotte has her argument rehearsed. In a way, the fact that she represents the breaking of two rules at once makes the one cancel out the other: she is a monarch, but she is a woman. She cannot easily overstep. Her husband is the King of Naples, and the Queen will swear a solemn oath never to breathe a word about magic to the King.

But she can give the magisters of Naples access such as they have never had – such as no magisters have.

This is where she told Caramanico that, as queen, she intended to make the court of Naples the centre of the diplomatic world, as it ought to be, with men such as the prince given key positions. What wonders magic could work in spycraft – but of course, few have ever been able to attempt it, because of the rules against monarchs knowing anything about magic. It would take someone bold and intelligent to put magic to use in ways no one ever has. A departure, certainly, but are these not extraordinary times?

This is where she told Lunardi that in this golden age, magic ought to work in concert with the other arts and sciences. Charlotte explained her intention to make the court of Naples a beacon to the world's best artists, writers, composers, and natural philosophers – and she would need Lunardi's help in that. Perhaps magic could be put to use in unrolling the ancient papyrus scrolls found in Herculaneum – the King would have to agree to grant access, of course. Perhaps a new Academy of Sciences, with Lunardi as royal adviser?

Cagliostro, who seems to want nothing but to defraud fearful housewives, presents a more difficult problem. Charlotte swallows, turns back to look at him. 'And of course we must do something about the charlatans with their oils and nostrums, preying on the simple. I understand, of course, that you, Count Cagliostro, are nothing of that kind, despite appearances.'

'I use my gift to help people,' he says, his voice thick and cautious.

'Just so. But as you are known for your gift with elixirs, you might very well be caught up in the King's efforts to rid the city of such people, unless you had someone at court willing to ensure your name was kept off all the lists.'

Cagliostro downs what remains of his champagne and sets the crystal flute back on the table. 'The King has no interest in anything but hunting and whores. He doesn't care about me or anyone else, so long as we pay the right bribes. He might be very interested to find that his little German wife fancies herself a witch.'

The world stops, spools, tangles. Caramanico agreed, kissed her hand, went out through his door to the gallery. Lunardi agreed, kissed her hand, went out through his door to the anteroom.

Cagliostro isn't meeting her eye, and not out of respect. He simply can't be bothered.

'Let me be plainer still,' she says. 'The King is occupied with the business of state, and I am the business of state. The King loses a great deal if he loses me: good relations with the Habsburg Empire, for one thing. My position is not at risk, but yours is, Count. I will make it my business to hunt down every peddler of superstition in Naples, if you try to thwart me.'

She's shaking now; it's a brazen lie, or close to it. Without more magic, Charlotte will remain powerless, and Ferdinand could well make her life even more miserable than it is. She can only hope Cagliostro will think she's shaking out of anger. He does look at her then, still exuding a cultivated arrogance, but she can tell he's uncertain now.

'If the people look to their superstitions for a little hope,' he says, 'a little distraction, is that such a bad thing?'

'We will replace their counterfeit hopes with truer stuff,' she says.

'We,' he repeats.

'I am already welcome among your "Brothers" here in Naples. I brought you here as a courtesy and to give you a warning. If you cause me problems, I will cause you problems. I think you may find that a queen makes a better ally than an enemy, *Count.*'

He pauses, and then nods, just briefly. 'Indeed, Your Majesty. I have never put much stock in the hidebound rules of our Order.'

'No, I thought not.' She smiles, trying not to show her relief. 'How did you come to be a Brother?'

'Ah,' he says, bowing. 'We magisters must keep some secrets, even from each other. I will expect Your Majesty at the next meeting, then. If Caramanico, Lunardi, and Hamilton have already agreed, who am I to cause trouble?'

Charlotte nods tightly, thinking furiously. Hamilton? There is another member of the Order of 1326 in Naples. A Brother she didn't work into her plans, who has no reason to accept her. No reason not to treat her as the Order treats any other rogue.

William Hamilton has been the British envoy to Naples for several years. His official residence is in Naples, but he also has a beach house in Posillipo, and a villa at Portici, on the slopes of Vesuvius, close to the ruins of Herculaneum. He spends a lot of time at the ruins, it's said, and so Charlotte takes an interest in them. This is, apparently, the sort of thing a young queen is supposed to want to do, and when she asks to go, she encounters no trouble about carriages or guards.

Running into him at the ruins will also help avoid any misconceptions on Hamilton's part, or on the part of any onlookers. This is not a diplomatic matter.

The Roman town, buried since the eruption of AD 79, now looks like a building site, with ramps carved out of the dirt, and bits of pediments and other masonry lying here and there as if waiting to be set in place. There are trees on the slopes nearby, but here everything is open, between Vesuvius and the sea.

Hamilton's a sharp-faced man, middle-aged, his coat dusty. He scrambles up out of a shallow hole with a bit of broken pot in his hand. But he doesn't look surprised to see her.

'I have expected you, Your Majesty,' Hamilton says evenly. 'Caramanico told me.'

She shades her eyes against the sun, to see him better. 'Can we speak here?'

'Oh, certainly.' He gestures at the open space around them. The nearest person is Charlotte's footman, waiting back at the carriage. 'This place used to be a hive of activity, but since the discovery of Pompeii, everyone has moved there – shallower, you know. I don't mind. They've left me all sorts of wonders. This was a temple, I'm certain of it.'

She peers into the hole. 'May I see it closer?'

He taps the bit of pot against his hand. 'I should like to know, Your Majesty, whether you have any plans to undermine our Order, to spread its secrets abroad, or use it to work against the interests of King George.'

'I do not.'

'Then by all means.' He steps down into the hole and offers her his hand. There's not much more she can see, only some stones that seem to form the bottom of a wall. She takes his hand, but she's on her guard.

'Mr Hamilton, you seem remarkably unconcerned about the fact that I've asked to join the Order.'

He smiles. 'I would not say that, Your Majesty. But it seems the choices before me are few, and none of them good. I am not an assassin or a fanatic. I joined the Order because I am interested in all aspects of the natural world.'

'Do you think of magic that way?'

'Of course!' He puts a hand onto the ruined wall. 'It's all one: magic, science, even religion, or at least the stories thereof.'

'Surely the Church is not—'

He waves his hand. 'The Church is quite opposed to magic, whenever it is forced to acknowledge it exists. For everyone's sake, we try to prevent that from happening as much as we can. But the stories – "In the beginning was the Word", we're told in the Gospel of John. Words are will, intention, decision. Many cultures have a story about language as a medium of creation, or destruction for that matter. Magic is, fundamentally, the first law of nature.'

Charlotte's reading has tended more to political philosophy than natural. 'Hobbes says the first law of nature is peace,' she ventures uncertainly.

'Rot,' says Hamilton, shaking his head. 'That's the first law, the only truth. Rot. Decay. When anything is left to itself, it decays, and changes into any number of possible states. Some of those states are more likely than others. Magic is, simply, the choice to force a highly improbable condition. But there is, in all things, an equilibrium. Forcing one possibility, at the expense of others, has a cost: the sacrifices decay. And so, to some degree, does the magister who made those sacrifices. So perhaps Hobbes is right after all. Perhaps decay is a kind of peace. Some people think a volcano is violent, but I think it is the most peaceful thing there is.'

She looks towards Vesuvius. An insect is trilling in the trees nearby. She feels, suddenly, a kind of homesickness, a lost feeling, like nostalgia soured, but she has nothing to be nostalgic for. Everything is ahead of her, and nothing is behind.

'Thank you for explaining,' she says, turning back to him. 'I have a great deal to learn about magic.'

'Will I see you at the next meeting, Your Majesty?'

She nods. 'I wasn't sure you were in the habit of attending. My spies did not see you.'

'Ah,' he says. 'That's because I am careful. Underneath Naples, there are tunnels – no one knows how many. Some were quarries, so the builders could get tufo – not this stuff, this is mostly ash, here – but the volcanic rock, you know, oddly light. Some were aqueducts. Some were for secret doings. There is an entrance to the cavern beneath the Masonic lodge through the tunnels.'

'And if I were also to find my way through the tunnels, would I find the entrance there open to me?'

'One simply speaks the password,' Hamilton says. '"*Omnia mea mecum porto*". There are doors into the tunnels throughout the city. There was even an entrance beneath what is now the Palazzo Reale, so it is said. Don Pedro, a viceroy of the sixteenth century, mentions in his letters a "vexatious stair" that was uncovered during building work – it must have interfered with his plans, but he was loath to brick it up, in case he needed it to make an escape from the people he ruled.'

She nods with what she hopes looks like mere polite interest. No need for Hamilton to know that the Queen is desperate to find a way in and out of the palace that doesn't require permission.

CHAPTER TWELVE

*Secrets of the Palace — Under Naples — The Moon
Waxes — Rituals — Rules Are Broken*

———————— ❧ ————————

Caterina shows no outward sign of surprise or curiosity when
Charlotte asks her about the stair to the tunnels. They each
have needlework in their laps, and there are other ladies
scattered about the room. So they speak in low voices, as if
they are gossiping.

'There's no such stair that I know of, Your Majesty, and I
would venture to say that I've had occasion to sneak into
every dusty staircase and dim corridor in the palace.' She
smiles a little at that, thinking no doubt of her Austrian lover.
Then she adds, as her needle moves, 'Well, except one.'

'Except one?'

'The Haunted Staircase. Haven't you heard the stories?
The ladies love to frighten each other with them. Young
courtiers used to dare each other to run up it, I'm told, but
it's been locked for years anyway.'

'*Up* it?' Charlotte repeats.

Caterina nods. 'It can't be your stair to the tunnels. It's in the
undercroft, beneath the chapel, but it leads up, back to ground
level. It probably led to a vault or a sacristy; perhaps someone
started the haunting story as a way to discourage theft.'

'Well, if it's the only staircase you haven't seen, let's have a look.'

It's easy enough to go to the chapel that evening, and neither Ferdinand nor Tanucci are ever there outside their obligatory appearances at Mass. In fact, the place is quite empty, and Caterina and Charlotte slip behind an arcade and into the plain door that leads down to a small stone undercroft.

There are several heavy wooden doors, all with locks. Caterina strides to one, picks the padlock with a hairpin (Charlotte does not comment) and it swings open.

The pale stone steps do indeed rise, straight into a brick wall. Charlotte sighs. She tells Caterina she will just test the bricks, and she steps onto the first riser.

And the staircase inverts, Charlotte lurches down; the world is a ship in a storm. She clutches at the walls and feels as though she's about to tip forward.

'What's wrong?' Caterina whispers.

'It's magic,' she says. 'Look!'

'I don't see anything.'

Charlotte turns, and looks up at Caterina – while Caterina is looking up at her. It's quite impossible, and makes her dizzy.

'The stairs do lead down after all. They were here two hundred years ago, Hamilton said, but I suppose they must have been built long before that. The Order must not know they're here, or it would have covered it up with something better than a flimsy lock and a story. Come, you'll see!'

She stretches out her hand, steps down, and Caterina puts her foot on the first step. Then she nearly falls on Charlotte, begging her pardon and laughing with embarrassment.

Instead of a brick wall, these stairs go on and on, down into depths too dark to see. When the time comes, they'll need to bring a light.

But they have three weeks to wait. The meetings of the Order follow the phases of the moon. There is, from what she can tell, no magical reason for this inconvenience, no real reason whatsoever.

Every morning, Charlotte wakes up grateful that no one has slipped a knife between her ribs, and she runs over her memories of magic, of Antoine, to make sure they are intact. Soliman and Rohan may have been ready to kill her for her knowledge, but these magisters are not. She has gambled and won.

She has not yet told Antoine, for fear her sister will worry. Once she is a member, and safe, she'll write all about it.

On the appointed night, she and Caterina both retire early, then meet in the chapel. Charlotte does not think she will be in physical danger, but she brings a stiletto and a number of other useful items in her enchanted pocket, nonetheless.

They open the lock, and Caterina holds up a lamp to the stairs that seem, once again, to rise.

'There is no map of the tunnels, but I know some of them already, and I have friends who know others, and it didn't take me long to find a route,' Caterina says. 'We will never have to go near the street. How funny that the Order meets beneath a Masonic lodge. If Tanucci sends his thugs to investigate, he'll find nothing but silly men comforting themselves with empty rituals.'

'While beneath the surface, there are silly men comforting themselves with empty rituals,' Charlotte says, smiling slightly. 'And performing magic.'

'Are there rituals?' Caterina says with mock nervousness that may be partly real.

'Something the prince said led me to think so. We are to be initiated, Caterina. But just think of everything we'll learn. They must have more spells. Everything they've kept so carefully hidden. I intend to put all of it to good use.'

They walk into the darkness, Caterina carrying the lamp and walking ahead. Charlotte doesn't look into the darkness behind her.

Some of the tunnels are built of hewn stone, with archways

to rival any village church. Some are carved roughly out of the rock itself, with ancient wooden lintels marking what passes for a ceiling. Some are mining shafts, with ciphers of workers long dead scratched into the stone walls. The city of Naples is built on this volcanic yellow stuff, and built out of it.

They come at last to a dead end, a mere hollow in the rock. Water drips from above.

'"*Omnia mea mecum porto*",' Charlotte mutters. For a moment, she thinks the password Hamilton gave her was a feint, and that they've been tricked, that they'll be trapped here, underground.

But then the rockface dissolves into an open archway.

This is the world she's always known must exist, and it is real, and she is entering it as a magister and as a queen.

Charlotte steps over the threshold.

In a cavern lit by torches stand Hamilton, Caramanico, Cagliostro and Lunardi. But tonight, they are dressed in black robes, and all are wearing red silk caps, loose at the top so that they droop in little peaks. They would look ridiculous anywhere other than this cavern, where they are dressed in shadows too.

'Your Majesty,' says Caramanico a little nervously. 'We have broken with long practice here tonight, but we hope to build a better world, and a stronger Brotherhood in Naples.'

He speaks a smooth, cosmopolitan Italian, not the Neapolitan of the palace. She wonders about that last bit, and it occurs to her that they agreed to her proposal to join them rather easily, and that four magisters does not seem very many for a city this size. Then again, what does she know about this Order of 1326? There is only one way to find out.

They bow, Cagliostro more slowly than the others, and she looks at them each in turn, trying to get the measure of them. Charlotte realizes that Lunardi has two other caps in his hand. She takes one, and hands the other to Caterina. They fit uneasily over mounded hair, and they itch.

'There's a ritual, to begin with,' whispers Hamilton with an avuncular smile.

Caramanico, looking annoyed at Hamilton's lack of solemnity, addresses Charlotte: 'These are ancient symbols, and we begin the meeting with the ancient rite. Do you come in darkness, and leave in silence?'

It seems to be the moment for her to take her vow. Should she elaborate on what she intends to do? She thinks not, somehow. 'I do,' she says, and Caterina repeats it.

'Then I admit you to the Order of 1326. From this moment you are bound to keep its secrets, to protect its ancient knowledge, and to serve the greater good of mankind.'

They stand in a loose circle, and Caramanico produces a goblet from somewhere. He spits in it, says, 'I give this to my Brother magister,' and hands it to Cagliostro. He does the same and passes it to the Lunardi, who follows suit and passes it to Charlotte, who does not look at the contents of the goblet. 'I give this to my Brother magister,' she says, and spits, hard, to make sure nothing dribbles. She feels more than a little ridiculous, more like a schoolboy than a queen, and more than a little concerned that there will at some point be an expectation to drink. She passes the goblet to Caterina.

When Caramanico has taken it back, he pulls a piece of bright blue silk out of some pocket, flourishes it, and lays it on the floor. It's a large star made of silk, woven in blues and reds and trimmed all around with silver thread. The lines that make up the pentacle are silver too. It's quite beautiful.

Caramanico dips a reed into the goblet and places three drops of the liquid inside into each of the five points of the star, intoning, 'From seven to five to three to one, the harmonies of the universe indivisible. The gifts of my Brothers' bodies I have taken for my own gifts. Every drop of my Brothers' blood I treasure. I give them now, to purify our craft, to keep it eternal, to keep it undimmed, to keep it for those who honour its mysteries.'

He's still speaking a variety of Italian, the words rolling out of him in a way that makes Charlotte shiver despite his pomposity. But there's nothing in the middle of the star; if he's trying to work an enchantment, what is he working it on?

'I give these sacrifices,' he whispers.

Charlotte flinches as an orange flame rises with a pop in the centre of the silk star. The star itself is the item, she realizes, with a sick drop in her stomach as the flame eats black-rimmed holes through the gorgeous weaving. The smell – like burning hair – is stronger than whatever odour of decay might come from a few drops of spittle. In moments, the star is nothing but a pile of dark ash on the floor.

Lunardi stoops and, with a little straw whisk, brushes the ash carefully into a silver pan. He hands them each a squat glass vial, into which the prince pours the ash using a little silver funnel.

'We have spells to share, and work to perform,' says Hamilton, 'but none of that is as important as the historic step we have taken here today. Her Majesty is now one of us, and no doors are closed. We must proceed with wisdom, carefully, but it is a moment for joy. A moment of possibility.'

He turns to her, and Charlotte has the unusual sensation of realizing that people are waiting for her to speak. 'I will keep the Order's secrets, and work for the betterment of my Brothers and for all mankind. And it begins here, today, underneath the city of Naples.'

As if to illuminate her point, the torches on the wall flicker. She rehearsed that speech, and it came off rather well.

She glances up at the wall, where a skull is embedded – somehow – in the rock, grinning down at her. How perfect, and how ridiculous. What would that skull see? A soon-to-turn-eighteen unsatisfactory bride, whose chin tends to double but whose lip never trembles. She glares at it.

'For today's business, I believe Count Cagliostro has a report,' Caramanico says, turning to him.

'The trouble is taken care of,' Cagliostro says.

There's a pause.

'You can speak freely among your Brothers,' Caramanico reminds him.

Cagliostro heaves a sigh. 'It was as we suspected. The midwife was a rogue magister. She will do magic no more. I took a few papers from her, and it includes a spell we did not have before. For enchanting a dog collar so that the dog never runs away. It could be useful to us, especially if it works on things other than dogs.'

'Could it be a trap?' Lunardi says. 'Remember what happened to our Brothers in Turin.'

Hamilton explains for Charlotte and Caterina: 'The rogues of Turin planted a spell that filled the room with a poisonous gas when the Brothers of that city tried to use it.'

'I have tested it,' Cagliostro says.

As odious as Cagliostro is, the prospect of shared spells makes Charlotte eager. 'Where are the Order's spells kept? Is there a library?'

'Oh indeed, Your Majesty, of a sort.' Hamilton smiles, and makes a gesture like a man pulling a cloth off a birdcage, but there is no cloth. Still, once he has finished, Charlotte sees a small dark table standing beside him, and, on it, a book thicker than a bible. 'This is the *Reconditus*. It is a single book, that exists in every place where there is a chapter of magisters. It cannot be removed from this cavern; the Freemasons' lodge was put here to disguise a place that already existed.'

'May I . . .?' Charlotte walks to the book, puts her hand on its cover. It is plain yellow leather, with no words or markings.

She puts her finger on the edge of the cover, but the book will not open. Then her whole hand, but she can't prise it apart, and is hesitant to use more force.

'It requires at least two magisters,' says Vincenzo Lunardi, stepping forward with a slight smile. 'May we show you?'

He takes the book, then looks past Charlotte to Caramanico, and asks, in an odd tone of voice, 'What is the virtue of five?'

'The virtue of five is to point in no direction,' Caramanico says, and steps forward to put his hand on the cover next to Lunardi's.

'Who is at the bottom of the grave?'

'The head, the heart, the hand, the eye, the voice.'

'What is the call?'

'The call is chaos.'

'What is the call?'

'The call is creation.'

'What is the call?'

Nobody says anything for an uncomfortably long time, and Charlotte wonders whether she is meant to say or do something. She shifts, opens her mouth, and Lunardi puts his finger to his lips.

Then there is a faint sighing: a creaking sound, as if somone has opened an old door very far away. The two men remove their hands and step aside, and gesture for Charlotte to open the book.

It opens smoothly, and the vellum pages turn stiffly in her hands. She sees all sorts of writing, from plump medieval majuscule to delicate copperplate, in all shades of ink. She sees German, and Russian, and some round languages she doesn't recognize.

'The Five Questions are a sort of key or password,' Hamilton says. 'In fact, the *Reconditus* only appears in a place for the first time when each of the Five Questions are asked by a separate magister. Once any magister has participated in calling the *Reconditus* into existence, that magister can never do so again, and any manifestation of the *Reconditus* can never be moved. This is why each chapter of the Order is to have five members.'

They all look around, at the six people gathered in the cavern.

Caramanico puts his hand to his mouth and coughs lightly; then he says, 'Having already broken with the traditional ban on magical monarchs, we saw no reason to restrict our numbers in these difficult times.'

'The Naples chapter has so much work to do,' Lunardi adds. 'The challenges we face are new, and so our response must be too.'

'Challenges?' Caterina asks mildly.

'Rogue magic is proliferating out in the world,' Hamilton explains with a vague, sweeping gesture. 'But within the Order, we hold ourselves to rules that hamper us to no good purpose. The original intent, I suspect, was to help keep magic secret, but in Naples, the effect of the rule of five has been to keep our numbers lower than they ought to be, as we lose members to other places quite often.'

In response to her questioning expression, Caramanico says, 'Because Naples, and in particular intellectual Naples, is a city of travellers. Perhaps that will change soon.'

Charlotte decides to accept this answer, and turns the pages of the *Reconditus*. Spell after spell that she has never seen before. What wonders could she perform! It makes the embroidered book look like a sampler.

She has so much to learn, but first she wants answers to basic questions, such as how the spells relate to the words from which they are derived, and how that can be when humanity speaks so many languages. Most of the spells seem to be in French or Latin.

Lunardi explains that the letter-substitution is a way of translating intention, that most magisters can only use spells derived from languages they speak.

Every answer begets more questions, but the relief of finally having answers at all makes Charlotte giddy.

'And how can it be a single book, in more than one place at once?'

'The magic is old and beyond our knowledge to replicate,' says Caramanico uneasily. 'When any of our Brothers, anywhere, writes a spell in it, the book grows to accommodate it. We may copy spells from it, but not, of course, remove the book.'

'Impossible to move the book,' Cagliostro mutters, and he rather looks as though he's tried.

'New spells will appear in our copy, but only when we add one of our own. Cagliostro, it's your turn to add a spell. Your dog collar one will do nicely.'

Cagliostro coughs. 'I thought we might keep it out of the *Reconditus* for a little while, Caramanico. Give Rome a little surprise.'

Rome? Charlotte thinks at first they mean the Holy Father, and she's seized with a worry that the Order's relationship with the Church might be more openly hostile than Hamilton had led her to believe.

'It isn't in the spirit of the Order to keep spells out of the *Reconditus*,' Lunardi says.

'It isn't in the spirit of the Order to steal magisters away, but that's what Rome has done to us,' Cagliostro snaps. 'Three of our best magisters in the last year.'

'They use Naples to get into the Order,' Caramanico explains, 'and then they go to Rome, where the five members might as well be five hundred, as they'll share the contents of the *Reconditus* with anyone claiming to be a Brother.'

Ah. Charlotte thinks. *There it is. A rivalry between chapters of the Order.*

'They didn't steal them,' Caramanico says smoothly. 'Those magisters left of their own accord. They found Rome attractive. As many magisters will find Naples attractive, especially now that we have many reasons for magisters to come here, reasons beyond dog collars.'

They all look at Charlotte.

'Perhaps,' Cagliostro says. 'Perhaps the other chapters would be interested to know about Her Majesty. If, that is, they don't try to kill her, which would be unfortunate.'

Caterina steps closer to Cagliostro. 'You'll keep her presence here a secret, or you'll find yourself in a collar of your own.'

Caramanico raises his hand. 'There are no secrets among Brothers, Marchesa. The other chapters will learn soon enough, but there is nothing to fear now that you have both taken the oath. I'm sure of it.'

No secrets among Brothers. Charlotte thinks of Antoine: a secret she has no intention of divulging to any Brother.

'All the same,' Charlotte says uneasily, 'perhaps for now—'

'At least one chapter is already aware,' Caramanico says. 'Brother Angelo will be arriving in a few days from Vienna.' Caramanico looks around at all their faces. 'If we are to restore Naples to her former position in the Order, we must demonstrate that we will not be trifled with. Cagliostro, you need not worry. The Brothers of Rome will be knocking on our door soon enough.'

Caterina is quivering like a harp string, and Charlotte feels sick. 'Brother Angelo,' she says. 'Angelo Soliman?'

'The very same.'

CHAPTER THIRTEEN

A Tragedy and a New Name — The Alchemist —
A Visitor to Naples — Factions — Confessions

———— ❖ ————

16 *June 1770*
Antoinette to Charlotte

Dear Charlotte,
You have no doubt heard about the accident with the fireworks display that greeted us in Paris. One hundred and thirty-two people trampled or burned to death. My husband and I have agreed to pay all our personal allowance over to the families of the dead, and I have been visiting their families. It isn't enough, but I don't know what more to do.
Surely magic must exist for some good purpose. In that terrible fire, the screams and the burning, everyone was powerless. Could they have saved themselves if they had enchanted their clothing to be fireproof, or enchanted the fireworks themselves not to be faulty? What if the manufacturers of fireworks, the smiths who shoe horses, the bakers of bread, what if they all could do everything with just a little more certainty of success? I can't solve their problems for them — I am nobody — but I am their dauphine,

and I wish I could do something for them. I wish I could understand more of our spells, or learn some new ones.

Don't worry; I won't stop being careful. I am doing as we agreed, and burning all your letters that refer to magic, never trusting to encryption alone.

What can I tell you that is happier? I admit I smile to see the words 'my husband' above in my own handwriting! The Dauphin seems very nice. He has been very gentlemanly towards me, and, though he doesn't talk much, when he does he always speaks to me like a true friend. I feel quite sorry for Louis (as he has agreeably asked me to call him in private), since he lost both his parents. His grandfather, the King, is very cheerful and brilliant but quite intimidating. The wedding and the journey were tiring for both my husband and me, and there was no rest when we arrived at Versailles. We must eat our meals, many of them, with people watching.

Mama will want to know that Louis has truly made me his wife but I'm afraid nothing of that kind has occurred. I don't know what to tell her. I suppose there is some mercy in the fact that she will know without me telling her; I have no secrets here, other than magic.

After all of this settles down, I'm sure the Dauphin and I will be very content together.

You asked me about Louis de Rohan. I did see him briefly as we went through Strasbourg, and we stayed in his uncle's house there. He was friendly towards me and I think he's satisfied that I am not a magister.

Which brings me to my confession. I didn't want to keep this from you, and I began to write this so many times on the journey, but I couldn't see a way to begin. So if it is disjointed, or makes no sense, just remember how jumbled I get when I'm nervous.

Courage!

In Vienna, I met another magister. Nobody else knows. Her name I swore to keep secret, but I don't even know all

*of it anyway, or where she is now. I wanted to tell you
but I was afraid . . . I don't know of what. That you
would send someone to keep her away from me or something.
I wanted to find out all I could about her. She is not a
member of that Order of 1326 – she said they would call
her a rogue.*

*She guessed my secret, but I didn't tell her anything about
you.*

*She was a friend to me when I needed one most, and
gave me a way to keep my spells close and safe.*

*Not that it matters; I can't seem to find a way to be
alone for ten seconds at a time, so I have made very few
sacrifices since I left home. Versailles is full of people, all the
time, even in our very rooms. I have nowhere to do magic,
or even to think.*

I'm very lonely, sister, and I'm making so many mistakes.

> *All my love,*
> *Antoinette*

*P.S. I've been told I must sign Antoinette now, being
French. I almost forgot, which was why the pen blotted.*

A few days after the meeting in the tunnels, Caterina brings
Charlotte news that a widowed old countess is telling
everyone that she is plagued by a mischievous spirit, that
not even the indefatigable Count Cagliostro's repeated
attempts to communicate with the spirit and send it away
have prevented strange occurrences in her house. The spirit
has taken several of her most treasured possessions, to
torment her. But Cagliostro has sworn to defeat it, and really
he has proven himself to be a powerful alchemist, and so
kind-hearted.

'Cagliostro will just grow bolder in his crimes now,'
Caterina says. 'He thinks he has royal permission.'

He does not have Charlotte's permission. It wouldn't help
him much if he did; she has very little power to protect her

friends or harm her enemies. She can't imagine what she can do about Cagliostro, other than continue to warn and threaten him. And in the meantime, she has a greater worry on her hands.

Angelo Soliman is in Naples.

He calls upon the Queen, as though he were simply a visiting scholar from Vienna calling upon the local Habsburg. Charlotte receives him alone in her antechamber, the better to protect Caterina, if it comes to that.

Soliman once made it his business to make sure that Charlotte knew nothing about magic. Now he knows that he failed in that task, and he may have a new solution to the problem in mind. Perhaps he won't appreciate the Naples chapter taking matters into its own hands. Hamilton has told her that there is no head or centre to the Order, that every chapter is equal to all the others, at least in theory. But the way the Brothers of Naples speak about the Brothers of Rome, and the way they speak about Vienna with a mixture of resentment and reverence, tells her that the truth is more complex.

Soliman kisses her hand and takes the seat she indicates for him. She sits opposite, back straight, and has a look at him. For the first time, they are meeting as two adults. He looks a little older now – he must be nearly fifty. There are a few bits of grey escaping his black turban.

Well, she thinks. *The only way out is through.*

'Have you come to Naples to kill me, Dr Soliman?'

At that, he laughs with genuine surprise, although his eyes are still sad. 'I have not, Your Majesty.'

'But the Order has rules against magister-monarchs.' She says it defiantly, plainly, poking at the sore spot. She wants to test precisely where she stands with him.

'We do. However, we also have strict rules against causing bodily harm to members of our Order, of which you are now one, I understand. Besides, the deepest purpose of our Order is to prevent magic from coming to public notice and changing the course of nations. The assassination of a queen would be, as it were, an even greater mess to clean up. If you'll forgive me for speaking plainly.'

'Please do speak plainly, always,' she says, and means it. For a moment, she considers mentioning Antoine, to ensure her safety too, but if Soliman has not asked, perhaps it's better to leave it. Antoine – Antoinette, she must get used to that – does not have the protection of the Order, after all.

'Then if you are not here to kill me,' she says, 'why have you come?'

'I have come to reckon with the consequences of mistakes I made.' His face is grave, his hands folded on his knees. 'I intend to make sure that this set of circumstances does not tear our Order apart, or cause harm to innocent people. I have come to make sure, frankly, that it does not ruin me. I am, you may have gathered, the senior member of the Vienna chapter, and there are many both in Vienna and outside it who would like nothing better than to see me ruined. For more than one reason. And I have a wife, now, to protect.'

'I never did have a chance to congratulate you on your marriage,' she says.

He inclines his head. 'Magdalena is the joy of my life. We have set up house in Vienna – I left Prince Wenzel's service, as you know. But I have begun tutoring the prince's nephew, and Magdalena is kept busy getting our house in order.'

The room they are sitting in has nothing of Charlotte in it. The walls are covered in patterned, burnt-orange silk, hung with gloomy landscapes of places she's never seen. She likes the marble chequerboard floor. But she feels wistful at the idea of *getting a house in order* – a magister's house, full of books and enchantments.

'Your wife knows nothing of—'

He shakes his head. 'Nothing. The Order's rule of secrecy is absolute.'

'So is its rule against magister-monarchs.'

'Indeed.' He sighs. 'It goes right to the heart of what the Order does. Do you know why it's called the Order of 1326?'

'Hamilton told me the Order was formed in that year.'

'Yes, when Pope John XXII issued a bull declaring witchcraft to be heresy. Before that, you see, Europe had its sorcerers and witches, all sorts of rituals and beliefs. Most of it was mere folklore or superstition, but not all. When magic became heresy, a secret Order took shape in Europe, with the goal of protecting scholars of magic, by keeping its study out of the public eye. It codified one particular way of working spells, and it improved its methods year over year. The Order has been, for reasons that may be obvious, the dominion of very powerful men; either they came into the Order because they were powerful, or they gained power because of their membership in it. Some very powerful men indeed.' He pauses. 'But not royalty.'

Charlotte shifts her arms, clutching one elbow protectively. 'Why not royalty?'

'Because magister-kings have proven to be dangerous. It had something to do with Sviatopolk the Accursed, in the eleventh century. For a long time, though, the Order was fairly lax about it, and succession being a difficult game to predict, some men who were already magisters became kings. One of your ancestors, Frederick III, had the motto AEIOU. Have you ever wondered why?'

She has seen that on family plaques, tapestries and portraits, but never drew a connection to the letters used in her spells. 'He was a magister?'

Soliman nods. 'And a king, because the Order didn't expect him to become king and didn't put a stop to him. He wasn't a very good magister, but after him, we became more careful. Rudolph II had some inkling about magic, from somewhere, and spent his life trying to find the truth, but we made sure he never did.'

Charlotte gets up, and he stands as well. She hasn't offered him anything; after all, he might have come to do her harm.

But he came as a friend, or as a potential friend, at least. Soliman makes her think of Joseph, of books and maps and the conversations of men. She pours brandy into two heavy cut glasses that fracture the light. She hands one to Soliman, and they stand near the window, with sunlight catching tiny motes in the air between them. How ridiculously grown-up it is to be here offering her brother's friend brandy and talking of societies and emperors. She sips to stop a nervous smile, to feel the warm sting on her tongue.

'I have no desire to become the sort of monarch who is called "the Accursed",' she says at last. 'I want to use magic to improve – I think we have a duty to use it for the good of humanity. To use it in service of science, education, agriculture. Don't you agree?'

'I do.'

He says it simply, without the slightest surprise. All those years he was watching her, checking to see whether she was working magic. He must have seen that she shared his friend Joseph's interests and ambitions. He gave her Montesquieu's book, after all.

'But you said you came to make sure that this set of circumstances – and by that you mean me, I take it – does not tear the Order apart.'

He sighs. 'The Order has never been completely successful in hiding magic here in Europe, but there was a time when it was fairly easy to find rogue magisters and prevent them from doing any harm. That time has gone. Ships crisscross every ocean, carrying people to and from this continent every day. There are those in Vienna – most notably, the doctor Anton Mesmer – who say it's no longer possible or even wise to put all our efforts into keeping magic contained to our little groups of five. Mesmer says we should develop new rules, for a new world. But many see him as a—' He stops, and smiles. 'Well, as a sort of heretic, one might say. As the senior member of the Order in Vienna, I've tried to keep the peace between the Brothers there as much as possible, but I admit I incline to the Mesmerite view. If we cannot control magic entirely, how can we best ensure it's used safely and to good purpose?'

'Exactly,' she says, waving her glass of brandy in her excitement. 'I have so many things I want to do. I don't see why magic should be used only for the benefit of a few learned men.'

He coughs. 'Well, yes. But the conservatives in the Order argue that there are good reasons why we keep magic out of the hands of the mass of people, and though I disagree with their insistence on following every rule laid down centuries ago, I admit they have a point. Magic is dangerous.'

'Why is it more dangerous for a rogue magister than it would be for you?'

'I have been trained to know the costs, and I am protected by the Order. I am not driven by desperation. The temptation to sacrifice beyond what is wise, for example. Imagine a poor woman, desperate, hungry, with mouths to feed. Imagine she found a spell that required some terrible sacrifice.'

Charlotte considers this. 'But even if the people were ignorant of it, magic could be put to secret use for their benefit. And perhaps one day, with the proper controls, more people could use it themselves.'

He nods slowly. 'Precisely the sort of approach I think we must take. You are a queen. You are a magister. What secret uses might you consider? What do you intend to do with your magic? That is the question I came here to ask.'

Charlotte has notebooks full of facts and problems, though she has very few solutions to any of them. But there is a fat book in a cave below the city, full of spells, and surely some of them must be of more use than the few tricks Charlotte and Antoinette managed to learn. What would Joseph do, if he could do anything he wanted?

'I want to show the world that it is possible to feed a nation without the use of forced labour or serfdom.'

Soliman nods again, a tutor's nod. 'Yes.'

She gazes into the distance, thinking of her other siblings: of Josepha, of Amalia. 'I want to make sure no woman ever has to marry without her consent. I want wars to cease. And all children to be educated and – to live. To be free from disease. To begin with.'

She snaps her gaze back at him, afraid she's being childish in the scope of her ambitions, but he doesn't laugh at her.

'I can't promise you any of that is possible,' he says. 'But this is a new age, with new arts and new sciences. And new magic, perhaps! The Order is ossified, weakened by its own fears. Perhaps a magister-queen can show it the way forward into the modern world. I think perhaps you are in a good position to start. I know that your husband is, if I may say so, rather tractable.'

He might have said rotten, rather than tractable. He might have used any number of words. But he doesn't know yet how Charlotte feels about her husband. She keeps that to herself, for now.

'But I don't even have a seat on the Council yet. Bernardo Tanucci controls everything. And I gather these Brothers of Naples are dilettantes.'

'Ha, yes. Alas. The ambitious magisters in Italy go to Rome, or to Turin. Those chapters have lost members recently, because rogue magisters have turned to violence to try to steal spells. So they tempt magisters from elsewhere. The ones who stay in Naples put their own interests above the Order's rules, as you've already discovered. But it also means Your Majesty is working with dull clay here.'

'And with at least one member who'd stick a letter-opener in my ribs the first chance he got,' she says.

'Cagliostro?'

'Cagliostro. He wants to be left alone to prey on old ladies, and sees me as a threat to that. He resents me and will try to turn the chapter against me, but I can't just ignore him.'

'No indeed. His reputation has reached Vienna. One of Prince Wenzel's great-aunts has made over her will to him in gratitude for his recognition that she is the incarnation of the goddess Isis, and the family is not taking it well.'

Charlotte makes a fist. 'He will attract attention and hamper all my plans.'

'And the Naples chapter will be distracted and ineffective,' Soliman says.

He explains that he has seen the effect of dissension within the Vienna chapter: not because of a charlatan, but because of a theatre director and scion of minor nobility named Theodore von Graben. Graben is a traditionalist who argues that if the Mesmerites get their way, rogue magic will spread like a rash across Europe. In search for evidence for their point of view, Graben and an easily led Vienna Brother have started seeing rogues behind every curtain: every irritating neighbour, every rival at court, every upstart prodigy must surely be a dangerous rogue magister. They recently concocted a conspiracy theory about the Mozart family and managed to stop the performance of the boy's opera. All Soliman's efforts to bring the chapter to a consensus have failed. For some time, he has suspected that the only way to bring peace to Vienna is for one side or the other to take over the chapter – and he knows which side he would prefer.

Now, he says, Charlotte has forced the question.

'Mesmer will see this as an opportunity, as I do. A chance for the Order to evolve. And I dare say Mesmer would sway the rest of the chapter if it weren't for Graben. Graben will never accept a magister-queen. He's a conduit for the conservative views of his friends in Paris.'

She frowns. 'Paris?'

'Prince Louis de Rohan is intent on preserving magic as a secret privilege. He can do as he likes in Paris, but I've had enough of his influence on Vienna.'

Charlotte is not so sanguine about Rohan, given that his path is likely to cross Antoinette's frequently. 'Are the Brothers of Paris all very traditional, then?'

'They're all the sons or grandsons of former Brothers. It's

become an inherited privilege, in Paris, and so perhaps they cling to it differently. But it's not the same elsewhere in France. In Marseille, the Brothers are quite scholarly, and take no interest in political debates. I think it would be the safest place for someone like Cagliostro. He could do little harm to the Order there. I could prevail on the Brothers I know in Marseille to summon Cagliostro, to replace a Brother who died last year.' Soliman stops, and thinks for a moment, tapping one finger against his brandy glass. 'We may be able to help each other, Your Majesty.'

He explains that Theodore von Graben has an invitation to go to Stockholm to run a new theatre there, but he's resisted because the Order in Stockholm already has its five Brothers. It would be a great relief to get him out of Vienna, Soliman says. The Stockholm chapter already inclines to Graben's views, but they're so enmeshed in the mess of Swedish politics that they won't bother too much about the rest of Europe.

'The lone Mesmerite in Stockholm is a young man named Isaac Lars Silfversparre, who has been miserable there. If Your Majesty would consent to welcome Silfversparre to Naples, Stockholm would have room for Theodore von Graben.'

'Why not simply bring this Silfversparre to Vienna, Dr Soliman? An even trade for Graben?'

'If Graben suspects I've had anything to do with it, he'll stay in Vienna out of spite. Silfversparre is about the age for the Grand Tour, so it will all seem perfectly natural if he comes to Italy. I think he could be a great help to you here.'

Charlotte nods. 'All right, then. Isaac Lars Silfversparre to Naples, Theodore von Graben to Stockholm, and Cagliostro to Marseille.'

With a smile, she thinks of how nervous she was when Soliman arrived. Even within the Order, there is politics – and she is good at politics. At last, she sees a path ahead. She has allies and plans.

She considers asking more about Paris and Louis de Rohan, but then decides she does not want Soliman's thoughts tending to Antoinette. She trusts him now, but Antoinette's secret is her own to keep.

14 August 1770
Charlotte to Antoinette

My dear, I have a confession. First, let me tell you that there's no reason to worry about me, though I know you will! I met with Angelo Soliman recently. He now knows I am a magister, and so do five others, here in Naples. The Order of 1326 has a chapter here, and they have admitted me.

Sweet sister, I did not make this decision lightly. This palace is a prison: my husband is a lout and his chief adviser stops me at every turn. I need to learn more magic or I'll be useless here, and useless to you. I need to learn what I can, about magic and about the Order, so I can keep you safe in France. Please forgive me, Antoinette, but believe that I'm safe and I've done what I think is best for both of us.

I have sworn to keep the Order's secrets. I consider that vow to cover its rituals, its spells, and its magical processes, but I will tell you anything else I can, of course! I haven't told them you're a magister, and I don't intend to. But as the other chapters across Europe learn about me, new suspicion is sure to fall on you. I'm sorry about that. Please be careful, especially if you encounter Prince Louis de Rohan. I don't think they will hurt you – and I will do whatever I can to keep you safe – but be careful. I'll find out what I can about the state of things in Paris.

My heart hurts when I think of how overwhelmed you must be in your new life. How I wish I were there to help you.

One last bit of advice: surround yourself with mirrors wherever you can. Mirrors have a scattering effect on magic, which can keep a room safe from outside magical influence. It isn't a sure protection, but it helps.

Apparently most of the kings of Europe, including Mama, have been advised to use mirrors by people they thought were decorators.

Be well. I will be thinking of you on your journey. You are never alone.

Your sister,
Charlotte

CHAPTER FOURTEEN

The Queen's Pocket — How Spells Are Added to the Reconditus — The Brothers of Naples — The Problem of Tanucci — Honesty

---

Under her panniers, the Queen of Naples wears a capacious pocket, a pale rose-coloured pouch of linen. Inside, depending on the day, she may have: her white gloves, an enamelled pot of rouge that will not fade until it is touched with a rose petal, a gold snuffbox that buys favours, a silver-handled hairbrush for taking memories, a rosewood box of face powder, a comb of ivory that enhances her ability to do arithmetic, a velvet mask that makes it difficult for people to recognize her, a silver-handled folding knife, a map of the world, an earring that lets the wearer understand any language spoken, and other things.

She is not the girl who left Vienna.

The summer of 1771 arrives, and the court moves to the sprawling Caserta Palace, a few hours' carriage ride outside the city. It always reminds Charlotte of childhood summers at Schönbrunn. Up on a high hill, and the skies overhead as dramatic as those of a fresco. The gardens are so vast that she almost gets lost in them.

Half the rooms at Caserta have chickens and ducks running

through them at all hours of the day and night, and the other half have Ferdinand's mistresses lurking behind the screens and tapestries.

But Charlotte has some privacy now, thanks to the spells in the *Reconditus*.

She has an enchanted candlestick that will gutter three times if someone comes into a room while it is lit: a guard against intruders. Another spell, on a candle itself, can dampen the sound in a room. She has seen a spell for a sword that will point to any hidden passageways; Charlotte, alas, does not have a sword, but she can work on that.

The firescreen spell seems the most useful of all: a way to hide a room. It requires a treasure sacrifice, but Charlotte still has a few things from her trousseau that no one will miss but her, including a gold and sapphire brooch in the shape of a cross, which belonged to her grandmother. It breaks before it decays; the sapphires roughen, darken, and crack, as the gold pits and darkens into a lump that lasts a long time, while her little bathroom smells like the deepest, darkest pit in the world. It's three in the morning, and no one will come unless she calls. All the same, her heart is pounding.

But then there is nothing but a stain where the brooch was, and nothing but void where she had written 'I hope to see Antoinette again'. The sacrifices are gone; the spell worked; the room is hidden. For a price in treasure and hope, Charlotte has a little privacy.

The firescreen is one of her own embroidery projects, a pastoral landscape with apple-cheeked farmers, inside a simple wooden frame. It isn't very large and not very good at keeping the heat and sparks off, but it's very portable. She can take it to any room and that room will suddenly drop out of everyone else's memory, as if it never existed.

The Palace of Caserta has rooms to spare. Ferdinand's father was jealous of Versailles, and undertook to build a palace so enormous that it is still under construction two decades later, with some wings filled with dust and the shouts of workmen – but no noisier than the habitable sections, with Ferdinand's standing invitation to the local animals and his many bosom friends. The painted ceilings soar; every room could be a cathedral. The walls are covered in patterned silk from the nearby factory at San Leucio, in yellows, greens, reds.

At first, she places the enchanted firescreen in her state bedroom, forgetting that it would make it impossible for servants to get to Ferdinand's adjoining rooms that way. They all went the long way around, causing incredible delays in his routine one night, which made her smile, but realize that she must be more careful.

So for her secret room she chooses a small boudoir at the very corner of the palace, a room that no one would pass through to get anywhere else, a room that connects only to her own apartments. The walls are bordered with mirrors. Gilt candle sconces jut out from them like wizened branches, beckoning the unwary on a forest path. On the floor of multicoloured stone, she draws an ashen star.

No one knows this room exists; she can come here and perform magic without being disturbed. She can take the firescreen with her when the court goes to the Naples or Portici palaces. She has a place of her own.

She may not have a child yet, or the respect of the King, or a seat on the Council of Naples. But she has magic and magisters to help her.

And since Ferdinand is usually either hunting or with his mistress, she has time to work.

In the mornings, she reads the reports of Ferdinand's ministers, procured for her in secret by Caterina using a duplication enchantment. In the evenings, she reads whatever Soliman sends her to further her education in all things, although she prefers the books on statecraft. This summer she is reading the *Nakaz*, Catherine of Russia's new statement of principles for a modern nation.

In between, she practises using her gloves, persuading her ladies-in-waiting to do small things with no consequence: to put their embroidery down and look out of the window, or to say something about the weather. She's getting better at it.

She's also studying spells from the *Reconditus*.

It is a book that takes sacrifices. Since new spells from other magisters in other parts of the world only appear when it is fed, every magister must take a turn, at each monthly meeting. Caterina doesn't hunt rogue magisters, the way that Cagliostro and Caramanico do, but she seems to find spells nonetheless; she has friends everywhere, and sources for everything. Charlotte takes her turns every sixth month, adding a spell from the embroidered book. (The unreliable shoe and the doll pin are already there.) Many of the spells that Countess Ertag found somewhere, which the Order did not know about, were women's spells: thimbles that divide, ribbons that mend, pockets and fans and gloves. What might Ertag have taught her, had she lived?

But Ertag did not have the spells in the ever-growing *Reconditus*. The strength of the Order is not in the individual magister. And so Charlotte makes her sacrifices, so that she can learn more and more and more.

In a letter, Soliman told her there have been magister-scholars who spent their lives travelling from city to city, noting down the order of the spells in each manifestation of the *Reconditus*, tracing the pathways of magic through the generations. The debate about which spell was the first to be placed in the *Reconditus* has grown so heated over the years that at least one magister's death in a duel can be attributed to it. Likewise the infamous rivalry between the chapters in Barcelona and Madrid, he writes darkly, saying no more about it.

Thanks to the *Reconditus*, Charlotte has so many new spells now, and she reads them over and over, making notes about what sacrifices she might make for each one.

The Brothers of Naples come to Caserta frequently, between official meetings, to sit in the gardens and discuss magic and gossip. Charlotte likes this better than the damp cavern with the silly red hats and rituals; the only reason she can see for visiting it every month is to check for new spells in the *Reconditus*. Instead of being an interloper at the palace, now she can play host, and she likes seeing her Brothers here: Hamilton with his battered notebooks, the sleek and sophisticated Prince of Caramanico, Vincenzo Lunardi pacing excitedly and examining the limestone walls in the grotto for fossils.

And the new member, the replacement for Cagliostro, whom Soliman successfully spirited away. Isaac Lars Silfversparre is a blond man in his early twenties, with a soldier's bearing and a gift for the violin. Sometimes in the evening, he plays for them, setting the instrument between his chin – always gilded with stubble – and his broad shoulders. Caterina is quite smitten with him, but Charlotte is merely grateful. He is a committed Mesmerite and wants nothing more than to put magic to some use – apparently the Brothers of Stockholm have been nearly as fractious as those of Vienna, and Silfversparre is relieved to be among people who, as he puts it, 'want to do more with their time than lock up midwives and fortune tellers'.

At every meeting of Brothers, Charlotte argues that Naples must demonstrate to the rest of the Order how magic can be put to use in a state project. No other chapter can do that. It would be a clear signal that Naples is the future of the Order.

To begin, she wants to turn the former Jesuit schools into royal institutions, with proper uniforms and teachers and books. And students, for that matter. Even the Jesuits had trouble convincing the parents in the poorest villages that their older children ought to study rather than work. Unlike Maria Theresa, Charlotte has neither the power nor the inclination to solve the problem with a mandatory education decree. The Brothers will have to find some way to compensate and support the families, and persuade them to send their children. Lunardi is excited to try something he calls a 'Pied Piper spell', so Charlotte leaves that with him.

She has enough to worry about: Charlotte needs the King to agree to use the school buildings. She will need to do something about Tanucci.

The Red Room at Caserta is one of her favourites.

Here they come to drink coffee in the evening with Tanucci sometimes, when Ferdinand has decided he should check on what's happening in his kingdom. Usually, this follows a letter from his father, the King of Spain. Ferdinand approaches these conversations resentfully, knowing that Tanucci only humours him when it comes to matters of state. But it is something he forces himself to do. And he invites Charlotte, more and more. At first, she thought it was so that he'd have someone to make feel small. But increasingly, he invites her because she asks clever questions of Tanucci, and so takes the pressure off him.

Tonight she watched her husband, all through dinner, gearing himself up for it.

Tanucci and Ferdinand are drinking port in chairs facing each other.

She sits to the side, with her needlework, maintaining a demure posture.

Charlotte's needle finds the hidden space in the weave, pricks apart the weft, leaves behind its scarlet thread. She is embroidering her monogram, to adorn a cushion. She will put her monogram on every surface she can find in this palace. She will brand this place with her mark.

As Tanucci runs through his list of new grievances against the Church and his worries about expenses, Charlotte stays quiet.

'Well, what are we going to do to bring in more money, Tanucci?' Ferdinand asks, covering his lack of intelligence with brusqueness as he always does.

'Luckily, Sire, the confiscated Jesuit property should bring in some income, once it's sold. I've written up an inventory.'

'What about the schools?' Charlotte asks mildly.

'Everything can be sold,' Tanucci says.

Charlotte clears her throat. 'There are so many children in Naples—' she begins.

Ferdinand interrupts. 'Of course there are! Most men in Naples don't have frigid Germans for wives!'

Tanucci smiles indulgently while Ferdinand laughs. Charlotte's face burns. She thrusts her needle into the cloth and leaves it there for the time it takes to breathe in and out.

'It is a question of how best to invest what the state has recovered from the Jesuits, it seems to me,' she says. 'You have exiled the Jesuits; you say they taught superstition and cant. Fine. Then we should put in new teachers. More schools. I don't see why the schools can't continue just as they are, with secular instruction.'

Tanucci smirks. 'Your Majesty is newly arrived here, and unfamiliar with our customs. The poor children of Naples learn best from their masters, where they have them, and from Nature, where they do not. They are simple people.'

'They have been kept that way,' she snaps. 'Do you want a nation of masters, or a nation of the mastered? I wonder.'

Then she takes her white gloves off the armrest of the gilded chair and draws them up over her arms. She tugs the ends of the gloves up over her elbows, smooths the satin over the backs of her hands.

Charlotte has never been one to move her hands as she speaks. She generally holds herself still, aware always that she was born to be an image, painted and posed, meeting the gaze of the world's unblinking curiosity. But now, deliberately, she waves her hand.

'Tell us the truth, Tanucci. Tell us what you want.'

And he does.

'What I want is for all you Bourbons and Habsburgs to go

off and amuse yourselves and let me do as I see fit in Naples,' Tanucci says. As his mouth forms the words, the rest of his face contorts, as if he's having some kind of stroke. His eyes go wide and a vein bulges in his forehead. He claps his hand over his mouth, like a child, and Charlotte can't help but laugh, louder and longer than she's laughed for a long time.

Ferdinand stares at Tanucci, and then stares at Charlotte.

Tanucci says, 'I didn't mean – Your Majesty, I didn't mean to say that.'

Ferdinand growls, 'This Bourbon wishes to use the Jesuit schools for the good of the kingdom and make the people love us. See that it is done, Tanucci.'

Tanucci nods, his face red. 'Excuse me, Your Majesty. I must – I am unwell.'

He stands and stumbles out of the room.

Charlotte smiles. All the practice with the gloves was worth it. At nineteen years old, at last, she sees the life that she was born to live stretching out in front of her.

CHAPTER FIFTEEN

Vincenzo Lunardi Is Frustrated – A Visit to San Leucio –
The Smell of Wet Silkworm – Ethics – A Letter
from Vienna

———— ⋇ ————

Having Ferdinand agree to use the Jesuit schools as secular institutions was only the first step. How much easier it would be if she had a seat on the Council! But for that, she needs to bear Ferdinand a son, and despite the depressing regularity with which he visits her bed, she isn't pregnant yet.

So Charlotte has to find a way to ensure someone hires the teachers and stocks the schools with supplies. It takes some magical duplication of ledgers and letters – with a few key alterations – and some subterfuge on the part of Caterina, but at last the Brothers manage to get some funds into the hands of Vincenzo Lunardi, who now appears as head of the education programme in the official documents, if anyone were to look. Lunardi grumbles somewhat at the work, but it gives him a chance to try his Pied Piper spell and to test a few others, such as a memory spell. And the Prince of Caramanico makes it very clear that such a position would be beneath him, and Hamilton is a foreign envoy, and Charlotte needs Caterina by her side.

The schools open and, bit by bit, the plan is a success.

But Lunardi is frustrated. It isn't enough, he says, to persuade the children and their parents (through magical means or otherwise) that they ought to be in school. The older children can't leave their jobs, not only because their families need the money but also because someone has to do that work.

So Charlotte decides to pay a visit to some working children, to see what might be possible.

The village of San Leucio is just a short drive north of Caserta, up in the hills, where the water runs down to the palace in a long aqueduct. There's a stately hunting lodge, a square of creamy buildings set against the olive-green hills, with palm trees in the courtyard overlooking a wide view down to Vesuvius.

Ferdinand's father, finding himself richly endowed with hunting lodges, decided to put the place to better use. He planted mulberry trees and founded a silk factory there, converting parts of the old lodge into lodging for the families of the workers.

Charlotte is well aware that gossips at court refer to the silk-works as her husband's 'harem'. Like most of the gossip about Ferdinand, it's plausible because of his character, but overestimates his energy. She hasn't known him to go up to San Leucio once. But it's obvious why the rumours started. Many of the weaving and twisting tasks are the domain of teenage girls from destitute families. They work en masse, separated from their family members who are out doing the other labour to maintain the silkworms and keep the colony running.

Charlotte can come and go as she likes these days, between her new skill with the white gloves and the fact that Tanucci seems less eager to cross swords with her. She drives to San Leucio with Caterina. They take a cold lunch in the drab, underused royal apartment, and after the dusty drive, Charlotte wishes she could take a proper bath, but doesn't relish the idea of a wooden tub and servants she doesn't know. Perhaps she could build a bathhouse here on this open hillside, in an ancient style, with frescoes on the walls.

In the meantime, there is work to be done. The superintendent takes them out of the main complex and shows them one of the connected cottages, with a little loom in the front room, and a kitchen in the back, bedrooms upstairs. The cottage's occupants, a family of four, stand quietly during this inspection. The youngest girl gives Charlotte a posy of orange blossom, the little white flowers shining as tightly as silkworm cocoons.

The cocoons themselves do not smell as nice. There's a strong, fishy smell of dead silkworm in one of the long, low buildings attached to the old lodge. Girls pull the shining white threads onto bobbins, and younger children run back and forth, resetting parts of the machines.

A matching building holds the big looms. It's a place of wooden gears and metal hinges, of girls in drab dresses, punctuated by swathes of bright woven silk: yellow fleurs-de-lys on a red background, bottle-green with dark vines, deep robin's-egg blue. It's as if parts of other rooms, in other places, have intruded here.

At least two dozen girls work the looms with strong arms and set expressions.

'As you can see,' says the superintendent, a minor noble who must have done something to annoy Tanucci to be given this job, 'the whole process is here, from the trees to the cloth. It's a self-contained world; the families have garden plots, and their marriages are even performed in the church.'

'And where are the school buildings?'

'The children are trained alongside their older siblings.'

'But where do they learn to read and write?'

The superintendent gives her a tight smile. 'The priest runs a small school once a week to help them with their names and that sort of thing.'

That won't do, Charlotte thinks. In Prussia they've had universal primary education for nearly a decade; it is not impossible. Parts of the lodge are empty, and can easily be converted to school buildings. But she's already having trouble supplying the former Jesuit schools. Creating more schools for these factory children means yet more money Charlotte will have to redirect from the state finances, hoping that no one notices. Tanucci may be a corrupt incompetent but the cold fact is that he's not wrong about the state of Naples' coffers.

There is one spell that could help: the duplication spell in the *Reconditus*, which Caterina uses to copy documents. It's a simple one, and can multiply nearly anything, but it requires a little sacrifice every time. To multiply a ream of paper or a bottle of ink, one would have to sacrifice a small quantity of blood, and the human body only has so much blood in it at any one time.

If they had more magisters – or if the students could manufacture their own supplies . . . A self-contained world.

She looks at the girls working the loom, those hard-working girls who have nothing but their labour and the glints in their eyes. Charlotte has said all along that she wants to use magic for the benefit of all. But the problems of government are problems on a scale that dwarfs the sacrifices any single magister – or even a half-dozen magisters – could make. To remake the world using magic, she will have to remake the way the world does magic.

1 October 1771
Angelo Soliman to Maria Carolina

Your Majesty,
Your question about having non-magisters perform small sacrifices for the public good, without full understanding of what they were doing, is an interesting one. It may not work at all; intention is key. Leaving that aside, what are the ethics of it? Can an action be good if it treats a human being as a resource, even if no material harm comes to that person?

David Hume would argue that 'public utility is the sole origin of justice'. We can say that an action is good if its consequences are good.

That last point is key, I think. The rule against non-magisters knowing anything about magic is there for good reason. A desperate person may make a desperate sacrifice, and so knowledge of magic could do harm. Which brings us from philosophy to the rules of our Order, of course, which we have already begun to break, and to change, and to re-form. Is this such a rule? Can the very bodies of the people be put into the hands of their sovereign?

One might say that they already are; the roads in some countries are built by their labour, which is taken as due and necessary. Sovereigns require their people to kill and die; why not require them to contribute to the public welfare? Informed consent would be, arguably, a greater danger to them than ignorance, until the Order and the world evolve.

If the question is not mere philosophy, I urge you to be careful. The idea holds many risks – and if you embark on it, you must take pains to make sure no Brothers outside your trusted circle know about it. A desperate person may make a desperate sacrifice, as we have discussed, and the same is true of a desperate magister, who may choose to denounce Your Majesty over something like this – or worse, to copy it, but without safeguards.

I suggest you take some time to consider these questions, and not act too hastily.

With my sincerest respects,

    Yours in fraternity,
    Angelo Soliman

CHAPTER SIXTEEN

*Married Life — The Grand Corps — How to Walk at
Versailles — A Planned Encounter — An Unplanned
Encounter — The War Room*

———————— ✤ ————————

Antoinette's mornings begin with a dozen strangers dressing her. The Comtesse de Noailles, her *dame d'honneur*, supervises all of this with thin lips. Madame Etiquette, Antoinette calls her, although she doesn't mean it unkindly. And Madame Etiquette corrects Antoinette several times a day, although she doesn't mean that unkindly.

And every day ends as every day begins, with strangers stripping her and watching her wash. Antoinette stands rigid as the court takes its due from her body.

Sometimes she feels as helpless and manipulated as she did when Charlotte used her gloves on her, that moment on stage when she was unable to move except as directed by an outside force. What is left of her, here? She is a doll to be dressed and undressed, a marionette.

For the briefest of moments, undressed and in bed, she is almost alone. But she hears footsteps. She takes a breath.

Louis comes to her bed as his attendants close the door on them. It is a ceremony, every time he makes the attempt, although now that a year has passed since the wedding, the mood of the attendants is more funeral than charivari.

They lie next to each other in their night clothes by the light of one candle, the sheets tucked over their chests.

Antoinette leans on one elbow and looks into her husband's face. She tries to look beguiling without looking intimidating.

'My dear, you are so lovely,' Louis says.

He caresses her hair: her real hair, unpowdered and loose, darker than it was when she arrived in France, now more brass than gold.

It is not exciting, but it warms her. Antoinette snuggles closer to him, puts her hand on his chest. Beneath the night-dress, his chest is soft, not well muscled. It is her husband's chest, her dear husband's.

'Shall we try?' she whispers.

In answer, he kisses her, and she rolls onto her back. He rolls on top of her and fumbles at their two nightdresses until they are both up to their chests.

She feels the pressure of his penis against her. With her hands on his back, she holds him to her, rises against him.

He rolls off. 'I'm sorry. Not tonight.'

She swallows, nods. For a little while, they lie next to each other in silence, watching the candlelight flicker across the carved ceiling. Antoinette has done everything she can think of to make herself lovable, and yet here she lies, unloved.

After a while, Louis kisses her cheek, bids her goodnight and uses the semi-secret passageway to go back to his own room, and she is alone in the dark.

31 October 1771
Maria Theresa to Marie Antoinette

My daughter,
In two days' time, you will be sixteen years old. I look often at the miniature you sent, though I see there someone

without the blush of youth that you had when you left Austria. You will never be able to rely on beauty, so you must use the other gifts God has given you, such as sweetness, charm, and patience.

My ambassador, Count Mercy, writes that you put those gifts to good use among the circle of courtiers that you call friends, that you have a gift for making everyone think you are speaking directly to them, with every remark you utter. This is all to the good, but he also writes that you never speak a word to important people, and that when the crowds come to watch you at mealtimes, you eat little and say nothing. You must take care that people do not lose the esteem they had for you on your arrival, when you made such a favourable impression. They will forget, so easily, if you let them.

Where is the full list of the books you are reading? I hope you are getting good advice in that matter. You mentioned your husband's love for David Hume's History of England; yes, I think that would be fine for you to read, if only to please the Dauphin, although you must remember it was written by a Protestant.

Joseph has been travelling for weeks, trying to see what can be done about the famine; we have had three years of crop failure, and I fear that whatever we do, many will die. Meanwhile, I watch very pretty manoeuvres and hope that our troops will not be needed for another war. I don't know how much you know about the current difficulties over Poland – you do not meet with the ambassador often enough. I have taken back a few small territories on the edge, which were once part of the Kingdom of Hungary. The rest of the country will soon be divided between Austria, Prussia, and Russia.

Your task is to ensure that this does not threaten our alliance with France, which has a friendly relationship with Poland, and may look unfavourably on the partition – a partition that is absolutely necessary to check the growing power of Russia, which has absorbed so many lands from its Ottoman war. The warm feeling between the Bourbon and Habsburg families may be all we have to prevent another conflict in which so many young soldiers would die on the field, come home wounded or diseased; in which the already barren fields of the Empire would be stripped bare. Your sister in Naples would find herself in the territory of the enemy.

Speaking of Charlotte, I will share with you how overjoyed I am that Ferdinand has made her his wife, completely, right from the wedding night. My contentment at the affairs of all your siblings is overshadowed by my concern for you. I do not think you understand the seriousness of your situation – or you choose not to understand it.

Sending you my best wishes on your birthday,

I remain,
Your loving mother

10 November 1771
Charlotte to Antoinette

My dear Antoinette,

I have wonderful news: I'm expecting a child at last. If it is a boy, I will have my seat on the Council, and an official role in the governance of Naples.

My dreams have been terrible, and no wonder, as I try to sleep wrapped around one pillow to save my poor hips and with my head propped on three more so I can breathe through a nose that seems to have swollen at least as much as my feet have.

(If only there were spells for all these aches, for the heartburn. I suppose magisters have focused on more important matters; or, at least, the magisters whose spells ended up in Ertag's hands and in those of my fellow Brothers.)

My heart aches to hear that you have nowhere to do magic, nowhere to be safe. Please do not ask where I learned these spells, and you must not tell anyone else about them, not even your rogue friend. I have enclosed the firescreen spell for the secret room. And the spell for the candle that dampens sound in a room when lit, but it requires a significant memory sacrifice, and of course the candle burns to nothing like any other, so do use it sparingly. After all, I have three years and three months more memories than you do, little sister.

I have the utmost faith that you will conceive, Antoinette. The difficulties with your husband will solve themselves soon enough. He is young and awkward, that's all.

Enjoy your peace while you can.

Your loving
Charlotte

Antoinette knows she has to reconcile with Madame du Barry, to start with. In fact, it piques her a little that there's a need to reconcile at all; she's been too nervous to speak to the woman, with her impertinent little smile and the cultivated blankness of her stare. But everyone thinks there's a feud, and that will make the King unhappy with Antoinette. Perhaps even unhappy enough to send her home, with the marriage still unconsummated.

She worked herself up to speak to Madame du Barry one day in the presence of the King, when all the courtiers were milling about. But all Antoinette could think to say was, 'There are a lot of people at Versailles today.'

How cold the Dauphine is to the Comtesse du Barry, people think! But it is not coldness; it is a terrible heat, a burning inadequacy. It, whatever it is, has taken on a life of its own.

And her husband's aunts, who bear no love for the royal

mistress, supplanter of their influence with their father the King, have done their best to help nurture it.

Twice, Antoinette has been scheduled to meet with Madame du Barry, and twice, Madame Adélaïde has helpfully created some minor emergency and called Antoinette to her rooms. Only afterwards, when Antoinette arrived pink and flustered, did she recognize the conspiracy.

So, on this evening, Antoinette has prevented that by asking Madame Adélaïde and her sisters to assist her while she gets dressed for the encounter. They assist by sitting on chaises, watching and making comments.

She tries very hard always to think of them as Mesdames Adélaïde, Victoire and Sophie, although the entire court calls them Aunt Rag, Aunt Pig, and Aunt Grub.

The King's daughters might have lost the childish nicknames that he gave them, had they married and moved away to other countries, other courts. Antoinette, after all, lost her name, and chose another. But Mesdames never married.

Adélaïde decided she was too good for any foreign prince, and as there was no French man other than her brother or her nephew high-ranking enough for a daughter of France, that was that.

Victoire and Sophie, two nervous rabbits raised in a nunnery, do what Adélaïde tells them to do.

All three aunts are married, in a sense, to the court: they know Versailles not only at the superficial level of etiquette, as Madame de Noailles does, but in its guts and workings. While the aunts are present as Antoinette prepares for her meeting with Madame du Barry, it's Madame de Noailles who dresses her.

'Such white skin,' says the *dame d'honneur*, lacing her into her stays. 'One can hardly tell where it ends and your chemise begins. It would show through the stays so nicely, in a *grand corps*.'

Antoinette sighs at the mention of the French instrument of torture, the corset that puts other corsets to shame.

'I can't move my arms in a *grand corps*,' she says.

'Well, one doesn't need to move one's arms a great deal,' says Madame Victoire.

The other aunts titter. In reaching middle age unmarried, they have achieved a sort of dispensation that allows them to flout the fashions of the court. Many days they spend in their adjoining rooms wearing comfortable old mantuas. When the time comes to greet the King, in moments when etiquette demands it, they step into panniers, tie a sort of false train around their waists with strings, and throw black taffeta cloaks over everything. Antoinette envies them.

'The *grand corps*', says Madame de Noailles, 'might help with the shoulders.'

The blasted shoulders. Despite all the pain she went through with the painting, or perhaps because of it, there's still something not quite right about them, it seems, and all of Versailles can see it.

'Oh, yes,' all the aunts say at once. 'The shoulders.'

Madame de Noailles frowns. 'Mesdames are teasing you, Your Royal Highness. After all, they are past thirty.'

The aunts groan and pretend to be offended.

'But His Majesty is very strict about the dress and figures of young women at court,' the *dame d'honneur* continues. 'He follows the rules set down by the Sun King.'

'Louis XIV had very particular ideas about the figures of young women,' says Madame Sophie.

Antoinette sighs as the *dame d'honneur* puts the final pin in her bodice. 'Well, luckily I am not off to see the Sun King tonight. I am only going to speak for a few minutes with Madame du Barry before bed. A chance encounter.'

'I hope you're prepared,' says Madame Adélaïde. 'She will be.'

It is fitting that this very carefully arranged chance encounter is to take place in the War Room, on the far side of the Hall of Mirrors from the Dauphine's apartments. They have chosen a moment late in the evening, when the activity of Versailles is concentrated in the smaller rooms, and the Hall of Mirrors is empty save for a few guards. Madame de Noailles follows – Antoinette hardly ever moves through Versailles alone – but at a long remove, to give Antoinette an opportunity to speak to the Comtesse du Barry woman to woman.

The corridors of Versailles are perilous to the absent-minded, but Antoinette has perfected the art of avoiding dog dirt and scraps of food. A woman walking in panniers is liable to waddle, unless she perfects a certain gliding stride.

Antoinette, taking no chances, wears a new set of shoes she enchanted that allow her to walk on just a quarter-inch of air. When they were very young, soon after they received the embroidered book, Charlotte used the same spell to make Wolfgang Mozart trip. It was a prank; the girls had learned for themselves that walking in the shoes takes practice. Mozart was a child of six, and didn't seem to mind falling into Antoinette's arms. She and Charlotte used the shoe spell to help them sneak into each other's rooms. Here in Versailles, Antoinette finds it useful for helping her walk gracefully, room to room, past the liveried ushers and uniformed guards. She never tangles in her skirt and she never waddles.

An unusual effect, though, is that she makes no sound of footsteps when she walks. She's never noticed it before now; usually there are so many people around, so many wooden heels on wooden floors. Tonight, she glides like a ghost towards the War Room, and she can see through the arch that the du Barry is not alone.

She's with the King, and another man, seated at three sides of a small table. None of them are facing the Hall of Mirrors, so they don't see her approach.

Their voices carry so far that she hears them before she's even at the door.

'She doesn't wear the *grand corps*.' Madame du Barry's velvet voice. 'Her shoulders are a disaster. Is it that one is higher than the other? I'd heard that about her and I swear it's so. I don't know why she doesn't wear the *grand corps*. Her figure is going to rot.'

'She doesn't wear it because she couldn't give a shit about Versailles, or about her husband, or about France,' says another voice, and Antoinette's hand goes to her throat. It's Rohan!

She'd heard that Louis de Rohan and Jeanne du Barry were friends. Why is he here? Charlotte has promised to tell Antoinette if the Order learns about her knowledge of magic; she has promised that Antoinette need not worry about them. But perhaps Charlotte doesn't know everything there is to know about everything. Unlikely, but Antoinette has to admit the possibility. It seems so reckless of Charlotte to reveal herself to the very Order that spied on them as children. Charlotte has said that Rohan and the other Brothers of Paris have no power over her, but they do know Charlotte's a magister.

'Husband, ha,' Rohan is saying. 'We all know it's in name only. And can you blame the boy, really? With her dressing like a country countess, and getting a matronly stomach without ever being a real wife?'

'But can she be sent back?'

The worst blow of all: the King's voice. The King! Antoinette looks down at her *robe a l'anglaise*; it's a beautiful shade of yellow, but it's not formal enough for a meeting with the King.

'Anything is possible,' says Rohan. 'The boy's revulsion for his bride may be a blessing. Gives us a chance to annul, now, before it's too late.'

The usher is trying his best to pretend he hasn't heard a thing. She could turn and leave. She could return to the aunts, to Madame de Noailles's dour ministrations. She could accept that she is unloved and unwanted, that she has failed in the one thing she came to France to do.

Antoinette sweeps into enemy territory.

Being inside the War Room is like being inside a sculpture of dark marble and bright gold, with soaring paintings overhead and an enormous bas-relief of the Sun King dominating one wall. It's a terrifying place, even without these people in it.

'Ah,' says the King as she enters and curtseys. 'My grandson's lovely bride. Please, come in, Antoinette. I was just wondering whether you've heard anything from your mother. I haven't had a letter lately, and I wondered if all was well.'

No one says anything about the fact that this was to be a meeting with Madame du Barry alone. The mistress's face is the usual mocking mask. Is it a trap, or simply a misunderstanding? In any case, if they won't acknowledge it, then neither will Antoinette.

Antoinette does not let her voice waver. 'Your Majesty, I had a letter just this morning and she is very well.'

'Ah. Good, good. I thought if anything were wrong, you'd be the first to know.'

The du Barry makes a face Antoinette cannot interpret; or maybe it's just the weight of her hair.

'Indeed, Sire,' Antoinette says slowly. 'My mother would not let three days pass without a long list of instructions to me.' She sucks in her stomach and wishes she could see herself in a mirror to know whether her shoulders are aligned.

But she has said the wrong thing, after all; Rohan's eyes roll upward, and then towards the King, as if she's said something horribly significant. And then she realizes it: they do not want her receiving instructions from Austria. She's confirmed their fears.

She looks from face to face. The old King's pitying grimace; the Prince de Rohan's sneer; the Comtesse du Barry's wide-eyed disinterest.

And there, above them all, the pale bas-relief as round and big as the sun, the Sun King on horseback, crushing his enemies.

It was he, a century ago, who put all the rules in place that govern Antoinette now: the hierarchy of ladies who take her clothes off and put her clothes on, the titles and forms of address, even the clothing (the dreaded *grand corps*; she should have worn it). He was all stage glamour and cheap tricks, but his ghost cannot be dislodged from this place.

Well, she won't be dislodged, either. She won't be a ghost before her time. *Be so good that the people of France will say I have sent them an angel,* her mother said. Antoinette isn't Charlotte; she doesn't know how to make people respect her.

She only knows how to make them love her.

Antoinette can't go back to Austria, a failure, a disgrace. Louis might never make her a wife, but by God, she will be a queen anyway. So they want her to wear better clothes? She will wear *such* clothes. A country countess, indeed. She will make all the people love her. It can be done. She has so much left to sacrifice.

'Your Majesty, you are most kind,' she says, carefully looking only at the King, as though Madame du Barry and Louis de Rohan do not exist. 'I hope you will come to one of my card parties some day. I have made it my goal to beat the Comte d'Artois at whist, and it will be a moment to remember.'

She smiles her most brilliant smile at her enemies.

CHAPTER SEVENTEEN

*The Hairdresser — Antoinette's Wardrobe Book — A Card
Party — Gifts and Wagers — The Chevalier Plays
the Violin*

———————— ❖ ————————

Léonard Autié is a legend among hairdressers. The Marquise
de Langeac claims him as her lover but can't lay claim to his
exclusive services; Madame du Barry, apparently, receives
him in her bath.

Antoinette has several hairdressers already, and the
morning ritual is daunting enough. But now she must have
the most fashionable hairdresser, the best dresses. She must
become perfect.

*She couldn't give a shit about Versailles, or about her husband,
or about France.*

None of these accusations is true. The trouble is that
Versailles, Louis, and France don't care enough for her. She
has not made any of them fall in love with her. She has
failed, and the alliance hangs in the balance. But she will not
fail for much longer.

Versailles is the easiest territory to conquer. She has been
too dowdy, too plain. Very well: she will become the most
fashionable woman at court.

She is awake, sitting on the edge of her bed in her morning

gown, when Madame Etiquette and the court ladies arrive to perform the rituals. Antoinette holds up her hand, then points at one of her ladies-in-waiting.

'Madame Campan will help me arrange my hair first, in my private dressing room,' she says. 'And I have sent for Léonard Autié to join me there to assist.'

Madame Etiquette goes beet red.

Campan, though, is smiling. 'You've destroyed her, Your Highness,' she whispers as she closes the door on the little antechamber, all robin's-egg blues and whites.

Antoinette laughs. 'She is indestructible.'

Monsieur Léonard arrives only a little late, breathless. Deliberately so, probably: maintaining his reputation for being always in demand, and always fleeing husbands. He looks like a performer of some kind – a stage magician perhaps. Between his sharp nose and chin, a curling red mouth. On his head, a wig of layered, fat white curls.

He bows low, and the wig does not shift.

'Your Royal Highness,' he says. 'I thought this day would never come.'

He speaks with the round, deliberate syllables and thick consonants of southern France, so different to the broad, smooth Parisian accent.

She inclines her head. 'I didn't want to impose on you. I know you're busy.'

'Never too busy for Madame la Dauphine.'

'Have you always worked at Versailles, Monsieur?'

He shakes his head. 'I came to Paris from Bordeaux, penniless, only two years ago.'

'Two years! From penniless to the most sought-after hairdresser at court!'

He steps forward and whispers. 'I have a secret.'

'Indeed?'

'When I arrived, I had nothing, and no prospects. But then I had a stroke of luck. I found something on the street, discarded. A tortoiseshell comb. It was pretty, so I picked it up and washed it. It was fate, you see.'

'And that comb inspired you?'

'More than that. It was magic. I swear it was. It gave me abilities, ideas, I never had before. You will laugh, Madame.'

'No,' she says, but not too seriously. 'I do not laugh. So, it is this magical comb that creates these wonderful coiffures?'

'The comb began it. It gave me confidence. It showed me what was possible. It taught me. The comb may have been magic, but I—'

'Yes?'

'Well, I am the magician.'

He looks self-satisfied, and she can't help but smile. 'Good. Tell me, then, magician. If I were to say to you, do whatever you like to my hair – create whatever you like – what would you do?'

He puts one hand to his lips, and cocks his head. Then he opens the black bag he brought, and pulls out a long piece of pink gauze.

Antoinette has taken Madame Etiquette's instruction on the proper thing to wear each day. No longer. She has her ladies bring her a wardrobe book each morning, page after page with little snippets of cloth from each of her dresses pasted in, and notes written beside the fabric about the style of the dress. She sticks a pin into the one she chooses. Sometimes it's a tentative stab, as she used to do with the Pandora doll when she wanted to speak to Charlotte. Sometimes it's deliberate and workmanlike, as though she's putting her needle back into a pincushion. Some mornings, it's almost savage.

Her hair and clothing are only part of the problem. She has made too many enemies, because she prefers the company of sweet, loyal women like Lamballe over the gossips and wits like Philippe d'Orléans.

How could Antoinette not love Lamballe? She's twenty-two, six years older than Antoinette, but she's never snooty. And she's always, eternally, cheerful. She was born in Turin; at seventeen she was packaged off to France to marry one of the Sun King's grandsons, a cad who made her miserable for a year before dying of the libertine's disease. Instead of the romance she deserves, the princess has had only fearful marriage and careful widowhood. And yet her smile has no bitterness in it. Only sweet love of life.

But Lamballe has no influence, so she doesn't count. Very well, then. Antoinette will go out of her way to befriend the people who gossip, who intrigue, who most clearly don't like the Dauphine.

As for her husband, she is at a loss. She had thought perhaps that his sixteenth birthday would be the moment he would consummate the marriage, but he did not. Mama is adamant that if Antoinette increases her caresses and adoration, all will be well. Patience and charm, Mama says. Very well: she will be patient and she will be charming.

France poses its own problems. Many people see Antoinette at Versailles, at the public dinners and presentations, and sometimes at affairs of state. She travels a little, to Fontainebleau or the Tuileries. But the common people have not truly seen her since her journey through the country to the wedding. *They will forget, so easily, if you let them.*

If only there was a love spell in her golden watch!

There is a spell of Geneviève's, though, about a lute-key that will turn music into a reminder. If nothing else, she can make sure the people who hear it will think of her. They will remember her, and they will remember her arrival, when they all cheered so loudly. Who would dare to send away one whom the people of France have welcomed so warmly?

There's an underused bathroom in the queen's apartments, very cold and damp, no one uses it now, there being no queen, and no one passes through it to get anywhere else. There, Antoinette enchants a firescreen; there, she is hidden from view at last.

After long labours, she finds a way to adapt the lute-key spell, to make it work on a violin bow. The enchantment on the bow is a simple one, and most of the sacrifices are minor memories. She is sixteen and has memories to spare. Now she only needs a violinist, and she has one in mind. She invites the Chevalier de Saint-Georges to a card party. And after a moment's thought, she invites Philippe d'Orléans too.

Antoinette's anteroom is lit with twenty-four candles and twelve lamps with golden glass shades. Everyone at the card party looks beautiful, and everyone is.

The Chevalier de Saint-Georges is the sort of handsome that crackles through the air of whatever room he enters. And he enters all the rooms. That's why she needs him; he travels all through France, and he plays his violin.

'Madame la Dauphine and I were discussing the Sun King earlier,' says Saint-Georges. 'I think I see a little of him in your face, Monseigneur.' He looks at Philippe.

Philippe snorts. 'You should. I'm descended from him on both sides. When my father dies, I'll become First Prince of the Blood: next in line.'

'After my husband and his brothers,' says Antoinette.

'Of course,' says Philippe. He looks down at his cards. 'Why are we talking about this? So tiresome, all these titles and bullshit.'

'We weren't,' says Lamballe mildly. She's practically family to Philippe: his wife is the sister of her late husband. 'Bad hand, Philippe?'

'The worst.' He throws it down, looks up at Antoinette, smiles. 'Why don't you sing, Madame? Sing for us.'

Antoinette shakes her head. 'It's kind of you to ask, Philippe, but I'm not in form tonight.'

'Not in the mood, you mean.'

'Isn't it the same thing?'

'We have the best musician in the world with us,' says Lamballe, saving her. 'Oh, do play for us, Chevalier. I'm sure we can procure a violin for you. Or will you only play your own?'

'Saint-Georges could get a tune out of anything,' says Philippe, his teeth shining in the candlelight. 'Bring him a bit of sausage casing and he'll play you a sonata.'

Saint-Georges smiles. 'No need for that, Monseigneur. I was bold. I brought my violin.'

But Philippe isn't finished. 'In fact, I will make you a wager, Monsieur. I will wager that you can't play a perfect scale using . . . a horsewhip for a bow. Footman, fetch us a horsewhip!'

Antoinette and Lamballe look apologetically at Saint-Georges, but he smiles.

'I am used to being the subject of wagers. I grew up proving myself in the streets of Paris. I can prove myself in Versailles quite happily.'

'Proving yourself, Chevalier?' Lamballe asks.

'The other students bullied me, called me mulatto, taunted my mother in the streets.'

'And your father did nothing?' Philippe asks.

'My father?' the chevalier snorts. 'I don't think the man who enslaved and raped my mother cared about what unkind things people might say to her. He left her to watch over my education in Paris and then went back to Guadeloupe.'

Antoinette hardly knows what to say; her conversational-etiquette training prepared her for such pinched and narrow circumstances and sets of people, and she's never had a friend like the chevalier before. 'I'm sorry, Chevalier. Is your mother still alive?'

'She is. And I learned to fence so I could draw the blood of anyone who insults my mother.'

The footman returns with a horsewhip on a red cushion. Philippe takes it, and holds it out to the chevalier, looking a little chastened. It's a rich, black-handled thing, with the whip wrapped around the bottom unused, by the look of it.

Lamballe laughs and claps her hands. 'Yes, let's see it!'

Saint-Georges obliges. The whip-handle rubs against the strings, bouncing awkwardly. The first note is uncertain, and the second squeaks. But every note is true, and on the eighth the chevalier plays a grace note, hops away from the group a little, and then brandishes his whip with a crack while the final note is still sounding.

'You see?' Philippe crows. 'I knew it.'

'Shall I play something with my real bow, now?'

'Wait a moment, please, Chevalier,' says Antoinette. She runs over to the side table, pulls out a long drawer that holds the enchanted bow.

For a moment, she holds the bow in her hands. The weight of it. The smoothness of the dark wood, the perfect tautness of the horsehair. With this bow, the chevalier will play in every city and town in France. He will play for every mayor and factory owner.

And with every arpeggio, every grace note, people will find themselves thinking of Marie Antoinette, the Dauphine. They won't know why. But they will think of her. She will be in their thoughts, and she will not be dislodged.

She turns and presents it to him. 'A small gift, if it would please you – I know musicians are very partial to their old instruments, but perhaps – It was made by the best, I'm told.'

'What a wonder!' The chevalier takes it from her with a short, chivalrous bow. 'I thank you, Your Royal Highness.'

'I hope it won't interfere with your playing.'

'Let's find out.'

Saint-Georges puts the bow to the strings with a little bounce, and then starts in on a low, slow tune Antoinette does not recognize. The sound of love stirring in the gut, the sound of an unrequited lover turning in cold sheets. And then a high note comes in, and the tune speeds up, until it is a whirl, a dance, a flirtation, a long deep chord.

The bow comes away from the vibrating strings and the chevalier holds it for a moment. No one claps; no one says a word. Antoinette realizes she has been staring, unfocused, at the floor. She looks up and sees Philippe staring at her, and Lamballe, and Saint-Georges. They have never stared at her that way before. She has been lost in the music, and they have been lost in thought – about her.

The enchantment works.

She claps and, as if it breaks a spell, the others applaud, too. Philippe puts his hand on Saint-Georges's broad shoulder.

'Do you like it, Chevalier?' Antoinette asks. 'It would bring me great joy to know you were using it, as a reminder of our friendship, even when we're far apart.'

'I think it will suit me very well,' Saint-Georges says. 'I'll use no bow but this one, from today forward, so long as I can do so without breaking my obligations.'

He will play, and people will think of the Dauphine. And, as Mama said, she made such a good impression when she first arrived. Just let Louis de Rohan and Jeanne du Barry try to send her away, when she has a home in the hearts of the people of France.

> *15 March 1772*
> *Antoinette to Charlotte*

My beloved Charlotte,
I have succeeded in adapting a spell meant for one sort of musical instrument to another, and then I thought, if I can adapt the item to be enchanted, why not adapt the enchantment as well? The rogue I met in Vienna told me that this is how most rogues in Europe get their spells: they trade among themselves when they can, but also, they invent them. Once one knows, for example, that both 'c' and 'n' can be replaced with 'o', or with 'i', it is possible, through a great deal of trial and error, to hit on a combination of sacrifices that will translate the magister's will in the magister's language.

I have been having very little luck and getting rather wet with 'fontaine de jouvence' so I think I'll try my hand at 'surprendre'.

I'm wearing these horrible French corsets and dressing my hair more fashionably. Mother will complain about my décolletage and my 'frivolity', but I can't win. She tells me to do what the French court expects? Well, this is what the French court expects. I need to do more than be a good girl to make them love me here. I have decided to take the Sun King as my model, and shine so brightly that without my presence the plants in the Versailles gardens would wither. Do you think I can do that? It's that or disaster, I think, so it had better work.

My little card and music parties have become quite the success. My husband's youngest brother, the Comte d'Artois, is very good at cards and we are friends already. As yet, I have not found anything in common in the Comte de Provence, the King's other brother, but his youngest sister, Élisabeth, is a charming child with the sweetest nature. How lucky I am in both of my families!

No consummation of my marriage.

I kiss you, my beloved.
  Antoinette

CHAPTER EIGHTEEN

Little Caps and Shoes, Done in White Lace — Hunger and Want — Letters and Plans — Ambitions — Many Small Sacrifices

———————— ❖ ————————

1 July 1772
Joseph to Charlotte

My dear Charlotte,

I was overjoyed to learn of the birth of your first child — I had just returned to Vienna after another journey into Bohemia, of which more in a moment — let me be brother first and emperor second. I know that you hoped for a boy — we all did — but the day will come, and you will take your place as the mother of the heir to the throne, and your seat on the Council of Naples. I would give my life in a moment for one more glimpse of my darling daughters, and I never wished them other than what they were.

And of course you have named your firstborn girl, as we all have, for our mother — it was very good of you, though I admit I suspected you might follow Amalia's path and put another name ahead of it! Amalia has stopped writing to Mama altogether, and has surrounded herself with young male bodyguards instead of ladies-in-waiting. She is by all accounts the real ruler of Parma. Your Ferdinand and hers are of a kind, I gather: two of the worst men the House of Bourbon has produced.

The news of the arrival of your little Teresa was a moment of hope amid great sadness. For months, I have been saying that the situation among the serfs is untenable, that we must curb the rights of the landholders. Three years of drought has left our empire barren, and now the mice and worms eat what is left. You must take care in Naples – grain will be dear everywhere, I suspect. In India, I hear, there are millions dead from famine – they can blame that vampiric British East India Company, but here in the Holy Roman Empire we can blame only our own bureaucrats. Mama has finally sent a commissar to take note of the situation – when she might have saved the man time and bother by simply listening to me.

What we need to do, most urgently, is distribute food and other aid. The supplies and the methods of distribution will occupy us for some time, while many die, and I anticipate uprisings before too long.

I cannot spend too long in Vienna – I am off to see our friends the Turks, increasingly our bulwark against Russia.

Mama has built a new gloriette in the gardens at Schönbrunn, and I have asked for another showing of Salieri's latest opera – it is very popular. Perhaps we all need a little comedy in such times.

I have sent some of my own Teresa's little caps and shoes, done in white lace.

With love,
Joseph

Caterina has told Charlotte about the famine that hit Naples and Sicily in 1764, a few years before Charlotte arrived. People died of hunger, and Tanucci tried to divert anger away from the King by blaming local merchants and officials, saying they were storing grain to try to make a profit. This caused violence in all the towns, and people stormed the storehouses, only to find them empty anyway. Then the gallows went up, to try to restore order.

Eventually, the kingdom bought enough grain from elsewhere, but the laws keeping the prices down had killed the local market, and so many people wanted to leave Naples that Tanucci brought in penalties to prevent emigration.

It is, Charlotte thinks, precisely the example of how not to run a country. She has that example before her, and she has the example now to the north of her mother and brother, trying in vain to feed an empire.

But she is not her brother or her mother. She has magic.

The question of whether to have people perform sacrifices without their knowledge has been haunting her thoughts for months. Ultimately, she sent a single teacher to San Leucio, deciding that it wasn't worth the risk just to save money.

But famine is another matter. If there is simply not enough food in Europe, surely that is a problem Charlotte must solve. The duplication spell, on a vast scale, would do it. It would simply require the same sorts of sacrifices that any labour requires: a little time, a little wear on the body. It won't hurt the unwitting magisters, and it may save their lives.

She makes the decision. The copying spell will become the loaves-and-fishes spell, and ensure her kingdom will not suffer as the other nations of Europe are suffering. Never again will Naples suffer a famine, not if Charlotte is here to prevent it.

In the centre of each pentagram on the hidden factory floor at San Leucio, a flour sack slumps. Each student is enchanting their sack to refill once it is empty.

Charlotte leans against the railing of the raised platform that runs the length of the factory. Her second pregnancy weighs heavily on her.

'How many sacks, now?'

'Five hundred,' says Caterina.

'That's enough. Any more and they'll drive down the price. You know what to do with them?'

She nods. 'Yes, Your Majesty. I have a man who picks up the empty sacks and delivers them to a place of my choosing nearby, where I have someone else pick them up a few days later.'

The flour must be put to market, or it will spoil, and they will have five hundred bags of spoiled enchanted flour, always refilling. They learned that early on, after a batch went bad. But no one must know of the magic, and they can't disrupt the ordinary flour market to any significant degree.

She's found a way to improve education and the food supply. Charlotte is on her way to becoming the secret King of Naples. Being a secret king is probably not nearly as satisfying as being a real one, but for her, for now, it will have to do.

'Good,' she says. 'Good. Next week, you can start the students on the beans, if you think they're ready.'

'They're ready.'

The girls file out of the factory and into a room where their supervisor, a prim lady Caterina found somewhere who sees nothing, directs them to clean themselves for dinner, where each of them must (by order of the Queen) brush their hair with a hairbrush they've been supplied. A hairbrush enchanted to remove a very particular strand of memory each time.

And each morning, they return to their posts at the looms to find the day's instructions waiting.

It is all managed with great care.

Charlotte and Caterina walk out into the dirt courtyard. It's warm for March, even for Naples. A bead of sweat trickles down her temple.

A movement draws her gaze: a student walking the path to the privies. A young woman, hair bundled into a cap, gaze low, clothing as simple as an oblate's.

They must have little to give up, these girls. But the spell doesn't ask for much. Each sack of flour takes one set of fingernail clippings, a coin, and a kiss on a handkerchief. The Crown pays them the coins in advance and supplies the handkerchiefs. They lose nothing.

And in return, the girls gain a place to live, two meals a day, classes in reading and arithmetic.

Charlotte has been able to write to Soliman and tell him they have a real experiment to consider, now. To test the question of how an enlightened monarch can direct their subjects' sacrifices.

Charlotte guides her belly down the steps after Caterina.

Charlotte's second daughter, Luisa, comes into the world at the cost of great pain to her mother, and the recovery takes weeks. But at last the day comes when Ferdinand decides he's waited long enough to visit her bed.

Ferdinand comes down on her like a lamprey. She dodges his lips, tucks her chin up at his shoulder while he pounds away at her. He whispers in her ear: 'Charlotte. Charlotte, you make me want to be better.'

Damn, if only he wouldn't talk. She flips him over and gets on top, finishes him off. Then she gets off the bed as fast as she can. He has never hit her after sex, but there is a first time for everything, with Ferdinand.

She turns away from him and pulls on her stockings. She's been repressing a shudder for the last twenty minutes, and she is trying to repress it just a few minutes longer, long enough to get herself dressed enough to make it to the privy closet, but her shoulders shake and she gags on nothing. Perhaps he doesn't see.

He lies, panting. 'You know, the courtesans have no trouble kissing me. It's only the low-class whores that turn their faces away. Like you.'

Ferdinand crawls naked out of the bed and picks up the white glove lying on the back of her chair. She reaches for it but he holds it up, teasing her with it.

Then he opens the window and throws it out, cackling. Her white glove. She'll have to retrieve it, or make another. Damn him.

A few more days of him coming to her room for their monthly reproductive duty. After this, he'll be some other woman's problem for a few weeks. It is an arrangement she can live with; an arrangement she can survive.

30 August 1773
Charlotte to Antoinette

My best beloved sister,

Your letter of 30 July arrived safely. I can't tell you how much I look forward to each one, Antoinette. You must write to me as often as you can, even if it's only a few words. I read every letter ten times or more, not counting the deciphering!

The new baby, Maria Luisa, is a healthy little thing. Her sister loves her dearly and calls her 'doll'. Teresa can say seven words now. (I write each one down on its own sheet of paper. I am such a miser: I hoard memories I hope never to spend.) She and my Luisa will be as close as you and I were, I'm sure, although perhaps they will get into less trouble. There is plenty of trouble to get into here. The ducks and pigs run through half the rooms of the palace, and Teresa was nearly mauled by a goose last week.

Sometimes I'm sure I will teach my girls magic, when they are old enough to keep the secret. But would it be wise to add a reason someone might want to hurt them? I'm not enough like our mother, I suppose.

You might have your heir before I do, if I keep having girls. Any progress on that score? Is the General still arriving with its usual promptness?

Wouldn't it be wonderful if we could have children without the interference of husbands? What sacrifices would that spell require, I wonder?

I'm so lonely here, my dear Antoinette. I'm able to see friends now, and have been gathering people, holding salons when I can. But most of my friends are scholars or diplomats, and I cannot deal with either at the moment. The world is on fire, and they argue about the temperature of the flames. I want to see you.

With love,

Your sister,
Charlotte

CHAPTER NINETEEN

*A Masquerade – A Duel – The Mysterious Swede –
An Attack*

———— ❖ ————

The carriage to Paris seats four: the Dauphin and Dauphine, and two chosen comrades: the Princesse de Lamballe and Philippe d'Orléans.

Antoinette still doesn't like Philippe; perhaps it's because he's several years older than her and Louis, and conveys the impression he'd have nothing to do with them if they didn't outrank him. But he's important at court, and Louis is wise – wiser than Antoinette used to be – in choosing his friends.

Not even Philippe's perpetual sneer can ruin this night. Day after day of being on display at Versailles, and tonight, for a change, she'll be behind a mask. A masquerade! At the opera house! In Paris! As the carriage rolls through the city streets, she peers out at the women walking in plain dresses with babies on their backs or baskets in their arms. They frown slightly at the carriage but nobody throws flowers or gawks, not tonight. Tonight the Dauphin and Dauphine are travelling incognito.

They are out, in glorious Paris, and nobody knows who they are. She can breathe; no need tonight for the *grand corps*. No need to say the right thing, to impress the court, to serve the alliance. She feels frighteningly free, as if anything might happen.

Antoinette dons the black feathered mask she enchanted with a dazzling spell – courtesy of Geneviève in one of her recent letters. It makes her identity harder to fathom. Philippe glances at her with a slight frown. She's getting something wrong, no doubt; she's always getting something wrong.

'Do you think it will be a good night?' Antoinette asks nobody in particular, brightly.

Lamballe lifts her chin, her slightly knobby nose high in the air. 'I think it will be a remarkable night,' she says.

Antoinette leans forward and puts her hand on the princess's knee, then glances at her husband.

Louis is nice. The warmth of him next to her is nice; it is January, and cold, despite the furs in the carriage. How fortunate she is to have a nice husband, when poor Charlotte has to live with a beast. Louis is stout and solid. His one passion is for locksmithing, of all things. He spends his days at his foundry when he isn't hunting. All things considered, he could be so much worse.

The carriage stops at last at the Palais-Royal, where the newly rebuilt opera house occupies one wing.

'They're all here,' says Philippe, peering out of the window at the bright people scattered all over the steps of the Palais-Royal. His breath fogs the glass. 'They know we're coming. They're waiting to attach, like leeches.'

Antoinette does not much like that *we*. But she says nothing. She does not have to like Philippe; it is of no consequence whether she likes Philippe.

The door opens, the cold air swirls in, and the Dauphine takes the footman's hand. People look at her, but curiously, not appraisingly. She could be anyone. She's taking up no more space than any other member of France's sprawling court.

She and Lamballe gambol hand-in-hand to a knot of people in harlequin silks and feathered masks, lounging on the steps of the opera house near a brazier. The heat of it ripples the air. One lanky character sits on the stairs, stretching his legs and whispering into the ear of the lady next to him. He'd be recognizable by his somewhat dark skin in any event – he's wearing only the slimmest of masks on his eyes, as if he doesn't care to bother pretending to hide – but there's also little mistaking the shapeliness of those legs.

'Chevalier!' Lamballe cries out as they approach. 'I know you.'

The Chevalier de Saint-Georges stands, and bows, and looks her over. Lamballe pirouettes obligingly.

'And I know you, Madame la Princesse de Lamballe,' he says. 'Which means this must be, ah, Your Royal Highness.' He bows to Louis. 'And Monseigneur le Duc. And Her Royal Highness the Dauphine? I would not have known you, Madame, if it had not been for your companions.'

Philippe nods absently; he's scanning the crowd, frowning as though he's looking for someone in particular, but not finding them. But, then, he always has that line between his brows; Antoinette resolves not to try to interpret it.

A snowflake kisses her forehead, and she looks up to see tiny pricks of white, falling from the black sky. They do not even hiss on the brazier; they melt before they touch the ground.

'We so seldom see you at Versailles these days, Chevalier,' says Lamballe. 'When will you play your violin again for us?'

'I beg your forgiveness. I've been travelling with Monsieur Gossec's orchestra.'

'I've heard you're very good, Chevalier,' says Louis encouragingly.

'Good?' says Antoinette, taking the chevalier's arm. 'I say today, with absolute confidence, that this man will be the next director of the Paris Opera.'

'I did not know Madame la Dauphine could see the future,' says Saint-Georges with a sad smile. There is something happening there; she will have to take him aside later and figure it out.

'Just the other day,' Lamballe says, 'I heard someone call you the Black Mozart.'

'My darling,' says Antoinette with a laugh, 'I have met Wolfgang Mozart, and I can say with confidence that he would be fortunate indeed to be described as the White Saint-Georges. The chevalier is the best violinist in France.'

'It doesn't seem fair,' says Louis, smiling, 'that the best violinist in France should also reputedly be the best swordsman.'

Louis's cheeks are red, not only from the rouge but also from the cold. Everyone is shivering but no one wants to go inside, not just yet.

'The best swordsman!' says Philippe with mock horror. They have his full attention, now, at last. 'Oh, no. You've gone too far. He knows you're not serious. It's cruel of you to mock him.'

He's smiling, but now the chevalier is not.

'I have never said I am the best anything,' the chevalier says.

'No, no, but your friends do. I admit your prowess with the violin, but I haven't yet had a chance to test the other thing.'

Philippe's rapier glitters in the light of the braziers and torches. Women gasp.

The chevalier bows low. 'Monsigneur. Forgive me. I cannot join swords with you.'

'Ah, you haven't the stomach for it. The quality of a musical performance may be argued, but there is no denying the victor in a duel.'

Saint-Georges sighs heavily. 'There is no way for me to win. I must not wound a prince of the blood, so I lose even if I win.'

'Then we'll fence for points. Come now, Saint-Georges. Surely you have enough control over your weapon to avoid spilling my blood?'

The chevalier cocks his head. 'It is not in me to refuse a challenge, Your Highness.'

He pulls his rapier free, and the two men clatter down the stairs to open ground. A crowd gathers with a great rustling of skirts.

For once, everyone is watching someone else, and Antoinette hangs back, one of the crowd. No one seems to recognize her; the enchanted mask is doing its work.

A red-cheeked young man beside her is staring at the duel, following every cut and thrust. His elbow meets her ribs and he starts.

'I'm sorry,' he says.

'Not at all,' she says, thrilled by anonymity. 'It's a dangerous sport. Who are you cheering for?'

'The chevalier, of course.'

'Of course. You are absolutely right. Are you a swordsman?'

He bows his head. 'I am a musketeer of the guard.'

'I had thought they were older!' she says.

'I'm sixteen, Mademoiselle,' he says, his cheeks getting redder. 'In fact, I'm about to be married.'

'Lafayette!' someone calls, and the red-cheeked boy turns his head. 'We're over here!'

The boy bows deeply, and he's gone.

She sees something at the corner of one eye: among the many powdered heads, a glimpse of a brown moth, embroidered on a lappet, hanging from a high white bonnet.

Her breath catches and suddenly, she can't breathe in the winter air.

There could be more than one such bonnet in the world. This is a masquerade, after all; people are wearing all sorts of strange costumes.

But Antoinette has only ever seen a moth like that on the bonnet Geneviève wore back in Vienna, in their secret meetings under the Chinese Cabinet Room.

Could it be Geneviève, here in Paris? Antoinette had a

letter from her just last week, and she made no mention of a visit here. She always says that she hates Paris.

Mumbling excuses, Antoinette jostles through the crowd, pursuing the bonnet as it bobs and dips away from her.

The opera house is nearly empty; everyone is outside, watching the duel. Antoinette moves easily through the empty foyer, past couples lolling against pillars. She glimpses the bonnet at the far end of the foyer.

Antoinette runs after it, down a small staircase.

An empty corridor.

On her right, a door is ajar. She pushes it open. The light from the candelabra in the corridor falls inside, casts a diamond of light. The room is painted with the same elaborate gilt and heroic frescoes as the rest of this vast place, but it's small. Too empty to be a dressing room.

Ah, there is a harpsichord near the back wall. A practice room, or something like that.

She peers into the shadows.

'May I help you, Mademoiselle?'

She steps back, surprised. A young man steps into the light from behind the door.

His French is good, his accent slight. Swedish, perhaps. It makes her conscious of her own regional accent, which she's worked so hard to purge. She knows some people call her *l'Autrichienne*, emphasis on *chienne*. The Austrian bitch.

'I was looking for a friend,' she says, which is the truth.

'You've found one.' He bows. 'I am at your command.'

She grins. A Swede, definitely. 'What makes you think I command my friends?'

'I am sure you don't, Mademoiselle. But I serve mine.'

'How far?'

'Unto death.'

She raises an eyebrow, wondering if the careful line of it shows above her mask. 'Then I hope for your sake, Sir, that your friends are few and good-natured. Why are you hiding?'

She looks again into the shadows, but there is no woman there – no man either.

'I needed a quiet place to think. It's very bright and noisy here.'

'Well, one does expect a little sound and light at a Paris ball.'

What a funny thing he is! Even with the mask over his eyes, he looks handsome as Saint-Georges, or nearly, and he seems to be Antoinette's own age.

To her surprise, he takes her hand, draws her into the room and pulls the door nearly closed again. It is very dark now but they are close enough that she can see the line of his face, and the rise and fall of his chest as he breathes. He's wearing a red and black damask coat, with brocade all down the front. His mask is black, shining silk.

'I beg your pardon, Monsieur. If you think—'

He puts his fingers to his lips. 'Someone is coming.'

'We have no reason to hide.'

'We do. You just don't know it yet.'

Her stomach flips. It isn't a sin, is it, to wish that some portion of this kind of fire might spark between her and her husband? The only man allowed to touch her, from now until the day she dies.

Antoinette drops her voice to oblige the stranger. 'I am married.' She didn't mean to make it sound like a complaint.

'I am not seducing you, Madame. As much as I might like to. Please, let us be silent for a moment.'

He's watching the door and seems to have forgotten that he's still holding her hand, not in the way of lovers, but in the way that one holds the hand of a child who can't be trusted not to run in front of a carriage.

She pulls her hand away.

Footsteps in the corridor.

The man takes her hand again and pulls her back, deeper into the shadows. He draws her behind the harpsichord and they both crouch down. She should be giggling, or, more wisely, leaving, but he seems so serious that she does neither. He smooths her voluminous skirts, pulls them out of sight. There's a slim gap beneath the lid of the harpsichord; Antoinette peers through it.

The door creaks open. A hand wraps around the edge of the door.

Antoinette sees a man standing there, dressed in black, sleek as a cat.

Prince Louis de Rohan.

She stops a cry of surprise in her throat. The Swede's arm comes around her shoulder, his hand over her mouth, gently. A reminder, not a threat.

Rohan has something in his hand, something black – a cross, made of gleaming ebony – no. No, it is a stiletto with a black hilt and crossbar, and the edge of the thin black steel hardly catches the light.

'My lord Bishop,' comes a voice from the corridor beyond. The stiletto disappears into Rohan's clothing as he turns.

'Monseigneur,' he says lightly.

It's Philippe's voice. 'I had thought you were in Vienna, finding out what you could about the partition of Poland and the proclivities of Viennese girls.'

Rohan chuckles, and closes the door, saying, 'I've recently returned. I was looking for someone.'

'Aren't you always?'

The door clicks shut, the room is dark, and their voices fade.

Antoinette waits in silence for several breaths, the Swede's hand slowly loosening at her mouth, the tips of his fingers grazing her cheek, and then he is no longer holding her. She turns and looks at him. His face is inches away.

Somehow, Rohan knows she is a magister. It's the only explanation. She feels as though she might vomit all over the handsome young man's shoes. Would Rohan have killed her?

'Thank you for hiding me,' she whispers.

The man looks at her. 'I would love to take credit for

216

gallantry, but the fact is, he was looking for me. An old enemy of mine. He set a trap for me, and I very nearly fell into it.'

She's astonished, speechless.

'It's best we get back out into the crowd,' he continues, standing up. 'Always the safest place.'

He walks forward, opens the door and looks out.

She stands, cursing the pins and needles in one calf, and staggers beside him, out into the room.

He takes her arm, and she blushes. Of all times!

'It's only pins and needles,' she says. 'You don't need to help me.'

He shakes his head with a grin. 'Unto death, remember?'

Her heart, her fool heart, is beating again. Let it beat.

They walk out into the corridor, and her leg finally comes to its senses. The Swede gestures for her to step out. For a moment, she almost takes his hand in their shared enterprise, but she stops as their fingers brush each other.

Lamballe comes running down the corridor, laughing, her face red. 'The chevalier won, of course – what is it?' she asks, seeing Antoinette, looking at the Swede. She was laughing: the duel with Saint-Georges must have ended without casualties. And with Philippe coming looking for her? Or for Rohan?

'Until the next time, Madame la Dauphine,' says the Swede with a small bow, and strides away from them, down the corridor.

Lamballe says portentously, 'I see you've met Axel von Fersen.'

Antoinette's face is hot, and she only realizes after he turns a corner and is out of sight that he should not have known who she was. Perhaps he recognized Lamballe, and put it together, as the chevalier had. Or perhaps he knew all along, while he was holding her hand and calling her Mademoiselle.

But if he knew all along, that means her enchanted mask didn't work on him.

CHAPTER TWENTY

The Newest Brother of Naples — A Puppet Show —
Expectations — The Empress Is Irritating —
A Game of Chess

———— ❖ ————

Charlotte holds the latest letter from her sister in both hands, willing her eyes to focus. She thought she could keep Antoinette safe by keeping her magic a secret, by saying that she, Charlotte, had been the only girl who learned magic at Schönbrunn. But this incident with the mysterious Swede and a knife-bearing Rohan has unsettled Antoinette, and no wonder. Louis de Rohan is a bishop, a prince, and a Brother of Paris. And he is skulking around in dark corners with a knife.

She puts the letter into the candle flame, then writes a short response, telling Antoinette not to worry, but to be careful. She writes another letter, even shorter, the quill leaping and jumping on the page, this one to Soliman.

At her signal, the usher shows in Isaac Lars Silfversparre.

The newest Brother of Naples walks into the room like a man of the world – a sailor, or something like that – though he's only twenty-one, and the only travel he's done is between Sweden and Italy. He's here to report on his work making connections with the intellectuals of southern Italy, but Charlotte's glad to see him for other reasons. He's more cautious than Caterina, better connected than Lunardi, and more pragmatic than Caramanico. He has just the sort of circumspect confidence Charlotte needs right now, when she is ready to cut out a bishop's heart with sewing scissors.

More than all that, he's a Swede.

Silfversparre bows, and she gestures that he should sit. A footman brings brandy and two glasses, and then Charlotte dismisses him and the usher.

She sips, and says, 'How is our list of writers and musicians coming?'

'Very well. It's true that many of the bright young men of good family have gone elsewhere, lately, but if we look beyond the bright young men of good family, Naples has many people whose talents have been overlooked.'

What a good choice he was. She must remember to tell Soliman how grateful she is.

'I know this takes you away from your other work,' she says.

Part of that work is the hunting of rogues. Already the Naples chapter has shown itself to be more tolerant and enlightened, only concerning itself with rogue magisters who have shown themselves to be a danger: to themselves, to others, or to the state. And now, when they find them, her Brothers merely discredit the rogues, or remove their memories of magic with enchanted hairbrushes in the night. No killing, if they can help it.

There are, even so, enough dangerous rogues in southern Italy to supply them with spells, to feed the *Reconditus*, to keep it up to date. Sometimes, Charlotte wonders whether some Brothers – not in Naples, of course, but elsewhere – hunt rogues more out of a need for their spells than out of any principle. The *Reconditus* makes its demands. The rogues always seem to be coming up with new spells, while the Order has little practice with that.

'Searching for talented people to support is a pleasant change,' Silfversparre says wryly. 'I've found it fascinating, in fact, how many bright young artists and scholars there are in Naples. I have been meaning to bring to your attention Eleonora Fonseca Pimentel. She wrote a poem on the occasion of Your Majesty's wedding – you may recall.'

'A lot of people wrote poems on the occasion of my wedding,' she says grimly. 'Was hers particularly good?'

He shrugs. 'I think she has talent. She corresponds with Voltaire now, and he has dedicated a poem to her. She has a rich dowry, and has been engaged for years to her cousin, but I don't think that's going to come off. All in all, I think she ought to be at court.'

Charlotte considers. 'A correspondent of Voltaire's – I do find myself in need of a librarian. I am going to replace this monstrosity.' She gestures at the room around her, the old King's dusty and dismal nod to literature. 'But do you think appointing a woman would draw criticism?'

'A signal of enlightened ideas, of newness. I'll have her come for an interview, if you like.'

'Good. Soon Naples will be the light of the world. I hope you'll never regret leaving Stockholm to join us.' She smiles.

'I think that is most unlikely, Your Majesty. I didn't get along with the Brothers there.'

She looks down at her glass, swirls the dark brandy. 'Did you ever meet a young man named Axel von Fersen?'

Silfversparre stiffens. 'Has he turned up in Italy?'

She shakes her head, gauging him. 'In Paris. I heard some rumour of trouble between him and our Brother Louis de Rohan.'

'Ah.' Silfversparre sits quietly for a moment, thinking or remembering. 'Fersen was once like a brother to me. He comes from an old family – he's the field marshal's son. We joined the Order at the same time, in Stockholm. Barely more than boys. Our fathers are magisters, so we were made magisters.'

'He's a Brother, then?'

He shakes his head. 'Not any more. He left the Order

shortly before I came here. He was sympathetic to Mesmer's ideas, like me, and he never had the stomach for hunting down rogues. But Fersen is more hotheaded, and he never knew when to give up, or how to have patience. They made his life miserable in whatever ways they could, until one day he simply stopped coming to meetings.'

'*Can* one leave the Order?'

Silfversparre gives a little shrug. 'Not officially, though they don't consider him a member of the Stockholm chapter. And I suppose that's why they didn't bother him too much, or treat him like any other rogue they knew about. As far as they're concerned, he's a Brother, just not a very active one.'

He's holding something back; his jaw moves strangely.

'But you know otherwise.'

A breath, and then the shoulders relax under the blue jacket. 'Some rogues are organizing themselves. They're creating new magical societies, or at least loose associations. I'm not sure how far any of it has gone – it must be difficult to hold an orderly meeting when your magisters are peasant midwives, back-alley fortune tellers, God knows what else. But I have heard that Fersen was interested in that – in the possibilities. He's a Mesmerite through and through.'

'Some might say the same about our chapter,' Charlotte says quietly. 'Yet you didn't leave the Order.'

'I thought that if we worked and waited, the Order would begin to change. And I have been proven right. Not in Stockholm – not yet. But here, and in Vienna. While they round up witches in Sweden, here I round up musicians and writers, and study magic. I believe the Order can change. Fersen does not. In fact, he argued that the Order is fundamentally opposed to change, that preserving secrets is its only reason for existence. I can't say I blame him, but I don't feel the same. I believe the Order is what we make it.'

'Indeed.' Charlotte considers. 'And if not the Order, then what?'

'Fersen liked to talk about the possibilities of teaching magic to anyone who wanted to learn, without the restrictions of any Order. But he doesn't fully grasp the dangers. It may begin with food in the belly of the poor, but how long until the poor are sacrificing their blood and bone for money? If you give magic to all, whole cities could be ruined.' He pauses, and sips his drink. 'All the same, Fersen was my friend, and he was treated badly by the Order. I have never forgiven myself for not . . . I don't know. For not being a better friend to him, for helping him find his way. He went on the Grand Tour not long ago, I heard – that's why I thought he might have been here.'

'He may have been,' Charlotte says, thoughtfully. 'I don't remember every young man who comes through Naples. Handsome?'

'Successful enough with women, anyway.' He pauses. 'Come to think of it, that may be the explanation for any argument he would have with Rohan. I hear the good bishop is quite the philanderer. Or it's possible Rohan thinks Fersen is a danger. The Order in Paris is quite opposed to reform.'

The Brothers of Paris holding knives, rogues in Paris trying to organize themselves, and Antoinette caught quite literally between them. Charlotte suddenly feels older than her twenty-one years. She has done too many sacrifices lately; there are so many spells in the *Reconditus* that are useful to her.

Little Teresa, Charlotte's firstborn, is a darling at nearly two years old in the spring of 1774. She squeals in gleeful terror and points at the stage, where the Devil now sits on her father's right hand.

On Ferdinand's left hand, Pulcinella squats, oblivious. The boor in the white suit and black mask, the favourite puppet of every stage in Naples. The puppet looks up, down, in every corner of the stage except where the Devil is. Teresa stands on her chubby legs, approaches the stage, and touches the puppet.

Pulcinella turns, and sees the Devil, and the wooden spoon in his hand becomes a weapon. Thwack! The Devil bows beneath Pulcinella's blows, but still the masked man hits him, to the sound of Ferdinand's high-pitched giggles from behind the stage.

At last, the red Devil puppet slips off his hand and floats down to the floor, where Teresa picks it up. She runs as fast as her little legs will take her, around the edge of the stage, to show her father what she has found.

King Ferdinand emerges from his puppet stage, red in the face and crawling on all fours, and all the courtiers applaud.

The King's latest mistress, a black-haired dancer called Isabella, lets out a long, loud whistle, and stands, her skirts swishing.

Charlotte pats her belly. Not yet swelling, but she knows. If it's a boy, Charlotte will finally get her seat on Ferdinand's Council. She'll have influence. He can't deny her her place on the Council if she has a son; it's in the marriage contract.

She does love her two little daughters, though. Maria Luisa crawls on a mat on the floor, while Teresa laughs with her father.

The King picks up Teresa and twirls her around, kissing her and flipping her upside down. How Charlotte wishes he wouldn't do that! One day the oaf will drop her.

When Charlotte was eight, Father took the youngest children to a puppet show in the village near Schönbrunn Palace. Antoine and Max both gasped at the Faust puppet with his ratty grey beard, his beetling eyebrows, his sorcerer's robes.

'No,' laughed Father, lifting Antoine up so she could see better, 'Faust is not the frightening one. Look, see his scholar's hat? He is just a man. If you are frightened by Faust, what will you do when Mephistopheles appears?'

Antoine pouted, and hid her face in Father's neck. But Charlotte, standing a little behind, could see that her sister's eyes were dry and she was smiling. Antoine never saw the horned figure appear, not then. But Charlotte watched it all, because she was a bigger girl, and Father's shoulder was already occupied.

Ferdinand puts his daughter down, and holds his back with an exaggerated groan, play-acting as if he were a much older man. Then he looks straight at Charlotte, the only adult in the room not standing.

His face is as serious as her own and his expression is a command.

So she smiles, bows her head, claps.

He smiles back, and leads his parade of fools to dinner.

Maria Theresa's weekly letters demand that Charlotte do something about Antoinette.

Antoinette, whose husband is not yet *truly* her husband. As though Charlotte could do anything about that! Worse, word reaches the imperial ears of ridiculous hairstyles and late-night card parties. All eyes in Paris are fixed on Antoinette, watching for the slightest pretext to tear her apart in print. *In print, and perhaps more.* Doesn't Charlotte know there have been riots in France? Right up to the doors of Versailles? What will Antoinette do about that? What will Antoinette do next?

Charlotte has no intention of changing Antoinette's mind about anything. Let Antoinette be. Let her live.

Meanwhile, Joseph explains that Mama, always so intent on her subjects' moral character and industry, has made education mandatory for all children in her dominions – despite the lack of schools and teachers, something he's been warning her about for years. Mama may not have educated her daughters to rule but she's a constant example of mistakes to avoid.

Charlotte's letter to Antoinette reassures her that the disagreement between Rohan and Fersen had nothing to do with Antoinette, and warns her sister to avoid them both and continue to keep her magic secret. Charlotte shakes pounce onto the letter to set the ink, taps it off in a fine cloud, folds it, lights her sealing-wax taper and pours a scarlet drop. Presses her seal. Done.

She glances up at Ferdinand, huddled over a chessboard, alone but for dregs of wine. He's playing a game with his father, King Carlos of Spain, by mail. In every letter, one move. Ferdinand is losing, of course.

He's had his father's last letter for a week but hasn't sat down to make his move until now. There's a pestilence in Naples and everyone has gone to ground, leaving Ferdinand without much company but his wife's.

Charlotte stretches her neck to see the board better.

'Christ on the cross,' Ferdinand mutters. 'I'm buggered in this game, I think. More wine!'

She stands, walks over to the board. Ferdinand's lost a lot of blood in the game, but he's far from doomed.

'You see?' he moans. 'I can't move anywhere good.'

'You could move your knight here.' She points to an open area at the edge of the board, within striking distance of King Carlos's knight.

Ferdinand glowers up at her. 'Are you mad? It threatens nothing there and would be completely unprotected. His knight would take mine and I'd get nothing in return.'

'But then you could take that pawn on the other side; the knight he moved to take yours wouldn't be protecting it any more.'

He scoffs. 'A fucking pawn.'

'But that gap puts you into a better position to get at your father's king. It makes him vulnerable.'

'Hmm,' says Ferdinand. He sees it now, sees how the sacrifice could be worth the cost; he would be clever if he weren't so resentful of anything that spoils his fun. He leans back and laughs as the footman pours wine into his cup.

'Isn't it astonishing?' he gestures, addressing the footman. 'My wife knows everything.'

This is one of his more dangerous modes, when he speaks

226

of Charlotte as if she were a prize addition to his menagerie. She takes a step back from the board.

The footman nods, retires. Charlotte's parents knew about the lives of all their servants and spoke with each of them privately, in interviews they scheduled. They never spoke to them while they were serving. Ferdinand is the opposite; he doesn't know any of the servants' names but he talks at them whenever he needs an audience.

'I'm tired of these games with my father,' says Ferdinand, and walks over to the mantel, lifts the lid off a box of snuff. 'Tired in general. And I have to meet those tedious Americans tomorrow. Remind me what they want, Charlotte.'

'The tedious Americans are about to go to war with the British, which serves your father's purposes. If the British Empire gets one or two of its tentacles lopped off, the whole world will breathe a little easier.'

'Oh, well, if Father wants it,' Ferdinand says sardonically.

There's no point in talking to him, but sometimes he's the only one in the room.

'There is such a thing as the national interest,' she says.

He's not listening. 'Do you know what Isabella said the other day? It was adorable. She said she thought the wars had ended, and now there was peace, we should look upon Britain as our ally. Do you know, as innocent as she is, I see a kind of wisdom in it?'

Charlotte's throat closes. She doesn't disagree with that, as far as it goes. And she is content – happy, even – to let Isabella into Ferdinand's bed. But the woman must not worm her way into his counsel. Charlotte has weakened Tanucci's position in Ferdinand's confidence; once she bears a son, she'll replace him completely. None of the King's mistresses can be allowed to step into that gap instead.

She must say something, do something. It is dangerous to chide Ferdinand, or even to disagree with him, but she must take the chance.

'I suppose when a woman learns statecraft on her back,

it is natural that she should get things backwards,' she says mildly.

'You are jealous, my wife,' says Ferdinand. The look on his face is a warning. She chooses to ignore it.

'Pfft,' she says. 'I don't care who you fuck. Just remember that the King is fucking her; the state is not.'

She has seen him move like this twice before, with this terrifying speed, over the past five years, and she knows what is coming.

Ferdinand grabs her arm, hard, and pulls her towards him, as if she were a child who will not obey. If she were a child, her arm might break when he twists it, bending the elbow the wrong way. But her bones are strong.

He pulls her close to him so that she can smell the wine on his breath. Even a queen knows there is always one man in the world who could hold her like this, hurt her like this. A queen has to obey her king; a wife has to obey her husband. Those are the rules and the rules are set.

'You do not tell me what to do,' he says. But there's doubt in his face; he is ashamed, now. She has indeed told him what to do and he is just clever enough to know it.

Charlotte is running the schools. She's collecting the brightest young minds. She's controlling part of the food supply. She reads all the diplomats' reports and knows more than anyone about how matters stand in Europe and around the world. One day, soon, Ferdinand will wake up to find that he is the King of Naples in name only, that his wife is the true king, and there won't be a damn thing he can do about it. On that day she will dance.

CHAPTER TWENTY-ONE

The Departure of Madame du Barry — The King Is Ill —
Louis and Antoinette — Changes

———— ✦ ————

11 *March 1774*
Geneviève to Antoinette

My dear friend,

    I am sorry to hear that you were so badly frightened by that villain Rohan. He's on his way to England, I'm told, and I'll keep an eye on him while he's here.

    And you needn't worry about Axel von Fersen, either. He is a friend of mine, and was in Paris at my behest. The trap they laid — the gall of anyone copying my bonnet! — was for him, not you.

    Let them do their worst. The days of the Order hunting us down are numbered. We — my friends and I — are working on great things, my dear.

    But so are you! I am impressed with that perfume spell you invented — the idea of different scents creating different emotions is genius. However, I wonder if it's too difficult to control? After all, we can't always know who might be smelling us, or even our letters or flowers. What if you found a way to put it into food instead?

I look forward to your next letter. In the meantime, I'm enclosing a spell of my own, for a bottle of ink that will make your letters rearrange themselves into ciphers as you write them. I know ciphering gives you a headache! But be warned that it doesn't make very much, and takes a heavy sacrifice, so you must save it for the days when you are very tired.

I embrace you,

Your friend,
Geneviève

What Antoinette likes best about the exterior of the château of Versailles is not the sensuous grey stonework, or the red brick that glows like the cheeks of a freshly scrubbed schoolboy, or even the golden fleurs-de-lys that rise from the railings against the azure sky. No, what she likes best are the windows. Sometimes they are as dark as deep water; sometimes, at a certain angle, they shine in jagged white, reminding Antoinette of the sugar on a slice of *Gugelhupf*, the cake Papa used to love.

And sometimes, like now, the sun glazes them golden, opaque, like the top of a *Linzertorte*. It makes her smile.

Out in the royal courtyard, little knots of people walk in the gentle sun of an early May morning. And her coach is waiting, its robin's-egg panels painted with mythological scenes, and four white horses ready to go visiting.

On a day like today, she cannot believe that Prince Louis de Rohan or anyone else wishes her harm. He's gone to England, anyway. Everything may not be for the best in the best of all possible worlds: her marriage is unconsummated and Mama is always disappointed in her. But the sun shines on Versailles.

Antoinette lifts one sage silk shoe to step into her coach, when one of the four horses snorts and the other stamps. Another coach comes rattling past, passes by Antoinette's and then rolls to a stop.

It shines in black and gold, the horses roan and bay, their coats glossy.

The footman opens the door, and out comes the Comtesse du Barry, in a dark green polonaise, with a *bergère* straw hat tilted down over her face. When she turns her gaze on Antoinette it looks wide-eyed and dazed, rather than, as is usual, studiously blank.

'The King is dying,' she says.

Antoinette steps back down to the grey stones of the courtyard. The King has been ill with smallpox for more than a week, but everyone said he was improving.

'Surely—'

'He has sent me away, so he can confess all his sins without the little additional sin of me on his conscience. Oh, I know, he did that with another mistress once, but this time I think he won't recover, and I won't return.'

'May God help him,' Antoinette prays. But what will happen if the King dies? Now? Today? 'The Dauphin – he's in his foundry.'

'They'll send someone to tell him. Now that I'm out of the way.'

Antoinette doesn't know what to say. 'His Majesty's love for you—'

'Ha,' the comtesse interrupts, staring at something invisible just over Antoinette's shoulder. 'Ha. For Louis, love flowed one way, like taxes. He collected as much as he could from as many as he could and he's still dying bankrupt.'

Madame du Barry looks at Antoinette then, just for a moment, and turns and gets back into her lacquered coach.

The shoes that carry Antoinette elegantly over the floors of Versailles don't manage well on uneven ground. She skids across silvery stones. Up the stairs to the Marble Courtyard, where the black and white diamonds unbalance her. It's crowded. She's trying to find Louis, her Louis. Nobody seems to know where he is, or to quite care.

She sees Madame de Noailles and runs to her.

'Your Highness,' the *dame d'honneur* says, and for once she doesn't flinch from Antoinette's embrace.

'Do you think it's really true?'

Madame de Noailles nods, and whispers, 'They say the King's face is as dark as bronze from the disease.'

'I must find my husband.'

'The Dauphin is in your rooms, waiting for you.'

Dear Louis! The last place she would have looked.

The King's valet comes trotting out into the courtyard, his face red with rouge and activity. 'The Comtesse du Barry!' he gasps. 'His Majesty calls for Madame du Barry.'

'Gone,' someone says.

'Her coach just left,' Antoinette says. 'I saw it. She can't have got far.'

The valet shakes his head. 'There isn't time.'

But there is time, as it happens. For several hours, Antoinette and Louis sit with a few of their closest servants and friends, and no one comes to advise them. The doctors want no one in the room with the King for his final breaths; they don't want the contagion to spread. Louis examines the workings of a barometer. Antoinette writes to Mama, to Charlotte, to Amalia, to her brother Joseph. She reads out loud for a while from a novel, *L'Histoire d'Ernestine*, but she can tell that Louis isn't listening, and she stops, letting the book fall onto her lap. She looks out of the window.

'Do you think that I should write to anyone?' he asks at one point. 'The King of England, or the King of Spain, or—'

'I'm sure someone will tell you what is best,' she says.

'Mmm.'

Louis, who can always eat, calls for bread and cheese.

The sunlight moves across the patterned carpet on the floor until mid-afternoon, when they hear a noise like thunder: it is dozens of hard heels tromping across the Hall of Mirrors, running from the rooms of the dead King to the room that holds the living one.

She and Louis take each other's hands and stand ready.

The door opens and the people rush through. There are a few murmurs of *'Vive le roi!'* And Madame de Noailles greets them both as majesties.

Antoinette doesn't remember, later, which of them moved first to kneel, but both she and Louis were on their knees, hand in hand still. And Louis, King at nineteen, said, 'May God guide us and protect us. We are too young to rule.'

The labour pains start just after the new year celebrations that welcome 1775, when it seems everyone other than Charlotte in the Caserta Palace is asleep with a headache a sick stomach. Charlotte walks up and down the empty idors; the walking distracts from the pain, although it does not soften it. She prays for her baby.

She writes instructions to the doctor that every bloody sheet, the placenta, the cord, must all be kept. In the event of her death, the cord is to be kept in a lead box and bequeathed to the baby, should he live.

He?

Yes, *he*, after a short but painful labour that gives Charlotte enough of her own blood for many spells. A little scowling duke, with tiny balled fists.

The doctor orders broth for Charlotte and hands the little bundle to the wet nurse – a potato-faced woman, matter-of-fact, with eyes only for the baby. Charlotte likes her at first sight.

When Ferdinand comes, he takes his son gently out of the nurse's arms, holds him up in the crook of one arm to have a look at him.

'Carlo,' he says.

Charlotte nods. The name was never in question: as their

first daughter was named for Charlotte's mother, their first son is named for Ferdinand's father. Their children are not merely children; they are states in waiting.

'Naples has an heir,' she says. He is, in a way, the fulfilment of duty, but those tiny fingernails, the smallest things in the world, require a greater duty still.

'And you have a seat on the Council,' he says, smiling at her in a way that is not quite friendly, but not cruel either. The smile of a stranger who doesn't quite understand. 'I wish you joy of it. Tedious, but I know you wanted it. This little one has changed your status, wife.'

'All my children have changed me,' she says.

She calls for Teresa and Luisa and her two girls, rising three and two, toddle in, each holding the hand of their nurse. They meet their brother, and kiss his little furrowed forehead. Teresa says he smells like cake, and Charlotte smiles. Her ladies are fussing to put pillows behind her back but shoos them away. No need for that; she doesn't care. She watches her children, three healthy children, and she doesn't care about anything else.

A day's rest. And then she gets to work. During her confinement, she has people bring her the records of the Council to read. Now that she doesn't have to rely on Caterina finding and copying only the most important, she wants to read everything. And there is so much to study! All the financial records are a mess, probably by Tanucci's design. There are so many complaints: reports of subjects seeking justice and receiving nothing for months on end, presumably until they bribed their local officials. The schools are improving, but the university needs support if it's to keep any of its scholars. The country's manufacturing and agriculture are thirty years behind the times. And then there are foreign matters: the American colonies have stopped all trade with Britain and there will be war before long, which could drag in Spain and, perhaps, Naples too. She can't make a wrong step once she takes her Council seat. This is her one chance to do what she's good for, and at last nobody can tell her not to do it. She is queen, and magister, and minister, and she's going to set all the wrongs right.

PART THREE

1775 TO 1777

CHAPTER TWENTY-TWO

The Baker's Wife — A Hope Sacrificed — The Comtesse de Polignac — The Petit Trianon — Private Life

———— ❖ ————

Now that they are king and queen, Louis and Antoinette are always on display. Some of their dinners together are public performances, and even the private dinners have people coming and going: not only servants but nobles clinging to their rights to wait upon the King, because personal service as a mark of royal favour is codified to the smallest degree at Versailles. Everyone at court is anxious to make sure they won't lose anything, under this new sovereign.

The nobles have reason to worry. Louis appointed Jacques Turgot as his minister of finance. Turgot is a reformer, and has already replaced forced labour with taxes on property owners, cut spending everywhere, and abolished many of the expensive sinecures that keep the privileged loyal to the Crown.

But the reform that shook the whole country is free trade in grain, because bread is everything.

It has long been the duty of the King of France to make sure there is bread on the table. Farmers grow approved amounts of wheat, and sell for an approved price, to the approved people, at the approved times, by order of the King.

Philippe tells her that the common people call the King 'the Baker', and her, Antoinette, they call 'the Baker's wife'. He mentioned it, she suspects, to puncture some of her happiness over the way the people have shown their love through paintings and poetry and letters, during this first year of her husband's reign.

At least there are no murmurs now that Antoinette will be sent away. She asks Geneviève what rumours she hears from England; she asks Charles and the Princesse de Lamballe what people say in the salons. Nothing. It has all faded away, the talk of getting rid of her. A dauphin's stumble into an annulled first marriage with a forgettable foreigner would be a minor embarrassment; it's unthinkable for a king beset with problems, whose wife is the subject of gossip and speculation in every village in France, thanks to the chevalier's violin. She has survived.

The newspapers call her beautiful, and indeed, on the coronation day, she knows that she was. She and Louis shone in the rays of God's approval.

But Maria Theresa's approval has been harder to win, especially since Louis keeps choosing advisers who are wary of the Austrian alliance. And what is Antoinette to do about it? She is just the Baker's wife; she does not set policy.

Turgot argues that the best way to ensure a steady supply of grain is to allow landowners to make profits, some of which they will invest, allowing France to produce more grain.

'It might still work,' Louis says glumly, pulling her bed sheets up over their legs for warmth. 'If this year's harvest is better than the last.'

Sometimes Louis comes to Antoinette's bed with intentions to consummate the marriage, though it never happens. They sit in their night clothes, backs against her lace pillows, and discuss the business of the day. It's the only time they really can talk, alone.

The first harvest of Louis's reign was a disaster. With a

shortage of wheat and Turgot's policies in place, the grain suppliers stockpiled and sold only to those who could pay the highest price. Louis bought grain from other countries; he opened the royal storehouses, set caps on prices once again. Still the people starved, and there were riots in the spring, all over France. In Versailles salons, people called it 'the Flour War'. Turgot, once so insistent that the police should have better things to do than enforce the price of wheat, ordered the police to restore order.

'It seems to me that it doesn't matter what might work in theory,' she says, gently, not wanting to overstep. She likes the fact that Louis talks to her about politics. 'What matters is what happens in practice.'

Louis sighs.

The next day, Louis's sister-in-law, the Comtesse d'Artois, goes into labour. Anyone with any rank is expected to attend the birth, so Antoinette is there, watching, as her poor sister-in-law screams and sweats and bleeds in front of everyone. She is there when the baby is born: a healthy boy, named Louis-Antoine.

There is a boy for the royal family, and Antoinette is no longer quite as necessary. She turns in one direction and sees something on Philippe d'Orléans's face: an expression of empathy? How dare he try to make common cause with her over this? She does not begrudge her sister-in-law her happiness, not one jot of it. She's not envious. She is worn out from being useless.

She whirls in the other direction and walks out through room after room after room, into the Hall of Mirrors. There are always crowds at Versailles – anyone who's dressed decently can come into some parts of the palace – but on a day like today, with a royal birth, the place is packed from wall to wall. A knot of plainly dressed women calls after her as she walks. 'When will it be your turn? When will you give us a boy?'

She doesn't breathe until she reaches the enormous, panelled guardroom that marks the entrance to her own chambers. She wipes her tears – a waste – and her shoes carry her on an inch of air into her secret room.

She collapses onto the floor, here where no servants can see her. How can they be angry with her, these strangers, for something that is not her fault? Why do they take such delight in taunting her?

The women of every market square in Paris expect only one thing from their queen, and that is something Antoinette cannot provide. Her body is of little use to France. She is not a mother, and even her occasional utility as a pretty spectacle is fading in these hungry times. Turgot has made it clear the state coffers have already been scraped bare. She is omnipresent in the thoughts of everyone in France, but what do they think of, when they think of her?

Antoinette slows her breathing. She is not without skills. She may not understand politics but she knows hearts, and Louis likes to confide in her. But every word Antoinette speaks in favour of a policy or a politician is as good as poison; she is *l'Autrichienne*, a foreign influence.

She is no Charlotte but she needs allies and plans of her own. It is time to stop losing her breath and her wits over what she cannot change. Some hopes are better sacrificed.

Antoinette goes to the little writing desk her mother gave her. She keeps it in her secret room because its many drawers hold small treasures and pots of ash. Under the gold watch are her notes about the new emotion spell: not perfume but, as Geneviève suggested, something to eat. She has a little sack of flour, given to her on a goodwill tour of a mill the month before, a mill that had been the target of a mob. Perhaps it wasn't wise, when so many are hungry, but she couldn't very well refuse. She told the miller it was a treasure greater than any riches, and she meant it. Antoinette had asked to keep the flour herself, and everyone seemed to forget she had it.

She could ask for cakes to be made of it. Louis's chief trouble is that his advisers squabble among themselves over their pet theories; what if magic made them all a little more tractable, compassionate, pragmatic?

But every time she has tried to enchant the flour, the sacrifices do not decay. She hasn't been able to bring herself to write down a hope that would suffice. Perhaps Antoinette has hardly known what to hope for, these days.

The one hope she has clung to, she will sacrifice willingly now. She will throw her vision of herself as mother onto the fire and watch it burn. Why hold onto the hope for a child, five years into an unconsummated marriage? What good does it do her? It only hurts.

Antoinette writes it down and places it in the star. Three coins for treasure, and one affection. The fifth sacrifice is of the body. There's a bag of hair clippings out of the desk. She's been collecting them every time Léonard cuts her hair. She shakes them out onto the floor, where they look sad and dirty and alien. For good measure, she takes her silver scissors out of her desk drawer and cuts one long tress, near the crown, where it won't show when her hair is dressed, then it curls down on top of the rest, a slightly different colour because of the powder.

She places the sack in the centre of the star, thinks for a moment of the housewives fighting each other for flour in Paris, and steps back, covering her nose.

'I give these things.'

The sacrifices do not vanish. It is not enough; she has not given enough. Her most painful hope has been found wanting. Is that it? Or is it the body? Has she not punished it sufficiently?

She grasps a chunk of hair from the top of her head and yanks it out. The ripping sound of it is what stuns her, astonishes her, stops her face from contorting into thwarted sobs. Her head stings and her fingers trail long powdered strands, a fistful of hair, a sacrifice from the root.

She throws it onto the point of the star as if it were a spider, and as the last strand floats down onto the pile, the paper with the hope written on it begins to curl, the coins to rust, the hair to rot. There's a smell like dead animal and Antoinette stands, numb. The desire for a child is in her memory, a thing that she used to want. But time passes, doors close, and some things will be only for others, not for her.

16 September 1775
Geneviève to Antoinette

My friend,

I must admit I received your last letter with a mixture of pride and trepidation. You write that you wish to do more with magic; well and good, so long as you're careful. You ask me for the names of rogues you might befriend. There, I can't help you. Paris may be full of rogues but none of them are friends I trust, and even the ones I know of aren't the sort of people who could visit you at Versailles without attracting attention.

Rohan's travels in England and Austria are at an end, I hear, and he is determined to ingratiate himself with your husband. He's ambitious in his own right – or greedy, anyway, and certainly won't take well to Turgot's reforms. And the Paris chapter of the Order no doubt wants to get its tentacles into everything, to make sure they can find and discredit any rogues in the army, the scientific and artistic academies, anywhere they might appear. So Rohan is even more dangerous these days, and you mustn't do anything to make him wonder whether Soliman was wrong about you all those years ago, whether your sister is not the only magister in the family.

Count Axel von Fersen, by the way, is quite chagrined about drawing you into danger that night at the opera house. Yes, I know you were probably thinking of him when you asked me about rogues, but he can't be your ally in Paris, as he's stopped travelling for the moment too. He's returned to Sweden, and is working to protect some friends there from the Stockholm chapter, which has become especially vicious in the last few years. I've told him to stay away from you anyway, to prevent any more close calls, and now the poor man is afraid even to write to you, lest he cause you any danger by association. But he asked me to give you the spell I've enclosed, for a candle that dampens sound in a room. An offering in apology for endangering you, he says.

If you wish to have magister-allies, my dear, you will have to create them. Find some people you can trust, people of high enough birth that they'll have access to you and you to them. Find a safe place where you can meet.

Antoinette, you told me once you wanted to be worthy of France, and I am not surprised that you haven't dropped that ambition. You are stubborn, in your own way! But remember that being worthy of France, and being welcomed by it, are different things. Nobody will take kindly to a queen meddling, and the Order has spies everywhere.

I remain,

> *Your friend,*
> *Geneviève*

Antoinette orders cakes to be made of her enchanted flour that will make whoever eats it more compliant, temporarily. She's eager to try another batch; perhaps one to make Louis's advisers wary of new schemes and persuasive rhetoric. At last, she may be able to have some influence, to help nudge things in useful directions for Louis even when he can't himself. She may be able to help Louis's advisers stop pulling the cart in six different directions, each of them arguing only for their own pet projects. Even Turgot may learn to be a little more practical.

But the cakes will only work on the people she can feed them to, and her circle at the moment does not include many people with the ear of the King, or even the ears of his advisers. She has to be careful about how people perceive her. Perhaps it's because she's a daughter of Maria Theresa, or for some other reason, but she knows that Versailles is always liable to interpret her smallest move as an attempt to take power away from her husband.

So she needs allies, which, it seems, means telling a few people about magic, and teaching them how to do it. A thrilling and terrifying thought! And she needs somewhere to speak to those people, where they won't be overheard. Her little secret room at Versailles, hidden by the firescreen, is quite unsuitable and it would attract too much attention to have people disappearing inside.

When Antoinette was a child, and not yet destined for France, the old King began construction on a retreat for his mistress at the time, Madame de Pompadour. It was not finished when she died, but it was ready and waiting for the new mistress, Madame du Barry, to occupy as she occupied everything else. Then the King died, and Antoinette's husband became Louis XVI, and the Comtesse du Barry was packed off to an abbey to cool her heels.

King Louis XVI has no mistress, nor any desire for one. He has had to stop people from putting women forward for the position. Antoinette occupies the positions of both wife and mistress; or, rather, she occupies neither.

And thus, the Petit Trianon falls to Marie Antoinette.

If one meanders through the gardens, keeping the Palace of Versailles at one's back, veering to the right and walking down a tree-lined road, one comes upon it almost by accident. It is a simple, classical rectangle, five windows at the front and five at the back, adorned with columns and pilasters, and a balustrade around the top. There is a bit of open lawn beside a stream, behind, which looks like a good place for children.

So it is there that she invites Gabrielle de Polastron, Comtesse de Polignac, and her two young children, to enjoy some lemonade made with fresh juice from the greenhouses at Versailles.

The daughter is seven, and the son is four, and they are charming, with red cheeks and dark curls and polite expressions. When they have permission to run and play, they go to the stream and bend over a pile of rocks, happily oblivious.

Antoinette and Polignac sit on a sheet of white muslin and drink lemonade. Here they are free, not only from Versailles's gossips and spies, but also from its tedious etiquette.

Polignac looks perfectly comfortable, her long legs folded beneath her, her simple lavender dress the same colour as her eyes. She has a calming presence, with the same lovely dark curls as her children, and a stillness to the way she holds herself – not taut, not slack, simply present.

Polignac is second on Antoinette's list of people she may be able to trust with the secret of magic. The Princesse de Lamballe is at the top, of course. But Lamballe has always moved in the same rooms Antoinette does, and knows what Antoinette knows. Polignac is different. Though Antoinette doesn't know her well, she finds her fascinating and would like to know her better. And Polignac seems like a rather clever choice as a magister-ally, Antoinette thinks a little smugly. She has deliberately separated herself from the daily intrigues of court life, and doesn't seem to care about politics.

Polignac is the last person anyone would suspect of meddling in the government's affairs.

'I suppose the late King must have planned these gardens,' says Polignac politely. Between the little slope where they're sitting and the building, there are rows of black earth, line after line, with a hodgepodge of plants.

'They're botanical. The arrangement is a bit ugly, isn't it? More like a classroom than a garden. Do you have gardens at Claye, Madame?'

Polignac smiles a little. 'Mainly for vegetables. It's a very simple place, Your Majesty, but we are – how shall I say it?

Self-sufficient there. We have, over the last few years, sunk into the habit of hardly ever coming to court.'

'I hope there's nothing keeping you from us. If I can resolve anything, I will.'

'Oh, no. Thank you, Your Majesty. We're simply happy where we are, and we are quite on the other side of Paris, of course, so it is a drive to Versailles. It seems a world apart, sometimes. We have a quiet life.'

'Do you not miss the parties and dances?'

'I do not miss the scheming and sniping. Our private life may be dull but at least it's not painful. I protect myself, and my children. That's the main thing.'

Antoinette nods, looking over at the children under an overhanging willow. 'I envy you. I have no private life here. I am dressed in public, I pray in public, I eat in public, and I sleep in public. I have found . . . little ways to carve out space in Versailles, and I guard my little ways like a miser.'

'Kings and queens must carve out their private lives for themselves, if they are to have any at all,' the countess agrees. 'That is why this place is here, isn't it? A private place for a mistress. But now it is yours, Madame. And you have no mistress.' The violet eyes twinkle.

'No, indeed, though some of the pamphleteers spread all sorts of rumours about Lamballe!' Antoinette smiles, all the way to her eyes. It's true, she thinks, that the Crown now pays Lamballe, as new Superintendent of the Queen's Household, precisely what the King used to lavish on Madame du Barry. 'I suppose at least I can come here myself to be alone from time to time. What I want is not loneliness, though, but a small piece of private life, like the one you've managed to create.'

'I think you could do that here, Your Majesty. It would need some work, of course, but you could have a few friends here, for days at a time if you liked. It's distant enough from the palace that one could be quite informal here. It's a place for secrets, after all.'

It's a place for secrets.

'You're right, Madame,' she says, trying to keep her excitement out of her voice. 'I do have a place of my own, now. And it's mercifully small – so small I could only have an intimate circle of friends at any one time. One would have to do something about the gardens, but at night – with lanterns – it would be lovely here.'

'Sometimes it takes a little work to fall in love,' says Polignac indulgently. 'Armand! You're getting your knees wet.'

How clever the Comtesse de Polignac is! How capable!

'It takes sacrifices, too,' Antoinette says, testing.

But Polignac's expression doesn't change; her shoulders don't tighten. She merely nods, still gazing after her child. 'We make our choices.'

'And I believe our choices can remake our worlds, or at least our own small parts of it. To help us do our duty better.'

'My duty is there,' Polignac says, looking out at her children.

'And so is mine,' Antoinette says with cold determination. 'My duty to God and to France is to ensure that every child is protected from harm, that every mother can feed her babies.'

'That is the duty of us all, surely,' Polignac says, turning to her with a kind smile. 'But some of us can run away from it more easily than others. Most days I don't think beyond protecting my own family, my friends.'

'Then your friends are very lucky to have you.' Shyly, she adds, 'I would like to count myself among them.'

Polignac's smile brightens, as though she's amused. 'Your Majesty, I am at your service.'

'But you must have some rooms at Versailles, so you can be here with me sometimes,' Antoinette says, in a rush. 'I'm sure we can find something suitable. For you and your family.'

Polignac inclines her head. 'I thank you, Your Majesty,

but I'm afraid it's very expensive to live at Versailles. There are other reasons I don't come to court. I did not attend the wedding of the Comte d'Artois because I couldn't bring myself to spend the money on a *grand habit*. Anyway, I don't see why I should have to. Terrible, painful things.'

'You should not have to,' Antoinette says with feeling. 'How I wish I had your courage! You must have rooms at Versailles – not for your own benefit but for mine. I need your help – to carve out my private life here. Will you agree? I'll take care of the money – it is not for your benefit, but for mine.'

Polignac looks away, and for the first time, Antoinette sees a frown cross her face. 'I'm not sure the gossips would like a mere countess being given rooms at Versailles out of the Queen's budget.'

Antoinette shrugs. 'Then I shall make you a duchess.'

The little girl, Aglaé, comes running up to her mother. 'Mama, look, I found the perfect stone!'

She's holding it in her palm, a smooth, round, pink pebble.

'The perfect stone for what, dear?' Polignac asks, cupping her daughter's hands.

'Simply the perfect stone, that's all,' the girl says. 'May I take it home, Mama?'

'You must, as my gift,' Antoinette says, leaning forward. 'You are a clever girl, to find the one perfect stone in all the world.'

CHAPTER TWENTY-THREE

Secrets at the Petit Trianon — The Paris Opera —
Two Impossible Sights — One Singular Duty

———— ✤ ————

On a spring morning in 1776, Antoinette invites three friends
to the Petit Trianon: Polignac, Lamballe, and the Chevalier
de Saint-Georges. She brings them to the little room beside
her bedroom on the second floor, where Antoinette has
installed mirrors on movable panels over the windows.

It's a small space, but there are only four people. Three
friends, each of them with different circles of influence and
different talents, but all loyal to her.

'I have something to tell you all,' she says. 'It is something
wonderful, but it is something dangerous. The knowledge
may put your lives in peril. I will love you no less if you
choose not to know.'

The chevalier stands stiffly and looks wary, but then he
always looks wary, these days. He's had a difficult few years.
Antoinette favoured a bid proposing him as the new director
of the Paris Opera. He was the obvious choice: he's not only
a brilliant soloist and composer, but he's also proven his skills
as concertmaster and director of smaller orchestras. But two
singers and a dancer gave her a petition declaring that they
would find it beneath them to take orders 'from a mulatto'.

Antoinette wanted to ignore the women's petition, but while she hesitated, Saint-Georges formally withdrew his name from consideration. A few months ago, Louis put the operations of the opera under his own supervisor of entertainments, to avoid further scandal.

All in all, she feels that her friendship has been as much an irritant as a help to Saint-Georges, lately. For years, he has been performing magic on her behalf – unwittingly. She owes him a great deal, and let it start with some honesty.

Polignac has her face cast down and her violet eyes cast up, her face serious. Since Antoinette brought her to Versailles, she's been an asset and an inspiration in every way, quietly asserting the Queen's independence and resisting the old strictures of etiquette.

Lamballe looks perfectly relaxed, curious, and trusting. Lamballe is here because there is nothing she won't do for her queen.

These are her chosen confidants, her friends, her allies. The Queen's inner circle.

Antoinette takes a breath.

Out of her pocket, Antoinette pulls two pieces of letter paper, and a third, battered sheet with the *tabula recta* on it, in Charlotte's handwriting. She takes her bottle of ink, and then walks to the writing table in the corner of the room and dips in a quill.

'If you'd like to know, then you must all watch me write,' she announces, and they come closer, obeying. They are nearly over her shoulder.

'Someone give me a keyword.'

There's a pause, then Polignac says, '*Jonquille.*' Antoinette smiles. There are daffodils scattered down the slope beyond the windows, though they can't see them now because of the mirrored shutters.

'Perfect!' She writes 'jonquille' carefully on the first sheet of paper, to teach the ink.

On the second sheet of paper, she writes, very slowly: 'bienvenue dans le cercle social privé de la reine.'

By the time her quill reaches the first 'n', the initial 'b' shivers, and the ink seems to wick strangely into the paper. The 'b' opens into a 'k'. The 'i' doubles, triples, into a 'w'. Saint-Georges shifts. Lamballe gasps. Polignac takes a step back.

'What is it?' Polignac asks.

'Magic,' the Queen says simply. 'It's magic. The ink is enchanted.'

The rest of the ink has soaked into its enciphered shape, a string of letters, undecipherable to anyone without the keyword.

Lamballe claps, smiling. 'I knew it! I knew there was magic in the world. How wonderful!'

Antoinette looks at each face, at the emotions there. She has not felt this way since she and Charlotte did magic together. What a joy it would be to tell Charlotte about this, but Charlotte is a member of the Order, and Antoinette can't ask these people to join her and then put them at risk.

'May I try it, Your Majesty?' Polignac asks.

Antoinette hesitates, looking at her little bottle of brownish ink, so dearly bought with sacrifices. But what else can she show them? So few of her enchanted items have any immediate and visible effect. It occurs to her for the first time that most spells have been made by people who wanted to hide their magic – rogues hiding from the Brothers, or the Brothers themselves hiding magic from the world.

She puts her hand into her pocket, and feels the lorgnette there, one she enchanted with a spell Geneviève sent her: one of the spells she used to work the Mechanical Turk.

The lorgnette is a slim brass tube, wider at one end like a spyglass, just like anything a lady would take to the opera – only this lens does not see what it's pointed at.

'Come with me, Marie-Louise,' she says and, taking Lamballe by the hand, leads her to the Queen's bedroom, next door. Antoinette unscrews the tortoiseshell cap from the end of the lorgnette, places it carefully on the washstand, and positions Lamballe in front of it, saying, 'Just stand there, dear, and when you hear me call your name, wave at the washstand. I know it sounds ridiculous.'

Lamballe does not question. She never does.

Back in the boudoir, Antoinette hands the lorgnette to Polignac.

'What shall I look at through it?'

'Anything. It doesn't matter.'

Polignac takes the lorgnette to the window, peers through the lens. She steps back with a start, examines the lorgnette, looks through again.

'Marie-Louise, you may wave,' Antoinette calls.

At that, Polignac drops the lorgnette and it rolls on the floor. Polignac picks it up, stares at it for a moment as if it were a grenade, then hands it to Antoinette. 'Your Majesty, I have never seen anything like it.'

Saint-Georges looks next, and then they call Lamballe back in, and then Lamballe looks while Saint-Georges goes next door, until finally they've all seen it: they've seen Lamballe, in the next room, because the lorgnette shows whatever its cap sees. It has not proven very useful, since its cap needs to be close by, just as Geneviève said years ago, but Antoinette keeps it with her, because it reminds her of her friend.

'How astonishing!' Lamballe says, picking up the bottle of ink. 'Where did you get such things?'

'I made them,' Antoinette says. 'And so will you.'

When she has answered the first of their questions, and showed them how to make a star, she warns them they must not tell anyone.

'Are there no other of these "magisters" in Paris?' Polignac asks.

Antoinette shrugs. 'In Paris, there are vagabonds and charlatans and sorcerers. How many there are, and how many are the right sort – I mean, for us to work with – I don't know. But more importantly, there is a group of magisters: the Order of 1326, they call themselves. They exist to keep magic secret and prevent anyone outside the Order from doing it.'

She explains that they must all take the greatest care to prevent anyone learning what they do together.

'If this Order exists to keep magic secret, and we hide it away, are we not doing their work for them, Your Majesty?' Saint-Georges asks.

'We'll share our knowledge, but carefully, under their noses,' she says, mildly flustered. 'And we'll keep ourselves and any other magister safe from their attacks. They may undermine us, spread stories about us. They may try to take our memories. They may even try to kill us. They think no one should be allowed to do magic unless they are members of their Order and follow their rules. I *do not* accept this. I believe that each of us – each human on this Earth – has only one duty, to ourselves, to our fellow man, and to God – one singular duty, which is to do our best. It sounds so childish, doesn't it? But how can we do our best if we are forbidden from using the tools we have to make beautiful and useful things?'

'Are there magical weapons, Your Majesty?' Saint-Georges asks. 'Magical food? Shelter?'

Antoinette is at a loss. 'I don't know yet what is possible. Yes, there are magical foods. In fact, I have an enchantment for flour that has an effect on the emotions, and using it I hope to resolve the civil war that's been brewing among my husband's advisers. We've seen how badly they've served him in the first two years of his reign: Turgot wants to prove his theories at any cost to king and country, and those whose privileges Turgot is taking away will do anything to save them. Nobody is thinking of the good of France, of the King. But we can. Working in secret, we can change hearts and minds and put an end to the riots, the hunger, the discontent. I believe we could do a great deal. I hope we find out together.'

Saint-Georges nods slightly, thoughtfully.

She considers telling him about his violin bow, but can't think how to explain.

Instead, Antoinette ducks behind a table, and emerges with three scrolls of paper tied in blue ribbon. She hands one to each of her friends, saying, 'Here are all the spells I know. The Petit Trianon is a safe place, and here we can learn together. I've kept this secret here alone for so long, and wished that I could do some useful work with it. Now the time for wishing is over.'

CHAPTER TWENTY-FOUR

King Ferdinand Goes Hunting – Charlotte Is Forgetful –
Sicily – Habsburgs of Old – The Inquisition

Ferdinand isn't good at anything, and he takes no chances when he goes hunting, which is almost daily. He had an enclosure built at Portici in which everything is artificial; even the trees are planted in holes blasted one by one into the volcanic soil and filled with less unpredictable loam. The hunting enclosure is so small that Charlotte can see the far end of it, a smudge of fence against the horizon.

Yelling quickly in Neapolitan, Ferdinand sends two dozen of his beaters to flush out the game with nets and bring them back to him, so he can shoot them and congratulate himself.

Usually Charlotte has the energy to resist when Ferdinand decides he wants her and the children as part of his entourage, but on a September day in the year 1776 she is tired. Her latest childbirth, for Marianna, was taxing: her second birth in a year, and even months later she still feels exhausted. So the family is here, as he demanded: Teresa and Luisa are playing with dolls on a quilted blanket in many colours, and one-year-old Carlo and baby Marianna are sleeping, swaddled and perfect, while the nurse knits beside them.

To make it even harder for Charlotte to say no, Ferdinand

has insisted that all the other members of the Council of Naples attend the so-called hunt today as well, so that he can call it a meeting. Ferdinand's father in Spain says he must meet with the Council once a week, but doesn't specify where.

So Charlotte is here, with a scarf around her head and shoulders to keep the sea air at bay, and the half-dozen men who served as Ferdinand's regents and who are now his Council. Tanucci's men, all of them, but only by default. When she manages to keep Tanucci quiet, the old men all listen to her. She wears her white gloves to every meeting. She could enchant another pair but she would prefer not to; she's getting frugal with her sacrifices, now that she's twenty-four years old.

The white gloves do look out of place here where everything is brown and red. Ferdinand is dressed in his favourite floppy hat, with his beaver-fur stockings, and a leather apron and pouch for his instruments of death.

Everyone who isn't running around with nets for Ferdinand is sitting on blankets on the ground: Ferdinand's friends, of the male and female varieties, lean on their elbows, eating grapes and laughing.

The other councillors looks similarly uncomfortable, at least. Princes, dukes, all of them old, sit on large stiff cushions, their legs awkward in front of them.

They are used to Ferdinand, though; they do nothing but shake their mournful jowls at him and wait to be dismissed. Tanucci has no use for a council at all, as he has been making decisions for seventeen years with no one to contradict him save his true master, the King of Spain.

Charlotte sometimes feels sorry for her husband. A little sorry. At eight years old, his parents went off to rule Spain and left him here with these regents and tutors. Left him with his older brother Filippo, who was deemed unfit for the kingship because of his mental condition. Filippo lives at Portici, and he is with the beaters now, running headlong, and for once, no one is mocking him.

'If we are to have our meeting of the Council, I have some things to discuss,' Charlotte says.

Tanucci's face looks as if she's proposed something ridiculous. 'Here?'

'We meet at the King's pleasure.' She gestures. 'We see before us the King's pleasure.'

He changes his expression to one of long-suffering indulgence. 'Indeed, Your Majesty.'

'Then I propose we begin our work.'

'The true work of the Council', Tanucci lectures, 'does not happen in meetings. We are not a parliament, thank God. We implement the King's will.'

'Which king, I wonder?' Charlotte snaps, and she waves her white glove so she can shut Tanucci up for long enough that she can talk about the Academy she wants to found. The white gloves do come in handy; she lets herself smirk a little at the sight of Tanucci's jowls in motion as he begins to speak, and stops; begins to speak, and stops; begins to speak, and stops.

Charlotte has the floor. Or would, if there were a floor.

But as if he's been summoned, Ferdinand comes sauntering up, covered in blood. He's holding a small dead boar under one arm, like a travesty of a child, and in his other hand he has a long, curved knife.

'Look what I caught,' he says, and throws the newly dead boar down onto the dirt. His friends applaud, and the councillors smile indulgently. A few nicks of Ferdinand's knife by the boar's hamstrings, and he runs an iron bar through the legs, and hangs the beast up.

'Watch, wife,' he says, huffing from the exertion. 'Watch, girls.' The sharp knife circles the legs, separates the black, hairy hide from the pink and white beneath. He peels the hide down and makes a long cut down the middle of the boar. And then with ungloved hands he pulls the entrails out, holds them high like a trophy and throws them into the dirt. It's all done so quickly; Ferdinand is good at something after all.

Charlotte covers her nose, while her daughters squeal and groan dramatically. Teresa is four and Luisa is three.

'I was just about to inform your councillors that I've completed my list of recommended names for the first investiture of the Royal Academy of Sciences and Humane Letters,' she tells Ferdinand.

'What's that?' he asks incuriously, wiping his knife on his leather apron, as though the apron weren't already coated in blood.

'Well, it doesn't exist yet,' she says. 'But we're creating one, so I've made a list of names, having taken advice from many learned people.'

'Again?' Tanucci asks. Damn. The gloves only work to keep Tanucci quiet if she remembers to use them constantly. Hang Ferdinand for distracting her! 'There were quite enough names on your first list, Your Majesty. Or have you rethought some of your choices?'

She stares, stunned. The first list? A chill creeps up her arms and she can feel her eyes widen as she tries desperately to think faster than this old fox.

She's lost a memory, somewhere. She handed over the names already, and she's forgotten.

Perhaps it coincided with some event where Ferdinand was particularly beastly. Charlotte tries to sacrifice memories of Ferdinand, when she's working an enchantment that requires a sacrifice of memory. It is a double victory: she is able to work the enchantment, and life with Ferdinand becomes a little easier to bear. But she knows it is dangerous to forget too much – she has nightmares of her future self greeting Ferdinand with an innocent smile, unaware, unguarded.

One has to sacrifice something. And now she's forgotten some small matter, and Tanucci is looking at her as though she's hanging on a slaughtering hook herself.

'Well, whatever you both think,' Ferdinand says. 'Tanucci,

perhaps you can send someone round to find some eggheads, eh? What about Caramanico, eh? He knows all the smart people.'

For all his bluster, Ferdinand is quite intimidated by philosophers and artists, but he always wants to be thought enlightened. It's one of the reasons Charlotte chose the Academy as a project; she knew that Ferdinand, at least, would not oppose it.

Tanucci makes a face. 'Many of the friends of the Prince of Caramanico may find themselves out of Naples altogether before long. We know all about the Masonic meetings that continue to take place despite His Majesty's wise edict against them. Whom will we find when we surprise one of them, I wonder?'

Surprising a meeting of Masons! Tanucci has been railing against the Masons for years but everyone's largely ignored him, including the Brothers of Naples, who still use a Masonic meeting as cover for their activities. Several lodges have simply flouted the edict Tanucci somehow induced Ferdinand to sign.

Tanucci is gloating, seeing the expression on Charlotte's face. 'Oh, did Your Majesty forget about that? There is no cause for concern. We'll make sure it's a meeting with none of the nobility present.'

Between her memory sacrifices and the white gloves, she's managed to make herself dangerously ignorant of what Tanucci is up to.

Baby Marianna cries; the nurse soothes her back to sleep but now Carlo has woken, and the nurse stands, walking with him. His cry banishes all other thoughts and Charlotte puts her arms out to take him, magnet to magnet. To enfold him in her body and make all well.

Ferdinand steps closer to her, pinches the top of her breast through the fichu. 'He's hungry, or he's pretending he is. Don't I understand it! I'll have some later.'

He roars, and his friends roar with him. Charlotte scowls.

She had barely stopped bleeding after Carlo's birth when he came to her bed and thrust himself on her, without so much as asking, and she was pregnant again: two babies within ten months.

'Women are made for the joys of private life,' says Tanucci, beaming at the scene of Charlotte holding the baby. 'A gentler life than the one of statecraft, without so many tedious things to remember. I am quite envious.'

Let Tanucci have his wish, she thinks, violently. Let him find the joys of private life. She sees, suddenly, a way to trap him, a way to be rid of him at last.

'I will consult the Prince of Caramanico about the Academy, while you move against the Masons,' she tells Tanucci, and relishes the look of confusion on his face. 'I think surprising one of their meetings is an excellent idea.'

Charlotte throws open the curtains and looks out over Palermo. Ferdinand is King of Sicily as well as Naples, but they don't get to the island frequently enough for her taste. She turns away from the view, past columns of bright marble and palm trees to low, neat gardens in every kind of green.

Far beyond, Charlotte can just make out the busy port, the masts of ship after ship. Every one of them taking something to or from her people: olive oil, wheat, silk, wool, sulphur, and wine. Sometimes she feels separate from the business of humanity, as though it would carry on much the same no matter who sat on the throne, or who whispered behind it. But she reminds herself it is not so: there would be fewer ships or more in the harbour; they might be bound for other places; they might be carrying poorer things; they might be swarmed by poor and starving people; they might be ships of war or of piracy. Civilization is resilient but not immutable.

When they landed in Palermo three days ago, the first thing she saw was the cages. Hanging from the parapet of a great stone edifice, the Holy Office of the Inquisition. Three iron cages, their rust staining the walls. Cages that once held those who fought against Charles V, the last Habsburg to rule both the Holy Roman Empire and Spain, as well as much of Italy. She comes from greatness; she comes from barbarism.

But she is not Charles V. She came with Ferdinand this time to tell the Grand Inquisitor – a good, thoughtful man, given his job as a punishment for thinking aloud – that the Holy Office of the Inquisition is ended in Sicily. She can do it, too. The Crown maintains the prisons, and the Crown can, and will, abolish them.

The Crown has long been compensated for its part of the business, receiving one-third of the goods confiscated from heretics. But heretics are thin on the ground, these days. Nowadays, most prisoners of the Holy Office are bigamists – usually wives who've left their rotten husbands and taken up with new men. Old women accused of witchcraft, men accused of sodomy. All sold to the Inquisition by nasty neighbours hoping for reward. And Tanucci has encouraged those neighbours, because every accusation means money for the Kingdom of Naples.

It is an abomination, and she has put a stop to it. The few remaining prisoners, all old and unwell, will be found new places, places they will be cared for. Most prisoners were subjected to the *toca*, a form of interrogation in which the mouth and nose are covered with cloth, and several pitchers of water poured onto the face, so the subject feels as if they are drowning. The Grand Inquisitor seems relieved it is over. But the Holy Father in Rome may object to Maria Carolina meddling in religious matters, and some of the more old-fashioned believers may object too. Tanucci, who has lined his pockets with the goods taken from prisoners, would certainly object. But Tanucci will soon be a problem no longer.

Slowly, Charlotte turns away from the window, looking towards the bed where her husband sleeps. The whole room smells of sour vomit, but she suspects it is just the smell coming through Ferdinand's pores, as his body tries to rid itself of a quantity of strong spirits consumed at great speed.

She opens the window.

Ferdinand blinks, and puts his arm over his eyes. 'I wasn't to be disturbed.'

'I know,' she says soothingly, apologetically, walking over to his bedside. 'I would not have let them disturb you for anything less than an emergency, but this—'

He sits up, his shirt falling half off his shoulder. At least he's alone this morning.

'The children?' he asks, awake now, alarmed.

She shakes her head. 'They're all fine. It's more an emergency of state.'

Relieved, he waves her away. 'Tanucci can handle—'

'I'm afraid Tanucci's the one who's created the mess. And this time, I don't think there's any way he can clean it up.'

She sits on the edge of his bed, gingerly, and passes him the sheet of paper in her hands.

Ferdinand's brows bunch in the way they always do when he reads. '"Luigi Seno. The Prince of Ferolito. Don Paolo Moccia. The Prince of Francavilla. The Duke of Maddaloni. The Duke of San Demetrio. The Duchess of Termoli. Niccolò Piccinni."' He stops, although Charlotte knows the list continues. He looks up. 'Is this the list for your Royal Academy?'

'It is not, although several of the names might appear on that list as well, might they not? No, this is the list of the people apprehended by Tanucci's thugs at a Masonic meeting in Naples a few nights ago. They are all in his custody, although he has had the good sense not to dungeon any of them. I believe he has them sitting in your opera house. What he intends to do with them now, I cannot say.'

It was such a small matter, once she'd decided to do it. An innocent question to another member of the Council, to determine where and when Tanucci planned to send his thugs. And then, invitations to a soirée at that lodge, that night, to all the great and good of Naples.

Invitations that could, quite literally, not be refused. There is a spell in the *Reconditus* for summoning magic, a spell that Soliman says has been neglected, as every magister eventually realizes that it doesn't mean summoning a familiar, a demon, a ghost, or even someone long lost or in hiding. It simply summons the person who agrees to touch the paper. Charlotte finds it very useful, even if her brethren do not.

Ferdinand's eyes go as round as oranges. 'But he said there would be no nobility! And these – these are some of our best writers, best musicians. The list – how many?' His voice is a whisper.

'Thirty-nine. The question at this moment, my husband, is whether you would rather explain to your father why all these luminaries have left Naples – as they surely will, if they are further insulted – or whether it is time for the old bull to go out to pasture.'

Ferdinand runs his hands through his short, sweaty hair. He looks, for a moment, younger than his twenty-five years, younger than Charlotte's twenty-four. A brat, a bully, and a fraud. He has no choice, and he knows it. But he has never had to be the one to make decisions. When his father left to take the throne of Spain, Tanucci was there to tell him what to do. Tanucci has always been there for him.

'But what would we do about the Inquisition?' he asks.

She's taken aback momentarily, that his mind should run there – he doesn't know what she's been doing here while he whores and hunts. But he is not a man who sees past the end of his long Bourbon nose: the Inquisition, with its declining revenues, is his most proximate worry, here in Sicily. And Tanucci has always been the one to manage it.

'I'll take care of it,' she says.

Ferdinand looks up at her. 'Will you?'

'Certainly. It's better if the King doesn't get involved in disputes over holy matters.'

'That's true. And you like to keep busy.'

'I do,' she says, sitting beside him on the rumpled, stinking bed. She waits.

'Give me a pen and paper, will you, Charlotte? I will write Tanucci's dismissal now.'

CHAPTER TWENTY-FIVE

War in America — An Inconvenient Performance of
The Barber of Seville — The Peace Room — La Hire and
the Queen of Hearts — A Secret Meeting

— ✥ —

In February 1777, Versailles reeks of wood smoke and
everyone repairs to the smallest rooms, where the outmoded
fireplaces stand a chance of doing some good. When the
Marquis de Lafayette is announced, Antoinette sees him in
her private cabinet room, much smaller than the two state
antechambers. The decor is dark and heavy; all these rooms
were vacant for years, when there was no queen to occupy
them. The walls seem to have a patina of age on them, or
perhaps that's only the soot. There's work to be done here.
But for now, she focuses on the face of the young man in
front of her, blotchy not only from the cold but from indig-
nation too.

They both stand; Lafayette does not have the rank to sit
in her presence. She's seen him here and there, since she
met him that night at the opera, when she saw Rohan with
the knife, and Fersen. Lafayette is always gallant and has
rescued her more than once from a tedious dance or conversation. He's not the best dancer, but his timing is always
good.

'You are so certain that the cause in America is just?' she asks him. 'You'd risk your life for these rebels? I've heard some say the Americans are simply angry that King George won't let them take more land from the natives in the west. I'm not sure why any Frenchman should take up arms to encourage spoiling the Americas.'

The magisters who meet at the Petit Trianon have all been using enchanted flour – and other spells for spying and persuasion – to gently sway the consensus at Versailles towards incremental reforms, to keep the peace and prevent unrest. It worked better than Antoinette dreamed, with the unforeseen consequence that Turgot became as unpopular at Versailles as he was in the rest of the country, and the King dismissed him.

But the new minister of finance, Jacques Necker, is just as opposed to a costly war in America as Turgot was.

'I'd risk my life to prevent King George deciding anything for all the world, as he seems determined to do,' Lafayette says. 'I understand why His Majesty had to be seen to forbid any Frenchmen from going to fight in America. Publicly. But privately . . . If I could slip away, you see, and know that I had His Majesty's secret permission to do so . . .'

'And you would like me to obtain that secret permission?'

'I would, Your Majesty. I know that the King listens to no one so much as he listens to you.'

She spreads her hands. 'Lafayette, my husband is walking the edge of a knife, as you must know. We cannot risk yet another open war with England. In the last one, I am told, we lost our navy, most of our colonies in India and America, and much of the treasury.'

'And I lost my father,' says Lafayette, thin-lipped. 'These are all reasons why France should be doing its utmost to help England's enemies now.'

'The King already went along with Monsieur Beaumarchais's scheme to run weapons across the Atlantic.'

Beaumarchais, who has been a clock-maker, a harp teacher

at Versailles, and a playwright, has been trying his hand at spycraft lately. He was in England, trying to negotiate the return of a rogue French spy, the Chevalier d'Éon, and he's been talking to the American delegates desperate for French support in their war. He invented a company that delivers French supplies to rebels without implicating the French King.

'It was Beaumarchais who thwarted me!' Lafayette paces in anger; then he stops himself with a jolt, realizing he turned his back on the Queen for a moment. 'We were in Le Havre. We were there! I was on the ship! We were ready to sail for America, and no one knew. Then Beaumarchais gets wind of a local production of *The Barber of Seville*. He cannot resist going to see it, and then when he thinks they are staging it wrong, he steps in to direct it himself! With everyone talking about that, it wasn't long before the English got wind that he had three ships laden with supplies and fighting men, and sent a protest to the King. Beaumarchais has ruined everything.'

Antoinette can't help but smile. 'Not everything, surely. Lafayette, you have a young wife here at Versailles, don't you? And a baby?'

The familiar expression crosses his face: the awareness, not quite guilt and not quite pity, that Antoinette herself has no child. She has seen it cross so many faces.

But when Lafayette speaks, it is not about his wife and child. 'Your Majesty, I was raised in the south of France, by my grandmother, after the English cannonball killed my father. My ancestor fought with Joan of Arc! And I was stuck out in the countryside, hunting the fabled beast of Gévaudan with a stick by day, and eating stewed beef with a kindly old lady at night.' He laughs shortly. 'I couldn't avenge my father.'

'You were a child,' she says gently.

'And now I am a man, with a dull sword at my waist. My whole life, I have wanted only to take up arms in a good cause. That's all I ask.'

KATE HEARTFIELD

She considers. 'I cannot ask my husband to put this country's peace at risk.'

He casts his face down, nods. 'Of course, Your Majesty.'

'You could . . .' she says.

'Yes?' He looks up, hopeful again.

'You could go to England. Visit someone there – find some pretext. Then sail from there.'

He nods. 'Throw the dogs off my scent. But the trouble is that the ship I bought is docked in Bordeaux.'

'The ship you *bought*!'

'Oh yes,' Lafayette says, grinning. 'Did I forget to mention that? After Beaumarchais ruined our plans in Le Havre, I bought a ship in Bordeaux. But the trouble is that the King has men watching my ship, day and night. He's had to, to placate the English, and then also my father-in-law is so set against my plans . . .'

'I don't wonder,' Antoinette says, thinking of Lafayette's young wife. She'll have to make sure the young woman is provided for, once Lafayette leaves.

Because Lafayette will leave, and Antoinette is going to help him. Here is a chance for Antoinette to help France's interest in secret. To help her husband, and to be of some use to her people.

Besides, why shouldn't a young person be able to act boldly, to prove his worth through his courage, in a cause he believes to be just?

'Wait here,' she says, and she walks through the panel into the secret room, the *arrière-cabinet* with the enchanted firescreen. She enters it brazenly, knowing Lafayette will forget it is there, just as everyone does.

She returns with a hat in her hand. A black tricorne that she wore for her portrait in riding clothes, six years ago. Her mother's favourite portrait of her, despite the fact that Maria Theresa disapproves of women riding.

For years, Antoinette has been trying to work out the enchantment for the 'cap of Hades' in the embroidered book,

270

the one that promises to 'steal shadows'. She was sure it would confer invisibility, and she was right. Finally, she found the right sacrifices. She was desperate for a way to walk unseen, a few weeks after she had to walk through the Hall of Mirrors the day her nephew was born. The hat seemed to make people's gazes slip off her. She has used it a few times since, but she can always enchant another. She hesitates, suddenly nervous that the marquis will mock her, disbelieve her, but this is a man who spent his childhood hunting a legendary beast.

'You must swear to me now, on your honour, to keep the secret I'm about to tell you,' Antoinette says, holding out the hat.

Lafayette, looking slightly confused, swears passionately.

'This hat has an enchantment on it. When you wear it, people will not notice you. They might be able to see you, if they look straight at you and concentrate very hard, but when they aren't doing that, you can slip right past them. As if you're in a deep shadow.'

So many expressions pass over his face that she can't tell what he's thinking.

'I'll show you,' she says. 'Look out of the window for a moment, and try to think about something else. Count to one hundred, then turn back and look for me.'

He turns slowly, and she jams the hat onto her hair, cringing at what Monsieur Léonard will say when he sees what she's done to this morning's creation. She walks to the far side of the room, and waits. Lafayette turns, looks at the spot where she had been standing. Then he lets his gaze roam, but doesn't see her.

She takes the hat off her head with a triumphant flourish, and hands it to him. 'This ought to get you past my husband's hounds.'

He looks down at the hat. 'An enchantment.'

'Yes.'

He looks around the room again, as if to convince himself that what he just saw – or didn't see – was real.

'I've never seen such a marvel.'

'It's not the only such marvel in the world,' she says. 'But you must promise not to mention that to anyone. For my sake as well as yours.'

'I will keep this, and the secret of it,' he says, his voice low. 'I will honour the gift you've given me, Your Majesty.'

She ought to feel nervous, exposing her secret again. Instead, she feels exhilarated. Another friend and ally. Lafayette is young and honourable, and she trusts him to do what he thinks is right.

'Just come home to your wife, Lafayette.'

By April of 1777, Lafayette's departure is the talk of Versailles. He went to England for a few weeks, and his family thought he was still there when they received his farewell letter. He sailed to Spain, and then disembarked so he could go back to Bordeaux and write once more to Versailles to plead for permission. Antoinette half suspects he just hasn't had a chance to use her hat of shadows yet and is desperate for the King's men to chase him.

But at least it is now clear to everyone that he's an ungovernable young man, and there is no case for England to go to war over him.

The Peace Room, which connects the Queen's Apartments to the Hall of Mirrors, is painted in scenes of plenty and grace, supported by walls of swirling grey marble and delicate gold. It is a room of glories and triumphs.

It is, in short, the perfect room for a game of cards.

On a little marble table to one side are pink- and green-glazed petits fours, made by the Queen's own chef with flour Antoinette enchanted – the Queen explained that she wanted to make good use of the flour given her by France's millers. It's an experiment, tonight: she's trying some new emotions. The pink ones should induce good humour and the green ones suspicion.

The trouble with the experiment is that everyone has been

eating the cakes that already accord with their personalities. Antoinette's partner for whist tonight is Louis's merry brother, the Comte d'Artois. He could very well end up being the father of the nation if Antoinette does not manage to give France a dauphin, but he's so gracious and good-natured that she can't begrudge him. He's had a pink cake, though she can't tell the difference.

Their opponents are Adélaïde and Victoire, or as the court still calls them, Aunt Rag and Aunt Pig. A green cake each.

'Do you think Jacques Necker will last?' Adélaïde asks, to nobody and everybody. 'I think he's much more reasonable than Turgot. Not such a fanatic.'

'Mmmm,' says d'Artois, picking up his cards and frowning at them.

Antoinette has a red ribbon to wear in her hair that enhances her own short-term memory – she uses it on busy court days – but she does not wear it to play cards. Antoinette is many things but never a cheat.

She focuses on her own cards. The first one she sees is the Jack of Hearts. This card always depicts La Hire, the French hero of the Hundred Years War, but this is a strange deck: instead of La Hire's name printed down one side, it has a motto: 'Jusqu'à la mort'.

Unto death.

She shudders, and remembers the night she met Axel von Fersen in Paris, in their masks, when he used those very words.

And – how odd – the drawing of the Jack looks very like him. Uncannily like him.

'Are you with us, Your Majesty?' Adélaïde asks, and Antoinette looks up to meet the aunt's shrewd gaze.

If Adélaïde were a magister, with enchanted ribbons of her own, that might explain her eccentric style. Why in God's name would she wear that ecru lace shawl over a striped pink-and-green *robe à la polonaise*? She looks a fright. She is forty-five now, twice Antoinette's age. Somehow,

Antoinette can't imagine ever being that old. It would be charitable of Antoinette to lend Adélaïde her dressmaker, Rose Bertin, or Léonard Autié for her hair – but Adélaïde would no doubt take it wrong, just as she did when Antoinette asked her to take charge of the orphan boy Antoinette recently adopted, after her carriage nearly ran him over in the street. Antoinette had thought it would be seen as a mark of great favour, but a week of flattery was required to convince Adélaïde of that.

'How is little Armand this week?' Antoinette asks breezily. 'Is he still having trouble learning his multiplication?'

'He doesn't see why he should, and I'm inclined to agree with him,' says Adélaïde. 'What point is there in teaching a child of his background things he'll never put to use?'

'He might put them to use,' says Antoinette, flicking the corner of the Jack of Hearts in her hand. 'Why shouldn't he? Perhaps he'll invent something using the multiplication tables. A flying machine. Or a new kind of . . . oh, I don't know. Bridge, or gun.'

'The day your protégé invents a flying machine is the day I fly to the moon,' murmurs Victoire.

Antoinette is unreasonably offended on Armand's behalf. Or perhaps not so unreasonably. She was not supposed to learn magic, but she did, and she has discovered a dozen new spells since she came to Versailles, useful spells that weren't even in the embroidered book. And she's willing to bet some of them, at least, were not in any magister's book. What might little Armand do, if he had a spellbook? What does it cost the world to keep him ignorant and incapable? He might invent a new kind of bridge. The world always needs better bridges.

Antoinette draws the Queen of Diamonds, and though it ought to be the Biblical Rachel, the picture on it looks exactly like Marie Antoinette.

And the motto is not the name Rachel, but four words: 'Cour de la Reine'.

The Queen's Courtyard. There is a Queen's Courtyard here at Versailles, in the midst of her private chambers. It's dark and dismal and no one ever goes there.

No one ever goes there.

She slides the Jack and Queen cards to one side of her hand and looks at the next: another Jack, this one the Jack of Clubs. Lancelot. Only he, too, looks uncannily like Axel von Fersen. And there is only one word on this card: 'Minuit'.

Unto death.

The Queen's Courtyard.

Midnight.

Antoinette pushes her chair back and stands, gripping the table with one hand and throwing her cards onto it with the other. She realizes too late that she's thrown the cards face up, but now that they're on the table, the words have changed back to their usual forms, and the pictures too.

The message, if it was a message, was for her alone.

The Queen of France is in possession of a particular coverlet that she requests on certain nights, a coverlet that creates the impression, if one does not examine it too closely, that she is underneath it.

She is also in possession of a new hat of shadows, this one small and made of straw, with a jolly blue ribbon. It doesn't go with her lace dressing gown at all, but then no one will see her in it, will they? That's the point.

Unless, of course, her suspicion is correct and there is someone waiting in the courtyard. Which is why she has worn a particularly nice, and particularly modest, lace dressing gown. Her hair is brushed, braided and unpowdered, and she is wearing no rouge or face powder. The light of a single candle is forgiving, or so she hopes.

When she steps lightly down the stone steps and sees the dark courtyard empty, lit only by a patch of moonlight, she is taken aback by her own disappointment. All the windows are dark; the parts of the palace that stay up after midnight do not face onto the Queen's Courtyard, and neither does the room where her guards are stationed.

It is dark, empty, and cold: just barely April, and midnight. She has been ridiculous.

She turns, hears 'Your Majesty', and nearly jumps out of her skin.

Axel von Fersen steps out of the shadows, holding a tricorne hat.

'It is you,' she says, which is not the right thing to say but it will have to serve. 'And I see you have ways of going unseen. Count von Fersen, if one wishes to be presented to the Queen, there are less uncomfortable ways.'

'I'm perfectly comfortable. Are you uncomfortable, Madame?'

He's teasing her; she gives him a look. 'I thought you had forgotten all about me.'

He glances away from her into the darkness. 'I beg your forgiveness. I have been occupied elsewhere.'

'I know,' she says, happy to have more information than he may realize. 'Our mutual friend Geneviève told me you were working together. She told me you were nothing to worry about.'

'Did she?' He looks at her again, smiling now. 'I'm not sure I like the sound of that!'

'Geneviève is a very discerning woman. Where is she now? Is she well?'

'She is very well. As for her discernment, well, you ought to know that she warned me about you.'

'Did she really? What harm could I possibly do to you?'

'Much,' he says, but he punctuates it with another wry little smile. They're standing inches apart now, but he's not the same young man who grabbed her arm so easily at the opera house. He's a few years older, he's got a day's growth of stubble and his eyes are tired, but perhaps that's only the effect of the candle in her hand.

'I'm glad you decided to make your appearance at last,'

she says. 'Though I do still think you might have asked for an audience.'

'I'm not in France at the moment. Not officially. I'm here to see some friends, to pass on some messages that I couldn't trust to anyone else. The Order thinks I'm in Sweden and I wish them to continue believing that. I came here to tell you that the war in America is more important than you may realize.'

'I understand the importance of the American war, Count von Fersen.'

'Of course. Forgive me, Your Majesty. What I mean is that it is important in another way, too. The Order – you know all about the Order, I think?'

'I do.' She thinks of Charlotte, and knows he is thinking of Charlotte too.

'It has kept itself out of politics, out of all affairs of the world, for centuries. But the situation in America has rather forced its hand. It has very little presence there – all its copies of the *Reconditus*, its book of spells, are on this continent. It is finding it difficult to suppress rogue magisters in Europe's colonies, and it worries that an independent America may become a training ground and haven for rogues.'

'What does this have to do with me?'

'Just as many Brothers are fighting on the side of the British, many rogues are fighting on the side of the rebels. Not all of us – there are rogues on both sides. But there are more on the rebels' side. So the more chance we can give the rebels, the more chance we have of breaking the Order's grip on magic for good.'

'And you think I can influence my husband.' She thinks of her group of magisters, already so practised in shifting opinion at court.

He looks awkward. 'Anything you can do, even the smallest thing.'

She hesitates. She has already done one small thing. 'Do you write to any of these rogues who are fighting in America?'

'I do.'

'Will you ask them to keep one eye on the young Marquis de Lafayette? He is a friend.'

He says nothing for a moment; then he chuckles. 'I wondered how he made his escape so easily. All right. I will make sure he has friends among the rogue magisters. As do you, Your Majesty. But please be warned. The Order is changing its ways, but it remains dedicated to hunting rogues. I know of your connection to the Order in Naples—'

She frowns. 'I wouldn't put it that way.'

'Just be sure you don't count on that connection to keep you safe. Every chapter of the Order makes its own decisions, and the Brothers in Paris are zealots.'

'I have spent many years being careful and discreet,' she says.

Fersen doesn't smile. 'I'm not sure discretion will be any protection now. We will all need our friends, and as much powerful magic as we can muster.'

A peal of distant laughter from a window above – Antoinette looks up, but there's no light to be seen. Just the life of Versailles.

When she brings her gaze back down to earth, Fersen is gone.

CHAPTER TWENTY-SIX

Too Much of a Coincidence — Count Falkenstein Arrives
at Versailles — Hairstyles — Antoinette Continues
to Disappoint — A Frank Talk

———————— ⁂ ————————

2 April 1777
Louis de Rohan to Maria Carolina

Your Majesty,

In gratitude, I received your letter of congratulation on
my elevation to the position of grand almoner of France, and
I must humbly agree with your assessment that if I am soon
made a cardinal, it will be of great utility for our Order. God
will dispose as he sees fit, but in the meantime, I am
making all arrangements I can.

Though I disagreed with the decision of the Brothers
of Naples to admit a monarch — I made no secret of it —
I have always hoped that we would be able to work together
to fight the scourge of rogue magic, which is proliferating in
Paris despite our best efforts. I regret to inform Your
Majesty that I have recently become aware that this scourge
has entered the very heart of Versailles.

Over and over, I have reassured my Brothers here that if
the Queen of France had been a magister from childhood,

Your Majesty would surely not have concealed such a danger from us. It is inconceivable that Your Majesty would be so reckless; it would be treason against the Order. Of course, I can't argue against them when they point out that much of the magic that seems to be afoot in Versailles bears a striking resemblance to the effects of Your Majesty's white gloves, which are celebrated throughout the Order – so few magisters have managed to use that spell to any good purpose, though it has been in the Reconditus for generations.

How astonishing, then, that the court of Versailles turned, almost overnight, against Monsieur Turgot, so that one moment he was hailed as a visionary, and the next, exiled in disgrace. For months, the Order here has been trying to ascertain how it happened. We have traced the change of heart of every courtier, every adviser. And each trail comes back to one of four people: the Queen of France herself, or one of three friends, including her two favourites, the Princesse de Lamballe and the Comtesse de Polignac. The whole of Versailles knows how the Queen meets with her intimate friends at the Petit Trianon.

It all seems too much of a coincidence, and if magic is indeed being used to steer the ship of state, I hope you will share my alarm and tell us anything you may know about the activities of your sister. Perhaps you have been as surprised as I by all of this, given your earlier reassurances that Her Majesty was not a magister.

Please accept, Madame, my sincerest salutations, and be assured I remain,

> *Yours in fraternity,*
> *Prince Louis de Rohan*

In the unforgiving light of a morning in April 1777, Antoinette's face in the mirror is unpowdered, unrouged, imperfect. She is twenty-one and has been married for seven years – half married. Is her face doughy around the jaw?

She would like to lean forward, to look more closely, but Monsieur Léonard has her by the hair.

This Monsieur Léonard is not the same as the one she usually uses. This is Jean-François Autié, Léonard Autié's brother. The original Monsieur Léonard has been so successful at Versailles that he sent for Jean-François as an assistant. While the original is apparently the one who develops new styles, they both implement them perfectly well. Somehow, they have arranged it so that whenever anyone calls for Monsieur Léonard, the brothers send whichever of them is at liberty.

They also dress alike, and look nearly identical, and speak the same Gascon French, pronouncing letters that the Parisians leave silent. There are already stories circulating about one brother creating an alibi for another so they can carry on affairs.

But at the moment, Monsieur Léonard looks very sober, almost dour, with tongs in his hand.

She is slowly getting used to the Queen's Bedchamber, this enormous temple of rose and gold, divided into the parts where she is displayed, and the parts where the people may come to see her. The bed itself is an enormous stage on which the last drama to be played was the death of the previous queen, her husband's grandmother, two years before Antoinette arrived in Versailles. Beside the bed are panelled doors where the women of the court stream in every morning to take their roles in dressing her.

When that's done, it's not a bad place to receive visitors, while Monsieur Léonard does her hair. But today, mercifully, is quiet, as her brother is coming and she has refused to see anyone else. It's only Antoinette, and Léonard, and Lamballe. While Monsieur Léonard works his magic, Lamballe plays the harp, quite beautifully.

'Your Majesty's hair is growing back,' says Monsieur Léonard, dividing it into locks. He – they – took the missing clump of hair as a personal affront, and have been dressing her hair with customized pieces and wigs and elaborate ribbons to cover it up.

Lamballe walks over to her with a click click click on the polished floor, leans forward and takes a pot of rouge off the table. She dots each cheek with it, using her finger. These little intimate touches – to make Antoinette feel that she is just a young woman in a room with friends and pretty things – they're deliberate, of course. Antoinette would like to put her arm around her, but she can't move at the moment, without risking Monsieur Léonard's irritation.

'Tell us some gossip, Monsieur Léonard,' Lamballe says brightly.

'I never gossip, Your Highness. That's my brother.'

'I command you,' Antoinette murmurs, keeping her head perfectly still for him, giving Lamballe a little smile with only the corners of her mouth.

'Well,' he says, but does not pause long enough to make a convincing show of searching his memory, 'have you heard about the Chevalier d'Éon?'

Who has not? A dragoon and a spy, who blackmailed the late King with some secret papers, and so has been living in exile in England, until now.

'I've heard d'Éon and my husband the King have come to an arrangement, that d'Éon has agreed to hand over the letters and behave, and come home to France. Quite the development!'

'Ah, but you haven't heard the most wonderful part!' says Monsieur Léonard joyfully, having abandoned all pretence of reluctance to gossip. 'D'Éon is the chevalière now, not the chevalier.'

'What do you mean?'

'She says she is a woman,' says the hairdresser, 'and always has been.'

'I had heard that d'Éon dressed as a woman to sneak into Russia—'

'This is no disguise, Your Majesty. She says she *is* a woman.

She only agreed to come home after His Majesty agreed to pay for a new wardrobe of women's clothing. She also wants to go to America to fight. In a dress, one assumes.'

'A *robe à la polonaise*, for the freedom in the skirts,' says Lamballe, smiling.

'Oh yes.' Léonard laughs. 'A *robe à la française* would be completely unsuitable for fighting.'

'I think I could fight,' Lamballe says.

Antoinette laughs in her turn. 'My dear, you swoon at the sight of blood. Don't you remember how we had to revive you when I cut myself on a bit of broken glass?'

'Other people's pain, yes, but my own doesn't bother me a bit. I just think about embroidery.'

'Embroidery!'

'It's very calming. I imagine the needle going in and out, the snick of the thread through the cloth, the colours. I don't know why. It's a trick I picked up as a child.'

Antoinette smiles at her beautiful friend. Lamballe has proven quite talented with magic, and always seems to know precisely how to substitute sacrifices for the old spells that make so little sense to anyone else.

Monsieur Léonard fits the metal frame of the pouf onto the crown of Antoinette's head and stuffs the triangular cork shape inside.

'How marvellous this is, about the Chevalière d'Éon. Don't you think it's marvellous, Monsieur Léonard? I am looking forward to meeting her, even if she did spy on my family, once upon a time. Perhaps I should give her one of my dresses.'

'It would probably make a scandal.'

'Oh, probably. But it would give me pleasure.'

He draws a lock of her stumpy hair through the frame, adds a lock of false hair from his kit. 'Tch,' he says, and pulls it out again. 'I am afraid nothing is going right.'

'Do your best, Monsieur Léonard,' she says, with another smile. 'It is all any of us can do.'

Madame Campan opens the door, glides over to them and says, 'Count Falkenstein has arrived at Versailles.'

She claps her hands together. Joseph!

'Count Falkenstein, Your Majesty? I don't know the name,' Léonard murmurs.

'My brother. The Emperor. That's the name he travels under.'

Even as a child, Joseph bore the world on his shoulders. He stoops a little now. Thirty-six and twice a widower, his people hungry and war at his borders. No wonder he looks dyspeptic.

He kisses her hand, and Lamballe's, as Monsieur Léonard bows.

'I don't know what you hope to achieve by travelling incognito,' Antoinette says. 'You can't help looking like who you are.'

'It saves on expense and wasted time, that's all, not having to go through all the ceremonies and rigamarole when I visit a place as the Emperor. And you look – well, I won't say like a queen, unless queens are constructed of wire and cork now. I had heard your hairstyles were ridiculous but this . . .'

'This, Your Imperial Majesty, is exactly how queens are constructed,' says Lamballe loyally. 'We are in the queen-making factory. And Monsieur Léonard is the manager of the factory.'

'I hoped to have a moment with you alone,' Joseph says, looking at Antoinette.

'I am never alone, so you might as well say what you like. I can no more be separated from Lamballe than I can my very soul. She knows everything anyway. And don't worry about Monsieur Léonard. He only gossips at the Queen's instruction.'

Joseph raises his eyebrows. 'All right then.' He pulls a gilded chair forward, sits on the sky-blue cushion. He looks sprightly, as if he might rise at any moment on a matter of state. He leans forward. 'Mother is worried,' he begins.

'Of course she is. She is a martyr to it. Is it my hair? I have told her that a *pouf sentimental* is simple good taste here.'

'Because you have made it so. You set the fashion and then you complain that you're a victim of it.'

'Joseph, when I tried to wear a corset that didn't make me numb to the fingertips, they nearly sent me away from this place in disgrace. If I kiss a friend on the cheek, it is a scandal. If I step off the garden path to see a butterfly, I am not behaving like a queen. The only freedom I have is excess.'

Lamballe replaces the pewter lid on the rouge pot, punctuating the end of Antoinette's little speech.

'Your freedom costs the treasury dear. Surely you could reduce your dress budget a little. It's unseemly.'

'If I reduced my dress budget, two hundred people would immediately find themselves out of work, and people would hate me for ruining the French economy and failing to comport myself like a French queen. I tried it. I know.'

Monsieur Léonard takes the cloth snake from his dressing table and climbs up on the stepladder to wrap it around her hair.

'Good lord, it that a snake?' Joseph asks.

'It's the serpent of Asclepius, silly. There will also be a club, a sun and an olive branch. Can you guess the riddle?'

He shakes his head.

'It's a celebration of smallpox inoculation,' Antoinette explains. 'Since we women of Versailles started wearing it, after the disease struck the late King, inoculation has become a fashion here. My hair saves lives, Joseph.'

He rolls his eyes. 'I can't tell when you're being serious.'

'Well, I'm a Frenchwoman now.'

'Apparently. But don't forget the reason you are a Frenchwoman. You are here to hold Europe together, not to indulge your whims. And it isn't only your hair that has Mother on her knees praying for you every moment she gets. Antoine, you have been married seven years now.'

'Ah,' she says. 'That.'

'Yes. That. What in God's name is wrong? Is it—' He glances at Monsieur Léonard, and then at Lamballe, who has occupied herself in arranging the brushes on Antoinette's dressing table. 'You're sure you wouldn't rather we spoke about this later?'

'All the world knows my husband does not have – how do the pamphlets put it? No, perhaps we'd better put it another way. Does not have congress with me.'

'Well, why not? Is there something wrong with him? He's what, nearly twenty-three now? We can't put it down to youthful shyness any more. There must be something.'

She cannot move, not with Monsieur Léonard attaching the white-spotted red ribbon, his new touch for *poufs à l'inoculation*. She cannot shrug or cock her head.

'He has been examined, and the doctors say no operation is necessary. He can – he can, you see, but he doesn't. He simply doesn't like it.'

Joseph makes a noise of exasperation, waves his hand. 'He ought to be whipped like a donkey – that might do the trick.'

Lamballe snorts with laughter, but then puts her pretty hand to her mouth. She and Antoinette make wide eyes at each other.

'All right,' says Joseph, more calmly. 'I'll talk to him. Antoine, I wish you were happier here.'

She stares straight into the mirror. 'Do you remember what happened at my marriage? How all those people died, trampled to death, during the fireworks display? I thought the people would hate me for it. But they didn't. And then at our coronation, in Reims, when the people had no bread, and there was so much misery. Still they came to see us. They lined the streets and they cheered. My marriage makes them happy. And that makes me happy. Really, it does.'

He nods, and bows his head. When he raises it again, his tone is gentler than she's ever heard it. 'Then you must give them a future, Antoine. You must give them a dauphin.

France is in trouble. More trouble than you know, I think. The King needs an heir, or he – and you – may very well be replaced.'

'Replaced! You mean my baby nephew? Or perhaps Philippe d'Orléans? Wouldn't he like that.'

She blinks as Monsieur Léonard's ministrations draw tears from her eyes. Her hair is done, rising above the top of the mirror. She puts the cone over her face and Monsieur Léonard applies the powder, as Joseph stands and steps a few feet away to protect himself. She has put a little of her enchanted flour into the hair powder – the one for goodwill – to see whether it might have some effect even if it is not ingested. So far it is difficult to say.

'Next,' she says. 'everyone comes in to watch me apply the rouge.'

The doors open and in come the courtiers, in order of precedence, gliding past the dais where she and Joseph sit. She watches his face in the mirror: there is nothing like this in Vienna. Here she is on display. He needs to understand that. He needs to understand how she is loved.

When her face is covered in white cream and powder, with two circles of red on her cheeks, she turns to Joseph.

'What do you think? Is the edifice complete?'

'I think you look like a harpy, decorated in the blood of your victims.'

She smiles, and now she can cock her head, carefully, judging the angle.

'That's only because you're standing so close to me,' she says. 'From a distance, I look lovely.'

CHAPTER TWENTY-SEVEN

The Austrian Woman — Hunters in the Woods —
An Offering of Love — The Emperor's Advice

———— ⚜ ————

One benefit of Joseph's travelling as Count Falkenstein is that there is no need for a state dinner. He occupies himself for his first few days, trying to arrange a meeting with Benjamin Franklin without annoying the British. Louis takes Joseph to the smithy where he spends so many hours making his locks and keys. He invites Antoinette, as he always does, but she makes her usual excuse: 'Venus does not visit Vulcan's forge.'

For her part, she invites Joseph to come and see the Petit Trianon.

Here, she does not have to put up with courtiers and commoners alike, all crowding in, each to hand her an article of clothing or gawk or show their position or brag to their friends. All these worthless rewards they fight for like chickens scrapping over corn in a yard. All inventions of the Sun King. He made the French court the way he needed it to be, so he could survive. He could not have known the consequences for an Austrian archduchess a hundred years later, and he certainly would not have cared.

It is the kind of bright clear morning in which it almost

seems that life itself might be enough. Joseph arrives and she is ready for him, playing cards with Lamballe, Polignac, and Saint-Georges on the patio. The princess is in a *robe à la polonaise*, her perfectly round pink overskirt raised and swagged over a robin's-egg petticoat. But Antoinette is in her riding costume: brown breeches, red redingote, black hat.

'Good God,' says Joseph, looking her up and down. 'Is there a fancy-dress party?'

'You said you wanted to go riding, brother.'

'Yes, but with my sister, not a musketeer.'

'Amalia dresses like a man all the time, so I hear.'

'Yes, well. Amalia is another of my problems.'

They take their leave of the other three, who do not seem sorry to see them go – they are eager to practise. They have each got a little pot of ash and their scroll of spells. As she rides away with Joseph, she can see Saint-Georges, Lamballe, and Polignac walking into the woods behind the Trianon, their heads low, chattering away.

Antoinette and Joseph ride out through the woods in the cool glancing sunshine, on two long-necked bay mares. The formal gardens and waters of Versailles stretch out behind the palace like a long cross, surrounded by thousands of acres of forest. This was a hunting lodge before the Sun King made it the centre of France. The Petit Trianon is on one edge of the estate, and it takes only a few steps to be out on the criss-cross network of the beaten roads and narrow deer paths, all shaded by oak, birch, linden, and chestnut.

'Have you arranged your meeting with Monsieur Franklin?' she asks.

'Mmm, it's proving difficult, but I'm sure we'll pull it off. I'd like to see Rousseau while I'm here, if I can. And Voltaire on my way home, though it would send Mama to an early grave if she heard of it.'

'I wonder if Rousseau the man is as comforting a companion as his books are,' she says.

'You find his books comforting? I didn't know you were even reading them.'

'Well, I have them read to me,' she says, with a sly smile, and quotes: '"Let us leave to others the task of instructing mankind in their duty, and confine ourselves to the discharge of our own."'

'Mmm. That would be comforting, I can imagine.'

'I do try to do my duty,' she says. 'I know you don't believe it, but I try very hard.'

'I do believe it.'

They turn the horses onto one of the main roads that lead through the woods, past the gardens. In the distance they can hear shouts and the barking of dogs: Louis and his brother, hunting.

'I had a talk with Louis,' Joseph says, his horse walking next to hers. 'It's all a matter of confidence. He had a few bad moments and it's put him off the whole business. I never knew such indolence. And in a king!'

She remembers how Joseph left his second wife alone in misery, not sharing her bed or even her table, but she says nothing. It is beside the point.

'Now, I know it must be difficult for you, too, not having any experience,' Joseph says. 'If only one of you were a fumbler, well, but with Louis being as he is, you have to take the initiative, Antoine. You're not a fourteen-year-old girl any more. It could be forgiven, then. There was time. And matters stood differently in Europe.'

If only he would stop. She doesn't need the lecture. Hasn't she tried? Hasn't she tried everything she can to make herself desirable to Louis? She has sacrificed her memories and hopes for straight teeth and clear skin. She has eaten just enough to swell her décolletage but not enough to inhibit the strictures of the *grand corps*. She has flirted, caressed, cuddled. She has been submissive and sweet, and she has tried to be a partner.

She has even tried to find some hint of a spell that would

work, some magical solution to make the whole business less distasteful to her husband.

'I believe he's got the right idea about it now, anyway,' Joseph says. 'I think, if you—'

She is saved from more lectures as a single rider approaches on the horizon. God help her, it's Prince Louis de Rohan.

He rides right up next to them, on a heavy grey horse with a white mane.

Antoinette smiles.

Rohan removes his hat and bows his head. 'Your Majesties.'

'You recognize me then?' says Joseph warmly, although she hears the falseness behind the warmth, and Rohan doubtless does too. Rohan may be a hedonist and a hypocrite but he is not a fool.

'I am afraid it's no good travelling incognito here,' says Rohan smoothly. 'Gossip, you know. I try to get away from it, but it is everywhere.'

'I wish you a good morning,' Joseph says impatiently.

'A good day for hunting,' Rohan replies, gazing off at the pale sky in the direction of the baying of hounds.

'Hunting! I did not know you enjoyed that sport,' says Antoinette. 'And you're not dressed for it.'

'Oh, I am perfectly dressed for the sort of hunting I am doing.'

'A woman, then.' Joseph's voice is cold; he does not even pretend to be boisterous or encouraging. Rohan, it is well known, has been trying to get himself named a cardinal, and he seems to be about to manage it, with the help of the King of Poland. The fact that he is still notoriously debauched doesn't seem to be an impediment.

'I must keep my secrets, Your Imperial Majesty. We all have our private conversations. With God.' He turns to Antoinette with a smile. 'I don't suppose you've seen a young woman, clad perhaps a little inappropriately for the weather?'

'Knowing your reputation, I would not be a very good

queen if I helped you find the lady,' she says, smiling with teeth.

'Alas, it is an axiom that Austrian women are never able to help Frenchmen recover what they've lost. No matter. There's better hunting in the area, I would imagine. Everyone hides their friends away in the little houses, and I know full well there are some small and intimate parties happening nearby. As I said, no one goes truly incognito here. I shall delay you no more.'

As they watch Rohan ride away, Joseph says, 'You caught that, I hope?'

'What's that?' Antoinette feels stunned, and has to clear her head to respond. 'Oh, yes – the Austrian woman. He means Mother, and the French colonies. Many in this country still blame the Austrian alliance for the fact that we lost New France, you know.'

'Well, many in Austria wonder what help France has been to us. We lost Silesia, for our part.'

'Joseph, don't pick a fight with me. You know I am always an Austrian in my heart, but now I'm Queen of France.'

'Indeed. You're the glue that holds this alliance together. And every year that your marriage to Louis is open to question is a year in which that odious man and all his ilk get more powerful. If they can split the two of you apart, they can split Austria and France apart, and then Britain will rule the world.'

But Antoinette is hardly listening. She is thinking of what Rohan said next, about the intimate parties. She is thinking of her three friends, their magical bundles in hand, walking into the woods.

And Rohan was riding directly towards them. It wasn't a woman he was hunting at all. All these years, he's been suspicious of Antoinette. He's never stopped watching. And now he's riding towards her friends.

'Race me,' she yells to her startled brother, and she turns her horse to the side, finds a narrow deer path through the woods that will bring her back to one of the cross-angled roads and thence to the Petit Trianon, she hopes, in time. She has always been a good rider.

Does he know, or does he merely suspect?

If the latter, his suspicions would only be confirmed if he arrived at the Petit Trianon to find an out-of-breath Antoinette there with her friends.

She must stop him from reaching the house altogether.

If she can circle around, she can head Rohan off before he reaches the little road that leads to the Trianon; she is galloping, and he was not. He doesn't expect her to do anything to stop him. He expects her to be afraid, to be silent – or perhaps to make an error. As perhaps she is about to do.

Antoinette urges her horse onward. When she meets him, what then?

The gold watch and all her papers are in the drawer of her writing table, but Antoinette has a good memory, and a little jar of ash in her pocket. She needs something that will distract him. Deter his horse. Something loud – but what? But what?

It comes to her as her horse emerges at a little crossroads near a stand of white-skinned birch trees. If she can manage to make a tree fall at just the right moment, she can frighten his horse.

She dismounts quickly, ties her own mount at a little distance. She draws a shaky star of ash in the dirt around the tree nearest the road, its leaves golden despite the newness of the year. She has been working on adapting the spell for mending into a spell for breaking. She thinks she has the right sacrifices at last, but she's never been able to use it because of the terrible simplicity of the sacrifice required. The letter of love is 'o', and this spell is: 'ooooo'.

The letters all together mean one single point in the star; it cannot be divided into five. A great love. No mere affection or fondness will do; she must snuff out a true, deep love.

She begins to write Charlotte's name but a sob chokes her before she reaches the 'l' and she crosses it out, digging into the ground.

Who, then? She is setting out to consummate her marriage. Would it not be easier to bear that if she didn't love another man? For of course she loves him.

She writes his name, full out in a fresh point of the star: 'Hans Axel, Comte de Fersen'.

So official. As if there would be any doubt of whom she means, if she means it.

Antoinette stops, and balls her fists, and breathes in hard. She must break the tree, block his path, and be gone.

'I give these things,' she whispers, screwing her eyes shut, believing she means it . . .

. . . she does not.

There's a deep sound, a thud like the unbalancing of the world, so deep she isn't sure whether she heard it at all or only felt it.

The breeze smells of rot, and when she opens them, the bark has peeled and blackened on the birch trees all around her star, as though blasted by the thwarted forces of decay, by her wavering intentions.

But the name of Fersen remains, in the love-point of the star. The tree remains. Her will wasn't strong enough to see it through.

And she can hear hoofbeats, now. He is coming.

She crawls to the point, wipes tears out of her eyes, and gets dirt in them. She rubs out his name with the heel of her hand, and writes in a third point: 'Marie-Thérèse Louise de Savoie, Princesse de Lamballe'.

Dear Lamballe, who loves her so. But what does it matter if Antoinette loves her back? Friendship out of duty is just as good as friendship from the heart. Antoinette will always take care of her, and that's what matters.

She can see Rohan now, riding up the road.

'I give these things,' she says.

Rohan is near, now; he'll see her, or the horse, any moment now.

She does not think of Fersen; she doesn't think about him, very hard. She thinks of Lamballe, rescuing her, putting her hand on her shoulder.

'I give these things!'

A crack, a rushing sound, a whinny from Rohan's horse. The tree breaks, halfway up, and its golden branches fall onto the road and shake. Rohan's horse does not spill him, but only because he is a good rider. He wheels away, the frightened horse running in the other direction. Antoinette scrambles up onto her own horse, and rides hard to the Petit Trianon.

By the time a bewildered Joseph finds her there, still muddy, laughing about having fallen off her horse, wouldn't Mama scold her, she is always telling Antoinette it isn't safe to ride like a hoyden – by then, she has told Lamballe, Polignac, and Saint-Georges that Rohan is roaming the grounds, that he must not find them doing magic.

Antoinette, Polignac and Lamballe return to Versailles that day, and Saint-Georges returns to his house.

After all Antoinette's attempts to find some magical solution to the problem of her marriage bed, some way of changing herself to make her husband change, it seems Joseph's lecturing has had some effect. Madame Campan tells her the King is coming to her bed.

Antoinette does not hope, but she prepares. When Louis comes in, through the not-so-secret passage that connects their rooms, Antoinette is already wearing her best chemise, all Belgian lace, and has her hair down, her real hair. It almost brushes her shoulders. Monsieur Léonard was right; it has been growing in.

He walks in, stands, looks at her.

They stare at each other for a moment, and Antoinette readies her little speech about duty – when Louis speaks.

'The Emperor made me see that I have been selfish,' he says, his voice thick. 'I can abide a little discomfort, if it must be. I thought – I thought it would not be such a tragedy if the Dauphin were one of my brothers' children, you see. That is the good in having brothers! Charles already has a little boy. I thought that was enough. But your brother made me see that malcontents might use my childlessness against me, try to push me off the throne. It would create instability.'

Antoinette nods. 'I am here to be mother to France. And Joseph spoke to me, too.'

He gestures towards the bed, as if he were helping her to her seat at the opera, and she sits on top of the covers. He sits beside her and puts his arms around her, kisses her neck.

She holds herself still, forces herself to stretch her neck out longer, not to shrink, not to move her shoulder up to discourage him.

He will want to be gentle, for himself if not for her. But she wants him to just get it over with. She tries to think of a way to convey this, but the only idea she can think of is to seem eager, which could alarm him and make him think she's more experienced than she ought to be.

At last he unties his breeches and moves his hand inside her chemise, up her thigh. She takes that as a signal to lie on the bed.

She helps him with it, swallowing, trying not to think of anything. Keeping her mind blank.

It is not that she does not feel affection for him; she does. She loves him, even, as her king – for she does now think of herself as a Frenchwoman – and as a husband. As one of the very few people in Versailles who respects her and treats her not with awe or with disdain, but with simple, friendly courtesy.

She kisses him on the mouth, and feels him hard against her. Feels the skin on his legs tighten as he flinches – but he does not cry out, and he pushes against her, inside her.

They are both trying hard to remember not to hold their breath.

He moves a little inside her – this must have been Joseph's instruction.

'Is it all right?' she whispers.

He nods, biting his lip, and then, to her surprise, laughs in one short bark. 'Better than all right,' he whispers. 'And for you?'

'Better than all right,' she lies, holding him close.

After a little while, he shudders, and cries out softly, and lies on top of her.

She wishes it were something either of them wanted, but they want the result, and that will have to be enough. Poor Louis.

Louis eases himself up to sitting. 'I am going hunting early and don't want to disturb you, so I'll leave you.'

She blinks, startled, and then nods.

Antoinette wakes alone, which is nothing new. It is perhaps not what she expected of the night she consummated her marriage, but then she did not expect to be seven years married when it happened, either. And perhaps her expectations were skewed by being the child of Francis and Maria Theresa, who always spent their nights together whenever they were in the same house. There was no resident *maîtresse en titre* at Schönbrunn or the Hofburg. Francis saved his affairs for his travels. Vienna was a world apart from Versailles.

Now, at last, Antoinette is the King's mistress as well as his wife. The two most powerful offices a woman could occupy at Versailles, united in her person. And yet, she wakes alone.

Truth be told, she has always relished mornings by herself, before the noise when everyone comes in to dress her and wash her and ogle her. But, on this morning, these quiet moments she would like to share with someone.

She is alone when Madame Campan comes in and whisks away the bedsheet before Madame de Noailles can get hold of it and parade it before the princes and princesses of the blood, as etiquette no doubt demands.

Campan is kinder, although Madame de Noailles believes her strictures are a greater kindness in the long run, saving Antoinette from herself. She is probably right.

Everyone is grinning from ear to ear and they pamper her as though she were ill. It is a macabre combination, this delight in the wifely duties they seem to treat as an affliction. Today she does not feel like dressing to the nines; she wants to lie in a linen dress and look out of a window and think about Fersen. She wants to drink orange-water with Polignac and sit quietly and talk about things that have nothing to do with Versailles. But today of all days, she must be Queen of France. Today is her true coronation day.

So she sucks in her breath as the *grand corps* swallows her, and she can barely lift her arm enough to take three letters off the salver when they come.

One from Joseph on his way back to Vienna, saying that things went poorly with the Benjamin Franklin business. Thanking her for the hospitality and needling her, once more, about her feathers and furbelows. He, too, means it as a kindness. So much kindness, all around her, like drowning in goose down. She will have to send him a letter to thank him for convincing Louis to try – but first she must tell Maria Theresa, who will fly into a rage if anyone outside France finds out about the consummation before she does.

The second letter is from Charlotte, warning her that Louis de Rohan is suspicious of her. Chiding her for being careless. Reassuring her that Charlotte has written to Rohan, insisting that Antoinette cares nothing for politics or ideas and is far too frivolous to be involved in any such thing, and if there are any magisters involved in the ever-shifting winds of opinion at Versailles, it is ludicrous to connect them with Marie Antoinette.

Somehow, Antoinette does not find Charlotte's letter to be a comfort.

The third letter she reads is also enciphered, and bears no name.

All my thoughts are of you.

I assure you that those who truly love you will love you unconditionally. Remember that, if you forget all else.

There is so much work to do, to make this world worthy of the wonders in it. Write to me when you can, please. In the meantime, I think you will soon meet a mutual friend.

Your obedient servant, always, unto death.

Even the deciphered letter is still coded, still safe: he does not say where he is now, or mention magic. He does not even say he loves her. Not quite.

If she were not watched by seven pairs of eyes, Antoinette would weep. Instead, she smiles and lets the letter drop to her lap – this piece of paper that she will treasure so dearly that it would make a three-letter sacrifice – and she contrives to look bored.

CHAPTER TWENTY-EIGHT

Inoculation — Fear and Death — New Dangers —
Franz Mesmer's Reputation

---❖---

At the end of a long, hot summer, Charlotte gives birth to her fifth child. Francesco is a tiny red bundle, full of screams, and she adores every particle of him. She wraps herself up in the smell of him. Another boy. This time, though the cannons fire, no orchestras march through the streets of Naples to celebrate. Or perhaps they do, but Charlotte would not hear them anyway; they came to Caserta for the birth, to be as far away as possible from Portici. Filippo, the King's brother, has been ill for weeks with smallpox there.

A month after the birth, Ferdinand comes into her room, where she sits in bed with the baby. He walks over and touches the sleeping boy on his temple, just lightly, and rests his other hand on her shoulder for a moment before abruptly removing it.

She's made him promise that he'll leave her alone in her bed for a few months; she has no need or desire to be pregnant again, with five healthy children, two of them boys. But it's a promise with no weight behind it and there's nothing she can do if he decides one day to dishonour it. For some reason he seems to interpret her request to mean that he cannot touch her at all, and while that baffles Charlotte, it's a happy side effect.

'Filippo is dead,' he says.

The poor man! The last time she saw Ferdinand's older brother, he was laughing uproariously as he instructed one of his servants to put several gloves on one of his hands, one after the other. He got it up to seven before they wouldn't go on any more. Filippo dead, alone save for his physicians. When she first met him, he told her, 'I am the oldest and should have been king, but I'm sick.' Sick all his life, with an unnamed affliction. And now dead of one whose name is spoken every day, all over Europe.

'God rest his soul,' she says. 'Is the smallpox spreading beyond Portici? Is it in the city?'

'It's always in the city. If not this year, then next year. We can stay here a few more weeks, though, to be safe.'

Safe. In her arms, Francesco purses his tiny mouth, as if he doesn't trust the word either.

'My sister writes that everyone in Paris is having the inoculation, after the death of the old King,' she says. 'Perhaps we should have it. And the oldest children too.'

Letters from Antoinette have been infrequent, lately. Perhaps Charlotte shouldn't have told her that she has been reassuring the Order of her sister's frivolity and self-absorption. But what would she have Charlotte do? If Rohan thinks the Queen of France is a threat, he'll act on it. He's made that clear.

Ferdinand pulls a face. 'Ugh, inoculation. It's terrifying. Don't you think? Having a doctor open a wound and put pus into it? I don't think I could do it.'

'You wouldn't have to *do* anything. Just sit there.'

'Just sit there, and be ill for weeks or months afterward, and possibly die. Well, it's not going to happen, anyway.'

'Why not?' She cranks her neck to look up at him. 'What do you mean?'

'My father's forbidden it. It's an offence against God's will.'

'Your father! Is your father the King of Naples, then?'

'No,' he says, tersely. 'He's the King of Spain. And the head of my family.'

'These are my children,' she replies, holding Francesco closer. 'And the doctors say that the chance of dying from inoculation is much lower than the chance of dying from the natural illness, which, as you say, is always in Naples. We live in a port city, for God's sake, with all and sundry coming through our very house day after day. No. I will keep them safe. I will write to my brother Leopold today, and ask him to send me that doctor in Florence. Angelo Gatti.'

She does not ask permission any more, not of Ferdinand, and certainly not of his father.

Three straight, deep cuts across her children's arms. Bright blood welling, impossibly red. Teresa is five, and old enough to sit with her jaw and fists clenched tight, while tears pour down her cheeks. Luisa whimpers and Carlo, only two and a half, wails piteously, his chubby arms reaching out for Charlotte, blood dripping from one. She went first, to show the children it was safe, but it only alarmed them. Beyond a screen of Chinese silk lies a young woman, a seamstress. They can't hear her, but they can hear her sniffle as the lancet pierces her, draws the poisonous pus from her so Dr Gatti can push it into the wounds he's made in the royal family.

And then they wait.

2 November 1777
Charlotte to Antoinette

My sister, my Antoinette, my dear,
   I wish you a very happy twenty-second birthday! How strange it has been to go six weeks without writing to you. But Dr Gatti insisted that the contagion could spread that way, and so we've kept ourselves apart from the world. From the two smallest children, as well. Six weeks in which we

could not see them. That was the hardest, Antoinette. My Francesco cried when I took him in my arms, and he wanted to go back to the nurse. My own tiny baby, and I could not nurse him or hold him or watch him breathe.

Everyone is well now: Ferdinand and I and all the children. I should tell you that at the start. I had a difficult recovery. I suppose I was still weaker than I realized from the birth, and the inoculation gave me the most horrible headaches.

And then the fevers. I kept seeing three red lines – the wounds in my children – and I would wake from half-dreams convinced that they were dead.

I used to sit straight up and stare at the wall for hours in that state, my heart racing, unable to think properly. I tried to focus on Dr Gatti's reassurance that his particular inoculation technique, because it uses unripe matter from an inoculation patient rather than a pustule from the natural illness, was much less likely to cause a full-blown infection. Some say it confers less immunity, too – there was a duchess in France who caught the natural infection after being inoculated by Dr Gatti, wasn't there?

I intend my new Academy to study these matters, and I have asked Dr Gatti to stay here in Florence. I am convinced now, more than I have ever been, that only I can protect both my family and my kingdom, that no one else will do it for me.

I was jealous to read of your visit from Joseph. I wish our brother happiness – no, not happiness. I don't think he'd welcome it; I think he's grown the scars on his heart on purpose, and I don't begrudge him them. I wish him peace.

I wish peace for us all, my sister, and rest after our labours are done.

In hope and affection,

    I remain your
    Charlotte

3 November 1777
Angelo Soliman to Maria Carolina

Your Majesty,

I was overjoyed to learn of the delivery of His Highness the prince, and I hesitate to burden you at such a time, but I know you, like me, always prefer knowledge to the lack of it. I have written just now to Isaac Lars Silfversparre, William Hamilton, and Caterina de San Marco to warn them of what seems to be a coordinated rogue effort to steal spells and undermine the Order, here in Vienna. I cannot say whether Naples is also at risk.

Franz Mesmer, you may recall, has long been using magic to increase our knowledge of nature and physiology. It has suited his purposes to be seen as a charlatan, a wizard of a slightly more sophisticated sort than our old friend Count Cagliostro. Mesmer has performed what seem to be exorcisms, and even some healing, using a half-invented theory of magnetism as a cover for the magic. The true method of healing is a spell that enchants a musical instrument – Mesmer uses a glass armonica, I suspect because it sounds so eerie and convinces the credulous that something scientific must be afoot.

One of his patients was a talented composer and pianist by the name of Maria Paradis. She is quite blind, and Mesmer was attempting to heal her using magic (under cover of his theory). I have heard varying accounts of how successful he was, and indeed I wondered about the wisdom of the attempt. As it turned out, it was unwise for reasons I never considered.

Fräulein Paradis used to take notes during their sessions using an ingenious writing device, in which the letters of the alphabet correspond with shapes she could feel. Each time she pressed a letter, a tiny printing press would imprint it onto the page. An invention of Wolfgang Kempelen's. (You may have heard of the Mechanical Turk that was so *popular here a few years ago. It was a marvel – I could hardly beat it in a game myself, and I could find nothing magical about it.)*

Now, though, I wonder.

The writing device seems to have been enchanted somehow to copy nearby papers: when Paradis brought the machine near any written matter, the enchantment allowed it to absorb the information in the form of a sequence of letters, which she could then recreate later on a fresh sheet of paper. Mesmer was careless in leaving his notes and spells in the room near Paradis – I suppose since she was blind, he didn't consider it a danger. We know that she copied several of his spells, in whole or in part, including the spell for the glass armonica that can heal certain wounds when played near the patient. More dangerously, Paradis may have copied an incendiary spell, the spell for unbreakable sealing wax, the ancient bezoar spell, and, perhaps, the one we've taken to calling the 'loaves-and-fishes spell', the duplication enchantment Your Majesty has put to such good use in San Leucio.

Mesmer abruptly stopped treating her, and she is going on tour, I believe. The damage to Mesmer's reputation as a healer here in Vienna has been severe, as Paradis has not recovered and he had to pretend failure to explain the sudden break in their relationship. Whether he would have succeeded, in time, I can't say. His armonica is a wonder but it is slow and uncertain in its effects.

The damage to the secrecy of the Reconditus may be incalculable.

In haste and great anxiety,
I remain,

> *Yours in fraternity,*
> *Angelo Soliman*

CHAPTER TWENTY-NINE

*The Return of d'Éon — An Old Friend — A Walk
in the Gardens — Choosing Sides*

———————— ❖ ————————

Like everyone else at Versailles in the autumn of 1777, Antoinette is anticipating the return of the Chevalière d'Éon, the prodigal spy. The problem with d'Éon, as far as Versailles is concerned, is that she has not been presented, now that she is the Chevalière. Women of quality who wish access to the court must first appear before the King and Queen at Versailles, and be introduced according to a precise ritual. Of course d'Éon has been to Versailles many times, in the years before her exile, before Antoinette came to France, before Antoinette was Antoinette. But d'Éon is a woman; d'Éon has not been presented; and so d'Éon is still in a kind of exile, even though she's home in France at last.

This second exile lasts several months in mid-1777. For one thing, Antoinette and Louis are not at Versailles for much of the autumn; they are at Fontainebleau. For another, d'Éon needs time to prepare. A dancing master must teach her how to walk and curtsey forwards and backwards in a *grand habit*. And then there is the *grand habit* itself, that torturous construction of panniers and train and corset: it must be new, it must be expensive, it must be black, and it must be from Rose Bertin's shop in Paris. That last item is not, of course, in the rules set down by the Sun King, but by 1777 it might as well be.

Antoinette sends a set of her own diamonds to the Chevalière, and a new fan 'to replace your sword', and she pays for the *grand habit*. Madame Bertin writes that the Chevalière has selected a very lovely embroidered satin, in pure white, and to the objection that debutantes must wear black unless they are in mourning, responded, 'I am forty-nine years old and have friends in eleven countries. I am always in mourning.'

The day arrives at last: one of those crisp days in November when Versailles smells almost pleasant: the smoke and stale air of the winter is yet to come, and the stink of the close-stools and sweat has faded. A Sunday, when the King and his family go to Mass, and anyone who likes may come to Versailles to watch them walk through the palace to the Royal Chapel, dressed in their best. At noon, the Queen and her attendants leave her state apartments and walk into the Hall of Mirrors, where Louis and his brothers and sister are coming from the council chamber midway through, and they all walk through that long room together, the guards holding the people back.

After Mass in the grand, soaring chapel, they walk back, Antoinette's enchanted shoes gliding above the parquet. She has had to enchant ten different pairs now, but luckily they seem to keep the enchantment even if the shoes get a new buckle, a new bow. It makes her wonder what part of an object holds its enchantment and whether an enchanted shoe is like the ship of Theseus: if the heel, the sole, and every other part were replaced, when would the enchantment vanish?

But, so far, all of her shoes still help her walk more gracefully than ought to be possible, and that's the main thing.

And then, after Mass, the presentation.

Versailles is particularly crowded today; word has gone

out that this is the day for d'Éon's arrival. Antoinette takes a glass of sherry and arranges herself in the chair in the Nobles Room, her main antechamber. She waits. Her dove-grey silk skirt, pinned with golden tassels, spreads around her. D'Éon will have to go first to the King, and then come here.

She's announced by a flurry of shouts and footsteps in the Hall of Mirrors, and then a commotion in the Peace Room, and the guard throws open one of the double doors (both doors are opened only for people of high rank) and d'Éon enters.

The white *grand habit* is dazzling, and the diamonds on her neck catch the light. Antoinette smiles to see that d'Éon is wearing the Cross of St Louis on her breast; she may be a woman but she has not given up the honours she earned. She curtseys, very well, and steps forward.

She looks familiar. Her face – the second curtsey – Antoinette puts a hand to her mouth to stop from crying out.

Geneviève. The woman who visited her in Vienna, who hid beneath the Chinese Cabinet, who has been writing to her all these years.

The third curtsey, and Geneviève manages to pull off her glove and take Antoinette's hem to kiss it. Antoinette is, at this point, supposed to pull back, to graciously refuse the kiss, to stand and offer her cheek. But she's so dazed that it takes her a moment, and Geneviève is left holding the hem for a heartbeat, until Antoinette stands, flustered.

'It's you,' she says, aware of the half-dozen guards and dozen princesses and duchesses behind her, all of them gazing at d'Éon.

'I thank Your Majesty for sending the carriage for me and for the lovely gifts,' says d'Éon.

'You play the violin, I hear,' Antoinette says, her voice dull, as if from very far away or underwater. 'Will you come and play at one of my salons?'

'Gladly,' says d'Éon. 'My disagreements were with the late King. I hope you understand, Your Majesty, that I am glad to be back in France, and hope to be a friend to you and your husband.'

'I should like nothing better. And I understand His Majesty has set a decree, for any who may be in doubt, that you are a woman.' She smiles, hoping that was the most delicate way to broach the subject.

'Yes, Your Majesty. Although, I wonder . . .'

'Yes?'

'Well, the decree requires me to always wear dresses, on pain of losing my estates.'

'And that is not acceptable to you?'

She spreads her arms wide. 'Sometimes I like to wear breeches! I don't like to always be caged like this.'

Antoinette laughs. 'Sometimes I like to wear breeches too. Riding, particularly. My mother hates it. All right, I'll see what I can do about that. And I have some corsets and things that I would like to give you, if you don't mind.'

The chevalière smiles, as if satisfied. 'I would be most grateful, Your Majesty. I have come to understand that my former wardrobe will not be suitable in France.'

There are chuckles behind them, but Antoinette knows that that former wardrobe contained several old-fashioned mantuas and at least one white bonnet with two moths on the lappets. Were they for helping d'Éon in her spycraft, somehow?

Antoinette thinks hard and fast. Tonight is the usual gambling party, and d'Éon could come to that, but it would be hard to find a place to speak alone. The best place to be alone, at Versailles, is outside.

'Later there will be the dinner, but I am at liberty before that. I will rest and change my clothing, and you may do the same, if you like. Will you walk with me in the gardens, Chevalière?'

D'Éon inclines her head, and then manages the three

backward curtseys – one must not turn one's back on the Queen, even if one is wearing a cumbersome train – and then she is gone, and Antoinette stares, astonished.

All of the orange trees in their pots have been moved inside for the winter, so the parterre is a vast landscape broken only by the occasional sculpture and by the swirls and whorls of pathways cut into the lawns. Anyone could see Antoinette and d'Éon here, walking in their *robes à la polonaise*, but it doesn't matter if they're seen, so long as they aren't over-heard.

'When I met you, in Vienna—' Antoinette begins, stumbling over too many questions.

'When was that, 1770? Yes, there was a tiresome campaign in London to determine my sex in those days – wagers and kidnapping attempts and everything of that sort – and I got in the habit of disappearing for weeks or months and visiting my friends in other places.'

'How does Master Kempelen work his Mechanical Turk without you, I wonder?'

'Ha. I send him an assistant whenever he wants to trot it out. He's proven useful. I had him build a printing device for a rogue in Vienna, who used it to copy out and steal some of the Order's spells. I'll send them to you. There's something that ostensibly will start a fire out of nothing, though we can't make it work. And Mesmer's healing spell, though one needs a glass armonica for that.'

'Hardly very useful, then,' Antoinette says with a smile.

'All spells are useful. They help us learn how to make more. There's one that would be very useful indeed – a duplication spell. We think the Order has been using it in Naples to replicate food.'

'Food!' Antoinette stops walking. The harvest of 1777 has been a good one at last, thank God, but no one knows when another bad year might come, with the cattle walking like skeletons, and the crops hanging yellowed and dead, and the market women screaming at the gates of the palace. 'Could we use it to make more flour? More bread?'

'We could, if we had it. Our rogue friend only managed to copy half of it before she was caught. We know it exists in the Order's great spellbook, but we don't know the sacrifices for it.'

She pauses, and Antoinette, thinking hard, walks on.

'I allowed myself to be convinced to come to France largely because of you, Your Majesty,' Geneviève says after a while. 'I have had worries I didn't want to entrust even to ciphered letters. I have reason to believe the Order knows your secret.'

'Yes,' Antoinette says, thinking of Rohan on his horse. 'So do I.'

'The Order in London, at least, now seems to believe that Your Majesty, while a magister, is too . . . simple, in heart and mind, to make any use of it but for frivolous things. I don't know where they got that impression.'

Antoinette does: from Charlotte. But she says nothing, setting her jaw. 'Were you a Brother of the Order once, as Fersen was?'

D'Éon snorts. 'Far from it. They wouldn't have me as a member anyway. I don't meet their standards. Oh, I'm rich enough, but in all other ways entirely unsuitable. Which suits me quite well. But I have my spies, and I know what the Order thinks, and I am worried about them, too. For centuries, they have kept magic to themselves because they hold the general mass of humanity in contempt. But now they have seen what your sister is doing in Naples, and they have begun to dream of a magical empire – where not only magic is under their control, but *everything*. They see an empire ready for the taking: the greatest empire in the world.'

Antoinette blanches. 'Do you mean King George—'

'The King of England is not a magister. I'm sure of that much. But his advisers are Brothers, or in the power of Brothers, and they grow bold. A king whose power cannot be checked, not even by force of arms, is the worst possible evil.'

'Do all rogue magisters in England take the part of the Americans?'

'We take the side of whoever will destabilize the Order. It has never been as powerful as it is now. It is a European order, and for centuries that limited its reach. But now, where is Europe? Europe is everywhere, like smallpox. The Brothers of the London chapter view England's colonies with a mixture of greed and terror. They have so little control there, but they are eager to expand their great book of magic. They have started trying to acquire, and then suppress, the magic of their colonies from America to India. And the Spanish and the Dutch Brothers do the same, to a degree.'

'And in the French Empire?'

D'Éon snorts. 'A few years ago, I would have said yes, and haven't you wondered why I made myself an enemy of the King I once served? But now I suspect it is an academic question, as the French Empire is much diminished, isn't it? The empire on the ascendant now is the British one.'

Antoinette has always wanted to do her best, to use what she is given, to serve her family by making herself worthy of the love of the people of France. If that is too simple a wish, then let them call her simple.

'Count von Fersen told me many rogues are on the Americans' side.'

'Rogues are on no one's side. That's been one of our difficulties all along. By nature, we are disorganized. We thrive in chaos, and America is chaos. It is – possibility. An object poised at the moment of sacrifice, a reality that might decay into any number of possible states, and some of those states could be better than anything that has gone before. Perhaps!'

'Or worse.'

'Or worse.'

Antoinette sighs. 'Fersen wants to go. To America.'

'Yes, many rogues with radical notions are fighting the British. Your Philippe d'Orléans got his naval commission for a reason.'

Antoinette is shocked wordless for a moment, and stops, with a swishing of silk skirts. 'Philippe! You mean to say that Philippe d'Orléans is a magister!'

'And quite a radical-minded one.'

'Of all people! Well, that is a surprise.'

'We have all been working in our own small ways to keep ourselves safe and to stop the excesses of the Order. But now I think that will no longer be enough. Now, I think, the risks of secrecy are greater than the risks of exposure. The risks of living in a world in which kings and queens use magic to extract all they can out of people who are already starving and hungry. Now, I think, we go to war. So, the question becomes: what part will you play in this war?'

Antoinette stops, looks back at the palace of Versailles, a grey hulk against a grey sky. 'I could teach my husband magic. I could teach the King.'

'Do you think that's wise?'

She casts her gaze down, then, tries to think. Searches herself. 'I don't, really. I trust him with my life, with everything. But he has to rely on his counsellors, and I don't trust all of them. I have a feeling some would take the Order's view of things, and we've learned it's quite difficult to change people's minds, predictably and without attracting notice.'

'Indeed,' says d'Éon appraisingly, and Antoinette notices that she's changed the diamond earrings for a set of little amber drops, each one containing something small and feathery – the wing of a moth?

'You seem to know what I'm going to say before I say it, d'Éon.'

She shrugs. 'I'm a good listener. I listen to the whispers before the words: the glances, the frowns, the smiles, the sighs. Right now, for example, I am listening to you considering whether the magisters you've been training at the Petit Trianon might play a part in the American war.'

Antoinette laughs. 'You heard me say that with my eyebrows, did you?'

'Well, I know how you've been occupying your time lately.' Geneviève adds, her voice lower, 'And what I know, the Order suspects.'

'We are in danger,' Antoinette says, and lifts her chin. 'I know that. I do not forget that my first governess died at the hands of the Order, inside a royal palace. And Prince Louis de Rohan has made it clear he is never going to stop threatening me, or my friends.'

D'Éon cocks her head, and the amber earring swings. 'Now perhaps Your Majesty understands why I wear the white of mourning. A war is on the horizon. A much bloodier and dirtier war even than the rebellion in America. A war fought in secret, with lies and murders. And it is time for every magister to choose a side.'

PART FOUR

1777 TO 1779

CHAPTER THIRTY

Dinner with William Hamilton – War and Diplomacy –
A Request – Volcanoes – Prince Caramanico
Finds Himself Short

―――――――― ❖ ――――――――

1 December 1777
Antoinette to Charlotte

My sister, my heart,

    How I have praised God that the famines which struck both the Holy Roman Empire and the Kingdom of France did not strike Naples in these last years, that your ports have been laden with goods and your people fed. In my own country, I have seen children begging in the streets outside the palace with skin stretched over their bones. Over the last few years, we've had more bad harvests than good in France, and the stores are depleted. Another bad year would mean a great deal of suffering.

    I won't thank you for telling your fellow Brothers that I am too frivolous to bother about. It may be the truth, but I do try, Charlotte, and I do care. Last year, as I told you, I adopted a small boy named Armand, and he is doing a little better now. I thought, perhaps I cannot feed them all but I can feed this one! My capabilities have never been adequate to the task, and even my magic is of so little use – and you tell me not to use it, to keep myself safe, to keep myself apart.

And all these years you have had access to the spells of the Order. Not once have I asked you to give me any. Little did I imagine that there would be a spell to create food – to create more food for the people! – and that you would keep it for yourself, knowing what has been happening in France.

I ask you now to share that spell with me. Don't ask how I know about it. Trust me to use it wisely and for the good of my people.

We can see, in America, that people will rise if their monarchs do not act in their interest. What does our old friend Angelo Soliman say about it? I envy you your friendship with him, but then I have quite enough Brothers in my life, with France's grand almoner chasing after me and my friends, as though we were his pretty domestics.

I ask for your help and I send you my love, which is always yours.

Antoinette

Charlotte always feels slightly circumspect about William Hamilton. They are members of the same Order, but his primary loyalty is to a foreign power. The Paris Brothers have recruited the American ambassador, Benjamin Franklin, to their cause. He pretends to champion the rebellion, but he's actually sowing confusion among the French about what, precisely, the colonies want. He's given the Marquis de Lafayette a sword, as a token of appreciation from America. What Lafayette does not know is that it is enchanted with what the *Reconditus* calls the 'cut-both-ways' spell, to make the owner prevaricate. The goal is to dull the young man's infamous reckless courage, but what effect it might have on a man as impulsive as Lafayette is reported to be, Charlotte can only imagine. Cagliostro writes to Silfversparre, who reports that Franklin is secretly working now to secure an America, and a world, in which magic is preserved for and by the Order. But so many of Franklin's colleagues and countrymen are rogues. It all makes Charlotte nervous.

Still, she enjoys visits to Hamilton's villa near Caserta, which is always full of antiquities he's collected, his papers on Herculaneum and Pompeii, and visiting poets and musicians.

He also has an excellent cook. On a chilly evening in January 1778, Charlotte is the only guest at his table. 'You have a wrinkle between your eyes that was not there when last we spoke,' she says.

'I am nearing fifty, Your Majesty,' Hamilton says in his pleasant rumble. 'Wrinkles will appear.'

Hamilton is indeed nearly twice her age, and can be avuncular, but has a plain-dealing manner with her that she appreciates, particularly in a diplomat; perhaps it is an English quality, or at least an English skill.

'I know the look of a foreign policy wrinkle,' she says, and picks up her fork. On blue-and-white china, there's a little bowl of red and white octopus.

'The Elector of Bavaria has died,' Hamilton says.

'Yes, my brother told me. Joseph wants that territory.'

'Prussia will not let him have it.'

Charlotte puts down her fork, and the servants bring plates of grilled swordfish and artichoke.

'The Prussians will be able to count on the support of Russia. And others?'

'And others,' Hamilton agrees cautiously.

'But my brother has allies too. France, for example.'

She thinks of Antoinette's letter, asking for the spell. How it tore at her heart!

'France will remain neutral,' Hamilton says. 'It won't support Austria, if Austria chooses to make this a war.'

Mama won't like that. Poor Antoinette; she'll have a barrage of letters to deal with.

'You have information to that effect?'

Hamilton does something with his eyebrows. 'The anti-Austrian sentiment in France is high. France would rather use its depleted forces to hurt England in the colonies than to enter another war within Europe.'

'You think my mother made the wrong choice, allying with France and Spain over Britain?'

'I could not think otherwise.'

The servants bring in hot, savoury rice *sartù*, one mound of rice for each of them, with English sausage and leek inside.

'Spain is helping the American rebels,' Hamilton says, and takes a sip of red wine. 'They may be of two minds about encouraging distant colonies to throw off their masters, but they cannot help but support the enemy of their rival. American privateers have access to the ports of Spain.'

'And to the ports of Naples and Sicily.' She smiles at him wryly; it is a sore point.

'And to the ports of Naples and Sicily. Do you think Spain will join the Americans and declare war against Britain?'

Charlotte dabs her lip with a napkin. 'I am not privy to the plans of Spain. Spain does not talk to me.'

'No, indeed. I have heard the King, your father-in-law, is furious about the inoculation, and says terrible things about you.'

Charlotte is surprised. Perhaps Ferdinand was right to be afraid of his father. 'Still? It was months ago, and everyone survived.'

'The King of Spain does not brook disagreement, and he regards Naples as part of his own kingdom. All of which means, my friend, that you and I could be at war before too long.'

The dessert course consists of blancmange with rose-petal jam, and rum babas – a food of Lorraine, Charlotte's father's home. She smiles; Hamilton pays attention to everything.

'If Spain goes to war with England,' she says, spearing the blancmange with her spoon, 'that does not mean Naples will follow. I would have Naples chart its own course.'

'Then, Your Majesty, it will need its own ships. What would happen to trade here if the Spanish did not keep piracy at bay? How does the Neapolitan navy stand now? A single ship of the line? A few galleys and frigates? A half-dozen xebecs, which are hardly any good in battle?'

She nods, blinking hard. 'You are right,' she says. 'It is a problem that becomes more urgent by the day.'

He leans back in his chair, silent for a moment, as if thinking. 'Before the coffee, would you like to see my new engravings of the Phlegraean Fields?'

Charlotte smiles. Some day, William Hamilton will retire from diplomacy, and he will spend his days digging up pottery and studying volcanic activity, and he will be perfectly happy.

When Soliman visits in February 1778, he is glum. Joseph has gone to war with Prussia, and Mesmer has gone to France. In the cavern beneath Naples, they meet, and there are new spells in the *Reconditus*, one from Constantinople that prevents sails from ripping, and one from Amsterdam that keeps powder dry. Charlotte is eager for both. But it is her turn to add a spell to the *Reconditus*, and she has finally run out of spells from the embroidered book. Silfversparre and Lunardi tend to get spells from the rogues they capture, and Caramanico gets them in trade for his secrets and favours. Charlotte is busy with governing.

She kneels at the little desk where they keep quill, ink, and paper, and hastily writes out the spell Antoinette sent her, the one about the flour that changes people's feelings when it's baked into little cakes.

'You can use this in your salons with your poets and philosophers, Caramanico,' she says. 'In fact, would you use it when you go to Florence next month? Invite some naval men, and make them trust you. I need to learn about building a fleet. If they won't eat little cakes, mix it in whatever they will enjoy.'

Caramanico approaches and looks over her shoulder, and

when he speaks, it's in a low voice, low enough that the others won't hear. 'I can't use that spell, Your Majesty, but I could take a bag of flour with me, if someone else were to enchant it.'

'You can't use it?' She turns to look up at him.

He looks embarrassed. 'The sacrifice – the love spell. I find myself short.'

She has never considered the possibility, and it turns her skin cold. 'Short of love? You have nothing left to sacrifice?'

He straightens his shoulders. 'But I believe I know just the man who can help Your Majesty – an Englishman, serving in the Tuscan navy. He managed a manoeuvre that's made him famous; no one knows better how a fleet behaves in these waters.'

'That will do nicely,' she says after a moment. She stands, and prepares to add her sister's spell to the store of the Order's knowledge.

The enchantment to add a spell to the *Reconditus* seemed silly to her the first time: write down the spell to be given, place it as a memory sacrifice, and it will appear in the book. Hardly a sacrifice at all; merely a transfer. But it still makes her feel slightly ill, every time: losing the memory of the spell for a moment, forgetting what she wrote on the paper that turns to dust. The book grows new pages as a salamander grows limbs, the sacrificed spell appearing first and then others, all in the handwriting of the magister who sacrificed them.

The familar smell of rot is barely a note beneath the cave's dampness. They ask the Five Questions, and open the book and find the spell written there, along with the spells for powder and sails.

'These spells have been used, and are safe?' Silfversparre asks.

Soliman nods. 'There was a powder explosion near Berlin not long ago, but on investigation, we found that was a different spell altogether. An attempt at the loaves-and-fishes spell by some rogue, I shouldn't wonder.'

'Who was the rogue working for?' Caramanico asks.

'Himself, probably,' Soliman says. 'Any rogue could make their fortune that way, and blow up the world while they're at it. The Prussian chapter doesn't know who it was. We in Vienna are in contact still with our Prussian Brothers, as much as we can, given the present state of war between Prussia and the Empire.'

'The Order has always held itself apart from worldly disputes,' says Caramanico.

'Yes . . .' Soliman agrees slowly. 'But more than that, we are beginning to use magic for the public good, inspired in part by what you have achieved here in Naples. It is a very cautious experiment. In Vienna, we are using the white-gloves spell to try to ensure that His Imperial Majesty's troops seldom engage with the enemy, and some like-minded magisters in Königsberg are using maps of confusion to do something similar. We hope to reduce the casualties, and make time for diplomacy to work.'

It was only a matter of time, Charlotte thinks. And the traditional members of the Order – the Rohanites, as people have started to call them – can hardly complain, given their conviction that the war in America is one that magisters must join. They argue that the American question poses a threat to the existence of the Order – but doesn't all war?

'A marvellous opportunity to use magic as an instrument of reason in the modern world,' says Lunardi.

'It will be,' Silfversparre grumbles, 'if we can keep the two armies from eating up the countryside and leaving dysentery and bastards in their wake while they dance around each other.'

'Empress Catherine won't let them dance for long,' Caramanico argues.

Soliman nods. 'We will do what we can. I believe that the Order will one day be a light unto the world. But for the moment, the rogues are not going to stop with one theft. There was an attack on another of our number a few days before I left – he found himself lost in the alleys of Vienna for more than a day, and we still don't quite understand what magic the rogues used against him, or why.'

'Perhaps it was gin,' says Silfversparre.

Soliman smiles, but shakes his head. 'I saw the man. Something of the nature of our map spell, but what, I don't know. Perhaps it was mere mischief, or a message – to show us what they can do.'

'Is there a *they*?' Lunardi asks. 'The rogues in Naples hold no meetings and have no ideas beyond their own little grimoires and amulets.'

'For now,' Soliman says. 'But you must be ready. There are rogues with ambition, who would rule their fellows if they could, who will form a sort of shadow of the Order and go to war against us. And if that happens, not only will we fail in keeping humanity safe from the knowledge of magic, but we may fail in keeping them safe from magic itself. What is to stop some common soldier with a half-dozen spells from declaring himself emperor, in any country where the monarchs don't have magic, where the Order is not powerful enough to stop him? A half-dozen spells, if they were powerful enough, could be a match for an army. It could even be a match for the Order here in Naples. We must not allow any more rogues to steal from us. We must draw the line here, or we fail in our duty to the past and the future.'

Charlotte swallows, and nods. She has known for weeks what she must write to Antoinette, and the time has come simply to do it. Hasn't it been difficult for Charlotte to regulate the flour and beans, to make sure she doesn't disrupt trade and agriculture? The French government is a mess; if it had to deal with Antoinette feeding mysterious stocks of food into the system, it would devolve into anarchy. Besides, Antoinette is too trusting, and she has rogues as friends. Rogues who might well use the spell to create gunpowder or worse – it would require enormous sacrifices, but there are people willing to do anything for a cause, or for money.

She must tell her sister that she can't give her the loaves-and-fishes spell. Will she accept Charlotte's reasoning? She will resent it, most likely. And Antoinette is too honest even to keep the secret of its existence. No, Charlotte must tell Antoinette that she knows of no such spell. She doesn't think she has ever lied to Antoinette before, but perhaps she has sacrificed the memory.

CHAPTER THIRTY-ONE

*A Gift for Charlotte, Signed with Love — An Inadequate
Fleet — Charlotte Borrows from Leopold — A New
Project for San Leucio*

———————— ✜ ————————

Antoinette reads the letter in which Charlotte refuses to provide the spell that could help her feed France. Her sister repeats that she can't keep Antoinette safe if Antoinette insists on doing things that will draw the attention of the Brothers of Paris, who are understandably concerned that the Queen of France has been influenced by rogue magisters.

With her jaw set and her lips tight, Antoinette sits down to respond to Charlotte.

She thinks about what she wants to write:

You have chosen your allies unwisely. And you've mistaken my affection for stupidity for the last time.

But she doesn't. She lets those sentences live in her mind and not in her pen.

The rogues do things differently, and Charlotte will never see the virtue in that. Saint-Georges and Polignac have already found other magisters in Paris, and Antoinette has told them they may of course share any spells they like. But Antoinette has no friends in Naples, the way Charlotte does in Paris. She has no way to take the spell that would help her feed her people. She asked for it, and Charlotte refused.

So Antoinette has enchanted a portrait of herself, only this time the magic has nothing to do with her appearance. This time, the portrait is an extension of herself, and if Antoinette tries, she can hear what's happening in any room where it hangs. It's an alteration of the same spell responsible for Geneviève's fan, and the lorgnette that so impressed her friends that day at the Petit Trianon. It took some time to make it apply to a painting. Antoinette tested it in a few places in Versailles, and heard things she wishes she hadn't.

She writes a gentle, brief, sisterly letter. She adds a note to the bottom, saying that she's sending a painting. She signs it with love.

A gift for Charlotte, from her sister: a portrait of Antoinette, as queen.

This portrait shows a woman with feathers riding in her hair, and strings of pearls wrapping the thick ringlets to her shoulders. Heavy-lidded eyes the same colour and clarity as the sapphire at her breast. A rosebud smile.

This woman looks nothing like the apple-cheeked girl in riding clothes, newly arrived in France. Certainly nothing like the terrified Dauphine, in one of the old-fashioned court dresses, her hair scraped back from her temples.

This young woman gazing at something just outside of the frame looks regal. More than that, she looks almost *happy*, but then Antoinette has cultivated the skill of looking happy, and painters lie. Still, Charlotte stares at it for a long time, wishing she could speak to the woman painted there, a woman ten years older than the weeping sister she left behind at Schönbrunn.

My dear Leopold,

I am writing to tell you that Dr Gatti has accepted my invitation to stay here with us in Naples, and so you have lost a doctor by lending him to me. What a good brother you are! I know you won't begrudge me. (Peace, peace. I'll make it up to you somehow.)

Shamelessly, I'm writing now to ask you for another favour, and possibly for another loan of a talented man, or two. The last time Joseph was here, he moaned and grumbled about the state of the Neapolitan navy, and I dare say he was right, but I had too much to occupy me. Now, I'm told on good authority that I have run out of time to procrastinate, and we can't rely on the Spanish to protect us any more. We are entirely open to the sea here, Leopold, and if your fraternal love for me is not enough to bestir you, consider that if Naples falls to one of Europe's naval powers, Tuscany won't be far behind.

The trouble is that I know nothing about building a navy — how many of which sort of ship, and of what designs, and who ought to build them, and all of that. This is one of many areas of my education our mother saw fit to neglect when she was teaching me embroidery and dancing. And Ferdinand, as you know, is useless.

Isn't there anyone there you could send me to advise me? My friend the Prince of Caramanico says wonderful things about your Englishman, John Acton, the one who commanded your frigates in the Algiers campaign.

Your nieces and nephews send you kisses. Kiss all of mine for me.

Your sister,
Charlotte

1 May 1778
Antoinette to Charlotte

My dear Charlotte,

I am glad to hear the portrait pleases you. I was very amused to read your letter about your new arrangement with your husband, and for your sake I hope you can stretch it a few more months. I wish you joy of your celibacy from this day onward! Surely he cannot insist, now that you have given him five children.

It seems God has disposed everything rather well, because I suspect I at last am with child myself. It may be nothing, but the General is very late and I am hopeful.

I shall have to order some new clothes, and I have already decided on a way to announce my condition to the people: I'll give 12,000 francs for the relief of the poor. I've asked for specific attention to be paid for those in debtors' prisons, and especially those whose poverty made them unable to pay their wet-nurses. I'm told there are a great many such people. To think of all the mothers who could not nurse themselves – or fathers or grandmothers raising babies whose mothers died in childbirth – what a terrible prospect it must be to know that the money will run out, and the child will go hungry. And then to be taken away to prison, where one can be of no more good to anyone!

The pamphleteers continue their fascination with me; I fear I may have wrought too well with my enchantment of the chevalier's violin, years ago. The people think of me, and when they have nothing to think about, they invent.

Oh well. God willing, when they think of me, soon enough, they'll think of a darling tiny dauphin.

Finally, I must tell you that I have no response to Rohan's 'concerns', as you put it, about my being influenced by rogue magisters. The fact that he is now Cardinal de Rohan means nothing; he's still a scoundrel. If you love me, the best you can do for me is trust that my own judgement

*is sound. You keep your secrets and I will keep mine.
I know you mean well, Charlotte, but they don't. You know
very well that I can be as stubborn as you, in my own way,
and I have no intention of changing my opinion on this.*

*Speaking of the family stubborn streak, Joseph's decision
to send troops into Bavaria in support of his claims there
created no end of difficulties for me here, as Louis was dead
set against it, and I found myself having to argue both sides
to the other. Again, I have given fuel to those who think
I care only for the fortunes of our family.*

*How can we be a family when borders and interests
divide us?*

> *All my love to you, my sister forever,*
> *Antoinette*

The *Reconditus* grows in fits and starts. As the threat of war
grows across Europe, some chapters go for months without
adding spells, hoarding what they know, uncertain now of
how magic may be used by governments. But always, eventually, new spells appear, as curiosity overcomes caution. To
stop adding to the *Reconditus* would be to stop learning from
the discoveries of other chapters. The Order is held together
by mutual greed.

The girls at the San Leucio factory have little to do at the
moment; the kingdom's stores of beans and flour are as full
as Charlotte dares to make them, without attracting notice
or disrupting the market. What is she to do with the extra
flour?

She thinks of Antoinette's little spell, for the cakes. She
could set San Leucio onto this new spell for a while instead:
enchanting flour not to duplicate it, but to create an emotional
effect in the people.

They will enchant the flour to induce doubt. In small
quantities, across the whole population of Sicily and Naples,
it may be enough to change the hearts of the people. To

reduce their certainty, to make them less vulnerable to dogma and cant, and more open to new ideas. To make them happy to leave the Inquisition and all the other civil power of the clergy in the Middle Ages where it belongs. To give Charlotte her sphere of influence, free and clear.

For various reasons – because she is a woman, like the workers at San Leucio; because Charlotte knows she can never betray her; because the others are busy – oversight of the project falls to Caterina. On the last day of 1778, she comes to Charlotte's study in the Palazzo Reale, to report.

Caterina looks tired as she lays out the problems she's had to solve. Unlike the duplication spell, this new enchantment on the flour requires more sacrifices than they can ask of any girl more than once or twice. It requires more girls, working on less frequent rotations. It's hard work, making sure that the girls don't really understand or remember what they're doing, making sure that they do it properly. And making sure they are recompensed with a good education and good wages for their work on the silk looms.

Charlotte listens, with gratitude, and looks at Caterina's face. She's asked a great deal of her friend these last years.

'Come,' Charlotte says. 'I'll show you a marvel.'

She draws back a Chinese screen and shows Caterina her new globe. It's a beautiful piece: the lines of the continents a delicate gold, the lines of the meridians solid and sure. It sits on its axis within a wooden stand.

Caterina walks around it, inspecting, clearly not wishing to give offence but unable to see what's so glorious about it.

'Look with this,' Charlotte says, and hands her a magnifying glass. 'Look at the ocean. Any ocean.'

Caterina bends over the Atlantic Ocean with the glass in her hand, frowns, looks closer. 'Ships! Good heavens, they're moving. Look, there's a British flag on that one.'

Charlotte claps her hands. 'You see? We can't affect the real world by touching the globe, so don't bother poking at them. But it shows us where the ships are. I am going to build a navy for Naples, and that navy will be the safest and the most dangerous on the seas, because it will know where every other ship is and where it will be.'

'Will be?'

'If we know where they are, we can guess where they're going. Look there, in the English Channel: thirty British ships of the line.' She goes to her writing desk and makes some calculations. 'If they carry on in their current speed and course, by the twenty-third of July they will be west of the island of Ushant, by, oh, a hundred miles? We'll make a wager, and see whether I'm right.'

'Is it a rogue spell? Or in the *Reconditus*?'

Charlotte shakes her head. 'One of Dr Soliman's inventions. He writes interminably about the problem of placing two enchantments on a single item: it so seldom works, without one enchantment slipping off or changing in some way. Soliman thinks the reason for this is connected to what he calls the "spell of spells", the formula that can determine the sacrifices for any enchantment.'

Caterina blinks, amazed. 'Any enchantment? Even one that has never been proven before?'

'That is his theory. Whether such a thing could really exist, I can't say. Soliman has been experimenting with multiple spells on single objects, and he sent this to me to see whether it made a difference when two different magisters worked the spells. It was my task to choose what I wanted to see, and I chose the ships of the line of all the nations of the world.'

Caterina walks around the globe, bending down now and then to peer at the little ships. 'And the cost?'

'The memories of twenty-five days – but not just any days. Twenty-five birthdays. And I just happened to have twenty-five birthdays to sacrifice.'

Caterina looks stricken, so Charlotte holds up a hand to reassure her.

'What are the memories of twenty-five days, over the course of a life?' Charlotte says. 'Birthdays were never terribly important back in Austria anyway; we made a bigger fuss over name-days.'

Caterina gives her a sad smile. 'It's an impressive device, Your Majesty.'

'And very useful too. I can tell my admirals precisely where to sail. Once I have the admirals to tell, that is.'

'But how will you tell your admirals what they need to know without telling them how you know it?'

'I'll simply give them orders, Caterina. I am queen, you know.'

CHAPTER THIRTY-TWO

*Lafayette's Travails in America — Conversations
at the Petit Trianon — The Problem of
Philippe — Naval Intelligence*

The Chevalière d'Éon leans back in her chair and crosses her legs. Here at the Petit Trianon, everyone has a chair rather than one of the stools that fill the rooms at Versailles, and the conversations go differently.

D'Éon clears her throat and snaps a piece of paper in one hand. 'Let me read from Lafayette's own letter. He writes: "There are a half-dozen magisters among the officers here in America, but I don't know what to do with them. Their spells are useless to me and one of them keeps trying to ignite a lantern through magic and setting his tent afire. He protests that there is a want of firewood, which is true, but there is a want of everything: men, money, food, uniforms, muskets, time. General Washington is in the north and I am here. My wound has healed and my health is quite good, if I do not starve. Please convey my best wishes, look after my wife, I remain, et cetera, et cetera."'

She pushes her reading spectacles down her long nose and peers at Antoinette. 'They are starving.'

Saint-Georges paces by the window, as he usually does,

whether there are stools or chairs or anything. 'I have found a few more spells to send him.'

'From your friends in the alleys around the Palais-Royal?' d'Éon asks.

'Spells are spells,' Saint-Georges says, turning. 'And who are we to turn up our noses at halfpenny conjurers, since we cannot manage anything useful on our own?'

'Speaking of the Palais-Royal,' d'Éon continues, 'Your Majesty, I really think we should bring the duke into our meetings here.'

The duke she means is Philippe d'Orléans. Antoinette still can't believe he's been a rogue magister all this time. The Orléans branch of the family is more wealthy and powerful than anyone in France save the King himself. Philippe recently received a gift from his father: the sprawling and increasingly misnamed Palais-Royal in central Paris.

It was at the opera house there that Antoinette met Fersen, a lifetime ago. The complex has been in the Orléans family for generations but now she can't go there for fear of being mobbed. Philippe has rented out the colonnade to shop-keepers of all kinds: booksellers, silk merchants, wig-makers, potters and cobblers, stalls jumbled with trinkets of dubious origin. It is his private estate, and there are no police. Cloaked men mutter in the shadows of the many little coffee houses that tuck into the marbled arcades. The voices of actors rise in the gardens, and the laughter and boos of their audiences. Polignac has told her all about it.

'I used to think he wanted magic only for his own benefit,' d'Éon says. 'But I hear he knows many rogue magisters, even some he's taught himself. Farmers and fishmongers, even. Actresses. All sorts of people. He may be able to find spells we can't, and act on things happening far from Versailles.'

'Farmers and fishmongers!' Antoinette says, astonished. 'Can they all even read?'

'I don't know,' d'Éon says, as though amused. 'They don't need to know *agricola, agricolae* to be magisters, I suppose.'

'No, but they need to know how to read spellbooks,' Lamballe says. 'Why teach these unfortunates to use something they can hardly understand?'

'If it were someone else, I would say it is because they are unfortunate,' Polignac says evenly. 'But this is Philippe, so I am sure he's doing it to be an ass.'

'Surely,' Antoinette responds, 'if he had anything useful to contribute to the state, he would have done so.'

She thinks of her own efforts to be of use to the state: the enchanted cakes, the winds of opinion shifting in ways they might have shifted anyway. How little she has done!

Polignac says, 'Philippe is a creature of Versailles, for all that the Orléans family thinks they occupy a world apart. He operates on favours. He may be waiting for someone to ask him.'

'If only we had the complete loaves-and-fishes spell!' Saint-Georges cries. 'Franz Mesmer is here in France, I've heard. Perhaps we could even sway him to our cause. He is the most liberal-minded of Brothers, so I understand.'

D'Éon shakes her head, her grey ringlets brushing her shoulders. 'He is liberal-minded, but I do not trust any Brother of the Order. Not now. The magisters of London are beginning to interfere in America. They never would have done such a thing ten years ago. This business in Naples has emboldened them – the more they see magic used for political ends, the more they convince themselves to abandon their own principles of secrecy and caution. But their core principle, the preservation of their own power, that they will never abandon.'

'We could steal the spell from him,' the Princesse de Lamballe says quietly. 'I would be willing to try.'

Lamballe sits in her chair as though it were a stool. Unloved, undemanding of love, her face shining.

It doesn't matter at all if Antoinette doesn't love her. Love is an action, isn't it? And if Antoinette acts as though she loves her, it will be no different than as if she truly did. She has very nearly convinced herself of this.

'My darling, it is too dangerous,' Antoinette says. 'Mesmer is new here, and on his guard now.'

'The Queen of Naples offered us nothing?'

Antoinette sighs. 'She will not give it to us. I know she has it.'

'Then perhaps we should take it from her,' Saint-Georges says, stepping away from the window. 'They will not expect us to strike in Naples. There are so few rogues who've escaped the Order's hunters there. No one left but confused old women and cheap charlatans.'

'No,' Antoinette says uncertainly. 'We would start a war.'

'Several wars have already started around us, it would seem,' Polignac says gently.

Antoinette thinks. 'I have my portrait in Naples, and I am listening. I hear things – snatches of conversation. It is only a matter of time before there is some discussion of the loaves-and-fishes spell, and the moment there is, I will write to Lafayette, and he can feed and clothe his men.'

'Mmm,' d'Éon says. 'It may be too late by then.'

'In the interests of France and in the interest of rogue magisters everywhere, we need to keep those soldiers alive to fight on,' says Saint-Georges. 'It was you, Your Majesty, who gave the marquis the means to go to America, gave him a glimpse of magic that fed his curiosity, and now he—'

'I know,' Antoinette snaps. Polignac looks at her warningly, and Lamballe anxiously.

She breathes, puts a hand on her belly. 'I am sorry. I am dyspeptic – the pregnancy.'

Saint-Georges bows his head. 'The fault was mine, Your Majesty. I do not like waiting and doing nothing.'

The interests of France. After the Battle of Saratoga, when the Americans showed they might be able to win against Britain, Louis was finally induced to sign treaties of agreement with the rebels. Britain had little choice after that but to declare war. But there have been no battles between the two countries; the war remains on American soil, for now.

But at sea, there are ships of both nations, circling, waiting for the order to attack.

She lifts her chin. 'I don't like doing nothing either. I will talk to Philippe. I'm not sure what to do about the fishmongers, but he's an officer of the navy, and there I think we may be able to work together.'

Antoinette meets Philippe d'Orléans alone in her private cabinet room. There are a few mirrors on the walls to prevent magical eavesdropping, and the doors are thick. Even so, neither one of them wants to speak of magic first. They exchange pleasantries and look uncomfortably at each other; Antoinette rearranges her hands several times.

Philippe is seated on a proper chair, his right as a prince of the blood.

At last she says, 'You should know that I have founded a little society of magisters. The Queen's Circle, we call ourselves.'

The word *magisters* hangs in the air, and he slowly nods. 'At the Petit Trianon.'

'Good heavens. If they're that obvious to you, I should take better care, or the Order will be at our doors.'

'Indeed, Your Majesty.'

Antoinette smiles at Philippe in a way she hopes is disarming. 'I learned magic when I was very young. D'Éon tells me the same was true for you.'

He looks at her warily. 'I was fifteen. My father sent me to a courtesan. Rosalie Duthé. You might have heard of her.'

Duthé had affairs with half the men in Versailles. Antoinette merely raises an eyebrow.

'She, too, was very young,' Philippe continues. 'Pimped out by an aunt. She'd been expelled from a convent for practising magic; I don't know where she first learned it.

Anyway, she taught me.' He leans forward, his elbows on his knees. He's wearing a coat of naval blue with gold lapels, over scarlet breeches. 'For all the good it's done me, or any of us.'

'I've heard that you are sailing out soon to help keep French waters safe, and I thank you.'

'Safe,' he says dismissively. 'The British will make short work of us, just as they're making short work of the Americans. The rebels starve and freeze, and we bob on the waves. We simply don't have enough ships.'

She pauses. D'Éon says they need him. And her friends deserve some sort of victory, some consolation for her failure to obtain the loaves-and-fishes spell. Antoinette has heard many conversations, through the painting she sent to her sister. Most of them are tedious: road repairs and taxes. What Antoinette hoped to hear – the loaves-and-fishes spell, or orders to act against rogues in Paris – she has not. But there are a few that might serve better purposes. At last she says, 'I cannot offer you ships, but I can offer you information.'

He raises an eyebrow.

'What if I told you that the British will have thirty ships of the line approximately one hundred miles west of the island of Ushant at noon on the twenty-third of July?'

He gapes. 'You're sure?'

'I trust the information. But you must promise me, Philippe, not to make it look as though you knew this in advance. Don't ambush them.'

He leans back, looks as though he would whistle. 'Well, I can't do anything about it anyway. Not unless I were made an admiral.'

'An admiral!' She shows her surprise, and he scowls. 'But you're already a lieutenant-general, Philippe. To be made an admiral so soon—'

'The King could see it done. If he chose.'

'Ah.' What confidence he has! What must it be like to be so certain that one is equipped to lead, to rule! 'Philippe, I can't ask the King to make his cousin an admiral, particularly when that cousin has very little military experience. You do see that I can't do that?'

He gives her a nasty smile. 'I see. Of course. I had to ask. I'll go off to sea, with my little squadron and your information, and hope for the best. Your Majesty.'

He nods, and she stands to let him know their audience is over. 'We are working together, Philippe. We are on the same side.'

He takes her hand, and performs the proper motions of affection.

CHAPTER THIRTY-THREE

Summer at Portici — John Acton Arrives in Naples —
A Gift from Joseph — Rogue Attacks — Shipbuilding

In the summer of 1778, the palace of Portici no longer contains the spectacle of poor Filippo, mocked by the people sworn to serve him. The children love the palace. It is right on the slopes of Vesuvius, near the ruins of Herculaneum and Hamilton's villa, and the breezes are good.

A blight threatened the grape harvest for the second year in a row, but then Charlotte had an idea, and went rifling through her notebooks. A few years ago, Antoinette sent her a spell she devised to make vines and clinging plants grow more quickly. Charlotte could almost hear her voice in the letter, laughing at the fact that so many of her spells prove useless to her, wondering whether this one might be of use to Charlotte?

Antoinette does not send her spells any more.

Soliman sends letters full of philosophy, expounding on the lessons to be learned from the Mughal emperors Jahangir and Aurangzeb, or from Peter III of Russia. She reads his letters carefully, happily. There's something comforting in their abstraction.

And Leopold, the long-suffering dear, sends her John Acton

to build her a navy. He was born in France to a wandering Englishman, and he followed an equally wandering uncle into the Tuscan naval service, where he distinguished himself in an otherwise disastrous Spanish campaign against Algeria.

Charlotte meets Acton in her study at Portici. He looks very English: slightly pink, and more than slightly smug. He takes her hand, looking uncomfortable.

'I understand you are the reason Spain got away from its latest adventure with any men left alive,' she says.

He bows his head. 'I would not say that.'

'But is it true?' she snaps. 'I want a plain speaker for this job, General Acton. I have quite enough people who will tell me what they think I want to hear.'

He swallows. 'Your Majesty, it is true in the sense that I made one or two decisions which proved to have been the right ones. But I was not the only one on our side who made quick decisions that day, so I don't think it's right that I take the credit.'

'Hmm.' She walks around him, appraising, while he stares straight forward, military. 'Our side. Our side. Do you think, then, that Tuscany and Naples and Spain all form a single side, so to speak?'

'I think that Your Majesty's brother is Grand Duke of Tuscany, and that Your Majesty's father-in-law is the King of Spain.'

'That is not an answer.' She stops her inspection. He's a man like any other: tall, a bit narrow in the shoulders in his dark-blue soldier's coat. 'I am, foremost, the Queen of Naples. Any man who works for me works only for me. I expect total loyalty and total silence. That includes any members of my family, here or in other countries. No other members of the Council of Naples. No one at all, here at court or elsewhere. Is that plain?'

'Plain indeed, Your Majesty. I am not a man who enjoys life at court, and I should be happiest left to my own devices, out with the workmen, overseeing the job.'

'Left to your own devices.'

He nods. 'Tell me how many ships are required, and how much money I can spend, and how much time I have to do it in, and Your Majesty will hear no more of me until they are built.'

She smiles. 'Perhaps I will like you, John Acton.'

For her twenty-sixth birthday in August 1778, Joseph sends Charlotte a mahogany desk with a great wheel mounted on top of it, like a paddlewheel, twice the height of the desk itself. Each of the dozen paddles of the wheel is a little desktop that can tilt to any angle she likes. Charlotte can have a different set of papers or a different book open on each, and when she wants to switch from one task to another, she merely spins the wheel. An inkstand sits on the desk proper, below the moving parts.

'A piece of furniture to match your mind,' Joseph writes. 'Keep it oiled. I will visit when I can.'

She finds the desk a great help with the work of the Council. Charlotte often works by candlelight in the small hours, pregnant again, with Francesco fussing at her breast; she did not allow a wet-nurse this time. For a year, she's had breast milk to use in her sacrifices.

In the palace of Caserta, her library is coming along nicely. She uses one of its rooms as her study. Here she has hung the portrait of her sister; here she installed the great desk.

One night, with Francesco dozing fitfully in her lap, she finds herself staring at a document, the words mere shapes on the page. Reports from the bishops, about the current state of things as regards the Crown's relationship with the Holy See in Rome. Charlotte will need to know all of this. She is eager to separate religion and the state into their own spheres. Montesquieu's books are adamant on the point, and her own mother has demonstrated over and over the dangers of state religion, with her costly schemes to move Protestants around the empire, her persecutions of the Jews, her narrow-minded fears of enlightened philosophy. But Charlotte is walking on a knife's edge, after bringing the Inquisition to an end. There are pamphlets about her, grumblings that come to her ears through Caterina and Ferdinand. So many people are still in the grip of supersitition. How can a nation reach Enlightenment if its people refuse to question?

Meanwhile, Lunardi is convinced a rogue is behind the broken wheel that sent his carriage flying off the road the other day and could have killed him. And maybe he's right. The rogues of this city, those who have survived with their memories intact, must know the stories of the shadowy Order that forces them to hide. Is it so surprising that some rogues have learned the names of the Brothers of Naples, and are seeking revenge? It is a constant danger. They wouldn't even need to use magic. A knife in the ribs can kill a magister as easily as it would any man.

The words swim on Charlotte's page and her eyes fill with tears for no reason she can understand. They are sore from too much reading and too little sleep.

She looks up at the portrait of Antoinette. 'I can't do this,' she whispers, not sure what 'this' is. 'Nobody wants me to do this. And I'm so tired. I could retire to a country estate. Hell, I could even go to a nunnery.'

She reaches out with her right hand, the hand not cradling Francesco, and gives the wheel a violent spin. Papers fly off: reports of the Council; the spell to keep powder dry, which hasn't accepted her sacrifices yet; a letter she's ciphering. Everything scatters.

'I need you to tell me it's worthwhile, or isn't,' she tells the portrait. 'I could always tell, just by looking at you, when I was in the wrong. When I was trying to prove my cleverness, or have my revenge, instead of doing what was right. I need you and a letter won't do. I need to hear your voice.'

The baby screws up his face and wails, and Charlotte grits her teeth and blinks away her tears. She can't travel with the baby, doesn't dare leave the children behind, in the care of others. And the French King and his wife never leave France. The portrait stares, silent.

A summer night, and the King and Queen hold one of their parties, under strings of Chinese lanterns. As it has for months, the volcano emits a constant, narrow pillar of pale smoke, like a snuffed candle.

The courtiers stream through the corridors. In the dining room, chairs line the damask walls, and a table in the middle groans under mounds of food. Charlotte glides through a little crowd of genuflectors and hem-pluckers. The more piggish courtiers are already seated, their plates on their laps, heaped with macaroni and roast pork and meat pies.

Ferdinand is at the far end of the room, desperately embracing some wench, so Charlotte aims for a chair at the near end. It's cooler here, by the door. Everyone swirls around her, not around Ferdinand. She watches them eddy, watches them watch her.

A footman comes to her elbow before she sits.

'Madam, the Englishman is here,' he whispers. 'He wants a word, in private.'

'William Hamilton, you mean?' She feels befuddled by the wine and the heat, and the wearing of the mask.

He shakes his head. 'The general, from Tuscany.'

She claps her hands. Acton. Her navy.

'All right,' she says, and hands the man her plate. She isn't hungry, anyway. She feels as though she is liable to vomit – it could be the heat, the smoke of the torches, the noise.

The footman offers to bring Acton to the coffee room adjacent to the dining room, where the white-coated servants are readying their bottles of liqueurs, but Charlotte does not want him to get the idea he can come to her parties unbidden; nor does she want the guests gawking. She walks, sweating, to her study.

The Englishman, Acton, does not look as if he feels the

heat. He lounges in her study, leaning against a wall and somehow managing not to look at himself in any of the mirrors.

Her study is the same, or nearly the same, in every one of her palaces. Wherever the Queen goes, the portrait of her sister goes with her. Every study must have mirrors on the walls, always.

'Your Majesty,' he says, so primly that it's practically insolent.

She's warm, flushed, and he probably assumes she's drunk. Or perhaps he is still getting used to the idea that the Queen is the power in Naples. The only power. The Brothers listen to her. And the Council, too, and bit by bit the Council shows itself more interested in governing. She wears her white gloves (a new set) in every meeting, which helps. She has persuaded them to listen to her ideas about prison reform. They are starting to understand that it is in the state's interest to feed and clothe all the prisoners, not only those whose families can pay the bribes. When they come out, the poor prisoners will no longer wear old smallpox-infested clothing. And they'll be strong enough to work.

She has learned to appeal to their cupidity. But she needs more than sound arguments and white gloves. She needs guns and ships.

'Acton, you told me I would not see you again until the work was done. But it's only been a few weeks. Surely you're not a magician?' She means it to be a joke, but is relieved when nothing shows on his face but a kind of grim resolve.

'There is very little good timber to be had anywhere,' he says. 'From Milan to Palermo, wherever I send a man to enquire, he finds that all the good oak has been bought, and what remains is only available at an exorbitant cost.'

She narrows her eyes. 'I took a carriage to Caserta last month and saw plenty of trees on my way.'

'There are very few big oaks and pines left – so much timber comes from the Americas, and the war there has slowed everything down. And, of course, now that the British and French fleets are engaging in European waters, there will be damage to repair, new ships to build, so I can't imagine the prices will go down.'

'The British and French fleets have engaged? Where? When?'

'Last month, Madame. I've just had the full reports. It seems the French surprised the British in the English Channel. Madame, what I will need, to be plain, is more money. Or to build fewer ships.'

She peers at him. So dour. Keeping his own counsel.

Leopold said she could trust him. *Acton hates parties and gossip*, he said, and Charlotte took that to mean: he won't talk. But now she sees herself as he must see her, flushed and silly, and, even at twenty-six years old, very young. If he hates parties and gossip, he hates her ridiculous court. He can't see the use of it.

'You'll have your money,' she says. 'You'll have whatever I can give you.'

Charlotte catches a glimpse of her reflection in the great golden-framed mirrors. Her face is beetle-browed, suspicious, and tending (she can never quite forget) to a double chin.

She turns away from the image, towards the more comforting image of her sister's portrait, which smiles down at her.

CHAPTER THIRTY-FOUR

The Tortoiseshell Comb — Where Emotions Live in the Body — Philippe Returns from Battle — The Hall of Mirrors — The Problem of Love Spells

———— ⊰⊱ ————

Monsieur Léonard Autié – the original – steps back, his favourite tortoiseshell comb in his hand, and pauses.

'What is it?' Antoinette asks, her voice sharper than she intends. She is tired; she has a headache.

'Madame, may I suggest an alternative to pulling your hair out by the roots?'

Her arms go cold with gooseflesh; his face swims in her mirror. 'It has been falling out again, has it?'

The hairdresser walks around to the side of her dressing table, to face her.

There are ushers at the door, and Madame de Noailles and another lady are sitting on stools in the corner, chatting and watching the coiffeur.

Monsieur Léonard cocks his head, and whispers. 'Your Majesty, if you require hair for magic, I can cut some off, if it must be.'

She swallows, uncertain. He could be a spy.

'I told you years ago, Madame, I am a magician. I know all about it.'

'But I didn't think you were serious!'

'I am always serious.' He smiles, his mouth curling up around his sharp nose. 'Anyway, the *pouf sentimental* is so common now. It is overdone. I suggest a simpler fashion, with short hairs, curled charmingly around the face, tied with a ribbon. Young and fresh.'

Somehow, a hairdresser telling her she'll look young and fresh makes her feel very much the opposite. 'Monsieur Léonard, I don't understand. You are . . . not a member of a magical order, by any chance? Forgive my ignorance.'

'Your Majesty has no ignorance to forgive. Certainly, I am not a member of any order.'

'Then how . . .?'

'I found a comb, as I believe I once mentioned. It seemed quite clear to me that there was something magical about it. I was content with my good fortune, but my brother was consumed with curiosity about how such a thing could be. He spoke with every alchemist and conjurer in the alleys of Paris, asked if they too had magic objects, and he traded and haggled for whatever he could find, until at last we had a little store of things with unusual properties. One day, a man came looking for us, to buy something from our collection, and what he traded for it was not an object but a spell.'

She's astonished. She remembers Countess Ertag, her careful collection of spells. How many enchanted objects did she have? The Order must have taken them when they killed her. But the Order didn't know about the embroidered book; perhaps it missed other things too. All these centuries, the Order has not quite succeeded in stamping out rogue magic. There must be so many magical items out in the world to be found, in attics and storerooms, their uses perhaps forgotten, secrets taken to the grave by their owners.

The hairdresser says, quite proudly, 'My brother and I have seven spells now, altogether. He bought the last one from His Serene Highness, he says, and that was what made me suspect that Your Majesty's hair was – have I overstepped?'

His Serene Highness. Philippe d'Orléans knew that at least one Léonard brother was a rogue magister and didn't see fit to tell her?

'No, you were quite right to speak, Monsieur Léonard, but you must say nothing to anyone, not about me and not about Philippe d'Orléans either. And you must not assume that I know everything he knows. He doesn't like me.'

Monsieur Léonard tucks his comb into his breast pocket and folds his arms across his chest. 'Your Majesty, any Queen of France would find the same. The Orléans family was founded by the brother of the Sun King. How much resentment that man must have had!'

'You think such feelings are passed down in the blood?' She smiles, a little. Monsieur Léonard's theories are always amusing.

He gives a small shrug. 'Emotions live somewhere in the body. They must, or the hair powder would have no effect.'

She should not be surprised, but she is. Her pots of enchanted hair powder are right there on the dressing table, the alteration of the flour spell to induce emotions for anyone who gets close enough. Has he known all this time what they do?

'Siblings have such strong feelings,' says Monsieur Léonard sadly. 'My own brother is a trial to me – he was a libertine and a thief before I taught him how to arrange hair. But I love Jean-François all the same.'

For so many years, Antoinette felt alone with her secret, sharing it only with d'Éon and Charlotte by letter. Now, it seems, there have been magisters around her for years, and she simply didn't know it. And, as the Order's power fails, there will be more and more.

On a Sunday in the Hall of Mirrors, Antoinette prepares to congratulate Philippe d'Orléans. He's been back in Versailles for a few days, and brought news to the King of a victory they are calling the Battle of Ushant. After a few days dancing around each other, the French engaged some English ships, and though there were losses on both sides, the French forced the English to scurry away. Philippe has been the talk of the town.

But when he comes into the hall, there are titters, and he goes red in the face. Oh God, Antoinette thinks. Can he have got himself into another scandal with some woman? His poor wife.

Philippe takes Antoinette's hand and bows. There are people all around, so she can't ask what she wants to ask. And she wishes she could make people stop laughing at him. Whatever he's done. So she steers the conversation to his military success.

'I was so pleased to hear of your bravery, cousin,' she says.

His frown deepens and he goes redder than ever, and someone guffaws. 'You have not heard, I take it, Your Majesty, or you have, and you mock me.'

'Heard? Heard what?'

'The English fleet was vulnerable, and the admiral ordered a full French attack to finish them off. But the signals' – there's a general roar of giggling – 'the signals were unclear. What I saw, and what the admiral conveyed, were two different things.'

He looks at her significantly, and she understands: there must have been a Brother of the Order on the French ship, using magic to confuse the signals.

'And so,' says Louis, beside her, 'the English got away, when they might have been destroyed. These things happen, Philippe. There will be another chance. And we did make them run.'

Louis, who has been trained to be king, looks out at the hall full of people, many of whom are there to have their exchange of a few words with the royal family: soldiers, visitors, country cousins. Antoinette follows his gaze and sees Axel von Fersen, looking at her.

And for the first time in their lives, they speak to each

other in the sight of others, and Antoinette can't think of what to say, so she says, 'Oh, look, it's an old acquaintance!'

Philippe fades away, having done his duty, and Antoinette is left looking at Fersen's face in the sunlight, in the daylight, in full view of everyone. Louis turns to say a few words to a group of sailors, and Antoinette takes a few steps away from him.

Fersen congratulates her on her pregnancy – now known across Europe, and starting to become evident in her choice of corsetry – and she invites him to her card parties.

And then, for three weeks in a row, he sends his regrets, his excuses, and stays away.

At last, she sends him an enciphered note saying that if he wishes to see what her protégés have done, he will dine with her at the Petit Trianon in three days' time.

In the little mirrored room there, she shows him every tiny jar of enchanted flour, her latest variations. He politely lifts the lid on each, as though attempting to see or smell the difference between approval and suspicion, ambition and satisfaction.

'It's a brilliant idea,' he says. 'You discovered the proofs yourself?'

'Yes, after tears and blood, literally,' she replies, and the lamp seems to flicker along with her laughter. 'The trouble is, it's hard to do in any quantities, because the sacrifices don't go far. But with a half-dozen of us, we have been making progress.'

He glances over all the labels. 'I don't see love here,' he says mischievously.

'No, alas. I've never been able to find a love spell.' She rushes onward, so she won't blush. 'What time is it, I wonder?'

'Nearly midnight, I should think. Tomorrow I'm expected in Rouen.'

'Ah. You come and go so quickly.'

He says softly, 'No matter where I go, I will write, and

send whatever help I can to you, whenever I can, so long as I'm alive.'

'And what will the King of Sweden say about your allegiance to France, Count von Fersen?'

'I owe no loyalty to the Queen of France. But I swear to you that, to my last breath, I will be loyal to Marie Antoinette.'

She can feel the blood heat her cheeks. 'Why?' she whispers.

'One reason is that I have been following all the news about you, since the night we met. To make sure you were not an enemy. I've been putting together a little story in my mind of the sort of person you must be, from these things that anyone could read, and from what Geneviève would tell me. I almost convinced myself I knew you, even before I ever came to Versailles. It was a fool's dream, perhaps.'

'And what sort of story did you tell?'

'Two years ago, you adopted a peasant boy to raise as though he were your own son. Armand, is that what you call him?'

She glances down. 'Yes.'

'There. You see? That's part of the story. You care about people,' Fersen says.

She snorts a little laugh. She hasn't visited Armand in over a week; she's been busy. Remiss.

'You think too much of me, sir. The ugly truth is, I want the people to love me. I need them to love me.'

'Your interests are their interests. That's true of all kings and queens, but most monarchs don't have the . . . what? The imagination? The compassion? . . . to realize it.' His voice drops, even though they are alone. 'To use magic for the good of all.'

'You said that was one reason for your loyalty. What are the others?'

'I think I should keep those to myself.'

She watches the corner of his lovely mouth, just there, where it always dimples as though he is about to smile.

'What a pity you're immune to magic,' she whispers. 'I should like to read your thoughts, if I had such a spell.'

He swallows, and now it is his turn to blush. 'For my part, I am very glad you can't.'

'Count von Fersen,' she says, 'have you ever seen the sun rise at Versailles?'

The path of white stones leads them through the dark night. At some point, Antoinette's enchanted shoe catches on something and Fersen takes her hand. She laces her fingers between his; neither of them are wearing gloves. She didn't even take a shawl. It's a little cold but they are walking fast.

'Once the sun rises, you'll see what I have to work with. I'm going to clear away these paths and flowerbeds and put an English garden in here,' she says. 'Something more natural.'

'I have seen beautiful gardens in England,' he says.

They walk silently for a while, and she can't think of anything but his hand in hers, the way he brushes his thumb against hers, so lightly. They've crossed it now, the barrier between what she is allowed to do and what she must not. They've stepped over it as though it were a mere crack in a marble floor. She opens her mouth as if to speak and instead exhales, just once, and her ribs shudder within the stays beneath her gown.

'Will you tell me something?' she asks.

'Anything.'

'A memory. Tell me which memory you will never sacrifice, no matter what spell requires it.'

He shakes his head, and stops walking. They're nearly at the end of the garden here. It's too dark to see more than the outline of the grassy berm that marks the edge of the flowerbeds and, beyond it, still blanketed in darkness, a meadow where the palace sheep graze.

'I'm sorry,' she whispers. 'I shouldn't have asked.'

His mouth twists. 'Once, I nearly sacrificed my memory of the night I met you.'

She can't breathe.

'I keep a diary,' he says, apologetically, although she can't tell if he's ashamed of having nearly done it, or of preventing himself. 'I would have known what happened. That night. But I wouldn't have been able to remember what you said, or how you looked, or what I was thinking.'

'And what were you thinking?'

A slow smile transforms his face, and his eyebrow quirks.

'I've told you enough already. You tell me. What were you thinking?'

She cocks her head. 'I could see your mouth, below your mask. I remember thinking that whoever had the honour of kissing that mouth would be a very fortunate person.'

And now he laughs, throwing his head back, and there is no one to hear him laugh but her and the nightingales.

'You're mocking me.'

'I'm not! Look, I'll prove it to you.'

She steps closer to him and closes her eyes. His lips part against hers and she stands on tiptoe and presses her body against his. She unbuttons his coat and pulls it off, and pulls his shirt up so she can run her hands against his skin.

'You aren't wearing your uniform,' she says into the hollow of his ear. 'I'd like to see a Swedish uniform.'

'I'll wear it the next time,' he says.

'You have made me a promise.'

As if in response, he puts his hands to the hook between her swollen breasts that holds her *robe à la polonaise* together. 'I have made you all the promises.'

Her robe falls to the grass, and they press against each other as he unties her stays at the small of her back. She lets her petticoat float down as they walk farther into the meadow. It's so dark here, away from the lights of the palace. If anyone were to see her walking in her white chemise, and Fersen in his white shirt, they would think the figures were ghosts.

He pulls her down into the long grass. They have no cause

to worry, she thinks with some distant part of her mind: she is already pregnant.

She pulls him against her, and gives herself over to slow kisses. Louis always stops the kisses at some point, as if afraid of what will happen if they continue, but Fersen does not stop. By the time he presses himself between her thighs she wants him, pulls him towards her – and then, for just a moment, flinches, because this part, she thinks, will be familiar: there will be a small shock of pain, then discomfort, then a few minutes of gentle labour.

Instead it is quite different.

'Let's make an agreement,' she says, as the sky lightens and she traces a pattern on his chest. 'This memory. Tonight. This. Neither one of us will ever sacrifice it. It is sacred. No matter what.'

'No matter what,' Fersen says, and takes her fingers in his hand and brings them to his mouth. 'This is sacred. I promise.'

She is a traitor. An adulteress. Everything the libel pamphlets say, about the *l'Autrichienne* and her revels at the Petit Trianon – all true.

'I'll build a temple here, to remind us, and I'll worship you here every day,' she says, and then her voice cracks, taking her by surprise. She can't cry. She'll look blotchy if she cries.

'I love you madly,' he says. 'You need build me no temples.'

'It's for me, not for you.'

At that he laughs. For a long while, they say nothing, and Antoinette lies as still as she can, eternal in an eternal world.

'When I learned about magic,' Fersen says hoarsely, breaking the silence, 'when the Brothers of Stockholm made me one of them, I thought that I knew what my life's purpose was. And then, as the months passed and I felt more and more sick about their entire project, I felt alone. As though I were broken, because I could not be what they wanted me to be. What I wanted me to be. I sought out other rogues because I wanted so badly to be a part of something. I found a few people who wanted to change things, but I found many more who wanted nothing but to live their lives in ease and die in luxury. It took a long time for me to find Geneviève and the others who had more desire than fear, who cared about justice and progress and truth. But I still felt like a wanderer, like someone without a home or a creed. Until now.' He traces her eyebrow. 'You may build all the temples you like, but I have found mine.'

She kisses him deeply and wraps her arms around him. Holds him to her.

'I must go, very soon,' he whispers in her ear. 'But I will come back.'

'You must write to me.'

'What shall our keyword be? For the cipher?'

She thinks for a moment. He said that this night would be sacred.

'*Sacré*,' she says.

He does not kiss her; he nods, gazing into her eyes until she can't bear it and looks away.

CHAPTER THIRTY-FIVE

The Queen Needs Air — No Less Dear to Me —
Charlotte Is Desperate — Tiny Fingernails

In the middle of December, Antoinette gets her labour pains. In the middle of the night, Lamballe goes from room to room, informing everyone who has a right to know; the list is long. She sends messengers to the Palace of Saint-Cloud to tell Philippe, who has a right to be present, as a prince of the blood. Louis's siblings, the aunts. All of them crowd into the Grand Bedchamber. Beyond the walls, as the sun comes up, Antoinette can hear the hum of onlookers who have not been invited, but who crowd into the Hall of Mirrors none-theless. This place is their place; the Sun King deemed it so.

She is not required to lie in the enormous golden bed, thank God, but in a little one covered in white linen, linen that is soon soaked with blood. Louis arranges the tapestry screens himself so that all his family members in the room are at least not peering at his wife, although by this point, Antoinette would not care if they were. Her body is splitting apart and when they announce the birth, she is glad that at last she can die, she can rest, she can go away. She's shiv-ering and in so much pain.

When she wakes, they tell her that she fainted. The room

is freezing – to help revive her, someone opened the windows to the December air – and at last they bring her the baby. Her little Marie-Therèse Charlotte. She cradles her close and says, 'Poor little girl, you were not what was desired, but you are no less dear to me on that account. A son would have belonged to the state. You shall be mine.'

In the middle of December, Charlotte's son Carlo gets a fever. He's nearly four, and his limbs are so long now, the arms and legs of a child, not an infant. Charlotte remembers her first glimpse of his tiny fingernails, how she felt, as she feels with every birth: the marvel of a new person in the world who is of her and yet his own. And yet, God's. She spends hours watching him and cooling his face with cloths dipped in water while the doctors bleed him and tut. She wets his tiny lips, so pale and cracked.

'But it is not smallpox,' Charlotte says as she stands in the shadows with Caterina, just far enough from the bed that Carlo will not hear their whispers. 'It's malaria, they think. If we can only break the fever. Keep some water in him. For God's sake, Caterina, Antoinette rearranged her shoulder bones. There must be some way we can bring the boy's fever down. I refuse to believe that a simple fever is more powerful than the Order and all its magisters.'

Carlo moans, a small, pitiful sound.

'There is nothing in the *Reconditus*,' Caterina says. 'Nothing that would save him.'

'But there are new spells all the time,' Charlotte says, clenching her fists. 'Soliman invents them by accident. Write to him. Bring him here.'

'It will take a week for him to arrive, Your Majesty, and by then—'

She shakes her head, looking at her child. 'I would sacrifice anything. Do you hear me? Anything it takes. Write to Soliman. Write to every chapter in Europe. Find me a spell, no matter the cost.'

Charlotte sits, enclosing her little boy's small limp hand in her own, while Ferdinand sits on the far side and sings to the boy a little. Soon Ferdinand too is silent. And they sit in a room with nothing but the shuddering, terrible breathing of two parents' lungs, as Carlo is gone from them forever, his small body cooling at last.

CHAPTER THIRTY-SIX

*Lafayette Returns – Antoinette Has Measles – A Visit
from the King – A Conversation Overheard – Philippe
Goes to Italy*

———— ⚜ ————

Lafayette returns in February 1779, a man of twenty-one now. For eight days, Louis keeps him under house arrest as punishment for leaving the country like a fugitive, but on the ninth he invites Lafayette to go hunting, and, from then on, the young marquis is the toast of Versailles. He wears the uniform of a major general of the Continental Army.

Antoinette thought he might limp – she's heard the stories of his boot filling with blood at Philadelphia – but he doesn't seem to bear any marks of his time at war, or none that she can see.

The young marquis returns to a wife still grieving the loss of their first child. It is a pain Antoinette cannot imagine, though she tries, knowing what her sister has been through. For three weeks at the beginning of 1779, Antoinette didn't hear Charlotte's voice at all. She was doing no business, or at least none in her study where the portrait hangs. When Antoinette wrote her condolences to Charlotte on the death of poor Carlo, she received a very short letter in response.

Lafayette hasn't been able to convince George Washington

to attack Quebec and return it to French control – Louis receives this news with composure that borders on open relief. The King listens to Lafayette's pleas for a fighting force to turn the tide of the war. The King, as he is wont to do, considers them at length.

An easy victory for England would clear the way for the Order to assert its dominance outside Europe, and increase its power everywhere. There isn't much Antoinette and her circle of magisters can do to affect the outcome of battles across the sea, but they can make sure Lafayette doesn't return empty-handed. So Polignac and Lamballe get to work, using whatever persuasive magic they have to maintain enthusiasm for the war effort at Versailles. D'Éon sends intelligence about British plans, garnered through magical means, to Philippe, who gets it to the proper people. Saint-Georges and Lafayette spend long hours together, discussing military uses for magic.

Antoinette comes down with the measles.

She goes to the Petit Trianon to be away from the rest of the court, and particularly the baby. After the first few days, her fever and sore throat pass, and she misses her blue-eyed darling painfully, but she can't return to the court.

For three weeks, she lives away from people. Her mornings are quiet affairs, with only Madame Campan to help her dress, and in the afternoons she often sits and listens to the sounds of the birds, the distant calls of workmen, the crackle of evening fires.

And then she gets bored.

She invites her friends – only those who have had measles before – to the Petit Trianon to play cards. She includes her brother-in-law, the Comte d'Artois, whom she refuses to shun, despite a recent outbreak of obscene poems about the two of them in Paris. The very idea.

She makes sure to invite the Princesse de Lamballe, as though she were still her favourite. And indeed, Lamballe is as important to Antoinette's affairs as she's ever been. At

Antoinette's suggestion, Lamballe has become a member of the Freemasons, joining the Adoption Lodge of Saint-Jean de la Candeur to make connections – discreet connections – with other rogue magisters.

One Sunday, Antoinette is surprised by a commotion in the courtyard. She opens the bedroom window to see her husband, gazing up at her, with nervous courtiers around him.

'What is it? What's wrong? Is it Mousseline?'

Her nickname for tiny Marie-Thérèse, whose cheeks are as soft as the finest muslin. Is there something wrong with the baby? But no, Louis is smiling.

'I just wanted to see you, but they say you're still infectious. I miss you.'

She smiles at him and sits on the chaise by the window and rests her chin in her hand. 'Then send everyone away, and you stay there, and I'll stay here, and we can talk.'

He tells her about war and peace, and she tells him about trying to sing with a sore throat, until they come to take him home again.

A letter from Fersen, addressed on the outside to Joséphine, his code name for her:

My heart,

The King of Sweden has granted permission for me to travel to America to join the war there. I cannot tell you when exactly, but it will be soon. Remember that I have promised to come back to you and I plan to do so. And I will see you again before I go, God willing.

I don't worry about you, because I see how you have made yourself queen. Yes, you have done it yourself. It was not your marriage or your husband's coronation, but your own determination to make yourself worthy of your people. Against an army of busybodies who wanted you gone, wanted you destroyed, you stood firm, and you are queen, truly and completely, and no one can take that from you now.

It will not be easy to have an ocean between us but the more we work, the harder we fight, the sooner we will have a world without tyrants choosing who may make sacrifices, and who may not.

Believe me your own
F.

She reads it over too many times to count, sitting outside in her courtyard. Once, she and Charlotte went bathing in a lake with Countess Ertag, as children, and she swam out too far and could not touch the ground for a moment, just a moment, before her governess took her by the arm. Antoinette feels like that now, as though the ground has disappeared from beneath her feet. She watches the sky sink into violet, the distant, dark shapes of sculptured trees against a flat horizon. The spring evenings are cool, but she stays sitting, reading Fersen's letter, until she is shaking with cold and Madame Campan comes tutting with a shawl and a cup of chocolate.

She's shaken out of her reverie by the sound of her sister's voice in her mind – and Angelo Soliman's:

Marianna is still prone to fevers, but the doctors say she is in no immediate danger.

I am glad to hear it, Your Majesty. I regret I was not able to be here in December, but there is no spell I know that could have saved your son.

Thank you, Dr Soliman. What matters is that we carry on the great work, and that we don't allow anything to interfere. It seems every letter you send me has news of some fresh rogue plot or attack.

Many rogues have taken it upon themselves to support the French and American side in the current war with Britain.

And so it falls to us to make sure they don't succeed, Dr Soliman. What are they doing, exactly?

A great deal of spycraft, in the main. They seem to have got word of where the British ships would be, giving the French the advantage at the Battle of Ushant. Rohan insists this could only have been magic, and he's vowing to squeeze the life out of every rogue in Paris until he finds the culprit.

Rohan has been seeing rogues around every corner for years now. Yes, Your Majesty.

Still, he could be right. I wonder.

Whether he's right or wrong, he scents blood.

There's a long silence.

Antoinette clutches the blankets and thinks, suddenly, of the Pandora doll, but it is in the main palace, and anyway what good would it do to give Charlotte a sore hand, all the way in Naples? Charlotte, Brother of the Order, who is currently discussing how to deal with the danger that is Antoinette?

Dr Soliman, I have not added it to the Reconditus, *but I have a spell to enchant flour, to induce certain emotions. In the factory at San Leucio, we have been enchanting bags of the stuff, to sow suspicion. If I were to offer some to the Brothers of Paris, and suggest they use it to undermine the reputations of known and influential rogues, might they consider that as an alternative to violence?*

It's worth trying, Your Majesty. Do you have enough to send some to Paris?

The voices trail off. Charlotte and Dr Soliman must have walked away from the painting.

Every year Antoinette and her husband watch the harvests in fear, because Charlotte refuses to send the loaves-and-fishes spell. And now she learns that Charlotte has so much flour to spare that she can enchant it and send it to France. To use against her. To make Antoinette's own people mistrust her even more than they already do.

Antoinette throws off the bed covers, calls for help to get dressed, to return to Versailles, to warn her friends and make a plan.

At the card tables, in the salons, everyone is soon whispering about the great insult that Marie Antoinette has given Philippe d'Orléans. It happened like this, the gossips say: Philippe asked to rejoin the fleet; the Queen wrote to Philippe in the name of the very busy King informing the duke that he must stay in Paris instead. Anyone can see that 'you are needed in Paris' is what one says to a military liability in a time of war. Philippe went to his hideaway at the Palais-Royal in a foul mood, until the King at last sent word that he should go to Italy, to amuse himself. A peace offering and a way to be rid of him.

And so Philippe's journey to Italy is explained.

His real purpose is to find the flour Charlotte has enchanted, and destroy it. It must never reach France and sow suspicion against *known and influential rogues*, as Charlotte put it. While Philippe and Antoinette were arranging things to prevent court gossip, Geneviève was writing to everyone in southern Italy who owes her a favour.

She's learned that the enchanted flour was taken away from the factory in San Leucio, and is being stored in a bakery in Naples.

All the magisters of Versailles meet in the Petit Trianon to plan the operation.

'But must we destroy the enchanted flour?' asks Jean-François Autié, the second Monsieur Léonard. He sits next to his brother in the mirror room at the Petit Trianon, and it is a strange sight to see both of them together. They have the same high foreheads, long noses and powdered curls, but there are differences, clear enough when they're sitting right next to each other.

Still, so few can tell the brothers apart that they won't be missed at Versailles. They can be in two places at once if they choose. Jean-François, who was once a thief, is perfect for this job. He'll accompany Philippe.

'Would you rather use the flour, Monsieur Léonard?' Polignac asks. 'Surely you don't want your ladies to grow suspicious of each other. It can only do harm.'

'The flour could do a great deal of good in America, fed to the other side,' Philippe says. 'But getting it there would be a feat indeed.'

'So be it, then,' Jean-François says. 'We trick the guards, we take the flour, we dump it. Where?'

'Bury it,' says Lamballe. 'Or put it in the sea.'

The Chevalière d'Éon shakes her head, her curls shivering. Like Antoinette, she has adopted the newly fashionable short hairstyle. 'If they bury it, it could affect the crops. If you scatter it in the ocean, it could affect the fish.'

'Does it matter if fish are suspicious?' says one of the Léonards.

'It matters if people eat the fish,' d'Éon snaps.

Antoinette rubs her temples.

'Presumably the people eating the fish of Naples would be the people of Naples,' Philippe says.

Saint-Georges shakes his head. 'The less of it there is in the world, the better. It's dangerous.'

It was Antoinette's spell, originally. Her little cakes. She never thought it could be used to do any more than prevent Louis's advisers from riding off too quickly on their ideological hobbyhorses. And now there is a bakery full of the stuff, and if it goes in the sea it will poison the fish, and if it goes in the ground it will poison the crops, and Philippe and Jean-François both look as though they're likely to stuff it in their own pockets. No. This is her mistake – and Charlotte's. It must be put right.

'We are not the Order,' Antoinette says, firmly. 'We are trying to protect ourselves from their magic, not use it to undermine them at the cost of harming innocent people.'

'We could burn it, I suppose,' Philippe says. 'They must have enough flour to make quite the bonfire. I could set fire to the bakery. That would send a message.'

'And possibly catch the whole neighbourhood on fire?' Antoinette says, her interlaced fingers tight. 'I want no deaths on our conscience. Just destroy it. Bury it if you must, but far from any farmland or water. Write and let me know when it is done. And be careful.'

9 July 1779
Antoinette to Charlotte

Charlotte,

Your letter arrived. How worrying that your little Marianna is still suffering so much from fevers. I pray every day that she will be healthy again soon.

You're with me here, every moment, although you may not know it.

I have enclosed a lock of my baby's hair. A small treasure for you. If you sacrifice it, I'll try to send another. You don't know this – it was too early to announce yet – but I had hoped to have another little head of curls soon. I miscarried a few days ago, after reaching up to close a carriage window. I've been afraid to tell Mama.

I have suffered other losses too, and fear to suffer more. But I don't ask for your help. I know it's useless. You have cast in your lot with murderers who act against France, against my friends, and against me.

So the gifts I can entrust to you now, Charlotte, are mundane things. A lock of hair from the little head I love best. A sacrifice to you, and to nothing else but you. No magical items and certainly no spells. I won't have my own spells used against me.

I have begged you for years to stop trying to affect matters in France, and concentrate on your own affairs.

I beg it again, not for my sake now but for yours.

I remain,

    Your sister,
    Antoinette

CHAPTER THIRTY-SEVEN

*The Party Is Too Hot – Hamilton's Monkey –
A Terrible Theft – Tunnels – Pillar of Fire – Rescue*

A party at the Palazzo Reale.

This room, like every room in this palace, like all of Naples, is too busy: the floor is all tiles of red and green, squares within squares to a dizzying horizon, where wallpaper vines come down to meet it. Old Testament patriarchs gambol overhead, pointing with wrinkled fingers to apple-breasted sinners full of regret.

It makes her dizzy.

Charlotte arranges herself against a Chinese screen, settles into her skirt and crosses her arms at the wrists. Her head is turned gracefully, just so. Ferdinand stands just behind her. Her five children – Teresa, now seven, holds the baby, Little Mimi. Luisa holds a struggling Francesco on the other side. Marianna, three years old, pale and tired from long struggles with fever of late, stands with Luisa and Francesco. It would be a perfectly even, triangular composition – like the Holy Family – if her sixth child, Carlo, were not in heaven now. Her silk gown shines in robin's-egg blue, in its folded shadows shimmering rose.

The Queen is present. This is her family, and her palace, and her kingdom, and every party is her party.

Acton approaches and bows before her – before the King, one should say. The difference in angle is slight and anyone would forgive a sailor with his sea legs still under him. She finds herself noticing Acton's arms, sleeved in a thick blue coat. She imagines the pale skin under it, the golden hairs.

Charlotte looks up, and glances to the right. Ferdinand is looking at her, his mouth mocking, triumphant. He's always said there was something between her and Acton, and he's always been wrong. Still is wrong. It was only a passing thought.

Acton is looking at her too – everyone is looking at her – but Acton does not look triumphant, not in the least. His search for masts for her ships must not be going well; he'll tell her that, the next time they are able to speak alone. The navy, that must be it; that must explain the slightly tragic expression on her Englishman's face. Hers, only in the sense that they are all hers, because she is queen. If there is emotion on his face, it isn't yearning, the way the gossips would have it. It's business.

She leans, like the tower at Pisa, all of a piece, and speaks to a footman concealed behind the screen.

'It is hot,' Charlotte murmurs. 'Bring me my fan.'

William Hamilton has acquired a monkey. He's from India, a lanky creature with dark fur and a pale mane. The first time Charlotte saw him, he bared his teeth, but she is still inclined to like him. Hamilton has deliberately trained him to act like an antiquarian, looking through lenses and examining everything he picks up. It amused his owner. The monkey also has a habit of grabbing the testicles of Hamilton's manservant as though it were a great joke, so Hamilton tends to bring the creature everywhere he goes, for the sake of not losing a good manservant.

When the guests have all been greeted, and the children run off to play under tables with Hamilton's monkey,

Charlotte goes looking for Caramanico and finds him with Hamilton himself. Caramanico nods politely while Hamilton talks excitedly about volcanic activity. She steals Caramanico away with a smile, and tells him she is sending him to England.

'As His Majesty's ambassador?'

She nods. 'As mine, yes. We need a strong relationship with Britain.'

'We, the people of Naples? Or we . . .'

'Both.'

Caramanico glances into the crowd and she follows his gaze. But Acton isn't here; he's off in Castellammare, not far from Pompeii; he wants to build a shipyard there.

'Your Majesty.' It's Caterina, at her shoulder, her face drawn.

'What is it?'

Caterina gestures for her and Caramanico to come away from the crowd, into a recess near a statue.

'The flour at the bakery near the San Gennaro gate. It's been stolen.'

'Stolen! How could it have been? Were there not protections?'

Caterina's mouth is tight. 'Protections, and disguises too. I don't think this is any ordinary theft.'

'Rogues,' Caramanico says, his hand at a dress sword that looks far too pretty to do much good.

'Our man there discovered the theft this morning, but it could have been days ago,' Caterina explains. 'We disguised it with enchantments. We made the baker forget he had flour in that room at all. Forty-eight sacks, all gone.'

Someone knew it was there. No ordinary rogues, then. Silfversparre, Lunardi, and Caramanico have worked hard to purge Naples of any rogues who might be a threat. And why would rogues care about the flour anyway? That flour wasn't even meant to be used here. It was meant to go to Paris, to help Rohan discredit the rogues there.

She feels cold, dizzy. 'We must meet tonight in the usual place,' Charlotte says. 'We will need a strategy. Tell the others. I'll say I'm tired and leave the party early.'

Caterina and Charlotte make their way underground. The familiar smell of damp rock, tallow candles, and plain wood, smoothed and darkened by time and running feet. Then, into the darkness, lit by brooches that glow with magic.

Down, down, down stone steps, and the smell of damp makes Charlotte feel as if she's about to sneeze. They take a passage she has never taken before, squeezing through a crack in the rough rock.

'A different route, I think,' Caterina says.

Charlotte stops, her hands holding her skirts. 'Why?'

'Someone knows more than I'd like about our business. Perhaps they know our usual way of traversing the tunnels too.'

'If they know that, surely they'll be waiting at the cavern.'

'That's one possibility. Silfversparre went early to check. This way, Your Majesty. Don't worry. I know these passages better than anyone.'

When did that happen? Charlotte wonders.

Through a dank passage that smells of cat urine, where a water drop falls onto her earlobe and another on the back of her hand. Then it opens up, a tall archway overhead made of dressed stone. They walk through an arcade, where she can almost imagine the denizens of this now-deserted underground city hawking oysters or measuring cloth. Only rats and ghosts live here now.

Then they come into a rougher section again, but this time the ceilings soar high above, elongated domes stretching up like Pulcinella's hat.

Charlotte's legs ache from the uneven slopes. She runs her hands over the tunnel wall, where chisels carved Greek letters long ago: the writing of slaves, perhaps, or magisters. Underground Naples has long been a place for secret doings.

Through a narrow passage and into an oblong cavern. The air is fresher here; there's a change in the quality of the darkness, too: a shaft in the cavern ceiling. Charlotte looks around, and gasps: encased in the walls of the cave are seven headless skeletons, their white bones just barely breaking through the yellow rock.

'There have been cults of the dead in Naples for a very long time,' Caterina says, lifting up a wilted paper flower lying against the cave wall. 'This close to the flaming fields, people thought they stood on the threshold of the underworld.'

Indeed, it feels warm in this room – and she is puffing a bit from the long walk. What is today, 8 August? In five days, she'll be twenty-seven years old. Too young to be puffing, but the air down here is unwholesome and she's put on a little weight, truth be told. After seven children, is it any wonder? Wait – 8 August—

Wait – she needs a moment; she needs to catch her breath, to think, to count the days.

She's late. She ought to be bleeding by now. She keeps track so carefully, to ensure she doesn't have a night with Ferdinand at unnecessary times, when it can't make her pregnant. He's back in her bed now, her respite over. And last week was the one for the General to arrive, but there has been so much to think about, with the masts and the war in America and the operations at San Leucio and the distribution of the flour and the Paris chapter needling her about her sister.

'Your Majesty?'

Wait, wait – just a goddamn second, she is trying to count the days – six days, seven beyond where she should be? The General is usually so prompt.

Another child, then. She bites her lip to keep from thinking about little Carlo, the warmth of his head against her cheek. Another child. She has sliced her heart into a million pieces, to offer to the nations of Europe one by one as offerings, the ones Death does not gobble first.

Caterina is frowning slightly. 'Your Majesty, are you well? It's a ghoulish place, I know, but quite safe. No one would think to find us here.'

She nods curtly. 'I'm quite well. Just needed a moment to rest.'

A flash of light fills the cavern.

She puts her hands before her, helplessly, leaning on the damp wall, wishing, for one futile moment, for something she doesn't have time to name.

But the flash subsides, and she is still alive. Caterina puts her hand on her arm. The cavern is much darker than it was when they walked in. Another flash, a smaller one.

'It's lightning,' says Caterina uncertainly.

Lightning. Charlotte looks up at the shaft in the cavern's ceiling. Somewhere far above, there is a storm. It rumbles around the walls of the cavern.

The ground shakes and a fine, acrid dust falls on her from the cavern ceiling, stinging her face. She puts her hand into her pocket and rummages – her hand touches a dozen items of no use to her. But this is no storm. Charlotte puts her hands to the cavern walls; they're trembling.

The cavern fills with silent red light, not a flash this time, but a new dawn.

'We have to get out,' Caterina says, taking her by the arm. Charlotte turns on her heel and they run together.

As they get further from the air shafts, the tunnels are again lit only by their brooches, flashes of gold, with a bit of green from the emerald in Caterina's. Which way? Which way? The tunnel forks, and along the left-hand fork she can see another corridor branching off again. She can't remember, can't turn herself around in her mind enough to think which way they came, what it might look like from this side. Caterina is around the corner, ahead, out of view except for the occasional flash on the walls.

She runs farther, past more branches and intersections.

A lump of rock, large enough to brain her, falls from the ceiling just one pace ahead.

She runs faster, and her foot hits a patch of wet rock and she lands, hard, on her tailbone. It takes her a moment to right herself and she can hear Caterina: 'Your Majesty, please, it isn't safe that way! Up here – there's an exit—'

Caterina takes her hand, and they run up a half-dozen uneven steps towards a crack of grey light. It's a wooden door, hanging ajar, and it takes them out to an alley, the stone walls leaning in on either side. The air is thick with grey clouds of ash. Charlotte's shoes slip on the flagstones.

'Come this way, Your Majesty, there's a—'

Caterina's voice is lost under a loud crack that shakes the whole world, and a blast of air comes out from the tunnel door behind them with a great whoosh. It knocks Charlotte to her knees. She struggles to breathe, the air thick with stinking dust.

She is pushing aside her filthy skirts so she can set her hands and push herself back to standing when the wall falls on her.

She is face down on the street, pressed down, buried alive. Her scream hurts her ribs. Every breath brings great pain, all down the side of her body. The ground stinks of damp rock, a rotten smell, like bad eggs, and this damned grit in her eyes she cannot blink away.

She'll die. So will the child who might be growing in her womb, barely larger than a thought. The only one of Charlotte's creations she has not yet unleashed on the world, the last thing to survive in Pandora's box.

Little Teresa: someone must make sure she marries properly. Leopold's boy, he would be the best. Has Charlotte discussed this with Ferdinand? She can't remember. Charlotte did not plan to die.

Her arms are pinned; she can't reach her pocket.

And the Pandora doll is not in her pocket, anyway.

What made her think of that?

It is, suddenly, horribly bright. She can hear Caterina at some distance, screaming for help.

Her eyes sting; she closes them, and prays. She does not pray to God, she finds, to her amusement, but to Antoine, the child Antoine, the beloved imp, the patron saint of impossibilities. The being who exists for Charlotte only in letters now, and in paintings.

The hand that invades her armpit and pulls, stretching her side like a broken accordion, is a man's hand, on a man's arm: pale, the hair coated in golden dust.

Coughing breaks her body, and the man is still pulling her, without regard for the fact that her legs are not budging – perhaps he thinks she is a corpse already. But she is coughing. Surely he must hear that she is coughing.

Then there's a face near her own, and he's speaking. He's speaking German, accented German.

'I can't pull you out, not without causing you even more pain. I'll have to shift some of these bricks first.'

She blinks, and swallows to stop coughing, and he seems to take it as assent because now she finds that she can see only the man's legs. Good legs, fine legs, in blue culottes.

It's Acton. Her English general. How strange that she should recognize him by his legs.

He's saying something about the volcano. The volcano will erupt – it has been smoking. He wants to get her farther away before— No.

The volcano has erupted. That is why the wall fell, why the— Why won't her brain work? The stink of it.

As a great weight rolls off her side, the pain, somehow, gets worse. She gasps.

Acton is there, his hand under her arm, his hand at her back. Slowly she rises.

'Caterina,' she coughs.

'Already safe.'

She is standing now, holding her ribs, bent but standing.

She walks a little farther into red clouds, and then she can't get another breath, and her legs weaken under her.

Someone is carrying her through the corridors of Schönbrunn Palace, and her nightdress is dragging to her knees. Not Papa – he never carried her; not Joseph either. Who is it? Who is carrying her? And where is Antoine?

For three days and nights, Vesuvius burns.

Charlotte's children tell her exitedly that they saw a pillar of fire, three times the height of the volcano itself. That must have been the red light she saw. William Hamilton climbed up onto a garden wall to watch it, with his monkey at his side and the children pointing and calling to each other. There was a rain of stones and then a storm, and the water was warm on their cheeks. They could see the smoke rolling in like a black blanket that covered the sky, and then Sir William told them to go inside, and the monkey started to dance and gibber.

Meanwhile, John Acton was riding north from Castellammare, rushing back to the palace, when he heard Caterina's screams for help for the Queen. She and Caterina had nearly made it home. All the same, it was a stroke of good luck that Acton found her. And a stroke of bad luck that she was in the tunnels when Vesuvius rumbled. Is that all it is? Luck? Her mind wants to make connections; she is having trouble trusting that anything is luck these days.

The smoke rolls like waves through the streets of Naples. For three days, there is wailing as people smash in doors, steal everything they can, fight for no reason. It's as if the smoke has poisoned their souls. Charlotte and Ferdinand, for once, agree completely on what must be done. They send out soldiers to keep the peace and clear the rubble, to find homes for the people who escaped from the slopes, whose houses are running with lava now.

They take Charlotte to Caserta, where the air is a little fresher. A story goes out that she and Caterina were walking in the palace gardens when the ground shook and the Queen fell. Acton does not ask why she was out in the streets, and says nothing to contradict the official story.

Angelo Soliman travels over the Alps again, to see her.

Charlotte receives him alone in her rooms at Caserta, propped up on a chaise longue.

She has not bled, still. But she has not mentioned to anyone, not even the physician, that she might be pregnant.

'You have seen Caterina?' she asks after he kisses her hand.

He nods. 'She is still hoarse from the pumice dust. And afraid, as everyone is afraid. It makes me wonder. We don't know where the rogues took the flour that they stole. Flour that was enchanted to sow suspicion. I wonder – I wonder if there might be something in these infernal clouds of ash that is working on our emotions as well as on our lungs.'

She's shocked. 'You think they put the flour into the volcano? Who would do such a thing? Why?'

'Rogue magisters working to disrupt our plans. Who else?'

She pauses, grasping at a last hope. 'It could have been a Rohanite faction, unhappy with the ways we have been using magic in Naples.'

Soliman shakes his head. 'I don't think so. Theft would not serve their purposes. We were going to give that flour to Rohan anyway! But we know the rogues will steal from us. They have before.'

'How would they know about the flour?'

He makes a little movement of the shoulders in agreement. 'I am not easy in my mind about that. I have been trying to determine how they stole from Mesmer's papers, how their machine worked. I haven't stopped searching for the spell of spells, the key to making any enchantment we can imagine. Although it eludes me, all my trial and error has resulted in several new spells of late. I found one that leaches the contents of a book, so that a blank book of mine filled with writing, and, in Madras, a rogue's spellbook turned blank. I had to buy it very dear. I have not spoken or written of that, or of my search for the spell of spells, to anyone but you, Your Majesty. I think perhaps your fears about concealed spies were not so far-fetched, although it amazes me, here in this room surrounded by mirrors.'

Another silence, and then she breathes in deeply, for strength. 'Dr Soliman, you told me, years ago, that magisters have difficulty with action at a distance. That is why, for example, a king cannot simply send a fireball to smite his enemies, and why we need not worry about someone listening to us from three miles away.'

He nods. 'It's true. That's one of the areas that has proven most frustrating, all down the centuries – that and the area of killing and healing. My spell with the books is interesting in that regard; it suggests there is something unique about information. But I have begun to wonder whether everything that exists can be said to be information, in a manner of speaking. And this raises interesting possibilities.'

He thinks she's asking about metaphysics but she just wants to keep herself safe. 'Could a magister enchant an object, leave it in, say, my study, and then use it to spy on our conversation? What if it were already in the room, and in plain sight, and thus the mirrors would be of no use in keeping it out?'

His face is grave. He sees her meaning. 'It's never been done, so far as I know.'

'That doesn't mean it can't be done.'

'No,' he says, frowning. 'That is the way of all science. Everything is impossible only until it is not. Some magister might have found such a spell. But he would have to be a very great magister.'

He? Charlotte thinks, and she smiles a painful smile, remembering a letter from Antoine some years before: *I think I'll try my hand at 'surprendre'*.

It did not register at the time that the French word for 'surprise' also means 'overhear'.

Charlotte paces. Her old habit; the servants at Caserta quietly replaced the green and gold Persian carpet in her study with cheap braided rugs. She must have walked the distance from Naples to Versailles many times over by now, pacing like this.

Her study is quiet. No papers on any surface of the desk. Ink in the inkwell, pounce in the powder-horn, sealing wax coiled.

On the wall, Antoinette stares down at her. Another queen. Another magister. She always had a knack for it. How good is she now?

Charlotte cocks her head and speaks to the portrait, in a whisper. 'At Christmastime, even though my own child was dying, I never stopped worrying about you, knowing that you might be in your first labour at any moment. I fretted that I'd given you bad luck, somehow. And then a few days after Christmas, the messenger came and said you were alive, the baby too. And I was so happy for you, Antoinette! Despite my grief. A girl, the messenger said, and I knew, of course, that you would name her for Mama, as we all have done so dutifully. All of us but Amalia, the only one of us with any guts.'

Her leg still hurts when she stands for any time. She paces again, back and forth, and stops again, just under the portrait. 'But then the letter came from Louis and he told me you named her Marie-Thérèse *Charlotte*. And he told me how difficult the labour was for you. That you were racked with pain, my dear heart, and bleeding and torn and near death and those French fools! They gaggled around you and watched! As if you were a pantomime. I remember' – she looks over at the floor by her desk – 'I remember that I stopped reading the letters and I lay down on the floor, just there, and I sobbed so hard that my voice was sore for days, until I barely had any throat to scream with.

'And now I wonder whether you listened to those sobs. Whether you heard them, because it is you listening, isn't it? Your portrait is listening. *You* knew about the fleet of British ships, a hundred miles west of Ushant. I don't know if you have been working against me, or if you have simply been working for your own selfish goals without considering how it might affect me. I don't care which it is. You listened, and you knew. Just as you knew what we were doing with the flour, and where to find it. You sent your friends to poison my kingdom.'

She stops, out of breath, her throat hoarse.

'I miss you so terribly. I see Leopold every year or two, and Joseph comes when he can. But oh, I am so alone, Antoine. I've wanted to talk to you.'

She looks up at the painting. 'You thought, no doubt, that no matter what you did, that I could never hate you. You were wrong. I don't think I have ever hated anyone as much as I hate you now.'

Charlotte climbs up onto the chair and grabs the gilt frame in both hands, pulling it off the wall. It's heavy and awkward but not beyond her ability to carry it under one arm.

She will take it to the kitchens, throw it on the biggest fire she can find, breathe in the sour fug of smoking pigment and varnish and gilt.

Through the corridors, ignoring the servants' proffered hands, ignoring her little Teresa, seven years old, chasing after a family of peacocks escaped from the menagerie. Ignoring the courtiers' exclamations, the tittering of the Prussian ambassador at the sight of the Queen carrying a painting through the palace.

She passes the door to the kitchen, pausing just for a moment.

Then she climbs a servants' staircase, up to the storeroom where they keep the presents nobody wants. Automata that frighten the children; unfashionable furniture; portraits of relatives unpopular or unsound.

The portrait of Marie Antoinette, Queen of France, goes against the wall.

Charlotte throws a thick black cloth over the painting.

'It's war between us now, sister.'

PART FIVE

1781 TO 1785

CHAPTER THIRTY-EIGHT

The Forgotten Days — Attacks in Paris — Death of
Maria Theresa — Duty Fulfilled — Philippe
Is Determined

Nobody knows which day it is, the day the Dauphin is born.

The words for the months and the days of the week have vanished from memory, and though people do try to guess the date, it always seems wrong. Within the palace, people started naming the days after small events to keep track of them, such as the Day of the Ladder when a workman fell to his death, or the Day of the Wineglass when one shattered in the Salon of Mars, leaving a thousand shards scattered on the parquet for the god to gaze down at. After a while, it became a sign of status to know the story behind the name of the day, or to pretend to know. The clever people compete to see who can make the most absurd or banal name stick: the Day of Onions, or the Day of the Stockings. Polignac was goaded into it by the Comte d'Artois one day and came up with the Day of the Rowlock, which somehow captured the character of that day precisely.

No one quite acknowledges that they can't remember the real dates. It's simply that the fashion for creative and hilarious names is so charming.

The *Gazette de France* and the *Mercure de France* take their dates very seriously, as do the other major newspapers across the country. Their editors have taken to consulting teams of philosophers who calculate the days according to the evidence they can find, though they disagree more often than not. Some of the smaller scandal sheets and opinion pamphlets have done away with dates altogether.

The last time anyone was sure, it was June. Around the time that the Palais-Royal burned.

The Orléans family has two main residences. Philippe's father prefers the château at Saint-Cloud, and so Philippe has the Palais-Royal for his own use. On the day of the fire, the opera house there had shown *Orphée*, by special request from Marie Antoinette, who wanted to see more people appreciate the music of her old teacher Christoph Gluck.

She had not even been there that night. But somehow, Philippe blamed her for the Order's attack, and perhaps he's right. When the actors were still in their dressing rooms, a great serpent of fire coiled around the opera house, and breathed sparks down on the houses below, like fireworks in reverse.

Philippe himself helped put out the blaze, with the help of nearby workmen and, strangely, some Franciscan monks. Their efforts saved the Louvre and God knows how much more of Paris, but they couldn't save the opera house or the dancers in their dressing rooms. They found a dozen bodies after the fire. The newspapers say that porters were carting costumes out of the wreckage and one of the men put on a purple robe and a crown; he clambered up onto a box, and demanded to be called king, and the people laughed.

There is no doubt it was the work of the Order. The Brothers have grown bolder, because there is not much point in trying to hide the evidence of magic any more, not since the war in America with all its impossibilities: disappearing cannons in Salem, a spectral hand that prevented a British officer from shooting at George Washington, the rebels' impenetrable fortress at Bull's Ferry. The Order confused the correspondence between Rochambeau and Washington, freezing the French troops on Rhode Island for a year. But the rogues have always matched the Order with better, newer magic. Antoinette sent a tiny French village made of wood across the ocean with the American John Laurens, a village that grew where it was planted into French-style bakeries and taverns, and fooled the British into thinking the French troops were going one way when in fact they were going another. Going to Yorktown, where, Antoinette knows from a certain portrait in miniature kept in a certain soldier's trunk, the Americans have just turned the tide of the war.

There is too much magic to snuff out. So the goal of the Order now is to frighten anyone who tries to see that evidence with their own eyes or think about it with their own thoughts.

Rohan and the other clergy preach against the black arts and the corruption of the elites. Mesmer, it seems, has completely broken with the Order and is curing people with magic quite openly. He brought Saint-Georges back from the brink of death after an attempted poisoning, but he wants nothing to do with the Queen's Circle. He is one of a growing number of unaligned magisters in Paris, most of whom have their own agendas, or none whatsoever.

And amid it all, the pamphlets continue, most of them coming from Jacques-Pierre Brissot, a Frenchman based in London who used to be content to accuse Marie Antoinette of debauchery. Now he accuses her of debauchery and sorcery – not in so many words, but the words grow fewer and sharper with each hideous publication.

The thing that Charlotte feared most is coming to pass. The Order is losing control of magic.

The thing that Antoinette feared most is coming to pass too. She could be cast out, condemned – a witch, a harpy, a demon. Rohan, in his cardinal's red, rails against clandestine goings-on at the Petit Trianon. He emboldens the Church against Versailles, and Versailles needs the Church very badly. It needs the Church to tolerate the tax reforms that might pull France out of utter bankruptcy.

It was the Order that lit the Palais-Royal on fire, although rogues burned St Petersburg.

It was the Order, all on its own, that caused much of humanity to forget the names of the days and months. D'Éon, who has spies everywhere, says that the Order has been trying to steal magic from all the people it has feared for so long: those in Europe who worked spells other than the Order's, and those around the world with their own ways of rear-ranging reality. They have tried to steal it from every colony, desperate for new weapons to use against their enemies. It is rumoured that they found something they didn't know how to use, a spell they thought would make everyone but them forget magic entirely. It didn't work. Instead, the wags of Versailles go about talking about the Day of the Onions.

D'Éon says the effects are fading, that people's minds, like the palace, have hidden rooms, which they will remember soon. There is no need for this day to be anything else than the day the Queen gives birth.

Antoinette bunches the bedclothes in her sweaty hands. How has Charlotte done this eight times, faced this pain and this terror? It feels entirely wrong, more like death than birth. The bands of cramps around Antoinette's lower back, and nauseating twinges in her abdomen, the sensation of her body being slowly ripped in pieces. But then she will put herself back together afterwards, as Charlotte always does.

Louis makes sure the windows are open, this time, and that the room has only a half-dozen ladies in it. Lamballe is one of them and she is so very good, staying quiet, and making sure Antoinette has what she needs for her comfort. There can be no comfort, in the moment, but when the little white bearing-bed is soaked with blood and the cries of a baby echo through Versailles, she feels tired but not ill the way she was with Marie-Thérèse.

They whisk the child away, saying nothing to her, and she waits, patiently, for Louis to come in and tell her.

He comes at last, bearing the child in his arms, and he says with the endearing formality he adopts in the face of emotion: 'Madame, you have fulfilled my wishes and those of France. You have borne a dauphin.'

He is to be named Louis-Joseph Xavier François, and his godfather is her brother Joseph. And he is to be christened by her great enemy, Louis de Rohan, Cardinal and Grand Almoner of France. His position gives him the right to perform the Mass for the royal family, and their baptisms. But there is nothing she can do about that, and he can't hurt her in public.

She has a little boy. She has done the one thing she was sent to France to do, eleven years ago. At last, she has proven she is worthy to be their queen.

Madame de Guéméné, the governess, carries the child in a cushioned basket all through Versailles and Antoinette can hear the applause, now from this direction, now more distantly from that one. Cries of 'A dauphin, a dauphin, can you believe it?' As though it's a miracle, and many will think it's been accomplished by the age-old methods of miraculous births, knowing the King's troubles in the bedroom. But she doesn't care. Let the pamphleteers say what they like about her; they will talk and talk about her, in the four corners of France and beyond, and there's nothing she can do about that now. Today all is well.

She smiles a million private smiles, while far away on a rolling sea, a ship carries news to France, news that she knows already but cannot say: the Americans won a great victory over the British at Yorktown. She knows it the way she knows, suddenly, that today is 22 October 1781. Her little portrait travels with Fersen, and hears what he hears.

France has a victory, a dauphin, a future. She closes her eyes for a moment, and thinks of the day she left Austria and came to France, how alone she felt. Her mother's constant letters, telling her not to ride, what to wear, how to speak to her husband. Her mother's dream that Antoinette would accomplish one thing with her life: seal the family alliance that will bring Europe peace.

But now she cannot write to her mother to tell her the goal is accomplished, because Maria Theresa is dead. In the autumn, Antoinette had a letter from Leopold, saying that he had visited Vienna, that Maria Theresa was heavier, breathing with difficulty when she walked any distance at all, and irascible out of embarrassment. Forgetful and confused. And then, before Antoinette had a chance to respond, they brought her the news of her mother's death.

No more letters from the Empress enquiring about her monthly courses; no more instructions from the ambassadors. Across Europe, the children of the Empress free at last. Joseph has lost no time: he's freed the Empire's serfs and declared a new edict of religious tolerance. And Charlotte?

Antoinette suspects she is the only person who understands the shapes that Charlotte's grief will take. But she does not write about such things to Charlotte now. They hardly have any need of a cipher any more. The letters are their own ciphers. Antoinette will write to tell her sister that France has a dauphin, a potential husband for one of Charlotte's daughters, perhaps. And she will receive a polite letter of congratulation and statecraft in return.

The year changes: 1782. Antoinette recovers from the birth. She appoints Polignac – the Duchesse de Polignac, now – as governess.

Perhaps it is the tightness of her corset, but the theatre feels warm. Antoinette puts a fingertip to her brow and wipes a drop of sweat, casually, as she looks around her.

The Queen takes an interest in the construction of theatres. They always make her think of cabinet houses, those little curios the Duchess of Devonshire likes so much. Or perhaps the little model village, the plaything for her Mousseline, that Antoinette enchanted and sent to America to fool the British. Missing walls that show people in their little boxes, level upon level. Façades, revelations. She recently built a little theatre of her own at the Petit Trianon, all blues and gold, grey silk and gilt carving.

This theatre – a new private one, belonging to Philippe's stepmother, Madame de Montesson – is warmer and heavier. Rich wood and rich curtains, heavy chandeliers, and cherubs on the ceiling. She smells her own rosewater perfume, weighted by warmth.

Like cabinet-house people, the people inside a theatre are all on display. Especially the audience. Especially the Queen in her box. She catches the eye of the Chevalier de Saint-Georges as he walks out to applause. No one applauds more vigorously than she does, but he glances away from her, quickly, and looks almost annoyed. He has a fresh scar over his eyebrow.

Saint-Georges lifts his baton, and with four majestic, repeated notes of horns and strings – one two three FOUR – the overture of *L'Amant anonyme* begins, and then a skirl of violins lift the melody to sweetness, and carry it to sadness, and then the oboes bring defiance to finish the passage. How does the chevalier manage it? She leans forward in wonder, as far as her stays and ostrich feathers will let her, forgetting everything else while the music lasts.

In the crowded salon behind the theatre, she walks with her ladies, acknowledging the bows and greetings as she makes her way to Saint-Georges. Polignac at her side always grounds her.

Saint-Georges is standing against a wall, holding a glass of wine, and Philippe is skulking and scowling next to him.

When the Queen approaches, they both bow, though Philippe takes his usual moment of hesitation.

'Your Majesty,' Saint-Georges says. 'Thank you for coming.'

He seems slightly pained, and she rushes to reassure him.

'It was an utter triumph. That music – I'll be thinking about it for some time. How one was never sure what it was doing until it was done, and then it was inevitable.'

They're surrounded by other people, so she can't say anything about the shiny red gash over Saint-Georges's eye. But Polignac, who is sharp, attaches herself to Madame de Montesson and draws her aside, talking in an animated fashion about something or other, and leaving Antoinette, Lamballe, Saint-Georges, and Philippe more or less alone in a corner of the loud room.

'This orchestra deserves a better room,' Philippe says.

'I've heard work is going very well at the Palais-Royal,' Antoinette says.

He scowls.

She pulls herself back, draws herself up inside her gown: cool silk on the outside, chemise damp with sweat on the inside. The ostrich feathers in her hair dip into her view for a moment. Philippe seems to be in an even more Philippe mood than usual.

Saint-Georges says, 'I am grateful, Your Majesty, that you chose to attend tonight, and I regret that I can only perform in small private theatres these days, places where we know the exits and entrances and can put precautions in place.'

'True safety', Philippe argues, 'will be in daylight. Not in private theatres, but in public ones. I am building more than a new opera house. I am building coffee houses, arcades, entertainments at the Palais-Royal, where everything beautiful the world can produce will be on offer.'

'Are you going into business as a shopkeeper, then, Philippe?' Lamballe asks with a little laugh.

She doesn't mean anything by it; she never does. But it hangs in the air, and he squares his shoulders, looks at them through those eyes that always seem so pained and vulnerable, down the long nose that reminds her which family he comes from.

'Why not?' he asks. 'There is more nobility of character

in the shopkeepers of Paris than there is in the drawing rooms of Versailles. The Order of 1326 is no match for a city that has chased away wolves and barbarians. The safety of magisters, the safety of all people, is in the daylight. That's where I put my trust.'

'I don't think the Order will be afraid to attack me in public,' Saint-Georges says grimly. 'They don't need serpents of fire, or fits of dancing, or anything magical at all. They send mere ruffians against me, because everyone expects men to attack me.'

'They can blame jealous husbands,' Philippe says, smiling a little to show that his argument with Saint-Georges is a friendly one.

'Or other motives,' Saint-Georges adds.

'Be careful,' Antoinette says. 'It's not only the Order we have to fear now. Since the war in America it seems the world is full of half-taught magisters, with their own ambitions and their own goals.'

'They are not our enemies,' Philippe says. 'They are our allies. The more we spread magic to the common people, the sooner the day will come when the Brothers find that if they want to kill all the rogues, they'll have to kill everyone.'

CHAPTER THIRTY-NINE

Earthquakes — Sad Paintings — Interruptions
in Trade — Portrait of the Royal Family

———— ❖ ————

Charlotte is afraid.

The rogues are no longer scattered; they have organized; like everyone else in 1782, they have an ideology. Every attack on the rogues brings retaliation, and helps recruit new members to the rogue cause. Even the old methods of discrediting them are gone or failing.

The only path to a world in which governments alone can wield magic is through magic itself, through power and its uses. Through Soliman's spell of spells, perhaps. Through the San Leucio factory. Through the Kingdom of Naples, a place of honour, to draw all the talented and thoughtful magisters to the new Order, and relegate the rest to the margins of society.

She writes to Soliman every day, urging him to help her find some way to dissipate the fog. The fog, the fog! She can't see the city when she looks out of the window. She tries to imagine it, the city of honour she is building: rising out of the sea on slopes unbroken by the fires of hell, its ports bustling with trade in all languages, its people living in harmony, its children happy and fed, its dreams unbounded, a haven of beauty and light calling all travellers home.

But the fog makes the city vanish when she rubs her eyes, like one of those phantom castles in the sky above the horizon she has seen once or twice in the Straits of Messina that the sailors call a Fata Morgana.

Soliman does not care. He writes excitedly about Joseph and his new laws, the Enlightenment that spreads across the Holy Roman Empire now that Maria Theresa is dead.

Naples has not seen the light, not for more than a year.

Soliman's suspicion has been proven right: the rogues who stole the flour dumped it into the already smoking Vesuvius. How could anyone be so wicked as to inflict that on a kingdom? As the months passed, the smoke darkened, thickened, spread. The warm weather of this false summer brought with it stinging dampness, and the clouds never dissipate now. The enchanted flour spread over the land, in the air, a miasma of mistrust.

At the edges of the fog, in France and Poland, Libya and Turkey, it is a mere haze, its psychic effects barely noticeable, in this age of uncertainty.

But here in Italy, no one can see the sun or trust their neighbour.

Caserta Palace is at least up on a hill, outside of the city, and though no place is free of the fog, Charlotte is glad of the breezes and of a chance to spend time in her library, with its walls of green and gold, its leather books and marble busts.

She spends time with her six living children, especially her eldest, nearly ten years old. She has given birth to eight children, but smallpox took Marianna, and now she is in the ground with Carlo.

Every morning at Mass her head rings and she finds no peace. Caramanico and Lunardi are in England, where Caramanico goes to parties and Lunardi performs experiments; he wants to fly in a balloon. They write her letters assuring her that the fog cannot be so bad. It has, after all, spread doubt, which was always the flour's intention. The Inquisition remains quietly etherized in Sicily. Charlotte's new age of secular justice has begun.

And what a task it has before it.

The fog darkens the days and turns the sun blood red. Everyone hates each other and there are brawls every night in the city below, the piazzas like battlefields come morning, dead bodies in the fountains.

Elsewhere in Europe, there are discoveries. New wonders. A new metal, named as tungsten! An entirely new planet!

In Naples, the philosophers drive stilettos into each other's ribs over nothing at all.

And Charlotte's enemies gather. Enemies everywhere! Even in her own house. The Council appointed Acton as minister of war, which simply made sense, as he understands the current state of Naples' growing fleet better than anyone. But her husband has grown paranoid about Acton, accusing Charlotte of adultery before the whole court whenever he gets a chance. He has drawn Spain into it, now, and informed Charlotte that his father demands Acton's removal. How he, the whoring ignorant carbuncle, could dare.

And who does she have at her side? Silfversparre is drinking. He goes out hunting for rogues, as he always did, but he does it now as a sleek housecat hunts for mice, out of habit. He says magisters are everywhere: at the court of Tsarina Catherine in Russia and in the alleys of every seaside town. There are pamphlets everywhere, asking why the powerful do nothing useful, why they squander the knowledge that they have hidden from the common people for so long. Do they refer to magic? Sometimes Charlotte thinks they must, and sometimes she thinks she can't trust her own mind.

Magisters with ambition could seize control.

She can't get a clean breath into her lungs.

Charlotte stretches out her fingers, both hands wide. These hands must grow big enough to get a grip on the world.

She begins by summoning her husband.

⁜

Ferdinand takes an indecent half-day to respond. It's probably for the best. She's not shaking any more. Her anger at the morning's message has resolved into icy numbness. The shock – that he would dare order Acton removed from office, now of all times, when Naples is in a state of permanent riot barely contained – has only hardened her the way a wasp sting hardens an oak.

He looks afraid when he arrives.

'Acton,' he says, sinking into a leather chair, although she's still standing. She leans one fist on an ebony-inlaid table.

'Acton, of course. How dare you slander him? He's the best minister of war this kingdom has ever had. It's ridiculous. Juvenile.'

'My father doesn't trust him.'

'Your father! He doesn't like the English, I suppose.'

'He doesn't like the fact that all Europe is talking about your affair.'

He says it flatly, almost sadly. Charlotte breathes in hard.

'All Europe? As though anyone in Spain knows anything about what happens beyond its borders. Where does this nonsense come from? Why so much gossip about him, for God's sake? I will have a painter paint the man. I will have a bust made of John Acton, and send it to Spain, and then your father will see whether he cuts the sort of figure to turn a woman's head. Unlikely.'

Ferdinand's mouth twitches in half-hearted agreement. He doesn't believe her. Nobody believes anyone.

'My husband,' she says, walking around the table to him, and standing in front of him. 'I can't think of any way to convince you of what I know to be the truth. Nothing has happened between John Acton and me. I have not had an affair with him. Not even a night with him. Not a kiss, not an embrace, not a flirtatious word. Why won't you believe me? It hasn't happened.'

'Oh, I know it hasn't happened,' he says, waving his hand

dismissively. He pushes himself out of the armchair and wanders to the bookshelf, examining a bust of Voltaire there. 'You're too perfect to ever do anything you're not supposed to do. I've always known that.'

'You've known?' The anger makes her shudder again, as though she has a fever. 'You've known? You've accused me of adultery, in public and in private, for the last year.'

'Because you wanted to,' he says quietly, still not looking at her. 'It's the same thing. Isn't that what the priests say? You wanted it in your heart. You still want to. I knew that night at Portici when you were talking about Diderot. Seven or eight people all standing around in a circle, talking about some bullshit, I can't even remember, and then he said something about Diderot and you turned to him and you turned your back on everyone else. You forgot everyone else was there.'

'What?' She is genuinely befuddled. 'I've never had a conversation with Acton about Diderot. We talk about ships and rations and ambassadors, when we talk about anything. You're making this up.'

'Oh, for God's sake!' he says, turning to her now. 'You were there. It was hardly six months ago. You talked to him for a quarter of an hour, with your backs turned to everyone else. Don't treat me like a fool.'

Her face fills with heat. He's sure of the memory, and she doesn't remember the conversation at all. She must have sacrificed the memory. It must have been important to her.

'I had too much wine,' she says weakly. 'That night. I don't remember.'

'Convenient,' he mutters. As though she's done something wrong by talking about great matters with her minister of war. As though he doesn't have another woman in his bed every month.

'Why do you care?' she asks suddenly. 'You have your lovers. You have never loved me. Why do you care if I talk to the man?'

'Because it's humiliating!' he yells, his body and attention fully turned to her now. 'Because you're my wife and people gossip about you. And him. And where am I in all this? The fool. The butt of the joke.'

She's angry now, and grateful to be angry. He knows, and wants, no other way to deal with his resentments than to inflict them on her. Her woman's body is there to bear the bruises he makes. He will never learn to be secure in himself, because he never has to. Because everything will always be her fault, and when he fails to be anything but a worm, that will be her fault too, simply for being there. It will always be like this. She's never expected him to change, but it's still sour, the taste in her mouth, the loneliness of being the only one in the room who understands what's happening.

She draws herself up. 'Sending him away will only make people believe that the rumours are true.'

He shrugs.

'As you like, then,' she says, throwing up her hands with frustration that is only partly calculated. 'Dismiss John Acton. Find your kingdom a new minister of war. Go to lunch with the English and Austrian ambassadors and discuss foreign policy. Explain to the minister of finance why the new minister of war needs more money for the fleet, which he will, because no one knows how Acton managed to do so much for so little. Go do all of this, and you won't have to suffer from knowing some people might stop spreading certain entirely false rumours about your wife. Give them a chance to make up new stories. And give me a little peace.'

He hangs his head, and shakes it. But he has nothing to say, because she's right. Without Tanucci, without his father, he can't govern his kingdom. He needs her.

Ferdinand grasps the white bust of Voltaire in his long fingers and holds it up to the light from the window. Her first thought is that he will throw it against the wall, that it will smash, that it is new, that Voltaire is not long dead and it would be a shame to see his image smashed. But a grin breaks across Ferdinand's face.

'He is ugly, isn't he? A lot like this fellow.'

He means Acton, she realizes after a moment. If anything, Voltaire's thin smirk and long, pointed nose are mirrors of Ferdinand's own face. Acton's nose is highly ordinary, serviceable, lived-in, like all his features. Acton doesn't smirk, not ever. His expression is wary, never arch. A sailor's expression.

But she nods, and smiles a little, to agree with Ferdinand. 'Terribly ugly.'

'It's hilarious, really, that anyone would think—'

'Isn't it?'

He nods, still looking at Voltaire, and then nods again, decisively, as if he and the late philosopher have made a pact. He replaces the head on the shelf and, without looking at Charlotte, crosses the room to the door. Just as the usher moves to open it, he holds up a hand, and turns to Charlotte.

'I'm going hunting.'

February 1783 brings three earthquakes in three days, destroying towns and killing thousands in Sicily and all across the toe of the Italian boot. In the cities, buildings fell and candles fell, and the candles started fires, and burned the cities to ash.

Then Poseidon rode up over the beaches, drowning the people in their houses, leaving fetid pools where the dead still float. Mountains crumbled and cracked, damming the rivers, and their sandy banks boil like volcanoes. Pestilence rises from the waterlogged and broken land.

All across the Kingdom of Naples, the unlucky survivors of all these disasters sicken with fevers.

At night, the sky glows, greenish pale, so people can walk abroad without lanterns. Philosophers in Rome argue about the glow: whether it is electric in origin. The Pope calls for prayers. There are stories of people in Milan and Turin walking around with orange slices to their noses, or the beaked masks of plague doctors filled with cloves and camphor.

In Naples, where the people are used to foul odours and dim skies, despair kills all entertainments. No plays are performed, as if by common consent. There are no Pulcinella shows or masquerades.

Charlotte spends hours staring into the middle distance, moving letters in her mind, idly wondering whether she could make a spell to count the bodies. Buildings are ruined, villages are broken, and whole fields have slid into the sea. So many were buried alive, and so many have suffocated on the surface. As if southern Italy is a hellmouth determined to devour its people, one way or another.

Volcanoes, earthquakes, fog. Soon her reign will rival Pharoah's for the sheer number of plagues. These disasters must have been the work of rogue magisters. Difficult though it is when she's breathing this unholy fog day and night, Charlotte strives for reason and empathy. She is prepared to believe that the earthquake could have been an accident: a tunnelling spell gone wrong, perhaps. In her darker moments, she is sure it was all a deliberate act of violence. She sends Silfversparre looking for the rogues responsible, whether they died in the attempt or not. He reports that he can find no evidence of rogue involvement. He thinks these were merely acts of God. But Charlotte has no quarrel with God, while the rogues stole her flour and poisoned her air and turned her sister against her.

One of the few things Charlotte used to like about the Palazzo Reale were the views.

'I can only paint sad paintings now,' says Angelica Kauffman, sitting with Charlotte and drinking Turkish coffee, looking out at the bleak sky over the bay, where only small fishing boats dare venture. 'For so many years I wanted to be taken seriously as a historical painter. No other women are, you know. They're all portraitists, because we aren't supposed to paint people in the nude. No gods or goddesses for us. But I did. I do. I learned it all, and made the world despise me. And now? It all seems terribly silly and pointless, all my sentimental figures in their skimpy clothing. I start, and then I can't finish.'

Charlotte pushes the air with a silk fan, but it doesn't freshen. Her newest pregnancy has swollen her body and makes her breath come short.

'I would like you to paint my family, Signora Kauffman,' she says. 'There's nothing sentimental about us, I can assure you. And then you would have to finish.'

The Swiss woman turns a pair of hard, bright eyes on her. 'It would be my honour. We can begin the sketches when-ever it pleases Your Majesty, and leave space for the baby, when he arrives.'

'In a few weeks, then, we'll start,' she says. 'That will give Gennaro and Giuseppe time to recover.'

For there is another calamity: smallpox has come to the palace at Caserta. The older children have been inoculated but the physicians said the procedure was not safe for the little ones. Two-year-old Gennaro was very ill indeed, his blond curls sticking close to his pale face, but the doctors say he will recover. She wants to believe them, though she has trouble believing anything or anyone these days. Gennaro, her darling: she remembers the day she realized she was pregnant with him, the very day the volcano erupted.

And now one-year-old Giuseppe, her youngest child, is ailing, covered in sores.

She does not visit the earthquake zone, because she can't leave her children while they're sick. She goes to Mass, she presides over the Council, and in all the other waking moments she holds onto Giuseppe, sitting in his bed every day. She holds onto him so tightly, his warm head resting on her arm. She does not let him go until his hands are cold, and the doctors tell her he has no pulse.

She writes in her diary about the loss of her third child,

gone to join Carlo and Marianna: 'Three parts of me that are cold and in the ground.'

Kauffman begins her sketches. Charlotte does not wear mourning for her children, not in the painting. Kauffman paints her stomach flat as a girl's, and paints a baby in the chaise, for the baby will be born by the time the painting is finished.

Between the first sketches and the modello, Charlotte's baby is born in blood, born dead, too soon. There are more earthquakes in the south. And though each of them sat separately for their portraits, the royal family is gathered together in the modello. Out in the garden, in simple dress, with three of Ferdinand's godforsaken dogs, and a harp for Teresa. Francesco with another little dog, and Little Mimi at Charlotte's knee. Luisa holds Maria Amalia, and Gennaro plays at her feet, all of them in a wheeled chaise which also holds the ghost of the baby who only ever lived in the painter's imagination, barely visible beneath the veil Kauffman has painted over the image.

The painting depicts happiness the way an artist who has never seen an elephant might paint an elephant; it comes out odd.

It's all false.

The sky behind the painting is dark and smoky.

Charlotte cocks her head, and says, 'We'll need a new version. Paint the baby out entirely.'

'Of course.'

'And make me look older.'

'Older? You look – you look quite beautiful here.'

'Yes, I do. I look like a shepherdess. Dress my hair higher, and make me less sweet altogether. And the sky—'

'Yes?'

'Too dark. Paint it blue and bright.'

Kauffman delivers the final portrait and Charlotte asks her to stay on as court painter, as her friend. Kauffman promises, politely, to consider it.

Everyone is polite. The merchants who have broken off all trade with Naples, because the fog threatens their ships, send the Queen their sincerest regrets. The kings who have recalled their frightened ambassadors after one too many reports of imminent rioting. She does not want their politeness. She wants their respect, their gold, their trade. She must do something.

CHAPTER FORTY

Fersen Returns — The Cardinal's Stockings — Flight —
The Muslin Dress — Natural Philosophy —
Fersen Departs

In June of 1783, Axel von Fersen returns to France. Antoinette has been working to get him the colonelcy of the Royal Swedish Regiment, which is perhaps a reckless public indication of her fondness for him. But although it seems everyone knows or suspects at court (including Louis, probably), the obscene pamphlets have her paired with everyone but Fersen. He never factors into the public speculation about who fathered her children. She isn't quite sure why that is – perhaps it's Fersen himself, working some magic. Or perhaps, she sometimes half thinks, it's Charlotte, showing sisterly love in a Charlotte sort of way. She won't stop the horrible lies the Order spreads, but she might well make sure they don't hit near the mark. That would be like Charlotte.

And Antoinette won't ask about that either, not least because her portrait remains silent, and the letters between the sisters are few and perfunctory now.

She misses the sound of Charlotte's voice.

Fersen's voice, though, has been in her mind for the last

two years, though the only image of his face she's seen has been the little miniature he sent. Three years, he's been away. Why should she be nervous? They spoke last night, when he disembarked at Brest. He's on his way to her. He said, just last night to her own listening portrait, that he loves her. So why should she be nervous?

But she is. She will see him at court, first, and receive him as queen, standing next to her husband. So she is in court dress.

She wears the full apparatus of panniers and terrible corset less frequently now. At the Petit Trianon, she and the other ladies go about mostly in one-piece gowns of white muslin tied with sashes. The fashion was born not long after her daughter, her little Mousseline, but she can't quite remember now whether the nickname followed the fashion or the other way around.

But some days, there is no help for it: the court dress must be worn.

Fersen is in his French uniform, though soon he will trade it back for his Swedish one. Surrounded by courtiers in the Hall of Mirrors, they stare at each other, drink each other in. It feels strange to see him and not to hear his most private thoughts, as though she is further from him now that he is in her presence. They stare at each other, but they give nothing away.

His hair is a little thinner about the temples, unpowdered and tied at his nape. He looks like an American. The uniform sits well on him – his body is leaner than it was. Hers is not; her battles have been the birth and care of children, which leave different traces on the body. She draws her chin higher, self-consciously. Perhaps he will find her ridiculous, in her wide court skirt and high powdered hair. Perhaps he will find her ugly. Perhaps all this time they were speaking to each other's portraits, they were clinging to those images of themselves, to ghosts.

The discomfort doesn't disappear when they're alone

together, later, in her little secret room. He sits on a settee in the window, looking at her, while she paces.

'I didn't see Cardinal de Rohan at Versailles today,' he says.

'He didn't have an invitation.'

'Neither do hundreds of the people here on any given day.'

'No, but he is smarting from an insult. A few months ago, he came to a masked ball to which he was absolutely not invited. He was in disguise, and he must have enchanted his mask – the way I did, you remember—'

'I remember.'

'I didn't recognize the Cardinal at all, but Lamballe recognized him by his red stockings and then he felt a fool. I've tried to have him removed as grand almoner, but then I'm accused of misusing my influence. One can't be rid of him, though he and his comrades never stop trying to hurt us. How long are you in France this time?'

'For the summer, I hope, if King Gustavus can spare me.'

'You must be eager to be home.'

'France is my home now. My sister wants me to be married, but—'

They look at each other. 'But,' she whispers, and traces a line on the walnut table where she works out her spells. Where she works out the words to say what she wants to say, or something close to it. 'When one is young, love feels like a magnet, doesn't it? As though resisting the pull to the other person would kill you, as though your bodies are drawn together. I admit I have missed that feeling, as excruciating as it was. I didn't know it wouldn't always be that way. But now we are nearly thirty, and for three years you have been at war, and perhaps – if your affection for me is something else now, then that's all right. I know—'

And her words run out there, and she coughs.

He stands and comes to her, takes her hands. She looks up at his face, defiantly, noting the new lines, the new sadness in his eyes.

'Do you not feel the magnet, then?'

She casts her eyes downward. The smell of him! She could sink into it. She could sink into the hollow of his collarbone, trace a thousand words on the ball of his shoulder with her fingers. She doesn't touch him.

'Yes, for three years I have been at war,' he says, his voice heavy and soft. 'It is a horrible neverending moment and it feels as if the rest of one's life has become a dream.' He takes one hand away from hers and holds it by her cheek, as though he will touch her skin, but he does not – not quite. Just holds his hand there as though framing the image of her face. 'But I felt the magnet, every moment. I felt it all the way across the Atlantic, and it drew me back to you.'

She puts her own hand to his, takes it to her mouth. Puts the tip of his fingers to her lips and closes her eyes. She has remembered the smell of him well.

When she opens her eyes again, he has an expression she's never seen before.

'What happened, in America?' she asks, hoarsely. 'What didn't you tell me?'

'Memories I am most eager to sacrifice.'

'Let me take them from you.' She kisses the corner of his eye, kisses the hollow of his neck, unbuttons the French uniform. 'Give them all to me.'

A cannon booms, and everyone in the courtyard at Versailles freezes. Everyone save Antoinette: she does not startle easily, and she uses the moment to watch everyone else. Her little girl, her Mousseline, puts her small hand into hers. The vast crowd stills, but the faces move as her gaze sweeps across them.

Fersen is dutifully not looking at her. He's looking at Benjamin Franklin, who's dressed in his usual rustic costume.

Another cannon booms! Lamballe puts her hand to her heart, but it is four-fifths performance.

The three aunts, Mesdames Victoire, Adélaïde and Sophie,

stand looking at the great balloon as if it is something disagreeable.

It takes Benjamin Franklin only a moment to recover his avuncular expression. He looks like a boiled potato in his ill-fitting brown coat, gazing up at the great balloon that looms over the crowd.

The golden suns painted on it are reminiscent of the Sun King, and the letter 'L' also in gold is for her husband, who is manifestly not. If the sun were shining, the balloon would be dazzling.

But the sun is not shining. The sun has not shone in months. All summer, this strange darkness and a faint odour of brimstone. A volcano is erupting in Iceland, and the wind is wrapping its fumes around the world. But Antoinette thinks it's more than that. The air in France has had a strange smell to it for years. A smell of rot and rust; a smell like magic. Antoinette is almost used to the faint headache, the slight thickness in the air, which sometimes seems to make it difficult to understand people.

Her little Mousseline has never known a world without it. A soft hand rests in Antoinette's as they speak their word-less language to each other. They are on guard; wary; in control. Her daughter understands her as no one ever has, not even Charlotte once upon a time. To her left, the little Dauphin pouts regally; his hand in Antoinette's is sweaty. What perfect children she has.

She knows that she has been lucky, that other parents lose their children at all ages. She remembers all the lives she wasn't able to save: her sisters, her brothers, Joseph's daughter. She has read Charlotte's increasingly curt letters telling her of the deaths of Carlo, Marianna and, earlier this year, Giuseppe. Antoinette knows that any day could be the day that takes a child from her, but that is a thought she cannot entertain, because it will break her. She cannot consider breaking, not even for a moment.

There are so many things Antoinette must not do, big and

small, every day, lest she be seen to be too emotional, not maternal enough, too Austrian, too dowdy, too extravagant. She has learned that a painting of her in a muslin dress has been added to her catalogue of errors.

The portraitist Élisabeth Vigée Le Brun made her debut at the Salon this summer, and among her paintings was one of Marie Antoinette in simple white, in a garden with a rose: a picture of the Rousseauian ideal. It began as a triumph: the Royal Academy of Painting and Sculpture controls nearly everything when it comes to teaching and exhibits in Paris, but it has been exceedingly reluctant to admit women. Antoinette loves Vigée Le Brun's work, and she has had quite enough of closed societies of men setting arbitrary rules. She managed to use her influence (magical and otherwise) to have Vigée Le Brun admitted, which means she can exhibit at the Salon in the Louvre.

But the triumph was soured by the reaction to the painting of Antoinette in the muslin dress. People said the Queen had herself painted in her nightgown, that it is a sign of her moral decadence, that she hates the silk-makers of France and would rather wear muslins that come from Bengal.

She never knows which of her choices will be seized upon as unwomanly, or too womanly, or both.

So Antoinette stands tall, and does not embrace her children.

Her gaze roves to the Chevalier de Saint-Georges, and to Philippe d'Orléans standing beside him. They are speaking to two men. The older one she knows, and it takes her a moment to remember from where. When Philippe went to Naples to destroy the flour, he returned with information about the Order in Naples, and the members thereof. He showed them a little engraving of the Prince of Caramanico. That's him, that stern, sleek man with a neat wig. The younger man, with wild natural curls, must be Vincenzo Lunardi. But she thought they were both in London.

Two Brothers of Naples, here in Paris, and speaking with Philippe.

Mousseline shifts beside her, and Antoinette realizes she's been gripping her children's hands too hard. She forces her gaze away, so she won't be caught staring at her sister's spies – for what else could they be? Philippe must be up to something.

There is Étienne Montgolfier talking to Franklin, now; there is a lot of back-slapping but Montgolfier looks nervous. He is the more presentable Montgolfier brother, people say, but the other was the genius who first had the idea for the hot-air balloon. It reminds her of the Messieurs Léonard and she wondered, at first, if they were magisters, but Fersen says not.

So many learned men and women in France in 1783. She watches them in the crowd: Joseph-Ignace Guillotin, the physician. Nicole-Reine Lapaute, the astronomer. Antoine Lavoisier and his wife Marie-Anne, both chemists. So many students of the natural world are Freemasons, and the Masonic lodges have long been covers for the Order, though there are rogues among the Masons too, now. Men of science have been petitioning the King to call a commission into Mesmer's work; Mesmer, of the remarkable instrument with healing powers, and the odd theories that don't quite explain his results. There are so many fronts to the magical war.

A cheer goes up as Montgolfier lights the brazier under the balloon.

'Won't it catch fire?' Mousseline asks quietly.

'They have coated it in alum,' Antoinette responds. 'If it lifts up and lands unexpectedly on a building, though, it could catch. We have *pompiers* ready to douse it if so. Versailles will be safe, little one.'

'And the balloon?' the Dauphin asks, solicitous. He is always anxious.

At her gesture, Montgolfier walks to them, wiping sweat from his forehead.

'Monsieur, the Dauphin wishes to know whether the balloon will survive the journey,' Antoinette says.

Montgolfier smiles. 'Your Majesties, I certainly hope it will. It may get a tear. It may be singed. But it should survive.'

'What about the passengers?' little Louis-Joseph asks.

'There are no people,' says Mousseline gravely to her brother. 'Only animals.'

'I hope the animals will be all right,' Antoinette says.

'Wouldn't we learn more about the effects if we sent up people?' asks the King gruffly.

'We don't know what flight will do to the human body, Your Majesty. The air is thin. No one has ever been there before. We have plenty of volunteers, ready to go up as soon as the balloons have been tested with animals. For now, today, we have a very willing sheep, a rooster, and a duck.' He looks down at Mousseline. 'The duck, you see, should be accustomed to the air, so he will show us whether anything that happens to the animals happens because of the atmosphere or for some other reason. The rooster is similar in its body to the duck, but does not fly. And the sheep will tell us, really, whether humans can fly. If a sheep is unharmed, I believe a person would be.'

Mousseline nods. 'What are their names, Monsieur Montgolfier?'

'What, the animals?' Montgolfier chuckles, forgetting for a moment he is addressing the royal family. He bends down, closer to Mousseline. 'I don't believe they have names. Would you like to name them?'

Mousseline considers. 'The sheep should be Montauciel, because he is going up to the sky.'

'A very good name,' says Antoinette, and squeezes her hand. 'And the birds?'

'Louis-Joseph may name the birds,' Mousseline grants.

'What shall the birds be called, Monsieur le Dauphin?'

Louis-Joseph frowns. 'What about Pierre and Jacques? Would that be all right?'

'Very suitable,' says Louis. 'Are you tying the animals down in the basket, Montgolfier?'

Montgolfier nods. 'For their own safety, Your Majesty.

They're ready now. It only remains for Your Majesty to give the signal.'

Louis raises his hand, a long red ribbon fluttering from it, and brings it down again.

The crowd cheers, although nothing has happened yet with the balloon. Men bustle around it, and Montgolfier stands on his tiptoes so he can see. He has patches on the bottoms of his shoes.

The balloon jostles, and then it is up. It is up! Rising above the heads of the people, who crowd around it despite its tail of dark smoke. The blue and gold orb rises higher, higher, and floats over rooftops covered in people trying to get a better view.

Antoinette gently uncurls her fingers from her children's hands so she can applaud, and they do too. Louis claps louder than anyone. She turns to him and smiles. He so dearly loves it when things work.

'What do you think, Mr Franklin?' Louis calls to the American. 'What's the use for such an invention?'

He makes a non-committal face. 'What's the use of a newborn baby, Your Majesty? It has potential. What that potential is, often the inventors themselves do not know.'

Her smile goes as tight as her bodice across her belly. The use of a newborn baby, for her, is not mere potential. The Dauphin is delicate, and no one will be satisfied until he has a brother. She does not look at Fersen. This new baby is certainly Louis's, *mathematically* Louis's, but that hasn't stopped the libel pamphlets from speculating about the Comte d'Artois, even, despite the impossibility, the Duchesse de Polignac.

The pamphlets, too, are a front line. The ships have come home from America but the war among magisters is far from over.

Fersen sits at a table in her bedroom in the Petit Trianon, writing letters by candlelight. She watches him. Every so often he looks up, frowning, and then writes again.

'Is it a difficult letter?'

'Hmm? No, it's a plain missive to my sister. About the itinerary.'

Tomorrow, he leaves again. King Gustavus of Sweden has called on him to be the captain of his bodyguard. And Gustavus is on his way to Italy, on a state visit.

'Then perhaps the itinerary is making you pensive.' She doesn't know quite what to say about the fact that Fersen will see Charlotte in a few months. She's jealous of both of them, and angry at Charlotte, and worried about everything.

He's left a streak of dark ink on his forehead. She laughs, and goes to him with a kerchief, and wipes it off.

He takes her hand, rests his cheek on it for a moment; then he looks up at her, his face illuminated by the candle.

A summer in France has put some of the light back into Fersen's eyes, although it has not smoothed the tiny lines around them. A summer together, they've had at last. A summer without sunlight, but they didn't care about that.

To Naples.

'You must not let her persuade you of anything,' Antoinette says, biting her lip.

They are in her bedroom in the Petit Trianon. She feels safe – they have surrounded the room, and the building, with magical traps and alarms – but she also feels like a prisoner on the eve of execution. Tomorrow he leaves her, for who knows how long.

'Your sister? Do you think she's going to try to pull me back into the Order?' he asks, amused. 'No fear of that, my love.'

She shakes her head. 'No, I suppose I— Just be careful. She'll interfere. She always interferes. If I had to guess, she'll try to convince you that you should stay away from me, for my benefit.'

'No fear of that, either.'

'She's very . . .'

'What?'

'She's very Charlotte.'

He chuckles. 'I'll survive. I want to give some aid and comfort to the rogues of Naples, and see what I can find out about what the Order is up to.'

'Write to me every day.'

'Every day.'

'And will you – will you write to me about her too? My sister. Tell me how she is, how the children are. Amalia and Leopold and Joseph tell me a little, when they visit her, but they don't know her as I know her. And Charlotte still writes occasionally, for the sake of appearances, but nothing real.'

He kisses her cheek.

'I will write every day, long, long letters with everything I can tell you in them. And I will come back to you. Always. Unto death.'

They won't sleep tonight.

They were by turns shy and passionate, the first few nights after he returned. She peeled his uniform off him as if she could peel off the war. They were not innocent – not any more – but uncertain, as though they were natural philosophers studying some new wonder.

Now she turns to Fersen, glowing as he undresses in her bedroom like a husband. Takes off his breeches and puts his shoes under the bed. So comfortable. She steps towards him, and lets out a little gasp.

'What is it?' Fersen worries so easily, now. The carefree libertine has gone, despite the stories she hears of the women who throw themselves at him. What are stories? There are pamphlets full of pornographic tales about the Queen and her ladies, all through Paris.

She puts her hand on her belly, and her hand can't feel it through the corset but her gut feels it again, the little punch outward.

'The baby's quickened,' she says, breathless.

He wraps his arms around her and unlaces her bodice, down her back. She is unused to the court dress, these days, but the balloon demonstration demanded it. His fingers open her dress as she pulls down her skirts, standing on a sea of petticoats like Venus on the foam. At last she's in her shift, and he puts his hand on her belly. They laugh together at the strangeness of it, as her skin ripples under his hand. He leaves it there, warm and solid, while his other hand lifts her shift, and she gasps again.

'I'll write every day,' he whispers in her ear, and lifts her to the bed.

CHAPTER FORTY-ONE

The Future that Charlotte Fears — The Treaty
of Paris — Disagreements and Libels — The Ways
Women Fall to Pieces — The Painter

———————— ❖ ————————

It's becoming crowded, this little mirrored room in the Petit Trianon. Antoinette needs another place for rogues to meet, even quieter and more private. But for now, they gather here, behind the mirrored walls and windows.

She's uneasy, and not only because she never quite feels safe here now, and not only because Fersen has been gone for weeks, on the way to Naples. The world feels uncertain, as though it's about to tilt, but in which direction, she cannot say.

So she fusses while they take their seats.

Polignac pulls the lever to bring down the window-coverings. Marvellous devices, with mirrors on their interior sides. Somehow, the pamphleteers heard about the mirrors – servants gossip – and it furnished the worst of them, Brissot, with a new pornographic story to tell about Antoinette and Lamballe. *Why do you give them these gifts?* Louis asked her, plainly frustrated, and wounded. *But it's a marvel of engineering, dear,* she told him, pretending not to understand.

Antoinette would not choose Lamballe as a lover anyway.

Polignac, now, that is more believable – she has a way about her. Antoinette smiles, and turns to her friends, her comrades. Lamballe and Polignac lounge on a chaise; Lafayette paces; Saint-Georges stands near the door.

'I've heard this fog is much worse in Italy,' says Philippe. He's thrown himself into one of the carved chairs at a louche angle, his legs crossed and his gorgeous thick-heeled shoes swinging. He always finds some way to show his complete disdain for Antoinette's position, under the cover of their secret fraternity.

'Did you learn that from Caramanico and Lunardi? You were speaking with them at the balloon launch,' Antoinette says.

'I was,' Philippe lobs back. 'And so was the chevalier.'

'Are they here as spies, do you think?' Lafayette asks, pacing with a little less than his usual energy. Perhaps he's tired; he's been occupied with politics: with the aftermath of the Treaty of Paris that ended the American war, making peace between the British and French. 'Or are they here to help Rohan and his bunch with some new operation?'

'They're turning against the Order,' Saint-Georges says. 'Not officially. Not yet. But they will.'

'Taking our side?' Antoinette feels irrationally ill at ease, knowing of traitors to Charlotte and saying nothing.

'Taking their own side,' Philippe drawls. 'As all men of ambition are, now that the possibilities are opening up. Why should any magister now take his orders from a stuffy old cult, or from a queen? Or both at once, as is the case in Naples.'

'When will Fersen be in Naples?' Lamballe asks, shifting the conversation, as she does.

They all look to Antoinette for the answer.

'Not until the New Year. For the moment, he and King Gustavus are in Florence. My brother – the Emperor – is there, and an old friend of my family, Angelo Soliman, is travelling with him. Fersen reports Soliman's been talking with every scholarly magister he can find, and mathematicians too. Fersen thinks he's trying to crack a new spell.'

'I could have told him that, and saved him the business of travelling,' Philippe says. He stops, says nothing, enjoying their surprise.

'Well then, Your Highness, do tell us,' Lafayette says, half teasing.

'Lunardi told me about it. You see? Some good comes of having eyes and ears open. The men of science laugh at Soliman's notion – he calls it the "spell of spells".' Philippe adds a pseudodramatic wave of the hand. 'It's an axiom that would allow a magister to create any enchantment they wanted, without the bother of years of trial and error, or having to trade with other magisters.'

Saint-Georges shakes his head. 'If such a thing were possible, surely someone would have hit upon it already.'

Lamballe looks up languidly. 'Many things that were not possible have become so. We watched a sheep, a rooster, and a goose go up into the air in a balloon.'

'A duck,' Antoinette mutters.

'Your Majesty?' Lamballe asks.

'It was a duck,' she repeats a little louder. 'This idea of Dr Soliman's may be quixotic, but he is not a fool.'

Philippe sits up straighter. 'You think – Your Majesty, do you think there's something in it? If he is right, if such a thing is possible, the magister who had it could do almost anything.'

Antoinette acknowledges his point with a curt nod. 'Yes. If Soliman thinks it is possible, I would not discount it. And if it is as Lunardi described it, well, the Order would be able to do almost anything. And they would not hesitate to use that power against us.'

'Anyone with such a spell at their command would be the most powerful man on Earth,' Lafayette says.

'Or woman,' Antoinette corrects. 'Angelo Soliman is a close associate of my sister, as I'm sure you're all aware. It cannot be allowed to happen.'

'Leave it with me,' Philippe says. 'I have some associates in Naples.'

'I don't want Angelo Soliman killed,' Antoinette says.

'We are not the Order,' Philippe says. She hears a mocking echo of her words before she sent him to Naples to destroy the flour. 'We don't kill magisters. We create them, and teach them. It's time to teach the people to do magic. Our only safety is in numbers.'

'But before we get the numbers, we have to keep ourselves safe,' she responds.

Lamballe says, 'We have enchanted enough corpse liquor now to protect dozens of rogues, and I can make more. That's a start.'

Paris's overpopulated cemeteries have become notorious for hasty reburials to deal with collapsing walls and eroding soil. It gave cover for some of Philippe's less savoury rogue friends to dig more recent burials without anyone asking questions. The Circle has been enchanting corpse liquor to protect as many rogues as it can from the Order – an idea that came from Philippe in the aftermath of the Palais-Royal fire, but Lamballe has taken it on with diligence. She should be grateful for Lamballe, as she is for Polignac. She has always found strength in the friendship of other women, and she should remember that.

Philippe throws up his hands. 'A start. Always so cautious! We will die of caution. Every man, woman, and child in Paris has seen magic done in the last few years. What are we waiting for?'

'Yes, they have seen magic done!' Antoinette retorts. 'And most of them know it for what it is, but we tell them to cross themselves and keep walking, or tell them it is some new form of science. If the great mass of people learn that they too can do magic, all at once, what do you think will happen? Imagine how many poor, desperate people would sell their livers, their wombs, their toes, arms, legs! Imagine if all the love in the world were sacrificed, and all the memory too, while humans dodder on to the end of days like chimpanzees in enchanted clothing, forgetting all history and language, all love and virtue.'

That is the future that Charlotte fears. Antoinette understands that, has always understood that.

'You sound like a Brother of the Order,' Philippe says. 'Your Majesty.'

Saint-Georges pushes himself off from the wall impatiently, and leans on the back of a sofa. 'There is so much good we could do, with all that we know.'

'We have done good already,' Lafayette puts in, but he's uncertain. There was a time, not long ago, when Lafayette would have been the first to argue for the most dramatic course. As with Fersen, time in America has tempered him.

'When I was last in London,' says Philippe, 'I met Jacques-Pierre Brissot.'

Lamballe and Polignac don't look at him; neither do they look at the Queen. They stay perfectly still, frozen, their eyes just a bit wide. Antoinette stays frozen too, her gaze on Philippe, her smile in place.

'The pamphleteer?' she asks, mildly. 'The one who writes such imaginative things about me and the Princesse de Lamballe?'

'I was curious about him. He seemed to come out of nowhere. I wondered if Brissot might be a magister – all those pamphlets, so thick on the ground that one can't walk in Paris without them sticking to one's heel. He is not a magister. I'm certain of it. But after I got him in his cups, he confided something in me. He believes he has an enchanted pen. Enchanted? I said. Surely magic cannot be real? He shrugged and said all he knew was that after he started using it, his pornographic pamphlets about the Queen of France – forgive me – started selling. He is going to start writing real essays with it, he promised me, open letters to the Emperor, that kind of thing. And I think he means it, and if you scratch his surface you might find a decent man.'

Antoinette raises her eyebrows, and her wig shifts uncomfortably on her skull.

'A decent man. Indeed.'

'Misguided, and over-passionate. The pen, I thought, might well be mere superstition, but it turns out it was a gift. From William Hamilton.'

Antoinette draws a breath as sharp as a dagger. 'The British ambassador to Naples.'

'The very same,' says Philippe.

Antoinette turns to look out of the window, and sees only herself, reflected in the mirror, and realizes that instead of hiding her expression from her companions, she has shown it.

They look alarmed.

She whirls back to face them, dropping all pretence of calm. 'Well, I cannot make a spell for my sister to love me, though that would solve everything. So, I suppose we must deal with the traps she lays for me.'

'But what His Highness intends, I think,' says Saint-Georges, 'is that perhaps we can recruit this Jacques-Pierre Brissot, use him to spread some useful spell with his magic pen. He has argued against slavery, and one of the pamphlets he has in his mind is an essay on emancipation. What if he could teach as well as argue? We won the war in America. There are more rogue magisters using the Order's magic than there are members of the Order now. Surely this is the moment to show the world what we can do.'

'You know I am opposed to slavery too,' Antoinette protests, and it sounds weak even to her ears. It is one thing to be opposed, and it is another to oppose. 'I want to free magic for the benefit of all people. I just don't think we can trust a man who received his magic pen from my sister.'

'We are expending all our magic here, in London, and in New York, on fighting the Order—'

'Because if we do not, the Order will keep the people of the world under their heels forever,' Lafayette says.

'What does it matter whose heel you're under, if you're ground into the earth?'

Silence stretches out between them. Antoinette says, at last, 'We have to stop the Order from attacking us, and keep an eye on Soliman and his notion about the spell of spells. We have to grow our numbers, but carefully. It may not be enough but it's what I can do, here in Versailles, and I will do it alone if need be.'

Lamballe crosses to her, takes her hands. The princess's facial features have seemed such a jumble lately, as if she becomes a different stranger in every angle and every light. Just looking at her gives Antoinette vertigo, so she looks down at their hands, at Lamballe's little lace gloves, with a smidge of dirt on the edge of one pinkie.

'Not alone,' Lamballe says.

'Your Majesty is never alone,' Lafeyette agrees. 'We are all working together. Saint-Georges, if you want to see where you can get with this Brissot, I see no reason why you shouldn't. You and His Highness both can keep an eye on him.'

'I'm glad to have something to do,' Philippe mutters. 'Better a pornographer's babysitter than a grave-robber.'

She has been too hot-headed with Philippe, she knows. She's failed dismally at earning their love. As usual.

The ways in which reality falls to pieces may be myriad, but Antoinette can count on one hand the ways she has seen women decay. She understands the Princesse de Lamballe, who has settled into an angelic arrangement of the pretty and the good. She understands the Duchesse de Polignac, who has settled into wary and remote sophistica-tion. She knows the ways they can sit in rooms, or walk in and out of them, and the sorts of rooms that contain them. They chose these paths the way they might choose a portraitist from sample paintings, or a dress fabric from a Pandora doll.

Somewhere there are other rooms, with other women in them. Women who have much worse choices, or no choices at all. And women who have managed to arrange reality in ways that Antoinette cannot.

Élisabeth Vigée Le Brun is not anyone's painted image. She wields the brush. As an artist, she goes into all the sorts of rooms that Philippe, Saint-Georges, and Lafayette can enter, and hear conversations the Queen of France never can, because they stop when she appears.

Vigée Le Brun grew up across the street from the Palais-Royal. She has told the Queen how happy it made her, in childhood, to go into the brightly lit gardens at night with her parents. People would spill out of the opera house and sing and play instruments. Her whole life, the painter has been surrounded by brilliant people and new ideas.

Today, Vigée Le Brun lives on the other side of the Palais-Royal, but still not far from its cafés and art exhibits (the Orléans family collection alone, open to the public, is massive, and the nearby Louvre Palace is mainly used these days to house the royal collection). Now that Philippe has expanded the Palais-Royal, the neighbourhood is noisy with arguments in the cafés and the private salons in the houses of painters and philosophers.

Ideas are brought to Antoinette in stamped leather books; even the ones that are banned, the ones for her private library, are presented, made official, and sanctioned. Noted in ledgers.

Ideas are not presented to women like Vigée Le Brun; they breathe them like air and they create them. Antoinette wants such a woman in her Circle, someone who might be able to enter all the rooms that the men enter, but who can see women as something other than paintings.

The portrait of the Queen in white muslin may have damaged Antoinette's reputation, but not Vigée Le Brun's, whose talent is not in question. She is fierce at her work, and only lets a laugh play around her lips when she is not looking at her canvas. Why this should suggest to Antoinette that the painter is trustworthy, she does not know. But it does.

So when the painter arrives for the Queen's next sitting, in the Queen's bedroom, the Queen is ready to invite her into the world of magic. An even trade of knowledge and access. With every day that passes, Antoinette becomes more certain that Philippe's loyalties are not with the Circle. She wants to know whom he meets and what they talk about. In fact, she wants to know what all the rogue magisters of Paris are talking about. Polignac and Lamballe are loyal spies at court, but Antoinette has no one she can rely on in the Palais-Royal, no one who is hers. Lafayette and Saint-Georges are good men, but they are not *hers*.

It is the eve of Antoinette's twenty-eighth birthday. Lamballe is with her for the portrait sitting, and knows what Antoinette has planned. She is stiff with excitement. Antoinette can see it, although Lamballe sits demure on her cushioned stool, perfectly still, patronizingly aristocratic in the presence of the painter. How strange, to know someone so well, and yet gain no comfort from familiarity.

Vigée Le Brun has a blowsy scarf around her shoulders and she walks slowly, one hand on her lower back, obviously pregnant.

Then the painter trips, and the pine box in her hand opens and her brushes go everywhere, skittering across the floor. She laughs, and grabs the back of a chair to lower herself to the ground.

Antoinette crosses to her, one pregnant woman to another, and takes her elbow, righting her. 'No, you must not,' she says. 'Sit here, please, and let us do it.'

Lamballe is already gathering the brushes and Antoinette takes a bundle from her, picks up the remaining few. She hands the box to Vigée Le Brun.

'Your Majesty is too kind,' says the painter. 'I am sorry for being so clumsy.'

'Nonsense. I know how it is,' says Antoinette. 'You have one child already, isn't that so?'

'A little girl. The light of my world.'

'Tell me, how is the Academy treating you, now that you're a member?'

When Antoinette used all the persuasion in her arsenal to make the fusty Academy admit Vigée Le Brun, she had a feeling, even then, that this painter's love would be worth the cost – and anyway, she is the only artist who shows Antoinette as she really looks, and somehow makes her look beautiful anyway. It's a kind of magic of its own.

'We shall see,' the painter says. 'I must thank you for speaking on my behalf, Your Majesty.'

'Your talent speaks for itself,' Antoinette protests. 'I love all of your work. Your portrait of Lamballe captures her perfectly.'

Vigée Le Brun nods warily. 'Her Highness was a very obliging subject.'

Lamballe beams.

'I'm sure,' says Antoinette. 'She is a very obliging person. But you've caught how pretty she is, that little pointed nose, those languid eyes, that chin—'

'You're naming body parts, now, my dear,' says the princess. 'Everyone has them.' She looks at Antoinette with sad confidence, like a maiden aunt looking at a roué.

Suddenly, horribly, Antoinette understands that Lamballe knows. She knows. She can see that the Queen no longer loves her back. Of course she knows. She's not a fool.

'But not everyone has yours, Marie-Louise,' Antoinette stammers. She must keep up the pretences; everything will crumble otherwise. 'And other painters have not captured them properly. You have an eye, Madame. You see the world as it is, and you see its beauty. Two qualities that don't exist in the same person very often.'

'Your Majesty does me great honour,' says the painter. 'I'd be pleased to create another portrait.'

'And so you shall. But I brought you here today for another conversation, for something else I would like to offer you, and to ask of you.'

Vigée Le Brun looks from Lamballe's face back to Antoinette's, patiently. Antoinette does not know quite how to begin – she never does, with a new magister.

'Have you heard strange stories over the last few years? Rumours of magical occurrences? The clock tower that walked in London, Dr Mesmer's healing instrument, the man who couldn't shoot George Washington . . .'

The painter looks cautious. 'These ideas spread like fashion, don't they? Or like the old stories of werewolves and revenants. I admit I've seen things that I can't explain.'

'But perhaps I can,' Antoinette says. 'As an artist, you understand that there is a kind of power in objects, that they carry meaning and possibility. A crucifix, a child's tooth, a box of paints. Some people have learned a way of increasing that power. Of making objects carry certain invisible qualities.'

'Is it science, Your Majesty?'

'Some view it that way,' says Antoinette, thinking of Mesmer. 'It is a kind of experimentation, although no one understands quite how it works. But we call it magic. As a kind of shorthand, perhaps: a word for a thing we don't understand.'

She watches the painter's face. The reactions are perfect: shock, and slight confusion. If Vigée Le Brun is a spy for the Order of 1326, she is the best actor Antoinette has ever seen. The word *we* echoes in the room.

The painter looks at Lamballe, as if for confirmation.

'It's true,' says Lamballe, pouring tea out of a silver pot. 'We – Her Majesty, and I, and other people – are magisters. Magicians. Sorceresses.'

She carries the cup of tea to Vigée Le Brun, hands it to her kindly.

'Here,' says Antoinette. 'I'll demonstrate.'

She pulls a hairpin from her wig and holds it between thumb and forefinger. It is slim, smooth silver, with a single round chrysoprase, green with black veins, set on the end. She aims it at the far wall, at a bit of wallpaper she has never liked, and a bolt of lightning strikes it. The wallpaper smoulders. She looks at Vigée Le Brun.

Vigée Le Brun's eyebrows are as high as they can go. Then they drop; she frowns. 'Your Majesty, why tell me this? Why take me into your confidence?'

'Because a painter of your talents would be an excellent worker of magic, I feel sure. Because I trust you. And because you may be able to befriend other magisters, tell me what they are saying, in Paris.'

'Other magisters?'

Antoinette swallows. 'First, I must tell you that there are dangers. There are some magisters who want a world in which only they can do magic. I will tell you who they are, but you must always take care, and you may choose to keep your abilities secret.'

The painter nods grimly. 'You wish me to spy on them?'

'No, my friend. I am not sending you into a lion's den. I would like you to, well, to befriend my own friends. My colleagues. Men and women of science, and art, and members of the nobility, all of whom are magisters too. They speak to me as the Queen of France, and I need someone who will speak to me as a friend. And so many of my friends' – she glances at Lamballe – 'are here at Versailles, with me, and can only see what I see.'

The painter is still frowning. She looks again at the wallpaper, and then back at the Queen.

'Well? What do you say? This is not an order from your queen, but a request from your friend.'

Vigée Le Brun looks sombre. Good; she's decided to do it.

'I'm honoured, and I'll do what I can. I – Everything I believed to be true is in question. Forgive me. I would ask—'

'Yes?' *Name your price, and make it a good one.*

'I would ask for as much instruction in magic as Your Majesty can give me.'

Antoinette claps her hands. 'What did I tell you, Marie-Louise? I thought she would say that.'

'And I agreed, as I recall,' says Lamballe mildly.

Antoinette feels something unpleasant rising in her chest, bile or heartburn. It feels like punishment, but it's only the pregnancy.

Then Antoinette buckles.

The cramps are like the ones she had with Mousseline, that awful day, with all the court watching – but it is too early, this baby cannot come yet.

She screams, and Lamballe grabs her skirt, looks at it, at the blood there. Then both Lamballe and Vigée Le Brun call out, some words that Antoinette does not hear.

CHAPTER FORTY-TWO

Visitors to Naples – A Cancelled Party – A Splinter –
Specious Taxonomies

❖

Joseph visits Naples in January 1784. 'Count Falkenstein' arrives with Angelo Soliman, who is limping from some wound in the foot and cannot attend at court, and with a retinue of a dozen servants in false livery. Joseph likes the work of being Holy Roman Emperor but not the pomp. He is the opposite of Ferdinand, who bows low to Joseph, refusing to play along.

'My dear brother-in-law,' Ferdinand booms. 'Naples welcomes you. We have prepared a marvellous reception for tomorrow night. We have fruit ices carved like hot-air balloons, all the rage in Paris. We have little sausages, because I know how you Germans like sausages, eh? I know my wife does, don't you, Charlotte? We have – we even have seven hundred and thirty-nine starlings in cages in the under-kitchen, ready to be killed and baked in pies with wine and tarragon.'

Charlotte smiles sympathy at her brother. Behind her shoulder, she can hear Acton's soft breath. Her six living children flank her, all but the wilful baby Maria Amalia (so like her namesake) dutifully smiling at their uncle, the Holy Roman Emperor.

'These children are a marvel,' says the childless Joseph, looking at each one as if he were inspecting troops. They reward his attentions by standing straighter. Teresa is eleven now; her marriage is one of the topics Joseph is here to discuss.

Joseph turns back, looks at Ferdinand. He does not return the bow or the greeting. 'Why seven hundred and thirty-nine?' he asks.

'What?' Ferdinand says.

'The starlings, sir.'

'I don't know!' Ferdinand laughs. 'You know everything, Acton. Tell me. Why seven hundred and thirty-nine starlings?'

'Because His Majesty asked for a thousand,' Acton replies.

Charlotte tries not to smirk. Acton doesn't mean to be impertinent; it isn't his fault he sees the worst in everything. It's one reason he's so valuable.

'Yes, my wife's minister is right,' says Ferdinand with a wild little laugh. 'Nobody in Naples does anything properly. We do it half-arsed, or we do it as if it's the only thing that matters. Nobody works in Naples, unless they feel like it.'

'A great many people work in Naples,' snaps Charlotte. 'We eat the bread they bake every morning. Naples' problem is not laziness but corruption.'

'We may run short on the pies,' says Ferdinand, as if she had not spoken, 'but we will have a marvellous masque, Joseph. Some of the actors will be nude. It's a nature piece. Rousseau and all that, you know. Nipples everywhere.'

Charlotte breathes, evenly, keeping the blood out of her face. Ferdinand no longer calls Acton her lover but he calls him her minister in the same sort of tone. He's been more horrible than ever, lately, and she has simply stopped visiting his bed every month. To hell with it. She has given Naples enough children. The last time she saw him at night, he was drunk, and he had come back from the hunt. She told him he would be needed at the hand-kissing ceremony the following day and he whacked her across the chest with one of his hunting gloves. That was two days ago. He is the King, and he is her husband, and there's nothing she can do under her religion about either of those things, but by God she won't see him alone again, the bastard.

'I thought I might have a tour of Calabria later,' says Joseph as they walk to the Hall of Mirrors. 'See some of the damage first-hand. Are the roads passable?'

'You can ask my wife about that,' says Ferdinand, and he walks ahead. 'She knows everything. Beatrix, heavenly creature, what the hell are you wearing in your décolletage? Is that a miniature between your gorgeous breasts? Let's see it.'

He runs forward, and for a moment Charlotte remembers the child Wolfgang Mozart, running through the halls at Schönnbrun, before he tripped and fell into Antoine's arms. A performance, she thought at the time, and still does.

Joseph rolls his eyes at Ferdinand's antics. He probably remembers Mozart too.

'You won't find the roads passable,' Charlotte tells her brother. 'I travelled there in the autumn, but now, with this cold snap, it's all frozen muck. The horses can't get through.'

'How are the people getting food? Supplies?'

'By boat when they can, although one out of every three founders in this horrible fog. Is the fog as bad in Vienna?'

'No. No, not quite this bad. It is a blight, though. Some of my schools report that the children cough so pitifully through their lessons that the instructors can't teach. How are your schools coming, Charlotte?'

'Very well. We've converted many of the old monasteries and every peasant child can attend for free.'

'If their parents can afford to lose them at home.'

'Yes, of course. Rome wasn't built in a day, Joseph.'

'But your navy was, or so I hear.'

'Not at all!' She laughs. 'I did as you suggested, brother. I built a navy the likes of which no one has ever seen. But it was not overnight. It took years of hard work and we had to bribe or intimidate every mast-wright south of the Alps to get it done. Here, Joseph, this is General Acton. The glory of the new navy goes to him.'

Joseph nods. 'I've heard all about you, sir.' He looks back at Charlotte, as if appraising whether the rumours are true.

'Acton can show you around Naples, if you like,' she says hurriedly. 'You'll find no better guide.'

'Surely he has better things to do than show a visitor the sights.'

'Acton serves at the pleasure of His Majesty,' she says. 'In other words, he does what I tell him. Even if what I tell him to do is impossible.'

'It would be my honour, sir,' says Acton. 'Perhaps tomorrow, before the reception.'

Joseph nods. She walks with her brother through the corridors to the coffee room, for a real conversation. Acton follows, a few steps behind.

Then her brother pulls her to one side, behind a marble statue of Diana. He's frowning; his face is so much older since the last visit. 'What's that on your shoulder?'

She pulls her fichu over to cover her collarbone. 'It's nothing. A bruise.'

Joseph takes her by the wrist, as though she were not a queen, and walks her a few steps away. Acton steps towards them but she glances at him, tells him what to do with her eyes, and he obeys. He stops, and waits, and watches.

'Is he hitting you?' Joseph hisses. 'That godforsaken boor of a husband. Does he strike you, Charlotte?'

She breathes in, breathes out. She sees no point in lying. There is nothing Joseph or anyone else can do about it anyway. What the late Empress Maria Theresa joined together, no man can put asunder. Joseph knows that better than anyone.

'He has hit me, yes. When I first arrived, and had no one here to help me, and nowhere to go. Then he stopped for a while. This is, I think, the fourth time he has hit me, in our years together.'

'Christ.' Joseph scowls. 'I'm not going to that man's party. I don't want to see him again, not once while I'm here. He can eat seven hundred and thirty-nine starlings by himself.'

'Good. I'll cancel it. He'll mope and go off whoring and gambling for three days and I'll have three days of peace.'

'Why don't you – Why don't you do something about it?'

'And what shall I do about it, Joseph? Tell me.'

'Where does he hit you?'

She shakes her head. 'In our bedroom. In the carriage, twice.'

'No, I mean – is it on the face? Where it shows?'

She cocks her head and looks at him. What a disappointment men are. 'Thank you for your concern, brother. He has never hit me on the face.'

He lets go of her wrist. 'Well, thank God for small mercies, anyway. Slip a knife between his ribs, Charlotte, the moment your boy is old enough to take the throne.'

He smiles wanly, to show that he's only mostly serious. Charlotte makes a face in response that Joseph is free to interpret any way he likes. She's thought about it. She thinks about it every day.

But Charlotte is not Catherine of Russia, though by God some days she would like to be. She won't kill her husband. She will use the tools at her disposal to keep him away from her. She is the one who sets the schedule, who determines which members of the royal family will be in which palace on which days. She has six living children, though God knows it would be better if she had more than two boys. Still, Francesco is strong and healthy, and her seat on the Council is secure in any case – no one would imagine running the government of Naples without her. And her daughters will make good marriages. She need never be in the same room alone with Ferdinand ever again.

They cancel the party. She and Joseph spend the rest of

his visit in easy, quiet work, drinking coffee and scheming. They plot Teresa's marriage; like her, he favours a match with Leopold's son, who will be the Habsburg heir, and Joseph's heir too. It's settled.

'And what about Antoinette's little Marie-Thérèse? What does she call her? Mousseline?' Charlotte asks. 'She'll be marriageable soon enough.'

Joseph groans. 'The Bourbons have all sorts of plans, as usual, and most of them are out of the question. But don't worry. There's time for many things to change.'

The Emperor says this almost grimly, as though he's determined to make up for the years he spent ruling alongside Maria Theresa. His sudden, sweeping modernization schemes have had unforeseen consequences: even something as simple as changing the official language of the Empire to German rather than Latin has made all the non-German-speakers fear that they're being pushed down, pushed out. The more he tries to unify the Empire, the more it fractures.

And as for the Bourbon–Habsburg alliance that Maria Theresa made the goal of her daughters' lives? Bourbon France and Spain have only been reminded of their common interests, now that they've humbled Britain in the American war. And Joseph is turning not to Bourbons for allies, but east to Russia, and even to their mother's old enemy Frederick of Prussia.

Joseph's right. Many things are changing. And that leaves room for her kingdom to make its own choices.

Caramanico returns to Italy. After several years of service in England, she's recalled him; it is not good practice to leave the same ambassador anywhere for too long, lest they become part of the furnishings of the place, as William Hamilton has with his fossils.

With Soliman in Naples too, Charlotte invites the two men to a salon in the palace, protected by enchanted firescreens.

The next meeting of the Order is not for some weeks, and anyway, Angelo Soliman's foot is still too sore for him to walk through the tunnels. But she wants to get a sense of how the Order stands across Europe.

The prince comes through the door in a plain brown coat and his natural brown hair tied neatly in a Quakerish ribbon.

'You look like an American,' Charlotte says as the prince kisses her hand.

'Everyone looks like an American now, in England, or else they look like a hot-air balloon, all puffed up,' he says. 'There is no middle ground in 1784.'

'You left your daredevil secretary in England, I take it?'

'Yes. Lunardi's work is going well, speaking of hot-air balloons. Combining magic and science, drawing crowds wherever he goes, and proving all sorts of things possible.'

Charlotte isn't sure she would call this going well; it seems reckless in more ways than one. She opens her mouth to say so, when Caramanico turns at the sound of the door opening.

'Ah, I see I was not misinformed after all, and Dr Soliman does grace Naples with his presence.'

It's good to see Soliman. Charlotte is surprised by the relief she feels at having him there in person, and not merely at the other end of a letter. But he is pale, leaning on a cane, a line of sweat above his ear.

It began, he tells them, with a splinter.

An ordinary splinter. A black line no wider than a hair and no longer than a thumbnail. Wood, perhaps, or a sliver of some metal. The day they arrived in Naples, it slid into the sole of Soliman's foot and stayed there.

He did try to get it out himself, with tweezers, with a needle, even with a knife. When it remained stubborn, he put a poultice of honey and turmeric on it to draw it out, and then a poultice of salt, bread, and milk, and then of coltsfoot and lard.

After a few days, he was hobbling about with a bandaged

foot, and had purple lines running up his leg, a great ulcer on the sole.

'Good Lord,' she says. 'Sit here, this is the best chair. Some brandy?'

'I'll keep my wits about me, for now. Thank you, Your Majesty.'

'You're sure it's not enchanted?'

'It seems a strange way to attack someone,' Caramanico says, 'wasting sacrifices on leaving a splinter about, on the chance that one person would step on it just so.'

Soliman holds out his hands. 'As you say, a strange attack indeed. We can assume it is an ordinary bit of bad luck, then.'

If anyone had ever made a spell to draw out a splinter or heal an infection, it is not in the embroidered book – or in the *Reconditus*, which now holds all the spells in the embroidered book along with its many others.

'My physicians will have a look. Do you know, there are a number of female doctors in Italy? The bourgeois families send their daughters to the University of Bologna.'

'We might consider some for the Academy, Your Majesty,' says Caramanico.

'Mmm,' she says. 'Though most men and women of science have had enough to occupy them, with this unwholesome fog. I had hoped, Dr Soliman, you might have some ideas for me about how to dispel it.'

He bows his head. 'Your Majesty, when your brother the Emperor does not need me, I have been working day and night to find the spell of spells. When I do, it may provide a way forward.'

'You believe you will find it, then,' Caramanico says, stepping towards him.

She examines Soliman's face, this face she's known since she was a child. One of the few faces she's come to trust. 'You have such faith in it. Such faith that the answer exists, that you can find it.'

He considers. 'Faith? I am a philosopher, not a monk. But I learned from old books written by scholars who sought to understand the natural world as an expression of something less tangible. It is as if the ancients knew there was some great truth beyond their horizon, like their land of Prester John or their earthly paradise, but they didn't have the tools to get there. And now we modern scholars have those tools but we have forgotten that the far land exists. Magisters always knew, and could have been searching. How does magic work? If we understood that, what a world we could create! But instead of searching for answers, we have spent so many centuries developing signs and rituals to shield the truth from the uneducated. And then we came to believe in these signs and rituals ourselves, and we have come to fear the truth. We may practise magic but we fear it as much as any peasant fears his superstitions.'

'By we, you mean the Order,' Caramanico says.

'Of course,' Soliman responds, surprised.

'I thought perhaps you meant the magic practised in savage lands.'

'I did not, but I have been seeking answers from other lands, as much as I can, to see what principles underlie all forms of magic. What little I have been able to glean has been instructive but inconclusive, at least as regards the question of the spell of spells.'

'Perhaps those forms are merely inferior,' Caramanico says. 'Being from hotter climates, where the need for invention is not so immediate, and so the people have evolved to be inferior. If there are taxonomies of humanity, why not taxonomies of magic?'

Caramanico does not look at Soliman, but Charlotte does, and can see on his face what he thinks about 'taxonomies of humanity'. His letters over the years have criticized such ideas in David Hume's writing, and even in their beloved Montesquieu.

Caramanico rushes on, filling the silence. 'Surely the Order's forms have reached the highest expression, and the others are, perhaps, imitations. Degraded and corrupted forms, half learned from rogue magisters. Or primitive attempts, perhaps. Perhaps more rudimentary societies are, as Rousseau would have it, closer to nature. If there is a great truth in the natural world, a truth that governs magic, perhaps they have some instinctive understanding of it.'

'I cannot say,' Soliman says curtly.

'But you believe you will discover the spell of spells,' Caramanico says.

'I believe it exists, and I must believe that if I am given enough years, I can find it, not through prayer or poetry but through numbers and hard thought. And I believe that one day, the world will be the better for it. The perfection of humanity does not lie in innocence we have lost but in wisdom we have not gained. Rousseau looked backward; I look forward.'

Charlotte would call that faith, but his faith is not like her mother's simple beliefs: that reward follows virtue, intercession follows prayer, and punishment follows sin, and if the consequence fails then the cause was not what it appeared. Maria Theresa's faith of smoke and muttering was always obscure to Charlotte, but Soliman's faith in the future shines so brightly she almost wants to reach towards it with him.

He seems to have the same effect on Caramanico, who walks towards Soliman and puts his hand on his shoulder. Soliman winces, perhaps from the pain in his foot. 'Then I will help you, now that I'm home in Naples again. I fully support your ambitions, Dr Soliman. It is a new world, and we will need new ideas to make our way in it.'

'You have enjoyed your time in England, I see,' Charlotte says dryly.

He bows his head. 'So many opportunities for men of talent to make their own mark, to lead. One may encounter great men so easily, simply by walking in St James's Park, or going to any coffee house, or the grand new Freemasons'

Hall, or the daily demonstrations of electricity and micro-scopes. But there are opportunities here, too, and I am glad to be home. And glad to be able to be of some assistance, Dr Soliman. While you are unable to go and interview scholars yourself, I will be your errand-boy. I know everyone in Italy these days. I can get you any books you need, and carry any letters.'

Soliman inclines his head. 'Thank you, Your Highness, but I expect His Imperial Majesty will be travelling north again soon.'

'You cannot travel with such an injury,' Charlotte protests. 'You will stay here until you are healed, and my brother will agree.'

Emperor Joseph leaves, King Gustavus of Sweden arrives; the court turns, shuffles partners, bows, begins again.

The currency of the court of Naples is proximity to the King and Queen. Physical proximity. If you are anyone of note – a lord, a minister, a courtier – you will be invited to one of the hand-kissing ceremonies that occur throughout the year. You will be invited to kiss the monarchs' hands in the order of your importance. You will stand on the starkly patterned marble floor like a pawn on a chessboard, waiting to move forward to assert some small measure of power.

At other court events, the important people stand as close as they can to the King and especially, in these last few years, the Queen. Charlotte often finds it claustrophobic, having so many other bodies crushed around her wide panniers and stopping her from moving without calling out her intentions, like a peddler in a carnival.

But on the day of the arrival of King Gustavus, she finds herself grateful for the squirming wall of sweat and rosewater, brocade and silk. It insulates her, makes it unnecessary to so much as acknowledge the presence of Count Axel von Fersen.

She couldn't very well disallow him. He's the captain of the King of Sweden's guards, and the King of Sweden is here on a state visit. Still, she has no intention of letting him believe he's entitled to the slightest toleration. The lover who made her sister prey to a doomed cause. A traitor to the Order, Silfversparre says. She ought to kill him where he stands. Run a dagger through his ribs.

But there's nothing clean about murder.

So she simply does not look at him, though he's there at Gustavus's elbow. The King of Sweden is nearly forty and has an actor's mobile face under his wig of fat grey curls. He looks self-satisfied; perhaps any sovereign would, who'd managed to leach power from both parliament and nobility.

He speaks with Charlotte about the Russian–Danish alliance, about what her brother Joseph might do in the event Sweden tries to acquire Norway. She supplies the careful, precise answers that she and Acton crafted in advance, and meanwhile she is aware of Fersen, watching her, unsmiling.

'May I present the captain of my guard, Your Majesty? Count Axel von Fersen.'

Gustavus's words slice through the fog in her mind, and she refocuses her eyes. 'Hmm?'

'Count Axel von Fersen.' He gestures to the count, who bows perfectly.

'Count,' she says. 'How wonderful. I get so little news of my sister in Paris, and I hoped since you spend so much time there, you might tell me how she is.'

He smiles.

'Have I said something amusing, Count?'

'Forgive me, it's only that Her Majesty asked me to report the same regarding you and your children, Your Majesty.'

Charlotte inclines her head. 'Did she? Then you may tell the Queen of France we are all quite well, God be thanked.' She pauses. Her spies tell her things, but they never tell her what she really wants to know. 'And *is* my sister well?'

'She would teach the torches to burn bright,' he replies, his dark eyes flashing. It stops her breath, and she understands, suddenly, that he truly loves her. That Antoinette is

450

loved. And that she probably loves him. He is not merely a dashing rogue; he is everything to her, and she is everything to him. It makes her ache, seeing that possibility. How terrible and wonderful it would be to have someone who would quietly and without hesitation lie down and die for you, not out of duty but out of pure love.

She glances back at the King, becomes aware suddenly of the crush of courtiers all around them, the hush as they listen.

Charlotte laughs lightly. 'So you quote Shakespeare, among your other charms,' she says lightly, weakly. 'She would teach the torches, wouldn't she? How gallant you are, Count. I see why my sister keeps you close. She would teach everyone and everything to do more and be other than they are. She wants the world to be perfect and everyone in it to be happy. And her friends indulge her naivety, I'm afraid, exposing her to harsh judgement by the cynics and the pamphleteers. If she would only act—'

'Her Majesty does not act at all,' Fersen says. 'I have never met anyone more natural in all their dealings.'

'How anyone can be natural at Versailles is beyond me,' Gustavus says smoothly. 'There is such rigour in everything there. I'm always afraid to open my mouth.'

Everyone laughs politely. The rest of the Swedish visit goes smoothly, though Charlotte does not speak to Fersen again. When they go, she feels not relieved but bereft, as though she missed a vital opportunity.

Charlotte loves the sky at Caserta. It's a green, gentle part of her kingdom, untouched by the calamities of the fog and the earthquakes. The massive complex, rivalling Schönbrunn and Versailles, is set on gently sloping ground, so when she walks uphill in the gardens behind her palace, she can see for miles. Charlotte has commissioned a series of mytho-logical fountains to mark each stage of the glittering canal that rises in pieces, guiding the walker towards a man-made waterfall that leaps out of the green hills. Everything is man-made: the stones from ruined Pompeii and the ancient-looking temples set into the woods, even the paths that seem on the brink of being overgrown, and the English garden she is building near the top of the hill, just beside the fountain that shows Diana being surprised by the hunter Actaeon.

But in this spring of 1784, there is no view. The fog has lingered for more than a year. People have forgotten what the sky was like before. Now she looks down the long avenue towards the palace and sees nothing but garden melting into grey mist. This is not the damp, cool fog of a summer day. It doesn't make the greens richer. It blocks the sunlight, and the grass is yellow.

She feels hemmed in tight. She wants to run the length of these pathways, and breathe freer air. To feel something bigger than anxiety and exhaustion.

Charlotte turns to Acton, who holds his papers in his hand and waits for her to finish gazing and thinking. She has made him prime minister, and he manages the country with the same calm capability he showed in creating her navy.

'Is there anything else?' she asks.

'There is always something else. If Your Majesty is tired, we can address it tomorrow.'

It is a long walk, though there's an optical illusion that makes it look much shorter when you set out. The end of the park is two miles from the palace, which is one reason Charlotte likes to walk here with Caterina, or the other Brothers of Naples, or Acton. She learned as a child that the most private place in a palace is outside it.

'No,' she says. 'I'm not tired. Let's do it now.'

'All right. The cook at the city palace is concerned about a flock of birds.'

It surprises her into a laugh. 'Birds?'

'Apparently they have been in cages in an under-kitchen for some time. They were to have been eaten at the party for your brother's visit, and the party was cancelled.'

She laughs, a loud sound here in this birdless, grey garden. 'The starlings! The seven hundred and thirty-nine starlings.'

He looks at his notes. 'Six hundred and four now. Some must have died.'

'But why are the starlings still there?'

'His Majesty has not requested starlings since.'

She laughs again. 'All right, so it's starlings for dinner, is it? But why is the cook so impatient? Surely they can't eat much seed.'

'These particular birds – these starlings – have a habit of imitating the sounds around them, I'm told. Every time a bell rings at St Mary's, the starlings repeat it, at some length.'

She laughs again, and claps her hands together. 'Marvellous. This I must see. Under no circumstances is anyone to eat these birds until I have had the chance to hear that for myself. In fact, let's send for them. Bring them here to Caserta. They'll pine less in the country, surely.'

He smiles his tight sailor smile and folds his papers, putting them into his waistcoat pocket.

'I am sure the birds will find it lovely here, Your Majesty.'

The garden doesn't look lovely at the moment. It looks leached and sere. They approach the top of the hill, where a grove of mulberry trees makes a deeper shadow in this grey new world.

'It's hard to be happy since the fog set in, isn't it, Acton?'

'Yes, I suppose it is.'

'You suppose?' She turns and looks at him, and finds he is looking at her, and blushes. How foolish to blush – there's nothing wrong with looking, not even at a queen.

'I don't concern myself with happiness. It isn't a – I don't have a philosophy against it, nothing like that. Just the way I was made, Your Majesty.'

'Ah. I'm the same way, I think. I am content, or I am not. I am working, or I am not. Happiness seems like a bother. A chimera.'

'Yes.'

They look at each other, and Charlotte remembers Fersen, glaring at her in her own throne room, quoting Shakespeare about her sister.

'The rumours have stopped, I think,' she says in a voice so contained it strains her throat. 'About you and me, I mean.'

He nods, not pretending he doesn't know. 'These things will pass, when there's nothing behind them.'

'Of course.' It's cold, suddenly. She would like to be by a fire, with a book, alone. She would like to forget ever having wanted anything. 'It's hard to know where it even started.'

'Oh, that much I know. It started because I am not Naples' prime minister, and everyone sees that. I'm yours.'

'Are they not the same?'

He shakes his head, almost sadly. 'They are very much not the same. But you are Queen of Naples, and so I serve Naples, because I serve you. You are right to worry about the fog,' he says, looking away and biting his lip. 'It is a problem for trade and for the harvest. I'm relieved to see the mulberry trees are thriving, at least.'

The mulberry trees planted by Ferdinand's father, when he founded the silk factory just up the road at San Leucio. Food for the worms.

'I have spent a great deal of time in San Leucio,' she says, wishing for a moment she could tell him all about her secret work, how much good she's done in the shadows. 'It's a fortunate little village. Everything they need is there: farmland, water, good air. The roads to Rome and Naples are good but it is far enough away that they live quietly, without any politics or ferment.'

'Utopia, then.'

'It could be,' she muses, leaning against a tree. 'We could make it one, Acton. Bring all the jobless and walking wounded from Calabria and Sicily. All their wages would go into a common fund to make sure their needs were provided for. They could elect a council of elders to oversee the daily business of the colony—'

'It's a colony now!' He laughs, the laugh of a friend. He leans on the next tree over, a few feet away, one knee bent.

'Yes, a colony,' she says, smiling approvingly at him. 'A perfect society. The women and the men would be equal. No child marriages. No dowries, no incentives for families to marry off their girls to boors.'

She doesn't know how to cross the distance between them. He's looking away from her, down the avenue, at nothing. At ugly grey mist. At the future.

'Do you know of the late Jacques Vaucanson?' he asks. 'The one who built that grotesque duck automaton?'

Acton's questions are never predictable; he carries on conversations like a ship at sea, into the wind, coming out of the fog when you least expect it. This one makes her nervous; Vaucanson was a rogue magister, and many of his devices were enchanted. Soliman has told her all about it. The famous duck was able to nibble food out of someone's hand, and even produced excretions that Vaucanson claimed were evidence of a sophisticated chemical device that perfectly replicated digestion. In reality, it was an enchantment, used to gull spectators out of money for the chance to see it work. How disgusting that anyone would use magic for such a purpose.

The Brothers of Paris got nervous and had Vaucanson killed two years ago – the Rohanites have been more violent of late. Vaucanson willed his collection to the French King, and apparently the King's philosophers are bewildered by the fact that so many of his creations do not work after his death.

It is one more piece of evidence that what everyone insists on calling 'the new science' is slipping outside of science's grasp, or was never there. Magic is loose in the world. The common people call it by its name.

And what can the Order do, now that the genie is out of the bottle? Recruit and discredit, as it's always done, but more and more, destroying some people and welcoming others into the fold, for the right reasons and the wrong ones.

'Yes, I've heard something about it,' she says. 'I don't see the appeal, myself. My sister Antoinette has a new life-sized doll that plays the dulcimer. One day we will wake up and find that these automata have taken over Europe in our sleep.'

She imagines the Pandora doll, sitting somewhere in a box, moth-eaten. Does Antoinette still have hers? Charlotte had terrible stomach pains one night in the fall and she thought for a moment it was the Pandora doll – it felt the same – but the next day, the General arrived.

'Nobody could take the throne of Naples from you,' he says, and pauses for a long time before he adds, 'Your Majesty.'

For a fey moment she wonders what Acton would say if she told him that she had the power to enchant objects, that she is a magister. A sorceress. A witch. Perhaps he would think that all her success was down to magic, to mere trickery. And perhaps he would be right.

But she won't trick him. And she won't ever give him reason to stop believing she is wonderful.

A breeze skirls down the mulberry avenue and she shivers in her thin sleeves.

'You haven't told me about Vaucanson and his duck,' she says.

'He also made a loom, in which the pattern can be controlled using a stiff card punched with holes in a particular pattern. It isn't widely used, yet, but if we had such looms here, we could have the jobless of Calabria at work within a week, without training them.'

She imagines her kingdom dotted with enchanted looms, clacking under the hands of women. She doesn't embroider much any more; she works on a bigger scale now. Perhaps the embroidered book should have gone with Antoinette after all. Charlotte has become a weaver instead.

She turns her head, lolling still against the tree. Acton is looking at her steadily.

'Tell me something, John Acton,' she whispers. 'Are you mine? Really mine?'

He swallows, his Adam's apple moving under his pale skin. 'I am yours.'

'Then I have two requests to make of you. Second, please help me build the perfect society at San Leucio.'

'And first?'

'First, please come closer to me,' she says. She cannot cross the distance but she can order him to do it. And he does. He takes two steps towards her, while she turns to him, her back still against the mulberry tree.

'Please, please come closer,' she whispers as his rough cheek rests against hers, as their arms clutch each other.

They are impatient, both unlacing his breeches at once. He lifts Charlotte against the tree and she wraps her legs around him, her petticoats bunched against his brass buttons. She grabs onto the branches of the tree and kisses him to keep from crying out.

CHAPTER FORTY-THREE

The Queen's Hamlet — The Effect of an Opera Performance — Terror in the Night — A Visit to the Cardinal — Antoinette Makes a Purchase

———— ⚜ ————

Élisabeth Vigée Le Brun's second pregnancy ended in grief not long after Antoinette's own miscarriage. When their bodies had recovered, the two women took a quiet cup of tea together in a private corner of the Trianon. In the spring of 1784, Vigée Le Brun paints the royal children in the gardens at Versailles; the painter insists she is ready to work. Antoinette's daughter is neither Mousseline nor simply Marie-Thérèse today; today she is Madame Royale in striped gold-and-blue satin. She has a wise face for a five-year-old, and she collects her little brother in his blue suit, puts her arm around him. On her breast there is a pink carnation, and on his the medal that shows him to be a member of the chivalrous Order of the Holy Spirit.

The children are wearing straw hats, partly because the Messieurs Léonard are nowhere to be found. Though Antoinette knows full well where they are: there is a group of shopwomen in Marseille – milliners and haberdashers – who had been practising magic to keep their accounts, create impossible new dyes and hats that do not obey gravity, and set traces on their goods in case of theft. The Brothers took their memories – the women were unknown to the Circle and not immune to magic – but they did a botched job of it, and the poor women have been roaming the streets screaming nonsense about sorcery, their shops burning down. They are discredited, which is good enough for the Order; they are one more piece of evidence for those who insist, in the face of mounting evidence, that magic is not real, is a conspiracy of the government, or a corrupt plaything of the elite. If the shopkeepers prove persuasive in their rantings, then the Order will simply kill them. It is only a matter of time before the women are destroyed, or destroy themselves.

So the two Messieurs Léonard have gone to Marseille with their hairbrushes, to do the job properly, and show mercy to the women. Antoinette does not want attention drawn to their absence, so she suggested the hats.

On Mousseline's lap, there's a bird's nest. Empty and abandoned; Antoinette doesn't know where Vigée Le Brun found it.

'That nest is a bit dismal, isn't it?' Antoinette peers forward at her children, her embroidery in her lap.

'In the painting, it will have birds in it,' Vigée Le Brun responds, setting out little jars of yellowish oil and turpentine on the shelf of her easel.

Antoinette leans back in her cushioned armchair. 'That smell must be convenient for covering the smell of enchantments.'

'In Paris, everything stinks,' Vigée Le Brun says wryly, pulling drawers out of the paintbox she has set on the little table beside her.

'And what can you tell me of the Palais-Royal?'

It's a quiet spot, at the wilder edges of the gardens, with the sound of a fountain at a little distance. Out here, they can speak freely, as even the children are at enough distance that they will only catch a word or two. Vigée Le Brun has spread colours on her palette, and is sketching in the shapes of the children in straight, bold strokes of brown.

'Oh, the Palais-Royal is very exciting. Did you hear about what happened the other night, Your Majesty?'

'I heard Salieri's latest opera put everyone to sleep.'

The mention of opera makes her think of her brother Max, who writes to her dutifully, usually of music, which is all he cares about. She cares about it too, so why does she find it so hard to remember to reply? Can it really still be because she sacrificed her love for him, all those years ago? If they were together in person, they would be friends, she's sure. Maybe she would even gain new affection for him. They would go to the opera together.

'It did indeed put everyone to sleep.' Vigée Le Brun steps back and examines the portrait, while the Dauphin wriggles his feet. 'Everyone. The entire audience, and the orchestra, and the singers too.'

Antoinette grips her chair. 'Another attack?'

'So it would seem. But it was stymied. A soprano came out from behind the wings, with a glass of wine in her hand, already singing. Her spell reversed the effect of the magic, and everyone woke up, with only the haziest memory of having nodded off.'

'Then most people don't know?'

She shakes her head. 'I heard it from Mademoiselle Dervieux herself.'

'That name is familiar,' Antoinette says, puzzled. 'Has she been to Versailles?'

'Unlikely, Your Majesty. She's the daughter of a washer-woman, and she's an actress, and . . . a courtesan. You may have heard her name in connection with certain scandalous affairs. His Majesty's brothers . . .'

'I see.' Antoinette gazes into the distance, at the figures walking in the orangery, and along the grand canal. 'So she is a magister. And she has a spell that can counter magic! I wonder where she got it.'

'From Philippe d'Orléans, she says.'

'What?'

Rogue magisters are under no obligation to share spells with each other; they are not the Order, and they have no great book or library. They trade spells, or buy them from each other, if they choose. But the rogues of the Circle have tended to share their spells, especially the major ones; they are working towards the same goals, after all.

'And I bought it from Dervieux. I'll write it down for Your Majesty.'

'I'm grateful.' Antoinette can hardly think of what to say. 'I suppose Philippe must have found it quite recently.'

Vigée Le Brun wipes her brush, as if thinking. Then she says, reluctantly, 'She told me of a number of spells that His Serene Highness has been using to create powerful protections against magical attack at his family's estate at Saint-Cloud, which he is starting to apply to the Palais-Royal as well. Spells that are not among those Your Majesty shared with me.'

'May we stand up for a little while?' Mousseline calls. 'Louis-Joseph is wriggling.'

The little French village that grew on American soil and fooled the English has now shrunk back to size; all it took was a word of command. Fersen brought it back across the ocean to Antoinette.

She hasn't known quite what to do with it. It seems a shame to leave it in a trunk. Mousseline has outgrown her love of tiny houses. The Dauphin already has a model of George Washington's house at Mount Vernon, a gift from an American town council or some such thing to mark the end of the war. He's not old enough yet to show much interest in it.

And Antoinette has long yearned for a place she can go with her friends and break spells, work enchantments, without fear of spying eyes. Somewhere bigger than the little mirrored boudoir in the Petit Trianon.

She raises her little hamlet not far from the Temple of Love she built six years before, which she can see from her window at the Petit Trianon. Beyond the natural English garden and the grotto. She had the whole area blocked off while the buildings grew over the course of a single day, but she watched it with Polignac, and listened to the groans of the wood stretching, the crackling sound of mortar multiplying. It still has a toy quality: it doesn't quite look like a real place. That's why it worked so well to fool the British into thinking these were buildings set up to support and supply French troops, she supposes: it looks like what a French village *ought* to look like, not like what one really does.

There is a tiny cottage, with one room. A windmill. Ovens and a dovecote. A farm, so that she can work on her own version of a loaves-and-fishes spell and other useful things. The spells don't work terribly well. It requires a quart of her blood to make one loaf of brown bread, which she serves with fresh cheeses, telling her rogue friends they are living in Rousseau's Nature now. She walks in a loose, simple white dress, and wears a straw hat over her hair, which has grown out long again.

Louis could visit any time but he considerately does not. She only invites trusted magisters, her children, and the peasants who run the farm, and who love her. No courtiers or gossips or ambitious servants.

There are no shadows on the ground, not with this haze still blocking the light.

Fersen returns from Italy, bearing gifts, most of them enchanted. Her favourite is a busk, a narrow dagger of carved teak that slides down the front of her corset. A lover's gift. The carvings on it are of dates, lines and lines of dates. The first is 30 January 1774. When she runs her finger over any date, she remembers every vivid detail that has slipped from her mind despite the fact she never would have sacrificed them: the smell of his neck or some little conversation they had about nothing. It is her favourite gift.

They have six weeks together, while the Swedish King talks politics with Louis. She is able to show Fersen everything she has done at the Petit Trianon and he laughs to see the magical village in its new place. Polignac's prediction was correct: Antoinette has made the Petit Trianon a place she can love. Before Fersen leaves, she invites a few friends to a party there on a July evening and instructs everyone to wear white.

And then the idyll ends, and Fersen returns to Sweden with his king. And Antoinette is left with her toy village.

She asks a gardener, one day in a reckless mood, what he would do if he had magic. He does not put down the basket of cabbages strapped to his back, but bows his head and stares at the ground. She waits for him to make a choice, as if she were a genie offering him three wishes in a story. A big house of his own? Enough sausages never to run out? A goose that lays golden eggs? And what would he sacrifice for such trifles?

'Your Majesty, I suppose I would stop the people I love from dying.'

She is taken aback; so would she. The smell of Mama's sickroom; the smell of the Habsburg crypt.

She staggers away from the gardener, who looks at her with an alarm she doesn't have the breath to dispel, although she's fine, she really is fine.

But he's not looking at her any more. He's looking just beyond her, and she hears hoofbeats.

It's a messenger, and for one heartbeat she fears that this is it, the possibility she has pushed away from her mind every moment of every day, that one of her children is dead.

But this messenger has not come from Versailles, which is mere minutes' ride away. He's dusty, and in brown clothes, not palace livery. And most important, his face is placid, nearly smiling. He slips off his pony and performs the obeisance of a man meeting his queen for the only time in his life.

'Yes?' she asks.

'Your Majesty's pardon. I went to Versailles but they insisted—'

He looks at her simple costume, glances at the gardener as if wanting confirmation that she is indeed the Queen.

She looks at the basket hanging from his saddle. 'You have a letter for me?'

He takes it from the basket. If Louis knew she allowed such access, if Fersen knew – but she has told the servants to send messengers to Polignac, and if Polignac is not here, then to her. They don't know enough to be properly alarmed by it, and they must assume it is part of her eccentricity, her desire to play at being ordinary here in her little artificial village. They are not wrong.

She takes the letter and opens it. Encrypted, and in Vigée Le Brun's beautiful handwriting.

'Would Your Majesty like to send a reply?'

Antoinette shakes her head. She needs to read this somewhere private, and think.

What can she give the messenger? She looks over at the gardener's basket and takes a cabbage, holds it out. 'A gift,' she says, realizing how foolish she's being, yet unable to stop. Too late, she realizes she could have told him to go to the kitchens for a coin.

He ducks his head down, probably to stop from grinning or making a face. He takes the cabbage.

The padlock on the door of her little house, her boudoir, opens at her touch – a name-day gift from Fersen a few years before. Inside, it still smells of sawdust and furniture oil, despite the little blue-and-white vases of forget-me-nots. She sits on the chair – beautifully carved but simply, and with plain blue upholstering – and lays the letter on the table.

There is no name at the top of the letter, although the messenger knew right enough where he was headed. Antoinette decrypts it onto a sheet of rough paper.

I have seen Cardinal de Rohan at the Palais-Royal often this week, and I was alarmed, thinking there might be another attack. So I have been following him as much as I can. I don't know the full import, but he has been meeting privately with Philippe d'Orléans. I fear I may have been seen – I write to tell you that I will not come to Versailles, therefore, for the next week – I did not want you to take alarm at my absence.

ELVLB

Antoinette crumples both papers, the original and the decryption. Then she goes to the mantelpiece and lights a candle from the tinderbox, sets both papers alight and puts them into the hearth to burn to ash.

Philippe d'Orléans hates the Order more than anyone; hates the idea of anyone telling him what he can and cannot do with his magic. He could not be a traitor, working for the Order.

Then what?

The Château de la Muette is closer to Paris than Versailles is, but it feels farther away from everything. On the edge of the Bois de Boulogne, on the bank of the Seine. The air is salubrious, people say, and so in summer Antoinette goes there with her children. She is pregnant again, and is increasingly desperate to retreat from court life as much as she can, to give this pregnancy every chance. To rest. Last year, she watched the first manned balloon flight here at the Château de la Muette, when she was recovering from the miscarriage.

In Lyon, this summer, a woman has flown in a balloon. She sang arias and leaned over the edge of the basket. How wonderful it must have been.

The clean air and green grass is also good for little Louis-Joseph, the doctors say. At nearly three years old, he's been sick with fevers, on and off, and the court has been whispering – oh, she knows – that the Queen needs to produce another boy, just in case.

She sits with Polignac – her children's governess – and watches her children. Mousseline will soon be six, and she strides around the gardens like a general, surveying everything and calling it hers. Louis-Joseph is quieter. Antoinette gazes at her boy playing on the grass with the toy soldiers that once belonged to his sister. He's a beautiful child, with blond curls and even features. Her angel.

At the Petit Trianon, Antoinette has a few small protections in place. Mirrors on the walls.

At the Château de la Muette, she's taken no such precautions. She does not meet with the Circle there. It's a retreat for her and the children.

But it is there, at the Château de la Muette, that the next attack comes.

In the night, Antoinette wakes to the sound of a woman screaming. She runs towards the sound in her nightdress, into her son's bedroom, past the lady of the bedchamber who screamed, and into his playroom next door.

The model house built to look like Mount Vernon, George Washington's home, sits on a table in the middle of the room. But there's something odd about the way it's shining in the candlelight, and about the way Louis-Joseph is standing, looking at it.

Then she realizes: he's holding the white cupola in his hand, as though he just broke it off. Polignac is kneeling beside him, trying to prise it out of his hands. But something crumbles onto the floor.

Antoinette is there, holding her son, pulling the mass of broken house out of his hand. Has he hurt himself? He seems calm, and there's no injury she can see.

Then she sees that his pudgy little hand is sticky with sugar, and that the bit of house that broke and fell onto the floor is brittle and nearly translucent.

'The whole house has turned to barley sugar,' Polignac hisses, wiping the Dauphin's pudgy hand. Why? Surely nobody would dare to poison—

'It wasn't before!' the stricken lady of the bedchamber says. 'It was wood – I know it was wood. I thought he was putting wood in his mouth – and then I saw it had changed!'

Antoinette grabs her son by the shoulders. 'Did you eat any, darling? Did you put any your mouth?'

He shakes his head dutifully, and Antoinette convinces him to open his mouth for inspection.

Breathless, she hugs Louis-Joseph close while Polignac goes to take away the nurse's memories.

The Dauphin is only two years old. He poses no threat to anyone.

Just last year, she daubed both her children with some of Lamballe's enchanted corpse liquor and made them immune to magic. Only magic with physical effects would have any effect on him. Whoever did this must have known that, chosen this clumsy display for that reason perhaps.

She holds her boy close, her darling boy, who has finally given himself permission to cry. She kisses his soft pale hair.

Anxious hours turn to anxious days. The magisters of Versailles search for the culprit. Antoinette wakes in the night, for weeks afterwards, to check on her son. She puts her hand on his back to feel him breathing.

On those nights, she holds Fersen's miniature and whispers to him, softly so as not to wake him, murmuring all her worries. Once or twice, he answers, saying he couldn't sleep either. The conflict between Sweden's King and parliament is reaching another crisis point, and he is lacking for allies among the rogues there. She says, *Tell me everything*, just so that she can lie back in the chaise in her son's bedchamber, and listen to her beloved's voice rather than her own fears.

When she is satisfied the Dauphin has not been poisoned, she turns her mind to preventing another attack.

The invitation Antoinette sends to Philippe d'Orléans is a summons, and she makes sure that is very clear. He comes to her audience room at the Château de la Muette, looking uncomfortable in the summer heat.

'I have heard that you have protection spells. That you can leach the magic out of a room, and set invisible alarms to warn you of the approach of anyone wearing a certain object, and perhaps other things too.'

He swallows. 'I have been attacked more than once, as Your Majesty well knows.'

'As have I,' she snaps. 'The Dauphin was attacked, here, in his very bedroom.'

'Louis-Joseph?' He turns to her, a line of concern on his brow. He is fond of children.

She nods, but she's suddenly relieved. She was half beginning to suspect Philippe of arranging it himself. He is always trying to convince her that they have been too cautious, too secretive, that the only way to protect themselves is to raise up an army against the Order and dismantle it. But he seems genuinely concerned.

'A gift from America was not all that it seemed, and changed into barley sugar after we took it into our house. The Dauphin tried to eat it.'

'Was it poisoned?'

She pauses, calms herself. 'Not in any way that we could detect, but we had to keep it quiet, you see. We have tried to trace the gift to the sender, but all the records have changed, and the people involved all remember it differently, how it arrived, where and when . . . He is unharmed. I can put mirrors up but that will not stop them from disguising objects that seem harmless. I need more protection for my children.'

Philippe paces while Antoinette sits, her hand resting on her leg, the stays holding the sore, taut skin of her pregnant belly.

'Many of the protections at Saint-Cloud are not mere spells one can perform. They are built into the architecture. I have been working on them for years.'

She breathes out, hard, in frustration. 'There must be some things you can give me, at least.'

'Of course.' He pauses, looking out of the window. 'Could it have been an innocent gift gone wrong? They haven't attacked children before.'

'They hadn't set fire to your opera house before they did,' Antoinette retorts.

'Fair enough.'

'The Cardinal likes to terrify me any way he can. He won't kill me outright.' Or at least, so she surmises. It would draw too much attention to the Order, perhaps. Or attention from Charlotte. 'So he tries to deter me, undermine my reputation, keep me afraid. I don't know how far he will go. The death of a child – even a dauphin – might seem less risky in his eyes than my death. Or perhaps he only meant to make him ill. Or the house was not poisoned, and it was all to make me wonder. I don't know.'

'Then perhaps it's time I had a talk with him.'

'Haven't you been talking with him already?' she snaps.

Philippe blanches. 'I see him from time to time. I try to reason with him, to bargain, to keep the two sides from blowing Paris to kingdom come. I am doing work on many fronts, Your Majesty.'

'He attacked my child.'

He looks away from her, balls his fists. 'The man is known for his appetites. Perhaps there's something I can offer to make him reconsider his approach.'

Antoinette looks at him for a moment. 'A transaction?'

He shrugs, and turns back to her. 'He can't attack the children. That cannot stand.'

'No, it cannot.' She allows her fingers to flutter on her leg, to drum a little while she thinks. An outward sign of her anxiety; a tiny intimacy for Philippe, to show him that she is more human than he wants to believe. 'I will come with you.'

'Your Majesty—'

'Philippe, he is my son. It was my home. I am coming with you.'

Cardinal de Rohan has invited Marie Antoinette to see him many times since she came to France, and every time she has snubbed him. His usher shows her and Phillipe into a salon, where a footman is just drawing a panel to close off half the room. Is the Cardinal in there? More likely one of his strumpets.

She stands, waiting, dressed in a formidable green *robe à la polonaise*, its skirts gathered behind her, its yellow-striped jacket trim on her stout and strong torso. The sort of dress for doing business in.

They can hear voices, somewhere near. Behind the panel? No, in the next room. He's in there, with someone, laughing. Keeping the Queen waiting. No doubt she's surprised him in a liaison and she is not the only female company the Cardinal has today.

She strides past the footman, opens the door into the next salon. It's all dark wood and red silk. There is Rohan, sitting on a settee in a black velvet waistcoat, and the person next to him is not a woman but a man in robes like a wizard's, midnight blue, all bedecked in spangles and stars, with a heavy golden pendant around his neck. His face is pink and jowled and his natural greying hair, though sparse on top, is long, curling around his shoulders.

He stands, looking as though he's been caught in something. Rohan stands more slowly, smooth as a cat.

'Your Majesty,' he says, bowing his head. 'May I present Count Cagliostro? He is staying with me, and I wanted to be sure he was comfortable and wanted for nothing before I entertained Your Majesty.'

'You come from Naples,' she says coldly. From her sister. Another Brother sent from Naples to France, to spy on the rogues, to keep the Queen in her place.

Cagliostro scowls. 'I have not been in Naples for some

years. My wife and I are wanderers. We make our homes where we find them.'

'I see,' she says, although she doesn't, but she doesn't much care, either. She taps one foot. 'Shall we talk here, then?'

Rohan holds out a hand and gestures to the adjoining room, so she sweeps through it again, past Philippe's frowns.

'Your Majesty,' says Rohan. He turns to Philippe. 'And Monseigneur. I have so hoped for this day, so hoped that we might become friends at last.'

She glances at the footmen at both doors, the one that brought her to this room, and the one that leads to Count Cagliostro.

'We have not come to exchange niceties,' Philippe says, standing beside her. For once, it feels as though they truly are on the same side. 'We've come to say that if the Order makes any attempt on the children again, then every Brother in France will die.'

Rohan raises his eyebrows. 'The children?' He speaks lightly, as though they're discussing the opera.

'Don't try to pretend,' she says, making a fist at her side. 'You attacked my son. Never, ever do it again.'

'Ah,' he says, and turns away from her. She frowns, and steps closer, as if he's a snake who might dart in any direction at any moment. 'Hardly an attack. A gift. A reminder that we are here. That we are everywhere. That's all. Is the Dauphin well?'

Her jaw is clenched so tight that it's making her head ring. 'He's alive. He will be king. That's all you need know. If you hurt any of my children, I will rain down vengeance on you. I can, you know. I will.'

'I don't doubt you can, Your Majesty. I am familiar with some of your spells. May I humbly suggest that the greater danger comes not from me, a man of God and a servant of the royal family, but from the innumerable rogue magisters in France, of varying levels of ability and moral character?

472

Perhaps not all of them are happy with the government.' Cardinal de Rohan walks towards her, his arms spread wide, as if in benediction. 'The role of the Order, you see, was to make sure that magic could never be used by the powerful to enhance their control over the less powerful. Magic was only to be used by those trained in its mysteries and devoted to using it for the good of humanity. But now? Anarchy. You've opened the gates. Let's see who comes out.'

She steps back, wary. He said *was*, in reference to the Order. Philippe is looking at the Cardinal thoughtfully.

'But Her Majesty is a magister now,' Philippe says. 'As is her sister.'

'The world tilts,' the Cardinal says, cocking his head with a false smile. 'How it will be corrected, I can't say, but I know it will be corrected.'

She's sick to her stomach. He's preaching her own destruction at her, and smiling while he does it.

'You attacked my son,' she says, her throat dry.

Rohan spreads his arms wide. 'Accuse me, then, Your Majesty. I have a feeling that a trial in which the Queen of France berates me for giving her son sweets would not go against me. Especially given that the Queen of France is not particularly well liked.'

'You are an enemy of France,' she says, 'and you will pay with your life.'

'No, Madame,' says Rohan. 'I think you will find that you are the enemy of France. I think you will learn that very soon.'

A sound, a rustling, this one coming from behind the panel. Another magister there? Are they surrounded?

Philippe's hand is at her elbow, and her hands have no weapons in them, nothing with which to cut out the Cardinal's heart. So she turns on her heel, hardly taking the time to think about what she is doing, strides over to the chinoiserie panel and pulls it aside.

The woman may or may not be a magister, but what is

certain is that she is in a state of undress on a chaise longue. She pulls a gauzy robe around her stays and petticoat, and stands up uncertainly. A woman of about Antoinette's own age, with pretty red lips, a great deal of rouge, and pearl earrings.

'Your Majesty,' she breathes. 'How lovely to see you again. We met before – I am Jeanne de la Motte, of the Valois family, a descendant of Henri Deux, I have proof of my ancestry—'

The Cardinal is at her side, but instead of being embarrassed, he's laughing. 'Jeanne, for God's sake, shut up, this isn't an audience.'

She does remember – Antoinette seldom forgets a name, thanks to her enchanted earrings – this woman from some offshoot of a defunct royal line, poor and poorly educated, desperate for a connection at court. It seems she found one.

Antoinette walks out of the door she came in, saying nothing further. She has nothing more to say to the Cardinal. It was a mistake to come.

Louis assures her the Château de la Muette is quite safe, but he doesn't know – can't know – what happened. It gnaws at her. If the Château de la Muette is unsafe, and the Petit Trianon is for the rogues, Antoinette needs another place where she can bring her children, where they can play on the grass without hundreds of townspeople and courtiers gawking at them, where they will not be attacked.

And the only place she can think of is the Château de Saint-Cloud, with its magical protections. Philippe has hidden them from her all these years, taken all the spells she gave him without giving her in return the spells she could have used to keep her children safe.

Saint-Cloud is on the other bank of the Seine. It's on high ground and the air is clean. It has an orangery, lovely gardens, even a grotto. And it does not belong to Philippe. It belongs to the Duc d'Orléans, Philippe's father.

It isn't often she tells Louis she wants something. So when she tells him she wants Saint-Cloud for the children, the King makes it happen. He negotiates the sale with the duke and gets a very good price.

And Philippe comes to call again, without being summoned, his face pink and shiny with rage. She is sitting in her ante-chamber, practising the harp in the company of Polignac, when they hear the royal guards in the next room stamp their feet twice, as they must every time a duke passes by, and somehow Antoinette knows before the usher tells her that the duke in question is Philippe, Duke of Montpensier and Chartres, and soon enough, when his father dies, Duc d'Orléans and First Prince of the Blood.

'The château was to come to me,' he says, after he has bowed with as little movement as possible. 'You have taken my inheritance. Have you not enough palaces, Your Majesty?'

'None that are safe, thanks to you,' she snaps. She has heartburn and she is not in the mood to be fair. 'I bought it. I did not take it. If your father wishes to sell his property, he can.'

'He did not wish to sell,' Philippe says, but he turns from her with a gesture that says he knows he's lost. 'If anyone other than his king had asked, he never would have done so. There can be no fair transaction when one side has power over the other.'

Sometimes she thinks she has been unfair to Philippe, that he simply has his own ways of showing his loyalty to her, to Louis, to France. But those times are becoming fewer and fewer.

CHAPTER FORTY-FOUR

*Riots – A Marital Agreement – If, If, If – A Mystery
Solved – The Fog Persists – Humility*

❖

Ordinarily, Charlotte's family would spend the summer at Caserta or Portici, and the winter in the Palazzo Reale in the heart of Naples. But Portici is still under repair from the rain of lava, and still too close to the volcano, which continues to smoke.

And at Caserta, there is no escape from the fog. The palace is set on a wide, gentle slope, and in ordinary times, its wide vista brings joy to the heart. Now it feels like an island surrounded by grey mist. In Naples proper, where everything is close, and the air is broken by buildings, walls, docks, and hillsides, it is harder to notice the fog, until one looks out to sea.

So when the riots begin in late summer, Charlotte feels no regret about ordering the family back to the Palazzo Reale early. It's smart politics, because staying at Caserta would seem like hiding. There are no state visitors to worry about, as the King of Sweden (and Axel von Fersen) have left, and Joseph is gone too, leaving Soliman behind to recover. The children will be as safe in the Palazzo Reale as anywhere, because Charlotte's presence is what keeps them safe. The *Reconditus* has been filling with new protective spells as an effect of the magical war; she has alarms set that allow only people in a specific livery to enter certain areas, and she changes the livery a little every few months. There are mirrors in places where they can be seen, and mirrors in places where they can't.

But none of the spells in the *Reconditus* can do anything about the fog.

Cagliostro writes to Silfversparre, and Silfversparre tells Charlotte that the Brothers of Paris are desperate: outnumbered and outranked by the rogues there. Charlotte greets this with a slight smile of pride, at first – of course, Antoinette is among them – but then her smile drops as Silfversparre reports that there is a spell in Paris that can take all the effects of magic right out of a room. The Palais-Royal is a den of witch-prostitutes and conjurer-thieves and the Order can no longer use enchantments to hunt them, because the royal family simply tells a woman to go and sing, and the magic disappears.

Charlotte is half inclined to dismiss this as yet another whine from the Paris chapter but oh, if they're right! A spell that could dissolve the effects of magic – if such a thing exists, she might not need to wait for Soliman to find his spell of spells, or for the wind to finally blow the fog away from Naples. If, if, if.

Meanwhile, everything tastes of fog, smells of fog. The mornings are full of reports of riots the night before; reports Charlotte doesn't need, because she heard them herself. Shouts, half revelry and half something else, fuelled by cheap rotgut.

The morning she finds she can't lace her corset any more is grey and damp, and the rioters are still shouting. Only a few – it's not anything as cohesive as a mob, just drunks who never went to bed. But they're restive, and she can hear them. It steels her. She needs to be steeled.

She is pregnant, with Acton's child. She is waiting for Ferdinand to come in for his new daily marital ritual: a glass of milk, for his health, and a barely polite enquiry after the business of the state, for his conscience. Then she will tell him.

He will know it's not his. She has not shared Ferdinand's bed since Maria Amalia was born in 1782, two years ago. She does not intend to, ever again.

For days, she fretted about how she might trick him. Her husband is immune to magic, but his lackeys are not, and she could have convinced a few of them that Ferdinand had been visiting her room at night while massively drunk. The massively drunk part would not be invention. So, after his hangers-on teased him a few times about needing to be half blind with wine to do his duty with his ugly wife, Ferdinand might well have come to believe the child was his own.

But the more she turned that plan over and over in her mind, the less interested she became. She is not a fifteen-year-old bride now, hopeful and powerless. She is, for all intents and purposes, the King of Naples. And if the titular King wanted to pack her off to a convent or find some other way to get her out of his life, he would be left with the thing he fears most of all: a kingdom to run.

And more important than all of that: she simply doesn't care to pretend. She is not ashamed, and he has no power over her.

Still, she clenches her jaw as she waits for him; the air is thick and musty, as she will not open the window to let that fog in. She stands behind her chair at the table where he always takes his milk, before he goes off to the hunt.

He comes in at last, shuffling over to the long, gleaming table. Charlotte doesn't send the usher at the door away; he's a young man, his palace livery neatly brushed, his sword hilt at his waist. On the far side of the doors stand two of the royal guardsmen, their halberds sharp.

'I'm pregnant,' she says, with no other greeting.

Ferdinand looks at her, confusion crossing his face. Then astonishment as he realizes what that means. Then resignation – or perhaps admiration? A trace of something almost comradely.

They say nothing to each other. Usher or no usher, he

might choose to rail at her, even throw something. To denounce her and the child. To have his friends go after Acton with a rope or a gun.

Instead, he nods, very slightly, a few times. He's thinking. She doesn't disturb him.

His chin lifts; he looks up to the ceiling with its blue skies, its cherubs, its old prophets glaring and pointing. A deep, loud breath in through his nose. Opens his mouth. Tilts his head back down.

'When?'

She thinks for a moment he means *when did you fuck him* and the answer is always, everywhere, many times. But he doesn't mean that. 'Before Christmas.'

She realizes then that he doesn't actually care who is in his wife's bed. He isn't jealous; after all, he has never loved her, and has more mistresses than names she can remember. (Early on, when she could remember their names, she tried a few times to sacrifice those memories but the spells never worked; they aren't worth enough to her, perhaps. Or the memories were too fresh; they were something other than memory.)

What Ferdinand cared about, when he cared, was the embarrassment of the rumours that went all the way to Spain. He cares about being seen as a cuckold. Now that those rumours are dead, the truth can't hurt him. And they could use more children, for state reasons. More boys – have they not had reason to know that no child's life is guaranteed? And more girls for state marriages. He knows all of that, though he doesn't make it his business. It would only become his business if she failed to manage it. Which she never will.

He sits down and drinks his milk out of a crystal glass, and sinks his teeth into a bun, chews. She stays standing, immobile.

'Christmas is a good time for a baby,' he says. 'One more, eh? We'll need a new nurse.'

*

She doesn't tell Acton whose child it is, and he doesn't ask. The child will be a Bourbon, and he knows that full well. He hands her a pillow for her back, halfway through a sentence about the price of whale oil, and it makes her smile.

Every morning, he sits in Charlotte's study and looks down at the paperwork in his lap, and she looks out of the window, and thinks this is an end to it, that she's exorcised whatever demon drove her to his arms. Then she turns, and sees him, and they lock the doors of her study.

Meanwhile, the fog prevents trade, and the cupboards of Naples are running bare. The looms at San Leucio sit idle for lack of anywhere to sell silk, while Caterina has the girls enchant more bags of beans and flour. Ferdinand comes to Charlotte and Acton one day and complains to them both that the palace cooks are running out of spices.

Angelica Kauffman complains that her paints are expensive, that no one wants to pay for her work. People write from France, from Austria, from Germany and Spain, that the fog is dissipating there. Even Rome is brighter than Naples. Kauffman wants to go north.

'Things will change,' Charlotte says, trying to keep her tone light. 'If it is dissipating there, it will dissipate here. I swear it seems brighter lately. The sea will open up and everything will be as it was.'

'I am sure that is so,' Kauffman says. 'In the meantime, I am starving for light.'

28 August 1784
Isaac Lars Silfversparre to Maria Carolina

Your Majesty,

I have appended a list of all the people I suspect of being magisters here in Bari. It being a port city, the list is liable to change by tomorrow.

My conclusion is that Caramanico's suggestion of establishing a Reconditus and a chapter of the Order here is a good one. The first five names on the list are those I would suggest recruiting into the Order; the rest, I can dissuade from practising magic, once I have Her Majesty's permission.

Before we take any action, though, there is another matter. The sixth name, I would draw your attention to. This woman is a back-alley purveyor of curses and charms, but she has some real spells in her book, and she sells them, for a price. She makes half her money, it seems, from blackmail, and to that end, she keeps a book with the names of her clients, and the spells they have bought from her.

Her book includes the name of the Prince of Caramanico, and records that soon after his return to Italy, he bought a spell from her to enchant a piece of wood or metal to produce the symptoms of infection. This spell is not in the Reconditus; if the prince has it, he has not shared it, which in itself is a violation of our rules. I note, as well, the coincidence of the illness that afflicts Angelo Soliman.

I am aware, though, that this woman's grubby little book may be falsified.

I will carry on here, amending my list, until I hear from Your Majesty.

> *Yours in fraternity,*
> *Isaac Lars Silfversparre*

Charlotte holds Silfversparre's letter in her hand, while Caramanico stands in her study. She has not asked him to sit. She has not spoken; the ways in which their friendship will decay hang in the air, waiting.

'You bought a spell from a rogue witch in Bari,' she says. It is not a question; if it were a question, he might falsely deny it, counting on a lack of hard evidence. 'A spell for an enchanted splinter.'

But the prince is not craven. He is a man of silk and marble, and completely sure of himself.

'Soliman is close to finding the spell of spells, or so he

says. What would that mean, if he could invent any spell he liked? He'd be the most powerful man in the world. Could he undo all our magic with it? Clear our memories with a snap of his fingers? Remove magic from the world, and hoard it all for himself? Why would any man give up that kind of power? We can't assume that when he finds this spell of spells, he will share that knowledge with us.'

'Of course he would,' Charlotte snaps. 'He is a member of our Order.'

Caramanico does not contradict her, or not exactly. 'In my travels, I have found that men of ambition frequently keep what they know to themselves, or use it to trade for power – inside the Order and outside it. And I should think a spell of as much power as this – if it indeed exists – would tempt any man to personal ambition. It would tempt me.'

'Would it.' She breathes once, in and out, her taut belly pushing against her *robe volante*. 'You have attempted to murder a Brother of the Order, and my friend. Tell me why I should not have you arrested.'

'Your Majesty!' He's shocked, at last. 'The enchantment only produces symptoms. It will not kill him. I have had all assurances. The intent was not to harm him, but merely to keep him here, where we could aid him in his work while also ensuring that work was not completed in secret, and perhaps provided to the ruler of a rival nation. Angelo Soliman is a friend to Your Majesty, but is he not an even closer friend to the Holy Roman Emperor? I could not know where his loyalties lay, so I kept him here. That's all. I have been helping him. And he is here, where I *can* help him, and not in Vienna.'

She could strip him of his title. Throw him into a cell. Throttle him with his cravat. He has been useful to her; but he has been greedy. Perhaps it's time to be rid of him. He's made himself a liability.

'The spell must not have had a love sacrifice,' she says. 'You have no love left in you, do you?'

His face drops, slackens. 'I have always clung to the belief, Your Majesty, that the sacrifices are all, to some degree, renewable. That love is a thing we may learn again, after we've lost it.'

And like a candle going out, her anger is gone. She has every right to feel nothing but contempt for him, but she understands him. Perhaps he does still have his uses after all. He has been a good ambassador. He slinks like a cat into every salon and palace. But she needs to get him away from Soliman.

'I shall send you back to France, this time as ambassador,' she says abruptly. His face registers shock again; he has a strange capacity for it, or perhaps it is only that he has so seldom been told what to do. His last jaunt to France with Lunardi was entirely on their own initiative, to talk to balloonists and men of science, or so the two men said. 'You can do the double duty of being my liaison to the Brothers of Paris.'

And while he spies on them, Charlotte has others on her payroll in France who will spy on Caramanico.

'Very well,' he says after a moment, as though he had any choice in the matter.

'But before you go, you will reverse the spell on Dr Soliman.'

He stammers: 'But there is no way to reverse it. Anyway,' – he rushes on, seeing her expression – 'anyway, there is no need! The spell does not cause death, and it will wear off before the year is out.'

'Whose assurances do we have for that? Those of the bead-curtain sorceress who took your money?'

'You have my assurances, Your Majesty.'

She stamps her foot to tell the usher to open the door. 'Go to France. Get out of Naples. Do not return until I send for you.'

She called Dr Soliman her friend, and she means it. Her oldest friend, come to think of it. How many others can she count in that number? She still trusts Silfversparre, as much as she trusts anyone. Acton, of course, but that's different. She has no allies, nowhere to turn for help.

Meanwhile, the fog seems thicker than it has ever been, as though it feeds on itself. She thought that it would dissipate over time, as it has in the rest of Europe. But here, where Vesuvius continues to smoke, there's no end to it.

Charlotte thinks back to the day Mama told her *it is Naples for you*. That moment of knowing that she'd lost, how terrible it was. But she accepted the defeat and turned it into a victory. She humbled herself so that she could triumph. She can do the same again.

The rogues of Paris have a spell that counteracts magic. Charlotte needs such a spell, now, to save her kingdom. To triumph over this fog, she is prepared to humble herself. A magister-queen is prepared to make sacrifices.

CHAPTER FORTY-FIVE

The New Ambassador Brings a Gift – A Cacophony
of Portraits – Charlotte Needs a Favour

The Prince of Caramanico is presented in the Hall of Mirrors, as the new ambassador from Naples. He catches Antoinette's eye, and she catches his, and they both know full well what the other is about. Louis is not the sort to give ambassadors the run of the place anyway; the prince may hang about the card tables and the theatre, and come to Mass and gossip, but then anyone can do that, and half the time Mass is conducted under the eyes of the Cardinal who is head of the Order in Paris. She does not fear Caramanico.

She is more unsettled by the gift that comes with him: a portrait of the Queen of Naples for her sister, the Queen of France. They roll it into the Hall of Mirrors and everyone turns to look politely, while Antoinette's smile ossifies.

D'Éon has been sending portraits all over Europe – and indeed the world – setting up galleries full of rogue magisters, all staring at each other, in private houses and in the dustiest rooms of royal collections. It's a way for anyone owning such a gallery to address several rogues all over the world, all at once, though the resulting cacophony in their minds has led them to establish strict rules of use. Antoinette has a room with the portraits of d'Éon, Fersen and a half-dozen others, and she presents a report there once a week.

A portrait of Charlotte cannot be a mere portrait. It must be enchanted.

What can Charlotte mean by it? Retribution for Antoinette's listening-portrait, or acceptance of it?

Antoinette watches the men undrape it. She prepares herself for magic, for a fright.

Instead her face betrays her in a way she could not have foreseen. She laughs in delight, and covers her mouth.

She has never seen a portrait of her sister like this. All the portraits of Queen Maria Carolina of Naples have been terrifying: a woman pinned to the background by enormous panniers and stiff corsets, hair powdered to a dark silver, an expression of ugly fury.

But this painting shows another woman altogether. This is Charlotte as Antoinette knows her. The colours are warm. She's sitting, relaxed, wearing a classical robe of white and gold, and her hair is golden too, loosely bundled and braided with pearls and lace, with a ringlet falling to her shoulders. She's almost *smiling*. She looks as if she's in conversation with a friend. Does she have any friends?

Antoinette turns to the new Neapolitan ambassador. 'Who is the painter?'

The prince smiles. 'Angelica Kauffman, Your Majesty. This is a copy. Her Majesty the Queen is a great patron of her work.'

'I can imagine,' Antoinette breathes. 'All right, let's have it in my private rooms.'

She tells them to hang it in one of her dressing rooms. She removes the firescreen so that the workmen can find the room, and replaces it after they have gone. Charlotte will hear nothing there, can spy on no one.

But she can't sleep, that night, wondering. Charlotte must know she has the painting by now, or will have it soon. But she hears nothing in her mind. What's the point, if Charlotte isn't going to use Antoinette's portrait to begin a conversation?

She huffs, annoyed, and throws the covers off. Throws her silk mantua on, and slips through the panel door into the passage, walks in her stockinged feet to the painting.

For a long time, she stares at it.

'So, sister,' she whispers. 'It is not enough for you to poison the world against me. You have decided to spy on me as well. But you might have chosen another method. I know about this one, you see.'

Antoinette does not really expect Charlotte to answer. She only half expects Charlotte to hear. Even if this painting is enchanted – as it must be – there is no reason to think Charlotte is even awake at this hour, much less standing in front of the painting's counterpart in Naples.

All the same, it does not really surprise her when she hears Charlotte's voice, though it brings a surprising little half-sob to her throat.

I didn't send it to spy on you. I sent it so that we could talk.

Antoinette stumbles backward. She hasn't heard Charlotte's voice in so long. Only the occasional rustling of rats or servants told Antoinette that Charlotte had not ordered the painting destroyed altogether.

Charlotte can hear her, just as Antoinette can hear Charlotte. They can speak to each other. Speak to each other, at last! Tears rise to her eyes, and she's grateful Charlotte can't see her.

Are you there?

'Yes,' she says; then more bitterly: 'Yes. I am here. I am here, despite your patronage of libellous pamphlets against me. Despite your Order's attack on my son.'

Your son? Is he hurt?

'If you cared about my family's safety or mine, you would stop these attacks. You choose your Order over me at every turn. What did I ever do to you to earn such hatred?'

Her voice betrays her and she puts her hand over her mouth, clamping down on the sobs.

I don't hate you. I spoke in anger, and I have regretted it every

489

day since, but you know it takes me time to swallow my pride. God, Antoinette, think! You've been working against me for years! You spied on me and used that knowledge to attack another nation. You covered my kingdom in fog!

'That flour was destined for France. To be used against me. My friends acted to protect the country, and to protect me. I had no idea how they'd destroy the flour, and none of us had any idea the fog would result. Not everything is about you, Charlotte.'

Of course it isn't about me. It's about whether we use magic to better the lot of humanity or to fuel its worst impulses. You've been using magic to get what you want, doling it out like a favour to your friends, letting the people glimpse what they cannot have, undermining the very foundations of governments, and then you pretend you've been wronged when there are consequences.

'I have not undermined the foundations of government. I have tried, over and over, to be a good queen. And because of these horrible, enchanted pamphlets, my people despise me, Charlotte!'

Not everything is about you, Antoinette! We're queens now, have you forgotten? For once in your life, stop caring whether everyone loves you.

The expression on the painting no longer seems friendly; it seems patronizing, arrogant. Her sister as she is.

'I know you do not love me,' Antoinette says, as calmly as she can. 'I don't even ask you to stop amusing yourself at my expense. Keep spreading your hatred of me as much as you like. I know full well there's nothing I can do to stop you. You have been undermining my reputation in any way you can for years.'

It was that or let them kill you, Antoinette! You're disobeying every law – how dare you? How dare you tell me that I do not love my own sister?

Antoinette puts her hands to her hot face and kneels on the ground, her silk robe falling around her, the muslin chemise doing nothing to keep the cold of the floor from her knees. It was a mistake, coming here. She should burn it.

Charlotte stands in front of the portrait, holding one hand out, palm first, as though she's trying to calm a horse. Antoinette is teaching people magic, spreading spells among the women of Versailles as though they were the latest fashions, supporting the most dangerous rogue magisters in Paris. So it is utterly fair and reasonable, more than reasonable, for the Order to keep attacking that reputation. It is the only real power Antoinette has.

It is utterly fair.

And Charlotte will not, cannot defend it.

'Are you there?' she asks.

Silence.

'Antoinette, I didn't send the painting so we could argue. I sent – I – So much has happened, these last years. My children – I miss you. I need your help.'

Silence.

'I hear the fog has thinned in France, that it's hardly noticeable now. I wish I could say the same for Naples. It is killing us, Antoine. My people are hungry, and there is war in the streets, war without armies, without goals, without even sides. I . . . I don't ask this for me. No, that's a lie. Of course it's for me. But I ask also for my people, because I owe it to them to spare no effort that can help. And I believe you can help. I believe you know how a magister dispelled magic in the Palais-Royal. If I could perform that enchantment, I could rid my kingdom of the fog. Undo this horrible thing we've done, and let Naples breathe free again.'

She waits, but there is nothing. No, wait: she cocks her ear. Breathing. Is someone breathing?

'Antoinette?'

Silence.

'Antoinette!' she hisses. 'Sister, for God's sake, take pity on me. I'm at my wits' end.'

Silence.

She walks out of the little room, locks the door with a golden key, and strides down the hallway, wiping her eyes.

CHAPTER FORTY-SIX

This Damnable Fog — Sarabande — Hope —
An Excursion with Hamilton — A Flight of
Starlings — Namesakes

————— ❖ —————

Ships founder. Merchants cannot trade. Market stalls that once sold squid and swordfish now sell eels and oysters for three times their former price. For two long weeks, there is no coffee to be had in Naples, and Acton gets a new line between his brows. The fog is no thinner, and the effects have now started to seem normal. Naples is not the shining city Charlotte saw in her mind. It's impoverished and sick.

And then at last, one morning, a messenger brings a plain letter, sealed with an old French coin. It's encrypted, all but the first two lines, which are plain French in Antoinette's hand.

The keyword is a monthly visitor.

It takes her only a minute to think of *General*, and lo, it works. The word the Habsburg girls used for menstruation. It's been so long since Charlotte and Antoinette exchanged encrypted letters – they send each other trivial, unencrypted niceties every month, to prevent rumours – that either Antoinette forgot they had been using Émilie du Châtelet's *Institutions de physique*, word by word, or she thought Charlotte would have forgotten. They had been on page eighteen.

Charlotte grabs her pen, dips it into the inkwell and sets to work decrypting the letter. There is no personal note from Antoinette. No acknowledgement, no rapprochement, no word of affection or even of anger. Just the spell 'for wine to sing away one enchantment'.

The enchantment is simple enough; the only trouble with it is the amount of hope it requires. Charlotte cannot muster enough. She puts a cask of wine in the middle of the star (wine, at least, is cheap these days; it is half the reason for the constant brawls in the streets). She arranges the other sacrifices in the points of the star: one of her own baby teeth; the memory of the thimble spell; and her enchanted copy of *Candide*, valuable as a treasure sacrifice because of the sacrifices she made for it, years ago. There is hardly any requirement for love; she writes the names of three of the children's pets of whom she's fond. None of that is too painful, in the grand scheme. She's sure they're enough.

But the hope sacrifice is beyond her. She tries, first, her wish that Teresa's marriage will be a happy one. The sacrifices remain. She adds her aspirations for all her children; for Francesco to rule a peaceable and prosperous kingdom well. She adds her desperate need for her boys to live. She adds her dreams of love with Acton and even, at the end, her hope that the fog will dispel. And then, at last, she writes one more note for the pile: her hope that she and Antoinette will reconcile.

Empty, she looks at the pile of wishes, and says the words. But the sacrifices do not disappear. The truth is that she can't bring herself to hope for anything while her kingdom is broken. Her dreams for a new era of enlightened magic seem farther away than they've ever been, and Antoinette is utterly lost to her. How can she hope when she can't believe any good things will ever happen again?

She gathers the bits of paper to her like a mother hen gathering chicks, before she burns them all.

Charlotte does not have enough hope in her to save her country.

The next day, she is woken before dawn, by Caterina. She tells her Soliman has a fever. He's raving.

She calls for a doctor.

'You, Angelo Soliman, once single-handedly saved a man from six attackers on the battlefield,' she whispers, sitting at his bedside. 'You have a wife and a daughter. You are the Grandmaster of the Masons of Vienna and the Senior Brother of the Vienna Chapter of the Order of 1326. I once watched you explain the mathematical problems of the Seven Bridges of Königsberg and make a room full of counts and duchesses actually care about what you were saying. You cannot be killed by a splinter.'

'Yes, Your Majesty.' He smiles wanly. Then his smile drops and he looks at the wall.

But another day passes, and Soliman does a very good impression of a dying man. His face is grey, and he slips in and out of lucidity. The doctor tells her he expects he will be dead within a day.

She will kill Caramanico herself, she vows. Angelo Soliman, whose belief in a better world has sustained her when she could not count on her own, this scholar who was so certain that he could find the answer to everything, to magic, to the nature of reality, that if one simply worked hard enough, if one simply cared beyond one's own life just a little, the world would be better. How she has failed him! And yet, even after all these years, he has never lost hope.

And as he lies on his deathbed, she decides that she will, at the end, take it from him. That she owes her kingdom everything now, more than she has to give.

She steels herself, and chooses one of his sharper moments.

She tells him that she knows of a spell that will drive the fog away, but it requires a hope sacrifice greater than she can give. Whatever gods or monsters pass judgement on the scraps of paper that magisters leave in their stars, they have decided that Charlotte's are insufficient.

'Dr Soliman,' she says. 'You have such hope. And no reason for it! It's baffling. Everything you've seen. And yet you still believe the world can be better.'

He turns his face to her, breathing roughly, making her say it. He won't help her do this.

'It would be a shame for that hope to die with you,' she says, ashamed. 'Wasted. When it could save the lives of so many.'

He turns away from her, and says nothing for many minutes. She thinks that's it, that he's refused, or that his mind is too far gone. But at last he croaks: 'Bring me the ash, and the small trunk I travel with.'

He sits on the edge of the bed, barely upright, while she draws the star. He writes the love, memory, and hope sacrifices in a shaking hand and folds the papers over, so she won't see them when she places them in the points. A vial of his blood; a small pinkish seashell, which she does not ask about.

He rasps the words and the sacrifices disappear. The wine in the middle is enchanted, ready for a singer.

She turns back and sees him: his face without hope is another man's face. Or perhaps, she consoles herself, that is the mark of death upon him.

But, as it turns out, she was right: Angelo Soliman cannot be felled by a mere splinter. And that damned villain Caramanico was right, and his back-alley sorceress too. The enchantment passes, and the fever breaks. Angelo Soliman does not die. Within a day, he's sitting up to eat, and within a week, he's walking. She didn't take the hope from a dying man, but from a living one.

If a singer can leach the magic from a room, how many singers would it take to leach the magic from the sky? Charlotte has no way to know, but she does have cages full of starlings.

She also has no way to know whether chirping counts as singing for these purposes. Despite Soliman's instruments and note-taking, magic is not a science; or if it is, it is a science so difficult to measure that one might as well try to count grains of sand.

So Charlotte takes no chances. She wants the starlings to sing.

Acton is away in Sicily, comforting the viceroy there, who's been tasked with wresting some of the nobility's control away from their old lands and reforming taxation.

She brings a starling back in a gilded cage to the room where Teresa practises her harpsichord, and tells the footmen she is not to be disturbed.

Charlotte is no singer; music was always Antoinette's gift. So she plays Handel's Sarabande from the Suite in D minor, the one Josepha used to play. Over and over, until the starling joins her.

She brings them in, in cages, in batches of a dozen at a time. After a month, she's taught all 334 of the surviving starlings.

Enchanted wine in their water dishes, a few drops each.

Acton comes to her in her study. How she has missed those arms, that face. She lays her head against his chest and breathes, for the first time in weeks.

He takes her face in his hands and kisses her. Then he looks at her, up and down. Kisses her again, his hand on her swollen belly.

'How is the fog now?'

He sighs. 'No better, I'm afraid.'

She clucks. 'You had a safe passage, though. Thank God.'

'Safe, albeit slow and gloomy.'

'And my viceroy in Sicily?'

'Mmm.' He unhooks her bodice, and pulls the busk out so he can kiss between her breasts. 'He's at his wits' end. So much land has reverted to the Crown through the new inheritance laws, and that is all to the good. But the old families see no reason to police what they no longer own. He needs more men to keep the peace.'

'I have given him more men.'

'But the lawlessness persists.'

'It's this damnable fog,' she mutters, and though he knows nothing more of magic than anyone in the street witnessing these strange times, he does not disagree.

'I had hoped to give him a well-earned break, and replace him with Caramanico. But then you sent Caramanico to France.'

She thinks she hears a chiding tone, a patronizing weight. She wraps her bodice back around her, suddenly wishing she had a blanket or a cloak to hide her shoulders from him. 'You would prefer to determine my policies, then.'

'No!' He spreads his arms wide. 'I'm yours. I'm true to you. And as I'm true to you, I won't act the sycophant. When I disagree, I'll tell you. You would not want me to do otherwise.'

'I want you to remember your place, Prime Minister.'

'I do. My place is here. I serve Naples.'

'No, you serve me.'

'Technically, I serve your husband.'

She turns from him, hot tears in her eyes. 'If you serve him, you are no good to me or to your country.'

He laughs, putting his hand to his cheek. 'This is not my country. I was born in France to an English father. My darling—'

'I am not your darling. I am your queen. You think because you fuck me that you can disobey me?'

He takes her hands. 'If you'll trust me . . .'

'I need a prime minister more than I need a lover. Go, and be my prime minister.'

He drops her hands. 'This is what you want?'

No, it isn't what she wants. What she wants doesn't matter. But she needs Acton's body: she needs more children; she needs him to hold her sometimes, to quiet her mind. She must remember that they are not partners, that's all. She has a cold feeling in the pit of her stomach, but she can distract herself from that.

'Come here,' she says, pulling him towards her roughly, kissing him and pulling off his jacket.

There is no need to wait for night to do secret deeds in Naples. The fog is so thick that it almost cuts Charlotte off from her guards and footmen, who walk behind her, or the porters behind them, pulling the carts. But she makes no effort to slow down for them. She keeps pace with William Hamilton, who can climb a gravel slope faster than any goat.

She asked Hamilton to accompany her for two reasons: first because no one knows these ever-shifting pathways up the volcano better than he does. Second, because he is lonely. His monkey died, and then his wife, and then his face looks older lately, his pale eyes rheumier, as he stares unseeing at his pots and statues, as if gazing into some country no one else can see.

He does not question her when she says she has found a way to dispel the fog, but it will require the release of 334 starlings from the top of the volcano. He is a man who appreciates performance.

A thin column of smoke rises from the mountain, dark against the lighter wreaths of fog and the white wisps of natural cloud that flit around the summit. Charlotte wraps her silk scarf around her mouth, but it cannot block the smell of brimstone.

'This is as high as is safe for the wagons,' Hamilton says. They stand nearly at the edge of the crater, the interior of which is simply grey smoke; the smaller inner cone that used to rise from the centre, when Charlotte first arrived in Naples, was obliterated by the eruption that created the fog.

At their feet, the mountain slopes away into a sea of grey, below which her people cough and weep, argue and lie.

Charlotte gestures to the footman, who gestures to the

porters. A dozen wagons, each bearing a half-dozen tall, segmented iron birdcages, each cage bearing four or five birds. They line up the wagons on the sloping path.

Somewhere close to here, the rogue magisters would have come, under cover of night, and dumped her flour, sack by sack, into the maw.

The Queen walks along the line of cages, opening doors. Each plump starling is singing for her already, its dotted plumage puffing out at the neck, whistling and calling. A few speak the words they learned from her, in eerily human voices: *'Encore! Encore! Encore!'* with the occasional *'Voyons.'*

Hamilton claps his hands in delight.

Like 334 singers in a round with 334 beginnings, the starlings sing the first notes of the song she taught them. She and Hamilton stand for a long time, watching the birds duck and glide in and out of the fog, away from the volcano, towards clearer air.

'It worked,' she says, standing in the doorway of Soliman's room, watching him write. 'Your sacrifice. The fog is lifted, as you'd know if you ever left your desk.'

He smiles wanly. 'I went for a walk just this morning, Your Majesty. The air is lovely.'

'The foot is not sore at all, then?'

He shakes his head. 'I am in nearly perfect health. Well enough to travel. And travel I shall.'

She opens her mouth to object before she realizes he is not asking her permission. 'Home to Vienna?' she says lightly, instead. She cannot hold him here and does not wish to. She is not Caramanico. But she will miss him, and she can't forget what she took from him.

'To Barcelona first,' he says, his voice tired. 'There are some books there that I think might contain some clues. My illness has delayed my search for the spell of spells, and I can't waste any more time. It is all I will work on, for the years that remain to me.'

She swallows, and sits on the little wooden bench by his door, her *robe volante* ballooning over her growing belly. 'You are always welcome here, should you wish it. Your family as well.'

'I am not a Neapolitan, Your Majesty. Not your subject.'

'No, but you are . . .' She starts to say *my friend*, and then fears the look that will cross his face if she does. 'You are a Brother of the Order.'

'Am I?' He laughs shortly, bitterly. 'I hardly know what that means any more, if I ever did. Rohan has been writing to me, alarmed by what Caramanico is telling him about our work here and in Vienna. The Cardinal is convinced that magic ought to be above any law, and out of reach of the state. Magic, and magisters. He thinks he is right, and I think I am right, and we both call ourselves Brothers. But I don't know how much it matters now. We live in a new world, and the institutions and ideas of the old world are of little use to it.'

Charlotte is thinking about all the ways in which she has failed, day by day. The Inquisition is gone but the jails are full of the petty criminals the fog has bred. The girls at San Leucio keep the nation fed, when trade cannot. They have new, enchanted looms, and the silk trade flourishes. And the girls? They are cogs in Charlotte's machine, and how far that is from the perfect society she is trying to make – just that one little village, and even that eludes her.

She is thinking of the day Soliman came to Naples, and chose to turn against the rules of his Order, to trust that Charlotte could do something no one had ever done before. She is thinking about the sacrifice he made then. She is thinking about the sacrifice he made a few weeks ago, at her request.

She deflates against the wall. 'But how?' she whispers. 'How can you carry on looking for this spell that might not exist? How can you believe a world is possible that has never existed before? How can you do that, without hope?'

'The future doesn't require me to hope,' he says. 'It only requires me to work.'

The next baby is born a fortnight before Christmas: an easy delivery of a bright-eyed girl. She is born into a city with clear air, where ships come and go again, and people smile at each other in the streets. The fog has lifted at last.

When they were children, and knew that one day they would be separated, Charlotte used to promise Antoinette that she would come to her rescue if she ever needed her older sister. But it is Antoinette who has rescued her.

Charlotte sings to her baby, so softly that no one can hear. She sings her the song that dispelled the fog. She names her Maria Antonia.

CHAPTER FORTY-SEVEN

*Antoinette Does Not Buy a Diamond Necklace — Traps
and Precautions — Les Cadavres — Motherhood*

———————— ⁂ ————————

The Dauphin has always been small for his age, and prone
to head colds. Louis prefers the children to spend their time
at Fontainebleau, la Muette or, now, Saint-Cloud, because
Versailles is always full of people, and therefore full of coughs
and fevers. Saint-Cloud, with its magical protections, is
Antoinette's preference. But Antoinette likes to have the
children by her, and she likes to have Polignac, their
governess, by her too. And Antoinette is, much of the time,
required to be at Versailles. Every week, she makes decisions
about where her children might be safest, and what is possible
for them and for her.

In the months following his third birthday, Louis-Joseph
seems . . . not ill, precisely, but pale and listless. Seventeen
eighty-four turns to 1785, and then the time comes when
windows are opened, the sheets hung out in the sun, the
tapestries beaten to billow out a winter's worth of fine dust,
the fireplaces scrubbed with wet sand. The world smells of
lye and manure. The sky is cloudless; the air is fresher than
it has been in years. But her little boy has a faraway look
in his eyes, and does not play.

'They've poisoned him,' she tells Polignac, who is calm as always and says there's no reason to think the boy's condition has anything to do with the sugar house. They don't even know whether he ate any. And all of that is true, but it doesn't comfort her.

Antoinette asks Vigée Le Brun to be on the watch for any whisper about poisoning or about the royal children, but the painter hears nothing of the kind.

She has mirrors on the walls and, at Saint-Cloud, traps on the grounds. There are guards everywhere, and only trusted people in the kitchens. Food-tasters would be pointless against a slow-acting poison.

One of the spells the rogues stole from Mesmer while he was still in Vienna was a bezoar enchantment, a way to convey properties to a stone so that if it were dropped into a glass or a dish of food, it would absorb any poisons therein. But it only works once, and there is no way to know when and where to use it. Besides, it's difficult enough to convince Louis-Joseph to eat, without placing a stone in his food. And the spell stipulates that the stone may not be broken into pieces after its enchantment, to allow it to be used more than once.

But what is a stone, really? Could a grain of salt be a stone? She used to wonder which part of an object held the magic, whether an enchanted shoe would still carry her an inch above the floor if every part were replaced, like the ship of Theseus. There are so many things she still doesn't understand. Nonetheless, she has always had a knack for adapting spells.

Antoinette locks herself in the Petit Trianon for three days, pleading headache and sore legs from her pregnancy. She works on permutations of proofs, trying to calculate what sacrifices would be needed to create a dish of salt that Polignac could keep with her at all times, so she could drop a grain or two into Louis-Joseph's food. The original proof, for a single stone, is 'oeee'. She works and works, trying to find some way to fold the magic into a new form, but she can't see a way that wouldn't require a king's ransom for the treasure sacrifice.

Antoinette has made her boy immune to magic. She cannot make him immune to violence, poison or disease – or at least, not all disease. There is something she can do about smallpox, at least.

So, she and Polignac and the physician gather around Louis-Joseph's bedside. He's three and a half years old, old enough for inoculation. And it's safest to do it now, before Antoinette's new baby comes.

The scalpel splits the skin on the inside of his upper arm, twice, and he bites his lip, his fingers curling around Antoinette's. She can't stop her sharp intake of breath as the doctor threads the sharp needle, coated in the pus of smallpox scars, through his flesh, from one hole to the other. Three times, he draws the red thread through, and there is no going back.

Louis-Joseph is perfectly well for a week. Then the fever takes him. For three nights, she holds him while he sweats and moans. Pustules appear on his arms and on his beautiful face, even his eyelids.

She lies beside him in his little bed, the curtains drawn all around it, and holds him, kissing his brow.

Children do die of inoculation. King George of England has lost two young sons to it in the last few years. She holds her boy and does not think about what she will say to Louis if his son dies.

On the fourth day, his fever breaks, and the pustules start to fade. He has come through this trial stronger. She has protected her boy as best she can.

In Lyon, a group of people called 'les Cadavres' is reported to be using ritual self-mutilation and handing out bread and salt to the people; alarmed, Louis sends troops, who kill two young men for coming at them with knives, and there's a riot.

Meanwhile, Louis has yet another set of financial advisers, and they are urging him to take bold action. Only by spending vast amounts of money can France right itself, they say. They resurrect the moribund French East India Company, saying: Look, look at the British! Their East India Company did not content itself with trade; it owns and taxes the land, tells the people what to grow, and sells what it likes where it likes. It sells opium to China and silk to France and nobody stops it. France still has a few holdings in India, a few ships. It still has an empire, and the time has come, they whisper, to make it pay.

Fersen writes that the British East India Company has been using the loaves-and-fishes spell to grow its arsenal. British politicians are alarmed; they are fighting among themselves. Rogues have gone to support the Indian magisters and other mages in fighting back, but there is no end to the carnage.

Vigée Le Brun says there's a steady stream of clerics going in and out of Cardinal de Rohan's palace, and they're all preaching about the devilry of the new sciences, about Lucifer's sin of pride, about Adam and Eve in the garden. They warn of witches and harpies, and then the pamphlets print engravings of Antoinette as a harpy, above rude poems about her and Polignac in bed. Who would believe that the Queen of France is a witch? Only the simple, surely, and the Cardinal has never said he believes it. But are there wealthy women who dabble in black sacrifices for their entertainment? Are there women at Versailles who will indulge themselves in every way possible? Of course. Have we forgotten the 'Affair of the Poisons' a century ago, the black masses, the amulets and charms that streamed in and out of the palace? It has always been a den of degeneracy.

Antoinette is in Versailles and out of sorts, heavily pregnant, when Charles Auguste Boehmer, the crown jeweller, requests an audience.

Under Madame Campan's stern eye, Antoinette is sitting with Polignac in a small salon, and they both have needles in their hands, cushion covers in their laps. The Queen is known for her needlework, her designs emulated throughout France.

There are many reasons why it is advisable to do needlework when the jewellers come to call. It sends the message that the Queen and her ladies (even Polignac, whose indifference to gossip at court has given her a reputation for haughtiness) are working women, after all, taking care of their household and making useful things. It gives them something to occupy their hands while others bow and scrape. It keeps the fingers strong and the eyes sharp, and the mind working.

And, in the end, one has an embroidered cushion.

Boehmer looks distraught. He's brought an assistant, and when they wheel a black velvet case on a table between them, Antoinette closes her eyes and takes three breaths to stop herself from screaming at them. She has more important things to do.

'Your Majesty,' Boehmer says, bowing low. 'Thank you for seeing us.'

'It must be a difficult time to be a jeweller in Versailles. We need ships and bread, not diamonds and gold.'

'It is of diamonds I have come to—'

'Surely you have not brought the same necklace that I have refused twice already? Even Our Lord was only tempted by Satan three times. I hope this will be the last time you force me to say no.'

The assistant lifts the lid as Boehmer hangs his head. She does pity him, a bit. Madame du Barry was the original target for this gaudy thing, back when she was still the old King's mistress, and now they've got no one to sell it to. Ropes and tassels of diamonds, worth a king's ransom. Worst of all, it's ugly, despite its price.

'It isn't my style,' she says, as gently as she can. 'Anyway, my jewel cases are rich enough. What money I have to spend, myself, goes to the Queen's Hamlet and now to my children's new home at Saint-Cloud. And I have already told the King he is not to buy it for me, and not to listen to anyone who tells him I want it. I do not want it.'

She hates to be blunt, but she must be clear.

'We thought perhaps – Madame Royale is such a beautiful girl. When she marries, she will take jewels with her. Or the Dauphin, when he takes a bride—'

'If I can give my children humility and virtue, those will be ornaments enough.'

'Of course.' The jeweller looks as if his dog has died. This piece will bankrupt him if he can't find a buyer. But these are not times for luxury. The drought of 1784 threatens a poor harvest in 1785, and bread is expensive again. Antoinette cannot afford to buy an enormous diamond necklace, and she can certainly not afford to be seen wearing it.

Antoinette turns to Madame Campan. 'Will you see Monsieur Boehmer out, please?'

The jeweller opens his mouth and closes it again, but he dutifully shuts the lid of the velvet case. He and his assistant follow Madame Campan's uncompromising figure out of the door.

Polignac sets her needlework aside and plucks a chocolate off the plate on the side table. She eats it thoughtfully, until Antoinette at last gives in and asks what's troubling her.

'The necklace would be incredibly valuable,' Polignac says. 'And yet you'd never want to wear it. Gaudy and ridiculous. Entirely unsuitable for the times.'

'You're thinking of the sacrifice for the bezoar spell to protect from poison,' Antoinette says quietly. 'It won't do, my dear. I can't afford the necklace unless I ask Louis to buy it for me, which I won't do. I can't be seen spending that kind of money on frivolous things, not now, with the treasury empty. If I acquire it for the crown jewels or for one of the children, it doesn't truly belong to me and the sacrifice won't work. Even if I could make it work, I'd have to account for its absence at some point. A replica wouldn't go undiscovered for long. It's a risk I can't take.'

Polignac cocks her head. 'If we could have someone else buy it for you, in secret, then poor Boehmer would get his money and stop bothering you, and you would own the necklace for long enough to sacrifice it.'

Antoinette doesn't like the feel of this, like drifting out into a lake and losing sight of shore. 'I can't accept a gift like that from anyone. Even if I knew someone who would buy it.' She is thinking of Fersen, whom she would never ask for such a thing.

'Of course you can't accept it. I almost have it . . . I can feel the answer, do you know what I mean? There's a game they play in England, where they light a bowl of brandy on fire, and float raisins in it, and one has to pluck the raisins out and pop them in one's mouth still alight. It feels like that, as if the answer is between my fingers but it keeps going out before I can get it onto my tongue.'

Antoinette leans her head to her shoulder, like a duck preening its feathers, maternally. She's very pregnant, now, and the weight of her belly grounds her. She watches Polignac pull a bit of thread through her cloth. 'I don't think there is an answer. God knows I would do anything to protect my children.'

'Yes,' Polignac acknowledges. 'Kings can wear armour, but we must find our own protections. Let me think about it. Sometimes one simply has to work at a problem.' She smiles dazzlingly at Antoinette, and holds up her cushion cover. A lovely purple thistle, surrounded by green leaves and gold ribbons.

Easter Sunday, pain wakes Antoinette before dawn, the cramping across her back sending her clutching for the bedpost every few minutes. When the Duchesse de Polignac comes with Louis-Joseph and Mousseline and sees the Queen kneeling on the bed, sees the look on Antoinette's face, she sends the children off with Madame Campan and kneels on the floor, taking Antoinette's hands in her own.

'The baby's coming,' whispers Polignac, who's had four children herself.

Antoinette drops her head in something like despair.

'I'll stay with you. It will be all right.'

'We'll have to tell everyone. Just . . . will you give me one more moment before you tell them and they all come in?'

Polignac snorts. 'I'll do more than that. We don't need them all in here. It's Easter; I'll keep it quiet until they're all at Mass, and then you won't have so many people crowding around.'

Antoinette kisses her friend's brow, leaning on her gratefully.

And Polignac, good as her word, keeps the room quiet until the little boy rips his way out into the world with a healthy cry. Polignac is the first person to hold the child. Antoinette and Louis have already spoken about the name. If it had been a girl, she would have been Charlotte. The boy is named Charles – well, Louis-Charles.

Antoinette loves him with all her heart, this squalling boy. She holds him close, clinging to the spider-thread that connects sister to sister even now, the thread they have chosen to preserve when it would have taken nothing but a thought to snip it and end it, and be enemies. She isn't quite sure how they managed it, she and Charlotte, or whether the thread itself is stronger than their wills and their regrets. She isn't quite sure what it will mean that, despite everything, they are sisters.

CHAPTER FORTY-EIGHT

The Summit of Happiness — Polignac's Plans — The Decay
of the Imperishable — Evidence Is Offered

———— ❖ ————

One day in July, a letter arrives for Queen Marie Antoinette on the usual silver plate, opened, unencrypted. Madame Campan opens all the letters that come to her through the usual post at Versailles; the secret messages come other ways, and they're always encrypted anyway.

This one is from Charles Auguste Boehmer, and as plain as day. Madame Campan hands it to Antoinette with a frown.

> *Madame,*
> *We are at the summit of happiness to dare to think that the latest arrangements which have been proposed to us, and to which we have submitted with zeal and respect, are a new proof of our submission and devotion to Your Majesty. We take satisfaction in knowing that the most beautiful set of diamonds in the world will grace the best of queens.*
> *B.*

Good God.

She grips the letter between finger and thumb; the paper snaps taut. They've taken some misconception into their heads – she tries to believe that for a moment, but in her mind's eye she sees Polignac's face, her determined little smile. Polignac. A betrayal. A loving betrayal, the worst kind.

Antoinette is frozen, as though under a spell. She's lost control, somehow. She is being manipulated.

She will have to breathe eventually. She will have to speak. She will have to make it clear to everyone that this is not what she wants, or what she ever wanted. But Polignac is a magister and a friend. The letter has been read.

Her thoughts grind, her nerves sizzle, her body wakes.

'What can it mean, Campan?' Antoinette laughs lightly, holding out the letter. 'You're so good at solving the riddles published in the *Mercure de France*. Perhaps you can solve this one for me. Is he still trying to sell me the necklace? Has someone made some suggestion to him for a new course of action to win my consent?'

Campan takes the letter and reads it over again. 'It must be something of that sort, Your Majesty,' she says uncertainly.

'Well, I won't spend any more time worrying about it. They'll come when they come, and I'll send them away again. He's the crown jeweller, a position he bought dearly, as I recall, so I'll just have to put up with him.'

She holds out her hand for the letter and twists it, hard, and puts the end into the lit candle for her sealing wax. It falls in cinders, and Antoinette brushes it all away with the toe of her shoe, not even bothering to keep the ash for spells.

Polignac is at Saint-Cloud with the children; Antoinette summons her to Versailles and waits, sitting, as the usher shows her in. She's flushed with summer heat and smiling. She walks towards Antoinette, hands held out.

'I didn't know they'd send you a letter. I wanted to wait until everything was concluded before—'

'Before you told me you were acting in the Queen's name without the Queen's knowledge?'

Polignac stops, her smile dropping. 'You had to be kept out of it.'

'And yet I was not. The jeweller seems to think he has an agreement with me. Will you tell me what I've agreed to do?'

'Nothing,' says Polignac, and a ghost of a smile returns to her face. 'That's just it. May I sit?'

'No.'

She's taken aback, and the flush deepens. She speaks now, unsmiling, hotter and quicker than she probably intends. 'Your Majesty, you are not implicated. The evidence shows it quite plainly.'

'Begin at the beginning, if you can.' Antoinette holds onto her anger, to the hard fact that her duty to her people is all that she is. She feels the desire to forgive creeping up on her, like that day years ago when Charlotte used her enchanted gloves to make her forget her dance step. How humiliated, how angry she was! But it melted away like sugar on the tongue, and she wanted to reach out her hand to Charlotte, just as she wants to reach out to Polignac now.

Polignac swallows. 'Cardinal de Rohan has a new mistress. Jeanne de la Motte. Do you know her?'

Antoinette remembers the half-dressed woman in Rohan's palace. 'Yes, we've met. What does she have to do with anything?'

'She's a money-grubber, desperate for anything that will give her and her husband – oh yes, she has a husband – a place in society. That's why she's sharing Rohan's bed, of course. It's certainly not out of affection for him; she hates him more than anything. So, I managed to show her that if she had money of her own, and her own estate, she could stop opening her legs for that lout. And I showed her a way to have her revenge on him for the way he treats her.'

'Revenge.'

'She persuaded him to buy the necklace for you, to lend you the money and act as your agent so you won't be implicated.'

'Why in God's name would he do any of that? He hates me.'

'Precisely. He's doing it not as a favour to you, but because he thinks it will discredit you. He thinks that you have requested the necklace as the cost of restoring him from his disgrace. Jeanne de la Motte told him that. And he thinks, once you have the necklace, that he will be able to reveal your scheming. He's received letters from you – he thinks. It's a spell where the handwriting changes depending on who's holding the paper.'

'These forged letters appear to be from me?'

'When *Rohan* reads them, they are unquestionably from your hand. When anyone else reads them, they're plainly forgeries that Rohan should have seen through instantly. Your name is signed wrong, for heaven's sake. No one will ever believe you were involved. But he does. He thinks he's trapped you. I had to find something that would work – Rohan is immune to magic. But magic isn't immune to him. When the paper feels the touch of his hand, and his hand only, the ink actually moves into different shapes, like your ciphering spell. And he can pass that very paper to someone else and say, "Look! It's clearly from the Queen!" and everyone will see what a fool he is.'

'And he's going to pay the jewellers for the necklace? Two million livres or something close to it, on faith that I'll pay him back? It's a great chance to take, just to make me look greedy. He's really going to pay for it?'

'He already has.'

Polignac reaches into the pocket under her skirt. An enchanted one, it seems. What she pulls out is a necklace too bulky to fit into any ordinary pocket.

It's an absolute mess of diamonds. Draped over Polignac's lovely arm, it catches the morning sunlight that streams through the shutters.

Antoinette lifts it with both hands. It's lighter than it looks and, suddenly, not as gaudy as it appeared in Boehmer's black velvet case. It doesn't even look like Madame du Barry's style. Antoinette can almost imagine how it would drape on her own décolletage, how 647 of Africa's best diamonds would capture and scatter the lights of Versailles just a little more brilliantly than even the best paste copy ever could.

'But he knows I have it!' she objects. 'If I sacrifice it—'

'Whether you sacrifice it or not, he will say you have it. He will show the letters, and look like a fool. Let them search the palace; they won't find it. It will be gone.'

Then she must sacrifice it. It drags on her hands; she can't be found with it. The people would riot if they knew she was spending the price of two ships on a necklace, when she already has so many.

She does not want to sacrifice it, now.

Which might be for the best. She needs to consider it hers, for the spell to work. She needs to treasure it.

If she says no, if she tells Polignac to return the diamonds, the jewellers may make noise about it, about the promises they've had, and the payment they expect. Returning the necklace would connect her to the jewellers more than sacrificing it would.

And sacrificing them – God, what a price – will give her a dish of salt that could save her children's lives. Her little baby, Charles, already immune to magic by her touch but not immune to the many evils of the world.

'So be it,' she says to Polignac, holding up the necklace. 'You have caught me in this net. I know you did it out of love for me and for the children.'

Or if not love, then stubbornness, which is so often the same thing, when it comes to the people we have to protect. Polignac's hard heart works a love of a different kind than Lamballe's, but it is loyal, and Antoinette understands her.

'We should make the sacrifice right away,' Polignac says.

'I will make the sacrifice alone.'

The spell requires a moderate love sacrifice as well, and Antoinette finds that the affection she bears for Gabrielle de

Polastron, Duchesse de Polignac, is sufficient, which perhaps is fitting. It is wise to harden her heart, but she feels a tremendous absence when the paper curls into nothing and her secret room fills with an odour of must. She is wearing a rose in her hair, and its petals fall, black and brittle, to the carpet, which is growing worn and mouldy.

Three of the points of the star are empty; the pile of dust that was the name of her friend in the fourth, and in the fifth, a necklace. A strand across the top, at the neck, although it has never touched her neck. Loops below it. At the sides, triple strands of diamonds. Two more triple strands cross at the bosom. All of it clear as ice and as hard as duty, seemingly indestructible.

But she has given it, and the force of decay is greedy. She kneels and watches the diamonds die.

The stones cloud over, as though covered in a film of grey dust, for what seems like a long time but is only a few breaths. And then, as though one of those breaths has become a wind, they collapse into piles of grey powder, shimmering just a little until nothing is left but a few specks of glitter, the sparkle of the diamonds like traces on the carpet. Beautiful even in death.

The room stinks of magic.

Antoinette lets herself lie down on the floor where the diamonds once were. She reaches out one hand for the little silver salt cellar in the middle, its crystals the only things in the room that still seem pure.

Life feels unlikely, in the days following Antoinette's sacrifice. It seems impossible that an object of such value could simply vanish from the world, like waking up to a world without Notre-Dame Cathedral in it. Some things are solid, and diamonds are among them. Be that as it may, the impossible happens, with more regularity than Antoinette would have believed when she was younger, even back when she wanted magic to solve everything. She is nearly thirty years old, a mother to three children, and she no longer requires the world to right itself, so long as she can bend some small part of it to be better, kinder, safer.

Still, she cannot lose the nightmare feeling, as if the world is decaying around her. The corridors of Versailles smell of mildew and sweat, though the salons are as glittering as ever. In Paris, the graveyards are overflowing and collapsing, and carts are taking bones into the tunnels beneath the city, turning them into ossuaries. A rearrangement of skeletons, a *danse macabre* with thousands of dancers.

Any day now, Rohan will make his move. He bought the necklace, he knows it's been delivered. He thinks he has her, and so he will pounce. That is the price she will pay. But how will he pounce? He will try to use the necklace to sway public opinion – that has always been her battleground. So that means he will use Jacques-Pierre Brissot, the man with the enchanted pen.

And Brissot happens to be living with Philippe at the Palais-Royal now. Where Philippe says he can keep an eye on him. As he was instructed to do. The Palais-Royal is no longer a rabble of brothels and shops, or no longer only that. Its cafés are more popular and influential than any salon, or so Vigée Le Brun reports.

Antoinette writes to Philippe, asking him to alert her immediately if any new rumours go out, if Brissot writes a new pamphlet. Polignac is ready to make sure the evidence of the Cardinal's gullibility gets into other pamphleteers' hands.

Philippe, insolent as always, does not reply to her letter. Fine. Let him be rude to her, so long as he does as she asks. She tells Polignac – who is eager to smooth over her relationship with the Queen – to keep an eye on the Palais-Royal.

But the blow does not fall how or where they expect. Rohan doesn't tell the public. He waits for the jewellers to tell Versailles.

Boehmer asks to see the Queen one day in August and

Antoinette, nervous, refuses. She says that she has already told the jeweller she will not be making any purchases, and that's true enough.

But then why is he coming to her? She mentions it to Madame Campan, lightly, making sure there are witnesses to her ignorance of the whole affair.

And then Madame Campan, wringing her hands, tells her Boehmer approached her as well, and told her that the jewellers believe they have sold the necklace to the Queen through an intermediary, but they have not been paid the agreed price of 1,600,000 livres. They delivered the necklace to that intermediary for only a small down payment, on his assurance that the Queen would repay the rest, gradually, so as not to raise suspicion.

Antoinette is shocked enough by this that she doesn't even have to pretend to be.

It makes her sick to realize that the jewellers are owed money, that Rohan took the necklace from them and gave it to Jeanne de la Motte, having no reason to think that Antoinette would ever pay for it and having every reason to believe otherwise. He's the one who made the arrangement; he's the one who owes the money. She tells herself this over and over, working the chain of justifications like a rosary, like stones on a string.

There's nothing Antoinette can do but let the court deal with it. Madame Campan, not wanting to bother the Queen with the jeweller's strange complaint, reports the affair to the minister of the royal household. It all has to be done quite properly.

And so it is that the King hears of it, and summons Cardinal de Rohan, and the Cardinal appears, ostensibly surprised on his way to Mass, sweeping in in his red robes.

Antoinette sits, stiffly, on a chair next to her husband.

'Your Majesty,' Rohan says, bowing to the King.

'What is all this about a necklace? The court jewellers are distraught.' Louis seems tired, his eyelids heavy. He's been melancholy for months; whenever he isn't meeting with his ministers, he's off hunting, or tinkering with his locks, or drinking. Antoinette can't blame him. He says the meetings with ministers are now just litanies of disasters. France spent an enormous sum on the American war, and gained very little. Once the Americans had what they wanted, they made a separate peace with Britain, and so nothing came of the Bourbon hopes of picking off parts of a humbled British Empire. Now, France is bankrupt. Louis's new minister of finance has been trying to get loans and mint coins to keep the state functioning, but it is clear that France can't survive without major new taxes on the nobles and the clergy. So Turgot's unpopular old reforms are on the table again, or something very like them.

Once upon a time, Louis XIV saved France by binding the nobles to him. Now, Louis XVI can only save France by making enemies of them. No wonder he looks as though he's about to collapse. And now he has to deal with this necklace nonsense. It never should have come to him.

'I received letters from Her Majesty,' Rohan says, and holds out a piece of paper, brazenly. 'I did as she asked of me.'

Ah, the letters. Polignac's magical ink. Has be been carrying around the letters everywhere he goes? This summons was supposed to come as a surprise to him. Polignac thinks they've trapped the Cardinal, but he doesn't look like a man who's walked into a trap. He looks like the hunter.

Louis takes the letter from him, reads. Antoinette is close enough to read it over his shoulder. It is in a handwriting similar to her own, but not so similar that anyone who knew her would mistake it. In the letter, she appears to be complaining about the price of the diamond necklace, which, the letter says, Rohan procured for her, after she promised to pay for it.

'This is signed "Marie Antoinette de France",' she says, handing it back accusingly. 'That is not how I sign a letter. That is not how any member of any royal family signs a letter. A person with the slightest familiarity with court would know that. You could have put some effort into this trick, Cardinal.'

She expects him to look confused, or at least surprised. The letter he has read is not signed that way, thanks to Polignac's enchantment. But he doesn't look surprised. He looks at her very calmly for a split second, and then he adopts a pained expression, like a man who's been fooled.

'I had no reason to suspect a trick,' he says. 'Especially not after the Queen herself met me in secret in the gardens, gave me a rose and told me she would put away her old disdain for me, if only I would buy the necklace on her behalf and manage the payments discreetly.'

'It's a lie,' she cries. 'Of course I never did such a thing. The King offered to buy the necklace for me, and I turned it down. I refused it three times. Why in God's name would I then go and buy it in secret? What good is a necklace that one can't wear?'

'It does seem preposterous,' Louis says, dear loyal Louis. She feels overwhelmed, for a moment, by gratitude for all that she has: for her husband and children; for Fersen; for Lamballe and for Polignac; for her brothers and sisters; even and especially for Charlotte, who understands, at least. Charlotte who has made her choices, and cast in her lot with the Order. Perhaps once she'd chosen to work with Soliman, a decent man and a scholar, it did not seem so impossible to work with men like Rohan and Caramanico.

Or the alchemist Cagliostro, who's now staying with Rohan. Just as Antoinette has an alliance of magisters around her who can spy and scheme, so does Rohan. He still has access to a book of spells greater than any rogue's. To the resources of the Order. Polignac has underestimated him.

Somehow, Rohan knows more than he should about Polignac's trap.

She can barely hear Rohan's snide whine; she catches up as he's saying, '. . . the person known as Jeanne de la Motte, who has disappeared along with the necklace. That is, unless the Queen has it?'

Louis frowns and looks at Antoinette.

'I do not have the necklace,' she says, as firmly as she can. It's the truth, but it is also not the truth. She needs to direct the conversation in another direction. 'Cardinal, isn't it true that Count Cagliostro, that notorious swindler, has been staying with you?'

The Cardinal straightens up. 'The count is a noted alchemist and healer, Sire.'

'Mmm,' says Louis, who has heard the stories of Cagliostro bilking money out of wealthy widows, the schemes he has pulled across Europe.

'It's an evident conspiracy,' says Antoinette.

'I tend to agree,' says the King, pink in the face. 'But as I have an interest in the matter, let's see what the Parlement has to say about it. In the meantime,' he says, addressing the captain of his guard, 'take Cardinal de Rohan into custody, and find this Cagliostro too and get him behind bars.'

The Cardinal seems genuinely shocked to be taken by the arms and led away, and that's some small consolation. A trial before the Parlement. Months and months of testimony. But what is to be done about it?

She never wants to see Polignac's beautiful face again. How can Antoinette keep herself safe from her enemies when her friends are more dangerous?

After Rohan has been taken away and they are left alone with only the footmen at the door, Louis mutters, 'You can't testify, Antoinette. That's one thing we must avoid.'

'You surely can't believe that a man as shrewd as Rohan was tricked by an actress and a forgery. He's known me all his life. He's playing some game.'

'Well, he can't be as shrewd as you think, my darling wife. He seems to have been taken in by Cagliostro, after all.'

'No,' she says firmly. 'I don't believe he's been fooled by anyone.'

CHAPTER FORTY-NINE

The Cardinal on Trial — A Prison Break —
Decay in the Heart of Versailles — A Separate Peace —
New Societies

———— ❧ ————

Antoinette paces by a second-floor window. Vigée Le Brun is late; the lamps are lit out in the courtyard, shining on the stones. Perhaps there was some disturbance after they pronounced Rohan guilty, some rough justice. Perhaps she isn't coming.

Louis forbade Antoinette to appear at the trial, even to be in the room. The King is synonymous with the state, he said; put the King on trial and the next step is anarchy.

Unspoken in his philosophy, but unquestioned in it, is that as his wife, *she* is indistinguishable from *him*, that she is part of his person. So she must not be involved in a trial at the Parlement. She has had to make do with the reports of Vigée Le Brun about the trial, and Lamballe's about court gossip. And Fersen writes worried letters from Sweden, promising to return soon.

At last, the usher opens the door and Vigée Le Brun strides in, her face serious. She curtseys, and Antoinette takes both her hands.

'No verdict yet, Your Majesty.'

Antoinette slumps in spirit, never in body. 'I thought it would be today.'

'So did we all. But the actress's testimony went on and on. She kept stopping to cry.'

The actress.

This whole affair should have come to nothing, or almost nothing. Rohan's letters are clear forgeries. But then a low-born actress who looks astonishingly like the Queen confessed to having impersonated Her Majesty in the gardens of Versailles, one summer night. Jeanne de la Motte hired her, she testified, and even provided her with a script to read, to persuade the Cardinal that the Queen wanted the necklace but did not want to be the one haggling over the arrangements.

The actress says the Cardinal seemed quite convinced by her performance.

'An actress indeed,' spits Antoinette.

The painter shrugs. 'Perhaps. But if it was all pretence, it was the best performance France has seen since Molière was a boy. I think she believes it, whether it happened or not. Perhaps she's been duped herself somehow. Her story helps to pin the blame on Jeanne de la Motte and make Rohan look innocent. But it doesn't help you.'

'I'm not the one on trial,' murmurs Antoinette.

Vigée Le Brun's expression is hard and cynical. 'This weeping actress has told the world a story about a too-trusting priest who was fooled because he believed it highly likely that the greedy, acquisitive Queen would meet a man in a garden by night, to make some shadowy arrangement to enrich herself. The same Queen who recently insisted on buying the Saint-Cloud estate from the Orléans family, despite the fact that she does not want for houses. This is how they will see it. They don't care that you weren't involved, Your Majesty. They only care that you could have been. That it was plausible. You are a character in a story to them – you always have been. An image in a painting. Now that story is about furtive, corrupt dealings. Lecherous clergymen in gardens; diamond necklaces that cost enough to feed all the starving. Stories don't need to be true, or even coherent, to explode like gunpowder. That is how gossip works.'

'Oh, how I wish I could speak for myself,' says Antoinette. 'How I wish Polignac had never guided me into this trap.'

Vigée Le Brun's cynicism is warranted. There are new mutterings against the Queen. The *libellistes* write pornographic pamphlets about *les bijoux de la reine*. The details don't matter; all anyone remembers is that Marie Antoinette was involved in some sort of shady deal involving diamonds, and clandestine meetings, and a trial at the Parlement.

'*L'etat, c'est moi,*' said the Sun King. If the King and Queen are the state, then in some fashion the state has just gone on trial, all over a great deal of nothing.

The Parlement believes that Rohan was duped. He and Cagliostro are acquitted.

Jeanne de la Motte is convicted. On hearing the sentence, she picks up a china cup on the desk of her jailer and cracks it against her face. She is stripped naked and beaten with rods, leashed to a halter, flogged and branded with the letter V for theft, a crime she did not commit, and put into the prostitutes' prison, Salpetrière.

But Antoinette knows full well that Jeanne de la Motte, while not precisely innocent, was not the architect of this whole affair. Rohan is a magister; he knows how to make sacrifices for what he wants. He has been scheming for years to discredit Antoinette and he finally found a way to do it. A trap within a trap.

She begins talking to Louis about finding a new governess for the children, says Polignac is too grasping, too ambitious, all of which is true.

And she asks her husband to release Jeanne de la Motte, but he refuses her, saying he must overrule her soft heart. How can he release the woman? Half the country already thinks that the royal family was somehow involved in the conspiracy. After all, where are the diamonds? Everyone knows how much the Queen loves beautiful things. How dazzling she is.

The Queen cannot visit Jeanne de la Motte.

But the Princesse de Lamballe can, bearing a few drops of oil that reshape stone. And when she hears that Jeanne de la Motte has escaped from prison and fled to England, Antoinette pretends to be surprised.

> *Francesco d'Aquino,*
> *the Prince of Caramanico,*
> *to Count Alessandro Cagliostro*
> *15 September 1785*

My Brother,

I greet you and I send my sympathies for your recent treatment. As I promised you, the actress's testimony served to free you as well as the Cardinal. I hope this reassures you as to the intentions of Philippe d'Orléans. The old allegiances don't matter; we are bonded now by common purpose. He wants what you and I want, what all men of courage want: a world in which magisters are not subject to the whims of kings and especially of queens. A world in which the true masters are the magisters, and a man of talent can lead, not follow.

I believe deep in my soul that this was the original intention of the formation of the Order, but now that Order has been corrupted by mundane power. It is only through working with like-minded magisters, no matter what pathways may have led them to magic in the first place, that we will establish a new order in the world, and take our place at the top of it.

Trust him, trust me, and give my regards to the Cardinal. The plans of our enemies betray them and serve us.

I am, dear count, most affectionately yours,
Caramanico

Antoinette, playing cards with Madame Campan in the evening, hears her sister's voice in her mind.

Come have a chat in an hour, if you can.

Antoinette loses the next two hands, excuses Madame Campan, says her prayers and slips into her secret room.

She notices, as she has not noticed for some time, that there is hardly any paper left on the walls other than a few blackened strips, that the plaster of the ceiling is rotting like cave stalactites, that the wooden floor is rotting into sawdust beneath the new carpet. Any given enchantment has very little discernible effect on its surroundings – except for the time she faltered in her intention in the woods, while she was trying to deter Rohan, and, like a damp squib, the forces of magic seemed to disperse oddly. But over time, there is an effect from the many spells of several magisters. Decay in the heart of Versailles.

She walks to where the portrait of Charlotte hangs behind a black cloth, as if her sister is dead. But she is not dead. It seems impossible to think of Charlotte dying, somehow. The world would stop spinning.

She stands for a few long minutes, staring at Charlotte's face, or the face of Charlotte as she was in 1783. What does Charlotte look like now, in 1785? Is she fatter? Probably, as Antoinette is herself.

'Good evening, Charlotte.'

Sister.

Antoinette speaks lightly, as though any part of this is normal. 'Your ambassador, the Prince of Caramanico, has invited me to tea. I will be on guard for poison. There are so many Italians in Paris these days.'

Don't go. He thinks he is my ambassador, but I don't trust him either. I intercepted a letter of his – that's what I want to talk to you about. It took me some time and cost me dear to decipher it, or I would have told you sooner.

She pauses. 'You spy on your own ambassador?'

I only sent Caramanico to France so I wouldn't be tempted to flense him with a letter-opener.

'He is a member of your Order. As is Cagliostro.'

Cagliostro! Cagliostro is a carbuncle on the Order. He is the worst of all possible worlds, a gold tassel on a cheap coat.

'A lecher and a cad.'

A boor. A shiny-faced fraud whose sins will go forever unexamined. I haven't spoken to him in years.

Antoinette nods, though of course Charlotte cannot see that. Luckily, she can't see her wipe away the tear at the corner of her right eye, either. Here they are, talking again, almost like friends.

But not allies.

'Cagliostro is free, but I am not, it seems. I will never be free. Your Order always manages to win.'

That's what I wanted to tell you. It was not the Order who helped Rohan, who set up that actress to tell that tale at the trial. It was Philippe d'Orléans.

'Philippe!' Antoinette says it too loudly, and claps her hand over her face. 'What game are you playing, Charlotte?'

No game at all. I have the evidence, in a letter from Caramanico to Cagliostro. Your Philippe certainly has no shortage of actresses at his command. There are Brothers and radical rogues making common cause against monarchy. They want to undermine the old structures so that they can rise to the top.

Antoinette leans against the wall. Fersen, when she tells him, will be livid. Could Charlotte be trying to fracture the unity of the Circle? But no, Antoinette must admit it. There is no unity left to fracture.

'Philippe has been meeting with Brothers, but I thought it was for our purposes,' Antoinette says. 'He befriended Jacques-Pierre Brissot, the man with the enchanted pen.'

I'm sorry. I was wrong about that.

Philippe has also become the patron of the Chevalier de Saint-Georges, who never seems free to come to Versailles any more.

Tell me, Antoinette, whose trap was it? Did Rohan set it?

She considers telling Charlotte about Polignac's role, about her one-time favourite being seduced by her own cleverness and duped in the end, but she is tired of thinking about friendships and alliances, betrayals and love. She says, simply and honestly: 'We both trapped each other. But I got the worst of it.'

What becomes of a war when each side turns on itself? Not quite peace, but perhaps a détente. A realignment. Antoinette's rogues and Charlotte's Order may still disagree on how to remake the world, but now they face a bigger threat and a common enemy: the rogues – and Brothers – who want to burn the world down altogether, so they can rise from the ashes.

Antoinette takes a deep breath. Will she and Charlotte be able to work together, to trust each other, now? At the very least, they're talking. 'I thank you, sister. I'll be wary. How are the children? How is little Maria Antonia?'

Thriving. Adorable to a fault. Just like her aunty. And my name-sake?

'Charles is a healthy little bear.'

I must go. Kiss my name-child for me.

Antoinette nods again, futilely, and reaches her hand out to the face of the woman in the painting, her fingers not quite brushing the varnish.

PART SIX

1789 TO 1793

CHAPTER FIFTY

Louis Stumbles — Where Philippe Walks — Vanity —
A Man Shouts at the Queen — Emptiness

———————— ❖ ————————

In the spring of 1789, Louis summons the Estates General, and everyone at Versailles pretends it is cause for celebration. It's been a century and a half since a French king had reason to call an assembly of the people, to be seen to ask for their counsel in a time of crisis. Unlike the Parlements, which have been resisting all of Louis's attempts at economic reform, the Estates General have no real authority. But also unlike the Parlements, which are fundamentally courts of justice filled with hereditary nobles, the Estates General represent all of the people. To call the Estates General is an act of mighty humility, a master stroke. It is dangerous, especially for a king like Louis, who actually cares what they might have to say. Antoinette prepares for the grand procession to mark the opening. She wears a gown of cloth of silver and Monsieur Léonard dresses her hair with feathers. No necklace. She accepts the mask for the powder with the ease of a dancer preparing for a performance at which she expects to be booed, possibly pelted with rotten fruit. Or worse.

A few weeks ago, Louis nearly fell to his death as he was

walking on the roofs of the palace, looking out over the gardens. He goes up there to think, when he can't get away to his locksmith's workshop. Antoinette has heard conflicting accounts of what happened: he was leaning on a ladder and it fell, something of that nature. She suspects a magister but of what tribe she can't imagine. The radicals among both the rogues and the Order might well want the King dead, but the most likely regent while the Dauphin is a child is Antoinette herself, which would not serve their purposes. Or would it? She goes over and over the logic of it in her mind, and wants to mention it to Lafayette, but Lafayette is not the sort of man who could discuss the attempted assassination of his king and not act. And action, at the moment, is dangerous. She feels as though they are all walking on a rain-slick precipice to which there is no ladder, with nothing but steep falls in all directions.

Her ladies take the powder mask and cape away, and she breathes.

'There,' says Monsieur Léonard, clapping his hands once. The original Léonard; Antoinette sees his brother less and less often at court these days.

He's showing his age and his worries, but his talents are still a marvel.

'You must not be so melancholy,' he whispers, and she recognizes it and appreciates it for what it is: not the plea of a friend but the exhortation of a theatre manager.

She thanks him, giving him her hand, and then she goes to her place beside the King. Louis smiles wanly at her. He, too, is dressed to shine, stout and determined in cloth of gold, with a sword at his waist. A procession is about being seen at a distance, being recognized for who and what they are, so that people can go home and say they saw the King, they saw the Queen.

She kisses Louis's cheek, daring more in front of courtiers than she would have in their newlywed days. She does love him. He bears everything without breaking. His fall on the roof – halted only by the quick arm of a workman – did not shake him at all.

Out into the May sunshine they walk, through the golden gates and into the town of Versailles. The procession is there waiting for them.

Behind the King and Queen, the delegates will walk, all wearing their prescribed clothing and walking in the order of their social position. The clergy are to wear their robes – she grimaces at the red of a cardinal, but Rohan has not come. Though he was stripped of his positions and exiled from court, the clergy elected him to the Estates General anyway, and there was some talk that he might come. He hasn't.

She's relieved, but Louis is frowning, looking out over the procession. He talks quietly to his brother, and frowns deeper.

'What is it?' she whispers.

'Philippe d'Orléans is here, but not in his place among the nobility,' he growls. 'Apparently he has chosen to walk with the Third Estate. Wearing plain black and without a sword. The buffoon.'

The Third Estate. The common people. Given double the numbers of the other estates, this time, in some recognition of their much greater population, although their voice will still only count as one of three.

Of course Philippe is play-acting as a peasant, though the death of his father in 1785 made him the Duc d'Orléans and he is wealthier than ever. She should have expected it. For months, there were whispers among the rogues of something called the Ladder Club – a new alliance of renegade Brothers and ambitious rogues. Vigée Le Brun was the one who got to the bottom of it: the Ladder Club meets behind an unmarked door in the Rue de l'Échelle, so called because of the pillory that stood there not long ago. It is very close to the Palais-Royal.

Philippe does not attend meetings of the Queen's Circle any more, and he would not be welcome if he tried. He does not come to Versailles at all. When the King convened an assembly to push forward the tax reforms, Philippe had himself elected president and turned the delegates against the King. Louis exiled some of Philippe's allies, but it hasn't stopped the growing discontent. The town of Grenoble rose up, and the King sent troops. A boy died.

Lafayette tries to keep a hand on everything, in France and abroad. When the American native leader Joseph Brant came to Paris, Lafayette met with him, and learned all about the land Brant has hidden from the British, using a combination of magister spells and his people's own traditions. Lafayette is a member of the same anti-slavery societies as Brissot, Philippe, and Saint-Georges, although he doesn't share Philippe's goal of removing monarchs and setting up magisters in their place.

And Saint-Georges? In London, he fought a sword duel with the Chevalière d'Éon – a friendly duel, to all outward eyes, and indeed they are friends. But Antoinette suspects, from d'Éon's letters, that the dispute over the course that rogue magisters ought to take is as fraught in England as it is in France.

Polignac's sojourn in England seems to have changed her. She returned carrying the best regards of the Duchess of Devonshire, who is an old friend, as well as a lingering cough and a strange new sympathy for the Order – or at least, the Order as it is in Naples. She argued that the principles of the rogues could not keep the monarchy safe against the revolutionaries – she used that word, *revolutionaries*, although no one else does, at least not within earshot of the King and Queen.

What good is magic, Polignac reasoned, if it does not support the monarchy? Beneath her words, Antoinette could almost hear her thoughts: what good is a queen who won't use magic to protect herself, her family, her nation? A government run by magic could restore France to its former strength. Fill its treasuries. This is what Charlotte has been working for, and perhaps she's been right all along. A new era, a golden age, when magic will solve all the people's problems.

'I have used magic in whatever ways I could, to be a better queen. What do you think I have been trying to do all these years?' Antoinette asked.

Polignac, for the first time in their friendship, set her jaw and her eyes, hard as gemstones, and said, 'You have tried to make yourself unassailable, yes. As if you could remake your person into such perfection that it would induce perfection in its turn. It is a chimera – a figment, a—'

'A what?'

'A vanity.'

So it goes. But she is sorry for Louis, who is solid and does not adapt quickly. Antoinette still adores his brother, her old friend and card-playing companion the Comte d'Artois, one of the few people at Versailles who made her feel welcome when she arrived as an unready child bride. But he's made life no easier for the King lately, greeting every egalitarian proposal with aristocratic disdain, like a mirror image of Philippe d'Orléans. D'Artois is known to be Antoinette's friend – indeed, he is the lover who appears in most of the pornographic poems and cartoons about her. And Philippe, the *soi-disant* man of the people, is the one who sells pamphlets denouncing her out of his shops at the Palais-Royal.

Fine. Let Philippe walk where he will. Antoinette walks beside her husband.

The people cheer as they walk past the lined streets, hanging out of windows, even up on lampposts. She hears several shouts of '*Vive le roi*' and though no one mentions *la reine* at all, it could be worse. She allows herself to breathe a little more freely.

Somewhere in this crowd, not far, is Axel von Fersen. Gustavus sent him to France to look after Sweden's interests, or so Fersen says; she doesn't know how he managed it but she is grateful.

Fersen has always been circumspect, compared with most of the other rogue magisters of Antoinette's acquaintance. These days, he is warier than ever. The rogues of Stockholm are as extreme as the Brothers of Stockholm, he says; one of them worked with Fersen for years on an enchantment to steal the Order's great spellbook, but then carried out the plan prematurely, alone, and managed to destroy the book and himself in the process. Fersen says a Brother of Stockholm named Theodore von Graben came to him in a great rage, saying there was nothing left of the *Reconditus* in Stockholm but a burnt and blackened star on the floor.

For many reasons, Fersen says he is done with Sweden. He has taken a house in Paris and has been busily working to find rogue magisters who might be allies. Antoinette is glad to have him near, even today, when he cannot be at her side.

The children, thank God, are not part of the procession. This is largely to avoid revealing the fact that the Dauphin can no longer walk. But they are waiting on a dais along the route, waving to their parents under the watchful gaze of their guards. Ten-year-old Mousseline is holding the hand of four-year-old Charles.

Antoinette's heart cracks when she sees their brother Louis-Joseph beside them, lying on cushions, cheering and clapping though he is so thin, his little face so pained. For two years now, the Dauphin has gone from one fever to another. Tuberculosis, according to the doctors, and they say that is what is twisting his spine and causing him such pain. A seven-year-old child should not know such pain.

She contemplated the painting spell to even out his shoulders and straighten his spine. D'Éon has used the painting spell more than once, she says, and she recommended a medical doctor from Holland, a rogue magister of Fersen's acquaintance. He said that the painting spell would likely do the child no good, that the pain was coming from within, from the effects of the disease. It might help him walk again for a little while, but not for long and not without pain, and why put the child through a gruelling procedure for that?

She is powerless, but she sends every drop of her heart's love to her child as she smiles and waves at him, Louis beside her doing the same.

And so she hardly notices that the crowd is pressing close around them and that a man is right next to her. His face is red. He looks in her eyes and screams, '*Vive le Duc d'Orléans!*'

She stumbles, almost into him, and Louis takes her arm to keep her from falling. She hears her husband shout at the guards to get the bastard away from his wife. She holds on.

Antoinette has moved the portrait of her sister into another hidden room in Versailles, one where the walls are still sound, and there is no smell of burnt silk or rotten velvet. A room not for doing spells in, but for speaking to her sister. It contains only one blue armchair, a footstool, and a table with a book on it to pass the time when Charlotte is late for their appointed conversations. (The book at the moment is *La Princesse de Clèves*, a novel by Madame de la Fayette, from another branch of the marquis's family.)

On the walls are two paintings: the familiar portrait of Charlotte, with her hair so golden . . .

. . . and one of Antoinette and her children by Élisabeth Vigée Le Brun.

The office of the royal household commissioned a portrayal of the Queen with her children, soon after the conclusion of the Diamond Necklace Affair. They had strict instructions about the clothing, the composition, and especially about the lack of any necklace on Her Majesty. The large jewellery case as a backdrop was also their idea, meant to imply that the four children are her true jewels, like Calpurnia of Rome.

Can a painting counter the pornographic poems, the cartoons showing Antoinette as a harpy with claws and tail, the vile essays that issue from the pen of Jacques-Pierre Brissot as he sits sipping coffee in Philippe's Palais-Royal?

The painting shows Mousseline, saucy girl, holding Antoinette's arm and gazing up at her mother. The Queen is upholstered in red velvet, lined with sable, and she is trying to keep a straight face. She clutches little Charles on her lap as he grabs for her breast. Louis-Joseph, unlike Mousseline, is taking the whole exercise very seriously, holding onto the bassinet and gazing at the interior with the indulgent smile of a big brother.

During the sittings, Antoinette's big pink baby Sophie was sleeping, breathing heavily, in the bassinet.

But the painting shows the bassinet empty, shadowed by a draped black cloth, for Sophie died, after a few days of terrible illness. Not a year old yet, not weaned yet, her cherub girl.

And the painting didn't hang at the Salon after all. An empty frame took its place. By the time the painting was finished, Louis's ministers were worried that any image of the Queen would only attract more ridicule, no matter how regal and matronly she may be, no matter how darling her children's faces. Just as Antoinette is the only person in the noisy tavern argument that has spread throughout Versailles who may not voice a political opinion, lest association with her kill the very thing she was trying to support.

The portrait hung in the palace, in the Salon de Mars, until Antoinette could no longer bear to have it where strangers might walk by and look at it, so she had it moved here, in the forgotten room where no one else ever comes.

She puts her hand out, touches the empty bassinet, a small ritual she performs every time. And then she hears her sister's voice.

CHAPTER FIFTY-ONE

Potemkin Villages — Grief and Loss — The Chief of Police — A Ship in the Bay of Naples — William Hamilton Takes a Mistress

━━━━━━━━ ✜ ━━━━━━━━

When she's at Caserta, Charlotte keeps Antoinette's portrait in an alcove off her suite of library rooms. Close enough that she can reach it when she needs to.

Sometimes she sits in her sister's silent company, long before the time appointed for their talks. She has a carved walnut armchair with a red seat that gives a little when she sits in it, in a homely sort of way. She starts leafing through the embroidered book, the crack and bend of its pages as familiar as her lover's body. More, because Acton has scars he won't talk about and, for the most part, she doesn't ask.

Page after page, the old familiar spells. Countess Ertag's book is the magic of sewing baskets and dressing tables. The world is bigger; the sisters' own magic is bigger. The last time they spoke, Antoinette admitted that the spell the Russian governor Potemkin used, to create whole villages out of nothing and then tear them down again to impress the Empress Catherine on a fact-finding journey, had been a spell of her own invention. The same one used to fool British

541

troops, years ago, and to build the Queen's Hamlet near the Petit Trianon. The spell spread beyond her Circle, as Antoinette's tend to do. The houses were wood straight through; toys made large.

Meanwhile, the Order's magic has been dealt a massive blow. The last time Charlotte, Caterina, and Silfversparre met in the tunnels beneath the Masonic lodge, they found the *Reconditus* had disappeared. It ought not to have been possible, and yet, somehow, somewhere, a rogue magister managed it. Then the letters came in from all over Europe, from all the remaining chapters of the Order. There are no copies of the *Reconditus* anywhere; it was, after all, one book, and stealing one of its manifestations means stealing all the others.

Soliman suspects the theft was in Stockholm, where the Order is weak, and there are ties of love and family between its members and the rogues. Charlotte suspects that Fersen had something to do with it.

I'm here, sister.

Charlotte closes the book, abruptly and with a bang, as though the painting were looking over her shoulder instead of merely listening.

'It's raining here. You might hear thunder. How is it there?'

Chilly today, but no rain. I have lily of the valley everywhere in my rooms; I love May. How are you, and the children?

It is a question with weight behind it, the warm soft weight of a hand on a shoulder. She had three more babies in three years: two girls and a boy, all of them Acton's. In December, Ferdinand's father died in Spain, and Charlotte felt a different weight lift from her. Her rule in Naples is untrammelled now. They had hardly got the news when smallpox came to the nursery again. Gennaro had survived smallpox once; they thought he was immune.

Ferdinand brought Gennaro fairy-tale books and read them to him in his overly formal, nervous reading voice. He performed a puppet show at the end of the bed until Gennaro gave him a weak smile. He smuggled in chocolates and other treats that sat untouched until the nurse removed them. None of it was enough to save him.

After Gennaro died, Charlotte had all the other children inoculated, and it was too much for the baby, who died at five months. She had named him Carlo, for the brother who died long before his birth, just as Charlotte herself was named for two of her dead sisters. Perhaps that is one reason she never thinks of herself as Maria Carolina, not even now, when she is thirty-six years old and has proven to the world that of all the children of the Empress with that name, it was she who laid claim to it, by surviving.

Are you there?

'Everyone's fine,' Charlotte says. 'Tell me about your family.'

Mousseline is learning to ride, and Charles looks at everything through those great big eyes, takes everything in, and then he wears himself out so that he's a wonderful sleeper. The Dauphin is still unwell. He did us proud at the procession today.

'So the Estates General have convened. And there will be more talk of taxes and trade.'

Yes. More talk.

'Are you safe?'

Of course. I'm in the Petit Trianon. There are mirrors and traps—

'And if the people rise against you?'

Quiet.

It will not come to that.

'Perhaps it's best if you and the children leave France for a while. You could come to Italy, and see me.'

The King can't leave now, you know that. It would be an abdication. And then who knows what?

'But the rest of you, you and the children—'

I will never leave the King, and I'm not sending my children away from me. They're not even as old as we were when we were packed off, and you know what that was like. My God. How little we understood of anything, then. How little I understand now.

'But it may not be safe for them there. Will you at least make a plan, to get them out if it becomes unsafe?'

Wouldn't the family help?

'Of course they will.' Charlotte bites it off. They'll help; she'll make sure of that. What is the point of being a Habsburg if you don't know every state in Europe will rise to your aid in times of direst need? That is, after all, what Mama had in mind, why she sent them away to bear the children of kings they'd never met.

Then I think we will manage.

'The family will help, but you need ways to get the children out. You will need to make plans.'

A pause.

I will make plans.

'Good.' Charlotte pauses in her turn, scratches her head, grimaces at her sister's face as though she's looking at a puzzle. They have not spoken of magisters and factions, and she considers what she might say about it. Then she hears Antoinette.

Good night, sister. I embrace you.

'Dream good dreams, Antoinette.'

The Queen of Naples sits alone on a gilt throne while her eight living children dance around her. They're wearing peacock feathers in their hair. The whole spectacle and its audience are on the deck of a ship in the Bay of Naples, so Charlotte is queasy.

She claps when the music stops and stands up, blowing a kiss to every one of her children. Teresa, her eldest, blowsy and flushed, nearly seventeen. By next year, she and Luisa will be married and gone: one to Austria and one to Tuscany, to preserve those alliances with Naples for another generation. Lucky Habsburgs – on both sides of both marriages.

Not only does she protect her children; they also protect her. Perhaps that's the way of things in all families, but for Charlotte, every child has meant more power on the Council, more power over her husband, more power in Europe. Here, encircled by her dancing offspring, she is safe on her throne.

The circle's harmony is marred a little by two gaps, two drops in the heights of the peacock feathers. The first, caused by the deaths of Carlo and Marianna, a decade ago now, so long ago that none of the younger children remember them. But Charlotte remembers them, as do the two eldest girls, and Ferdinand – who loves his children, for all his many, many faults.

After the gap comes sober Francesco, eleven years old, who will be nothing like his father if Charlotte can help it. Then happy, lithe Little Mimi.

Then the gap that means Gennaro and Giuseppe.

And then her four merry girls, the youngest three Acton's, though Ferdinand treats them as his own. Maria Amalia, Maria Antonia, Clothilde, Enrichietta. They can't seem to keep enough distance between them in their circle, can't keep their mouths from smiling. Her darlings.

She wobbles a little. It's the ship. *Her* ship: a ship of the line. Acton turns them out now like ducklings leaving the shipyard at Castellemmare. The sails are furled and they're anchored in the Bay of Naples for the party; flags in all colours run down the rigging and an orchestra plays on the poop deck.

Flanked by two guards in her livery, Charlotte walks towards the bow. The setting sun flashes into her eyes every time the ship's mast pitches to one side or the other.

People hold out their hands to her, to take her elbow. She refuses them all. There's Acton, father of some of her children, watching her. Slightly resentful, after all these years, of the passion between them that isn't quite love. But they work well together, nonetheless. He doubtless has reports to make, some criticism of the new ship. He's never satisfied. That's why he's such an indispensable prime minister, but in this moment she doesn't have the wherewithal to know what she wants to say or do with Acton, on this beautiful night, this night for lovers. She'll be fine – she's feeling more clear in her stomach already. She changes direction, walks towards her comrades in arms.

The last time she saw Isaac Lars Silfversparre, he was holding little Gennaro out in both his arms and spinning in the gardens at Caserta. He bows his head as he reports, and the other magisters, almost casually, gather from the far parts of the ship.

Caterina walks with the confidence of a sailor, her dark hair swept up with a rose at one side, a lace shawl around her shoulders.

William Hamilton is leaning on the gunwale, gazing at his mistress. Emma Hart arrived from England, as if by order, and Hamilton was lonely, so Charlotte says nothing about it. Still, this woman is young, and not his wife. She has not been presented to the Queen, which means the Queen does not speak to her. When Charlotte visits Hamilton, Emma is outside with her mother, or out in the carriage, or upstairs resting.

Charlotte, Hamilton, Silfversparre, and Caterina haven't had a ritual meeting of the Order in Naples since Vesuvius collapsed their tunnels; truth be told, they barely have enough of them for a chapter, most of the time, as Silfversparre is out hunting rogues in the rest of the kingdom, and Caterina is managing San Leucio.

The orchestra starts up, and it's noisy, so they can speak more freely.

'Caramanico and Lunardi have joined the Ladder Club,' Silfversparre says lowly. 'Rogue magisters and renegade Brothers. I've heard that, in Paris, they've taken to wearing red Phrygian caps.'

She snorts. 'Of all things, they've adopted the hats? Ridiculous things – always reminded me of folk stories, of gnomes and kobolds.'

She's developing an old lady's manners, abrupt and child-like, at thirty-six. But it's so loud, and the ship is rolling, and she's so tired.

Silfversparre has complained to her recently that he feels adrift. He wanted to make the Order better but instead the Order ate its own tail, and now the threats come from elsewhere. Charlotte told him that he has always been guided by decency, by honour, and that he can continue in that work whether the Order survives or not. He is still restless, though.

'We should recruit some new magisters,' Caterina says. 'Make up for our losses. My brother, Luigi de' Medici.'

Charlotte lets the frown cross her face. She's already made Luigi de' Medici her new chief of police; in his youth he was a street fighter, and now he's mellowed into a practical and solid man, with friends in all classes and ideas about lighting streets and numbering the houses. But to make him a magister?

Before she answers, William Hamilton says, 'My Emma—'

This startles Charlotte into forgetting to pretend his mistress doesn't exist. 'You want to make her a magister?'

The ambassador pauses, and looks at Silfversparre, who looks right back at him.

'She already is,' Hamilton says finally. 'She was before she came. Naples is full of rogue magisters now, and those we don't pull to our side will join the Ladder Club or some other group.'

'But the Order has always been strict about its membership,' she says. She, Charlotte, the first woman, the first monarch, to be admitted. She holds up her hand, says, 'I'll consider it. Not tonight. And, Silfversparre, don't go brushing anyone's hair over this.'

He smiles thinly. 'Your Majesty, if I tried to eliminate all the rogues in Naples now, I would never stop to eat or rest. It used to be that we would find them most in the back alleys, or the theatres. Conjurers and mountebanks and midwives.'

Or so-called alchemists, she thinks, remembering Cagliostro.

'And now?' Hamilton asks.

Silfversparre grimaces. 'Now, magic is spreading in the salons. The Ladder Club in Naples already counts among its members Luisa Sanfelice, Eleonora Pimentel, Mario Pagano, Domenico Cirillo.'

'And some of the nobility,' Caterina adds.

The nobility, and the intellectuals. Her Academy, her schools. But, of course, it was Caramanico who was her liaison with the Academy, and now he has turned his coat.

She steps away from the others for a moment, to get some air. Leans on the gunwale. Stares at the water, dark now as black glass. Men crawl on the ship's rigging to light the fairy lanterns.

Deep in the water, a shimmer of blue-green, glowing, like the reflection of some heaven much denser with stars than the one over her head. Sea creatures, tiny ones, that glow at night. She's seen them before. They shift back and forth, creating landscapes on the surface. Soliman believes there is a pattern behind everything, a grand truth, a web, a fabric. Sometimes nature seems to make his point for him.

She leans over farther, to watch the glowing creatures swim right under the ship, and then with no warning she opens her mouth and vomits over the side.

It's loud and liquid and, even over the din from the party, everyone hears. Someone is at her side, calling for a doctor, and someone else is screaming at Silfversparre, and there's a child crying somewhere. Bedlam. But her own Bedlam.

Then a strong, small hand is on her arm, and a woman is leading her away from the watching people.

'The Queen is fine, but she needs air,' she's saying.

Charlotte looks up and sees a sweet face, with red lips and limpid eyes. 'Miss Hart,' she says, recognizing Hamilton's mistress.

Emma Hart nods. 'Come with me, Your Majesty. I've been pregnant before, you know. I remember how it is.'

It's not the sort of thing the companion of the English ambassador should have admitted, even if everyone knew she was a mail-order mistress and a prostitute in London before that. Charlotte finds the forthrightness bracing, and doesn't bother protesting that, for once, she isn't pregnant. It's only the ship, and being so tired. She puts her hand on Emma's and walks with her, away from the rolling, glowing ocean.

1 June 1789
Emperor Joseph II to Maria Carolina

My very dear sister,
My health is a little better than the last time I wrote.
The doctors say I may never recover from that fall from my horse into the icy river at Karánsebes, though I count myself among the lucky that night. I still don't know how it was that the Austrian army was thrown into such confusion, seeing the enemy when there was no enemy there, and firing brother against brother in their panic.
Angelo Soliman tells me the Turks used some sort of device against us, to produce illusions. We were fighting no one. When the Turks actually arrived at the battlefield, they found only Austrian corpses, and I was wandering, lost, frozen, wet. I've sent him to the border to discover what this device was. Though he has written me a letter about it, I cannot claim to understand it.
Soliman is nearly seventy now, and perhaps I rely on him too much – he wants nothing more but to study his strange books and travel with his daughter. But where else am I to turn? Kaunitz served my mother as chancellor for decades, but now he doesn't even come when I summon him, and Austria is at war on all sides.
Truth be told, I prefer open campaigns, with soldiers and uniforms and gunsmoke, to the conspiring and sloganeering from secret societies in Liège – which may soon be in open revolt against the Empire – or the Austrian Netherlands. When the uprising happened there, I told Mimi and her

husband to come to Vienna, for their own safety, and so I could talk to them, impress upon them the necessity of our centralizing and rationalizing reforms. I told them what the Empress of Russia told me, that kings must do what is right, and pay no more attention to the cavils of the people than the moon pays to the dogs who bay at it. Since I sent them back home to rule last year they have managed to hold onto power, but they write that they are afraid. And they have reason to be.

This is why I think that persuading Antoinette to come to Naples or to Vienna, even for a family visit during the unrest, would be most unwise, and only guarantee a revolution in France. She writes to me that she must stay there, at her husband's side, and I agree. If she left, she might never be able to return, and it would be a capitulation to the forces of unrest all across Europe. It would put Mimi in danger, and Max, and Amalia, and Leopold, and you and me. We must support her through diplomacy, though God knows France does not look kindly on our ambassadors. The poor woman; my heart breaks over her letters and her descriptions of the Dauphin in his illness. I think that motherhood is the only role to which she was ever truly suited.

Charlotte, you are close to Leopold, and you have the most stalwart character of any of us: you must impress upon him that he may soon be emperor and must prepare himself to leave Tuscany. If my lungs give out, Leopold may very well find himself leading an empire at the heart of a continent in a state of general war. The war is everywhere – these societies, Charlotte, these clubs, these strange new weapons that strike at the heart of a nation, wielded by an invisible hand. You must be vigilant. You must not allow Naples to fall into the same peril.

I remain,

Your brother,
Joseph

CHAPTER FIFTY-TWO

Are There No Fathers Among Them? — Summer
at Versailles — Cockades — Soldiers and Women —
A Rainy Day

———————— ❖ ————————

Summer comes to France, and the Dauphin dies. This boy she could not protect and could not save. Her heart feels torn from her, and she cannot bear to talk to Charlotte because she would weep and weep and how would that be for Charlotte, who has lost so many children?

But now Antoinette has lost half of hers too.

Louis-Joseph dies in her arms on the morning of 4 June 1789. That afternoon, the court comes to her bedroom to pay its respects. She leans against the gilded balustrade that separates her bed from the rest of the room, and tries to remain standing. When everyone has gone, she goes to find Louis, and they sit together in silence.

The next few days are a nightmare of details and decisions. Lamballe tells her that they will drape the casket in cloth of silver, and she makes all the arrangements. Philippe d'Orléans, when invited to perform funerary functions in his role as First Prince of the Blood, refuses, claiming the work of the Estates General keeps him too busy. The Estates General are deadlocked, as the clergy and nobility try to prevent everyone else – the Third Estate – from dominating.

Every day, Louis turns away requests from the representatives of the Third Estate to speak to him about voting arrangements and rules of procedure. He asks wearily: 'Are there no fathers among them?'

The court leaves Versailles and its swirl of visiting delegates and political arguments, retreating to Marly for a week. It is a strangely private mourning, which is a relief in some ways, as the family (now two children and two parents) has a little time in peace. It's horrible in other ways; the death of a dauphin ought to be a national tragedy, despite the healthy little brother ready to step into a position the royal household has been subtly preparing him for over the last two years.

Jacques Necker arrives at Marly to tell the King that the Third Estate has revolted, and now calls itself a National Assembly.

Louis is sitting with his brothers, the Comte d'Artois and the Comte de Provence, and with Antoinette. He asks for their advice, while Necker looks on impatiently.

'This is treason,' says Provence. 'A complete challenge to royal authority.'

'What would you have me do, Necker?' Louis asks.

His prime minister looks as though he's never been more relieved to hear any question. 'I have prepared a set of reforms that will allow each of the three Estates dominion in their own sphere, while allowing majority votes on matters of national importance.'

'A compromise solution,' says the Comte d'Artois dryly. 'What does the Third Estate have to gain from compromise now?'

'The ability to get anything done in this country,' the Comte de Provence retorts. 'Not to mention their necks.'

'My dear?' Louis looks to Antoinette.

If only everyone in the country could see what a kind man he is. Even now, when his eyes are still red from weeping with her over their little boy, he only wants to do good. He only wants someone to tell him what that is.

'It seems to me that the main thing is for the King to speak to the Estates General, and help them to find common ground,' Antoinette says.

'Do the Estates General even exist any more?' the Comte d'Artois asks.

Necker hesitates. 'The Estates General convened at His Majesty's request.'

'Then make the preparations,' Louis says. 'The King will address the Estates General, propose a compromise, and put an end to this madness.'

By order of the King, the hall where the Estates General had been meeting is closed for a few days to construct the necessary seating and a dais for the King to make his speech. Somehow, the members of the self-declared National Assembly never hear of this plan. When they arrive at the hall to have their own meeting and find their way barred by the King's armed guards, they assume the King has simply ordered them disbanded.

So the Assembly convenes in a tennis court and vows that wherever its members meet, there the Assembly is. There is a new power in France, and it is not the King, nor by decree of the King.

When Louis and Antoinette return to Versailles, everything is in a muddle, and Louis's councillors give him contradictory advice. Some of them have been trying to work with the leaders of the new National Assembly, and everyone has a plan for how to salvage everything. But nothing can be salvaged. The King's brothers urge him to get rid of Necker and replace his council, which Louis does, hoping for a fresh start and a firm stand.

On the morning of 15 July, the women who dress the Queen are all chattering about the violence at the Bastille.

Antoinette nearly falls into Fersen's arms with relief when he arrives with news. They walk out into the gardens in the July heat, in a world of neat hedges and white stone paths.

'The pamphleteers and speechmakers have convinced the people that the King dismissed Necker because he intends to shut down the Assembly and put an end to all reform,' Fersen says. 'They say the King is going to war against the people.'

'It seems to me that the people are going to war against the King,' Antoinette protests. 'What on earth did they want with an old prison?'

'They thought they would find stockpiles of weapons and gunpowder. It didn't take them long to overwhelm the garrison and set free the few prisoners left inside.' He pauses. 'There are troops everywhere, even all through the town of Versailles. Sadly, because the King's council can't be sure of the loyalties of French soldiers, many of them are foreign regiments.'

'It's true, then,' Antoinette says, dazed. 'Louis was told it was a revolution. What should he do? Will you talk to him, tell him everything you have seen and heard?'

He nods, and turns to her, taking her by the shoulders. 'Of course I will. But we must think of your safety, and the children. Polignac is leaving France, and the Comte d'Artois.'

She shakes her head. 'The King can't leave, and I'm not leaving the King. Tell me, have you heard anything of Lafayette? I went to his portrait and spoke to him but I haven't heard anything.'

Fersen laughs ruefully. 'He probably hasn't had a moment alone. Lafayette has managed to get himself named the commander of the new National Guard, and he's writing a Declaration of the Rights of Man and the Citizen. He's helped design the revolutionary cockade: red, white, and blue.'

She frowns, first at the word 'revolutionary' and then at everything after. 'But those are the colours of the Duc d'Orléans.'

'Which no doubt makes Philippe very happy. But Lafayette

is loyal to you, my love, and to the King. He'll make sure the National Guard serves both the people and the King. He believes France can emerge from this a strong and peaceful constitutional monarchy.'

'And you?'

Fersen pulls her to him, holds her close.

The summer ends, and Antoinette does not want to go to a party.

She wasn't supposed to go, wasn't planning to go. She's bone-tired and the very last thing she wants to do is show her face anywhere. Since the storming of the Bastille, she has spent her days at the Queen's Hamlet as much as possible, working on loaves-and-fishes spells, trying to find a way to make enough bread, and damn the economics. She should have found a way to feed the people of France.

Polignac is gone, safe in Switzerland with her family. Antoinette wept when she said farewell, sincerely, grieving at last the friend she has not truly known in years. The Comte d'Artois and his family fled too, at the urging of the King. Antoinette is worried about her friends who do stay by her side – Lamballe, and especially Fersen – while at the same time, she is selfishly grateful for them.

Being away from court is not a dereliction of duty these days. The place is half empty. Many of the wealthiest families have fled the country, or at least gone to their own estates, far from the city. The King's councillors hate her, and the less she is seen in the palace, walking through the Hall of Mirrors, the better. No one objected to her seclusion. Louis meets with his advisers and goes hunting, and does not argue with her every Sunday after Mass when she says, 'One more week at the Hamlet for me, I think.'

It's all right. Antoinette has no intentions of opening up magic to Louis's carousel of advisers to squander as they have squandered all the gold and grain in France. And if he dismissed the advisers, and let his wife rule? Would the people love her as a sorceress-queen, when they have never loved her before? Or would they take the magic and leave the queen? She suspects the latter.

She loses people, one by one. Polignac is already making common cause with a faction of the Order in Switzerland. Saint-Georges has lost patience with the magisters of Versailles and cast his lot in with the radical rogues.

Radical Brothers and radical rogues all have the same immediate goal, it seems: tear down the moderates, clear them away.

Antoinette has at least found a new governess for Mousseline and Charles, who at four is now the Dauphin, after the death of his older brother. The Marquise de Tourzel is as upright and earnest as Polignac was sly and arch. The children call her Madame Virtue and she calls them her 'divinities'. She would probably not mind either if the royal family were to blast its critics to hell, and would not be surprised to learn they could shoot lightning from their fingertips. But unlike Polignac, Madame de Tourzel keeps her thoughts to herself.

Madame de Tourzel greets the news that the children are wanted for a party at Versailles using the same expression with which she would greet the news that giants had come over the border or that the weather was fine. The marquise has only one expression: placid contentment. 'All shall be well,' she says sometimes, even if no one has addressed any remark to her. They'll be watching the children perform a masque or a ballet, and Madame de Tourzel will clap her hands together and say *all shall be well*.

'Are you sure a party is the best idea, Louis?' Antoinette asks, quietly, as they eat a luncheon together. 'The bread shortages – it's not the time to have any sort of banquet.'

He takes a spoonful of the beef broth, and nods, as if he's agreeing with her. But then he says, 'The soldiers are clamouring to see us. They're loyal to us – they're singing songs in our praise. In your praise. It's like—'

'Yes?'

'It's like when you first came to France, and you travelled from town to town and everywhere there were crowds with tears of joy in their eyes to see the Dauphine. That's how these soldiers are, now.'

She remembers. She remembers the fireworks disaster and the panic too. There has always been horror lurking behind every joy. 'I'm not an exotic young dauphine now,' she says with a soft smile. 'I'm a thirty-three-year-old matron. I'm Madame Déficit, or so they call me in the pamphlets. I'm the Great Harpy.'

He shrugs. 'The soldiers want to love you. Look at' – he's about to say Fersen – 'look at Lafayette: he still loves us, though he serves under the command of the new Assembly. But we can't take their love for granted. We must go and show them we appreciate it.'

She nods. It's a foregone conclusion anyway; she's already in her white *robe à la turque*, with its close-fitted bodice and little lacy sleeves. White, the colour of royalty, although the jacket is striped in turquoise. She sets aside two white feathers for her hair, and calls for Monsieur Léonard.

Today, Jean-François comes with all his powders and tools in a black leather bag, like a doctor or a magician, and sets to work.

'Your Majesty, I must beg your permission to go away from Paris for a short time.'

'Go away? Of course. I shall have to make do with your brother.' She tries a smile. 'I'm sure he will manage.'

'He is a coward and an incompetent,' the hairdresser says, unsmiling. 'But it can't be helped. A few weeks, a month perhaps, if it must be.'

'I hope everything is all right. Is it family trouble? Anything I can help with, Léonard?'

He shakes his head. 'Thank you, Your Majesty. I'll return as soon as I can. In the meantime, I thought it best to tell you about your hair powders, so you can use them properly while I'm away.'

'Ah,' she says, smiling. 'Show me, then.'

He finishes tying an extension onto her wig and then comes around to face her. Out of his bag, he pulls a little tin case, full of squat circular pots. He opens the first one: pale pink.

'This one', he says, 'inculcates loyalty to the Dauphin. This lavender one, well, that's for friendliness to the Emperor and his policies, although I can't say it's very strong. The golden one, very subtle colour, so lovely, that's for loyalty to His Majesty the King, and the white is for loyalty to Your Majesty.'

She straightens her posture and composes her face. 'Put them all on, Monsieur Léonard. I need all the loyalty we can muster.'

She goes out to meet her husband and her two living children, lined up in their pastel dresses and jackets.

The first face she sees in the crowded Versailles opera house is Lamballe's. The princess of lost love, making her appearance at the party. Antoinette can't stand to look at her face, so she looks a little past her as they smile at each other, and two more Versailles smiles there never were.

Versailles was daunting when it was full of music and light; it is gruesome now when it is nearly empty, ghosts dancing through its chequerboard halls, no music, no sound of laughter, only the barking of dogs. The dogs frighten little Charles and she doesn't blame him.

As they enter the royal opera it's like stepping into the past: it's bright, and noisy, and everyone is pretending to have a good time. She is, once more, on display. They are demanding to love her.

At her side, the King. On his lapel, the new cockade designed by Lafayette: red and blue, the colours of Paris, combined with royal white. They are all revolutionaries now, and all royalists. Why not? There can be no traitors that way, and everybody lives.

Young Pauline de Tourzel, daughter of the governess, in her pretty bodice, so slim. She surveys the crowd as any young woman would, in any age, at any ordinary party.

Antoinette lifts Charles up – he's getting heavy, but she needs the warm weight of him.

A cheer – so many bright white uniforms and dark tricornes – and there beyond them all, like a groom waiting at the end of the aisle, waits Fersen.

Antoinette and her lover spend a quiet few days at the Petit Trianon. On the morning of 5 October, Louis is hunting. The children are playing with Madame de Tourzel. Fersen is sitting across a small table with a newspaper. There's drinking chocolate warming in the pot. He gives her a domestic smile, but she can see there's anxiety behind it. When she comes to him and kisses him on the forehead, he closes the newspaper almost absently, puts it into the box at his side.

She thinks: This is what I would like my life to be.

It's a foggy, grey day. They dress the children for a walk but by the time they reach the door, it's raining – hard, and from all directions. Antoinette's dog, Odin, yips and demands to be walked anyway; he was a gift from Fersen and she loved him to distraction. She sacrificed her love of the dog, though, to enchant a ring that shoots lightning. Now she can't bear to look at the dog, so she sends Pauline de Tourzel, the governess's daughter, to walk him during a break in the rain.

But the children are not so easily settled. Everyone is restless. Antoinette calls for the groom and orders the Dauphin's carriage to be hitched; the children can go for a drive, at least.

Then she turns to say something to Fersen, but he is not there.

She goes through the rooms until she finds him at last, at a garden gate, reading a note.

Fersen tucks the note into his pocket and takes her in his arms. 'We have to leave,' he says. 'Now.'

'Why? What's going on?'

'There's a mob in the streets – women, apparently, demanding bread. They're marching to Versailles. They'll be here sometime today.'

'They're marching in the rain?'

He arches one of his dark eyebrows.

'All right, all right, they're marching in the rain. We must tell the King.'

He nods. 'I'll send a messenger, but I suspect he'll know soon enough if he doesn't already. You must get out of here, Antoinette. Go to Italy or England. Go to Austria, for God's sake. The time has come.'

She shakes her head. 'My place is with Louis, and he won't leave.'

They hear hoofbeats.

'There's a carriage out front.' He walks around the corner of the house.

'I ordered the Dauphin's carriage hitched. I thought he could—'

'Take it, and go! Go now.'

'We'll take it, and we'll go back to Versailles. The family should be together. In the meantime, my love, what can we do? Is it bread they're asking for? The loaves-and-fishes spell. If I had enough of my blood—'

'It would take all the blood in your body to feed a hundred people, Antoinette.'

'And you think the life of one rogue magister is worth the lives of a hundred other people? Is that what we've come to?'

'When the magister is you, yes, I do believe that,' he says, and stops, and looks away from her. 'It isn't love talking, Antoinette. It's sense. There's no one in charge of this mob and nothing you can do would calm them. They're calling the soldiers' party an orgy; they're saying you and the soldiers . . . People are saying you threw some tricolour cockades on the ground and danced them into the mud beneath your feet.'

'No one could believe something so ridiculous,' says Antoinette, but all she hears is *it isn't love talking*. She's feared, for years, that one day he would sacrifice his love for her for some spell, some very important spell. Would she know if he had? Of course she would. Wouldn't she?

She piles obligingly into the Dauphin's carriage with the children and Fersen promises to follow on horseback once he gets the servants to safety. When they reach Versailles, the carriage drives through a knot of National Guard soldiers in their red and blue uniforms and Lafayette is there waiting to take her hand when steps out.

She nearly collapses onto Lafayette, out of sheer friendship and relief.

'You're here,' she says, almost a question, although she's not sure which one to ask.

'To protect Your Majesty,' he says, answering it. He pauses. 'To protect all of you, and to protect them, when they come.'

'So you're on everyone's side, Marquis,' she says, and it sounds more cutting than she intended.

He bows his head. 'These days, I'm on the side of anyone who isn't a murderous son of a bitch. Unless they're English, in which case I make a general assumption.'

He still looks young, somehow, although he's thicker about the chin. The hero of the American war. The war France paid for, is paying for.

She laughs. 'Good then. My husband isn't, you know. Murderous.'

'I know, Your Majesty. That's why I'm here.'

She walks towards the door, her children following with Madame de Tourzel. Then she stops, stricken suddenly, for no reason at all. Weak. As if someone somewhere has pricked a Pandora doll – but there is no pain anywhere, just pain everywhere.

She turns to Lafayette. 'Is there any hope?'

He cocks his head. 'I haven't spent all of mine yet.'

She nods, and glances quickly behind, at the children, at Mousseline so ladylike and tall already, at her brother so dignified and slender in his holiday clothes.

Antoinette walks into Versailles for the last time.

CHAPTER FIFTY-THREE

*Portraits and Preparations — The CarvedBusk — Family —
Lafayette's Position — Bring out the Queen*

❖

Antoinette and Fersen spend an hour in a room full of portraits, talking to rogues in America, in England, in Russia, in Austria and India and Turkey. Making plans for safe-houses for the moderates and aristocrats among the French rogues. At one point she has the impression they are surrounded by ghosts, as they pace in circles so they can talk to the walls.

When the last whispers scuttle away to silence, Fersen asks if there's anyone else she'd like to speak to. She shakes her head.

They don't speak about it, but she knows Fersen is thinking of the same thing she is: escape, and whether it's worth the risk. The expansion charm doesn't work on anything larger than a pocket, and while the pocket can hold a great many things, each thing has to be pocket-sized, to get inside. They could use a hat of shadows. Try to sneak away.

It would be a life of exile, if they survived. A life of decay in Moscow or Prague or London. And there would be no one to stop Philippe d'Orléans from taking the throne, as he's always wanted. A magister-king, ruled by resentment and cowardice. And Louis would never agree.

When they come out into the halls they hear the crowd outside, screaming something she cannot resolve into words, at first, and then she hears one clamour rise louder than the rest: '*Bring out the Queen.*'

Louis looks up and smiles to see her come in together with Fersen. They still don't talk about it, not ever, but he's glad of Fersen. Glad that Antoinette has someone. Glad, perhaps, that Antoinette's heart is one less thing he has to worry about. He holds out two hands, for each of them to take, and they bow their heads before the King.

Lafayette comes in and says, flushed, that the marching women have breached the outer gates. Versailles has no defences, by design; it was built as a kind of theatre, wide open to the people of France, a place for them to come and gawk at the Sun King and his less radiant descendants.

Antoinette has always hated being on display; she does better in smaller rooms. But she did what she must so the people would love her. She wore the torturous *grand habit*; she had the best hairdresser and the best dressmaker, made herself into the proper sort of spectacle. And now they hate her for it, hate her for her pleasure palace, for her fashion, for her ostentation.

Louis sets his chin. Little Charles is here with him, playing on the floor with one of his soldiers. Over by the curtained window Mousseline stands silently, watching. She will be eleven in a couple of months, old enough to be thinking of marriage.

A few years ago, early in their reconciliation, Charlotte suggested that Mousseline marry her son Franscesco, the eldest living boy, and heir to the throne of Naples. But Antoinette could not stomach it. To send a child of seven away to a foreign court would be to mar her childhood; to send her away at fourteen, as Antoinette was sent, would be to mar the rest of her life. Mousseline will marry one of her French cousins instead, and stay with her family.

And here the family is, all in the same room, for this

moment. It's quaintly domestic by Versailles standards, although nothing like a Habsburg Christmas.

'Marquis, what do you suggest?' the King asks.

'There are a few among them whose names I know. Intelligent women, writers and thinkers. They will use this opportunity to make names for themselves – if we bring them in to talk, they'll want to show the crowd how successful they've been.'

Louis pauses a moment. He has been so badly advised, in so many different directions, over the last twenty-five years. Fifteen years, and he still acts like a new king, an uncertain pupil whose time for education is running out. At last, he nods. 'Three or four,' he says. 'Half a dozen at most. And I alone—'

'No,' says Antoinette. 'They're women. Let them see me, and let them see the children.'

Louis shakes his head.

'Her Majesty is right,' says Lafayette. 'I'll be here. They won't take any weapons in.'

'Have they got weapons?' says Louis, furrowing his brow. 'I thought these were market women.'

'The mob looted the armoury at City Hall this morning. There are muskets and even some small cannon out there, in addition to whatever pikes, swords, pitchforks they started out with. It's wise to assume everyone has a knife, at least. But I won't let them bring anything in.'

Louis nods, but he doesn't look happy about it.

The King rises when the women come into the room. Three of them, dressed plainly but not in rags. About Antoinette's age. They don't bow. They don't curtsey. She's never seen anything like it – no one seems to know what to do.

Except Louis. He strides forward and takes them each by hand as if he were a roué and they were ladies at the opera. He lets each astonished hand drop, and then he sits at his desk.

'Tell me what I can do for my people.'

One woman steps forward, clears her throat. 'They're starving, Sire.'

Louis nods, ignoring her rudeness. 'I know. I've done all I—'

'You have full granaries, Sire.'

'The army must eat.'

'And the children?'

He nods, slowly. 'I will disburse some grain, right away. I am working on acquiring some more from outside France. As more grain comes into the country, it will flow out to the people.'

The factory in Naples that produces magical grain, one of Charlotte's oldest projects. If Antoinette had been more like Charlotte, she might have done something like that. But she never managed it. Charlotte should have been the one to marry Louis, just as Maria Theresa intended.

'Put it in writing,' the market woman demands, and the King asks for pen and paper.

The crowd gets smaller after sunset but it gets more aggressive. Lafayette says the delegation did convince many to go, but a well-armed and angry mob still shouts at the palace doors.

'At least now we know what we're dealing with,' Lafayette says.

'Can we get the Queen and the children away?' Fersen asks.

Before Antoinette can respond, Lafayette shakes his head. 'We're surrounded now. There is no way out.'

There is always a way out; that's what magic is. The question is only what one is willing to sacrifice. She and Fersen and Lafayette are all magisters, all friends, but she finds no comfort in their glances. Lafayette looks down his long nose at her. There's a line down the middle of his forehead and the corners of his mouth droop.

Mousseline is sitting in a chair, her ankles crossed properly, reading.

Antoinette walks over to her, drapes her arm around her shoulders and looks at the book. It's a collection of Shakespeare's sonnets, in English.

When Mousseline was born, Antoinette said her daughter would belong to her, and not to France. But she belongs to no one but herself. It is Antoinette who was transmuted into someone new, someone who loves without thinking of whether she is loved in return. She remembers the day they brought her the news that the Empress Maria Theresa had died. She was in the nursery, lying on the floor on her stomach, beside her daughter. Mousseline, not yet two, sitting with her chubby legs splayed, playing with her model village: a little windmill, a dovecote, a dairy, a bakery, all carved out of wood.

The village that became the Queen's Hamlet. If Mousseline recognizes it, she does not say so.

Mousseline was already tired of her toy village, and only liked it as a place to arrange her tin soldiers, a gift from her uncle Joseph. Mousseline's favourite was the miniature Frederick of Prussia, in flat, engraved tin, painted in blue and white and gold.

Antoinette read to her daughter from the little roll of paper that came in the box with the soldiers. '"The Battle of Mollwitz was the first great battle of Frederick the Second. During the war of Silesia" – oh, my dear, I know all about that one – "in 1741, the King was forced to leave the battle-field when it seemed his forces would be overrun. But his infantry rallied and drove the Austrians off the field."'

'What is Silesia?' Mousseline asked.

'Well, when your grandmother was first crowned—'

'I have her name.'

'Yes, my darling. The one you're named for. When she was made ruler of Austria and Hungary, this king chose that moment to invade her lands, and take a place called Silesia away from her.'

Mousseline frowned, and set the figure deliberately down, lying there as though he'd just conceded a game of chess. 'I don't like him then.'

'Well, he's a very great king. Your brother Joseph gets along well with him now.'

Antoinette felt lost, suddenly. Diplomacy was a dance to which she had never learned the steps, and she wanted Mousseline to know better. To be prepared, for whatever comes.

At that moment the door opened, and there was Madame Campan, her face already grim with the news that Antoinette's mother the Empress was dead.

The Empress once said to her, before she sent her away: *I thought I'd have time . . . you're growing up so quickly.* A painful conversation Antoinette never did sacrifice, and the sting has gone out of now.

She drops her voice low. 'I have a secret to share with you, Mousseline.'

'I'm good at keeping secrets, Mama.'

Antoinette points to the ring on Mousseline's finger. 'That is an enchanted ring,' she whispers. 'If you think hard, when you're wearing it, you can shoot lightning at someone. It hurts, though, so don't practise on your poor brother or anyone else. You can practise in the privy, shooting at the wall. Do you understand?'

Mousseline holds out her hand and examines the ring gravely. It's plain gold. 'Could it kill someone?'

Antoinette shakes her head. 'Unlikely. The lightning is not strong. But it will help you get away. If someone ever tries to touch you. To hurt you. But you must only ever use it as a last resort. Keep it secret.'

'You think the people will come inside the palace tonight.'

'Oh, no, we're quite safe,' Antoinette lies, rubbing her daughter's small shoulder. 'The Marquis de Lafayette is here. You used to think he was almost a god, when you were little.'

'Yes, but now I'm nearly eleven.' Mousseline sighs.

Madame de Tourzel takes the children to bed. Antoinette tells her to bring them to the King at the first sign of trouble. They'll be safest with him. People hate Louis a little less than they hate his wife.

Then she goes to bed herself around two in the morning, and listens to the crowd outside, the clattering, the booms of muskets being fired into the air, the screams.

At four o'clock, Madame Campan bursts into her room and says they're in the palace, they're down the hall. Antoinette is already dressed and prepared. She can hear them. She can hear the screams of the guards.

She grabs her expansive pocket from underneath her mattress, containing her gold watch, her little notebooks, and the Pandora doll, which barely fits inside it. The pocket looks empty, but it's heavy. She and Madame Campan run to the children's rooms. Mousseline and Pauline de Tourzel are standing guard near the door while Madame de Tourzel holds Charles in his bed, rocking him back and forth.

'We must go to the King,' Antoinette says. 'We should be together.'

But the King's door is barred, and his wife has to bang on it, screaming his name and her own, for what seems like an hour before his bodyguard lets her in, hurriedly. They can see red torchlight flickering on the flowered wallpaper, can hear the laughter of the approaching hunters.

'Wait,' says Lafayette, appearing with Fersen in the corridor behind Antoinette. A palace guard puts his hand on his sword, looks to the King, but Louis nods his head, gestures for Lafayette and Fersen to come in.

'I thought you'd left us, Marquis,' says the King.

Lafayette shakes his head.

They hear shouting in the hall, and a loud bang as if furniture has fallen, and little Charles wails at last.

'I'm ready to die to protect you, Sire,' says Lafayette. 'In service of the people of France.'

'Surely it won't come to that,' says Louis, frowning and glancing at the children. 'The children—' he says.

'Your Majesty, our only hope now is in escape,' Fersen says. 'There, perhaps I can help you.'

'My place is here,' says Louis. 'If I run away from my people, I may as well abdicate. But if you believe you can get the Queen and the children away—'

'If you send the Dauphin away, then you may as well abdicate too,' says Lafayette. 'The people need to see that you are not afraid of them. That you are still King.'

Nobody looks at Antoinette.

'Where my children are, there I will be,' says Antoinette. 'At my husband's side.'

Fersen sighs, but says nothing.

Lafayette nods. 'Then the only choice before us is to wait here for violence, or go out and address the crowd.'

Antoinette shakes her head. She walks away from the children, so she can speak softly to her friend, out of their earshot.

'Lafayette, they have guns.'

'Yes,' he says. 'It is very possible that someone will shoot the King if he goes out on the balcony. It is even more possible that someone will shoot or stab or behead the King if he does not. They are inside the building, Your Majesty. There's been blood, and there will be more if His Majesty does not act.'

Louis bites his lip, but she thinks it is out of sadness, not irresolution. 'Let's go, then,' he says.

They can hear the roar of the crowd coalescing into words. 'Bring out the Queen.' They don't want their King to address them, to make it all right. They want the Queen, the hated Austrian woman, Madame Déficit. They want revenge.

The King needs her; he needs her to use her magic now, as he has never needed it before. What does she have that can dispel a mob? Little pots of enchanted hair powder. Lavender, pink, gold, and white.

Lafayette walks with him to the door; then he glances back at Antoinette.

She runs to him, gives Louis a kiss, and then waits there so that Louis will walk on into the hall. As she embraces Lafayette, he whispers in her ear, 'Have you got something up your sleeve? I've bought you a little time, with this speech of the King's, but only a little.'

She pulls back, nods. 'Leave it to me,' she says.

'Bring out the Queen.'

She puts her hand into her capacious pocket to search for the pots of hair powder, and that's when she remembers. She wore all of her powders to the party; they are still on her dressing table.

She puts her hand to her throat.

'Bring out the Queen!'

'They are calling for me, and I am not dressed,' she says. 'I need to go back to my rooms. Get my things.'

Madame de Tourzel, for once in her life, disagrees. 'It is not safe,' she says.

'If I show myself as anything other than a queen, they will despise me,' says Antoinette, with genuine desperation in her voice. 'With unpowdered hair. In my night clothes. I can take the secret corridors. I'll be quite safe.'

But Madame de Tourzel's shocked face is looking beyond her, where the panelled door out of Louis's room has banged shut.

Young Pauline de Tourzel has gone. She's gone to get the things from Antoinette's room.

Antoinette opens the door and rushes after her, but Charles grabs at her leg, and she bends to kiss his little warm forehead, to brush away the tear on his cheek. By the time she detaches him and hands him, screaming, to a similarly distraught Madame de Tourzel, Pauline has been gone two minutes, perhaps three.

'Bring out the Queen.'

The Queen slips into the corridor, follows the path the

571

King has taken to her bedroom, to do his duty, all these long years. Around a dark corner, Pauline nearly runs into her. Her arms are full of clothes.

'Hurry,' says Antoinette, pressing against the wall so Pauline can get past her, back to safety.

Back in Louis's room, Pauline places everything on the bed. Tears are running down her cheeks.

'I saw . . .' she says. 'The rooms. They're all smashed, and there's blood. A body in the doorway – I couldn't stop to see who. I couldn't get your petticoats.'

Antoinette roots through the pile. Silk stockings. Her corsets, and her little case of busks. A *robe à la chemise*, simple; but that is the sort of dress that they all hated, when she wore it in a portrait. They hated her for wearing loose linen; they hated her for wearing diamonds. She hasn't worn any kind of necklace in years, not since 1785. There's a *robe à l'anglaise*, in white. It will have to do. She turns to Pauline, one silk mule in her hand. The other shoe isn't here; Pauline must have dropped it, or she only took the one.

'I don't see the hair powder,' she says. 'I need that more than anything. I must go back for it.'

Pauline shakes her head. 'It's gone. Everything was taken: the rouges, the powders. The mirror, smashed.'

'Gone?' Antoinette sinks down onto the bed, the shoe still in her hand. 'Gone? But what will I do? How will I make them love me?'

They can all hear the crowd chanting: '*Bring out the Queen!*'

She is going to her death; she is quite sure of it. She dresses as best she can, Madame Campan tying her corset and hooking her bodice over the carved busk that was a gift from the man she loves best in the world. In her last moments, she'll be able to think of Fersen, to remember him.

Louis comes in, looking shaken but alive.

She kisses him. 'They're calling for me.'

'We'll go out together,' he says.

She has tried to show them that she is a good mother. She gathers her children to her, takes Charles in one arm, and Mousseline stands staunchly by her side. They all walk towards the balcony – not close enough for bullets, but close enough for the crowd to see her silhouette, the shape of her family as if it were painted by Vigée Le Brun. The Madonna and children.

'No children!' people shout. 'Just the Queen!'

She puts her son down, and kisses the people who love her, and goes out to face these women who have been here all day and all night. There are more men among them now, by the voices; they've come from the towns nearby, no doubt, drawn here for the confrontation. She sees bayonets shine in the dawn sunlight. It's chilly, like any other October morning, and it makes her shiver in front of the world. So many things to worry about, and she worries about the lack of a shawl.

There's nothing she can do. No magic to help her. Any moment now, it will come: a musket ball, a crossbow bolt, even a rock. She is not far above her people, and they want her dead. She has tried everything to make them love her and she has failed. Like the little girl on the stage at Schönbrunn who's forgotten her dance steps, she freezes, and stares out at them.

They're screaming now, and some orange vegetable splatters on the balcony a foot from her. '*À la lanterne!*' someone shouts. She has read of the revolutionaries' favourite slogan, but she has never before heard it. To the lamppost, to hang the Queen.

She puts her hands on the balcony railing, moves closer to the line of fire. Let it come, and be over with, and this torture end! The noise is greater than anything she's ever heard.

She bows her head, just a little, very slowly, curving her body as much as the corset will allow.

Then she bows deeper. It's all over, and she's failed, and

she'll acknowledge it. She's failed. She's sorry, she's sorry, and if they would only stop screaming she would tell them so. But they're so loud. She can only stand silently, without magic, without any help, and bow her head, and admit her failure.

The roar dulls. Quieter, quieter, quieter. The Queen stands bowed before her people until she begins to wonder what magic somebody has done. Where is Lafayette?

At last she straightens up, and looks at their faces. Bemused, uncertain faces. It isn't love. But it isn't quite murder. Not tonight.

Lafayette is at her side, and he takes her hand and kisses it. As if he's broken some spell, a cheer goes up, uncertainly.

Louis walks out, then. 'We will go to Paris,' he shouts, and she thinks perhaps only she can hear just how dejected he is. 'The royal family is yours to command, and always has been. We will go to Paris to be closer to our people.'

'What did you do?' she whispers to Lafayette.

He shakes his head, and for a moment looks once again like the cocky, nervous sixteen-year-old she met at the Palais-Royal. 'Nothing.'

No magic at all, and yet the crowd went quiet. She has been looking for so long for the magic that would make her worthy to be queen. The only tasks that have ever come easily to her are simple acts of love, but she never thought that would be enough. And perhaps even now it isn't. Perhaps it's too late.

They bundle the children into carriages and ride, with the mob all around them, singing about the Baker and the Baker's wife. They ride slowly.

A head, outside her window. Bleeding from the neck, and under that, nothing but pike.

Antoinette gasps, her gorge rising. The head – one of the guards? – is garish with rouge and white cream, the hair frizzled and covered in powder. Her powder. Gold and white, pink and lavender. The head of one of the unfortunate guards, surely, but dressed up in her enchanted powder. If it has increased the loyalty of the drunken lout carrying the pike, what hatred must there have been in his heart to begin with?

Antoinette tucks her children's heads to her chest, so they won't see.

CHAPTER FIFTY-FOUR

The Tuileries — Rumours of War — Death of the
Emperor — Attitudes — Emigrés — A Library
in Vienna — A Discovery

———— ❖ ————

6 October 1789
Antoinette to Charlotte

Sister,

Don't worry; I'm fine. I couldn't take the portrait with
me so couldn't speak to you. I may be able to send for it.
The King, Mousseline, Charles, and I are all safe in the
Palace of the Tuileries — it is a mouldy old place on the
bank of the Seine, beside the Louvre. Its gardens have more
prostitutes than the Palais-Royal and they press their faces
against the windows to get a look at us. To make room for
us, our jailers are turning out the decrepit countesses and
valets' cousins and the rest who've made their home here for
decades. There is a whole wing inhabited by actors for my
brother-in-law's theatre, and little Charles found a room
full of enchanted, moving props and scenery that gave him
nightmares.

But we are in good hands. We do not have the royal
guards with us any more, but the Marquis de Lafayette has

577

*command over the National Guard soldiers, and I know he
will keep us safe. I will ask for mirrors. We are prisoners,
but the only way that will end is with patience and courage,
demonstrating to the French people that we are still their
servants.*

In haste, and knowing that this letter may be deciphered,

Antoinette

The portrait of Charlotte still hangs in silent halls. She heard
the terror on the night of 5 October 1789: screams close and
sharp, then muffled and distant, whimpers and shouts and
animal noises. She didn't sleep, or talk to anyone but God,
in the eight days it took for Antoinette's letter to arrive from
Paris.

Now Charlotte hears nothing but the occasional peal of
laughter, faint and far away, like malevolent fairies.

When Hamilton sends her a note saying that Antoinette's
court painter has arrived in Naples, Charlotte wraps a black
lace shawl around her shoulders, calls for her carriage and
is at Hamilton's villa within the hour.

Élisabeth Vigée Le Brun is not the first emigré from Paris.
Half of the Brothers of Paris have stayed. Some have taken
up the ideology of the Ladder Club, of tearing down all the
old rulers so magisters can take their place; they do not
respond to Charlotte's letters. Some respond with non-
committal expresssions of resigned distaste and talk about
the birth pangs of the new order. The few Brothers who
want to preserve both monarchy and the Order have fled,
not to Naples but to Russia. Charlotte suspects the Empress
Catherine is gathering magisters around her court, but the
wily old lady keeps her secrets close.

Vigée Le Brun, though, is an interesting case. Portrait magic
has been an important method of communication between
rogues over the last several years, and many of those portraits
were painted by her. She is, almost certainly, a rogue.

The painter is fresh-faced, wearing a simple kerchief around her pale brown curls. She strides across the wide raised garden that looks out on the sea, with the still-smoking volcano in the distance. She curtseys to Charlotte, and then Caterina joins them, and they are three women on just one side or another of forty. Three magisters.

Charlotte smiles at Caterina, one of her oldest friends, and the one whose loyalty is never in question. Caterina looks tired; there are fresh lines on her face, around her eyes. She's been working so hard at San Leucio, and, as with everyone else, these years of fog and suspicion have taken their toll.

'You are welcome in Naples,' Charlotte says to Vigée Le Brun. 'I am a great admirer of your work, and I would like you to paint the royal family. That is, if you intend to keep working.'

'I must,' she says with a rueful smile. 'My daughter and I left Paris with only eighty louis in cash and some brushes and clothing. My Julie is ten years old, and she'll need an education, a home. If I'm to provide for her, I must work. But I like working, so it's all right.'

'I have one of your paintings,' Charlotte says. 'It is of my sister. It is quite magical.'

Vigée Le Brun smiles at Charlotte. 'Thank you. I worked very long on it. Her Majesty is a difficult subject to capture properly. She has been very patient with me, and taught me magic. She said I would be safe here.'

Caterina and Charlotte glance at each other. 'You will be,' Charlotte promises. 'The Order in Naples is less concerned with who uses magic than with ensuring that it's used wisely.'

'Is that different?' Vigée Le Brun asks.

It is not a question Charlotte has an answer to, or at least not a short answer, for a woman she's just met. Caterina coughs, in the way she has of covering up a laugh, and Charlotte changes the subject. 'I worry for my sister and her family. I will be most grateful for anything you can tell me about them.'

Vigée Le Brun nods. She moves her hands when she speaks, as if she's painting her ideas. Those hands that painted Antoinette so many times, that painted the picture which allowed Charlotte to speak to her sister. 'France is in – I don't know what to call it. Not quite chaos. A brutal joke. The Assembly, or whatever they're calling it now, is meeting in the covered racecourse at the Palace of the Tuileries. Because the King is there, and the King accepts the reforms. Officially.'

Caterina cocks an eyebrow. 'And unofficially?'

The painter makes a non-committal face. 'I couldn't say, Marchesa. If he accepts the reforms, and everyone is friendly, why does he have to do whatever they tell him? What will happen if he does not?'

Charlotte says, as if trying to convince herself, 'But he is still the King.'

'For now,' says William Hamilton, walking to them, looking out at the purple sky over the sea. At his side is Silfversparre, a drink in the younger man's hand. 'Your Majesty, you have arrived just in time for the performance. Will you all come into the salon? She is ready.'

The salon is very dark, lit only with candles in wall sconces here and there. Silfversparre helps Charlotte to one of the armchairs set up to face a wall nearly filled with an enormous gilt frame. Inside, there is no painting; merely void.

Out of this void steps Emma Hart.

She comes from nothing, steps lightly over the bottom of the frame, her long brown hair trailing nearly to the ground behind her. She's in the sort of white that statues wear: white silk from San Leucio. The robe is draped impossibly around her breasts, and the shawl over her round shoulders. Her face, lit by the lamp in her husband's hand, shines like porcelain, save for her two dark-blue eyes, her curved mouth.

Then her shawl leaves her shoulders. Floats into the air as she reaches for it, in an attitude of longing. The shawl fills with air in the shape of an angel, reaching out as well, and the audience gasps, though some of them have seen this before.

A moment passes, and the shawl has taken the form of a child whom Emma is comforting. The stillness in the silk matches the stillness in Emma's posture, as though the room is frozen, and no one dares to move.

The final attitude is of Emma herself. The silk takes the form of its mistress so exactly that one would swear there was a second Emma inside it, looking back at her, as they cup their hands beneath their chins and peer at each other.

Then Emma plucks the shawl out of the air and it is a shawl again; the shape of the woman was made of nothing.

This is the third time Charlotte has seen Emma perform her Attitudes, and every time she feels stunned by the existence of a magister who has used her sacrifices to make art, and only art. But then, she reminds herself, it is not only art. Emma has come from the lowest classes of English society and now she is the mistress of the British envoy, and seems to have all she desires.

Vigée Le Brun says that she would like to paint her. Emma says she would like that very much. Hamilton pours the wine.

'Are there many artist-magisters in Naples?' the painter asks.

'There are artists who are magisters, but no one like Emma,' Caterina says.

'I should like to meet people here,' says Vigée Le Brun.

'And so you shall,' Charlotte decrees. 'There is a fashion for revolutionary ideas among the intellectuals these days. You can tell them what is really happening in France.'

'I cannot claim to know what is really happening, but I shall tell them what I can. But surely Naples has nothing to fear. It has escaped the famines in the rest of Europe. It has not indebted itself, the way that France has.'

'The people here have no reason to rise up,' Caterina agrees, uncharacteristically earnest. 'We disarm them by giving them nothing to fight against. Whenever my brother finds a new revolutionary society has started up, or that a writer has published a pamphlet, he invites them to dinner.'

'Your brother?' the painter enquires.

'My chief of police,' says Charlotte, uneasily rubbing the side of her wine glass. She is thinking about the pamphlets that rail against the Queen, that accuse her of sexual affairs with women – why always that, for her and Antoinette both? As though it might explain something that their enemies need explaining.

'Naples is as wonderful as I'd heard,' the painter is saying politely.

'It faces threats on every side,' Charlotte says.

'And we must be ready for them,' Hamilton says. 'There always comes a moment when one must stand on one side of a line or the other. Naples will continue to stand as a beacon to the world, no matter what happens. Indeed, many in England still hope that France will come out of this stronger, with a new constitutional monarchy, perhaps. It may achieve what England did, with less bloodshed.'

'I hope that is true,' says Vigée Le Brun. 'I hope it with all of my heart.'

It's frustrating, being able to talk to Antoinette's listening portrait but never hearing anything in response. The enchanted portrait of Charlotte still hangs in Versailles somewhere. At the Tuileries, Antoinette lives under guard. She insists, in her letters sent by special trusted couriers, that the captain of that guard, Lafayette, is still her loyal friend and protector. Antoinette has always been naive.

Meanwhile, Charlotte talks to Antoinette, whether Antoinette likes it or not.

When news arrives of their brother Joseph's death in Vienna in February 1790, Charlotte goes to her study, walking beneath the massive clock hanging from the ceiling: a golden birdcage with a clock face on its bottom. A gift from Antoinette: a congratulations for Charlotte's victory over the fog. She keeps a starling in the cage, and it sings the hours.

Charlotte sits near the portrait (she is pregnant again, and subject to dizzy spells). She begins with grief.

'I think he was quite alone, in his last days,' she says quietly. 'He seemed destined to be alone, our Joseph. And in his policies, too, always consolidating power. I would have done the same, I suppose, if I'd once had to share a throne with Mother. And Joseph wanted nothing more than the power to institute reforms for the sake of the people, but he had no allies. A gift for statecraft but no gift for politics. I will miss him, Antoinette, and I will miss Leopold, who will leave Florence and go to take his place as emperor soon.

'Poor Leopold inherits an empire in rebellion. Our sister Mimi is doing no better; she and her husband have had to leave the Austrian Netherlands again – the United States of Belgium, they're calling it. I believe they've taken refuge with Max. We must all be ready to help each other. I will urge Leopold to make it very clear that the Empire stands ready to defend you and your husband. If we waver now, we all fall.

'I will make you such a war, sister.

'I think often of Angelo Soliman. He tells me little in his letters now. He was so close to Joseph, for so many decades, and the Empire of today was as much his project as anyone's. I hope to see him when I go to Vienna, to see Leopold settled and the children married. I can't go until this baby is born, so it will be summer at the earliest. I wonder if I will find Vienna much changed.'

Charlotte insists that messengers find her on the road as she journeys north towards Vienna. She refuses to miss a single letter from Paris, even though every one makes her heart race as she opens it. At least the situation there seems to have settled into a tense equilibrium. The royal family lives fairly normally at the Tuileries and they've even been allowed to go to Saint-Cloud for the summer. Everyone goes along with the polite pretence that the King is as happy as anyone else to celebrate the anniversary of the storming of the Bastille prison. Antoinette reports that she wears red, white, and blue ribbons in her hair.

Vienna both is, and is not, how Charlotte remembers it. The city's gravity has shifted away from Schönbrunn; Joseph preferred the more austere and practical Hofburg, where he could be close to everything and not make such a great fuss about things. People are everywhere: walking in the parks, crowding the coffeehouses, waving newspapers at each other. The gentlemen of Vienna in 1770 stood up straight and wore velvet waistcoats; in 1790 they wear brown coat-tails and slouch against walls, with a tall felt hat pulled over the eyes, a pipe at a louche angle. People talk about the inner life the way they used to talk about garden design.

She finds Angelo Soliman's house at the end of a long and narrow green park. The house is gleaming, Palladian, with columns in the front and two great domes at either end.

She is admitted to a long room, in deep reds and sage greens, with golden bellpulls and vast dark paintings in gilt frames. A pretty young woman comes to her and curtseys.

'You must be Josephine,' Charlotte says. 'I am an old friend of your father's. If it isn't too much intrusion.'

'Not at all, Your Majesty. He's in the garden, if you'll come with me.'

They walk through several salons and anterooms, filled with strange machines and instruments on pedestals – like a mirror to Hamilton's villa, only instead of the broken marbles and old vases, Soliman's modern treasures gleam in brass and iron.

Then out, through heavy doors, into a long courtyard filled

with topiaries that turn to look at her. In the centre is a vast circle of marble, unadorned.

Soliman is there, pruning shears in his hands. She's used to seeing him in a turban, but today he's wearing an embroidered Turkish cap and a banyan gown, both in deep orange.

'Your Majesty. I heard you were on your way to Vienna.'

'Forgive me for intruding on you here, Dr Soliman. There is nowhere in the Hofburg that we could speak without being overheard.'

She looks around the courtyard. Josephine has left them alone.

'Come into the safest place in Vienna, then.'

He puts the shears down, and gestures for her to follow him. She follows him into the centre of the courtyard, and flinches when the light dims, the air changes.

They are in a library. A hidden library.

Soliman closes oak doors behind her. It's a world lit from a bright dome far above, and all the encircling walls filled with books. Shelves radiate from the centre, row upon row of calf-bound volumes, all stamped in gold.

She laughs. 'So this is where the books go, when you take them. Like the rogue in Madras whose spellbook turned blank.'

'Some of them are spellbooks. Most are simply books. All were acquired at great cost, one way or another.'

He shows her to a red settee.

'So, this is now the *Reconditus*,' she says.

'Nothing is the *Reconditus*, Your Majesty. This is only one building, and it could burn, like any building.'

'You keep it safe, though.'

'I keep it safe,' he agrees. 'As safe as any library can be. Not only the books but the library itself is a great joy to me. I'll show you: name any book that I might have in my collection.'

She considers; not for very long. '*The Spirit of the Laws*.'

'Ha. Of course. I have several copies.' He coughs, hand to

his mouth, then says, 'Show me the French edition of *The Spirit of the Laws*.'

As though a cloud is passing overhead, the light in the room shifts, consolidates, and a shaft of sunlight points down from the dome above. It narrows, and grows in strength, until it is a finger of light indicating one book among many on a far shelf.

'There it is,' Soliman says, pointing.

'Marvellous,' Charlotte says, clapping her hands together. 'I have such a cumbersome system in my own library at Caserta. I never thought of using magic. Since we lost the *Reconditus*, everything in Naples is scattered, and I never know what spells anyone has.'

'The Order has all but disintegrated in Vienna.'

'As it has everywhere,' she says.

'Yes. Our old friend the Prince of Caramanico has taken up revolutionary causes. He writes to me. I think he truly believes in it. I think he has found new ways to love.'

She wonders whether Soliman has found new ways to hope, but she feels as though she has no right to an answer to that question, not when she was the one who took hope from him.

'You sound as though you indulge his views,' she says lightly. They have not written to each other very often in recent years, and when they have, the letters have been impersonal and short.

'I indulge everything, because I have no energy to do otherwise. I will be seventy next year. I am of the age where most of my friends are dead.'

'I'm sorry about my brother. Your loss is as great as mine.'

He nods. 'I will miss him very much. The Emperor Leopold – he has some magisters on his staff.'

'Nearly everyone does, now. The new science, they call it. I have told him what I knew of each of his magisters, which he could trust and which he should watch. He gave me John Acton, after all. I owed him.'

'Do you think he will make a good emperor?'

She remembers the carriage ride, when she first came to Naples. How Leopold spoke to her as though she was worth speaking to. He did the same yesterday, when she arrived in Vienna so that they could marry their children to each other. He told her frankly that while he, Leopold, is of course worried about Antoinette, the Holy Roman Empire has no sister. She told him just as frankly that he was wrong. The Empire is not a territory but a family, and it stands or falls together. She pointed out that Vienna was filling with emigrés from France, that they would demand action, and that if Leopold would not provide it, then they would turn somewhere else. To the exiled Comte d'Artois, perhaps. The Empire would find itself circumvented, made irrelevant, while new armies took up arms and marched across it to answer the call in France.

'I will open discussions with Russia, Prussia, and England, about a possible invasion, should it come to that,' he agreed. 'Quiet discussions.'

'And if the royal family is forced to flee before that can happen?'

'If they flee, the Crown is lost.'

'Crowns can be restored; lives cannot. The Dauphin is only five, Leopold. We could protect him, keep him alive long enough to take the throne when this mayhem burns itself out. In Paris, what will they do to him?'

He nodded, rubbing his temple. 'All right. If they flee, I will have troops ready to help them at the border. But no farther, not without guarantees that the other nations of Europe will join me.'

Now, she tells Soliman cautiously: 'I think Leopold will be a wiser emperor than Joseph in some ways. He has no desire for war. And his instincts for reform are more, shall we say, democratic, which may be what the Empire needs to see it through to whatever lies on the other side of all this. He doesn't have grand visions, as Joseph had.'

'And as you have.'

'As I had.' She sighs. 'I trust Leopold, and I know he will do his best. Will you work for him?'

Soliman shakes his head. 'The new Emperor will have to do without me.'

'I'm sure your beautiful daughter will be pleased to have more of your time. I was sorry to hear of your wife's death.'

He bows his head. 'I remember your letter.'

'Yes, but I wanted to say it in person.'

She thinks, for the first time in a long while, of the embroidered book. Where did her long-dead governess find her spells? A woman in Vienna, in the old days, alone, collecting magic. She must have hoped to make Charlotte a magister too – why else would she have made sure Charlotte knew how to finish the embroidery? But what her goal was, her philosophy, if she had one, that Charlotte cannot guess. At that age, she didn't think of adults having goals or dreams, only rules and fears.

She reaches into her pocket, pulls out the embroidered book. 'This is why Countess Ertag died. All of the spells in it have long been in the *Reconditus*. Most are very minor spells indeed.'

'But you carry it with you. May I see it?'

She nods, and he takes it, flips through its pages with a scholar's care. The ink is blotted here, faded there. It seemed so magnificent once, but it is only one small book of magic in a world now choked with them. All that Soliman has, this vast collection, is only a small part. Spells spread and grow; they are passed from hand to hand on the streets of every city in Europe, probably every city in the world.

'These spells,' Soliman says, running his hands over the pages of the embroidered book. 'The wording of them suggests they may have come from the Order at some point, but I suspect this collection has been passed down and preserved among rogues for a long time. I don't think your governess knew many other rogues at all. Perhaps it was a family inheritance, and she was prepared to pass it along. If

I'd had the book-leaching spell then, if I'd been head of the Order in Vienna a little sooner, perhaps she would still be alive. Along with many others.'

And perhaps Charlotte would not be a magister. Or she would know the same small magics that her governess knew, and she would think that sufficient.

The gap of her years lived yawns at her feet, and she cannot step back across it. Whoever she was then is not who she is now.

'If there is any service I can render you . . .?' she says. 'There is nothing I am not prepared to sacrifice.'

'For your kingdom? I know that.'

She shakes her head, and blinks away tears she can't explain, and says, 'For hope.'

He closes the embroidered book, holds it for a moment. 'It's a very interesting little enchantment, the embroidery that hid this from the Order. I've never seen it anywhere else, though it's similar in its workings to my leaching spell. I wonder what she sacrificed to make this.'

He hands it to her. She stands up, and walks towards the door.

'Charlotte,' he says, calling her by her name for the first time.

She turns her head.

He looks reluctant, as though he already regrets saying what he's about to say. 'The spell of spells is not what I thought it was. Once I understood that, it was easy to find.'

'What?' She steps back towards him, her skirts in her hand. He has found it at last? The fabled method of calculating the sacrifices required for any spell, an end to the endless trial and error necessary to devise even the most useless of enchantments. It would change everything. She never really believed it existed.

'I found it in the work of Émilie du Châtelet, of all places. She died when I was a child, lived with Voltaire – her translation of Newton, well, she performed an experiment with balls in sheets of clay, and determined that the *vis viva*, the living force, is always conserved. The force used to enchant the object is always matched by the energy gained by the decay of the sacrifices. The answer is in the time of decay – it tells us the amount of sacrifice required. I have arrived at a set of tables, showing the time of decay required for various spells we know, and there is a harmony in it.'

She gasps. 'But that is astonishing! You said it was not what you expected. Is it not as powerful as you hoped, then?'

'Oh no, it is very powerful,' he says with a small smile. 'It's simply not the equation I expected. I went looking for a set of magic words and instead I found something bigger. The magic words are a mere memory of the thing I have discovered, like a children's rhyme or fairy tale preserving some great moment long forgotten. I have discovered something that no other scholar of magic has dared to postulate.'

She wants to be the student who once would have asked him questions about it, to care about something the way he cares. Instead she is thinking of what it would mean to be a magister powerful enough to end revolutions and win wars. Will he give it to her? If he won't, is there a way she could take it? Nothing has ever been more important.

'One thing has not changed, though,' Soliman adds. 'The more powerful the enchantment, the greater the sacrifice – this is true of every spell that can be devised. You and I have dedicated our lives to the idea that magic should be shared and put to wise uses. Now I wonder whether those two goals weren't contradictory after all. If this knowledge were to spread, what terrible sacrifices would we see? What forces of decay would cover the Earth? I don't know. I don't know what ought to be done.'

She swallows, chastened. 'I understand, Dr Soliman. Keep your discovery to yourself, if you think that is best. I have taken enough from you.'

He points at the embroidered book. 'My work. The tables are already there.'

She flips it open, all the way to the back, and finds several loose pages that he must have just tucked in behind the back cover. They're covered with his messy, angular handwriting, so familiar from his letters. Rows and columns. The tables remind her of Joseph drawing his neat lines when he taught her ciphering years ago.

She looks back at him, shocked.

'I know that there's no way to prevent you from taking it if you choose,' he says, and that makes her blood run cold, because it's true. 'I know better than anyone how easy it is to spy on a man, to steal a book's contents, and I know better than anyone that you will not hesitate to do what you believe to be necessary. Despite all my precautions, you might find a way. Or someone else might find a way, and if that happens, I would rather there be another magister in the world who could work against that person. So, I've saved you the trouble of using the leaching spell, should you ever decide my tables might be required. I hope that you will be prevented from using them recklessly, by the memory of everything you have already lost. Or whatever memory you haven't yet sacrificed.'

'I keep a diary,' she says hoarsely. She closes the book again, as though she's trapping a dangerous thing. 'I will remember. Thank you.'

'Don't thank me, Your Majesty. It isn't a light burden. But it's my life's work, and in the end, perhaps I want to know it will survive me, should anything happen to me or Josephine. I may go to my grave wishing I'd destroyed it, but destroying knowledge is not in my nature. One day, I hope – yes, I hope – humans will find a way to use it well.'

CHAPTER FIFTY-FIVE

Louis Makes a Decision — Arrangements —
The Nécessaires de Voyage — The Iron Cabinet —
Guests of Monsieur Sauce

———— ❖ ————

Sometimes Antoinette suspects that a relationship in which Charlotte talks to her and Antoinette cannot answer back is what Charlotte considers a perfect arrangement. Thanks to the portrait of Antoinette that still hangs in Naples, every day she hears Charlotte's voice in her mind, reporting on the state of diplomacy, on the possibility of rescue. And Antoinette tells Louis, who does not ask how she knows. People in France have always acted as though the Habsburgs had some eldritch connection.

Louis paces. 'We must tell our allies to wait. If Naples, Spain, Austria, and England invade now, what's the goal? You can't meet a mob on a battlefield. There is no treaty we can sign that will bind all these fractious rebels. At best it will come to nothing, and at worst it will end with France occupied, carved up. No, this is not what I want.'

'I don't think they've asked your permission, my dear,' says Antoinette mildly, standing at the open window. The King's rooms are on a higher floor of the Tuileries, where they don't have to shutter everything to keep people from looking in or throwing things. 'To be quite frank, I'm not even sure I'd call them *allies*.'

Antoinette and her husband talk about politics more now, just the two of them, or the three of them when Fersen is in Paris.

At first, Louis went along with reforms in the hope of staving off revolution. By the time he was forced to admit that the reforms *were* revolution, he was a prisoner. As are Antoinette, Mousseline and Charles. In the spring of 1791, more than a year after they were forced out of Versailles, all their movements are at the discretion of the Assembly. But for the first time in their marriage, they have some privacy. The King's room has candlesticks that Antoinette has enchanted on all the walls; when they are lit, as they are now, they cannot be overheard here.

Everything that comes in or out of their rooms is examined for magic, passed around from jailer to jailer to see whether it has any effects. But the jailers are not very competent magisters; she supposes it's beneath any former Brothers of the Order to take on such a position. They don't seem to know what they're looking for. Antoinette's friends have ways of hiding what they bring, and perhaps, like everyone else always has, they suspect the Queen of being too empty-headed to perform magic on her own. Louis, for his part, still has no idea his wife is a magister, and he has none among his advisers. He has a traditional streak, and has long been resistant to any talk of the 'new science'.

But one day, he showed her something that astonished her: at the touch of his hand, one wall of his room in the Tuileries transformed into the drawers of a cabinet.

Seven feet tall, three feet wide, the thing is massive evidence that Louis thinks deeper and stronger than anyone suspects. He commissioned it from Gamain the locksmith, who practically lives at Louis's old forge, who speaks to no one but the King. Louis's only friend. He's been allowed to visit the King here, and he brings locks and keys and tools and bits of scrap, all of which are duly examined and found to be quite ordinary. But on every visit, he was constructing the iron cabinet.

It opens only for Louis or Gamain. How long has Gamain been a practitioner of this new science? she asks. Louis shakes his head, says it is a new obsession, but at least in this instance a useful one.

Louis uses it now for information, for the correspondence he does not want to destroy. Memoranda, plans, maps, inventories. Names. Evidence. He has everything he needs to take back his country – except his freedom.

'The only way you can take control of the loyal troops is to be with them,' she says gently. 'And they're all on the border, at Montmédy. If you were there, you could command them. There would be no doubt who holds lawful power in France.'

'Lawful power. Sometimes I wonder. Have you heard that they let the Marquis de Sade out of prison, purely to spite me, because I put him in there?' Louis's jaw clenches. 'The man raped his servants. The poorest women. Widows, beggars, prostitutes. Children! Promised them jobs or money and then tied them up and poisoned them, tortured them. And now all he has to do is call himself Citizen Sade and they give him a seat in their Assembly.'

'The monsters are walking abroad,' Antoinette says. 'There's no one to reason with. At some point, soon, you must assert that you are still king, and for that, you need to be free, and in command of the army.'

He shakes his head. 'If I left Paris, you and the children—'

'We would have to come with you, of course. It's the safest place for them too, now. Right on the border, with the Austrian Netherlands on the other side. My family's territory. We'd all be safe there, if need be.'

He sighs. 'I don't know. I don't know what to do. Or whom I can trust. Thank God I have you.'

He walks to her and puts his hands on the back of her chair, kisses her linen-capped head. They dress simply here, so simply that she sometimes feels shabby in these white-and-gold rooms, so lavishly carved, and beneath the old paintings and tapestries that once gazed down on greater queens. What is the point of such beauty when there is no one to impress? It's a gilded travesty, but she does like the relative peace. The guards here may be as much to keep her in as to keep others out, but there has always been a guard at her door, since the day she arrived in France, naked but for her gold watch.

At night, though, they can hear the crowds not too far off, asking for the head of the Baker's wife.

In the daytime, the sounds of Paris are less alarming. Carts and horses, donkeys and dogs. Shouts of merchants, strains of street organs. Hammering, chopping, the flutter of pigeons on the roof.

But it occurs to her suddenly, coldly, that it has been days and days since she last heard church bells. Here, in the heart of Paris.

The revolution against religion is what drove Louis's aunts to leave, in February. They're on their way to Rome and, perhaps, Naples; she has told Charlotte to make them welcome. But Lafayette says their departure spooked the people of Paris, who are convinced the royal family is building secret tunnels to escape. Truth be told, Louis is also horrified by the subordination of the clergy to the new French government. The Pope has issued a condemnation, but the Pope is far away.

She's wondered what the line would be for Louis, if he even had a line beyond which he would not accept any more. It comes on the night when the people of Paris burn the Pope in effigy.

The figure rises into the air, borne up by magic – it could be any man, but the hat gives it away. The children look out of the windows at the sight, until Madame de Tourzel ushers them away to their prayers and their beds.

She thinks about what her mother would have thought of this spectacle, what the Sun King would have thought. The old monarchs always said that to turn against a king's religion was to turn against the King. Joseph thought otherwise, but Joseph, too, lost control.

Louis takes her hand firmly. 'We will prepare to go to the border. It is time to leave Paris.'

Antoinette will have to make arrangements for the people she's leaving behind. Over the last few years, she's adopted more children, finding them quarters in the palace and paying for their education and care. Most of them are nearly grown now, but they'll be at risk once there's open war between the royalist troops and the rebels. Armand, her first, has joined the revolution and wants nothing to do with her. Ernestine, the daughter of a Versailles chambermaid who died, she sends off to a country estate, much to the sadness of Mousseline, who is her friend. The Dauphin has also lost an adopted playmate. Antoinette adopted little Zoë just a year ago, the orphaned daughter of one of Louis's ushers. Her older sisters went to a convent, but she kept Zoë with them at the Tuileries. She will have to go to the convent now, to join her sisters.

Then there is Jean Amilcar. A French nobleman went to Senegal and returned with gifts for the Queen, including a six-year-old boy, intended to join her service. She refused to take a human being as a present and adopted him instead, making sure he was well cared for and well educated. She explained as much to Saint-Georges, the last time she saw him, anxious that he should understand.

'And why didn't you send him back home to his family, Your Majesty?' Saint-Georges had asked.

She was taken aback. 'He has the best tutors in the world here. More opportunities than he could ever have in Senegal.'

'Of course,' he said, but she was already losing him then.

Saint-Georges is in Lille, a member of the National Guard. And Lafayette is its commander.

Lafayette is keeping himself and his army neutral, when it comes to France's political future. Fighting on all fronts and under all colours, as if he could make peace simply by existing at the nexus. Sometimes she thinks of him, still, as the eager ginger-haired teenager she met that night at the Paris Opera. Despite all he's seen, he still believes in . . . everything. He still has such hope left. His sacrifices must not have tended that way.

And he loves her, has put himself between the mob and her three times, both at Versailles and here at the Tuileries. Loves her not for anything she's done or will do but purely because he does, because he's loyal. Because when England killed his father, Lafayette stole out of the country just for a chance to fight his father's killers, though he'd barely known his father anyway. That's the marquis. Her friend.

But also, now, her jailer.

He can't know about the escape plan. The only people who do, outside of the palace, are Fersen, of course, and Lamballe.

Because the Queen's favourite would be in danger from the mob once the royal family's absence is discovered, Lamballe agrees to go to her villa near the Swiss border for a few days, where she will slip out of the country, to meet Antoinette later in Brussels.

Bit by bit, the plan comes together.

On a morning in early summer, Madame Campan brings Antoinette her wardrobe book. So many patterns in red, white, and blue. She won't be needing those much longer; back to the greens and whites she loves.

Months ago, in the gardens at Saint-Cloud, Antoinette had Madame Campan add a few pieces of fabric that don't correspond to any of her clothing. Instead, each represents a plan in motion: a rescue attempt, an escape.

She sticks a pin in the powder-blue with yellow flowers, which means that the entire royal family will escape, and she hands it back to Campan.

Madame Campan stares at it, stares at the Queen, and then nods determinedly. She will be left behind; it's essential that there be no evidence that she knew anything about it, no scrap of conversation overheard. All the enchanted candlesticks are in the King's room, and she leaves them there. But Madame Campan deserves to know, after all these years.

'Your Majesty,' says Campan. 'There is talk that you've ordered several new *nécessaires de voyage*.'

'Indeed I have.' She frowns at her lady-in-waiting. The whole idea behind the code of the wardrobe book was to avoid such conversations.

But Madame Campan isn't digging for information. She looks worried. 'Is that wise, Your Majesty? Perhaps it could be . . . misinterpreted.'

What is wise, in these times?

She has commissioned, from several different manufacturers and under different names, seven exact copies of her own *nécessaire*: a neat box of walnut wood, and inside, a silver basin, travelling candlesticks with wide silver bowls on their bottoms, spoons, knives, chamberpot. Scissors, brushes, and mirrors. A dozen glass bottles and a collection of silver toiletry jars, for all the tinctures, oils, perfumes, and powders of a notoriously vain queen – or so the makers will think. In large part the makers would be right, but some of the bottles and jars are for blood and ash, nail clippings and hair, and small treasures. And a jar of Sydenham's anodyne drops, for pains and fevers should anyone take ill on the journey.

Her own *nécessaire* she will keep, for her own use, on the road. If all goes well, it will take a day and a night to reach Montmédy, and who knows where they'll go after that. If things get very bad indeed, she'll take the children to Brussels, to her sister Mimi.

But the *nécessaires* have another purpose, too. D'Éon has sent her a spell the rogues have been working on, in a collaboration that has taken years. An exact copy of an object can be twinned with it, so that once every full moon, they are, in a sense, the same object.

It means that if, for example, a little silver jar in one *nécessaire de voyage* were twinned with its replica, a person could place a message inside it and another person could open the jar to read that message, anywhere in the world.

It's a way to communicate when they can't be near enchanted portraits. The portrait magic is well known now, so even miniatures are liable to be confiscated.

One *nécessaire* is for Fersen and one is for Lamballe. One is for d'Éon and the rogues of London, and one for the rogues of Prague. One is for Amalia and one really is for Mimi, in case Antoinette should need to get something to her sisters quickly, as a last resort.

And after long thought, she has decided to send one to Naples, with no explanation. Let Charlotte worry over each of its 108 items, wondering which are enchanted and how.

'The *nécessaires* are gifts,' Antoinette says, smiling. 'Am I not allowed to send gifts, even now?'

'Of course, Your Majesty,' says Madame Campan, bowing her head. 'Everyone knows how you love to give presents.'

Monsieur Léonard Autié, the original of that name, looks down at the box of walnut wood in his hands.

Antoinette smiles encouragingly. 'The box is enchanted to dye the hands of any thief, but for your sake and mine, I hope that is never tested and you convey it to its destination without being bothered by anyone. You may open it, you know.'

He flips the catches on the *nécessaire de voyage* and opens it, sees the basin, the candlesticks, the chamberpot, the little bottles. Then his breath catches as he sees, nestled in every little pot and open space, her pearls, diamonds, the gold coins. Nearly everything that remains of her jewellery.

The crown jewels belong to the state, and the cursed diamond necklace is no more. She put a few things in the *nécessaire* for Charlotte, and she'll keep a few things herself. But she was stripped once on the border between Austria and France, and she will never be stripped of all her posessions again.

'I want you to take it to Brussels. To my sister Maria Christina, who is governor of the Austrian Netherlands – now that the revolutionaries there have been defeated again, thank God. If my children ever need money, and I am not able to provide it—'

He looks up, nods, and closes the case. 'I will guard it with my life, if it must be, and deliver it safely.'

'On the way, I need you to perform two more tasks for me. I know that I can trust you, Monsieur Léonard. Please travel through Metz, where you will meet the Duc de Choiseul, and through Montmédy, where you will meet the Marquis de Bouilly. They know to expect you. You will tell them the details of how they are to assist His Majesty, the children, and me in escaping this place and going to the border.'

His eyes go wide, and then he nods.

'I could not entrust this message to any letter,' she says. 'But I know I can trust you.'

And she knows that his absence will not be noted at the Tuileries. His brother is here, and most people can't tell them apart. But Antoinette knows his face, and his heart.

They wake the Dauphin just before midnight on the night of 20 June and dress him in girl's clothing. He says, sleepily, that they must be putting on a play.

Mousseline kisses him and says he looks beautiful. She puts on her plain dark dress and they both go with Madame de Tourzel, who is disguised in the other social direction, as a Russian noblewoman, with a passport to match.

They should be at the border before anyone in Paris knows they've gone.

Hats of shadows are well-known magic now, so the royal

family are allowed no hats except those their jailers provide, and those are changed at random. But nobody looks in the embroidery basket. Antoinette has embroidered linen caps for all of them, enchanted to let them slip out of the palace unseen. As with all hats of shadows, the invisibility is not complete: a guard looking straight at them in the light may see them. But it will keep them from catching the eye.

With their shoes removed, Antoinette, Tourzel, and the children tiptoe through the back corridors to the courtyard, through the long colonnades, waiting for the guards to turn their backs.

There's a small carriage waiting in the outer court, and for a moment Antoinette's gut lurches. Fersen was supposed to be here. Instead, there's a whistling coachman, a tobacco pipe stuck in his mouth.

The coachman turns then, and winks. At the sight of Fersen's wry face, Antoinette wants nothing more than to drop her children's hands and run to him, to put her head on his shoulder with his arms around her, to learn how he smells with tobacco smoke upon him.

She waits, though, until the children and Tourzel are in the carriage. Charles curls up to sleep on the floor under Tourzel's skirts.

Then she pulls Fersen behind the carriage and wraps her arms around him. Mousseline and Tourzel might be able to see through the carriage window but this is France, where people embrace their friends, especially on nights like this.

'I wish you didn't have to go back,' he whispers huskily.

'I must be in my rooms for the *coucher*. I'll be back but the King will be here first. Once he is here, if I don't come for any reason within half an hour, you must go, my love. Promise me. You'll have my children.'

'I promise,' Fersen says, and kisses her forehead.

The ritual of undressing, the *coucher*, has never seemed so shabby and ridiculous, but at least it is short and simple now, compared to the old days at Versailles. Louis's sister Élisabeth is among the few courtiers who undress Antoinette and watch her remove her tinctures and powders. Then Élisabeth stays behind and she and Antoinette dress each other in plain black for the journey. They wait by the window, watching the courtyard. There is Lafayette's carriage, and there is Lafayette himself, stepping down, striding into the palace. He comes for the King's official *coucher* every night, to check on his charge, to make his presence known. This may be her last glimpse of him, the man who has saved her life so many times.

And there, at last, is the King, in a slightly shabby hat and coat. He walks through the courtyard, not quite hurrying. And Antoinette and Élisabeth follow at last.

This time, she sees Fersen's face before he sees hers. She catches a glimpse of the frown he must wear for the rest of the world. It clears as she arrives.

'Thank God,' Fersen mutters, and takes her hand to help her into the carriage.

'Yes, thank God,' Louis echoes, and embraces her. He does not get jealous of Fersen, or at least not much. Still, he puts his hand over hers, while Fersen scrambles up onto the coachman's box.

They ride out past the city gates by circuitous roads, crammed into the tiny carriage. Antoinette tries to keep her face away from the window but it's hard not to look on Paris for what might be the last time.

Then they pause, pulling over to the side of the road in the dark night, and Fersen opens the door.

'This is where we'll meet the larger coach,' he says. 'But it's not here yet.'

He looks worried. The tiny carriage they're in, as well as being so cramped that the Dauphin has to lie on the floor, has no room for luggage and it won't hold up to the country roads.

But then the carriage drives up and they hurriedly pile into it. A big green and black thing, shining in the light of its own torches, yellow flashing on the wheels.

The drivers bow before them; all of them men Fersen trusts, loyal to the King and in on the plan.

'Here's where I leave you,' Fersen says, standing on the step, once they're all in. 'I'll send word once I reach Brussels.'

It's Fersen's task now to drum up support outside the country, to bring as many troops as he can for the coming civil war. The war that Louis so wanted to prevent; but better a civil war with Louis as king than an invasion with Louis as hostage.

Just after dawn, Antoinette wakes in the moving carriage. She reaches past the sleeping Mousseline, draws the curtains and watches the trees, the occasional houses.

Lafayette must know by now that they've gone. Will he blame her? Will he feel betrayed?

Louis peers out. 'Montmirail. I recognize that spire from drawings of it. We're a little behind time. But by mid-afternoon, the Duc de Choiseul and his officers will be ready to meet us at Somme-Vesle.'

When they reach Somme-Vesle, there are no officers there. She feels numb, as though she's in a dream, but there's nothing to do but go on. Perhaps everything will work out. *Ça ira*, as the revolutionaries sing. It'll be fine.

They roll on, keeping up their disguises and pretence at each town gate. Antoinette makes the children warm chocolate on a little lap table over the spirit burner from her *nécessaire*, and nearly catches her skirt on fire. At Clermont, at least, there should be 140 horsemen waiting to accompany them to the border.

They reach Clermont, and it is silent and dark.

The drivers go to their contact and find that all the horsemen have been sent home to bed, because the Queen's hairdresser rode through saying the whole plan was off.

Louis's face is utterly broken, and Antoinette does not know what to say. Monsieur Léonard would not have betrayed her. It's baffling. But what other explanation can there be?

There were supposed to be fresh horses here, too, arranged by Fersen, but nobody knows where they are.

At last they stop in a tiny town, at nearly midnight by Louis's watch.

One of the drivers opens the carriage door. 'We must have fresh horses, or we can't go on. They can barely lift their legs now, never mind pull this carriage.'

'Where are we?' the King asks.

'Varennes,' says the driver. 'A tiny place. Nobody here knows us or expects us. The best I can do is knock on doors and see if I can find six fresh horses.'

They doze as best they can while they wait for the drivers to return. Antoinette's forehead is tight and her stomach unsettled.

At last the drivers return with a little man, moustachioed and sweaty. He bows before the King.

'You recognize me,' Louis says, resigned.

Antoinette's stomach turns.

'Yes, Your Majesty,' he says. 'I am the procurator of Varennes. There are no horses to be had here.'

'No horses.'

'No, Your Majesty.'

'Well, we'll just have to press on, then,' says Antoinette. 'Go as far as we can. We can't stay here.'

'I'm afraid that won't be possible,' says the procurator, not looking at her. 'There is a cart overturned on the only bridge, and the ford is flooded. Quite impassable.'

She looks at Louis, looks at Mousseline, still lying in her lap, still with her eyes closed, but awake now, by her breathing.

'All right,' says Antoinette. 'There is an inn, is there? The children will need hot water and fresh sheets, Monsieur . . .'

'Monsieur Sauce, at Your Majesty's service,' says the procurator. 'The royal family will sleep in my house. It is the best house in Varennes. The sheets are clean.'

Antoinette puts the children to bed. She does not sleep; she and Louis make plans as best they can, listening to the sounds of the National Guardsmen surrounding the house.

At dawn, the men knock on the door and present the King with an order to return to Paris.

'Who are they to order their king to do anything?' she yells, angrier than she knew.

'There is no king,' says Louis with a sad smile. 'Not any more.'

On the way back, under escort, they pass a line of peasants chained to each other, standing in front of a line of ashen stars. A man in a velvet jacket walks down the line, cutting each wrist, streams of blood running down into the earth.

'Don't look,' Louis says.

'They're working enchantments,' Antoinette says, not caring that this is not something she and Louis talk about.

'I've heard about this,' he growls. 'The workers have all been freed, but they owe their former masters more than they can pay, so the masters are exacting it from their bodies.'

He turns and looks at her, and for a moment she thinks, foolishly, that he knows about magic, about Charlotte, when he says bitterly, 'But they say they can fill the silos with grain this way. Which was more than I could ever do.'

The Princesse de Lamballe left France for Brussels, as she was told. Antoinette hears her voice in her mind from time to time, as Lamballe speaks to the miniature portrait of the Queen she carries at all times, asking when she should return to France. Antoinette, with a miniature of her own, tells her to visit the French exiles in the Netherlands, in Germany, in England. She asks her to meet with Gustavus on the Queen's behalf. There are many things Lamballe can do for her abroad, she says. Where it is safe.

One month after the royal family's long, dusty ride back to ignominy, Léonard Autié presents himself in the Queen's single bedchamber. He looks worn down; he's wearing only his natural hair, greying a little, parted down the middle and lank on either side of his head.

He has the *nécessaire de voyage*, the one he was supposed to deliver to Mimi. He opens it, and shows her that the jewels inside are gone.

'Your Majesty,' he begins, looking down. 'My brother Jean-François has always wanted as much magic as he could find. He would steal it when he could. He sacrificed everything we earned, and soon he had long cuts down his arms from bleeding himself. Once we came to Versailles, I took all control of our money from him, and I thought that he had reformed. But he found other means. He learned that he could use magic to eavesdrop on the nobility, and blackmail them, and get more treasure to sacrifice. I don't know what sacrifice it was that cost him his soul, Madame, but I know that, at one time, he had one.'

She begins to understand. 'It was he who betrayed us on the road.'

He nods, his voice thick. 'He was spying on me, for reasons of his own, though I didn't know it. He met me on the road, tricked me, locked me in the basement of a farmhouse, stuffed the jewels in his pockets, although it never occurred to him that the *nécessaire* itself might have any value. Pretending to be me, he told the duke and everyone else to go home, that the plan was aborted. I assume he intends to collect a reward from someone for this.'

She sits for a moment, thinking.

'Where is he now?'

'In England, I think.'

'With my jewellery.'

He nods. 'Your Majesty, with your permission, I will go and find him. Track him down, and recover Your Majesty's property. Deliver him to justice.'

She feels empty. Defeated. What does justice matter now? 'You have my permission, Monsieur Léonard. If you want to find your brother, that is what you should do. Brothers and sisters should help each other, even when they don't deserve it, and even when they choose not to be helped.'

Fersen sneaks into the Tuileries through a side door. They aren't allowed such visitors, not any more.

She and Fersen hardly say anything before they make love on her bed, half dressed, mouths open on each other's cheeks and shoulders, collapsing into peace.

'What more have you learned?' she asks. Fersen can move about in the world, while she is here, ever more a prisoner.

There was nothing in the iron cabinet when Antoinette and her family returned to the Tuileries, under guard. All of Louis's secret plans and maps and letters with moderate rebels are gone, in the hands of the Assembly. Evidence, they say, of the King's plans for counter-revolution, and they are right.

The locksmith Gamain told them where to find the papers. The smith, the traitor, the King's best friend. Perhaps the only man Louis would have trusted to do magic for him. But everyone is dabbling in magic now, it seems, and everyone is making plans for where they will land when the horrible carousel of the revolution finally stops.

One betrayal might have been surmountable. Two were not.

'I have learned that the Princesse de Lamballe is in France and on her way back to Paris,' he says.

Antoinette props herself up on an elbow.

'What! She's said nothing to me.' Come to think of it, she's heard very little from Lamballe through the portrait of late. 'Why would she do such a thing? I wrote to her when she was in Germany, giving her the chance to resign her position in my household. She should have stayed outside of France.'

'She believes her place is at your side,' Fersen says. 'If you leave France again, she'll leave with you.'

'No more escape plans,' Antoinette says. 'Not for me. Did you deliver the *nécessaire* to Mimi?'

'I did,' he says. 'There is a rogue in her employ who knows about its enchantment. Her name is Eleanor. We can trust her.'

'Perfect,' she says, taking a roll of paper money out of her desk, trying not to think about whether Fersen has slept with this Eleanor. 'I am making some arrangements for Mousseline.'

She writes a short note to Eleanor and wraps it around the money, then opens the lid of the tiny teapot in the *nécessaire* to tuck it inside.

But there is something already there.

A locket: small, round, silver.

She opens the locket and sees a tiny miniature painting of her sister Charlotte. The brush strokes are rough. She looks angry.

Antoinette holds it up and stares at it for a moment. Then she says, 'Well done, sister. You figured it out.'

CHAPTER FIFTY-SIX

*Alarming Tidings — Only a Clothes Peg with a Bit
of String for Hair — Needles — Loyalty — Screams in
the Night*

———— ❖ ————

When a letter comes from Vienna at the end of March 1792,
Charlotte believes it will contain news of a declaration of
war with France.

Instead, it tells her of Leopold's sudden and inexplicable death.

Silfversparre answers her summons and stands very still
near the door of her antechamber while she paces.

'You must find out everything you can about the assassins,'
she says.

'*Was* he assassinated?'

'Oh, there is no doubt. A man of forty-four, in perfect
health? This was an attack!'

And she feels attacked herself, she realizes. For so many
years, Leopold was a source of comfort, a brother who treated
her as an equal and a friend. The man who sent her John
Acton when she needed him.

She is cut off from all support. She no longer has a brother
in Tuscany, or a brother on the imperial throne. Her generation
is falling away one by one, and she will be left without mentors,
only children and children-in-law, nieces and nephews.

And what does this mean for Antoinette?

After the fiasco of the French royal family's failed escape, Leopold took up the cause in the open at last. He managed to convince Prussia, Austria's old enemy, to sign a declaration warning that the sovereigns of Europe took a 'communal interest' in the fate of the French royal family and were prepared to act.

His son, the new emperor, will be less eager to start a war over the insults done to an aunt he's never met. Despite the fact that Francis is married to Charlotte's firstborn daughter, Teresa.

'The trouble will be that so many may have had a motive, and magic may be hard to trace,' says Silfversparre.

Charlotte reminds herself she still has a Brother, here in the room with her. She still has allies and family.

'Yes,' she agrees.

'I'll start by asking Dr Soliman if he knows of any plots,' Silfversparre says. 'But not even he knows everything that is going on in Austria these days.'

Charlotte writes to her daughter in Vienna. But her quill hesitates. Teresa is intimidating. She has an easy glamour about her: Charlotte remembers the day before they left for the wedding, standing, looking at family portraits with her shawl around her elbows. Something of the gifts of Antoinette, but more, Charlotte must admit, of the gifts of her father, Ferdinand. She looks comfortable with herself. It's a magic Charlotte never could fathom.

Charlotte always thought she would teach her children magic, but she put it off and put it off, fearing that they would tell their father, that it would be used against them somehow. It was only in the last months of their time together that Charlotte began to teach Teresa, slowly. So that their last conversation in Naples was about sacrifices:

'I was looking in the storage rooms for a little doll I used to have as a child,' Teresa said. 'A useful treasure. I could sacrifice it, and it's only going to waste here. But I can't find it. Do you have any idea where it might be?'

'What does it look like?'

Her daughter laughed. 'Oh, it's only a clothes peg with a bit of string for hair. Father bought it for me once, from a beggar in Rome,' she says.

'Why on earth would you treasure a clothes-peg doll? I gave you dozens of beautiful dolls when you were small, and you never seemed to care much about them.'

'Yes, but that was the only one Father ever gave me,' said Teresa with a small smile.

She writes to the new Emperor Francis, but she gets only a polite and dutiful response. Of course he is concerned about his aunt Marie Antoinette; who is not? The matter concerns all of Europe. Francis is young and did not expect to be emperor yet. He has so many things to occupy him.

The letter arrives the day after Charlotte's diplomats tell her that France's revolutionary government has declared war on Austria and Prussia. Jacques-Pierre Brissot and other men with poisoned pens have managed to convince his countrymen to go to war, now, when Austria is shaken.

Teresa must have been only three or four when her father gave her that doll. Charlotte doesn't remember the doll but she does remember her daughter's governess, a young countess from the south of Italy. She somehow knew, despite her youth, to expect obedience. Once, Charlotte watched the countess tell Teresa that she had until the count of three to pick her prayer book up off the floor.

'What happens when you get to three?' the Queen asked.

The countess shrugged. 'I've never had to, Your Majesty.'

'Seems a fragile kind of obedience.'

'Oh, it is. One day she will realize that she has a choice, that she could disobey. And on that day, I'll be in trouble. Today, I count, out of desperate hope that day is not yet here.'

By the time Teresa was nine years old, such tricks no longer worked, but there was no need for them either. She could govern herself, by then, and if she chose to disobey it wouldn't take the form of arbitrary petulance. She has always been a step ahead of everyone around her. Charlotte should have told her about magic sooner.

It strikes her that the bargains and tricks of the nursery are not so different from the compact monarchs make with their people. When the people obey, it is only because, so far, they have not yet chosen to disobey.

> *15 July 1792*
> *Count Axel von Fersen to*
> *Maria Carolina of Naples*

Your Majesty,

    With a heavy heart I write to provide whatever intelligence I can to your efforts to support the Austrian and Prussian invasion. Although we have differing views on magic, I know that we share a common interest – I refer not only to that person we both love, but also to the cause of peace. There is no hope now for the restoration of the monarchy without the full support of Europe. Whatever risk there is in action, the risk in doing nothing is far greater.

    My king, Gustavus, was eager to go to war against these French rebels, and had he not been assassinated in March, we would be in a very different place today. But while Sweden may have avoided the intended coup, it is in an uncertain situation and I fear we can now expect no help from that quarter. How terrible it was that in the same month, the world lost Your Majesty's brother, Emperor Leopold. These blows have fallen at the worst possible moment, just when Europe is called to act against forces that may destroy it. I don't know whether any magisters had a hand in either tragedy, but it has certainly all gone remarkably well for those who would see the world rid of monarchs.

    Here in France, the best hopes for the moderates to prevail died last year with the Comte de Mirabeau, whose name is now spoken with venom because of documents found in the iron cabinet showing he was in the pay of the King.

His rivals in the Jacobin club, a radical group of aggrieved deputies, have seized control of the country. They are fractious, and argue at least as much among themselves as with the rest of the world. Within this club, Jacques-Pierre Brissot and his so-called Girondins have the upper hand, and they preach war against Europe with all the fervour of true fanatics. They intend to spread their revolution everywhere. They are opposed mainly by deputies from Paris, such as Jean-Paul Marat and Maximilien Robespierre, who disagree only insomuch as they would prefer the people of France to take up arms here at home and direct their violence inward, against those they call enemies of the people.

I am sure you know that most former Brothers of the Order, including Cardinal de Rohan, have fled the country; even those who worked to bring down the monarchy have found it impossible to maintain a grip on power, given that they come from noble families. Most of the Jacobin magisters are rogues, but they are well taught, thanks in part to the leadership of Philippe d'Orléans, who remains in France for now, calling himself Citizen Égalité. He has taken to hiding in the Palais-Royal – or as a pitiful, roughly painted sign now calls it, the Garden of the Revolution – going to his theatre night after night. He has lost control over the rogues of Paris, if he ever had it.

So Paris is in the grips of a kind of nationalistic fervour, and there is more magic done every day; the smell of decay hangs in the air. If there is any hope for the royal family, it lies outside of Paris now: in the royalist parts of the country, and, especially, outside it.

May the Austrian troops be swift and victorious.

I remain,

> *Your Majesty's faithful and true friend,*
> *Axel von Fersen*

One night in August, Charlotte feels a twinge in her hand, a pinching. She rolls over in bed; that sometimes relieves her nerves in that arm. She's been working too hard, writing too much. Cramps come and go, and usually when they come, it's at night.

But this night, the pain doesn't go away.

The Pandora doll. Antoinette wants her. In the middle of the night.

Charlotte groans and sits up. They have been a mixed blessing, these conversations with her sister over the last few months. They are practical exchanges. About developments in France, where over the last year or so, Lafayette seems to have shown some resolution at last in his defence of the monarchy, though he has chosen to demonstrate it by shooting into a crowd. About the invasion which now even Antoinette wants, the war Charlotte is fomenting, quietly, far too slowly, among the fractious great powers.

Sometimes, the sisters talk about their firstborn daughters. Both Maria Theresas – their Mousseline and Teresa – are now magisters. Their namesake grandmother would be rolling in her grave, if she knew. Perhaps. Anyway, she has nothing to say about it now. Europe is populated with Habsburgs on every throne, just as Maria Theresa intended, and a fat lot of good it has done anyone. They may not be fighting each other but they don't have the power to fight the enemies rising up from within their own nations. Maria Theresa's strategems might have worked to prevent the evils of her own generation but in 1792 they are like bows and arrows on a battlefield full of artillery.

Others wage war; you, lucky Habsburg, marry.

She can't hear Antoinette, but Charlotte's portrait must be open, out of its case; she can hear something. Muffled voices or movements. Antoinette used the doll to wake her and is waiting for a response.

Charlotte holds her candle with one hand and opens the

door to the little room where Antoinette's portrait stares into the darkness.

'I'm here,' she says, half groggy, half worried.

There's nothing at first but more rustling, like furniture moving. Then her sister's voice, but distant.

They're coming. Charlotte—

'Yes? Antoinette, are you all right? Where are you?'

At the Tuileries, still. There are magisters – they are using all kinds of magic I've never seen. A guard – There were knives flying by themselves. I saw one sever a guard's head. They made the King wear a red cap, bundled him off somewhere. I should be with him, I – We are in a room on the second floor. Lamballe, the Tourzels and I. Madame de Tourzel and Pauline have seen me do magic, I'm afraid. Couldn't be helped.

Of all things to worry about. 'What magic? Have you got any weapons?'

They don't allow us any rings, anything like that, things they know about. We've got needles.

'Needles?'

They grow. We might be able to get out, when they come. They're coming.

'Get out now.'

We can't. We're surrounded. We need to get past them – Listen, Charlotte, I may only have a few moments. I put some money into the teapot in the nécessaire, for the children, if they make it out. You must look after them, Charlotte. Will you?

'Of course.' She has no will to protest or console. There is no time for that. 'What else do you need?'

Take care of Mousseline. She's wilful, and stubborn. She takes after her aunt.

'Yes, I always thought Amalia was horribly stubborn. What else?'

Nothing else. Only—

'Yes?'

I don't know what to say.

There's a crash and then screams, mostly male screams. Bangs.

'Antoinette?'

Gunfire.

'Antoinette!'

Nothing but crashes and bumps, and Charlotte forces herself to shut up. She sits before the painting until the candle gutters, and outside it is probably dawn but in the tiny closet it is pitch black. She listens to the inchoate sounds in her mind, punctuated now and again by children weeping, snatches of horrible songs. Blood-curdling yells.

She listens as a man she does not know tells her sister that they are taking her and the rest of the royal family to the Temple. The dark, medieval tower with the conical turrets that Antoinette has always hated. She listens to Antoinette reassuring her companions.

Then at last Charlotte says, 'Hold strong. Go where they tell you. Give them no reason to kill you. I'll get you out, as soon as I can.'

She opens a locket with Silfversparre's portrait in it, speaks a few words to tell him to go with whatever speed he can to Paris, to help her sister. The old alliances and factions are long broken, but perhaps she can still count on the loyalty of friends.

CHAPTER FIFTY-SEVEN

September in Paris — The Tocsin Rings — Madame Capet — Lamballe Is Courageous — An Escape

———— ❖ ————

Antoinette sits by the shuttered window, her embroidery on her lap. It is all that is left to her now: unpicking, stitching up. Her fingers are bruised with it, as though it's a penance, and yet the little shepherd scene is still not finished.

Lamballe sits in the chair opposite, as if they were back at the Petit Trianon and not in a set of small rooms, locked in a medieval castle with tall dark walls and pointed turrets. The princess is knitting a white scarf, her needles clicking. She always wanted a quiet life. Perhaps this imprisonment is not so bad for her. Or perhaps she is only taking it with the same fortitude with which she has greeted every other disaster.

Mousseline and Pauline de Tourzel, who have been eager to learn since they witnessed Antoinette use magic at the Tuileries, are working on a spell. Pauline has an aptitude for magic. She has already adapted a troublesome spell for unknotting thread — it tends to go too far, and make it so that the thread will never ravel or knit or hold in anything ever again. Pauline's version, with slightly different sacrifices, works much better.

Madame de Tourzel is knitting a cap for little seven-year-old Charles, who sits on the floor with his lesson book, writing out sentences his father has set him to learn. And Louis is reading a history of Charles I of England.

If only she could concentrate on her embroidery. How does Lamballe knit so steadily?

Antoinette has almost nothing left. The jailers at the Temple don't bother checking items for possible magic, and instead just take everything away. There is no hiding anything in pockets any more; she isn't allowed pockets here. Her miniature of Charlotte is gone. She still hears Charlotte's voice from time to time, speaking to Antoinette's portrait in Naples, assuring her that she will be rescued, that they will get her out. Telling her that the armies are coming at last to save France. But she has only a prayer book, pens and paper and ink. Blunt needles to work tapestries and embroideries, all of which are checked and many of which are removed. Two plain dresses, one blue and one pink. Linens.

And, of course, the invisible golden watch. Its spells are useless, though, with nothing left to sacrifice but memories, and fewer of them than she would like.

Once it seemed that Antoinette was the only magister in France. Now, she's one of the only people who can't do magic at all. It's everywhere, now, just as the Order feared. And just as the rogues dreamed – but not like this.

A strain of song comes up from under her window. It's shuttered, but she can still hear: '"The Queen goes up in her tower; will she come down again?"'

Pauline looks up from the spell she's studying with Mousseline – a little spell, the spell to enchant a lace to stay tied, or for mending. One of the first spells Antoinette learned.

'Can't we make them shut up?' Mousseline asks.

'It's only a song,' says Lamballe gently. 'They can't hurt us if we don't let them.'

But then the door bangs, and three men push past their guard. The guard does not object.

'We want the Queen's lover,' one shouts, and for a moment Antoinette's heart clenches when she thinks of Fersen, but he is not here – they mean the Princesse de Lamballe.

Another of the men is holding a bloody pike. Whose blood? Someone, down there in the courtyard or on the stairs, is still loyal enough to have died for the Queen. To have sacrificed themselves for her.

Another of the men holds out papers, and Antoinette snatches them, reads. A warrant for the arrest of Lamballe. On charges of treason, under the authority of the revolutionary tribunal, whatever that is.

The prison warden looks from the men to the princess, uncertain.

'When the Prussians and Austrians come, they will find no allies in Paris,' says the man with the pike. 'Traitors, priests, and foreigners must leave or face justice.'

Their warden cannot refuse, he says.

Antoinette grabs Lamballe's arm. 'She is not going anywhere.'

'Let me go,' Lamballe says, softly, taking Antoinette's hand in her own and lifting it off her arm. 'It's all right, my dear. If you cause a fuss, there will be violence, and we have to think of the children.'

Tightness in her chest, bitterness in her mouth. How can they take Lamballe? She's done nothing to anyone, her whole life long.

'My beloved friend,' she says to Lamballe, and as she forces herself to look at Lamballe's pretty face, she finds that she means it. 'Return to us.'

'The Tourzel woman too, and her daughter,' says a potato-faced man with papers in his hands. 'She was on the flight to Varennes. She has to answer for that.'

'I will come, and willingly,' says Madame de Tourzel. 'But why take my Pauline? She is innocent!'

'All three of you must come, on pain of death,' says the man with the pike.

At the sight of his beloved governess being taken by rough men, little Charles runs to her and grabs Madame de Tourzel's skirts, crying out. Antoinette takes him, pulls him back to her, and it feels like an act of violence.

Antoinette paces, listening to the roars of the crowd rise and fall. A week passes, perhaps more. Mousseline, not sleeping either, works at spells, using what little ash she's collected from burning rags in candle flames. But she can't make anything work. Charles thinks it's a game, and starts moving the sacrifices around in the points of the star, until his sister yells at him, and then weeps, her face in her hands. Mousseline is not yet fourteen. At her age, Antoinette was preparing to marry the Dauphin of France, and worried about her hairline and her pimples.

Antoinette is standing at the small and dingy window when the bell sounds.

To call it a bell – there is no word for it. It is like standing inside the huge bronze bourdon at the top of the tower of Notre-Dame Cathedral on Easter Sunday. It's a sound that kills all other sounds, and all thoughts, and every bone in her body shakes, her teeth grind, her skull splits apart.

It is coming from everywhere and nowhere. Insofar as she can think at all, she wonders briefly whether it's a sound in Naples, not here, but then she sees her daughter on the ground with her hands clapped over her ears, just as Antoinette's hands are on her own, trying to block what cannot be blocked.

She would do anything to stop the sound. Say anything, cut off any part of her body that would save her from it.

And then it stops.

And, outside the window, the screaming starts.

In the evening, a new guard comes on shift, stands at the door. He calls to her gruffly, 'Madame.'

The guards now call the King 'Louis Capet', after the

founding family of the Kings of France. She is 'Madame Capet', when she isn't being called something worse.

She stands and walks over to him, not hurrying.

He glances out of the barred window, then rushes her back away from the door.

'I am here to rescue you,' he whispers. 'I am a friend of the Queen of Naples.'

She doesn't recognize him. He's about her age, with blond hair and a strong, gilded chin. An accent like Fersen's. It is probably a trap, but what choices does she have?

'There isn't much time to lose, Your Majesty,' he says. 'I, uh, incapacitated the real guard, but it won't last long.'

She shakes her head, hands him back the little flask. 'We will go, but not yet,' she says. 'First, I need you to take this to the prison they call La Grande Force. It will be crowded with people; you should be able to get in, if you pretend to be a revolutionary. Free the Princesse de Lamballe, the Marquise de Tourzel and her daughter Pauline de Tourzel and get them safe in Naples. Then you can return for us.'

He takes a locket out from under his jacket, holds it between his thumb and finger, but doesn't open it. 'Your sister—'

'I won't go now, so there's no point in arguing,' says Antoinette, closing her hands around the locket and pushing his hand down. 'If you or my sister have the slightest regard for my welfare, you won't force me to abandon the people who love me, who are ready to die for me.'

Antoinette falls asleep at last, a sick, sweaty sleep born of sheer exhaustion. She wakes in the morning and feels a kind of peace. The guard on duty is one of the kinder ones; she asks him if he's heard any word about the fate of the Princesse de Lamballe.

'She's freed, I think,' he says, slowly. 'The tribunal acquitted her.'

She almost weeps with relief.

The family eats their plain breakfast and Louis asks his wife if she'd like to play backgammon. Of course, she says.

Charlotte's voice in her head: *You fool. Why didn't you come when he told you to? I didn't send him to collect your friends. This was the very thing I was trying to avoid. Listen, Antoinette, I know that you love Lamballe—*

That's the worst of it; she doesn't. Sometimes she thinks it's the very worst thing she's ever done, that sacrifice. She wants . . . not to expiate her sins, but to do what small acts of kindness she can, before they strip those from her too. Where is Lamballe now? Is she in pain? Is she thinking about embroidery, to help herself bear it?

Antoinette, you have to get out the moment he returns. It will be you next. You know it will. You must get out. I'll help you once you're here. It's not over. Do you even hear me?

Charlotte knows full well she can't answer, that there's nothing she can do. Antoinette has nothing left to sacrifice. She paces in front of the window. Mousseline is lying on her small bed, watching her.

And then Antoinette's knees buckle, and she grabs at the gritty stone windowsill.

Outside the window, a pale face that she thinks, at first, is a mask. The Princesse de Lamballe, her face scored and gashed, bloody where it isn't white with pallor or powder. The blood on her cheeks is mixed with roughly applied rouge and her hair frizzled and powdered in a way it has not been for months.

Her head is bobbing, on a pike, past the window.

Shouts from below. 'Kiss her! Kiss your lover's lips!'

The face, animated with something other than life, smiles, the lips cracking open. The eyes blink. Some sound, like the first notes of a song, gurgles through the streams of blood.

Antoinette crumples and her daughter catches her, eases her fall. She hears Louis screaming her name. The guard comes in, and it's one of the kinder ones, and he hurries them up to the King's room, to safety.

A letter arrives, flying through the bars of her window, folded into the shape of a bird:

5 September 1792
Axel von Fersen to Antoinette

My heart's only love, my queen, my all,

I write, first of all, to assure you that Madame de Tourzel and her daughter are safe. Madame de Tourzel has resources of her own, it seems; she somehow convinced the crowd to let her go free, although I can assure you she did not disavow you or the King. It was plain, simple, undeniable devotion to the children, I think; they wanted to believe that she would do anything for them, and thus they could excuse her staying with you.

Pauline de Tourzel is safe too, and for that we can thank Isaac Silfversparre. A fellow Swede, although he and I have not had dealings in many years. He remained a Brother, and I became a rogue, and so we were enemies. But we met outside the Grand Force prison as unwitting allies. I was on watch for some way of helping Lamballe and the Tourzels. He told me he was going in to get them, at your behest.

Lamballe and Madame de Tourzel insisted that Pauline go first, alone, because her face is not known. Their own faces would attract attention and they didn't want to endanger Pauline.

So I took her out, pretending to be a procurator of the Paris commune, aided by some enchantments. It took me a long time to get her through the mob, though. Over and over I had to argue that she was a peasant girl, there by mistake.

When I finally got her to safety and returned, both Madame de Tourzel and Lamballe had been taken into the courtyard. The crowd wouldn't let me pass. I arrived just in time to hear Lamballe say that she would never denounce you. Silfversparre was there, but wounded in some struggle or other. He will recover.

Everything is chaos, and fortune mocks us. The mob attacked the prisons and killed so many innocents, children even. The thirst for blood has fallen on this city like an evil enchantment. And perhaps it is an enchantment. Everything is decaying; the statues outside Notre-Dame look as though they've melted. The effect of so many spells, I suspect. Could it have an effect on our minds and hearts too? Or is it only that we are all so eager to sacrifice them?

If you hear of anyone who has turned against you, do not hate them. The mobs have forced them to stand on the piled bodies of their friends and relatives and shout, 'Vive la nation!' or else be torn apart with planks and rocks and ice picks.

The ones whose names they know, they keep alive as long as they can, to make sure they endure every torture.

There are so many enchantments: pikes that point to anyone hiding in cellars or alleyways. They have found spells that make the heads of the 'traitors' sing.

The cafés stay open, as though this bloody business were the normal course of affairs. And perhaps, now, it is.

I have never loved another and will love you until the end of time. Adieu for now, my heart.

Your own
Fersen

CHAPTER FIFTY-EIGHT

A Pact Founders – Civil Wars – The Gates of Hell –
The Sala Oscura – The Cost of Betrayal

———— ❖ ————

As the terrible year of 1792 draws to a close, there is little hope that 1793 will bring any mercy. The putative government of France sends Charlotte an ambassador; she refuses to see him. She refuses even to speak French; most of the court can get by in Neapolitan or German.

In December, Acton tells her a French fleet is sailing towards Naples.

'Let them come, then,' she says, spreading her arms wide. 'There's nothing I want more than war with these bastards. I've been trying to convince the cowards in Spain and Britain to join Austria and Prussia in a coalition against France. If they see France invading me, they'll have little choice.'

He takes a deep breath. 'Our navy has never been stronger. If we are forced to, we can mount a defence against this squadron.'

'But?'

'But I think we should avoid it if we can, nonetheless. The French have managed to turn back – to humiliate! – the Prussian army. It's astonishing. How can a nation in anarchy win so decisively on the battlefield, again and again? I don't understand it. No one understands it. Whether they have more of this new science that we haven't seen, or whether it's simply the fervour of revolution, they have struck terror into every part of Europe. The defensive pact in Italy has come to nothing. Even Spain, which ought to be at our side—'

She stops him. 'I understand Spain well enough. So you think we should negotiate?'

He nods. 'This does not strike me as an invasion fleet, in any case. Call it an intimidation fleet, to test us and see what we'll do. I think it's meant to answer your insult to their ambassador with a show of force, and perhaps to fan the flames of civil war here in Naples. Which is another reason I don't think we should be hasty to declare war on France.'

'Civil war!'

'In Saint-Domingue, the people have risen up, thrown off their French occupiers and formed a new government, outlawing slavery.'

'And I wish them all joy and success. Naples is not Saint-Domingue.'

'No, but there are examples for Naples to follow now. Saint-Domingue. France. America. Liège. The Austrian Netherlands. We are a hair's breadth from open rebellion in Naples, Charlotte.'

She frowns. She has been careful, since Leopold's death; she has tasters at every meal, and moves her apartments around within the palace every night. She has set magical traps. She has worried about assassination. But her chief of police – Caterina's brother Luigi – assures her that the unrest in Naples has been quelled.

Acton, though, sems less sanguine. 'Every month that passes with the French King in prison is another month that emboldens the republicans here. If we show too much sympathy – too much open sympathy, I mean – to the King and Queen of France, we may tip the balance for good, and lose control.'

She huffs, and turns away from him. 'Too much open sympathy.'

'Everyone suspects that the Queen's family helped her escape as far as Varennes. The Habsburgs stick together; everyone knows that. There are pamphlets claiming that you are conspiring to help her escape again, that you will bring the Baker and the Baker's wife to Naples, install them here while they plan their counter-revolution. At the expense of Naples' coffers, which have still not recovered from the earthquakes, from the volcano, from the building of the fleet, from your taxation reforms.'

'So if I help my sister,' she says, turning back to him with a cold stare, 'I could lose my country. If I blow the French ships back to the gates of hell, I foster resentment among those here who admire the revolution. If I let the French come here to *negotiate*, I let them spread their pamphlets and their speeches and whatever else, I will be safe?'

He nods. 'For now, we must be circumspect. And we must convince the French to turn aside. I suspect they will want to turn aside, will be looking for some small diplomatic triumph they can use as propaganda. We could meet them, somewhere away from Naples.'

She shakes her head. 'Let them come. It's time I found out where all my enemies are.'

Charlotte needs police she can control. Police with no ties, no loyalties, no ideas in their heads.

She recruits the least morally curious people in Naples and encourages them to believe that the tools she gives them are *scientific*.

She takes them from the brothels and prisons, uses them for a week at a time, takes their memories and sends them out free men and women. It's a mercy to everyone.

They don't need to be bright. All they need to do is watch, from doorways and servants' staircases, and hold onto a bit of glass while they do so.

Then they take their bits of glass to the Palazzo Reale.

Nobody but Charlotte and those she invites can get to her Sala Oscura – the dark room. It is dark in every sense of the word. There's a staircase where the Queen's rooms meet the bodyguard chamber between her rooms and the King's. That staircase leads, for people who are invited, to a golden door. (For people who are not invited, it leads to the floor above.)

Beyond the golden door is darkness.

The only furnishings in the room are a comfortable chair for Charlotte and a writing desk. There is a window, but it is curtained, and outside that window, it is always night.

It also holds an old magic lantern, delivered to the Queen from Vienna.

When her latest spy comes to report, he's holding five glass slides. Images he saw as he watched the front door of the rooms where the delegation of the French bastards is staying, while they make their displeasure known. Acton was right: it wasn't an invasion, but a batch of uninvited guests.

She looks at each slide in turn, the only light in the room the great circle of colour on the far wall.

There's a faint smell of magic, overlaying the smells of oil and varnish. Each piece of glass is framed in simple, cheap wood that feels solid between her fingers. Real evidence of moments that she could not witness in person.

Most of the slides show her the Frenchmen, entering their rooms and leaving them.

She notes a slide that shows a Neapolitan writer entering those same rooms. A traitor. She will have him arrested.

Out comes the slide, and in goes another, slotting in with comforting mechanical precision.

The next slide shows Luigi de' Medici, her chief of police.

And beside him, she sees the one person in all the world who ought not to be able to betray her. She sees Caterina de' Medici, Marchesa of San Marco.

⁜

Charlotte waits for Caterina in her rooms in the palace. All night long she waits. Sometimes she thinks she can still smell the fog in the palace, the remnants of it. The deep suspicion that soaked into every thread of every fabric, into every pore of her body. The edges of the windows are already rimmed with daylight when Caterina slips in through the door of her own anteroom, her fingers curling around the door, her footfalls silent.

'Does it hurt?'

Caterina's face is blank, a mask of whirling calculations. 'Your Majesty?'

'Betraying me. I enchanted you years ago, and I suppose it might not have worked. Or perhaps later, when you became immune—'

'It worked,' Catarina says, stepping forward and closing the door with a click. She doesn't sit; Charlotte doesn't ask her to. 'I hurt all the time. It took me some time, and some questions, to work out what the cause of the pain was. If you ask me, the magic is unjust.'

'Unjust, is it?' The gall. 'A small price to pay for betrayal.'

Caterina doesn't answer, looking away as she's gathering her thoughts. 'Someone has to keep asking questions about how the state ought to be, how justice ought to be disposed, how to achieve prosperity. You—'

'I don't have time, or the luxury,' Charlotte interrupts. 'We are at war, or will be very soon.'

'Indeed!' Caterina's face is clearly pained, Charlotte realizes, and has been for some time. She didn't notice. 'You don't have the luxury. But we do. We can be the ones to carry forward the ideas of virtue, of freedom, of justice. You call it betrayal but perhaps the best way I can serve you, now, is to betray you.'

How long has her friend been her enemy? To choose this moment, when Antoinette is in mortal danger, when Europe is at war. To sneak in under Charlotte's defences when she barely has the strength to withstand another loss.

Charlotte sinks into her chair and shakes her head. 'I wish no harm to you. But I cannot allow a secret society of Jacobins to flourish in Naples.'

'We are not Jacobins,' Caterina says defiantly. 'We're citizens.'

She wants things; how must that feel? Charlotte doesn't want anything any more. She only fears things. She is tired and her eyes are burning.

Charlotte has too much work to do: troops to mass, letters to write. It is coming to the time of the night when Charlotte speaks to her sister, alone, praying only that Antoinette can hear her. She would hate to miss that appointment.

'Go,' she says to Caterina, who hesitates, uncertain what this means. 'Go, before I change my mind. Go out of my service, away from the palace, this moment. And know that if you are caught again conversing with my enemies, you will be treated like any traitor.'

Nothing will happen now in Naples without Charlotte knowing about it. She will divide the city into twelve wards, and her secret police will report on every suspicious letter, every meeting of more than three people, every puppet-play and circus act that could be subversive.

There are to be no more meetings for philosophical discussion. No more Freemasons. No more salons; the time for such luxuries has passed. For now, at least, when the Jacobins are trying to get a foothold, Naples will be a place where everyone but the Queen must be always in the light.

CHAPTER FIFTY-NINE

Shouts — Farewells — Drums

———— ❖ ————

Before Christmas, they take Louis to a separate room in the prison, while they put the King on trial for treason.

Louis seemed somewhat consoled by the fact that his room in the tower is adjacent to a library. Antoinette can just barely hear him up there sometimes, reading Rousseau aloud to himself, muttering as if someone is listening to him. She can hear his footsteps.

They have been a help to each other, over the years, but in so many ways she and Louis have had to face their trials alone.

Mama had wanted Antoinette to be crowned queen alongside Louis, arguing that if she was not crowned, she would be vulnerable to the machinations of the anti-Austrians at court. But already, then, she and Louis knew that she would be despised for extravagance; that was during the years of the bad harvests. She did not argue when Louis's advisers suggested a single coronation.

'If we stay in Paris, people will think we're afraid,' Louis said. 'We will go to Reims. That is where the Kings of France are crowned. The people will see us, and they'll know that we are not afraid, and that we are working for them.'

To Reims they went, on bumpy roads built by the forced labour Louis's finance minister was trying to abolish. The coronation coach gleamed in the June sun, bearing angels and trumpets and two frightened young people north from Paris. Louis took Antoinette's hand from time to time, as if to reassure her, but the crowds lining the streets only cheered, though the bakeries bore painted signs in the windows saying 'No bread'.

Always, always, she was trying to make herself into an object to be adored, to be valued. She brought Monsieur Léonard with her to Reims, and instructed him to dress her hair in the towering new style known as the *pouf sentimental*. Even Louis gasped when he saw her, in a dress encrusted with sapphires and embroidered in gold, and the tall white feathers in her hair nodding.

In a special pavilion to one side of the cathedral, she took her place with the King's sister Élisabeth, to watch, making sure to smile. She watched the men weighted with blue and gold and canopies, and heard the ritual calls and responses. She pointed, like everyone else, to the sacred ampoule, the glass vial of anointing balm that was found in the sarcophagus of St Remigius.

Then the singing of the Te Deum transcended the vaults of the cathedral, and the skin under Antoinette's heavy gown shivered, and heaven and earth were filled with ineffable majesty, and her tears would no longer be dammed. She knew she must not cry; her face would puff up and go blotchy, and people would despise her. But she couldn't stop. It was too big for her; it was bigger than her. Her husband stood, girt with the sword of Charlemagne, grim with purpose, and even in his ermine and silk he looked very small in that great cathedral. She was small too, and grateful to be small, to be nothing and nowhere. She wept, tears she couldn't stop and couldn't catch, tears that were not calculated to endear or to manipulate.

Now she only wants to go and stand with her husband, and hold his hand.

The kindest jailers tell her a little about what is happening, so she knows when they pronounce him guilty. There is some talk, led by Mr Thomas Paine, of exiling the royal family to America, because America has not forgotten that it owes its birth, in part, to Louis, and that the debt he incurred in coming to the rebels' aid made it impossible for him to govern.

Then there is a death sentence, by a narrow vote. One of those who votes 'yes' to kill the King is the man who now calls himself Philippe Égalité. Antoinette's anger is like a ball of molten lead in her throat.

But there is talk still of a reprieve. Anything could happen. She doesn't tell the children much, and they don't ask. Mousseline sits and studies her spells with a tight mouth. Charles no longer writes his lessons, and no one has the heart to make him. He plays on the carpet with bits of bread and clay, toy soldiers or trains.

One evening in January, they hear a fresh tumult under their window. Shouts of 'Tomorrow, tomorrow, Louis Capet will die!'

Something breaks in Antoinette and it breaks in the children too, in Louis's sister Élisabeth, who still shares their captivity. They all slump like broken puppets, hands to their mouths, eyes red and wet. Perhaps it is only a rumour.

But the door opens, and the guards bring Louis in for the first time in weeks. His face is calm. She goes to her husband and holds him, with Charles holding both their hands and burying his face in their bodies, hiding the tears that shake his body. Mousseline, ordinarily so stoic, shrieks, her hands balled at her side.

'Perhaps now they will be satisfied, and let you all go,' he says in Antoinette's ear. 'Perhaps it is over.'

Antoinette shakes her head, still clutching him and her son. 'We have tonight,' Antoinette says, searching for words that make sense. This man has been in some ways a stranger to her as she has been a stranger to him, but they have been companions and allies and have never spoken in anger to each other, in all these years. She can't imagine a world without him; she tries not to imagine tomorrow's dawn.

'No,' he whispers, kissing her forehead. 'I must have some time alone, to prepare. I will come back in the morning. Let me go, children. In the morning I will be here. We don't need to say goodbye tonight.'

But he doesn't come back. They lie awake, Charles dozing fitfully, thrashing on his bed. The dawn comes, pale and merciless. Louis does not come. The morning stretches on, strangely quiet, until suddenly they hear drumming, and they clutch each other's hands, and there are horrible cheers in the streets below.

CHAPTER SIXTY

Emma Hamilton — Another English Naval Captain —
Victories of the French Army — Charlotte Calculates —
The Embroidered Book

———— ❖ ————

William Hamilton may have intended Emma to be his mistress, but she becomes his wife. She also becomes one of the few people in Italy to whom the Queen is simply 'Charlotte'. For Emma is amusing, brilliant, and useful – an English alliance may be the only hope now for an invasion of France, to free Antoinette and put out the fires.

Emma is also good at finding things out.

Charlotte berates Emma, mostly affectionately, when Emma tells her that an English naval captain is coming to Naples and will request an audience.

'I would have told you sooner, if my husband had known any sooner,' Emma apologizes. 'William says he's a little ugly man, but bright and ambitious.'

This is the moment. It took the execution of King Louis to force the nations of Europe into open war with republican France. Antoinette, Mousseline, and Charles are still alive. And England and France are finally at war again.

❖

Captain Horatio Nelson is not that ugly, really, but perhaps Charlotte's relief at seeing him and his tired but devoted men is colouring her view of him. He stares at Emma Hamilton as though he's never seen anything so wondrous, and William Hamilton beams with vicarious pride. Acton is there, of course, and Ferdinand, to lend his official approval to the conversation.

'They have taken my sister to a new prison, all by herself,' she tells the English captain. 'They have separated her from her children. And she has nothing but a prayer book, a table, and chairs. She can't even write to me.'

Charlotte's voice shakes despite herself at that last. She hasn't heard her sister's voice in so long; all she knows about her situation now comes from Fersen's letters, and he can only find things out in old-fashioned ways: bribing guards and gossiping.

Charlotte talks to Antoinette every night, even so, praying with her. Last night, she read her the latest letter from Soliman, in which he has laid out several new schemes for civic improvements (of course, she replies; she will get to them when she can) and also writes that his heart breaks for Antoinette and her children. It's the most personal thing she's ever seen Soliman write and Charlotte's voice wavers as she reads it out loud to her sister, hoping she is still alive to hear.

'What a pity that no escape attempt has succeeded,' says Nelson.

Charlotte shakes her head. 'She won't go now, not without her children. Our only hope is to destroy the fraudulent government and restore the monarchy, with her son Charles as king.'

'I am happy to report there are many in the city of Toulon, as in other parts of France, who share that goal,' Nelson says. 'The royalists can take Toulon, if they have help. I want to strike now, and I have my government's permission to do so, but there are no spare English troops close enough. So I am gathering what troops I can from our allies.'

Charlotte can hardly agree quickly enough. 'We have six thousand soldiers ready to sail.'

Nelson leans back, claps his hands. 'That's wonderful.' He glances at the King, as if for confirmation, but Ferdinand is playing with the Hamilton's spaniel, teasing it with the end of his steak.

'What?' he asks. 'Oh, of course, you must have the troops. My wife knows how many. You're saving us, Captain Nelson. Saving Italy. These French are monsters. Executing a king! Such a thing has never been done in the history of the world!'

'Begging Your Majesty's pardon, but we English have executed a king or two,' says Nelson with a little smile.

'Really?' Ferdinand leans forward. 'How barbarous.'

'There is no doubt that the French radicals will do whatever it takes to win,' Acton says. 'This plan for Toulon carries a great risk.'

'The French army has done remarkable things; I can't pretend that isn't true,' Nelson says. 'Extraordinary things. Nonetheless, I think I can win at Toulon.'

'But if you win, sir,' Acton says, 'then, within France, the royalist cause becomes a foreign cause, and the republican cause becomes a patriot's cause. You may win the battle and lose the war.'

Nelson nods slowly. 'I am not a politician,' he says. 'But I think we will definitely lose the war if we don't fight it.'

Charlotte claps her hands once. 'There you go, Acton, my prudent Acton. You've met your match at last. You will have my troops, Captain Nelson. I want to see my sister free.'

Nelson raises his glass, dark wine in crystal, but he says, 'I must be honest. I fear it may be too late to save the Queen. But not, perhaps, her children.'

Charlotte drinks her own wine down in one gulp. 'They will either learn to fear me, or they will know my revenge. I would like to see France pulverized, Captain Nelson, by the time this child in my belly comes into the world.'

⚜

A world full of magic, and some of it strange to her. A world full of magisters, and so many of them bent on destroying her sister. A French army that has, in ways that no one can explain, managed to strike terror into Europe. How many rogues are in that army, and what enchantments do they have?

But Charlotte has a weapon no one else has. She has the spell of spells – a way to disarm them all.

In a little, forgotten room in the Palazzo Reale, where the yellow silk wallpaper is frayed and rotting, Charlotte sits at a small writing desk and thinks.

The greater the spell, Soliman said, the greater the decay and the greater the sacrifice.

She pulls the embroidered book out of a drawer, flips it open to the dog-eared sheets of paper that bear Soliman's tables. There is the spell he used for stealing the spellbooks. There's the sacrifice he made for it. The tables include a multiplier, for making similar spells do more and greater works.

She could draw all the spells in the world into a book. It would cost a great deal – perhaps more than anything she can sacrifice. But even then, magisters would remember what they'd lost, and recreate it. It would be a blow, but not a victory.

Charlotte needs their memories too.

Even that will leave enchanted items in the world, but she hopes that if no one remembers they're enchanted, they'll be of little use to magisters. Objects that are thought to be broken, or haunted, or inexplicable. The spell will have to be massive as it is, to draw both spells and memories to her, without dealing with enchanted objects as well.

More calculations, and a second layer to the spell for the memories. She sits with Soliman's tables for hours, until she has worked it out in every possible way. For a spell of this size, there's a moderate body sacrifice. But the treasure and memory sacrifices are enormous.

What does she have? Money and jewellery – it can all go in. What does she need with jewels? Exactly the problem. She's already sacrificed every gift that meant anything to her.

She has to sacrifice a treasure she truly cares about, if there's anything left.

It is not impossible. It just means giving in to decay, giving in.

What memory is left to her to sacrifice? Everything that meant something to her, she has lost. She's kept only enough to allow her to remain queen, and even then, she leans on her diaries and luck. What memories would be a sacrifice that would hurt, but would allow her to remain in power, and remain Charlotte?

Only the memory of magic itself.

What treasure is left to her to sacrifice?

Her power as a magister.

From another drawer, she pulls out a fresh notebook: blank pages inside a soft, black leather cover bearing only her monogram, stamped in gold. She tears out a page, writes on it: 'All my memories of magic'.

A rough, uneven star on the floor, and the notebook in the centre. Tears are running down her face but that won't be enough for the body sacrifice, so she takes her desk scissors and chops off all her hair, lets it lie in a pile in the body point of the star.

Into the memory point, the scrap of paper. So simple, in the end.

Into the treasure point of the star goes the embroidered book, and all of Charlotte's notebooks, filled with spells from the *Reconditus*.

And then, she looks at the embroidered book, at everything it meant to her. The memory of her governess, of her sister. She is already giving up magic; must she give up this little remnant of the work of her childish hands, and the hands of the woman who died for her knowledge?

With a little pair of sewing scissors from the basket she keeps in her desk, Charlotte snips the embroidered cover off its binding. It comes away a bit frayed and with a few small holes, but she holds the embroidery in her hands, looks at the whorled vines and the friendly petals, and feels a moment of peace.

She intends to draw all the magic in the world into a single book, in one massive enchantment like the smaller ones Soliman performed so many times to make his library. Her plain notebook, with a page ripped out of it, will do the job. No one, not even Charlotte, will remember what that book contains.

Countess Ertag's embroidery, now cut away from its spellbook, fits loosely around the plain leather cover of the blank notebook. Charlotte tucks in its edges and pins it to the leather. There.

Then, the sacrifices. Into the star goes the spellbook that once belonged to two small archduchesses, now stripped of its embroidered cover. Into the star go the papers with Soliman's handwritten tables on them. For a moment, she thinks of all the other spellbooks there must be in the world: scraps of paper, thick leather books. Antoinette's gold watch. Soliman's library. He spoke of precautions, but could he have any precautions against this? She suspects not, and she ought not to hope for it – if she's going to do this, it must be complete. She must leave no magister standing. If any magister survives this, such a magister would be the only one left in the world, invincible. That is a chance Charlotte can't take. The world is broken enough as it is.

Charlotte kneels, her pregnant belly on her knees, her face wet with tears.

'I give these things.'

Nothing. Is it not enough? Does she need to bleed as well? Or perhaps did she not express a true intention?

She shuts her eyes violently tight, and imagines what she wants. Tries desperately to want it.

Let all the spells of all the magisters in all the world come into this book, in writing as tiny as the footsteps of ants. Let the paper blacken with ink, ink taken from every spellbook in the world. Let every spell fly through the air, faster than thought, and leave their pages blank.

Let all the spells in the world come to this book, and fill it with magic.

Let the memory of every spell in the world come to this book. Let every memory of magic, of the enchantment on any object, come into this book.

May this book fill with memory.

Charlotte opens her eyes and the hairs on her arms stand on end. The notebook is opening and closing, its pages ruffled by an impossible wind, the embroidered cover loosely pinned.

The pages that had been in the embroidered book are now a pile of rotten sawdust, slimy around the edges. The room smells of decay and of ink: a warm smell that has a tang like that of blood.

She thinks, *I'm sorry, Antoinette.* Sorry for . . . what? For the fear, the loss, for everything Antoinette has suffered. For not being there to rescue her.

Charlotte is tired, and her face is puffy with tears. Her head aches. She's on the floor in a room she can't quite place; there's something odd about it.

In front of her, a star drawn in ash, and in the middle of the star, a book with an embroidered cover, tacked on haphazardly with pins. She remembers that embroidery: Countess Ertag was working on it before she died, and Charlotte finished it when she was a child. The book was blank inside, as she recalls.

She crawls forward and opens it. The pages now are black with ink, heavy with ink, so much so that it comes off on her hands and the pages are stuck together.

There's something about it that terrifies her. She doesn't like this room; it smells of rot. There's an old firescreen but no fireplace. A writing desk. And the book with the embroidered cover and unreadable pages.

This is what comes of working so many hours and resting so little, especially during pregnancy.

Leaving the book on the floor, she stumbles out into another room, and another. Into her antechamber. Now she knows where she is. There are ladies-in-waiting looking at her with alarm, at her hands black with ink. Not to worry, Charlotte says, she only needs a rest. As she walks to her bedroom, Charlotte hears someone whisper, 'But where did she come from?' And realizes that she cannot remember.

CHAPTER SIXTY-ONE

Carnations and Letters — The Watch and the Seal —
A Woman in White — Knitters

———————— ❖ ————————

The Republic of France declares that the Austrian woman in the Tower must answer for her crimes. They take Charles away, and they don't let Antoinette see him. It's a blow she can't sustain. She coughs when she hears him cough, faintly, through the walls. She weeps, silently, when she hears him cry out. What are they doing to him?

Days pass, and his cries and sobs stop, and there's silence. That's worse. In the daytime, she presses herself to the window to see him as they take him outside for his exercise. He looks small, stoic. Eight years old. He never catches her eye.

Then they take her away from Mousseline and Louis's sister. She gives Mousseline as many instructions as she can, and kisses the tight, passive face that she knows so well. Her little bit of muslin, her friend. Daughter of France.

A muslin shawl comes with her into her last prison, and a black dress, a white cap. Her gold watch, a gift from her mother when she was young. The markings on it are strange and the gears complicated, and come to think of it, she doesn't remember ever using the watch to tell the time.

Some old-fashioned instrument that she was too flighty to understand as a child, no doubt, and in the intervening years the watch was a mere comfort, as it is now. Amazing that they let her keep it, all this time.

She had a miniature of Charlotte, she remembers, but they took it away. They tell her she can have one book, so she chooses Hume's *History of England*. It reminds her of Louis, and of Charlotte.

Even now, Antoinette is watched as she washes her face. Today, though, instead of a crowd of curious courtiers, it's a single guard. She does not meet his eyes, for his sake rather than hers. Let him keep up the pretence that she is not quite real, a display of a magic lantern.

She has written her letters to her sister-in-law Élisabeth and to Charlotte and Amalia. She has asked God's forgiveness, and stripped to nothing but the white dress she will wear to her death.

There have been attempts to break her out of prison. A ridiculous plot involving instructions pricked into the petals of a carnation. But she has made it known to everyone who has tried that she won't go. If she dies, there's a chance her children will live. If she escapes, they won't want any other members of the royal family left alive.

Her visitors are few, and mostly strangers, commoners sent to guard the Widow Capet and look after her basic needs. But she does get a few snippets of gossip. The Republic has a new calendar, she's told, with all the days of the week named not for saints or gods but for things like beetroot and barley. It reminds her of the ridiculous fashion for nicknaming days that swept through Versailles years ago. Where did such a notion come from?

She asks about her old friends: the Chevalier de Saint-Georges has founded a legion to fight for the French Republic, all men of colour. Not to be outdone, his old rival the Chevalière d'Éon has offered to raise a legion of women to do the same. It hurts to know that her friends obey the new government, but d'Éon's loyalty was always to France first and its king second. The new world will go on, despite the destruction of the old. Perhaps because of its destruction.

Lafayette, though, they've thrown into prison for being too moderate. Lafayette, moderate! She remembers him going off to America without permission – however did he manage that? There are gaps in her memory. Her hair has turned white. These last few years in captivity have made her old, and she's not well. She's been bleeding for weeks as though the General has gone to war against her too.

Antoinette writes out her last instructions. The gold watch, for some reason, she feels should go to d'Éon. She sends her seal to Fersen, with the motto 'All things guide me to you'. She writes a few letters, and saves one for last.

My dear sister, my wonderful Charlotte,

By the time you get this you will no doubt have heard of my death.

They have found me guilty of various crimes and I am to be killed in the morning. I want you to know that I go to my death with peace in my heart. They have given me pen and paper at last, but they won't let me write in code. Will this letter even reach you?

I did not think the trial could hurt me but it did, Charlotte. They accused me of incest and abuse of my son, my little Charles. What sort of imagination has such depths? I half suspected Brissot, but he's in prison, as is Philippe 'Égalité'. There are factions within factions inside the Revolution, and the newest to take power has branded Brissot and Philippe enemies of the people.

It doesn't matter.

Now, about the children.

Don't be angry at my Charles for the horrible things they made him say about me. He is a child, and frightened, and has been separated from me for months. Nothing could have hurt me more as a mother – even to put those perverse thoughts into a child's mind, they are monsters – but I know he loves me.

I ask his pardon for failing to keep him safe, and Mousseline's, too. I ask God's pardon, and the pardon of all who knew me, especially you, my dear sister, for all the vexations I caused you when we were children, and the years when we were not as close as we are now, for reasons I can't even remember.

I forgive my enemies and, above all, I ask you please to honour my final wish: don't avenge my death.

My God, it's hard to leave my children.

Antoinette

Marie Antoinette sits very straight in the back of the cart as it rumbles through the streets of Paris. She is dressed all in white, the colour of royal widows, the colour of women's power and women's sacrifice. On her head she wears a simple white cap. She feels old, although she is only thirty-eight. She feels naked.

The blueness of the sky is neither paint nor tint nor powder nor anything but itself; she stares and stares but cannot fathom it. The sun glints on the edges of the guillotine blade and she tries to gaze long enough at that beauty to have it, hold it, keep it. This moment is all the time she has, this now. It has never been enough. The shape of the blade was Louis's suggestion; even in the final years he tried to help, and he always had a talent for mechanical things. How she wishes she could have been with him in his last, terrible moments. But then he always managed to bear the weight on his own, when someone had to bear it.

Antoinette prays for a little of Louis's strength, to die properly, courageously. Death is something she has not trained for, though she has so many to show her the way. She goes to join Louis and their two lost children and all her other dead: Mama, Papa, Joseph, Leopold, her many brothers and sisters.

A memory surfaces, of Antoine and Charlotte, berating themselves for failing to save the lives of those they loved. Wishing they could find some magic spell or work a miracle. How innocent they were! A regret grabs Antoinette's heart, the years in which she and Charlotte grew distant, for reasons she can't recall, if there even were any. They were each in their kingdoms, occupied with their own concerns. But in recent years their letters have been warmer. She hears Charlotte's voice in her mind, so clearly, as though it hasn't been twenty-five years since they last spoke.

Charlotte would have been such a glorious Queen of France.

Antoinette tried her best, though it was never good enough. She gave herself to her new country, completely, though she knew she was a consolation prize. Stripped at the border, she stepped into her new gowns and new life as prettily as she could, trying so hard never to put a foot wrong. She gave herself to Fersen at first sight – how did he know it was her at that masked ball, when everyone else seemed fooled by her disguise? She doesn't remember now; she must have removed her mask with him, shown him who she was.

She offered her children what she could: her hand on Sophie's cradle, or on the hot brow of the ailing Louis-Joseph, or holding Charles's small hand in her own as they left Versailles, his small face so serious. Mousseline came into the world disappointed in her sex and Antoinette could do nothing about that but love her; *you shall be mine*, she whispered. And now Mousseline is a grim-faced young woman and Charles is a terrified little boy in the hands of their captors.

All Antoinette can give her children now is a death without shame or extra hurt. A few unfaltering steps across a stage, a stout heart, and faithful silence as she goes to God in the view of thousands of strangers who despise her. She can do it. Somewhere in her there is the strength.

Beside the scaffold, three women sit knitting, implacably. Long red scarves droop onto the floor of the scaffold, almost to the basket that will shortly catch Antoinette's head.

Women find their power where they can, and remember it in twisted threads. Misheard whispers. Embroidered and disguised.

As Antoinette mounts the six steps to the scaffold, one of her dirty white slippers falls off her foot to the ground; she pauses as she waits for someone to retrieve it, then remembers and turns to pick it up herself, but a hand on her arm urges her forward. She can't stop to collect her lost slipper; she has an urgent appointment.

The crowd is screaming; she hears laughter. A child's cry. She loves her daughters and her sons, the dead and the living, the adopted children too; her heart went out of her body a long time ago; she made a perpetual offering of it, the one thing she did without being taught, the one worthwhile sacrifice. What remains to her now is dross.

She steps on something, and realizes it's someone's foot. The executioner's foot.

'I beg your pardon,' she says. 'I didn't mean to do it.'

EPILOGUE:
DECEMBER 1798

If everything would only stop moving.

Charlotte puts her hand to the only space on the wall not covered in charts and drawings and Admiral Nelson's notes to himself. The Englishman gave his quarters on the *Vanguard* to the women and children of the royal family, while the men are in the wardroom.

This ship is all that remains of her kingdom, battered by stormy seas.

The French have declared Charlotte's kingdom a republic, the fools. A few short months ago she had Napoleon up against the wall in Rome, and now he's biting back, like the dog he is. She had no choice but to flee, to get the children and Ferdinand out.

Somehow, a common Corsican soldier has managed to overrun most of Europe.

The French took the Austrian Netherlands, and poor Mimi died earlier in the year in Vienna, powerless. Max is in Vienna too, no longer Elector of Cologne, since the French army overran his territory.

The Habsburgs and Bourbons did come together at last to fight their common enemy, but somehow this revolutionary rabble has beaten them all back and worked its way down the Italian peninsula. Amalia's Duchy of Parma is under French control. One by one, the children of Maria Theresa fall to Antoinette's murderers.

Antoinette's daughter Marie-Thérèse is now safely in Vienna at last. She is, reportedly, dour and prone to keeping her own counsel; Charlotte would be too. Antoinette's little son Charles died in prison of neglect and illness.

Everything is falling apart.

When Charlotte was a girl, she believed that she could help to build a golden age of reason. How she admired her brother Joseph, with his plans to spread tolerance, foster science, and abolish serfdom. How simple it all seemed then! And yet serfdom and slavery are rampant on both sides of the Atlantic. New discoveries only breed worse inhumanity, as knowledge is always the servant of power.

What moment did she miss? What opportunity did she lose? Sometimes she thinks she can almost remember.

She does remember the day Angelo Soliman gave her a book by Montesquieu. How he wrote her letters of guidance in her first years as queen.

When Dr Soliman died of a stroke at the age of seventy-five, the young Emperor Francis ordered his skin to be stretched over a wooden dummy and decorated with beads and feathers. Of all the hideous barbarities Charlotte's family has accomplished, over long centuries, this may be the most hideous of all. To no avail, his daughter Josephine has pleaded with Charlotte's nephew to have her father's remains.

And in Naples, Charlotte has been more and more her mother's daughter, ruling by decree, writing desperate letters to her far-flung children. Until at last the day came when not even Acton, not even her navy, not even her secret police could keep her kingdom safe. Napoleon is coming for her, and many in her own kingdom are gleeful at the prospect. The Corsican reportedly calls Charlotte 'the only man in Naples'. Ferdinand leads a separate life from her; they are seldom even in the same palace. He doesn't even pretend to take an interest in the business of state. That, at least, is a mercy.

Two days the *Vanguard* sat at anchor in the Bay of Naples, waiting for a storm to abate. Ferdinand acted as though he were waiting to be asked back, and a few boats did come once the wind died down. Acton refused them. The King will return, he said, when the people are loyal. When will that be? Not in these dying days of 1798, that seems certain.

The calm on the sea was short-lived, and the journey since has been rough. They're all terribly sick. The air smells of fish and vomit, and her poor six-year-old son Alberto is raving, when he wakes at all. His eyes are sunken and his breath is foul. If they can just get to Palermo, then Vienna, then revenge.

She opens the door out to the deck, taking care not to slip. Admiral Nelson is there, his uniform hastily pinned over his amputated arm. Her saviour. He's in close conversation with Acton and with Emma Hamilton, the woman everyone, including William Hamilton, now knows to be Nelson's mistress. She is the only one of the evacuees who is never seasick, and she has even contrived to look beautiful, somehow.

'Your Majesty,' says Nelson, turning. 'The crew are so sad not to be able to entertain the children today, it being Christmas.'

'There will be other Christmases,' says Charlotte. 'Will we make port in Palermo soon? Every day that passes is a day we lose ground against the French. We need to gather allies, and quickly.'

'Not far now, Your Majesty,' Acton says.

Emma crosses to her, walking steadily on the rolling planks. 'Your Majesty,' she says softly. 'Little Alberto is still doing poorly. His nurse says he doesn't drink water when she asks.'

Charlotte nods, to show she understands. 'All the more reason to get to Palermo as quickly as possible. But we must get something into him, for as long as he can keep it down.'

'I'll go to him,' says Emma, squeezing her hand. 'He'll do it for me.'

'Thank you, Emma,' says Charlotte. 'I'll be there shortly.'

She looks out, exhausted, and locks eyes with Acton, once her lover, now her co-ruler in all but name. Her friend? Maybe, once. He doesn't look as though he has any hope left in him, only resolve. Charlotte feels the same, much of the time. She had so much hope, once. Surely something better than this must be possible. Surely something better than the old world with its greedy kings, or the new world with its grasping demagogues.

Most of the men who sent Antoinette to the guillotine have now been fed to it in turn, but that brings Charlotte no satisfaction. What remains to her? What can she do in this world?

She can go to Vienna, and write letters. She will build such alliances that Europe will never again fall to an upstart tyrant. Like her mother on her black horse at the top of the hill, Charlotte can retake her kingdom at the head of an army. She will take her revenge, not only on the forces of chaos that killed her sister, but on this dying century that broke all its promises. Charlotte will study this new world as she studied the old one, until she understands how to tear it down and rebuild it better.

Charlotte turns away from Acton's hard gaze without saying a word. Then she climbs down into the hold, full of her large family's large trunks. She took only one portrait with her when they fled, one portrait out of all the great canvases in Naples. The 1778 portrait by Élisabeth Vigée Le Brun of her sister, Marie Antoinette, Queen of France.

She pulls a grimy brown cloth off that painting.

The expression on her Antoine's face seems to change every time she looks at it. Today it looks apprehensive, as though she can see something no one else can. Her hand rests on the voluminous silk skirts of twenty years past, and holds a single pink rose, upside down, as though she's forgotten she's holding it and may drop it at any moment.

The gilt frame still bears the words Charlotte scratched into it on the day she learned that Antoinette had died: 'I will seek vengeance unto the grave.'

The Queen leans against a trunk to steady herself as the ship rolls.

'It's Christmas, Antoine,' she says, as though she expects the portrait to hear.

ACKNOWLEDGEMENTS

This novel is the result of the hard work, encouragement, and support of many people over several years. My agent, Jennie Goloboy, has been an indefatigable champion and partner. Jack Renninson, my editor, knows every word of this book as well as I do, and I am so grateful for his vision and thoughtful labours. I thank Richenda Todd for saving me many times in copy edits, and the whole team at Harper*Voyager* for believing in this book and bringing it to readers. In particular, I thank publishing director Natasha Bardon, Andrew Davis for cover design, Holly Macdonald for cover direction, Terence Caven for internal design, Robyn Watts for production, Linda Joyce for proofreading, Emma Pickard and Fleur Clarke for marketing, and Fliss Denham and Amy Winchester for publicity.

The following people read early or partial drafts and provided feedback: Anaea Lay, Spencer Ellsworth, Tinatsu Wallace, Floris M. Kleijne, Anna Nicolle, Alan Heartfield, Linda Nicholson-Brown, Miriah Hetherington, Amanda Helms, Benjamin C. Kinney, Elinor Caiman Sands, Kate Dollarhyde, Erica Satifka, J. S. Bangs and Catherine Schaff-Stump.

Any missteps are, of course, mine alone.

This book is dedicated to my wonderful sister, Jennifer. I would not be a writer without the support of my whole family, including my brother Ian, my parents Alan and Cheryl, my partner Brent and my son Xavier.

I thank my writing-community friends, including the members of Codex and the East Block Irregulars, for always being there for advice, brainstorming, commiseration, and celebration.

Finally, I thank the many historians and biographers whose diligent work allowed me to ground my flight of fancy in such a fascinating period.